Charles James Lever

The O'Donoghue

A Tale of Ireland Fifty Years Ago

Charles James Lever

The O'Donoghue
A Tale of Ireland Fifty Years Ago

ISBN/EAN: 9783337122324

Printed in Europe, USA, Canada, Australia, Japan

Cover: Foto ©Andreas Hilbeck / pixelio.de

More available books at **www.hansebooks.com**

THE O'DONOGHUE:

A Tale of Ireland Fifty Years Ago.

BY

CHARLES LEVER,

LONDON:
CHAPMAN AND HALL, 193, PICCADILLY.
1862.

PREFACE.

DEAR READER,—It was a ramble through the wild and desolate scene in which this tale opens that suggested the story. The gloomy grandeur of the spot associated itself in my mind with the sombre history of those who had once dwelt there, and whose great names had now descended to the poorest peasants,—men whose personal energy and recklessness had carried down feudalism to the very last years of the past century, and in their half inaccessible fastnesses dared to set law and civilisation at defiance, and live the same lives of unbounded waste and unbridled tyranny that their ancestors had followed for centuries. My memory was stored with strange histories of their doings. Their barbaric splendour, their generous hospitality, their savage treatment of the peasant, and their open and avowed hate of the Saxon, were traits that had heightened many a story, the delight of my boyhood.

I thought how the last expiring embers of such a race would kindle up at the bare thought of a French invasion—how their hearts would throb at the prospect of anything like an equal-handed struggle with England—and with what enthusiasm they would hail the legions that were to aid them to achieve independence. If I attempted to typify the spirit in Mark O'Donoghue, I tried in the character of his brother to depict the less picturesque but higher traits which a wiser and better culture had developed,—the features, in short, of that new race of men by whom, in the altered condition of Ireland, the great gifts of the country were to be displayed, and its boundless resources carried out to their fitting destiny.

A chance traveller—an Englishman of station and fortune—suggested the portraiture of Sir Marmaduke Travers; not, indeed, that I wanted an individual to refresh my mind as to the crude, mistaken, but well-intentioned hints for the amelioration of Ireland which it has been the good pleasure of tourists to publish in our behalf for so many years past. I own to have felt it no uncongenial task to display the workings of a philanthropy totally unsupported by all knowledge—a benevolence so self-satisfied that it rejected every thought of the instincts, the traditions, and the nature of those it assumed to relieve.

The pleasant English delusion of confounding their own superior social advantages with a higher capacity for civilisation, I was content to leave to be dealt with by the Irish peasant, as often as he chanced to be interrogated by an English traveller; but I was not sorry to show that any real and effective good to Ireland must have its base in the confidence of the people.

So much for some of the characters of my tale. Of the story itself, I have only to remark that many of my intelligent friends have blamed the catastrophe. They have said that Kate O'Donoghue deserved a better fate than that for which I reserved her; that he to whose hands I have committed her future in life had given no guarantees of conduct. They may be right in their criticism; at all events, I am too conscious of even graver demerits in the volume to undertake any justification for this ending; in which it is yet possible some of my readers may concur with me.

And in this hope, I beg to remain,

Your very devoted and grateful servant,

CHARLES LEVER.

Casa Capponi, Florence,
    Dec., 1857.

CONTENTS.

vi CONTENTS.

THE O'DONOGHUE;

A TALE OF IRELAND FIFTY YEARS AGO.

——◆——

CHAPTER I.

GLENFLESK.

In that wild and picturesque valley which winds its way between the town of Macroom and Bantry Bay, and goes by the name of Glenflesk, the character of Irish scenery is perhaps more perfectly displayed than in any other tract of the same extent in the island. The mountains, rugged and broken, are singularly fanciful in their outline; their sides a mingled mass of granite and straggling herbage, where the deepest green and the red purple of the heath-bell are blended harmoniously together. The valley beneath, alternately widening and narrowing, presents one rich meadow tract, watered by a deep and rapid stream, fed by a thousand rills that come tumbling and foaming down the mountain sides, and to the traveller are seen like white streaks marking the dark surface of the precipice. Scarcely a hut is to be seen for miles of this lonely glen, and save for the herds of cattle and the flocks of sheep here and there to be descried, it would seem as if the spot had been forgotten by man, and left to sleep in its own gloomy desolation. The river itself has a character of wildness all its own—now brawling over rugged rocks—now foaming between high and narrow sides, abrupt as walls, sometimes flowing over a ledge of granite, without a ripple on the surface—then plunging madly into some dark abyss, to emerge again lower down the valley in one troubled sea of foam and spray: its dull roar the only voice that echoes in the mountain gorge.

Even where the humble roof of a solitary cabin can be seen, the aspect of habitation rather heightens than diminishes the feeling of loneliness and de-

B

solation around. The thought of poverty enduring its privations unseen and unknown, without an eye to mark its struggles, or a heart to console its griefs, comes mournfully on the mind, and one wonders what manner of man he can be who has fixed his dwelling in such solitude.

In vain the eye ranges to catch sight of one human being, save that dark speck be such which crowns the cliff, and stands out from the clear sky behind. Yes, it is a child watching the goats that are browsing along the mountain, and as you look, the swooping mist has hidden him from your view. Life of dreariness and gloom! What sad and melancholy thoughts must be his companions, who spends the livelong day on these wild heaths, his eye resting on the trackless waste where no fellow-creature moves! how many a mournful dream will pass over his mind! what fearful superstitions will creep in upon his imagination, giving form and shape to the flitting clouds, and making the dark shadows, as they pass, seem things of life and substance.

Poor child of sorrow! How destiny has marked you for misery! For you no childish gambols in the sun—no gay playfellow—no paddling in the running stream, that steals along bright and glittering, like happy infancy—no budding sense of a fair world, opening in gladness, but all a dreary waste—the weariness of age bound up with the terrors of childhood.

The sun was just setting on a mellow evening, late in the autumn of a year towards the close of the last century, as a solitary traveller sat down to rest himself on one of the large rocks by the roadside; divesting himself of his gun and shot-pouch, he lay carelessly at his length, and seemed to be enjoying the light breeze which came up the valley.

He was a young and powerfully-built man, whose well-knit frame and muscular limbs showed how much habitual exercise had contributed to make the steepest paths of the mountain a task of ease to him. He was scarcely above the middle height, but with remarkable breadth of chest, and that squareness of proportion which indicates considerable physical strength; his countenance, except for a look of utter listlessness and vacuity, had been pleasing; the eyes were large and full, and of the deep grey which simulates blue; the nose large and well formed; the mouth alone was unprepossessing —the expression it wore was of ill-humour and discontent, and this character seemed so habitual, that even as he sat thus alone and in solitude the curl of the upper lip betrayed his nature.

His dress was a shooting-jacket of some coarse stuff, stained and washed by many a mountain streamlet; loose trousers of grey cloth, and heavy shoes—such as are worn by the peasantry, wherever such luxuries are attainable. It would have been difficult, at a mere glance, to have decided what class or condition of life he pertained to; for, although certain traits bespoke the person of a respectable rank, there was a general air of neglect about him, that half contradicted the supposition. He lay for some time perfectly motionless, when the tramp of horses at a distance down the glen suddenly roused him from his seeming apathy, and resting on his elbow he listened attentively. The sounds came nearer and nearer, and now the dull roll of a carriage could be heard approaching. Strange noises these in that solitary valley, where even the hoofs of a single horse but rarely roused the echoes. A sudden dip of the road at a little distance from where he lay concealed the view, and he remained in anxious expectancy, wondering what these sounds should portend, when suddenly the carriage seemed to have halted, and all was still.

For some minutes the youth appeared to doubt whether he had not been deceived by some swooping of the wind through the passes in the mountains, when the sound of voices fell on his ear, and at the same moment two figures appeared over the crest of the hill, slowly advancing up the road. The one was a man advanced in years, but still hale and vigorous in look; his features, even yet eminently handsome, wore an air of mingled frankness and haughtiness; there was in their expression the habitual character of one accustomed to exert a degree of command and influence over others—a look which, of all the characteristics of temper, is least easily mistaken.

At his side walked one who, even at a passing glance, might be pronounced his daughter, so striking the resemblance between them. She did not seem above sixteen years of age, but through the youthful traits of her features you could mark the same character of expression her father's wore, modified by the tender beauty, which at that age blends the loveliness of the girl with the graces of womanhood. Rather above than below the middle height, her figure had that distinguishing mark of elegance high birth impresses, and in her very walk a quick observer might detect an air of class.

They both stopped short as they gained the summit of the hill, and appeared wonder-struck at the scene before them. The grey gloom of twilight threw its sombre shadows over the valley, but the mountain peaks were tipped with the setting sun, and shone in those rich violet and purple hues the autumn heath displays so beautifully. The dark-leaved holly and the bright arbutus blossom lent their colour to every jutting cliff and promontory, which, to eyes unacquainted with the scenery, gave an air of culture strangely at variance with the desolation around.

"Is this wild enough for your fancy, Sybella," said the father, with a playful smile, as he watched the varying expression of the young girl's features, "or would you desire something still more dreary?" But she made no answer. Her gaze was fixed on a thin wreath of smoke that curled its way upwards from what appeared a low mound of earth in the valley below the road; some branches of trees, covered with sods of earth, grass-grown and still green, were heaped up together, and through these the vapour found a passage and floated into the air.

" I am wondering what that fire can mean," said she, pointing downwards with her finger.

" Here is some one will explain it," said the old man, as for the first time he perceived the youth, who still maintained his former attitude on the bank, and with a studied indifference paid no attention to those whose presence had before so much surprised him.

" I say, my good fellow, what does that smoke mean we see yonder ?"

The youth sprang to his feet with a bound that almost startled his questioner, so sudden and abrupt the motion; his features, inactive and colourless the moment before, seemed almost convulsed now, while they became dark with blood.

" Was it to me you spoke?" said he, in a low, guttural tone, which his passion made actually tremulous.

" Yes——"

But before the old man could reply, his daughter, with the quick tact of womanhood, perceiving the mistake her father had fallen into, hastily interrupted him by saying,

"Yes, sir; we were asking you the cause of the fire at the foot of that cliff."

The tone and the manner in which the words were uttered seemed at once to have disarmed his anger; and although for a second or two he made no answer, his features recovered their former half-listless look, as he said,

" It is a cabin—there is another yonder, beside the river."

" A cabin ! Surely you cannot mean that people are living there?" said the girl, as a sickly pallor spread itself across her checks.

" Yes, to be sure," replied the youth ; " they have no better hereabouts."

" What poverty—what dreadful misery is this !" said she, as the great tears gushed forth, and stole heavily down her face.

" They are not so poor," answered the young man, in a voice of almost reproof. " The cattle along that mountain all belong to these people—the goats you see in that glen are theirs also."

" And whose estate may this be ?" said the old man.

Either the questioner or his question seemed to have called up again the youth's former resentment, for he fixed his eyes steadily on him for some time without a word, and then slowly added,

" This belongs to an Englishman—a certain Sir Marmaduke Travers—it is the estate of O'Donoghue."

" Was, you mean, once," answered the old man, quickly.

"I mean what I say," replied the other, rudely. " Confiscation cannot take away a right, it can at most——"

This speech was fortunately not destined to be finished, for while he was speaking, his quick glance detected a dark object soaring above his head.

In a second he had seized his gun, and taking a steady aim, he fired. The loud report was heard repeated in many a far-off glen, and ere its last echo died away, a heavy object fell upon the road not many yards from where they stood.

"This fellow," said the youth, as he lifted the body of a large black eagle from the ground—"this fellow was a confiscator too, and see what he has come to. You'd not tell me that our lambs were his, would you?"

The roll of wheels happily drowned these words, for by this time the postilions had reached the place, the four post-horses labouring under the heavy-laden travelling carriage, with its innumerable boxes and imperials.

The postboys saluted the young man with marked deference, to which he scarcely deigned an acknowledgment, as he replaced his shot-pouch, and seemed to prepare for the road once more.

Meanwhile the old gentleman had assisted his daughter to the carriage, and was about to follow, when he turned around suddenly and said,

"If your road lies this way, may I offer you a seat with us?"

The youth stared as if he did not well comprehend the offer, and his cheek flushed, as he answered coldly,

"I thank you; but my path is across the mountain."

Both parties saluted distantly, the door of the carriage closed, and the word to move on was given, when the young man, taking two dark feathers from the eagle's wing, approached the window.

"I was forgetting," said he, in a voice of hesitation and diffidence, "perhaps you would accept these feathers."

The young girl smiled, and, half blushing, muttered some words in reply, as she took the offered present. The horses sprang forward the next instant, and a few minutes after the road was as silent and deserted as before, and save the retiring sound of the wheels nothing broke the stillness.

CHAPTER II.

THE WAYSIDE INN.

As the glen continues to wind between the mountains, it gradually becomes narrower, and at last contracts to a mere cleft, flanked on either side by two precipitous walls of rock, which rise to the height of several hundred feet above the road; this is the pass of Keim-an-eigh, one of the wildest and most romantic ravines of the scenery of the south.

At the entrance to this pass there stood, at the time we speak of, a small

wayside inn, or shebeen-house, whose greatest recommendation was in the
fact that it was the only place where shelter or refreshment could be obtained for miles on either side. An humble thatched cabin abutting against
the granite rock of the glen, and decorated with an almost effaced sign of St.
Finbar converting a very unprepossessing heathen, over the door, showed
where Mary M'Kelly dispensed "enthertainment for man and baste."

A chance traveller, bestowing a passing glance upon this modest edifice,
might deem that an inn in such a dreary and unfrequented valley must
prove a very profitless speculation. Few, very few, travelled the road—
fewer still would halt to bait within ten miles of Bantry. Report, however,
said differently; the impression in the country was, that "Mary's"—as it
was briefly styled—had a readier share of business than many a more pro-
mising and pretentious hotel; in fact, it was generally believed to be the
resort of all the smugglers of the coast; and the market, where the shop-
keepers of the interior repaired in secret to purchase the contraband wares
and "run goods" which poured into the country from the shores of France
and Holland.

Vast storehouses and caves were said to exist in the rock behind the
house, to store away the valuable goods which from time to time arrived;
and it was currently believed that the cargo of an Indiaman might have been
concealed within these secret recesses, and never a cask left in view to attract suspicion.

It is not into these gloomy receptacles of contraband that we would
now conduct our reader, but into a far more cheerful and more comfortable
locality—the spacious kitchen of the cabin, or, in fact, the apartment which
served for the double purpose of cooking and eating—the common room of
the inn, where around a blazing fire of black turf was seated a party of three
persons.

At one side sat the fat and somewhat comely figure of Mary herself,
a woman of some five-and-forty years, with that expression of rough and
ready temperament the habits of a wayside inn will teach. She had a
clear, full eye—a wide, but not unpleasant mouth—and a voice that suited
well the mellifluous intonation of a Kerry accent. Opposite to her were two
thin, attenuated old men, who, for dress, look, age, voice, and manner, it
would have been almost impossible to distinguish from each other; for
while the same weatherbeaten, shrivelled expression was common to both,
their jackets of blue cloth, leather breeches, and top boots, were so precisely
alike, that they seemed the very Dromios brought back to life, to perform
as postilions. Such they were—such they had been for above fifty years.
They had travelled the country from the time they were boys—they entered
the career together, and together they were jogging onward to the last
stage of all, the only one where they hoped to be at rest! Joe and Jim
Daly were two names no one ever heard disunited; they were regarded as

but one corporeally, and although they affected at times to make distinctions themselves, the world never gave them credit for any consciousness of separate identity. These were the postilions of the travelling carriage, which having left at its destination, about two miles distant, they were now regaling themselves at Mary's, where the horses were to rest for the night.

"Faix, ma'am, and it's driving ye may call it," said one of the pair, as he sipped a very smoking compound the hostess had just mixed—"a hard gallop every step of the way, barrin' the bit of a hill at Carrignacurra."

"Well, I hope ye had the decent hansel for it, anyhow, Jim?"

"I'm Joe, ma'am, av it's plazing to ye. Jim is the pole-end boy; he rides the layders. And it's true for ye—they behaved dacent."

"A goold guinea, divil a less," said the other; "there's no use in denying it. Begorra, it was all natural, them's as rich as Crœsis; sure didn't I see the young lady herself throwing out the tenpenny bits to the gossoons, as we went by, as if it was dirt; bad luck to me, but I was going to throw down the Bishop of Cloyne."

"Throw down who?" said the hostess.

"The near wheeler, ma'am; he's a broken-kneed ould devil we bought from the bishop, and called him after him; and as I was saying, I was going to cross them on the pole and get a fall, just to have a scramble for the money with the gaffers."

"'They look so poor,' says she. God help her—it's little poverty she saw —there isn't one of them crayters hasn't a sack of potatoes."

"Ay—more of them a pig."

"And hens," chimed in the first speaker, with a horror at the imposition of people so comfortably endowed affecting to feel any pressure or poverty.

"And what's bringing them here at all?" said Mrs. M'Kelly, with a voice of some asperity; for she foresaw no pleasant future in the fact of a resident great man, who would not be likely to give any encouragement to the branch of traffic her principal customers followed.

"Sorrow one of me knows," was the safe reply of the individual addressed, who, not being prepared with any view of the matter save that founded on the great benefit to the country, preferred this answer to a more decisive one.

"'Tis to improve the property, they say," interposed the other, who was not equally endowed with caution. "To look after the estate himself he has come."

"Improve, indeed!" echoed the hostess. "Much we want their improving! Why didn't they leave us the ould families of the country? It's little we used to hear of improving, when I was a child. God be good to us! There was ould Miles O'Donoghue, the present man's father, I'd like to see what he'd say, if they talked to him about improvement. Ayeh! sure I mind the time a hogshead of claret didn't do the fortnight. My father—

rest his soul!—used to go up to the house every Monday morning for orders ;
and ye'd see a string of cars following him at the same time, with tay, and
sugar, and wine, and brandy, and oranges, and lemons.   Them was the raal
improvements !"

" 'Tis true for ye, ma'am.   It was a fine house, I always heerd tell."

" Forty-six in the kitchen, besides about fourteen colleens and gossoons
about the place ; the best of enthertainment up-stairs and down."

" Musha ! that was grand."

" A keg of sperits, with a spigot, in the servants' hall, and no saying by
your leave, but drink while ye could stand over it."

" The Lord be good to us !" piously ejaculated the twain.

" The hams was boiled in sherry wine."

" Begorra, I wish I was a pig them times."

" And a pike daren't come up to table without an elegant pudding in his
belly that cost five pounds !"

" 'Tis the fish has their own luck always," was the profound meditation
at this piece of good fortune.

" Ayeh ! ayeh !" continued the hostess, in a strain of lamentation, " when
the ould stock was in it, we never heerd tell of improvements.   He'll be
making me take out a license, I suppose," said she, in a voice of half contemptuous incredulity.

" Faix ! there's no knowing," said Joe, as he shook the ashes out of his
pipe, and nodded his head sententiously, as though to say, that in the miserable times they'd fallen upon anything was possible.

" Licensed for sperits and groceries," said Mrs. M'Kelly, with a sort of
hysterical giggle, as if the thought were too much for her nerves.

" I wouldn't wonder if he put up a ' pike,' " stammered out Jim, thereby
implying that human atrocity would have reached its climax.

The silence which followed this terrible suggestion was now loudly interrupted by a smart knocking at the door of the cabin, which was already
barred and locked for the night.

" Who's there ?" said Mary, as she held a cloak across the blaze of the
fire, so as to prevent the light being seen through the apertures of the door
—" 'tis in bed we are, and late enough too."

" Open the door, Mary, it's me," said a somewhat confident voice.   " I
saw the fire burning brightly, and there's no use hiding it."

" Oh, troth, Mr. Mark, I'll not keep ye out in the cowld," said the
hostess, as, unbarring the door, she admitted the guest whom we had seen
some time since in the glen.   " Sure enough, 'tisn't an O'Donoghue we'd
shut the door agin, anyhow."

" Thank ye, Mary," said the young man ; " I've been all day in the
mountains, and had no sport ; and as that pleasant old Scotch uncle of
mine gives me no peace when I come home empty-handed, I have resolved

to stay here for the night, and try my luck to-morrow. Don't stir, Jim— there's room enough, Joe: Mary's fire is never so grudging but there's a warm place for every one. What's in this big pot here, Mary?"

"It's a stew, sir; more by token, of your honour's providin'"

"Mine—how is that?"

"The hare ye shot afore the door yesterday morning; sure it's raal luck we have it for yon now." And while Mary employed herself in the pleasant bustle of preparing the supper, the young man drew near to the fire, and engaged the others in conversation.

"That travelling carriage was going on to Bantry, Joe, I suppose?" said the youth, in a tone of easy indifference.

"No, sir; they stopped at the lodge above."

"At the lodge!—surely you can't mean that they were the English family —Sir Marmaduke?"

"'Tis just himself, and his daughter. I heerd them say the names as we were leaving Macroom. They were not expected here these three weeks; and Captain Hemsworth, the agent, isn't at home; and they say there's no servants at the lodge, nor nothin' ready for the quality at all; and sure when a great lord like that——"

"He is not a lord, yon fool; he has not a drop of noble blood in his body: he's a London banker—rich enough to buy birth, if gold could do it." The youth paused in his vehemence; then added, in a muttering voice, "Rich enough to buy the inheritance of those who have blood in their veins."

The tone of voice in which the young man spoke, and the angry look which accompanied these words, threw a gloom over the party, and for some time nothing was said on either side. At last he broke silence abruptly by saying,

"And that was his daughter, then?"

"Yes, sir; and a purty crayture she is, and a kind-hearted. The moment she heerd she was on her father's estate, she began asking the names of all the people, and if they were well off, and what they had to ate, and where was the schools."

"The schools!" broke in Mary, in an accent of great derision—"musha, it's great schooling we want up the glen to teach us to bear poverty and cowld without complaining; learning is a fine thing for the hunger——"

Her irony was too delicate for the thick apprehension of poor Jim, who felt himself addressed by the remark, and piously responded,

"It is so, glory be to God!"

"Well," said the young man, who now seemed all eagerness to resume the subject—"well, and what then?"

"Then she was wondering where was the roads up to the cabins on the mountains, as if the likes of them people had roads!"

"They've ways of their own, the English," interrupted Jim, who felt jealous of his companion being always referred to, "for whenever we passed a little potato garden, or a lock of oats, it was always, 'God be good to us! but they're mighty poor hereabouts;' but when we got into the raal wild part of the glen, with divil a house nor a human being near us, sorrow word out of their mouths but. 'fine! beautiful! elegant!' till we came to Keim-an-eigh, and then ye'd think that it was fifty acres of wheat they were looking at, wid all the praises they had for the big rocks and black cliffs over our heads."

"I showed them your honour's father's place on the mountains," said Joe.

"Yes, faith," broke in Jim; "and the young lady laughed, and said, 'You see, father, we have a neighbour after all.'"

The blood mounted to the youth's cheek, till it became almost purple, but he did not utter a word.

"'Tis the O'Donoghue, my lady,' said I," continued Joe, who saw the difficulty of the moment, and hastened to relieve it; "'that's his castle up there, with the high tower. 'Twas there the family lived these nine hundred years, whin the whole country was their own; and they wor kings here.'"

"And did you hear what the ould gentleman said then?" asked Jim.

"No, I didn't—I wasn't mindin' him," rejoined Joe, endeavouring with all his might to repress the indiscreet loquacity of the other.

"What was it, Jim?" said the young man, with a forced smile.

"Faix, he begun a laughing, yer honour, and says he, 'We must pay our respects at Coort,' says he; 'and I'm sure we'll be well received, for we know his Royal Highness already'—that's what he called yer honour."

The youth sprang to his feet with a gesture so violent and sudden as to startle the whole party.

"What!" he exclaimed, "and are we sunk so low as to be a scoff and a jibe to a London money-changer? If I but heard him speak the words——"

"Arrah, he never said it at all," said Joe, with a look that made his counterpart tremble all over. "That bosthoon there would make you believe he was in the coach, conversing the whole way with him. Sure wasn't I riding the wheeler, and never heerd a word of it. Whisht, I tell ye, and don't provoke me."

"Ay, stop your mouth with some of this," interposed Mary, as she helped the smoking and savoury mess around the table.

Jim looked down abashed and ashamed; his testimony was discredited; and without knowing why or wherefore, he yet had an indistinct glimmering that any effort to vindicate his character would be ill received; he therefore said nothing more. His silence was contagious, and the meal which a few moments before promised so pleasantly, passed off with gloom and restraint.

All Mary M'Kelly's blandishments, assisted by a smoking cup of mulled claret—a beverage which not a château on the Rhône could rival in racy flavour—failed to recal the young man's good humour : he sat in gloomy silence, only broken at intervals by sounds of some low muttering to himself. Mary at length having arranged the little room for his reception, bade him good night, and retired to rest. The postilions sought their dens over the stable, and the youth, apparently lost in his own thoughts, sat alone by the embers of the turf fire, and at last sank to sleep where he was, by the chimney-corner.

CHAPTER III.

THE " COTTAGE AND THE CASTLE."

OF Sir Marmaduke Travers there is little to tell the reader beyond what the few hints thrown out already may have conveyed to him. He was a London banker, whose wealth was reputed to. be enormous. Originally a younger son, he succeeded somewhat late in life to the baronetcy and large estates of his family. The habits, however, of an active city life—the pursuits which a long career had made a second nature to him—rendered him both unfit to enter upon the less exciting duties of a country gentleman's existence, and made him regard such as devoid of interest or amusement. He continued, therefore, to reside in London for many years after he became the baronet; and it was only at the death of his wife, to whom he was devotedly attached, that these habits became distasteful; he found that he could no longer continue a course which companionship and mutual feeling had rendered agreeable, and he resolved at once to remove to some one of his estates, where a new sphere of occupation might alleviate the sorrows of his loss. To this no obstacle of any kind existed. His only son was already launched into life as an officer in the Guards; and, except his daughter, so lately before the reader, he had no other children.

The effort to attain forgetfulness was not more successful here than it is usually found to be. The old man sought, but found not, in a country life the solace he expected; neither his tastes nor his habits suited those of his neighbours; he was little of a sportsman, still less of a farmer. The intercourse of country social life was a poor recompense for the unceasing flow of London society. He grew wearied very soon of his experiment, and longed once more to return to his old haunts and habits. One more chance, however, remained for him, and he was unwilling to reject without trying it. This was, to visit Ireland, where he possessed a large estate, which he had never seen. The property, originally mortgaged to his father, was represented as singularly picturesqne and romantic, possessing great mineral wealth, and other resources never examined into nor made available. His agent, Captain Hemsworth, a gentleman who resided on the estate, at his annual visit to the proprietor used to dilate upon the manifold advantages and capabilities of the property, and never ceased to implore him to pay a visit, if even for a week or two, sincerely trusting the while that such an intention might never occur to him. These entreaties, made from year to year, were the regular accompaniment of every settlement of account, and as readily replied to by a half promise, which the maker was certainly not more sincere in pledging.

Three years of country life had now, however, disposed Sir Marmaduke to reflect on this long unperformed journey; and, regardless of the fact that his agent was then grouse-shooting in Scotland, he set out at a moment's notice, and without a word to apprise the household at the lodge of his intended arrival, reached the house in the evening of an autumn day, by the road we have already been describing.

It is but justice to Sir Marmaduke to add, that he was prompted to this step by other than mere selfish considerations. The state of Ireland had latterly become a topic of the press in both countries. The poverty of the people—interpreted in various ways, and ascribed to very opposite causes— was a constant theme of discussion and conversation. The strange phenomenon of a land teeming with abundance, yet overrun by a starving population, had just then begun to attract notice ; and theories were rife in accounting for that singular and anomalous social condition, which, unhappily, the experience of an additional half century has not succeeded in solving.

Sir Marmaduke was well versed in these popular writings; he had the " Whole State of Ireland" by heart ; and so firmly was he persuaded that his knowledge of the subject was perfect, that he became actually impatient until he had reached the country, and commenced the great scheme of regeneration and civilisation, by which Ireland and her people were to be placed among the most favoured nations. He had heard much of Irish indolence and superstition—Irish bigotry and intolerance—the indifference to comfort —the indisposition to exertion—the recklessness of the present—the improvidence of the future ; he had been told that saint-days and holidays mulcted labour of more than half its due—that ignorance made the other half almost valueless ; he had read that the easy contentment with poverty had made all industry distasteful, and all exertion, save what was actually indispensable, a thing to be avoided.

" Why should these things be, when they were not so in Norfolk nor in Yorkshire ?" was the question he ever asked, and to which his knowledge furnished no reply. There, superstitious, if they existed—and he knew not if they did—came not in the way of daily labour. Saints never unharnessed the team, nor laid the plough inactive; comfort was a stimulant to industry that none disregarded; habits of order and decorum made the possessor respected; poverty almost argued misconduct, and certainly was deemed a reproach. Why then not propagate the system of these happy districts in Ireland? To do this was the great end and object of his visit.

Philanthropy would often seem unhappily to have a dislike to the practical—the generous emotions appear shorn of their freedom when trammelled with the fruit of experience or reflection. So certainly it was in the case before us. Sir Marmaduke had the very best intentions—the weakest notions of their realisation; the most unbounded desire for good—the very narrowest conceptions of how to effect it. Like most theorists, no speculative difficulty was great enough to deter—no practical obstacle was so small as not to affright him. It never apparently occurred to him that men are not everywhere alike, and this trifling omission was the source of difficulties, which he persisted in ascribing to causes outside of himself. Generous, kind-hearted, and benevolent, he easily forgave an injury, never willingly inflicted one; he was also, however, hot-tempered and passionate; he could not brook opposition to his will where its object seemed laudable to himself, and was utterly unable to make allowance for prejudices and leanings in others, simply because he had never experienced them in his own breast.

Such was, in a few words, the present occupant of "the Lodge," as the residence of the agent was styled. Originally a hunting-box, it had been enlarged and ornamented by Captain Hemsworth, and converted into a cottage of singular beauty, without, and no mean pretension to comfort, within doors. It occupied an indenture of the glen of Keim-an-eigh, and stood on the borders of a small mountain lake, the surface of which was dotted with wooded islands. Behind the cottage, and favoured by the shelter of the ravine, the native oaks grew to a great size, and contrasted by the rich foliage waving in the breeze with the dark sides of the cliff opposite, rugged, barren, and immutable.

In all the luxuriance of this mild climate, shrubs attained the height of trees; and flowers, rare enough elsewhere to demand the most watchful care, grew here, unattended and unregarded. The very grass had a depth of green, softer and more pleasing to the eye than in other places. It seemed as if nature had, in compensation for the solitude around, shed her fairest gifts over this lonely spot, one bright gem in the dreary sky of winter.

About a mile further down the glen, and seated on a lofty pinnacle of rock, immediately above the road, stood the once proud castle of the O'Donoghue. Two square and massive towers still remained to mark its ancient strength, and the ruins of various outworks and bastions could be traced, extending for a considerable distance on every side. Between these square towers, and occupying the space where originally a curtain wall stood, a long low building now extended, whose high-pitched roof and narrow windows vouched for an antiquity of little more than a hundred years. It was a strange, incongruous pile, in which fortress and farm-house seemed welded together—the whole no bad type of its past and its present owners. The approach was by a narrow causeway cut in the rock, and protected by a square keep, through whose deep arch the road penetrated—flanked on either hand by a low battlemented wall; along these, two rows of lime-trees grew, stately and beautiful in the midst of all the ruin about them. They spread their waving foliage around, and threw a mellow, solemn shadow along the walk. Except these, not a tree nor even a shrub was to be seen; the vast woods of nature's own planting had disappeared, the casualties of war, the chances of times of trouble, or the more ruinous course of poverty, had laid them low, and the barren mountain now stood revealed, where once were waving forests and shady groves, the home of summer birds, the lair of the wild deer.

Cows and farm-horses were stabled in what once had been the outworks of the castle. Implements of husbandry lay carelessly on all sides, neglect and decay marked everything, the garden wall was broken down in many places, and cattle strayed at will among the torn fruit-trees and dilapidated terraces; while, as if to add to the dreary aspect of the scene, the ground for a considerable distance around had been tilled, but never subsequently restored to grass land, and now along its ridged surface noisome weeds and thistles grew rankly, tainting the air with their odour, and sending up heavy exhalations from the moist and spongy earth. If, without, all looked sad and sorrow-struck, the appearances within were not much better. A large flagged hall opened upon two long ill-lighted corridors, from which a number of small sitting-rooms led off. Many of these were perfectly devoid of furniture; in the others, what remained seemed to owe its preservation to its want of value rather than any other quality. Cracked looking-glasses —broken chairs, rudely mended by some country hand—ragged and patched carpets, were the only things to be found, with here and there some dirt-disfigured piece of framed canvas, which, whether tapestry or painting, no eye could now discover. These apartments bore little or no trace of habitation; indeed, for many years they were rarely entered by any one. A large square room in one of the towers, of some forty feet in dimensions, was the ordinary resort of the family, serving the purposes of drawing and dining-room. This was somewhat better in appearance: whatever articles of furniture had any pretension to comfort or convenience were here assembled; and here were met old-fashioned sofas, deep arm-chairs, quaint misshapen tables like millepedes, and fat old footstools, the pious work of long-forgotten grandmothers. A huge screen, covered with a motley array of prints and caricatures, cut off the group around the ample fireplace from the remainder of the apartment, and it is within this charmed circle we would now conduct our reader.

In the great arm-chair, to the right of the ample fireplace, sat a powerfully built old man, whose hair was white as snow, and fell in long waving masses at either side of his head. His forehead, massive and expanded, surmounted two dark, penetrating eyes, which even extreme old age had not deprived of their lustre. The other features of his face were rather marked by a careless, easy sensuality, than by any other character, except that in the mouth the expression of firmness was strongly displayed. His dress was a strange mixture of the costume of gentleman and peasant. His coat, worn and threadbare, bore traces of better days in its cut and fashion; his vest also showed the fragment of tarnished embroidery along the margin of the flapped pockets ; but the coarse knee-breeches of corduroy, and the thick grey lambswool stockings, wrinkled along the legs, were no better than those worn by the poorer farmers of the neighbourhood.

This was the O'Donoghue himself. Opposite to him sat one as unlike him in every respect as it was possible to conceive. He was a tall, spare, raw-boned figure, whose grey eyes and high cheek-bones bore traces of a different race to that of the aged chieftain. An expression of intense acuteness pervaded every feature of his face, and seemed concentrated about the angles of the mouth, where a series of deep wrinkles were seen to cross and intermix with each other, omens of a sarcastic spirit, indulged without the least restraint on the part of its possessor. His wiry grey hair was brushed rigidly back from his bony temples, and fastened into a short queue behind, thus giving greater apparent length to his naturally long and narrow face. His dress was that of a gentleman of the time : a full-skirted coat of a dark brown, with a long vest descending below the hips; breeches somewhat a deeper shade of the same colour, and silk stockings, with silver-buckled shoes, completed an attire which, if plain, was yet scrupulously neat and respectable. As he sat, almost bolt upright in his chair, there was a look of vigilance and alertness about him very opposite to the careless, nearly drooping air of the O'Donoghue. Such was Sir Archibald M'Nab, the brother of the O'Donoghue's late wife, for the old man had been a widower for several years. Certain circumstances of a doubtful and mysterious nature had made him leave his native country of Scotland many years before, and since that, he had taken up his abode with his brother-in-law, whose retired habits and solitary residence afforded the surest guarantee against his ever being traced. His age must have been almost as great as the O'Donoghue's ; but the energy of his character, the lightness of his frame, and the habits of his life, all contributed to make him seem much younger.

Never were two natures more dissimilar. The one, reckless, lavish, and improvident ; the other, cautious, saving, and full of forethought. O'Donoghue was frank and open—his opinions easily known—his resolutions hastily formed. M'Nab was close and secret, carefully weighing everything before he made up his mind, and not much given to imparting his notions when he had done so.

In one point alone was there any similarity between them—pride of ancestry and birth they both possessed in common; but this trait, so far from serving to reconcile the other discrepancies of their natures, kept them even wider apart, and added to the passive estrangement of ill-matched associates an additional element of active discord.

There was a lad of some fifteen or sixteen years of age, who sat beside the fire on a low stool, busily engaged in deciphering, by the fitful light of the bog-wood, the pages of an old volume, in which he seemed deeply interested. The blazing pine, as it threw its red gleam over the room, showed the hand-some forehead of the youth, and the ample locks of rich auburn, which hung in clusters over it ; while his face was strikingly like the old man's, the mildness of its expression—partly the result of youth, partly the character imparted by his present occupation—was unlike that of either his father or brother ; for Herbert O'Donoghue was the younger son of the house, and was said, both in temper and appearance, to resemble his mother.

At a distance from the fire, and with a certain air of half assurance, half constraint, sat a man of some five-and-thirty years of age, whose dress of green coat, short breeches, and top boots, suggested at once the jockey, to which the mingled look of confidence and cunning bore ample corroboration. This was a well-known character in the south of Ireland at that time. His name was Lanty Lawler. The sporting habits of the gentry—their easiness on the score of intimacy—the advantages of a ready-money purchaser, when-ever they wished "to weed their stables," admitted the horse-dealer pretty freely among a class to which neither his habits nor station could have war-ranted him in presenting himself. But, in addition to these qualities, Lanty was rather a prize in remote and unvisited tracts such as the one we have been describing, his information being both great and varied in everything going forward. He had the latest news of the capital—the fashions of hair and toilet—the colours worn by the ladies in vogue, and the newest rumours of any intended change—he knew well the gossip of politics and party—upon the probable turn of events in and out of parliament he could hazard a guess with a fair prospect of accuracy. With the prices of stock and the changes in the world of agriculture he was thoroughly familiar, and had, be-sides, a world of stories and small-talk on every possible subject, which he brought forth with the greatest tact as regarded the tastes and character of his company, one half of his acquaintances being totally ignorant of the gifts and graces by which he obtained fame and character with the other.

A roving vagabond life gave him a certain free-and-easy air, which, among the majority of his associates, was a great source of his popularity ; but he well knew when to lay this aside and assume the exact shade of deference and respect his company might require. If, then, with O'Donoghue himself he would have felt perfectly at ease, the presence of Sir Archy, and his taciturn solemnity, was a sad check upon him, and mingled the freedom he felt with a degree of reserve far from comfortable. However, he had come for a purpose, and, if successful, the result would amply remunerate him for any passing inconvenience he might incur; and with this thought he armed himself as he entered the room some ten minutes before.

"So you are looking for Mark ?" said the O'Donoghue to Lanty. "You can't help hankering after that grey mare of his."

"Sure enough, sir, there's no denying it. I'll have to give him the forty pounds for her, though, as sure as I'm here, she's not worth the money; but when I've a fancy for a beast, or take a conceit out of her—it's no use, I must buy her—that's it !"

"Well, I don't think he'll give her to you now, Lanty; he has got her so quiet—so gentle—that I doubt he'll part with her."

"It's little a quiet one suits him; faix, he'd soon tire of her if she wasn't rearing or plunging like mad! He's an elegant rider, God bless him. I've a black horse now that would mount him well; he's out of ' Divil-may-care,' Mooney's horse, and can take six foot of a wall flying, with fourteen stone on his back; and barring the least taste of a capped hock, you could not see speck nor spot about him wrong."

"He's in no great humour for buying just now," interposed the O'Donoghue, with a voice to which some suddenly awakened recollection imparted a tone of considerable depression.

"Sure we might make a swop with the mare," rejoined Lanty, determined not to be foiled so easily. And then, as no answer was forthcoming, after a long pause, he added, "And haven't I the elegant pony for Master Herbert there; a crame colour—clean bred—with white mane and tail. If he was the Prince of Wales he might ride her. She has racing speed—they tell me, for I only have her a few days; and, faix, ye'd win all the county stakes with her."

The youth looked up from his book, and listened with glistening eyes and animated features to the description, which, to one reared as he was, possessed no common attraction.

"Sure I'll send over for her to-morrow, and you can try her," said Lanty, as if replying to the gaze with which the boy regarded him.

"Ye mauna do nae sich a thing," broke in M'Nab. "Keep your rogueries and rascalities for the auld generation ye hae assisted to ruin; but leave the young anes alane to mind ither matters than dicing and horse-racing."

Either the O'Donoghue conceived the allusion one that bore hardly on himself, or he felt vexed that the authority of a father over his son should

have been usurped by another, or both causes were in operation together,
for he turned an angry look on Sir Archy, and said,

"And why shouldn't the boy ride? was there ever one of his name or
family that didn't know how to cross a country? I don't intend him for a
Highland pedlar."

"He might be waur," retorted M'Nab, solemnly—"he might be an Irish
beggar."

"By my soul, sir," broke in O'Donoghue—— But fortunately an interruption saved the speech from being concluded, for at the same moment
the door opened, and Mark O'Donoghue, travel-stained and weary-looking,
entered the room.

"Well, Mark," said the old man, as his eyes glistened at the appearance
of his favourite son, "what sport, boy?"

"Poor enough, sir; five brace in two days is nothing to boast of, besides
two hares. Ah, Lanty, you here—how goes it?"

"Purty well, as times go, Mr. Mark," said the horse-dealer, affecting a
degree of deference he would not have deemed necessary had they been
alone. "I'm glad to see you back again."

"Why—what old broken-down devils have you now got on hand to pass
off upon us? It's fellows like you destroy the sport of the country. You
carry away every good horse to be found, and cover the country with spavined,
wind-galled brutes, not fit for the kennel."

"That's it, Mark—give him a canter, lad," cried the old man, joyfully.

"I know what you are at well enough," resumed the youth, encouraged
by these tokens of approval; "you want that grey mare of mine. You have
some fine English officer ready to give you a hundred and fifty, or, maybe,
two hundred guineas for her, the moment you take her over to England."

"May I never——"

"That's the trade you drive. Nothing too bad for us—nothing too good
for them."

"See now, Mr. Mark, I hope I may never——"

"Well, Lanty, one word for all; I'd rather send a bullet through her
skull this minute, than let you have her for one of your fine English
patrons."

"Won't you let me speak a word at all," interposed the horse-dealer, in
an accent half imploring, half deprecating. "If I buy the mare—and it
isn't for want of a sporting offer if I don't—she'll never go to England—no
—devil a step. She's for one in the country here beside you; but I won't
say more, and there now"—at these words he drew a soiled black leather
pocket-book from the breast of his coat, and, opening it, displayed a thick
roll of bank-notes, tied with a piece of string—"there's sixty pounds in
that bundle there—at least I hope so, for I never counted it since I got it
—take it for her or leave it, just as you like; and may I never have luck

with a beast, but there's not a gentleman in the county would give the same money for her." Here he dropped his voice to a whisper, and added, " Sure the speedy cut is ten pounds off her price any day, between two brothers."

" What !" said the youth, as his brows met in passion, and his heightened colour showed how his anger was raised.

" Well, well—it's no matter, there's my offer ; and if I make a ten-pound note of her, sure it's all I live by ; I wasn't born to an estate and a fine property, like yourself."

These words, uttered in such a tone as to be inaudible to the rest, seemed to mollify the young man's wrath, for, sullenly stretching forth his hand, he took the bundle and opened it on the table before him.

" A dry bargain never was a lucky one, they say, Lanty—isn't that so ?" said the O'Donoghue, as, seizing a small hand-bell, he ordered up a supply of claret, as well as the more vulgar elements for punch, should the dealer, as was probable, prefer that liquor.

" These notes seem to have seen service," muttered Mark ; " here's a ragged fellow. There's no making out whether he's two or ten."

" They were well handled, there's no doubt of it," said Lanty, " the tenants was paying them in ; and sure you know yourself how they thumb and finger a note before they part with it. You'd think they were trying to take leave of them. There's many a man can't read a word can tell you the amount of a note just by the feel of it !—Thank you, sir, I'll take the spirits—it's what I'm most used to."

" Who did you get them from, Lanty ?" said the O'Donoghue.

" Malachi Glynn, sir, of Cahernavorra, and, by the same token, I got a hearty laugh at the same house once before."

" How was that ?" said the old man, for he saw by the twinkle of Lanty's eye that a story was coming.

" Faix, just this way, sir. It was a little after Christmas last year that Mr. Malachi thought he'd go up to Dublin for a month or six weeks with the young ladies, just to show them, by way of—for, ye see, there's no dealing at all down here—and he thought he'd bring them up and see what could be done. Musha! but they're the hard stock to get rid of ! and somehow they don't improve by holding them over. And as there was levees, and drawing-rooms, and balls going on, sure it would go hard but he'd get off a pair of them, anyhow. Well, it was an elegant scheme, if there was money to do it ; but devil a farthin' was to be had, high or low, beyond seventy pounds I gave for the two carriage-horses and the yearlings that was out in the field, and sure that wouldn't do at all. He tried the tenants for 'the' November,' but what was the use of it, though he offered a receipt in full for ten shillings in the pound ?—when a lucky thought struck him. Troth, and it's what ye may call a grand thought too. He was walking about

c 2

before the door, thinking and ruminating how to raise the money, when he
sees the sheep graziug ou the lawu forneut him—not that he could sell one
of them, for there was a strap of a bond or mortgage on them a year before.
'Faix,' aud says he, 'when a man's hard up for cash, he's often obliged to
wear a mighty threadbare coat, and go cold enough in the winter season—
and sure it's reason sheep isn't better thau Christians ; and begorra,' says
he, 'I'll have the fleece off ye, if the weather was twice as cowld.' No
sooner said than doue. They were ordered into the haggard-yard the same
evening, and, as sure as ye're there, they cut the wool off them three days
after Christmas. Musha! but it was a pitiful sight to see them turned out
shivering and shakiug, with the snow ou the ground. And it didn't thrive
with him; for three died the first night. Well, when he seen what come
of it, he had them all brought in again, and they gathered all the spare
clothes and the ould rags in the house together, and dressed them up, at
least the ones that were worst ; and such a set of craytures never was seen.
One had an old petticoat on ; auother a flannel waistcoat ; many, could only
get a cravat or a pair of gaiters ; but the ram beat all, for he was dressed in
a pair of corduroy breeches, and au ould spencer of the master's ; and may
I never live, if I didn't roll down full leugth on the grass when I seen
him."

For some minutes before Lanty had concluded his story, the whole party
were convulsed with laughter ; even Sir Archy vouchsafed a grave smile, as,
receiving the tale in a different light, he muttered to himself,

"They're a' the same—ne'er-do-well, reckless deevils."

One good result at least followed the anecdote—the good humour of the
company was restored at once—the bargain was finally concluded; and
Lanty succeeded by some adroit flattery in recovering five pounds of the
price, under the title of luck-penny—a portion of the contract M'Nab would
have interfered against at once, but that, for his own especial reasons, he
preferred remaining silent.

The party soon after separated for the night, and as Lanty sought the
room usually destined for his accommodation, he muttered, as he went, his
self-congratulations ou his bargain. Already he had nearly reached the end
of the loug corridor, where his chamber lay, when a door was cautiously
opened, and Sir Archy, attired in a dressing-gown, and with a candle in his
hand, stood before him.

"A word wi' ye, Master Lawler," said he, in a low, dry toue the horse-
dealer but half liked. "A word wi' ye before ye retire to rest."

Lanty followed the old man iuto the apartment with an air of affected
carelessness, which soon, however, gave way to surprise, as he surveyed the
chamber, so little like any other in that dreary mansiou. The walls were
covered with shelves, loaded with books ; maps aud prints lay scattered
about ou tables ; an oak cabinet of great beauty iu form and carviug oc-

cupied a deep reeess beside the chimney; and over the fireplace a claymore of true Highland origin, and a pair of silver-mounted pistols, were arranged like a trophy, surmounted by a flat Highland cap, with a thin black eagle's feather.

Sir Archy seemed to enjoy the astonishment of his guest, and for some minutes made no effort to break silence. At length he said,

"Ye war speaking about a sma' powny for the laird's son, Mister Lawler—may I ask ye the price?"

The words acted like a talisman—Lanty was himself in a moment. The mere mention of horseflesh brought back the whole crowd of his daily associations, and with his native volubility he proceeded, not to reply to the question, but to enumerate the many virtues and perfections of the "sweetest tool that ever travelled on four legs."

Sir Archy waited patiently till the eloquent eulogy was over, and then dryly repeated his first demand.

"Is it her price?" said Lanty, repeating the question to gain time to consider how far circumstances might warrant him in pushing a market. "It's her price ye're asking me, Sir Archibald? Troth, and I'll tell you: there's not a man in Kerry could say what's her price. Goold wouldn't pay for her, av it was value was wanted. See now, she's not fourteen hands high, but may I never leave this room if she wouldn't carry me—ay, myself here, twelve stone six in the scales—over e'er a fence between this and Inchigeela."

"It's no exactly to carry you that I was making my inquiry," said the old man, with an accent of more asperity than he had used before.

"Well, then, for Master Herbert—sure she is the very beast——"

"What are you asking for her? Canna you answer a straightforred question, man?" reiterated Sir Archy, in a voice there was no mistaking.

"Twenty guineas, then," replied Lanty, in a tone of defiance; "and if ye offer me pounds I won't take it."

Sir Archy made no answer; but turning to the old cabinet, he unlocked one of the small doors, and drew forth a long leather pouch, curiously embroidered with silver; from this he took ten guineas in gold, and laid them leisurely on the table. The horse-dealer eyed them askance, but without the slightest sign of having noticed them.

"I'm no goin' to buy your beast, Mr. Lawler," said the old man, slowly; "I'm just goin' merely to buy your ain good sense and justice. You say the powny is worth twenty guineas?"

"As sure as I stand here. I wouldn't——"

"Weel, weel, I'm content. There's half the money; tak' it, but never let's hear anither word about her here: tak' her awa' wi' ye; sell or shoot her, do what ye please wi' her; but, mind me, man"—here his voice became full strong, and commanding—"tak' care that ye meddle not wi' that

young callant, Herbert. Dinna fill his head wi' ranting thoughts of dogs and
horses. Let there be one of the house wi' a soul above a scullion or a
groom. Ye have brought ruin enough here; you can spare the boy, I trow:
there, sir, tak' your money."

For a second or two Lanty seemed undecided whether to reject or accept
a proposal so humiliating in its terms; and when at length he acceded, it
was rather from his dread of the consequences of refusal than from any satisfaction the bargain gave him.

"I'm afraid, Sir Archibald," said he, half timidly—"I'm afraid you don't
understand me well."

"I'm afraid I do," rejoined the old man, with a bitter smile on his lip;
"but it's better we should understand each other. Good night."

"Well, good night to you, anyhow," said Lanty, with a slight sigh, as he
dropped the money into his pocket, and left the room.

"I have bought the scoundrel cheap!" muttered Sir Archy, as the door
closed.

"Begorra, I thought he was twice as knowing!" was Lanty's reflection,
as he entered his own chamber.

CHAPTER IV.

KERRY O'LEARY.

LANTY LAWLER was stirring the first in the house. The late sitting of
the preceding evening, and the deep potations he had indulged in, left little
trace of weariness on his well-accustomed frame. Few contracts were ratified in those days without the solemnity of a drinking bout, and the habits
of the O'Donoghue household were none of the most abstemious. All was
still and silent then as the horse-dealer descended the stairs, and took the
path towards the stable where he had left his hackney the night before.

It was Lanty's intention to take possession of his new purchase, and set
out on his journey before the others were stirring; and with this object he
wended his way across the weed-grown garden, and into the wide and dreary
court-yard of the building.

Had he been disposed to moralise—assuredly an occupation he was little
given to—he might have indulged the vein naturally enough as he surveyed
on every side the remains of long past greatness and present decay. Beautifully proportioned columns, with florid capitals, supplied the place of gate-
piers. Richly carved armorial bearings were seen upon the stones used to

repair the breaches in the walls. Fragments of inscriptions and half obliterated dates appeared amid the moss-grown ruins: and the very door of
the stable had been a portal of dark oak, studded with large nails, its native
strength having preserved it when even the masonry was crumbling to
decay. Lanty passed these with perfect indifference. Their voice awoke no
echo within his breast; and even when he noticed them, it was to mutter
some jeering allusion to their fallen estate, rather than with any feeling of
reverence for what they once represented.

The deep bay of a hound now startled him, however. He turned suddenly round, and close beside him, but within the low wall of a ruined
kennel-yard, lay a large foxhound, so old and feeble that, even roused by the
approach of a stranger, he could not rise from the ground, but lay helplessly
on the earth, and with uplifted throat sent forth a long wailing note. Lanty
leaned upon the wall, and looked at him. The emotions which other objects
failed to suggest, seemed to flock upon him now. That poor dog, the last
of a once noble pack, whose melody used to ring through every glen and
ravine of the wild mountains, was an appeal to his heart he could not with-
stand, and he stood with his gaze fixed upon him.

" Poor old fellow !" said he, compassionately; " it's a lonely thing for you
to be there now, and all your old friends and companions dead and gone.
Rory, my boy, don't you know me ?"

The tones of his voice seemed to soothe the animal, for he responded in a
low cadence indescribably melancholy.

" That's my boy. Sure I knew you didn't forget me ;" and he stooped
over and patted the poor beast upon the head.

" The top of the morning to you, Mister Lawler," cried out a voice
straight over his head—and at the same instant a strange-looking face was
protruded from a little one-paned window of a hayloft—" 'tis early you are
to-day."

" Ah, Kerry, how are you, man ? I was taking a look at Rory here."

" Faix, he's a poor sight now," responded the other, with a sigh, " but he
wasn't so once. I mind the time he could lead the pack over Cubber-na-
ereena mountain, and not a dog but himself catch the scent, after a hard frost
and a north wind. I never knew him wrong. His tongue was as true as
the priest's—sorrow lie in it."

A low whine from the poor old beast seemed to acknowledge the praise
bestowed upon him; and Kerry continued,

" It's truth I'm telling; and if it wasn't, it's just himself would contradict me.—Tally-ho ! Rory—tally-ho ! my ould boy ;" and both man and dog
joined in a deep-toned cry together.

The old walls sent back the echoes, and for some seconds the sounds
floated through the still air of the morning.

Lanty listened with animated features and lit-up eyes to notes which so often had stirred the strongest chords of his heart, and then suddenly, as if recalling his thoughts to their former channel, cried out,

" Come down, Kerry, my man—come down here, and unlock the door of the stable. I must be early on the road this morning."

Kerry O'Leary—for so was he called, to distinguish him from those of the name in the adjoining county—soon made his appearance in the court-yard beneath. His toilet was a hasty one, consisting merely of a pair of worn corduroy small-clothes and an old blue frock, with faded scarlet collar and cuffs, which, for convenience, he wore on the present occasion buttoned at the neck, and without inserting his arms in the sleeves, leaving these appendages to float loosely at his side. His legs and feet were bare, as was his head, save what covering it derived from a thick fell of strong black hair that hung down on every side like an ill-made thatch.

Kerry was not remarkable for good looks. His brow was low, and shaded two piercing black eyes, set so closely together, that they seemed to present to the beholder one single continuous dark streak beneath his fore-head; a short snubby nose, a wide thick-lipped mouth, and a heavy massive under-jaw, made up an assemblage of features, which, when at rest, indi-cated little remarkable or striking; but when animated and excited, dis-played the strangest possible union of deep cunning and simplicity, intense curiosity and apathetic indolence. His figure was short, almost to dwarf-ishness, and as his arms were enormously long, they contributed to give that air to his appearance. His legs were widely bowed, and his gait had that slouching, shambling motion so indicative of an education cultivated among horses and stable-men. So it was, in fact; Kerry had begun life as a jockey. At thirteen he rode a winning race at the Curragh, and came in first on the back of Blue Blazes, the wickedest horse of the day in Ireland. From that hour he became a celebrity, and, until too old to ride, was the crack jockey of his time. From jockey he grew into trainer—the usual transition of the tadpole to the frog ; and when the racing stud was given up by the O'Donoghue in exchange for the hunting-field, Kerry led the pack to their glorious sport. As time wore on, and its course brought saddening fortunes to his master, Kerry's occupation was invaded ; the horses were sold, the hounds given up, and the kennel fell to ruins. Of the large house-hold that once filled the castle, a few were now retained ; but among these was Kerry. It was not that he was useful, or that his services could minister to the comfort or convenience of the family ; far from it, the com-monest offices of in-door life he was ignorant of, and, even if he knew, would have shrunk from performing them, as being a degradation. His whole skill was limited to the stable-yard, and there now his functions were unneeded. It would seem as if he were kept as a kind of memento of their once condition, rather than anything else. There was a pride in maintain-ing one who did nothing the whole day but lounge about the offices and the court-yard, in his old ragged suit of huntsman. And so, too, it impressed the country people, who, seeing him, believed that at any moment the ancient splendour of the house might shine forth again, and Kerry, as of yore, ride out on his thorough-bred, to make the valleys ring with music. He was, as it were, a kind of staff, through which, at a day's notice, the whole regiment might be mustered. It was in this spirit he lived, and moved, and spoke. He was always going about looking after a "nice beast to carry the master," and a "real bit of blood for Master Mark;" and he would send a gossoon to ask if Barry O'Brien of the bridge "heard tell of a fox in the cover below the road." In fact, his preparations ever portended a speedy resumption of the habits in which his youth and manhood were spent.

Such was the character who now, in the easy dishabille described, descended into the court-yard with a bunch of keys in his hand, and led the way towards the stable.

"I put the little mare into the hack-stable, Mr. Lawler," said he, "because the hunters is in training, and I didn't like to disturb them with a strange beast."

"Hunters in training!" replied Lanty, in astonishment. "Why, I thought he had nothing but the grey mare with the black legs."

"And sure, if he hasn't," responded Kerry, crankily, "couldn't he buy them when he wants them?"

"Oh, that's it," said the other, laughing to himself. "No doubt of it, Kerry. Money will do many a thing."

"Oh, it's wishing it I am for money! Bad luck to the peace or ease I ever seen since they became fond of money. I remember the time it was, 'Kerry, go down and bring this, or take that,' and devil a more about it; and lashings of everything there was. See, now! if the horses could eat peas-pudding, and drink punch, they'd got it for askin'; but now it's all for saving, and saving. And sure, what's the use of goold? God be good to us, as I heard Father Luke say, he'd do as much for fifteen shillings as for fifty pounds, av it was a poor boy wanted it."

"What nonsense are you talking, you old sinner, about saving? Why, man, they haven't got as much as they could bless themselves on among them all. You needn't be angry, Kerry. It's not Lanty Lawler you can humbug that way. Is there an acre of the estate their own now? Not if every perch of it made four, it wouldn't pay the money they owe."

"And if they do," rejoined Kerry, indignantly, "who has a better right, tell me that? Is it an O'Donoghue would be behind the rest of the country? Begorra, ye're bould to come up here and tell us that!"

"I'm not telling you anything of the kind—I'm saying that if they are ruined entirely——"

"Arrah! don't provoke me. Take your baste and go, in God's name!"

And so saying, Kerry, whose patience was fast ebbing, pushed wide the stable-door, and pointed to the stall where Lanty's hackney was standing.

"Bring out that grey mare, Master Kerry," said Lanty, in a tone of easy insolence, purposely assumed to provoke the old huntsman's anger—"bring her out here."

"And what for would I bring her out?"

"Maybe I'll tell you afterwards," was the reply. "Just do as I say, now."

"The devil a one o' me will touch the beast at your bidding; and, what's more, I'll not let yourself lay a finger on her."

"Be quiet, you old fool!" said a deep voice behind him. He turned, and there stood Mark O'Donoghue himself, pale and haggard after his night's excess. "Be quiet, I say. The mare is his—let him have her."

"Blessed Virgin!" exclaimed Kerry, "here's the hunting season beginning, and sorrow thing you'll have to put a saddle on, barrin'—barrin'——"

"Barring what?" interposed Lanty, with an insolent grin.

The young man flushed at the impertinence of the insinuation, but said not a word for a few minutes, then suddenly exclaimed,

"Lanty, I have changed my mind; I'll keep the mare."

The horse-dealer started, and stared him full in the face:

"Why, Mr. Mark, surely you're not in earnest? The beast is paid for—the bargain all settled."

"I don't care for that. There's your money again. I'll keep the mare."

"Ay, but listen to reason. The mare is mine. She was so when you handed me the luck-penny, and if I don't wish to part with her, you cannot compel me."

"Can't I?" retorted Mark, with a jeering laugh—"can't I, faith? Will you tell me what's to prevent it? Will you take the law of me? Is that your threat?"

"Devil a one ever said I was that mean, before!" replied Lanty, with an air of deeply-offended pride. "I never demeaned myself to the law, and I'm fifteen years buying and selling horses in every county in Munster. No, Mr. Mark, it is not that; but I'll just tell you the truth. The mare is all as one as sold already;—there it is now, and that's the whole secret."

"Sold! What do you mean?—that you had sold that mare before you ever bought her?"

"To be sure I did," cried Lanty, assuming a forced look of easy assurance he was very far from feeling at the moment. "There's nothing more common in my trade. Not one of us buys a beast without knowing where the next owner is to be had."

"And do you mean, sir," said Mark, as he eyed him with a steady stare—"do you mean to tell me that you came down here, as you would to a petty farmer's cabin, with your bank-notes, ready to take whatever you may pitch your fancy on, sure and certain that our necessities must make us willing chapmen for all you care to deal in ? Do you dare to say that you have done this with *me ?*"

For an instant Lanty was confounded. He could not utter a word, and looked around him in the vain hope of aid from any other quarter, but none was forthcoming. Kerry was the only unoccupied witness of the scene, and his face beamed with ineffable satisfaction at the turn matters had taken, and as he rubbed his hands he could scarcely control his desire to laugh out-right at the lamentable figure of his late antagonist.

"Let me say one word, Master Mark," said Lanty, at length, and in a voice subdued to its very softest key—"just a single word in your own ear." And with that he led the young man outside the door of the stable, and whis-pered for some minutes with the greatest earnestness, concluding in a voice loud enough to be heard by Kerry, "And after that, I'm sure I need say no more."

Mark made no answer, but leaned his back against the wall, and folded his arms upon his breast.

"May I never if it is not the whole truth," said Lanty, with a most eager and impassioned gesture ; "and now I leave it all to yourself."

"Is he to take the mare ?" asked Kerry, in anxious dread lest his enemy might have carried the day.

"Yes," was the reply, in a deep, hollow voice, as the speaker turned away and left the stable.

While Lanty was engaged in placing the saddle on his new purchase, an operation in which Kerry contrived not to afford him any assistance what-ever, Mark O'Donoghue paced slowly to and fro in the court-yard, with his arms folded, and his head sunk upon his breast ; nor was he aroused from his reverie until the step of the horse was heard on the pavement be-side him.

"Poor Kittane," said he, looking up suddenly, "you were a great pet : I hope they'll be as kind to you as I was ; and they'd better, too," added he, half savagely, "for you've a drop of the Celt in your blood, and can revenge harsh treatment when you meet with it. Tell her owner that she is all gentleness if not abused, but get her temper once up, and, by Jove, there's not a torrent on the mountain can leap as madly ! She knows her name, too : I trust they'll not change that. She was bred beside Lough Kittane, and called after it. See how she can follow." And with that the youth sprang forward, and placing his hand on the top bar of a gate, vaulted lightly over ; but scarcely had he reached the ground, when the mare bounded after him, and stood with her head resting on his shoulder.

Mark turned an elated look on the others, and then surveyed the noble animal beside him with all the pride and admiration of a master regarding his handiwork. She was, indeed, a model of symmetry, and well worthy of all the praise bestowed on her.

For a moment or two the youth gazed on her with a flashing eye and quivering lip, while the mare, catching excitement from the free air of the morning and the spring she had made, stood with swelled veins and trembling limbs, his counterpart in eagerness. One spirit seemed to animate both. So Mark appeared to feel it, as with a bound he sprang into the saddle, and with a wild cheer dashed forward. With lightning's speed they went, and in a moment disappeared from view. Kerry jumped up on a broken gate-pier, and strained his eyes to catch them, while Lanty, muttering maledictions to himself on the hair-brained boy, turned everywhere for a spot where he might view the scene.

" There he goes!" shouted Kerry; "look at him now; he's coming to the furze ditch into the big field. See, see! she does not see the fence; her head's in the air. Whew—elegant, by the mortial—never touched a hoof to it! Murther, murther! how she gallops in the deep ground, and the wide gripe that's before her! Ah, he won't take it; he's turning away."

" I wish to the Lord he'd break a stirrup-leather," muttered Lanty.

" Oh, Joseph!" screamed Kerry, "there was a jump—twenty feet, as sure as I'm living. Where is he now?—I don't see him."

" May you never!" growled Lanty, whose indignant anger had burst all bounds. "That's not treatment for another man's horse."

" There he goes, the jewel; see him in the stubble-field; sure it's a real picture to see him going along at his ease. Whurroo—he's over the wall. What the devil's the matter now?—they're away." And so it was; the animal that an instant before was cantering perfectly in hand, had now set off at top speed and at full stretch. "See the gate—mind the gate, Master Mark—tear and ages, mind the gate!" shouted Kerry, as though his admonition could be heard half a mile away. "Oh, Holy Mary! he's through it!" And true enough—the wild and now affrighted beast dashed through the frail timbers, and held on her course without stopping. "He's broke the gate to flitters."

" May I never! if I don't wish it was his neck," said Lanty, in open defiance.

" Do you, then?" called out Kerry. "Why, then, as sure as my name's Kerry O'Leary, if there's a hair of his head hurted, I'll——"

What the threat was intended for cannot be known; for his eye once more caught sight of his idol, and he yelled out,

" Take care of the sheep. Bad luck to ye for sheep, ye're always in the way. That's the darling—'twas myself taught you to have a light hand. Ah, Kittane, you're coming to rayson now."

" The mare won't be worth sixpence," muttered Lanty.

" 'Twas as good as a day's sport to me," said Kerry, wiping his brow with the loose sleeve of his coat, and preparing to descend from the eleva·tion, for the young man now entered the distant part of the lawn, and, at an easy canter, was returning to the stable-yard.

" There !" said Mark, as he flung himself from the saddle—"there, Kittanc, it's the last time you're likely to have a bold burst of it, or myself either, perhaps. She touched her counter on that gate, Lanty; but she's nothing the worse of it."

Lanty grumbled some indistinct mutterings as he wiped a blood-stain from the mare's chest, and looked sulkily at her heaving flanks and sides reeking with foam and sweat.

" 'Tis a darling you wor," said Kerry, patting her over from her mane to her hind-quarters.

" Faix, that cut is ten pounds out of my pocket this morning, anyhow," said Lanty, as he pointed to the slight scratch from which a few drops of blood still flowed.

"Are you off the bargain, then ?" said Mark, sternly, as he turned his head round; for he was already leaving the spot.

" 1 didn't say so," was the answer.

For a second or two Mark seemed uncertain what reply to make, and then, as if controlling his temper, he nodded carelessly, and with a " Good-by, Lanty," he sauntered slowly towards the house.

" Well, Mr. O'Leary," said Lanty, in a voice of affected politeness Irish-men are occasionally very fond of employing when they intend great self-respect, " may I trouble you to bring out that hack of mine ?"

" 'Tis a pleasure, Mr. Lawler, and no trouble in life, av it helps to get rid of you," responded Kerry, as he waddled off on the errand.

Lanty made no reply; perhaps he felt the encounter unequal—perhaps he despised his antagonist; in any case, he waited patiently for Kerry's appearance, and then, passing his arm within the bridle of each horse, he slowly descended the avenue towards the high road.

CHAPTER V.

IMPRESSIONS OF IRELAND.

IT was not without a feeling closely allied to disappointment that Sir Marmaduke Travers found the advent to his Irish estates uncelebrated by any of those testimonies on the part of his tenantry his agent, Captain Hemsworth, had often so graphically pictured before hîm. The post-horses were suffered to drag his carriage unmolested to its destination; there was no assemblage of people to welcome—not a bonfire to hail his arrival. True, he had come totally unexpectedly. The two servants sent forward to prepare the lodge for his reception only reached there a single day before himself. But Sir Marmaduke had often taken his Yorkshire tenants as much by surprise, and there he always found a deputation and a *cortége* of mounted yeomen. There were addresses, and triumphal arches, and newspaper paragraphs, and all the innumerable but well-known accompaniments of those patronising acts of condescension which consist in the visit of a rich man to his own home. Now, however, all was different. No cheering sounds broke the quiet stillness of the deep valley. No troops of people on horseback or on foot filled the glen. The sun set, calm and golden, behind the purple hills, unscared by the lurid glow of a single bonfire. Save from an appearance of increased bustle, and an air of movement and stir around the lodge itself, there was nothing to mark his coming. There, indeed, servants were seen to pass and repass; workmen were employed upon the flowergarden and the shrubbery walks; and all the indications of care and attention to the villa and its grounds easily perceptible. Beyond these precincts, however, all was still and solitary as before. For miles the road could be seen without a single traveller. The mountains seemed destitute of inhabitants. The peaceful solemnity of the deep glen, along which the cloud shadows moved slowly in procession, increased the sense of loneliness, and Sir Marmaduke already began to suspect that this last trial of a residence would scarcely prove more fortunate than the previous ones.

Age and wealth are uncomplying task-masters—habit and power endure restraint with an ill grace. The old baronet was half angry with himself for what he felt a mistake, and he could not forgive the country which was the cause of it. He had come expressly to see and pronounce for himself —to witness with his own eyes—to hear with his own ears; and yet, he knew not how it was, nothing revealed itself before him. The very labourers who worked in the garden seemed uncommunicative and shy. Their great respect and reverence he understood as a cautious reserve. He must send for Hemsworth—there was nothing else for it. Hemsworth was used to them, and could explain the mode of dealing with them. Their very idioms required translating, and he could not advance without an interpreter.

Not so his daughter. To her the scene had all the charm of romance. The lone dwelling beside the blue lake, the tall and peaked mountains lost in the white clouds, the waving forest with its many a tangled path, the bright islands that, gem-like, spangled the calm surface of the water, realised many a poetic dream of her childhood, and she felt that visionary happiness which serenity of mind, united to the warm imagination of early life, alone can bestow.

It was a fairy existence to live thus secluded in that lonely valley, where the flowers seemed to blossom for them alone; for them the summer birds sang their roundelays, and the fair moon shed her pale light over hill and stream, with none to mark her splendour save themselves. Not these thoughts alone filled her mind. Already had she noticed the artless habits of the humble peasantry—their gratitude for the slightest services, their affectionate greetings, the touching beauty of their expressions, teeming with an imagery she never heard before. All appealed to her mind with a very different force from what they addressed themselves with to her father's. Already she felt attracted by the figurative eloquence, so popular a gift among the people. The warm fervour of fancy she had believed the attribute of highly-wrought temperaments only she found here amid poverty and privation; flashes of bright wit broke from the gloom of daily suffering, and the fire which gives life its energy burned brightly amid the ashes of many an extinguished hope. These were features she was not prepared to meet among a peasantry living in a wild, unvisited district, and day by day they fascinated her more strongly.

It was not entirely to the difference between father and daughter that these varied impressions were owing. The people themselves assumed a tone quite distinctive to each. Sir Marmaduke they had always heard spoken of as a stern-tempered man, whose severity towards his tenantry was, happily, tempered by the personal kindness of the agent. Captain Hemsworth constantly impressed them with the notion that all harsh measures originated with his principal—the favours came from himself only. The exactions of high rents, the rigorous prosecutions of the law, he ever asserted were acts compulsory with him, but always repugnant to his own better feelings. Every little act of grace he accompanied by an assurance that he "hoped Sir Marmaduke might not hear of it," as the consequences to himself might prove ruinous. In fact, he contrived to mislead both parties in their estimate of each other, and their first acquaintanceship, it could not be supposed, should dispel the illusion. The peasantry, how-

ever, were the first to discover the error. Long before Sir Marmaduke had
made any progress in deciphering the mystic symbols of *their* natures, they
had read *his* from end to end. They scanned him with powers of observation no other people in Europe can compete with; and while *he* was philo-
sophising about the combined influence of their superstitions, their ignorance,
and their apathy to suffering, *they* were accurately speculating on all the
possible benefits which might accrue from the residence amongst them of
so very kind-hearted, but such a mere simpleton of a man as himself.

They listened with sincere pleasure—for they love any appeal to themselves—to the precepts he so liberally bestowed regarding "industry" and
"frugality," nor did they ever make the reply, which was ready at every lip,
that industry cannot be practised without an occupation, nor frugality be
pushed beyond the very borders of starvation. No; they answered with a
semblance of concurrence, "True for you, sir; the devil a lie in it—your
honour knows it well." Or, when pushed home by any argument against
their improvidence or recklessness, the ever-present reply was, "Sure, sir,
it's the will of God"—a piece of fatalism that rescued them from many a
difficulty when no other aid was near.

"They are a simple set of people," said Sir Marmaduke, as he sat at his
breakfast in the small parlour of the lodge which looked out upon the glen—
"very ignorant, very barbarous, but easily led—I see through them clearly."

"I like them greatly," said his daughter; "their gratitude knows no
bounds for the slightest services; they have a kind of native courtesy, so
rare to find amongst a peasantry. How that poor fellow last night wished to
climb the cliff, where the eagle's nest is, because I foolishly said I had never
seen a young eagle."

"They are totally misunderstood," said Sir Marmaduke, sententiously,
rather following out the train of his own reflections than noticing the remark of his daughter; "all one hears of their absurd reverence for the
priest, or the devoted adherence they practise towards the old families of
the country, is mere nonsense. You heard how Dan laughed this morning
when I joked with him about purgatory and the saints; and what a droll
description they gave of that queer household—the chieftain—what is his
name?"

"The O'Donoghue."

"Yes; I never can remember it. No, no, they are not so bigoted;
they are merely uninformed. We shall soon see many changes among
them. I have written to Bradston about the plans for the cottages, and
also the design for a school-house; and then there's the chapel—that reminds me I have not returned the priest's visit, he was here the day before
yesterday."

"If you like, we'll ride there; I have heard that the glen is beautiful
higher up."

" I was just going to propose it. That mare seems quiet enough—Lawler says that she has been carrying a lady these two years—will you try her ?"

" I am longing to do so. I am certain she is gentleness itself."

" Strange fellow that horse-dealer is, too," said the old gentleman, in half soliloquy. " In no other country in the universe would such a mere simpleton have taken to the trade of a jockey. He actually did not know what price to ask for his horse ; he left it all to ourselves. He'd soon finish his career in London, at that rate of going. But what have we got here ?—what, in Heaven's name, is all this ?" cried he aloud, as he suddenly rose from the table, and approached a small glass door that opened upon the lawn.

The object which so excited his astonishment was an assemblage of something more than a hundred poor people of every sex and age—from infancy to dotage—seated on the grass in a wide semicircle, and awaiting the moment when he should issue forth. Every phase of human misery which want and wretchedness can bestow was there. The cheeks of some were pale and haggard with recent sickness; others had but a few tattered rags to cover them; many were cripples, unable to move without assistance. There was wan and sickly childhood, and tremulous old age; yet the tone of their voices showed no touch of sadness ; they laughed and talked with all the seeming of light-heartedness; and many a droll and merry saying broke from that medley mass of suffering and sorrow. The sudden appearance of Sir Marmaduke at the door instantaneously checked all merriment, and a solemn silence ensued as he walked forth and stood in front of them.

" What do you want, my good people ?" said he at length, as none seemed disposed to open the proceedings.

Had their tongues been unlocked by the spell of a magician the effect could not have been more instantaneous—a perfect volley of speech succeeded in which Sir Marmaduke in vain endeavoured to follow the words of any single speaker. Their rapid utterance, their vehement gesticulation, and a certain guttural mode of pronunciation, quite new to him, made them totally unintelligible, and he stood confused, perplexed, and confounded, for several minutes, staring around on every side.

" Do, in Heaven's name, be quiet," cried he at last ; " let one or two only talk at a time, and I shall learn what you mean."

A renewal of the clamour ensued ; but this time it was a general effort to enforce silence—a process which eventuated in a far greater uproar than before.

" Who, or what are you ?" cried Sir Marmaduke, at last losing all temper at the continuance of a tumult there seemed no prospect of coming to an end.

" We're your honour's tenants, every one of us," shouted the crowd with one voice.

"*My* tenants !" reiterated he in horror and astonishment. "What ! is it possible that you are tenants on my property? Where do you live, my poor old man ?" said he, addressing a venerable old fellow, with a head as white as snow, aud a beard like a patriarch's.

" He does not talk any English, your honour's worship—he has only Irish ; he lives in the glen beyond," said a comely woman at his side.

"And you, where do you come from yourself ?"

"I'm a poor widow, your honour, with six childer ; and sorra bit I have but the little garden, and the grass of a goat; and sure, fifteen shillings every half-year is more nor I can pay, wid all the scrapin' in life."

Sir Marmaduke turned away his head, aud as he did so, his eye fell upon a poor creature, whose bloated cheeks and swollen figure denoted dropsy. The man interpreting the look into a compassionate inquiry, broke forth in a feeble voice, "I brought the nine shillings with me, yer honour; aud though the captain refused to take it, I'm sure you won't turn me out of the little place, for being a trifle late. It's the watery dropsy—glory be to God!—I'm under; but they say I'm getting better."

While the poor creature spoke, a low muttering of pity burst from those around him, and many a compassionate look, and many a cheering word, was expressed by those scarce less miserable than himself.

There was now a certain kind of order restored to the assembly ; and as Sir Marmaduke moved along the line, each in turn addressed his supplication or complaint. One was threatened with a distress on his pig, because he owed two half-years' rent, and could only pay a portion of the debt ; there was a failure in the potato crop, and a great famine the consequence. Another was only recovering from the "shaking ague," and begged for time, since if he thrashed his oats, now, they would bring nothing in the market. A third entreated liberty to cut his turf on a distant bog, as he was up to his knees in water in the place allotted to him.

Some came with odd shillings due on the last rent-day, and anxious to get leave to send their children to the school without payment.

Every one had some favour to look for—some mere trifle to the granter ; the whole world to him who asked—and, for these, many had come miles away from homes far in the mountains, a glimmering hope of succour the only encouragement to the weary journey.

As Sir Marmaduke listened with a feigned composure to narratives, at which his very heart bled, he chanced to observe a strange-looking figure, in an old scarlet uniform, and a paper cap, with a cock's feather stuck slant-wise in the side of it. The wearer, a tall, bony youth, with yellow hair, carried a long wattle over his shoulder, as if it were a gun, and when the old baronet's eye fell upon him, he immediately stood bolt upright, aud held the sapling to his breast, like a soldier presenting arms.

"Shoulder hoo !" he cried, and as the words were heard, a hearty burst of laughter ran through the crowd; every grief and sorrow was at once for gotten; the eyes wet with tears of sadness, were now moistened with those of mirth, and they laughed like those whose hearts had never known suffering.

"Who is this fellow?" said Sir Marmaduke, half doubting how far he might relish the jest like the others.

"Terry the Woods, your honour," replied a score of voices together.

"Terry the Woods!" repeated he, "and is Terry a tenant of mine?"

"Faix, I am proud to say I am not," said Terry, grounding his weapon, and advancing a step towards him; "divil a farthin' of rent I ever paid, nor ever will. I do have my health mighty well—glory be to God!—and sleep sound, and have good clothes, and do nothing for it; and they say I am a fool, but which of us is the greatest fool after all?"

Another outbreak of laughter was only quelled by Sir Marmaduke asking the reason of Terry's appearance there that morning, if he had nothing to look for.

"I just come to pay my respects," said Terry, composedly, "to wish you a welcome to the country. I thought that as you might be lading the same kind of life as myself, we wouldn't be bad companions, you see, neither of us having much on our hands; and then," continued he, as he took off his paper bonnet and made a deep reverence, "I wanted to see the young lady there, for they tould me she was a born beauty."

Miss Travers blushed—she was young enough to blush at a compliment from such a source, as her father said, laughingly,

"Well, Terry, and have they been deceiving you?"

"No," said he, gravely, as with steady gaze he fixed his large blue eyes on the fair features before him—"no—she is a purty crayture—a taste sorrowful or so—but I like her all the better. I was the same myself when I was younger."

Terry's remark was true enough. The young girl had been a listener for some time to the stories of the people, and her face betrayed the sad emotions of her heart. Never before had such scenes of human suffering been revealed before her—the tortuous windings of the poor man's destiny, where want and sickness lie in wait for those whose happiest hours are the struggles against poverty and its evils.

"I can show you the beautifullest places in the whole country," said Terry, approaching Miss Travers, and addressing her in a low voice; "I'll tell you where the white heath is growing, with big bells on it, like cups, to hould the dew. Were you ever up over Keim-an-eigh?"

"Never," said she, smiling at the eagerness of her questioner.

"I'll take you, then, by a short cut, and you can ride the whole way, and maybe we'll shoot an eagle. Have you a gun in the house?"

"Yes, there are three or four," said she, humouring him.

"And if I shoot him I'll give you the wing-feathers—that's what they always gave their sweethearts long ago; but them times is gone by."

The girl blushed deeply, as she remembered the present of young O'Donoghue, on the evening they came up the glen. She called to mind the air of diffidence and constraint in which he made the proffer, and for some minutes paid no attention to Terry, who still continued to talk as rapidly as before.

"There, they are filing off," said Terry—"orderly time," as he once more shouldered his sapling and stood erect. This observation was made with reference to the crowd of poor people, whose names and place of residence Sir Marmaduke having meanwhile written down, they were now returning to their homes with happy and comforted hearts. "There they go," cried Terry, "and an awkward squad they are."

"Were you ever a soldier, Terry?" said Miss Travers.

The poor youth grew deadly pale—the very blood forsook his lips, as he muttered, "I was." Sir Marmaduke came up at the instant, and Terry checked himself at once, and said,

"Whenever you want me, leave word at Mary M'Kelly's, in the glen below, and I'll hear of it."

"But don't you think you had better remain here with us? you could help in the garden and the walks."

"No; I never do be working at all—I hate work."

"Yes, but easy work, Terry," said Miss Travers, "among the flowers and shrubs here."

"No—I'd be quite low and sorrowful if I was to be staying in one place, and maybe—maybe"—here he whispered so low as only to be heard by her—"maybe they'd find me out."

"No; there's no fear of that," said she; "we'll take care no one shall trouble you—stay here, Terry."

"Well, I believe I will," said he, after a pause; "I may go away when I like."

"To be sure; and now let us see how you are to be lodged," said Sir Marmaduke, who already, interested by that inexplicable feeling which grows out of our pity for idiocy, entered into his daughter's schemes for poor Terry's welfare.

A small cottage near the boat-house on the verge of the lake, inhabited by a labourer and his children, offered the wished-for asylum, and there Terry was at once installed, and recognised as a member of the household.

CHAPTER VI.

"THE BLACK VALLEY."

ALTHOUGH deferred by the accidents of the morning, Sir Marmaduke's visit to the priest was not abandoned, and at length he and his daughter set out on their excursion up the glen. Their road, after pursuing the highway for about two miles, diverged into a narrow valley, from which there was no exit save by the mode in which it was entered. Vast masses of granite rock, piled heap above heap, hung as it were suspended over their heads, the tangled honeysuckle falling in rich festoons from these, and the purple arbutus glowing like grape-clusters among the leaves. It was a mellow, autumnal day, when the warmth of colouring is sobered down by massive shadows—the impress of the clouds which moved slowly above. The air was hot and thick, and, save when an occasional breeze came, wafted from the water, was even oppressive.

The silence of the glen was profound—not a bird was heard, nor was there in the vast expanse of air a single wing seen floating. As they rode, they often stopped to wonder at the strange but beautiful effects of light that glided now slowly along the mountains—disappeared—then shone again; the giant shadows seeming to chase each other through the dreary valley. Thus sauntering along, they took no note of time, when at last the long, low cottage, where the priest lived, came in sight. It was an humble abode, but beautifully situated at the bottom of the glen; the whole valley lying expanded in front, with its bright rivulet and its bold sides of granite. The cottage itself was little better than that of a poor farmer; and save from the ornament of some creepers, which were trained against the walls, and formed into a deep porch at the entrance, differed in no respect from such. A few straggling patches of cultivation, of the very rudest kind, were seen here and there, but all without any effort at fence or enclosure. Some wild fruit-trees were scattered over the little lawn in front, if the narrow strip of grass that flanked the river could be called such, and here a small Kerry cow was grazing, the only living thing to be seen.

A little well, arched over with pieces of rock, and surmounted by a small wooden cross, stood close to the roadside, and the wild-thorn that over-shadowed it was hung on every side with small patches of rags of every colour and texture that human dress ever consisted of; a sight new to the eyes of the travellers, who knew not that the shrine was deemed holy, and the tree the receptacle of the humble offering of those whose sorrows of mind and body came there for alleviation and succour.

Sir Marmaduke dismounted and approached the door, which lay wide open; he knocked gently with his whip, and as no answer to his summons was returned, repeated it again and again. He now ventured to call aloud, but no one came, and at last both father and daughter began to suspect there might be no one in the house.

"This is most strange," said he, after a long pause, and an effort to peep in through the windows, half hid with honeysuckle. "The place seems totally deserted. Let us try at the back, however."

As the old baronet wended his way to the rear of the cottage, he muttered a half upbraiding against his daughter for not complying with his desire to have a groom along with them—a want which now increased the inconvenience of their position. She laughingly defended herself against the charge, and at the same moment sprang down from her saddle to assist in the search.

"I certainly perceived some smoke from the chimney as we came up the glen, and there must have been some one here lately, at least," said she, looking eagerly on every side.

"This is indeed solitude," muttered her father, as he listened for some minutes, during which the stillness had an effect most appalling.

While he was speaking, Miss Travers had drawn near to a low latticed window which lay half open, and as she peeped in, immediately drew back, and beckoned with her hand for her father to approach, intimating by a cautious gesture that he should do so noiselessly. Sir Marmaduke came stealthily to her side, and, leaning over her shoulder, looked into the room. As both father and daughter exchanged glances, they seemed with difficulty to refrain from laughing, while astonishment was strongly depicted on the countenance of each. As they continued to gaze, their first emotion gradually yielded to a look of intense interest at the scene before them.

Seated beside the large turf fire of the priest's kitchen, for such it was, was a youth of some fifteen or sixteen years. His figure, light and well proportioned, was clad in a fashion which denoted his belonging to the better class, though neglect and time had made many an inroad on the costume. His brow was lofty and delicately formed—the temples marked with many a thin blue vein, which had given a look of delicacy to the countenance, if the deep glow of health had not lit up his cheeks, and imparted a bright lustre to his eyes. He held before him an open volume, from which he declaimed rather than read aloud, as it seemed, for the special delight and amusement of a small ragged urchin of about nine years old, who, with bare legs and feet, was seated on a little pyramid of turf right opposite to him.

Well might Sir Marmaduke and his daughter feel surprise; the volume was Homer, from which, with elevated voice and flashing eye, the boy was reading—the deep-toned syllables ringing through the low-vaulted chamber with a sweet but a solemn music. Contrasted with the fervid eloquence of the youth was the mute wonder and rapt attention of the little fellow who listened. Astonishment, awe, and eager curiosity, blended together in that poor little face, every lineament of which trembled with excitement. If a high soaring imagination and elevated tone of thought were depicted in the one, the other not less forcibly realised the mute and trembling eagerness of impassioned interest.

The youth paused for a few seconds, and seemed to be reflecting over what he read, when the boy, in an accent broken with anxiety, cried out,

" Read it again, Master Herbert. Oh, read it again. It's like the cry of the big stag-hound at Carrignacurra."

" It is the language of the gods, Mickey—finer and grander than ever man spoke," replied the youth, with fervour. " Listen to this, here." And then, with solemn cadence, he declaimed some twenty lines, while, as if the words were those of an incantation, the little fellow sat spell-bound, with clasped hands and staring eye-balls gazing before him.

" What does it mean, Master Herbert?—what is it?" said he, in panting eagerness.

" It's about a great hero, Mickey, that was preparing for battle. He was putting on his armour, a coat and a cap of steel, and he was belting on his sword."

" Yes, yes," broke in the little fellow, " and wasn't he saying how he'd murther and kill all before him?"

" Right enough," said the youth, laughing. " You guessed it well."

" Ah, I knew it," said the boy. " I saw how you clenched your fist, and your eyes wor shinin' like sparks of fire, and I knew it was darin' them he was, in the book there. What did he do after, Master Herbert? Just tell me that, sir."

" He went out in his chariot——"

" Say it like himself first, sir, av it's plazin' to ye," said he, with a most imploring look of entreaty. " I do be glad to hear it out of the book."

The youth, thus entreated, resumed the volume, and read on for several minutes without stopping.

" Oh, that's grand!" said the boy, in a burst of enthusiasm. " 'Tis for all the world the way the thunder comes down the glen—moanin' first, far off on the mountains, and then swellin' into a big roar, and afterwards goin' clap! clap! like a giant-clapping his hands. Did he kill the inimy, master dear?"

" No, he was killed himself, and his body dragged over the battle-field."

" Wirra, wirra, wirra!" broke in the child, while he wrung his hands, and burst forth into a torrent of tumultuous grief.

" He was killed, Mickey, and listen to the lament of his friends for his death."

Scarcely had the youth read a few lines, when Sir Marmaduke, advancing a little farther, his shadow fell across the chamber. The youth sprang up at once, and came towards them. The flush of surprise—it might be, too, of shame—was on his features; but there was less of awkwardness than many might have exhibited in the manner of his address, as he said,

"Father Luke is from home, sir. He has been sent for to Bally-vourney——"

" You are his relation, I presume ?" said Sir Marmaduke, without letting him finish his speech.

" I am his pupil," replied the youth, with a tone in which offended pride was clearly confessed.

" I ask pardon," said the baronet, hastily. " It was merely that I might convey my respectful greetings to the worthy father that I asked the question. Perhaps you will allow me to trespass so far upon you, and say that Sir Marmaduke Travers has been here."

While Sir Marmaduke was speaking, the youth's eyes were fixed with a steadfast gaze on the features of the young girl, of whose presence till then he seemed unconscious. Fixed and earnest as his stare was, there was nothing in it of rudeness, still less of insult. It was the unequivocal expression of astonishment, the suddenly-awakened sense of admiration in one, on whom, till that very instant, beauty had shed no fascination. His eyes were bent upon her, as Sir Marmaduke thus finished speaking, and the old man smiled as he saw the wonder-struck admiration of the boy.

" You will please to say Sir Marmaduke Travers," repeated he once more, to recal the scattered senses of the youth.

" And his daughter ?" murmured the other, as he still continued to stare at her.

" Yes, his daughter," replied Sir Marmaduke, smiling. " May I ask if there be no shorter road back to 'the Lodge,' than that yonder ? for I perceive it is full two hours later than I suspected."

" None for those on horseback. The mountain path lies yonder, but even on foot it is not without danger."

" Come, then, Sybella; let us lose no time. We must ride briskly, to reach home by daylight. We are late enough already."

" Too late, if you ride not very fast," replied the youth. " The rain has fallen heavily on the mountains this afternoon. See that waterfall yonder. I crossed it dryshod at daybreak, and now it is a cataract. This river rises rapidly, and in a single night's rain I have seen the valley all one lake."

" What are we to do then ?" cried Miss Travers, eagerly, for now she felt self-reproach at her refusal to take a groom along with them, and was vexed with herself, as well as uneasy for her father.

"Keep the left of the valley till you reach the tall black rock they call 'the Pulpit'—you know it, at least you must have seen it as you came along—then cross the stream, it will be fordable enough by that time, and make the best of your way along under the cliffs till you arrive at the broken bridge—the two buttresses, I mean. Re-cross the stream there, and gain the meadows, and in some hundred yards you are safe upon the high road. Away then; lose no more time, now; a minute is all the space between risk and safety." And with these words he sprang forward and lifted the young girl to her saddle, ere she had time or forethought to decline the service.

"May we not know the name of our kind adviser?" asked Sir Marmaduke, as he mounted his horse.

"Hark! there it comes!" cried the youth, pointing upwards to the brow of a cliff, over which a leaping torrent had just bounded. "The mountain lakes are flooded when Derrybahn is spouting. Away! away! if you care for safety."

They turned their horses' heads as he spoke, and with a hasty "good-by" they spurred forwards. Short as the time had been since they travelled the same path, the scene was wonderfully changed; the placid stream that stole along, murmuring over its gravelly bed, now rushed onward with a yellow current streaked with white foam; the tiny rivulets that came in slender drops upon the roadside, were now become continuous streams of water, hurrying on to bear their tribute to the river. The sky itself was black and louring, resting midway on the mountains, or drifting past in heavy clouds, while no breeze was stirring below. The many torrents as they fell filled the air with a low monotonous sound, like the noise of tree-teps moved by a distant storm.

"I thought I heard a voice calling to us," said Sir Marmaduke, as for the first time they slackened their pace, to clear several loose stones that obstructed the way; "did you hear it?"

"I half thought so too," replied his daughter; "but I can see no one near. There it is again!"

They halted and listened; but the swelling uproar of the waterfalls drowned every sound, and they spurred forward once more, fearing to loiter longer; yet both as they went thought they could trace the words "Come back! come back!" but from some strange dread of communicating fears that might not be real, neither told the other.

"He said the left side of the valley; but surely he mistook: see how the water has gained here, and the opposite bank seems dry."

"Let us follow the advice, father," cried Sybella; "we have no guidance save his; he could not—would not deceive us. Is it not grand! With all its danger, I can admire it."

As she spoke, a tremendous clap of thunder broke above their heads, and made the valley tremble with the sound, while, as if by the shock, the charged clouds were rent open, and the rain descended in torrents. With the swooping gush of the ocean spray, storm-lashed and drifted, the rain came down, wrapping in misty darkness every object around them. And now the swollen cataracts tore madly down the mountain sides, leaping from crag to crag, and rending the clayey soil in deep clefts and gashes. Again the thunder pealed out, and every echo sent back the sound, till the whole glen vibrated with the deafening clamour. Still they sped onward. The terrified horses strained every limb, and dashing madly on, mid rock and rushing water they went, now clearing at a bound the course of some gushing stream, now breasting the beating rain with vigorous chest.

The storm increased; the howling wind joined with the deep-toned thunder into one long continuous roar, that seemed to shake the very air itself.

" Yonder !" said the father, as he pointed to the tall dark pinnacle of rock known by the country people as " the Pulpit"—" yonder !"

Sybella strained her eye to see through the dense beating rain, and at last caught sight of the huge mass, around whose summit the charged clouds were flying.

" We must cross the river in this place," said the old man, as he suddenly checked his horse, and looked with terrified gaze on the swollen stream that came boiling and foaming over to where they stood, with branches of trees and fragments of rock rolling onward in the tide. " The youth told us of this spot."

" Let us not hesitate, father," cried the young girl, with a tone of firm, resolute daring she had not used before; " remember what he said, a minute may save or ruin us. Great Heaven! what is that?"

A terrific shriek followed her words, and she fell with her head upon her horse's mane: a broad flash of lightning had burst from a dark cloud, and came with vivid force upon her eyeballs.

" Father, dear father, my sight is gone !" she screamed aloud, as lifting up her head she rubbed the orbs now paralysed by the shock.

" My child ! my child !" cried the old man, with the piercing shriek of a breaking heart ; "look on me, look towards me. Oh, say that you can see me now—my brain is turning."

" Oh God, I thank thee !" said the terrified girl, as once more her vision was restored, and, dimly, objects began to form themselves before her.

With bare head and upturned eyes the aged man looked up, and poured forth his prayer of thankfulness to Heaven. The raging storm beat on his brow unfelt; his thoughts were soaring to the Throne of Mercies, and knew not earth, nor all its sorrows.

A clap of thunder at the moment broke from the dense cloud above them, and then, in quick succession, like the pealing of artillery, came several more, while the forked lightning shot to and fro, and at last, as if the very earth was riven to its centre, a low, booming sound was heard amid the clouds; the darkness grew thicker, and a crash followed that shook the ground beneath them, and splashed the wild waves on every side. The spray sprang madly up, while the roaring of the stream grew louder; the clouds swept past, and the tall Pulpit rock was gone! Struck by lightning, it had rolled from its centre, and fallen across the river, the gushing waters of which poured over it in floods, and fell in white sheets of foam and spray beyond it.

"God is near us, my child," said the old man, with fervour; "let us onward."

Her streaming eyes turned on him one look of affection—the emblem of a heart's love—and she prepared to follow.

To return was now impossible; the river had already extended the whole way across the valley in the rear; the only chance of safety lay in front.

"Keep by my side, dearest," said the father, as he rode first into the stream, and tried to head the terrified animal against the current.

"I am near you, father—fear not for me," said she, firmly, her bold heart nerved to the danger.

For some seconds the affrighted horses seemed rooted to the earth, and stood amid the boiling current as if spell-bound. A fragment of a tree, however, in its course, struck the flank of the leading horse, and he sprang madly forward, followed by the other. Now breasting the stream, now sinking to the mane beneath it, the noble beasts struggled fiercely on till near the spot where the Pulpit rock had left a space between it and the opposite bank, and here a vast volume of water now poured along unchecked by any barrier.

"To my side—near me, dearest—near me!" cried the father, as his horse dashed into the seething flood, and sank above the crest beneath it.

"I cannot, father—I cannot!" screamed the affrighted girl, as, with a bound of terror, her horse sprang back from the chasm, and refused to follow. The old man heard not the words—the current had swept him far down into the stream, amid the rent branches and the rolling rocks—"My child! my child!" the only accents heard above the raging din.

Twice did the heroic girl try to face the current, but in vain—the horse plunged wildly up, and threatened to fall back, when suddenly through the white foam a figure struggled on and grasped the bridle at the head;

next moment, a man leaped forward and was breasting the surge before her.

"Head the stream—head the stream, if you can !" cried he, who still held on, while the wild waves washed over him. But the poor horse, rendered unmanageable through fear, had yielded to the current, and was now each moment nearing the cataract.

"Cling to me, now !" cried the youth, as, with the strength of desperation, he tore the girl from the saddle, while with the other hand he grasped an ash bough that hung drooping above his head. As he did so, the mare bounded forward—the waves closed over her, and she was carried over the precipice.

"Cling fast to me, and we are safe !" cried the youth ; and with vigorous grasp he held on the tree, and, thus supported, breasted the stream and reached the bank. Exhausted and worn out, both mind and body powerless, they both fell senseless on the grass.

The last shriek of despair broke from the father's heart as the horse, bereft of rider, swept past him in the flood. The cry aroused the fainting girl ; she half rose to her feet, and called upon him. The next moment they were locked in each other's arms.

"It was he who saved me, father," said she, in accents broken with joy and sorrow ; "he risked his life for mine."

The youth recovered consciousness as the old man pressed him to his heart.

"Is she safe?" were the first words he said, as he stared around him vaguely ; and then, as if overcome, he fell heavily back upon the sward.

A joyous cheer broke forth from several voices near, and, at the instant, several country people were seen coming forward, with Terry at their head.

"Here we are—here we are, and in good time, too," cried Terry ; "and if it wasn't that you took a fool's advice, we'd have gone the other road. The carriage is in the glen, my lady," said he, kneeling down beside Sybella, who still remained clasped in her father's arms.

By this time some of Sir Marmaduke's servants had reached the spot, and by them the old man and his daughter were assisted towards the high road, while two others carried the poor youth, by this time totally unable to make the least exertion.

"This brave boy—this noble fellow," said Sir Marmaduke, as he stooped to kiss the pale high forehead, from which the wet hair hung backwards— "can no one tell me who he is ?"

"He's the young O'Donoghue," replied a half dozen voices together ; "a good warrant for courage or bravery any day."

"The O'Donoghue !" repeated Sir Marmaduke, vainly endeavouring in the confusion of the moment to recal the name, and where he had heard it.

"Ay, the O'Donoghue," shouted a coarse voice near him, as a new figure rode up on a small mountain pony. "It oughtn't to be a strange name in these parts. Rouse yourself, Master Herbert, rouse up, my child—sure it isn't a wettin' would cow you this way?"

"What! Kerry; is this you?" said the youth faintly, as he looked around him with half-closed eyelids. "Where's my father?"

"Faix, he's snug at the parlour fire, my darlin', where his son ought to be, if he wasn't turning guide on the mountains to the enemy of his kith and kin."

These words were said in a whisper, but with an energy that made the boy start from the arms of those who bore him.

"Here's the pony, Master Herbert—get up on him, and be off at once; sure there isn't a blackguard there, with lace on his coat, wouldn't be laughing at your old clothes when the light comes."

Sir Marmaduke and his daughter were a few paces in advance as these words were spoken, the old baronet giving directions for bestowing every care and attention on one he deemed his guest.

The boy, ashamed and offended both, yielded to the counsel, and suffered himself to be placed upon the saddle.

"Now then, hould fast, and I'll guide him," said Kerry, as elbowing the crowd right and left, he sprang forward at a run, and in less than a minute had disappeared in the darkness.

Sir Marmaduke became distracted at the loss of his benefactor, and message after message was despatched to bring him back, but all in vain. Kerry and his pony had already gained so much in advance none could overtake them.

"To-morrow, then, my child," said Sir Marmaduke—"to-morrow will, I hope, enable me to speak my gratitude, though I shall not sleep well tonight. I never rested with so heavy a debt unpaid before."

And with these words they slowly wended their way homeward.

CHAPTER VII.

SIR ARCHY'S TEMPER TRIED.

It was strange that, although the old man and his tender daughter should have sustained no other ill results from their adventure than the terror which even yet dwelt on their minds, the young and vigorous youth, well trained to every accident of flood or field, felt it most seriously.

The exertions he made to overtake Sir Marmaduke and his daughter, followed by the struggle in the swollen stream, had given such a shock to his frame, that ere day broke the following morning he was in a fever. The mental excitement, conspiring with fatigue and exhaustion, had brought on the symptoms of his malady with such rapidity that it was evident, even to the unaccustomed observers around him, his state was precarious.

Sir Archibald was the first person at the sick youth's bedside. The varied fortunes of a long life, not devoid of its own share of vicissitude, had taught him so much of medical skill as can give warning of the approach of fever; and as he felt the strong and frequent pulse, and saw the flushed and almost swollen features before him, he recognised the commencement of severe and dangerous illness.

Vague and confused images of the previous night's adventure, or visions of the dark valley and the tempest, occupied all the boy's thoughts; and though he endeavoured, when spoken to, to preserve coherency and memory, the struggle was unavailing, and the immediate impression of a question past, his mind wandered back to the theme which filled his brain.

"How was it, then?" said Sir Archy, who, as he sat beside the sick-bed, questioned the youth about his adventure. "You said something of a horse?"

"Yes; she was riding. Oh, how bravely she rode too! It was fine to see her as the spray fell over her like a veil, and she shook the drops from her hair."

"Whence came she? Who was the lady?"

"Take care—take care," said the youth, in a solemn whisper, and with a steadfast look before him; "Derrybahn has given warning—the storm is coming. It is not for one so tender as you to tempt the river of the black valley."

"Be still, my boy," said the old man; "you must not speak thus; your head will ache if you take not rest—keep quiet."

"Yes; my head, my head!" muttered he vaguely, repeating the words which clinked upon his mind. "She put her arm round my neck——There—there," cried he, starting up wildly in his bed, "catch it—seize it—my feet are slipping—the rock moves—I can hold no longer; there—there!" And with a low moaning sigh he sank back fainting on the pillow.

Sir Archibald applied all his efforts to enforce repose and rest; and having partially succeeded, hastened to the O'Donoghue's chamber, to confer with the boy's father on what steps should be taken to procure medical aid.

It was yet some hours earlier than the accustomed time of his waking, as the old man saw the thin and haggard face of Sir Archy peering between the curtains of his bed.

"Well, what is it?" said he, in some alarm at the unexpected sight.

"Has Gubbins issued the distress? Are the scoundrels going to sell us out?"

"No, no; it is another matter brings me here," replied M'Nab, with a gravity even deeper than usual.

"That infernal bond! By God, I knew it; it never left my dreams these last three nights. Mark was too late, I suppose; or they wouldn't take the interest. And the poor fellow sold his mare to get the money!"

"Dinna fash about these things now," said M'Nab, with impatience. "It's that poor callant, Herbert—he's very ill—it's a fever he's caught, I'm thinking."

"Oh, Herbert!" said O'Donoghue, with a tone of evident relief that his misfortunes had taken any other shape than the much-dreaded one of money-calamity. "What of him?"

"He's in a fever; his mind is wandering already."

"Not a bit of it; it's a mere wetting—a common cold: the boy fell into the river last night at the old bridge there; Kerry told me something about it; and so, maybe, Mark may reach Cork in good time after all."

"I am no speaking of Mark just now," said M'Nab, tartly, "but of the other lad, wha may be dangerously ill, if something be nae done quickly."

"Then send for Roach. Let one of the boys saddle a horse and ride over to Killarney. Oh! I was forgetting; let a fellow go off on foot, he'll get there before evening. It is confoundedly hard to have nothing in the stables even to mount a messenger. I hope Mark may be able to manage matters in Cork. Poor fellow, he hates business as much as I do myself."

Sir Archy did not wait for the conclusion of this rambling reply. Long before it was over, he was half way down stairs in search of a safe messenger to despatch to Killarney for Doctor Roach, muttering between his teeth as he went,

"We hae nae muckle chance of the docter if we canna send the siller to fetch him as well as the flunkie—eh, sirs? He's a cannie chiel is auld Roach, and can smell a fee as soon as scent a fever." And with this sensible reflection he proceeded on his way.

Meanwhile the O'Donoghue himself had summoned energy enough to slip on an old and ragged dressing-gown, and a pair of very unlocomotive slippers, with which attired he entered the sick boy's room.

"Well, Herbert, lad," said he, drawing the curtains back, and suffering the grey light to fall on the youth's features, "what is the matter? Your uncle has been routing me up with a story about you."

He ceased suddenly, as his eyes beheld the change a few hours had wrought in the boy's appearance. His eyes, deep-buried in their orbits, shone with an unnatural lustre; his cheeks were pale and sunken, save where a bright patch of florid red marked the centre of each; his lips were

dry and shrivelled, and had a slight tremulous motion, as if he were muttering to himself.

"Poor fellow," said the father, "how dreadful ill he looks. Have you
any pain, my boy?"

The boy knew the voice, and recognised the kindly accent, but could not
hear or understand the words; and, as his eyes glistened with delight, he
stole his burning hand from beneath the bedclothes, and held it out, all
trembling, towards his father.

"How sudden this has been—you were quite well last night, Herbert."

"Last night!" echoed the boy, with a strange emphasis on the only words
he had caught up.

"No, by the way, it was the night before, I mean. I did not see you last
night; but, cheer up, my dear boy; we've sent for Roach—he'll put you to
rights at once. I hope Mark may reach home before the doctor goes. I'd
like to have his advice about that strain in the back."

These last words were uttered in soliloquy, and seemed to flow from a
train of thought very different from that arising from the object before him.
Sunk in these reflections, he drew near the window, which looked out upon
the old court-yard behind the house, and where now a very considerable
crowd of beggars had assembled to collect the alms usually distributed each
morning from the kitchen. Each was provided with an ample canvas bag,
worn over the neck by a string, and capable of containing a sufficiency of
meal or potatoes, the habitual offering, to support the owner for a couple of
days at least. They were all busily engaged in stowing away the provender
of various sorts and kinds, as luck, or the preference of the cook, decided
laughing or grumbling over their portions, as it might be, when Sir
Archibald M'Nab hurriedly presented himself in the midst of them—an
appearance which seemed to create no particular satisfaction, if one were to
judge from the increased alacrity of their movements, and the evident desire
they exhibited to move off.

The O'Donoghue laughed as he witnessed the discomfiture of the ragged
mob, and let down the window-sash to watch the scene.

"'Tis going we are. God be good to us!"

"Ye needn't be cursing that way," said an old hag, with a sack on her
back large enough to contain a child.

"Eyah! the Lord look down on the poor!" said a little fat fellow, with
a flannel nightcap and stockings without any feet; "there's no pity now
at all, at all."

"The heavens be your bed, any way," said a hard-featured little woman,
with an accent that gave the blessing a very different signification from the
mere words.

"Blessed Joseph! sure it isn't robbers and thieves we are, that ye need
hunt us out of the place."

Such were the exclamations on every side, intermingled with an under-growl of the " Scotch naygur !"—" The ould scrape-gut !" and other equally polite and flattering epithets.

" This is no a place for ye, ye auld beldames and blackguards. Awa' wi' ye—awa' wi' ye at once !"

" Them's the words ye'll hear in heaven yet, darlint !" said an old fiend of a woman, with one eye, and a mouth garnished by a single tooth. " Them's the very words St. Peter will spake to yourself."

" Begorra ! he'll not be strange in the other place, anyhow," muttered another. " 'Tis there he'll meet most of his countrymen."

This speech was the signal for a general outburst of laughter.

" Awa' wi' ye, ye ragged deevils !—ye'r a disgrace to a Christian country !"

" Throth, we wear breeches an us," said an old fellow on crutches ; " and sure I hear that's more nor they do in the parts your honour comes from."

Sir Archy's passion boiled over at this new indignity. He stormed and swore, with all the impetuous rage of one beside himself with passion ; but the effect on his hearers was totally lost. The only notice they took was an occasional exclamation of,

" There it is, now !"   " Oh, blessed Father ! hear what he says !"   " Oh, holy Mother ! isn't he a terrible man ?"—comments by no means judiciously adapted to calm his irritation. Meanwhile, symptoms of evacuating the territory were sufficiently evident. Cripples were taken on the backs and shoulders of their respective friends ; sacks and ponches were slung over the necks. Many a preparatory shake of the rags showed that the wearer was getting ready for the road, when Sir Archy, suddenly checking himself in the full torrent of his wrath, cried out,

" Bide a wee—stay a minit, ye auld beasties—I hae a word to say to some amang ye."

The altered tone of voice in which he spoke seemed at once to have changed the whole current of popular feeling ; for now they all chimed in with,

" Arrah ! he's a good man after all. Sure, 'tis only a way he has,"—sentiments which increased in fervency as Sir Archibald took a tolerably well-filled purse from his pocket, and drew out some silver into his hand, many exclaiming,

" 'Tis the kind heart often has the hard word ; and sure ye can see in his face he isn't cruel."

" Hear till me," cried Sir Archy, aloud, as he held up a shilling before their wistful eyes, " there's mony a ane among ye able to earn siller. Which o' ye, now, will step down to Killarney, and tell the docter he's wanted up here wi' a' despatch ? Ye mann go fast and bring him, or send him here to-night ; and if ye do, I'll gie ye this piece o' siller money when ye come back."

A general groan from that class whose age and infirmities placed them out of the reach of competitorship met this speech, while from the more able section a not less unequivocal expression of discontent broke forth.

"Down to Killarney!" cried one. "Begorra! I wonder ye didn't say Kenmare, when ye war about it—the devil a less than ten miles it is."

"Eyah! I'll like to see my own four bones going the same road; sorra a house the whole way where there's a drop of milk or a pratie."

"That's the charity to the poor, I suppose," said the fat fellow of the nightcap. "'Tis wishing it, I am, the same charity."

"We wor to bring the doctor on our back, I hope," said a cripple in a bowl.

"Did ever man hear or see the like o' this?" exclaimed M'Nab, as with uplifted hands he stared in wonderment around him. "One would na believe it."

"True for you, honey," joined in one of the group. "I'm fifty-three years on the road, and I never heerd of any one askin' us to do a hand's turn afore."

"Out of my sight, ye worthless ne'er-do-weels; awa' wi' ye at once and for ever. I'll send twenty miles round the country but I'll hae a mastiff here 'ill worry the first o' ye that dares to come near the house."

"On my conscience, it will push you hard to find a wickeder baste nor yourself."

"Begorra, he won't be uglier, anyhow."

And with these comments, and the hearty laughter that followed, the tattered and ragged group defiled out of the yard with all the honours of war, leaving Sir Archy alone, overwhelmed with astonishment and anger.

A low chuckling laugh, as the sash was closed overhead, made him look up, and he just caught a glimpse of O'Donoghue as he retired from the window; for in his amusement at the scene the old man forgot the sick boy and all about him, and only thought of the ridiculous interview he had witnessed.

"His ain father—his ain father!" muttered Sir Archy, as with his brows contracted and his hands clasped behind his back, he ruminated in sadness on all he saw. "What brings ye back again, ye lazy scoundrels? How dare ye venture in here again?"

This not over-courteous interrogatory was addressed to poor Terry the Woods, who, followed by one of Sir Marmaduke's footmen, had at that instant entered the yard.

"What for are ye come, I say? and what's the flunkie wanting beside ye?"

Terry stood thunderstruck at the sudden outbreak of temper, and turned at once to the responsible individual, to whom he merely acted as guide, to make a reply.

" And ale ye tramping it too ?" said M'Nab, with a sneering accent as he addressed the footman. " Methinks ye might hae a meal's meat out o' the goold lace on your hat, and look mair like a decent Christian afterwards. Ye'r out of place, maybe."

These last words were delivered in an irony to which a tone of incredulity gave all the sting ; and these only were intelligible to the sleek and well-fed individual to whom they were addressed.

In all likelihood, had he been charged with felony or highway robbery, his self-respect might have sustained his equanimity ; any common infraction of the statute-law might have been alleged against him without exciting an un-due indignation ; but the contemptuous insinuation of being " out of place" —that domestic outlawry—was more than human endurance could stomach ; nor was the insult more palatable coming from one he believed to be a servant himself. It was therefore with the true feeling of outraged dignity he replied,

" Not exactly out of place jest now, friend ; though, if they don't treat you better than your looks show, I'd recommend you trying for a new situation."

Of a verity, Sir Archibald's temper was destined to sore trials that morn-ing ; but this was a home thrust, for which no forethought could have pre-pared him.

" I hope I am no going to lose my senses," said he, as he pressed his hands on either side of his temples. " May the Lord keep me from that worst of a' human calamities."

This pious wish, uttered with real, unfeigned fervency, seemed to act like a charm upon the old man's temper, as though the very appeal had suggested a calmer and more patient frame of mind. It was, then, with all the dignity of his natural character, when unclouded by momentary flashes of passion, that he said,

" What may be your errand here this morning ?"

Few and simple as the words were, there was that in their quiet, unassu-ming delivery, which in a second recalled the footman to a full conscious-ness of his impertinent mistake. He saw at once the immeasurable gulph, impassable to any effort of assumption or insolence, which separated them, and with the ready tact of his calling he respectfully took off his hat, and held forth a sealed letter, without one word of reply or apology.

Sir Archibald put on his spectacles, and having carefully read the super-scription, turned back towards the house without speaking.

" Here is a letter for you, O'Donoghue," said he, as he entered the par-lour, where the chief was already seated at his breakfast, while Kerry O'Leary, a short distance behind his chair, was relating the circumstance of the last night's adventure.

" Is it from Mark ?" said the old man, eagerly ; and then glancing at the writing, he threw it from him in disappointment, and added, "I am getting very uneasy about that lad."

"Had ye no better read the letter? the messenger wha brought it seems to expect an answer," interposed M'Nab.

"Messenger!—eh—not by post? Is Hemsworth come back?" exclaimed O'Donoghue, with an evident degree of fear in his manner.

"No, sir," said Kerry, guessing to what topic his master's thoughts were turning; "the captain is not coming, they say, for a month or six weeks yet."

"Thank God!" muttered O'Donoghue; "that scoundrel never leaves me a night's rest when I hear he's in the neighbourhood. Will you see what's in it, Archy? My head is quite confused this morning; I got up three hours before my time."

Sir Archibald resumed his spectacles, and broke the seal. The contents were at some length it would seem, for as he perused the letter to himself several minutes elapsed.

"Go on, Kerry," said O'Donoghue; "I want to hear all about this business."

"Well, I believe your honour knows the most of it now; for when I came up to the glen they were all safe over, barrin' the mare; poor Kittane, she was carried down the falls, and they took her up near a mile below the old bridge, stone dead; Master Mark will fret his heart out when he hears it."

"This is a very polite note," interposed Sir Archy, as he laid the letter open before him, "from Sir Marmaduke Travers, begging to know when he may be permitted to pay his personal respects to you, and express his deep and grateful sense—his own words—of your son's noble conduct in rescuing his daughter at the hazard of his life. It is written with much modesty and good sense, and the writer canna be other than a true gentleman."

"Travers—Travers," repeated O'Donoghue; "why that's the man himself. It was he bought the estate; he's Hemsworth's principal."

"And if he be," replied M'Nab, "canna an honest man hae a bad servant? There's nothing about Hemsworth here. It's a ceevil demand from one gentleman to anither."

"So it is, then, Sir Marmadude that has been staying at the lodge these some weeks past. That was Mark's secret—poor dear boy, he wouldn't tell me, fearing it would annoy me. Well, what is it he wants?"

"To visit you, O'Donoghue."

"What nonsense; the mischief's done already. The mortgage is foreclosed; and as for Carrignacurra, they can do nothing before the next term; Swaby says so, at least."

"Can ye no comprehend? It is no law document, but a ceevil way to make your acquaintance. Sir Marmaduke wad pay his respects to ye."

" Well, let him come," said O'Donoghue, laughing ; " he's sure to find me at home. The sheriff takes care of that for him. Mark will be here to-morrow or next day; I hope he won't come before that."

" The answer must be a written one," said M'Nab ; " it wad na be polite to gie the flunkie the response."

" With all my heart, Archy, so that I am not asked to indite it. Miles O'Donoghue are the only words I have written for many a year;" and he added, with a half bitter laugh, " it would have been as well for poor Mark if I had forgotten even that same."

Sir Archibald retired to write the answer, with many a misgiving as to the substance of the epistle; for while deeply gratified at heart that his favourite, Herbert, had acquitted himself so nobly, his own pride was mortified, as he thought over the impressions a visit to the O'Donoghue household might have on the mind of a " haughty Southern," for such in his soul he believed him.

There was no help for it, however; the advances were made in a spirit so very respectful, every line breathed such an evident desire, on the writer's part, to be well received, that a refusal, or even a formal acceptance of the proffered visit, was out of the question. His reply, then, accepted the intended honour with a profession of satisfaction; apologising for his omission in calling on Sir Marmaduke, on the score of ill-health, and concluded by a few words about Herbert, for whom many inquiries were made in the letter. This, written in the clear, but quaint old-fashioned characters of the writer's time, and signed " O'Donoghue," was carefully folded, and enclosed in a large square envelope, and with it in his hand M'Nab re-entered the breakfast-room.

" Wad you like to hear the terms of the response, O'Donoghue, before I seal it up ?" asked Sir Archy, with an air of importance.

" No, no; I am sure it is all right and proper. You mentioned, of course, that Mark was from home, but we were expecting him back every day."

" I didna make ony remark o' that kind. I said ye wad be happy to see him, and felt proud at the honour of making acquaintance wi' him."

" Damn me if I do, then, Archy," broke in the old man, roughly. " For so great a stickler for truth as yourself, the words were somewhat out of place. I neither feel pride nor honour on the subject. Let it go, however, and there's an end to it."

" I've despatched a messenger for Roach to Killarney; that bit of a brainless body, Terry, is gone by the mountain road, and we may expect the docter here to-night." And with these words Sir Archy departed to send off his epistle, and the O'Donoghue leaned back in his easy-chair, sorely wearied and worried by the fatigues of the day.

CHAPTER VIII.

THE HOUSE OF SICKNESS.

How painfully is the sense of severe illness diffused through every part of a household. How solemn is the influence it sheds on every individual, and every object; the noiseless step, the whispered words, the closed curtains, the interruption to the ordinary avocations of life, or the performance of them in gloom and sadness. When wealth and its appliances exist, these things take all the features of extreme care and solicitude for the sufferer ; all the agencies of kindness and skill are brought into active exertion to minister to the rich man in sickness ; but when poverty and its evils are present—when the struggle is against the pressure of want, as well as the sufferings of malady, the picture is indeed a dark one.

The many deficiencies in comfort which daily habit has learned to overlook, the privations which in the active conflict with the world are forgotten, now come forth in the solitude of the sick-house to affright and afflict us, and we sorrow over miseries long lost to memory till now.

Never since the fatal illness which left O'Donoghue a widower had there been anything like dangerous sickness in the house ; and like most people who have long enjoyed the blessings of uninterrupted health, they had no thought for such a calamity, nor deemed it among the contingencies of life. Now, however, the whole household felt the change. The riotous laughter of the kitchen was silenced, the loud speaking hushed, the doors, banged by the wind, or the ruder violence of careless hands, were closed noiselessly— everything betokened that sorrow was there. O'Donoghue himself paced to and fro in the chamber of the old tower, now stopping to cast a glance down the glen, where he still hoped to see Mark approaching, now resuming his melancholy walk in sadness of heart.

In the darkened sick-room, and by the bed, sat Sir Archibald, concealed by the curtain, but near enough to give assistance to the sick boy should he need it. He sat buried in his own gloomy thoughts, rendered gloomier as he listened to the hurried breathings and low mutterings of the youth, whose fever continued to increase upon him. The old ill-tempered cook, whose tongue was the terror of the region she dwelt in, sat smoking by the fire, nor noticed the presence of the aged foxhound, who had followed Kerry into the kitchen, and now lay asleep before the fire. Kerry himself ceased to hum the snatches of songs and ballads by which he was accustomed to beguile the weary day. There was a gloom on everything, nor was the aspect without doors more cheering. The rain beat heavily in drifts against the windows; the wind shook the old trees violently, and tossed their gnarled limbs in wild confusion, sighing with mournful cadence along the deep glen, or pouring a long melancholy note through the narrow corridors of the old house. The sound of the storm, made more audible by the dreary silence, seemed to weigh down every heart. Even the bare-legged little gossoon, Mickey, who had come over from Father Luke's with a message, sat mute and sad, and as he moved his naked foot among the white turf ashes, seemed to feel the mournful depression of the hour.

" 'Tis a dreadful day of rain, glory be to God !" said Kerry, as he drew a fragment of an old much-soiled newspaper from his pocket, and took his seat beside the blazing fire. For some time he persevered in his occupation without interruption; but Mrs. Branaghan having apparently exhausted her own reflections, now turned upon him to supply a new batch.

" What's in the news, Kerry O'Leary ? I think ye might as well read it out, as be mumbling it to yourself there," said she, in a tone seldom disputed in the realm she ruled.

" Musha, then," said Kerry, scratching his head, " the little print bates me entirely; the letters do be so close, they haven't room to stir in, and my eyes is always going to the line above and the line below, and can't keep straight in the furrow at all. Come here, Mickey, alanah ! 'tis you ought to be a great scholar, living in the house with his reverence. They tell me," continued he, in a whisper to the cook—"they tell me, he can sarve mass already."

Mrs. Branaghan withdrew her dudeen at these words, and gazed at the little fellow with unmixed astonishment, who, in obedience to the summons, took his place beside Kerry's chair, and prepared to commence his task.

" Where will I begin, sir ?"

" Begin at the news, av coorse," said Kerry, somewhat puzzled to decide what kind of intelligence he most desired. " What's this here with a large P in the first of it ?"

" Prosperity of Ireland, sir," said the child.

" Ay, read about that, Mickey," said the cook, resuming her pipe.

With a sing-song intonation, which neither regarded paragraph nor period, but held on equably throughout a column, the little fellow began :

" The prospect of an abundant harvest is now very general throughout the country; and should we have a continuance of the heavenly weather for a week or so longer, we hope the corn will all be saved."

As the allusion made here by the journalist was to a period of several years previous, the listeners might be excused for not feeling a perfect concurrence in the statement.

" Heavenly weather, indeed !" grunted out the cook, as she turned her eyes towards the windows, against which the plashing rain was beating. " Mike, read on."

" Mr. Foran was stopped last night in Baggot-street, and robbed of his watch and clothes, by four villains who live in Stoney-batter; they are well known, and are advised to take care, as such depredations cannot go long unpunished.—The two villains that broke into the house of the Archbishop of Dublin, and murdered the housemaid, will be turned off 'Lord Temple's trap' on Saturday next; this will be a lesson to the people about the Cross-Poddle, that we hope may serve to their advantage.

" Sir Miles M'Shane begs to inform the person who found his shoe-buckle after the last levee, that he will receive one and eightpence reward for the same, by bringing it to No. 2, Ely-place; or if he prefer it, Sir Miles will toss up who keeps the pair. They are only paste, and not diamond, though mighty well imitated."

" Paste !" echoed Mrs. Branaghan ; " the lying thieves !" her notions on the score of that material being limited to patties and pie-crusts.

" The ' Bucks' are imitating the ladies in all the arts of beautifying the person. Many were seen painted and patched at the duchess's last ball. We hope this effeminacy may not spread any further.—It is Mr. Rigby, and not Mr. Harper, is to have the silk gown.—Sir George Rose is to get the red ribbon for his services in North America."

" A silk gown and a red ribbon !" cried Mrs. Branaghan. " Bad luck to me, but they might be ashamed of themselves."

" Faix, I never believed what Darby Long said before," broke in Kerry. " He tould me he saw the Bishop of Cork in a black silk petticoat like a famale. Is there no more murders, Mickey ?"

" I don't know, sir, barrin' they're in the fashionable intelligence."

" Well, read on."

" Donald, the beast, who refused to leave his cell in Trim gaol at the last assizes, and was consequently fired at by a file of infantry, had his leg amputated yesterday by Surgeon Huston of this town, and is doing re-markably well."

" Where's the sporting news ?" said Kerry. " Is not this it, here ?" as he pointed to a figure of a horse above a column.

"·Mr. Connolly's horse, Gabriel, would have been in first, but he stopped to eat Whaley, the jockey, when he fell. The race is to be run again on Friday next. It was Mr. Daly, and not Mr. Crosbie, horsewhipped the attorney over the course last Tuesday. Mr. Crosbie spent the day with the Duke of Leinster, and is very angry at his name being mentioned in the wrong, particularly as he is bound over to keep the peace towards all members of the bar for three years.

" Captain Heavyside and Mr. Malone exchanged four shots each on the

Bull this morning. The quarrel was about racing and politics, and miscellaneous matters.

" It is rumoured that if the Chief Justice be appointed from England, he will decline giving persoual satisfaction to the Master of the Rolls ; but we canuot credit the report.

" The Carmelites have taken Ranelagh House for a nunnery."

" That's the only bit in the paper I'd give the snuff of my pipe for," said Mrs. Branaghan. " Read it again, acushla."

The boy re-read the passage.

" Well, well, I wouder if Miss Kate will ever come back again," said she, in a pause.

" To be sure she will," said Kerry ; " what would hinder her ? Hasu't she a fine fortuue out of the property ? Teu thousand, I heerd the master say."

" Ayeh ! sure it's all gone many a day ago ; the sorra taste of a brass farthen's left for her, or any one else. The master sould every stick an' stone in the place, barrin' the house that's over us, and sure that's all as one as sould too. Ah, then, Miss Kate was the purty child, and had the coaxing ways with her."

" 'Tis a pity to make her a nun," said Kerry.

" A pity ! why would it be a pity, Kerry O'Leary ?" said the old lady, bristling up with anger. " Isn't the uuns happier, and dacenter, and higher nor other women, with rapscallions for husbauds, and villains of all kiuds for childer ? Is it the likes of ye, or the crayture beside ye, that would teach a colleen the way to heaven ? Musha, but they have the blessed times of it—fastin' and prayin', and doiug all manner of penauce, aud talking over their sins with holy men."

" Whisht ! what's that ? there's the bell ringing above stairs," said Kerry, suddenly starting up and listening. " Ay, there it is again ;" aud, so saying, he yawned and stretched himself, and after several interjectioual grumblings over the disturbance, slowly mounted the stairs towards the parlour.

" Are ye sleepin' down there, ye lazy deevils ?" cried Sir Archy, from the landing of the stairs. " Did ye no hear the bell ?"

" 'Tis now I heerd it," said Kerry, composedly, for he never vouchsafed the same degree of deference to Sir Archy he yielded to the rest of the family.

" Go see if there be any lemons in the house, and lose no time about it."

" Faix, I needn't go far, then, to fiud out," whined Kerry ; " the master had none for his punch these two nights. They put the little box into a damp corner, and, sure enough, they had beards on them like Jews, the same lemons, when they went to look for them."

" Go down, then, to the womau M'Kelly's, in the glen, and see if she hae na some there."

"Oh, murther! murther!" muttered Kerry to himself, as the whistling storm reminded him of the dreadful weather without doors. "'Tis no use in going without the money," said he, slyly, hoping that by this home-thrust he might escape the errand.

"Ye maun tell her to put it in the account, man."

"'Tis in bad company she'd put it, then," muttered Kerry below his breath; then added, aloud, "Sorrow one she'd give, if I hadn't the sixpence in my hand."

"Canna ye say it's no for yoursel', it's for the house? She wad na refuse that."

"No use in life," reiterated he, solemnly. "She's a real naygur, and would not trust Father Luke with a week's snuff, and he's dealt there for sneeshin these thirty years."

"A weel, a weel," said M'Nab, in a low, harsh voice; "the world's growing waur and waur. Ye maun e'en gie her a shilling, and mind ye get nae bad bawbees in change. She suld gie ye twelve for saxpence."

Kerry took the money without a word of reply : he was foiled in the plan of his own devising, and, with many a self-uttered sarcasm on the old Scotchman, he descended the stairs once more.

"Is Master Herbert worse?" said the cook, as the old huntsman entered the kitchen.

"Begorra, he must be bad entirely, when ould Archy would give a shilling to cure him. See here, he's sending me for lemons down to Mary's."

Kerry rang the coin upon the table, as if to test its genuineness, and muttered to himself,

"'Tis a good one—devil a lie in it!"

"There's the bell again; musha, how he rings it!"

This time the voice of Sir Archy was heard in loud tones summoning Kerry to his assistance, for Herbert had become suddenly worse, and the old man was unable to prevent him rising from his bed and rushing from the room.

The wild and excited tones of the youth were mixed with the deeper utterings of the old man, who exerted all his efforts to calm and restrain him as Kerry reached the spot. By his aid the boy was conveyed back to his bed, where, exhausted by his own struggles, he lay without speaking or moving for some hours.

It was not difficult to perceive, however, that this state boded more un-favourably than the former one. The violent paroxysms of wild insanity betokened, while they lasted, a degree of vital energy and force, which now seemed totally to have given way; and although Kerry regarded the change as for the better, the more practised and skilful mind of Sir Archibald drew a far different and more dispiriting augury.

Thus passed the weary hours, and at last the long day began to decline, but still no sign nor sound proclaimed the doctor's coming, and M'Nab's anxiety became hourly more intense.

"If he come na soon," said he, after a long and dreary silence, "he need na tak' the trouble to look at him."

"'Tis what I'm thinking too," said Kerry, with a sententious gravity almost revolting. "When the fingers docs be going that way, it's a mighty bad sign. If I seen the hounds working with their toes, I never knew them recover."

CHAPTER IX.

A DOCTOR'S VISIT.

THE night was far advanced as the doctor arrived at the O'Donoghne's house, drenched with rain, and fatigued by the badness of the roads, where his gig was often compelled to proceed for above a mile at a foot pace. Doctor Roach was not in the most bland of tempers as he reached his destination; and, of a verity, his was a nature that stood not in any need of increased acerbity. The doctor was a type of a race at one time very general, but now, it is hard to say wherefore, nearly extinct in Ireland. But so it is; the fruits of the earth change not in conrse of years more strikingly than the fashions of men's minds. The habits, popular enongh in one generation, survive as eccentricities in another, and are extinct in a third.

There was a pretty general impression in the world, some sixty or seventy years back, that a member of the medical profession, who had attained to any height in his art, had a perfect right to dispense with all the amenities and courtesies which regulate social life among less privileged persons. The concessions now only yielded to a cook, were then extended to a physician; and in accordance with the privilege by which he administered most nauseous doses to the body, he was suffered to extend his dominion, and apply scarcely more palatable remedies to the minds of his patients. As if the ill-flavoured draughts had tinctured the spirit that conceived them, the tone of his thoughts usually smacked of bitters, until at last he scemed to have realised, in his own person, the conflicting agencies of the pharmacopœia, and was at once acrid, and pungent, and soporific together.

The College of Physicians could never have reproached Doctor Roach with conceding a single iota of their privileges. Never was there one who more stoutly maintained, in his whole practice through life, the blessed immunity of "the Doctor." The magic word "Recipe," which headed his prescriptions, suggested a tone of command to all he said, and both his drugs and dieta were swallowed without remoustrauce.

It may not be a flattering confession for humanity, but it is assuredly a true one, that the exercise of power, no matter how humble its sphere, or how limited its range, will eventually generate a tyrannical habit in him who wields it. Doctor Roach was certainly not the exception to this rule. The Czar himself was not more autocrat in the steppes of Russia, than was he in any house where sickness had found entrance. From that hour he planted his throne there. All the caprices of age, all the follies of childhood, the accustomed freedoms of home, the indulgences which grow up by habit in a household, had to give way before a monarch more potent than all, "the Doctor." Men bore the infliction with the same patient endurance they summoned to sustain the malady. They felt it to be grievous and miserable, but they looked forward to a period of relief, and panted for the arrival of the hour when the disease and the doctor would take their departure together.

If the delight they experienced at such a consummation was extreme, so to the physician it savoured of ingratitude. "I saved his life yesterday," saith he, "and see how happy he is to dismiss me to-day." But who is ever grateful for the pangs of a toothache?—or what heart can find pleasure in the memory of seutentiousness, senna, and low diet?

Never were the blessings of restored health felt with a more suitable thankfulness than by Doctor Roach's patients. To be free once more from his creaking shoes, his little low dry cough, his harsh accents, his harsher words, his contradictions, his sneers, and his selfishness, shed a halo around recovery which the friends of the patient could not properly appreciate.

Such was the individual whose rumbling and rattling vehicle now entered the court-yard of Carrig-na-curra, escorted by poor Terry, who had accompanied him the entire way on foot. The distance he had come, his more than doubts about the fee, the severity of the storm, were not the accessories likely to amend the infirmities of his temper; while a still greater source of irritation than all existed in the mutual feeling of dislike between him and Sir Archibald M'Nab. An occasional meeting at a little boarding-house in Killarney, which Sir Archy was in the habit of visiting each summer for a few days—the only recreation he permitted himself—had cultivated this sentiment to such a pitch, that they never met without disagreement, or parted without an actual quarrel. The doctor was a democrat, and a Romanist of the first water; Sir Archy was a member of the Scottish Episcopal Church; and, whatever might have been his early leanings in politics, and in whatever companionship his active years were passed, experience had taught him the fallacy of many opinions, which owe any appearance of truth or stability they possess to the fact that they have never advanced beyond the stage of speculative notions into the realms of actual and practical existence;—but, above all, the prudent Scotchman dreaded the prevalence of these doctrines among young and unsettled minds, ever ready to prefer the short and hazardous career of fortune to the slow and patient drudgery of daily industry.

If the doctor anticipated but little enjoyment in the society of Sir Archy, neither did the latter hope for any pleasure to himself from Roach's company. However, as the case of poor Herbert became each hour more threatening, the old man resolved to bury in oblivion every topic of mutual disagreement, and, so long as the doctor remained in the house, to make every possible or impossible concession to conciliate the good-will of one on whose services so much depended.

"Do ye hear?" cried Roach in a harsh voice to Kerry, who was summoned from the kitchen fire to take charge of his horse; "let the pony have a mash of bran—a hot mash—and don't leave him till he's dry."

"Never fear, sir," replied Kerry, as he led the jaded and wayworn beast into the stable, "I'll take care of him as if he was a racer;" and then, as Roach disappeared, added, "I'd like so see myself strapping the likes of him—an ould mountaineer. A mash of bran, indeed! Cock him up with bran! Begorra, 'tis thistles and docks he's most used to;" and, with this sage reflection on the beast's habits, he locked the stable door, and resumed his former place beside the blazing turf fire.

O'Donoghue's reception of the doctor was most cordial. He was glad to see him on several accounts. He was glad to see any one who could tell him what was doing in the world, from which all his intercourse was cut off; he was glad, because the supper was waiting an hour and a half beyond its usual time, and he was getting uncommonly hungry; and, lastly, he really felt anxious about Herbert, whenever by any chance his thoughts took that direction.

"How are you, Roach?" cried he, advancing to meet him with an extended hand. "This is a kind thing of you—you've had a dreadful day, I fear."

"D—n me, if I ever saw it otherwise in this confounded glen. I never set foot in it that I wasn't wet through."

"We have our share of rain, indeed," replied the other, with a good-humoured laugh; "but if we have storm, we have shelter."

Intentionally misunderstanding the allusion, and applying to the ruined mansion the praise bestowed on the bold mountains, the doctor threw a despairing look around the room, and repeated the word "shelter" in a voice far from complimentary.

The O'Donoghue's blood was up in a moment. His brow contracted and his cheek flushed, as, in a low and deep tone, he said,

"It is a crazy old concern. You are right enough—neither the walls nor the company within them are like what they once were."

The look with which these words were given recalled the doctor to a sense of his own impertinence; for, like certain tethered animals, who never become conscious of restraint till the check of the rope lays them on their back, nothing short of such a home-blow could have staggered his self-conceit.

"Ay, ay," muttered he, with a cackling apology for a laugh, "time is telling on us all. But I'm keeping the supper waiting."

The duties of hospitality were always enough to make O'Donoghue forget any momentary chagrin, and he seated himself at the table with all his wonted good humour and affability.

As the meal proceeded, the doctor inquired about the sick boy, and the circumstances attending his illness; the interest he bestowed on the narrative mainly depending on the mention of Sir Marmaduke Travers's name, whose presence in the country he was not aware of before, and from whose residence he began already to speculate on many benefits to himself.

"They told me," continued O'Donoghue, "that the lad behaved admirably. In fact, if the old weir-rapid be anything like what I remember it, the danger was no common one. There used to be a current there strong enough to carry away a dozen horsemen."

"And how is the young lady?" Is she nothing the worse from the cold, and the drenching, and the shock of the accident?"

"Faith, I must confess it, I have not had the grace to ask after her. Living as I have been for some years back has left me sadly in arrear with every demand of the world. Sir Marmaduke was polite enough to say he'd call on me; but there is a still greater favour he could bestow, which is, to leave me alone."

"There was a lawsuit, or dispute of some kind or other between you, was there not?"

"There is something of that kind," said O'Donoghue, with an air of annoyance at the question; "but these are matters gentlemen leave to their lawyers, and seek not to mix themselves up with."

"The strong purse is the sinew of war," muttered the inexorable doctor; "and they tell me he is one of the wealthiest men in England."

"He may be, for aught I know or care."

"Well, well," resumed the other, after a long deliberative pause, "there's no knowing how this adventure may turn out. If your son saved the girl's life, I scarcely think he could press you so hard about——"

"Take care, sir," broke in O'Donoghue, and with the words he seized the doctor's wrist in his strong grasp—"take care how you venture to speak of affairs which nowise concern you;" then, seeing the terrified look his speech called up, he added, "I have been very irritable latterly, and never desire to talk on these subjects; so, if you please, we'll change the topic."

The door was cautiously opened at this moment, and Kerry presented himself, with a request from Sir Archibald, that, as soon as Doctor Roach found it convenient, he would be glad to see him in the sick-room.

"I am ready now," said the doctor, rising from his chair, and not by any means sorry at the opportunity of escaping a *tête-à-tête* he had contrived to render so unpalatable to both parties. As he mounted the stairs, he continued in broken phrases to inveigh against the house and the host in a half soliloquy: "A tumble-down old barrack it is—not fifty shillings' worth of furniture under the roof—the ducks were as tough as soaked parchment—and where's the fee to come from—I wish I knew that—unless I take one of these old devils instead of it;" and he touched the frame of a large, damp, discoloured portrait of some long-buried ancestor, several of which figured on the walls of the staircase.

"The boy is worse—far worse," whispered a low but distinct voice beside him. "His head is now all astray—he knows no one."

Doctor Roach seemed vexed at the ceremony of salutation being forgotten in Sir Archibald's eagerness about the youth, and dryly answered,

"I have the honour to see you well, sir, I hope."

"There is one here very far from well," resumed Sir Archy, neither caring for nor considering the speech. "We have lost too much time already—I trust ye may na be too late now."

The doctor made no reply, but rudely taking the candle from his hand, walked towards the bed.

"Ay, ay," muttered he, as he beheld the lustrous eyes and widespread pupils, the rose-red cheek, and dry, cracked lips of the youth, "he has it sure enough."

"Has what?—what is it?"

"The fever—brain fever, and the worst kind of it too."

"And there is danger then?" whispered M'Nab.

"Danger, indeed! I wonder how many come through it. Pshaw! there's no use trying to count his pulse;" and he threw the hand rudely back upon the bed. "That's going as fast as ever his father went with the property." A harsh, low, cackling laugh followed this brutal speech, which demanded all Sir Archy's predetermined endurance to suffer unchecked.

"Do you know me?" said the doctor, in the loud voice used to awaken the dormant faculty of hearing—"do you know me?"

"Yes," replied the boy, staring steadfastly at him.

"Well, who am I then? Am I your father?"

A vacant gaze was all the answer.

"Tell me, am I your father?"

No reply followed.

" Am I your uncle, then ?" said the doctor, still louder.

The word " uncle" seemed to strike upon some new chord of his awakened sense : a faint smile played upon his parched lips, and his eyes wandered from the speaker, as if in search of some object, till they fell upon Sir Archy, as he stood at the foot of the bed, when suddenly his whole countenance was lighted up, and he repeated the word " uncle" to himself in a voice indescribably sweet and touching.

" He has na forgotten me," murmured M'Nab, in a tone of deep emotion. " My ain dear boy—he knows me yet."

" You agitate him too much," said Roach, whose nature had little sympathy with the feelings of either. " You must leave me alone here to examine him myself."

M'Nab said not a word, but, with noiseless step, stole from the room. The doctor looked after him as he went, and then followed to see that the door was closed behind. This done, he beckoned to Kerry, who still remained, to approach, and deliberately seated himself in a chair near the window.

" Tell me, my good fellow," said he, affecting an air of confidence as he spoke, " ain't they all broke here ? Isn't the whole thing smashed ?"

" Broke—smashed !" repeated Kerry, as he held up both hands in feigned astonishment; " 'tis a droll smash : begorra, I never see money as plenty this many a year. Sure av there wasn't lashings of it, would he be looking out for carriage-horses, and buying hunters, not to say putting the kennel in order ?"

" Is it truth you are telling ?" said Roach, in astonishment.

" True as my name is Kerry O'Leary. We offered Lanty Lawler a hundred and twenty guineas on Friday last for a match wheeler, and we're not off of him yet ; he's a big brown horse, with a star on his face ; and the cob for the master cost forty pounds. He'll be here to-morrow, or next day : sure ye'll see him yourself."

" The place is falling to ruin—the roof will never last the winter," broke in the doctor.

" Well, and whose fault is it but that spalpeen Murphy's, that won't set the men to work till he gets oak timber from the Black Say ? 'Tis the finest wood in the world, they tell me, and lasts for ever and ever."

" But don't they owe money everywhere in the country ? There isn't a little shop in Killarney without an account of theirs in it."

" Of course they do ; and the same in Cork—ay, and in Tralee, for the matter of that. Would you have them not give encouragement to more places nor one ? There's not one of those crayturs would send in their bill —no, though we do be asking for it week after week. They're afraid or losing the custom. And I'll engage, now, they do be telling you they can't get their money by hook or by crook ; that's it—I knew it well."

The doctor meditated long on these strange revelations, so very opposite to all he had heard of the circumstances of the O'Donoghues; and while his own convictions were strongly against Kerry's narrative, that worthy man's look of simplicity and earnest truth puzzled him considerably, and made him hesitate which side to credit.

After a long pause, from which the incoherent ravings of the sick boy aroused him, he looked up at Kerry, and then, with a motion of his thumb towards the bed, he muttered,

" He's going fast."

" Going fast!" echoed Kerry, in a voice very different from his former accent. "Oh, wirra! there's nothing so bad as death! Distress and poverty is hard enough, but that's the raal misfortune."

A dry, sarcastic grin from the doctor seemed to say that poor Kerry's secret was discovered. The allusion to want of means came too naturally not to be suggested by present circumstances, and the readiness of Doctor Roach's apprehension clinched the discovery at once.

" We'll go down, now," said the doctor; "I believe I know the whole state of the case." And, with these words of ambiguous meaning, he returned to the drawing-room.

CHAPTER X.

AN EVENING AT "MARY" M'KELLY'S.

IF sorrow had thrown its sombre shadow over the once proud house of the O'Donoghue, within whose walls now noiseless footsteps stole along, and whispered words were spoken, a very different scene presented itself at the small hostel of Mary M'Kelly. There, before the ample fireplace, a quarter of a sheep was roasting, while various utensils of cookery, disposed upon and around the fire, diffused a savoury odour through the apartment. A table, covered with a snow-white napkin, and containing covers for a party of six, occupied the middle of the room; cups and drinking-vessels of richly chased silver, silver forks and spoons of handsome pattern, were there also —strange and singular spectacle beneath the humble thatch of a wayside cabin. Mary herself displayed in her toilet a more than usual care and attention, and wore, in her becoming cap, with a deep lace border, a bouquet of tricolored ribbons, coquettishly knotted, and with the ends falling loosely on her neck. While she busied herself in the preparation for the table, she maintained from time to time a running conversation with a person who sat smoking in the chimney corner. Although screened from the glare of the

F

fire, the light which was diffused around showed enough of the dress and style of the wearer to recognise him at once for Lanty Lawler, the horse-dealer. His attitude, as he lolled back on one chair, and supported his legs on another, bespoke the perfection of ease, while in the jaunty manner he held the long pipe-stick between his fingers could be seen the affectation of one who wished to be thought at home, as well as to feel so.

"What hour did they mention, Mary?" said he, after a pause of some minutes, during which he puffed his pipe assiduously.

"The gossoon that came from Beerhaven said it would be nine o'clock, at any rate; but sure it's nigher to ten now. They were to come up on the flood tide. Whisht! what was that? Wasn't that like the noise of wheels?"

"No; that's the wind, and a severe night it is, too. I'm thinking, Mary, the storm may keep them back."

"Not a bit of it; there's a creek down there, they tell me, safer nor e'er a harbour in Ireland; and you'd never see a bit of a vessel till you were straight over her; and sure it's little they mind weather. That Captain Jack, as they call him, says there's no time for business like a gale of wind. The last night they were here there were two wrecks in the bay."

"I mind it well, Mary. Faix, I never felt a toast so hard to drink as the one they gave after supper."

"Don't be talking about it," said Mary, crossing herself devoutly; "they said it out of devilment, sorra more."

"Well, maybe so," muttered he, sententiously. "They're wild chaps any way, and they've a wild life of it."

"Troth, if I was a man, 'tis a life I'd like well," said Mary, with a look of resolute determination well becoming the speech. "Them's the fine times they have, going round the world for sport, and nothing to care for—as much goold as they'd ask—fine clothes—the best of eating and drinking; sure there's not one of them would drink out of less than silver."

"Faix, they may have iron round their ankles for it, after all, Mary."

"Sorra bit of it—the gaol isn't built yet that would howld them. What's that noise, now? That's them. Oh, no; it's the water running down the mountain."

"Well, I wish they'd come any way," said Lanty, "for I must be off early to-morrow; I've an order from the ould banker here above for six beasts, and I'd like to get a few hours' sleep before morning."

"'Tis making a nice penny you are there, Lanty," said Mary, with a quizzical look from the corner of her eye.

"A good stroke of business, sure enough, Mary," replied he, laughingly. "What d'ye think I did with him yesterday morning? I heerd here, ye know, what happened to the grey mare I bought from Mark O'Donoghue—that she was carried over the weir-gash and drowned. What does I do, but goes up to the Lodge and asks for Sir Marmaduke; and, says I, 'I'm come, sir, to offer a hundred and fifty for the little mare I sould you the other day for a hundred; 'tis only now I found out her real value, and I can get two hundred for her in Cork the day I bring her up; and sure your honour wouldn't prevent a poor man making a trifle in the way of his trade.' ' You're an honest fellow, Lanty,' says he—devil a lie in it, Mary, don't be laughing—'you're an honest fellow; and although I cannot let you have your mare back again, for she was killed last night, you shall have your own price for the four carriage-horses and the two roadsters I ordered.' With that I began blubbering about the mare, and swore I was as fond of her as if she was my sister. I wish you had seen his daughter then; upon my conscience, it was as good as a play. ' They have so much feelin',' says she to her father. ' For fun,' says I, to myself. O murther, murther, Mary, and them's the people that rules us !''

" Omadhauns they are, the devil a more!" interposed Mary, whose hearty contempt for the Saxon originated in the facility by which he could be imposed upon.

" That's what I'm always saying," said Lanty. "I'd rather have the chaytin' than the baytin' of John Bull, any day ! You'll humbug him out of his shirt, and faix it's the easiest way to get it after all."

" It's a mane way, Lanty," interposed Mary, with a look of pride—"it's a dirty, mane way, and doesn't become an Irishman."

" Wait till the time comes, Mary M'Kelly," said Lanty, half angrily, "and maybe I'd be as ready as another."

" I wish it was come," said Mary, sighing; " I wish to the Virgin it was; I'm tired heerin' of the preparations. Sorra one of me knows what more they want, if the stout heart was there. There's eight barrels of gun-powder in that rock there," said she, in a low whisper, " behind your back; you needn't stir, Lanty. Begorra, if a spark was in it, 'twould blow you and me, and the house that's over us, as high as Hungry mountain."

" The angels be near us !" said Lanty, making the sign of the cross.

" Ay," resumed Mary, " and muskets for a thousand min, and pikes for two more. There's saddles and bridles, eighteen hogsheads full."

" True enough," chimed in Lanty; " and I have an order for five hun-dred cavalry horses—the money to be paid out of the Bank of France. Musha, I wish it was some place nearer home."

" Is it doubting them ye are, Lanty Lawler?"

" No, not a bit; but it's always time enough to get the beasts when we see the riders. I could mount two thousand men in a fortnight, any day, if there was money to the fore; ay, and mount them well, too; not the kind of devils I give the government, that won't stand three days of hard work. Musha, Mary, but it's getting very late; that mutton will be as dry as a stick."

F 2

" The French likes it best that way," said Mary, with a droll glance, as though to intimate she guessed the speaker's object. " Take a look down the road, Lanty, and try if you can hear any one coming."

Lanty arose from his comfortable corner with evident reluctance, and laid down his pipe with a half sigh, as he moved slowly towards the door of the cabin, which having unbarred, he issued forth into the darkness.

" It's likely I'd hear anything such a night as this," grumbled he to himself, " with the trees snapping across, and the rocks tumbling down ! It's a great storm entirely."

" Is there any sign of them, Lanty ?" cried Mary, as she held the door ajar, and peeped out into the gloomy night.

" I couldn't see my hand forninst me."

" Do you hear nothing ?"

" Faix I hear enough over my head ; that was thunder ! Is there any fear of it getting at the powder, Mary ?"

" Divil a fear ; don't be unasy about that," said the stout-hearted Mary. " Can you see nothing at all ?"

" Sorra a thing, barrin' the lights up at Carriguacurra ; they're moving about there, at a wonderful rate. What's O'Donoghue doing at all ?"

" 'Tis the young boy, Herbert, is sick," said Mary, as she opened the door to admit Lanty once more. " The poor child is in a fever. Kerry O'Leary was down here this evening for lemons for a drink for him. Poor, Kerry ! he was telling me, himself has a sore time of it, with that ould Scotchman that's up there ; nothing ever was like him for scoulding, and barging, and abusing ; and O'Donoghue now minds nothing inside or out, but sits all day long in the big chair, just as if he was asleep. Maybe he does take a nap sometimes, for he talks of bailiffs, and writs, and all them things. Poor ould man ! it's a bad end, when the law comes with the grey hairs !"

" They've a big score with yourself, I'll be bound," said Lanty, inquiringly.

" Troth, I'd like to see myself charge them with anything," said she, indignantly. " It's to them and theirs I owe the roof that's over me, and my father, and my father's father before me owes it. Musha, it would become me to take their money, for a trifle of wine and spirits, and tay and tobacco, as if I wasn't proud to see them send down here—the raal ould stock that's in it ! Lanty, it must be very late by this. I'm afeard something's wrong up in the bay."

" 'Tis that same I was thinking myself," said Lanty, with a sly look towards the roasted joint, whose savoury odour was becoming a temptation overmuch for resistance.

" You've a smart baste in the stable," said Mary ; " he has eaten his corn by this time, and must be fresh enough ; just put the saddle on him, Lanty dear, and ride down the road a mile or two—do, and good luck attend you."

There never was a proposition less acceptable to the individual to whom it was made; to leave a warm fireside was bad enough, but to issue forth on a night it would have been inhumanity to expose a dog to, was far too much for his compliance; yet Lanty did not actually refuse; no, he had his own good reasons for keeping fair with Mary M'Kelly; so he commenced a system of diplomatic delay and discussion, by which time at least might be gained, in which it was possible the long-expected guests would arrive, or the project fall to the ground on its own merits.

"Which way will they come, Mary?" said he, rising from his seat.

"Up the glen, to be sure—what other way could they, from the bay? You'll hear them plain enough, for they shout and sing every step of the road, as if it was their own; wild devils they are."

"Sing is it? Musha, now, do they sing?"

"Ay, faix, the drollest songs ever ye heerd; French and Roosian songs —sorra the likes of them going at all."

"Light hearts they have of their own."

"You may say that, Lanty Lawler; fair weather or foul, them's the boys never change; but come now, be alive, and get out the baste."

"I'm going, I'm going; it's myself would like to hear them sing a Roosian song. Whisht! what's that? did ye hear a shout there?"

"Here they are; that's them," said Mary, springing towards the door and withdrawing the bolt, while a smart knock was heard, and the same instant a voice called out:

"Holloa! house ahoy!"

The door at the moment flew open, and a short, thick-set looking man, in a large boat cloak, entered, followed by a taller figure, equally muffled. The former dropping his heavy envelope, and throwing off an oilskin cap from his head, held out his arms wide, as he said,

"*Marie, ma mie! embrasse-moi;*" and then, not waiting for a compliance with the request, sprang forward, and clasped the buxom landlady in his arms, and kissed her on each cheek, with an air compounded of true feeling and stage effect.

"Here's my friend and travelling companion, Henry Talbot, come to share your hospitality, Mary," said he in English, to which the slightest foreign accent lent a tone of recitative. "One of us, Mary—one of us."

The individual alluded to had by this time dropped his cloak to the ground, and displayed the figure of a slight and very young man, whose features were singularly handsome, save for a look of great effeminacy; his complexion was fair as a girl's, and, flushed by exercise, the tint upon his cheek was of a pale rose colour; he was dressed in a riding-coat and top-boots, which, in the fashion of the day, were worn short, and wrinkled around the leg; his hair he wore without powder, and long upon his neck; a heavy riding-whip, ornamented with silver, the only weapon he carried, composed his costume—one as unlike his companion's as could be.

Captain Jacques Flahault was a stout-built, dark-complexioned fellow, of some four or five and forty, his face a grotesque union of insolence and drollery, the eyes black as jet, shaded by brows so arched as to give always the idea of laughing to a countenance the lower part of which, shrouded in beard and moustache, was intended to look stern and savage.

His dress was a short blue frock, beneath which he wore a jersey shirt, striped in various colours, across which a broad buff leather belt, loosely slung, supported four pistols and a dirk; jack-boots reached about the middle of the thigh, and were attached to his waist by thongs of strong leather—no needless precaution, apparently, as in their looseness the wearer might at any moment have stepped freely from them; a black handkerchief, loosely knotted round his neck, displayed a throat brawny and massive as a bull's, and imparted to the whole head an appearance of great size—the first impression every stranger conceived regarding him.

"Ah! ah! Lawler, you here? How goes it, my old friend? Sit down here, and tell me all your rogueries since we parted. *Par St. Pierre*, Henry, this is the veriest *fripon* in the kingdom"—Talbot bowed, and, with a sweetly courteous smile, saluted Lanty, as if accepting the speech in the light of an introduction—"a fellow that, in the way of his trade, could cheat the Saint Père himself."

"Where's the others, Captain Jack?" said Mary, whose patience all this time endured a severe trial—"where's the rest?"

"*Place pour le potage, ma mie!*—soup before a story. You shall hear everything by-and-by. Let us have the supper at once."

Lanty chimed in a willing assent to this proposition, and in a few moments the meat smoked upon the table, around which the whole party took their places with evident good-will.

While Mary performed her attentions as hostess by heaping up each plate, and ever supplying the deficiency caused by the appetite of the guests, the others eat on like hungry men, Captain Jacques alone intermingling with the duties of the table a stray remark from time to time.

"*Ventrebleu*, how it blows! If it veers more to the south'ard, there will be a heavy strain on that cable. *Trinquons, mon ami—trinquons toujours. Ma belle Marie*, you eat nothing."

"'Tis unasy I am, Captain Jack, about what's become of the others," said Mrs. M'Kelly.

"Another bumper, *ma mie*, and I'm ready for the story—the more as it is a brief one. *Allons donc*—now for it. We left the bay about nine o'clock, or half-past, perhaps, intending to push forward to the glen at once, and weigh with the morning's tide, for it happens that this time our cargo is destined for a small creek on the north-west coast, our only business here being to land my friend Harry"—here Talbot bowed and smiled—"and to leave two hogsheads of Bordeaux for that very true-hearted, kind, *brave homme*, Hemsworth, at the Lodge there. You remember last winter we entered into a compact with him to stock his cellar, provided no information of our proceedings reached the revenue from any quarter. Well, the wine was safely stored in one of the caves on the coast, and we started with a light conscience ; we had neither despatches nor run-brandy to trouble us— nothing to do but eat our supper, *saluer madame*"—here he turned round, and, with an air of mock respect, kissed Mary's hand—"and get afloat again. As we came near the Lodge, I determined to make my visit a brief one, and so, leaving all my party, Harry included, outside, I approached the house, which, to my surprise, showed lights from nearly every window. This made me cautious, and so I crept stealthily to a low window, across which the curtain was but loosely drawn, and, *mort de ma vie!* what did I behold, but the prettiest face in Europe. *Un ange de beauté.* She was lean- ing over a table copying a drawing, or a painting of some sort or other. *Tête bleue!* here was a surprise. I had never seen her before, although I was with Hemsworth a dozen times."

"Go on—go on !" said Lanty, whose curiosity was extreme to hear what happened next.

" *Eh bien*—I tried the sash, but it was fastened. I then went round the house, and examined the other windows, one after the other—all the same. *Que faire ?* I thought of knocking boldly at the back-door, but then I should have no chance of a peep at *la belle* in that way."

"What did you want with a peep at her ?" asked Mary, gruffly.

" *Diable !* what did I want ? *Pour l'admirer, l'adorer*—or at least to make my respects, as becomes a stranger and a Frenchman. *Poursuivons.* There was no *entrée* without some noise, so I preferred the room she was in to any other, and gently disengaging my dirk, I slipped it between the two sashes, to lift up the latch that fastened them. *Morbleu !* the weapon slipped, and came slap through the pane, with a tremendous fracas. She started up, and screamed—there was no use in any more delay. I put my foot through the window, and pushed open the sash at once ; but, before I was well in the room, bells were ringing in every quarter of the house, and men's voices calling aloud, and shouting to each other ; when suddenly the door opened, and whiz went a pistol-ball close by my head, and shattered the shutter behind me. My fellows outside, hearing the shot, unslung their pieces, and, before I could get down to them, poured in a volley—why, wherefore, or upon whom, the devil himself, that instigated them, can tell. The garrison mustered strong, however, and replied—that they did, by Jove !—for one of ours, Emile de Louvois, is badly wounded. I sounded the retreat, but the scoundrels would not mind me ; and, before I was able to prevent it, *tête bleue!* they had got round to the farm-yard, and set fire to the corn-stacks; in a second, the corn and hay blazed up, and enveloped house and all in smoke. I sounded the retreat once more, and off the villains scampered, with poor Emile, to the boat; and I, finding my worthy friend here an inactive spectator of the whole from a grove near the road, resolved not to give up my supper—and so, *me voici!* But come, can none of you explain this affair? What is Hemsworth doing, with all this armed household, and this captive princess?"

"Is the Lodge burned down?" said Lanty, whose interest in the in-habitants had a somewhat selfish origin.

"No; they got the fire under. I saw a wild-looking devil mount one of the ricks with a great canvas sail, all wetted, and drag it over the burning stack; and before I left the place the Lodge was quite safe."

"I'm sorry for it," said Mary, with a savage determination. "I'm sorry to the heart's core. Luck nor grace never was in the glen since the first stone of it was laid—nor will it be again, till it is a ruin! Why didn't they lay it in ashes when they were about it?"

"Faith, it seemed to me," said Talbot, in a low, soft voice, "they would have asked nothing better. I never saw such bull-dogs in my life. It was all you could do, Flahault, to call them off."

"True enough," replied Jacques, laughing. "They enjoy a *brisée* like that with all their hearts."

"The English won't stay long here, after this night," was Lanty's sage reflection, but one which he did not utter aloud in the present company. And then, in accordance with Jacques's request, he proceeded to explain by what different tenants the Lodge became occupied since his last visit; and that an English baronet and his daughter, with a household of many servants, had replaced Hemsworth and his few domestics. At every stage of the recital, Flahault stopped the narrative, to give him time to laugh. To him the adventure was full of drollery. Even the recollection of his wounded comrade little damped his enjoyment of a scene which might have been attended by the saddest results; and he chuckled a hundred times over what he suspected the Englishman must feel on this his first visit to Ireland.

"I could rob the mail to-morrow, for the mere fun of reading his letters to his friends," said he. "*Morbleu!* what a description of Irish rapparees, five hundred in number, armed with pikes!"

"I wish ye'd give him the cause to do it," said Mary, bitterly. "What brings them here? who wants them, or looks for them?"

"You are right, Mary," said Talbot, mildly. "Ireland for the Irish!"

"Ay, Ireland for the Irish!" repeated Mary and Lanty, and the sentiment was drunk with all the honours of a favoured toast.

For some time the party continued to discuss Flahault's story, and cal-culate on every possible turn the affair might give rise to; all agreeing, finally, on one point, that Sir Marmaduke would scarcely venture to protract his stay in a country where his visit had been signalised by such a reception. The tone of the conversation seemed little to accord with Captain Jacques's humour, whose convivial temperament found slight pleasure in protracted or argumentative discussions of any kind.

"*Que le diable l'emporte!*" cried he, at last. "This confounded talk has stopped the bottle this half-hour. Come, Talbot, let's have a song, my lad; never shake your head, *mon enfant.*——Well, then, here goes."

Thus saying, Flahault pushed back his chair a little from the table, and in a rich, deep, bass voice, which rang through the high rafters of the cabin, chanted out the following rude verses to a French vaudeville air, giving the final *e* of the French words, at the end of each line, that peculiar accentuation of *a*, which made the word sound *contrebanda*.

Though this information as to Captain Jacques's performance seems of little moment, yet such was the fact, that any spirit the doggerel possessed could only be attributed to the manner of the singer, and the effect produced by the intonation we have mentioned.

LA CONTREBANDE.

A bumper, " mes enfans," to swallow your care,
    A full bumper, we pledge, " à l'Irlande;"
The land of " belles femmes, le pays de bonne chère,
    Et toujours de la Contrebande."

Some like to make love, and some like to make war,
    Some of beauty obey " la commande;"
But what is a glance from an eye, " bleu," or " noir,"
    Except it be " la Contrebande."

When a prince takes the cash that a peasant can't spare,
    And lets him lie down " sur la lande;"
Call it as you like—but the truth is, I swear,
    " C'est bien pire que la Contrebande."

Stolen kisses are ever the sweetest, we're told,
    They sink like a " navire qui fondre;"
And what's true of a kiss, is the same, too, of gold,
    They're both in their way, " Contrebande!"

When kings take your money, they won't even say,
    " Mon ami, que Dieu vous le rende;"
While even the priest, for a blessing takes pay,
    " C'est partout et toujours Contrebande."

The good things of life are not equal, I'm sure,
    Then how pleasant to make the " amende;"
To take from the wealthy, and give to the poor,
    " Voilà ce que j'appelle Contrebande."

Yet, as matters go, one must not deem it strange,
    That even " la France et l'Irlande,"
If good wishes and friendship they simply exchange,
    There are folks who call that " Contrebande."

"*Vive la Contrebande, mes amis!*" shouted out Jacques, as he arose glass in hand, and made the room ring with the toast. And every voice repeated the words, in such imitations as they were able.

" 'Tis an elegant song, any way," said Lanty, "if one only understood it all—and the tune's mighty like the ' Cruiskeen Lawn.' "

" Well, Harry," said Flahault, slapping his friend on the shoulder, " will the song persuade you to turn smuggler? I fear not. You'd rather prac- tise your own ' Contrebande' among the bright eyes and dark locks of the capital. Well, there are worse ' métiers.' I have had a turn at it these fifteen years, and whether on the waters of Ontario, or Champlain, or scud- ding along under the fog-banks of the Scheldt, I never grew weary of it. But now for a little business talk : where is the *Padre?* where's Father Luke ? was he not to have been here to-night ?"

Mary whispered the answer in the captain's ear.

" Ah, *parbleu!*" exclaimed he, aloud—" is it so ? Practising a little ' Contrebande' of his own—trying to see a poor fellow safe over the frontier, into the next world."

" Fie for shame, Captain Jacques," said Mary, with pious horror. " That's not the way to talk of the holy offices."

" I wish I had old Maurice Dulang here, the priest of Trois Rivières, he's the boy could despatch them without trouble."

Neither Lanty nor Mary gave any encouragement to Flahault's new turn of the conversation, and so, addressing himself to Talbot, he went on,

" We were dining together one day at the little inn at Trois Rivières, when a messenger came from Lachégon for the Père to administer the last rites to a ' mourant.' Maurice promised to be there in half an hour, but never stirred—and though three other messengers came for him, the answer was all the same—until at last came word, ' *C'est trop tard, il est mort.*'

" ' *Trop tard!*' said Maurice, ' not a bit of it ; give me a pen and ink and some paper.' With that he folded a piece, note fashion, and wrote,

" ' MON CHER PIERRE,—Fais ton petit possible pour ce pauvre diable, qui s'est glissé hors du monde sans mes soins. Apparemment il était bien pressé ; mais tu t'arrangeras pour le mieux.

" ' Ton viel ami,

" ' MAURICE DULANG.

" ' St. Pierre, à la Conciergerie du Paradis.'

" ' Put that in his mouth,' said Maurice, ' and there's no fear of him.' "

" 'Twas a blessed gospel he gave him," said Mary, who did not compre- hend the French portion of the story, " and sure it's as good as anything."

" We all thought so, Mary. Poor Maurice related the story at Lyons, when he was led out to the guillotine; but though the Commissaire laughed heartily, and enjoyed it much, they had found a breviary in his portmanteau, and they couldn't let him off. Pauvre bête! To travel about the world with the ' pièce de convictiou' iu his possession. What, Harry, uo more wine ?"

" I thank you, no more for me, although that claret is a temptation."

" A bouquet, every glass of it ! What say you, Master Lawler—does it suit your palate ?"

" I begin to think it a taste cold or so by this time," said Lauty ; "I'm not genteel enough for wine, God help me ; but it's time to turn in, auy-how—and there's Mary asleep already."

" I don't stir till I fiuish the flask," said Jacques, firmly ; "aud if you won't drink, you needn't grudge me your company. It's hard to say whcu we meet again. You go northward, Talbot, isn't that so ?"

" Yes, and that's the point I wish to come to—where and how shall I find a mount ?—I depeuded on this priest you spoke of to meet me, but he has not made his appearance."

" You never fell upou your legs more fortuuately—here's your mau for a horse, all Ireland over. Eh, Lauty, what's to be had uow ?"

" Devil a thiug can be got for love or mouey," said Lauty. " If the geutleman only told me yesterday——"

" Yesterday, Mastcr Lauty, we were riding white horses iu the Western Ocean—but that's gone by—let us talk of to-day."

" My own hackney is here in the stable. If his honour likes him, I'll sell him ; but he's a fancy beast, and must have a fancy price."

" Has he strcngth aud speed for a fast ride," said Talbot, " and will his condition bear it ?"

" I'll answer for it—you may push ou to Cork in a hand gallop, if you give him teu minutes' rest and a glass of whisky at Macroom."

" That's enough—what's his price ?"

" Take a look at him first," replied Lanty, " for if you are judge of a beast, you'll not refuse what I ask you." With these words he lighted a candle, and placed it in an old iron lantern which hung against the wall, and opening a small door at the back of the cabin, proceeded, by a narrow passage cut in the rock, towards the stable, followed by Talbot, Flahault re-maining where he was, as if sunk in meditation. Scarcely, however, had the two figures disappeared in the distance, when he shook Mary violently by the shoulder, aud whispered in a quick, but collected tone,

" Mary—Mary, I say—is that fellow all safe ?"

" Ay, is he safe," said she, resuming her wonted calmness in a second. " Why do you ask now ?"

" I'll tell you why—for myself I care not a sou—I'm here to-day, away to-morrow—but Talbot's deep in the business—his neck's in the halter—can we trust Lawler on his account—a man of rank and large fortune as he is cannot be spared—what say you ?"

" You may trust him, captain," said Mary; "he knows his life would not be his own two hours if he turned informer; and then this Mr. Talbot, he's a great man, you tell me ?"

" He's a near kinsman of a great peer, and has a heavy stake in the game—that's all I know, Mary—and, indeed, the present voyage was more to bring him over than anything else. But hush, here they come."

" You shall have your money—you've no objection to French gold, I hope —for several years I have seen no other," said Talbot, entering.

" I know it well," said Lanty, "and would just as soon take it as if it had King George on it."

" You said forty pounds—fifty louis is not far off—will that do ?" said the youth, as he emptied a heavily filled purse of gold upon the table, and pushed fifty pieces towards the horse-dealer.

" As well as the best, sir," said Lanty, as he stored the money in his long leathern pocket-book, and placed it within his breast-pocket.

" Will Mrs. M'Kelly accept this small token as a keepsake?" said the youth, while he took from around his neck a fine gold chain of Venetian work, and threw it gallantly over Mary's. "This is the first shelter I have found, after a long exile from my native land; and you, my old comrade, I have left you the pistols you took a fancy to ; they are in the lugger. And so, now, good-by all; I must take to the road at once : I should like to have met the priest, but all chance of that seems over."

Many and affectionate were the parting salutations between the young man and the others ; for, although he had mingled but little in the evening's conversation, his mild and modest demeanour, added to the charm of his good looks, had won their favourable opinions ; besides that he was pledged to a cause which had all their sympathies.

While the last good-by was being spoken, Lanty had saddled and bridled the hackney, and led him to the door. The storm was still raging fiercely, and the night dark as ever.

"You'd better go a little ways up the glen, Lanty, beside him," said Mary, as she looked out into the wild and dreary night.

" 'Tis what I mean to do," said Lanty; "I'll show him as far as the turn of the road."

Though the stranger declined the proffered civility, Lanty was firm in his resolution, and the young man, vaulting lightly into the saddle, called out a last farewell to the others, and rode on beside his guide.

Mary had scarcely time to remove the remains of the supper, when Lanty re-entered the cabin.

" He's the noble-hearted fellow, any way," said he, " and never took a shilling off the first price I asked him ;" and with that he put his hand into his breast-pocket to examine once more the strange coin of France. With a start, a tremendous oath broke from him. " My money—my pocket-book is lost !" exclaimed he, in wild excitement, while he ransacked pocket after pocket of his dress. " Bad luck to that glen ! I dropped it out there ; and with the torrent of water that's falling it will never be found. Och, murther, this is too bad !"

In vain the others endeavoured to comfort and console him—all their assurances of its safety, and the certainty of its being discovered the next morning, were in vain. Lanty relighted the lantern, and muttering male-dictions on the weather, the road, and his own politeness, he issued forth to search after his treasure—an occupation which, with all his perseverance, was unsuccessful; for when day was breaking, he was still groping along the road, cursing his hard fate, and everything which had any share in inflicting it.

" The money is not the worst of it," said Lanty, as he threw himself down, exhausted and worn out, on his bed. " The money's not the worst of it—there was papers in that book I wouldn't have seen for double the amount."

Long after the old smuggler was standing out to sea the next day, Lanty Lawler wandered backwards and forwards in the glen, now searching among the wet leaves that lay in heaps by the wayside, or, equally in vain, sound-ing every rivulet and watercourse which swept past. His search was fruit-less; and well it might be : the road was strewn with fragments of rocks and tree-tops for miles, while even yet the swollen stream tore wildly past, cutting up the causeway in its passage, and foaming on amid the wreck of the hurricane.

Yet the entire of that day did he persevere, regardless of the beating rain, and the cold, drifting wind, to pace to and fro, his heart bent upon recovering what he had lost.

" Yer sowl is set upon money ; devil a doubt of it, Lanty," said Mary, as dripping with wet, and shaking with cold, he at last re-entered the cabin ; " sorra one of me would go rooting there for a crock of goold, if I was sure to find it."

" It is not the money, Mary, I tould you before—it's something else was in the pocket-book," said he, half angrily, while he sat down to brood in silence over his misfortune.

" 'Tis a letter from your sweetheart, then," said she, with a spice of jea-lous malice in her manner, for Lanty had more than once paid his addresses to Mary, whose wealth was reported to be something considerable.

" Maybe it is, and maybe it is not," was the cranky reply.

"Well, she'll have a saving husband, any way," said Mary, tartly, "and one that knows how to keep a good grip of the money."

The horse-dealer made no answer to this encomium on his economy, but with eyes fixed on the ground, pondered on his loss; meanwhile Mrs. M'Kelly's curiosity, piqued by her ineffectual efforts to obtain information, grew each instant stronger, and at last became irrepressible.

"Can't you say what it is you've lost? Sure there's many a one goes by here of a Saturday to market—and if you leave the token——"

"There's no use in it—sorra bit," said he, despondingly.

"You know your own saycrets best," said Mary, foiled at every effort; "and they must be the dhroll saycrets too, when you're so much afraid of their being found out."

"Troth, then," said Lanty, as a ray of his old gallantry shot across his mind—"troth, then, there isn't one I'd tell a saycret too as soon as yourself, Mary M'Kelly; you know the most of my heart already, and why wouldn't you know it all?"

"Faix, it's little I care to hear about it," said Mary, with an affectation of indifference the most finished coquetry could not have surpassed. "Ye may tell it, or no, just as you plaze."

"That's it now," cried Lanty—"that's the way of women, the whole world over; keep never minding them, and bad luck to peace or ease you get; and then try and plaze them, and see what thanks you have. I was going to tell you all about it."

"And why don't you?" interrupted she, half fearing lest she might have pulled the cord over-tight already—"why don't you tell it, Lanty dear?"

These last words settled the matter. Like the feather that broke the camel's back, these few and slight syllables were all that was wanting to overcome the horse-dealer's resistance.

"Well, here it is now," said he, casting, as he spoke, a cautious glance around, lest any chance listener should overhear him. "There was in that pocket-book a letter, sealed with three big seals, that Father Luke gave me yesterday morning, and said to me, 'Lanty Lawler, I'm going over to Ballyvourney, and after that I'm going on to Cork, and it's mighty likely I'll go as far as Dublin, for the Bishop may be there, and if he is, I must follow him; and here's a letter,' says he, 'that you must give the O'Donoghue with your own hands'—them was the words—'with your own hands, Lanty; and now swear you'll not leave it to any one else, but do as I tell you;' and, faix, I took my oath of it, and see, now, it's lost; may I never, but I don't know how I'll ever face him again; and sure God knows what was in it."

"And there was three seals on it," said Mary, musingly, as if such extraordinary measures of secrecy could bode nothing good.

"Each of them as big as a half-crown—and it was thick inside too;

musha, 'twas the evil day I ever set eyes on it!" And with this allusion to the lost money, which, by the adroitness of superstition, he coupled with the bad luck the letter had brought him, Lanty took his farewell of Mary, and, with a heavy heart, set out on his journey.

CHAPTER XI.

MISTAKES ON ALL SIDES.

THE occurrence so briefly mentioned by Flahault, of the night attack on the Lodge, was not so easily treated by the residents; and so many different versions of the affair were in circulation, that Miss Travers, the only one whose information could have thrown any light upon it, was confused by the many marvels she heard, and totally unable to recal to mind what had really taken place. Sir Marmaduke himself examined the servants, and compared their testimony; but fear and exaggeration conspired to make the evidence valueless, some asserting that there were at least a hundred assailants surrounding the house at one time, others, that they wore a kind of uniform, and had their faces blackened; some again had seen parties prowling about the premises during the day, and could positively swear to one man, "a tall fellow in a ragged blue coat, and without shoes or stockings"—no uncommon phenomena in those parts. But the butler negatived all these assertions, and stoutly maintained that there had been neither attack nor assailants; that the whole affair was a device of Terry's, to display his zeal and bravery; and, in short, that he had set fire to the rick in the haggard, and "got up" the affray for his own benefit.

In proportion as any fact occurred to throw discredit on the testimony of each, he who proffered it became a thousand times more firm and resolute in his assertion—circumstances dubious a moment before, were then suddenly remembered and sworn to, with numerous little aids to corroboration newly recalled to mind. To one point, however, all the evidence more or less converged, and that was, to accuse Terry of being the cause, or at least an accomplice in the transaction.- Poor fellow! his own devotedness had made enemies for him everywhere; the alacrity with which he mounted the burning stack was an offence not soon to be forgotten by those who neither risked life nor limb, nor were the taunts he lavished on their sluggish backwardness to be forgiven now. Unhappily, too, Terry was not a favourite among the servants: he had never learnt how much deference is due from the ragged man to the pampered menial of a rich household; he had not

been trained to that subserviency or demeanour which should mark the intercourse of a poor, houseless, friendless creature like himself, with the
tagged and lace-covered servants of a wealthy master. Terry, by some
strange blunder of his nature, imagined that, in his freedom and independence, he was the better man of the two; he knew that to do nothing was
the prerogative of the great; and as he fulfilled that condition to a consider
able extent, he fancied he should enjoy its privileges also. For this reason
he had ever regarded the whole class of servants as greatly his inferiors;
and although he was ready and willing to peril his life at any moment for
Sir Marmaduke or his daughter, the merest commou-place services he would
refuse to the others without a moment's hesitation. Neither intimidation
could awe, nor bribery bend him; his nature knew not what fear was in
any shape, save one—that of being apprehended and shot for a deserter;
and as to any prospect of buying his good offices, that was totally out of the
question.

Iu an Irish household Terry's character would have been appreciated at
once. The respect which is never refused to any bereavement, but in particular to that greatest of all afflictions, would have secured for him there
both forgiveness and affection—his waywardness and caprice would have
been a law to the least good-tempered servant of the family; but Sir Marmaduke's retainers were all English, and had about as much knowledge of,
or sympathy with, such a creature, as he himself possessed of London life
and manners.

As his contempt was not measured by any scale of prudence, but coolly
eviuced on every occasion of their intercourse, they, one and all, detested
him beyond bounds—most asserting that he was a thorough-paced knave,
whose folly was a garb assumed to secure a life of idleness, and all regarding him in the light of a spy, ever ready to betray them to their master.

When, therefore, one after another, the servants persisted in either
openly accusing or insinuating suggestions against Terry, Sir Marmaduke
became sorely puzzled. It was true he himself had witnessed his conduct
the night before; but if their version was correct, all his daring, energy,
and boldness were so many proofs against him. He was, indeed, reluctant
to think so badly of the poor fellow, but how discredit the evidence of his
entire household? His butler had been in his service for years—and, oh!
what a claim for all the exercise of evil influence, for all the petty tyranny
of the low-minded and the base-born, tracking its way through eaves-
dropping, and insinuating its venom in moments of unguarded freedom. His
footman, too——But why go on? His daughter alone rejected the notion
with indignation; but, in her eager vindication of the poor fellow's honour,
her excitement militated against success—for age thus ever prouounces upon
youth, and too readily confounds a high-spirited deuunciation of wrong with
a mistaken, ill-directed enthusiasm. He listened, it is true, to all she said

of Terry's devotedness and courage—of his artless, simple nature—of his single-minded, gentle character; but, by a fatal tendency, too frequent as we advance in years, the scales of doubt ever lean against, and not to the side favourable to, human nature, and, as he shook his head mournfully, he said,

"I wish I did not suspect him."

"Send for him, at least," said his daughter, as with an effort she restrained the emotion that agitated her; "speak to him yourself."

"To what end, my child, if he really is innocent?"

"Oh! yes; indeed—indeed he is," she exclaimed, as the tears at length fell fast upon her cheek.

"Well, then, be it so," said Sir Marmaduke, as he rang the bell, and ordered Terry to be sent for.

While Miss Travers sat with her head buried in her hands, her father paced slowly up and down the room, and so absorbed was he in his thoughts, that he had not noticed Terry, who had meanwhile entered the room, and now stood respectfully beside the door. When the old man's eyes did fall on him, he started back with horror and astonishment. The poor fellow's clothes were actually reduced to a mass of burned rags, one sleeve was completely gone, and there could be seen his bare arm, scorched and blackened by the fire, a bandage of coarse linen wrapping the hand and fingers; a deep cut marked his brow, and his hair was still matted and clotted with the blood, while his face was of the colour of death itself.

"Can you doubt him, now, father?" whispered the young girl, as she gazed on the poor fellow, whose wandering eyes roamed over the ornaments of the chamber, in total unconsciousness of himself and his sufferings.

"Well, Terry," said Sir Marmaduke, after a pause, "what account do you give of last night's business?"

"That's a picture of Keim-an-eigh," said Terry, as he fixed his large eyes, open to their widest extent, on a framed drawing on the wall. "There's the Eagle's Cliff, and that's Murrow Waterfall; and there's the lake—ay, and see if there isn't a boat on it. Well, well, but its beautiful—one could walk up the shepherd's path, there, where the goat is—ay, there's a fellow going up—musha, that's me—I'm going over to Cubber-na-creena, by the short cut."

"Tell me all you know of what happened last night, Terry," repeated Sir Marmaduke.

"It was a great fire, devil a doubt of it," said Terry, eagerly; "the blaze from the big stack was twice as high as the roof; but when I put the wet sail of the boat on it, it all went into black smoke; it nearly choked me."

"How did it catch fire first, Terry? Can you tell us that?"

G

"They put a piece of tinder in it. I gave them an ould rag, and they rubbed it over with powder, and set it burning."

"Who were they that did this ?"

"The fellows that threw me down. What fine pistols they had, with silver all over them! They said that they would not beat me at all, and they didn't, either. When I gave them the rag, they said, 'Now, my lad, we'll show you a fine fire!' and, true for them, I never seen a grander."

In this vague, rambling strain did Terry reply to every question put to him, his thoughts ever travelling in one narrow circle. Who they were that fired the haggard, how many, and what kind of appearance they wore, he knew nothing of whatever; for, in addition to his natural imbecility of mind, the shock of the adventure, and the fever of his wounds and bruises, had utterly routed the small remnant of understanding which usually served to guide him.

To one question only did his manner evince hesitation and doubt in the answer, and that was when Sir Marmaduke asked him how it happened that he should have been up at the Lodge at so late an hour, since the doors were all locked and barred a considerable time previous.

Terry's face flushed scarlet at the question, and he made no reply : he stole a sharp, quick glance towards Miss Travers, beneath his eyelids, but as rapidly withdrew it again, when his colour grew deeper and deeper.

The old man marked the embarrassment, and all his suspicions were re-vived at once.

"You must tell me this, Terry," said he, in a voice of some impatience; "I insist upon knowing it."

"Yes, Terry, speak it out freely; you can have no cause for concealment," said Sybella, encouragingly.

"I'll not tell it," said he, after a pause of some seconds, during which he seemed to have been agitating within himself all the reasons on either side— "I'll not tell it."

"Come, sir," said Sir Marmaduke, angrily, "I must and will know this; your hesitation has a cause, and it shall be known."

The boy started at the tones so unusual to his ears, and stared at the speaker in mute astonishment.

"I am not displeased with you, Terry; at least, I shall not be, if you speak freely and openly to me. Now, then, answer my question : what brought you about the Lodge at so late an hour ?"

"I'll not tell," said the youth, resolutely.

"For shame, Terry," said Sybella, in a low, soothing voice, as she drew near him; "how can you speak thus to my father ? You would not have *me* displeased with you ?"

The boy's face grew pale as death, and his lips quivered with agitation, while his eyes, glazed with heavy tears, were turned downwards; still h. never spoke a word.

"Well, what think you of him now?" said Sir Marmaduke, in a whisper to his daughter.

"That he is innocent—perfectly innocent," replied she, triumphantly. "The poor fellow has his own reasons—shallow enough, doubtless—for his silence; but they have no spot or stain of guilt about them. Let me try if I cannot unfathom this business; I'll go down to the boat-house."

The generous girl delayed not a moment, but hastened from the room as she spoke, leaving Sir Marmaduke and Terry silently confronting each other. The moment of his daughter's departure, Sir Marmaduke felt relieved from the interference her good opinion of Terry suggested, and, at once altering his whole demeanour, he walked close up to him, and said,

"I shall but give you one chance more, sir. Answer my question now, or never."

"Never, then!" rejoined Terry, in a tone of open defiance.

The words, and the look by which they were accompanied, overcame the old man's temper in a moment, and he said,

"I thought as much. I guessed how deeply gratitude had sunk in such a heart. Away! Let me see you no more!"

The boy turned his eyes from the speaker till they fell upon his own seared and burned limb, and the hand swathed in its rude bandage. That mute appeal was all he made, and then burst into a flood of tears. The old man turned away to hide his own emotions, and when he looked round, Terry was gone. The hall door lay open. He had passed out and gained the lawn—no sight of him could be seen.

"I know it, father, I know it all now!" said Sybella, as she came running up the slope from the lake.

"It is too late, my child: he has gone—left us for ever, I fear," said S. Marmaduke, as in shame and sorrow he rested his head upon her shoulder.

For some seconds she could not comprehend his words; and, when at last she did so, she burst forth,

"And, oh, father, think how we have wronged him! It was in his care and devotion to us the poor fellow incurred our doubts. His habit was to sit beneath the window each night, so long as lights gleamed within. Till they were extinguished, he never sought his rest. The boatman tells me this, and says his notion was that God watches over the dark hours only, and that man's precautions were needed up to that time."

With sincere and heartfelt sorrow Sir Marmaduke turned away. Servants were despatched on foot and horseback to recover the idiot boy, and persuade him to return; but his path lay across a wild and mountain region, where few could follow; and at nightfall the messengers returned unsuccessful in their search.

If there was real sorrow over his departure in the parlour, the very opposite feeling pervaded the kitchen. There, each in turn exulted in his share
of what had occurred, and took pains to exaggerate his claims to gratitude
for having banished one so unpopular and unfriended.

Alarm at the attack of the previous night, and sorrow for the unjust
treatment of poor Terry, were not Sir Marmaduke's only emotions on this
sad morning. His messenger had just returned from Carriguacurra with
very dispiriting tidings of Herbert O'Donoghue. Respect for the feelings
of the family under the circumstances of severe illness had induced him to
defer his intended visit to a more suitable opportunity; but his anxiety for
the youth's recovery was unceasing, and he awaited the return of each
servant sent to inquire after him with the most painful impatience. In this
frame of mind was he as evening drew near, and he wandered down his
avenue to the roadside to learn some minutes earlier the last intelligence of
the boy. It was a calm and peaceful hour; not a leaf moved in the still
air, and all in the glen seemed bathed in the tranquil influence of the
mellow sunset. The contrast to the terrific storm which so lately swept
through the mountain pass was most striking, and appealed to the old
man's heart, as reflecting back the image of human life, so varying in its
aspect, so changeful of good and evil. He stood and meditated on the
passages of his own life, whose tenor had, till now, been so equable, but
whose fortunes seemed already to participate in the eventful fate of a distracted country. He regretted, deeply regretted, that he had ever come to
Ireland. He began to learn how little power there is to guide the helm of
human fortune when once engaged in the stormy current, and he saw himself
already the sport of a destiny he had never anticipated.

If he was puzzled at the aspect of a peasantry, highly gifted with intelligence, yet barbarously ignorant—active and energetic, yet indolent and
fatalist—the few hints he had gathered of his neighbour, the O'Donoghue,
amazed him still more; and by no effort of his imagination could he conceive the alliance between family pride and poverty—between the reverence
for ancestry and an utter indifference to the present. He could not understand such an anomaly as pretension without wealth; and the only satisfactory explanation he could arrive at, to himself, was, that in a wild and
secluded tract, even so much superiority as this old chieftain possessed
attracted towards him the respect of all humbler and more lowly than himself, and even made his rude state seem affluence and power. If in his
advances to the O'Donoghue he had observed all the forms of a measured
respect, it was because he felt so deeply his debtor for a service, that he
would omit nothing in the repayment: his gratitude was sincere and heartfelt, and he would not admit any obstacle in the way of acknowledging it.

Reflecting thus, he was suddenly startled by the sound of wheels coming
up the glen; he listened, and now heard the low trot of a horse, and the

admonitions of a man's voice, delivered in tones of anger and impatience. The moment after, an old-fashioned gig, drawn by a small, miserable pony, appeared, from which a man had dismounted to ascend the hill.

"A fine evening, sir," said Sir Marmaduke, as the stranger, whose dress bespoke one of the rank of gentleman, drew near.

The other stopped suddenly, and surveyed the baronet without speaking; then, throwing down the collar of his great-coat, which he wore high round his face, he made a respectful salute, and said,

"A lovely evening, sir. I have the honour to see Sir Marmaduke Travers, I believe? May I introduce myself, Doctor Roach, of Killarney?"

"Ah, indeed! Then you are probably come from Mr. O'Donoghue's house? Is the young gentleman better this evening?"

Roach shook his head dubiously, but made no reply.

"I hope, sir, you don't apprehend danger to his life?" asked Sir Marmaduke, with an effort to appear calm as he spoke.

"Indeed I do, then," said Roach, firmly: "the mischief's done already."

"He's not dead?" said Sir Marmaduke, almost breathless in his terror.

"Not dead; but the same as dead. Effusion will carry him off some time to-morrow."

"And can you leave him in this state? Is there nothing to be done? Nothing you could suggest?" cried the old man, scarcely able to repress his indignant feeling at the heartless manner of the doctor.

"There's many a thing one might try," said Roach, not noticing the temper of the question, "for the boy is young; but for the sake of a chance, how am I to stay away from my practice and my other patients? And, indeed, slight a prospect as he has of recovery, my own of a fee is slighter still. I think I've all the corn in Egypt in my pocket this minute," said he, slapping his hand on his purse: "one of the late king's guineas, wherever they had it lying by till now."

"I am overjoyed to have met you, sir," said Sir Marmaduke, hastily, and by a great exertion concealing the disgust this speech suggested. "I wish for an opinion about my daughter's health—a cold, I fancy—but to-morrow will do better. Could you return to Mr. O'Donoghue's to-night? I have not a bed to offer you here. This arrangement may serve both parties, as I fervently hope something may yet be done for the youth."

"I'll visit Miss Travers in the morning with pleasure."

"Don't leave him, sir, I entreat you, till I send over; it will be quite time enough when you hear from me. Let the youth be your first care, doctor; in the mean while accept this slight retainer, for I beg you to consider your time as given to me now;" and with that he pressed several guineas into the willing palm of the doctor.

As Roach surveyed the shining gold, his quick cunning divined the old baronet's intentions, and with a readiness long habit had perfected, he said,

"The case of danger before all others, any day. I'll turn about at once, and see what can be done for the lad."

Sir Marmaduke leaned towards him, and said some words hastily in a low whispering voice.

"Never fear—never fear, Sir Marmaduke," was the reply, as he mounted to the seat of his vehicle, and turned the pony's head once more down the glen.

"Lose no time, I beseech you," cried the old man, waving his hand in token of adieu; nor was the direction unheeded, for, using his whip with redoubled energy, the doctor sped along the road at a canter, which threatened annihilation to the frail vehicle at every bound of the animal.

"Five hundred!" muttered Sir Marmaduke to himself, as he looked after him. "I'd give half my fortune to see him safe through it."

Meanwhile Roach proceeded on his way, speculating on all the gain this fortunate meeting would bring to him, and then meditating what reasons he should allege to the Donoghue for his speedy return.

"I'll tell him a lucky thought struck me in the glen," muttered he; "or what! if I said I forgot something—a pocket-book, or case of instruments—anything will do;" and, with this comfortable reflection, he urged his beast onward.

The night was falling as he once more ascended the steep and narrow causeway which led to the old keep; and here, now, Kerry O'Leary was closing the heavy but timeworn gate, and fastening it with many a bolt and bar, as though aught within could merit so much precaution. The sound of wheels seemed suddenly to have caught the huntsman's ear, for he hastily shut down the massive hasp that secured the bar of the gate, and as quickly opened a little latched window, which, barred with iron, resembled the grated aperture of a convent door.

"You're late this time, anyhow," cried Kerry. "Tramp back again, friend, the way you came; and be thankful it's myself seen you, for, by the blessed Father, if it was Master Mark was here, you'd carry away more lead in your skirts than you'd like."

"What, Kerry?—what's that you're saying?" said the astonished doctor; "don't you know me, man?"

"Kerry's my name, sure enough; but, artful as you are, you'll just keep the other side of the door. Be off now, in God's name. 'Tis a fair warning I give you; and, faix, if you won't listen to rayson, you might hear worse;" and, as he spoke, that ominous sound, the click of a gun-cock, was heard, and the muzzle of a carbine peeped between the iron bars.

"Tear and ounds! ye scoundrel! you're not going to fire a bullet at me?"

"'Tis slugs they are," was the reply, as Kerry adjusted the piece, and seemed to take as good an aim as the darkness permitted—"divil a more nor slugs, as you'll know soon. I'll count three, now, and may I never wear boots if I don't blaze if you're not gone before it's over. Here's one!" shouted he, in a louder key.

"The saiuts protect me, but I'll be murdered," muttered old Roach, blessing himself, but unable from terror to speak aloud or stir from the spot.

"Here's two!" cried Kerry, still louder.

"I'm going!—I'm going! give me time to leave this blasted place; bad luck to the day and the hour I ever saw it."

"It's too late," shouted Kerry. "Here's three!" and, as he spoke, bang went the piece, and a shower of slugs aud duck-shot came peppering over the head and counter of the old pony; for, in his fright, Roach had fallen on his knees to pray. The wretched quadruped, thus rudely saluted, gave a plunge and a kick, and then wheeled about with an alacrity long forgotten, aud scampered down the causeway with the old gig at his heels, rattling as if it were coming in pieces. Kerry broke into a roar of laughter, and screamed out,

"I'll give you another yet, begorra! that's only a true copy; but you'll get the original now, you ould varmiut!"

A heavy groan from the wretched doctor, as he sank in a faint, was the ouly response; for in his fear he thought the contents of the piece were in his body.

"Musha, I hope he isn't dead," said Kerry, as he opened the wicket cautiously, and peeped out with a lantern. "Mister Cassidy—Mister James, get up now—it's only joking I was. Holy Joseph! is he kilt?" And overcome by a sudden dread of having committed murder, Kerry stepped out, and approached the motionless figure before him. "By all that's good, I've done for the sheriff," said he, as he stood over the body. "Oh! wirra, wirra! who'd think a few graius of shot would kill him?"

"What's the matter here? who fired that shot?" said a deep voice, as Mark O'Donoghue appeared at Kerry's side, and suatching the lantern held it down till the light fell upon the pale features of the doctor.

"I'm murdered! I'm murdered!" was the faint exclamation of old Roach. "Hear me, these are my dying words, Kerry O'Leary murdered me."

"Where are you wounded? where's the ball?" cried Mark, tearing open the coat and waistcoat in eager anxiety.

"I don't know, I don't know; it's inside bleeding I feel."

"Nonsense, man, you have neither bruise nor scar about you; you're frightened, that's all. Come, Kerry, give a hand, and we'll help him in."

But Kerry had fled; the idea of the gallows had just shot across his mind, and he never waited for any further disclosures about his victim; but

deep in the recesses of a hayloft he lay cowering in terror, and endeavouring to pray. Meanwhile Mark had taken the half lifeless body on his
shoulder, and with the ease and indifference he would have bestowed upon
an inanimate burden, coolly carried him into the parlour, and threw him
upon a sofa.

CHAPTER XII.

THE GLEN AT MIDNIGHT.

" What have you got there, Mark ?" called out the O'Donoghue, as the
young man threw the still insensible figure of the doctor upon the sofa.

"Old Roach, of Killarney," answered Mark, sullenly. " That confounded
fool, Kerry, must have been listening at the door, there, to what we
were saying, and took him for Cassidy, the sub-sheriff ; he fired a charge of
slugs at him—that's certain ; but I don't think there's much mischief done."
As he spoke, he filled a goblet with wine, and, without any waste of ceremony, poured it down the doctor's throat. "You're nothing the worse,
man," added he, roughly ; " you've given many a more dangerous dose
yourself, I'll be bound, and people have survived it, too."

"I'm better now," said Roach, in a faint voice—" I feel something better.
But, may I never leave this spot if I don't prosecute that scoundrel O'Leary.
It was all malice—I can swear to that."

"Not a bit of it, Roach. Mark says the fellow mistook you for Cassidy."

" No, no—don't tell me that : he knew me well ; but I foresaw it all.
He filled my pony with water. I might as well be rolling a barrel before
me, as try to drive him this morning. The rascal had a spite against me for
giving him nothing ; but he shall hang for it."

" Come, come, Roach, don't be angry ; it's all past and over now ; the
fellow did it for the best."

"Did it for the best ! Fired a loaded blunderbuss into a fellow-creature
for the best !"

" To be sure he did," broke in Mark, with an imperious look and tone.
" There's no harm done, and you need not make such a work about it."

" Where's the pony and the gig, then ?" called out Roach, suddenly remembering the last sight he had of them.

" I heard the old beast clattering down the glen as if he had fifty kettles
at his tail. They'll stop him at last ; and if they shouldn't, I don't suppose
it matters much. The whole yoke wasn't worth a five-pound note—no,
even giving the owner into the bargain," muttered he, as he turned away.

The indignity of this speech acted like a charm upon Roach. As if galvanised by the insult, he sat bolt upright on the sofa, and thrust his hands down to the deepest recesses of his breeches-pockets, his invariable signal for close action.

"What, sir, do you tell me that my conveniency, with the pony, harness and all——"

"Have patience, Roach," interposed the old man; "Mark was but jesting. Come over and join us here."

At the same instant the door was flung suddenly wide, and Sir Archy rushed in, with a speed very unlike his ordinary gait.

"There's a change for the better!" cried he, joyfully; "the boy has made a rally, and if we could overtake that d—d auld beestie, Roach, and bring him back again, we might save the lad."

"The d—d auld beestie," exclaimed Roach, as he sprang from the sofa, and stood before him, "is very much honoured by your flattering mention of him." Then, turning towards the O'Donoghue, he added, "Take your turn out of me now, when you have me; for, by the Father of Physic, you'll never see Denis Roach under this roof again."

The O'Donoghue laughed till his face streamed with the emotion, and he rocked in his chair like one in a convulsion. "Look, Archy," cried he— "see, now!—hear me, Roach!" were the only words he could utter between the paroxysms, while M'Nab, the very picture of shame and confusion, stood overwhelmed with his blunder, and unable to say a word.

"Let us not stand fooling here," said Mark, gruffly, as he took the doctor's arm. "Come and see my brother, and try what can be done for him."

With an under-growl of menace and rage, old Roach suffered himself to be led away by the young man, Sir Archy following slowly, as they mounted the stairs.

Although alone, the O'Donoghue continued to laugh over the scene he had just witnessed; nor did he know which to enjoy more—the stifled rage of the doctor, or the mingled shame and distress of M'Nab. It was, indeed, a rare thing to obtain such an occasion for triumph over Sir Archy, whose studied observance of all the courtesies and proprieties of life formed so strong a contrast with his own careless and indifferent habits.

"Archy will never get over it—that's certain; and, begad, he shan't do so for want of a reminder. The d—d auld beestie!" and with the words came back his laughter, which had not ceased as Mark re-entered the room. "Well, lad," he cried, "have they made it up? What has Sir Archy done with him?"

"Herbert's better," said the youth, in a low, deep voice, and with a look that sternly rebuked the heartless forgetfulness of his father.

"Ah! better is he? Well, that is good news, Mark; and Roach thinks he may recover?"

"He has a chance now; a few hours will decide it. Roach will sit up with him till four o'clock, and then I shall take the remainder of the night, for my uncle seems quite worn out with watching."

"No, Mark, my boy, you must not lose your night's rest; you've had a long and tiresome ride to-day."

"I'm not tired, and I'll do it," replied he, in the determined tone of his self-willed habit—one, which his father had never sought to control, from infancy upwards. There was a long pause after this, which Mark broke, at length, by saying, "So it is pretty clear now that our game is up—the mortgage is foreclosed. Hemsworth has noticed the Ballyvourney tenants not to pay us the rents, and the ejectment goes on."

"What of Callaghan?" asked the O'Donoghue, in a sinking voice.

"Refused—flatly refused to renew the bills. If we give him five hundred down," said the youth, with a bitter laugh, "he says, he'd strain a point."

"You told him how we were circumstanced, Mark? Did you mention about Kate's money?"

"No," said Mark, sternly, as his brows met in a savage frown—"no, sir, I never said a word of it. She shall not be made a beggar of for our faults. I told you before, and I tell you now, I'll not suffer it."

"But hear me, Mark. It is only a question of time. I'll repay——"

"Repay!" was the scornful echo of the young man, as he turned a withering glance at his father.

"Then there's nothing but ruin before us," said the O'Donoghue, in a solemn tone—"nothing!"

The old man's head fell forward on his bosom, and, as his hands dropped listlessly down at either side, he sat the very impersonation of overwhelming affliction, while Mark, with heavy step and slow, walked up and down the roomy chamber.

"Hemsworth's clerk hinted something about this old banker's intention of building here," resumed he, after a long interval of silence.

"Building where?"—over at the Lodge?"

"No, here, at Carrignacurra; throwing down this old place, I suppose, and erecting a modern villa instead."

"What!" exclaimed the O'Donoghue, with a look of fiery indignation, "are they going to grub us out, root and branch? Is it not enough to banish the old lords of the soil, but they must remove their very landmarks also?"

"It is for that he's come here, I've no doubt," resumed Mark; "he only waited to have the whole estate in his possession, which this term will give him."

" I wish he had waited a little longer; a year, or at most, two, would have been enough," said the old man, in a voice of great dejection; then added, with a sickly smile, " you have little affection for the old walls, Mark."

The youth made no reply, and he went on: "Nor is it to be wondered at. You never knew them in their happy days! but I did, Mark—ay, that I did. I mind the time well when your grandfather was the head of this great county—when the proudest and the best in the land stood uncovered when he addressed them, and deemed the highest honour they could receive an invitation to this house. In the very room where we are sitting, I've seen thirty guests assembled, whose names comprised the rank and station of the province; and yet, all—every man of them—regarded him as their chief, and he was so, too—the descendant of one who was a king."

The animated features of the young man, as he listened, encouraged the O'Donoghue, and he went on : " Thirty-seven thousand acres descended to my grandfather, and even that was but a moiety of our former possessions."

" Enough of this," interrupted Mark, rudely. " It is but an unprofitable theme. The game is up, father," added he, in a deep, stern voice, " and I, for one, have little fancy to wait for the winner to claim the stakes. Could I but see you safely out of the scrape, I'd be many a mile away ere a week was over."

" You would not leave me, boy !" cried the old man, as he grasped the youth's hands in his, and gazed on him with streaming eyes—"you would not desert your poor old father. Oh, no—no, Mark ! this would not be like you. A little patience, my child, and death will save you that cruelty."

The young man's chest heaved and fell like a swelling wave; but he never spoke, nor changed a muscle of his rigid features.

" I have borne all misfortunes well till now," continued the father. " I cared little on my own account, Mark ; my only sorrow was for you; but so long as we were together, boy—so long as hand in hand we stood against the storm, I felt that my courage never failed me. Stay by me, then, Mark —tell me that whatever comes you'll never leave me. Let it not be said, that when age and affliction fell upon the O'Donoghue, his son—the boy of his heart—deserted him. You shall command in everything," said he, with an impassioned tone, as he fixed his eyes upon the youth's countenance. "I ask for nothing but to be near you. The house—the property—all shall be yours."

" What house—what property—do you speak of ?" said Mark, rudely. " Are we not beggars ?"

The old man's head dropped heavily; he relinquished the grasp of his son's hand, and his outstretched arm fell powerless to his side. "I was forgetting," murmured he, in a broken voice ; " it is as you say—you are right, Mark—you *must* go."

Few and simple as the words were, the utterance sank deep into the young man's heart; they seemed the last effort of courage wrung from despair, and breathed a pathos he was unable to resist.

"I'll not leave you," said he, in a voice scarce louder than a whisper, "there's my hand upon it ;" and he wrung in his strong grasp the unresist·ing fingers of the old man. "That's a promise, father, and now let us speak no more about it."

"I'll get to my bed, Mark," said the O'Donoghue, as he pressed his hands upon his throbbing temples. It was many a day since anything like emotion had moved him, and the conflict of passion had worn and exhausted him. "Good night, my boy—my own boy ;" and he fell upon the youth's shoulder, half choked with sobs.

As the O'Donoghue slowly ascended the stairs towards his bedroom, Mark threw himself upon a chair, and buried his face in his hands. His sorrow was a deep one. The resolve he had just abandoned had been for many a day the cherished dream of his heart—his comfort under every afflic·tion—his support against every difficulty. To seek his fortune in some foreign service—to win an honourable name, even though in a strange land, was the whole ambition of his life; and so engrossed was he in his own cal·culations, that he never deigned a thought of what his father might feel about it. The poverty that eats its way to the heart of families seldom fails to loosen the ties of domestic affection. The daily struggle, the hourly conflict with necessity, too often destroy the delicate and trustful sense of protection that youth should feel towards age. The energies that should have expanded into homely affection and mutual regard, are spent in ward·ing off a common enemy; and with weary minds and seared hearts the gentler charities of life have few sympathies. Thus was it here. Mark mistook his selfishness for a feeling of independence; he thought indiffer·ence to others meant confidence in himself—and he was not the first who made the mistake.

Tired with thinking, and harassed with difficulties, through which he could see no means of escape, he threw open the window, to suffer the cool night air to blow upon his throbbing temples, and sat down beside the casement to enjoy its refreshing influence. The candles had burned down in the apartment, and the fire, now reduced to a mere mass of red embers, scarce threw a gleam beyond the broad hearth-stone. The old tower itself flung a dark shadow upon the rock, and across the road beneath it, and, except in the chamber of the sick boy, in a distant part of the building, not a light was to be seen.

The night was calm and star-lit: a stillness almost painful reigned around. It seemed as if exhausted nature, tired with the work of storm and hurricane, had sunk into a deep and wearied sleep. Thousands of bright stars speckled the dark sky; yet the light they shed upon the earth but dimly distinguished mountain and valley, save where the calm surface of the lake gave back their lustre in a heaven placid and motionless as their own. Now and then a bright meteor would shoot across the blue vault, and disappear in the darkness; while in tranquil splendour the planets shone on, as though to say, the higher destiny is rather to display an eternal brightness than the brilliancy of momentary splendour, however glittering its wide career.

The young man gazed upon the sky. The lessons which, from human lips, he had rejected with scorn and impatience, now sank deeply into his nature from those silent monitors. The stars looked down, like eyes, into his very soul, and he felt as if he could unburden his whole heart of its weary load, and make a confidence with heaven.

"*They* point ever downwards," said he to himself, as he watched the bright streak of the falling stars, and moralised on their likeness to man's destiny. But, as he spoke, a red line shot up into the sky, and broke into ten thousand glittering spangles, shedding over glen and mountain a faint but beauteous gleam, scarce more lasting than the meteor's flash. It was a rocket sent up from the border of the bay, and was quickly answered by another from the remote end of the glen. The youth started, and leaning out from the window, looked down the valley; but nothing was to be seen or heard—all was silent as before, and already the flash of the signals, for such they must have been he could not doubt, had faded away, and the sky shone in its own spangled beauty.

"They are smugglers!" muttered Mark, as he sank back in his chair; for in that wild district such signals were employed without much fear by those who either could trust the revenue as accomplices, or dare them by superior numbers. More than once it had occurred to him to join this lawless band, and many a pressing invitation had he received from the leaders to do so; but still the youth's ambition, save in his darkest hours, took a higher and a nobler range. The danger of the career was its only fascination to him. Now, however, all these thoughts were changed. He had given a solemn pledge to his father never to leave him; and it was with a feeling of half apathy he sat pondering over what cutter it might be that had anchored, or whose party were then preparing to land their cargo.

"Ambrose Denner, belike," muttered he to himself, "the Flemish fellow from the Scheldt—a greedy old scoundrel too—he refused a passage to a poor wretch that broke the gaol in Limerick, because he could not pay for it. I wish the people here may remember it to him. Maybe its Hans 'der Teufel,' though, as they call him; or Flahault—he's the best of them, if there be a difference. I've half a mind to go down the glen and see;" and while he hesitated, a low, monotonous sound of feet, as if marching, struck on his ear; and as he listened, he heard the distant tramp of men, moving in what seemed a great number. These could not be the smugglers, he

well knew : reckless and fearless as they were, they never came in such
large bodies as these noises portended.

There is something solemn in the sound of marching heard in the stillness
of the night, and so Mark felt it, as with cautious breathing he leaned upon
the window and bent his ear to listen.   Nearer and nearer they came, till at
last the footfalls beat loudly on the dull ground, as, in measured tread, they
stepped.   At first, a dark moving mass, that seemed to fill the narrow road,
was all he could discern, but as this came closer, he could perceive that they
marched in companies or divisions, each headed by his leader, who, from
time to time, stepped from his place, and observed their order and precision.
They were all country people ; their dress, as well as he could discern, the
common costume of every day, undistinguished by any military emblem.
Nor did they carry arms ; the captains alone wore a kind of white scarf
over the shoulder, which could be distinctly seen even by the imperfect
light.   They alone carried swords, with which they checked the movements
from time to time.   Not a word was uttered in the dense ranks—not a
murmur broke the stillness of the solemn scene, as that host poured on,
the one command, " Right shoulders forward—wheel !" being given at intervals, as the parties defiled beneath the rock, at which place the road made
an abrupt turning.

So strange the spectacle, so different from all he had ever witnessed or heard
of, the youth more than once half doubted lest a wearied and fevered brain
had not called up the illusion ; but as he continued to gaze on the moving
multitude, he was assured of its reality ; and now was he harassed by conjectures what it all should mean.   For nearly an hour—to him it seemed
many such—the human tide flowed on, till at length the sounds grew fainter,
and the last party moved by, followed, at a little distance, by two figures on
horseback.   Their long cloaks concealed the wearers completely from his
view, but he could distinctly mark the steel scabbards of swords, and hear
their heavy clank against the horses' flanks.

Suffering their party to proceed, the horsemen halted for a few seconds at
the foot of the rock, and as they reined in, one called out to the other, in a
voice every syllable of which fell distinctly on Mark's ears,

" That's the place, Godfrey ; and even by this light you can judge of its
strength."

" But why is he not with us?" said the other, hastily.   " Has he not an
inheritance to win back—a confiscation to wipe out ?"

" True enough," said the first speaker; " but eighty winters do not improve a man's nerve for a hazardous exploit.   He has a son, though, and,
as I hear, a bold fellow."

" Look to him, Harvey : it is of moment that we should have one so near
the bay.   See to this quickly.   If he be like what you say, and desires a
command——" The rest was lost in the sound of their retreating hoofs,

for already the party resumed their journey, and were in a few minutes hidden from his view.

With many a conflicting doubt, and many a conjecture, each wilder than the other, Mark pondered over what he had seen, nor noted the time as it slipped past, till the grey tint of day-dawn warned him of the hour. The rumbling sounds of a country cart just then attracted his attention, and he beheld a countryman, with a little load of turf, on his way to the market at Killarney. Seeing that the man must have met the procession, he called aloud,

"I say, my good man, where were they all marching to-night, those fellows?"

"What fellows, your honour?" said the man, as he touched his hat obsequiously.

"That great crowd of people—you could not help meeting them—there was no other road they could take."

"Sorra man, woman, or child I seen, your honour, since I left home, and that's eight miles from this." And so saying he followed his journey, leaving Mark in greater bewilderment than before.

CHAPTER XIII.

"THE GUARDSMAN."

LEAVING for a brief season Glenflesk and its inhabitants, we shall ask of our readers to accompany us to London, to a scene somewhat different from that of our last chapter.

In a handsomely furnished drawing-room in St. James's-street, where the appliances of ease and luxury were blended with the evidence of those tastes so popular among young men of fashion of the period, sat, or rather lay, in a deep cushioned arm-chair, a young officer, who, even in the dishabille of the morning, and with the evident traces of fatigue and dissipation on his brow, was strikingly handsome. Though not more than three or four-and-twenty, the habits of his life, and the assured features of his character, made him appear several years older. In figure he was tall and well-proportioned, while his countenance bore those lineaments which are pre-eminently distinguished as Saxon—massive but well-chiselled features, the harmony of whose expression is even more striking than their individual excellence; a look of frank daring, which many were prone to attribute to superciliousness, was the most marked trait in his face, nor was the impression lessened

by a certain *hauteur* which military men of the time assumed, and which he,
in particular, somewhat prided himself on.

The gifts of fortune and the graces of person will often seem to invest
their possessor with attributes of insolence and overbearing, which are, in
reality, nothing more than the unbridled buoyancy of youth and power revelling in its own exercise.

We have no fancy to practise mystery with our reader, and shall at once
introduce him to Frederick Travers, Sir Marmaduke's only son, and captain
in the First Regiment of Guards. Wealth and good looks were about as
popular fifty years ago as they are in the year we write in, and Frederick
Travers was as universal a favourite in the circles he frequented as any man
of his day. Courtly manners, spirits nothing could depress, a courage
nothing could daunt, expensive tastes, gratified as rapidly as they were
conceived, were all accessories which won their way among his acquaintances,
and made them proud of his intimacy and boastful of his friendship. That
circumstances like these should have rendered a young man self-willed and
imperious, is not to be wondered at, and such was he in reality—less, however, from the unlimited licence of his position, than from an hereditary
feature which distinguished every member of his family, and made them as
intolerant of restraint as they were wayward in purpose. The motto of
their house was the index of their character, and in every act and thought
they seemed under the influence of their emblazoned inscription, "A tort et
à travers."

Over his father, Frederick Travers exercised an unlimited influence; from
his boyhood upward he had never met a contradiction, and the natural
goodness of his temper, and the affectionate turn of his disposition, made
the old man believe in the excellence of a system whose success lay less in
its principle than in the virtue of him on whom it was practised.

Sir Marmaduke felt proud of his son's career in the world, and enjoyed
to the utmost all the flattery which the young man's acceptance in society
conferred; he was proud of him almost as much as he was fond of him, and
a letter from Frederick had always the effect of restoring his spirits, no
matter how deep their depression the moment before.

The youth returned his father's affection with his whole heart; he knew
and valued all the high and generous principles of his nature; he estimated
with an honest pride those gifts which had won Sir Marmaduke the esteem
and respect of his fellow-citizens; but yet he thought he could trace certain
weaknesses of character from which his own more enlarged sphere of life
had freed him.

Fashionable associates, the society of men of wit and pleasure, seem often
to suggest more acute and subtle views of life than are to be obtained in
less exalted and distinguished company; the smart sayings and witty epi-
grams which are current among clever men appear to be so many texts in

the wisdom of the world. Nothing is more common than this mistake; nothing more frequent than to find that intercourse with such people diffuses few, if any, of their distinguishing merits among their less gifted associates, who rarely learn anything from the intercourse but a hearty contempt for all who are debarred from it. Frederick was of this school; the set he moved in was his religion—their phrases, their prejudices, their passions, he regarded as standards for all imitation. It is not surprising, then, if he conceived many of his father's notions obsolete and antiquated, and had they not been his, he would have treated them as ridiculous.

This somewhat tedious explanation of a character with whom we have not any very lengthened business hereafter, demands some apology from us; still, without it, we should be unable to explain to our reader the reason of those events to whose narrative we are hastening.

On the table, among the materials of a yet untasted breakfast, lay an open letter, which, from time to time, the young man read, and as often threw from him, with expressions of impatience and anger. A night of more than ordinary dissipation had made him irritable, and the contents of the epistle did not seem of a character to calm him.

" I knew it," said he at last, as he crushed the letter in his hand. " I knew it well; my poor father is unfit to cope with those savages; what could ever have persuaded him to venture among them I know not ; the few hundreds a year the whole estate produces are not worth as many weeks' annoyance. Hemsworth knows them well; he is the only man fit to deal with them. Heigho !" said he, with a sigh, "there's nothing for it, I suppose, but to bring them back again as soon as may be; and this confounded accident Hemsworth has met with in the Highlands will lay him on his back these five weeks—I must e'en go myself. Yet nothing was ever more ill-timed : the Queen's *fête* at Frogmore, fixed for Wednesday; there's the tennis match on Friday; and Saturday, the first day of the stag hounds. It is too bad. Hemsworth is greatly to blame; he should have been candid about these people, and not have made his Pandemonium an Arcadia. My father is also to blame ; he might have asked my advice about this trip ; and Sybella, too, why didn't she write ? She above all should have warned me about the folly." And thus did he accuse in turn all the parties concerned in a calamity, which, after all, he saw chiefly reflected in the inconvenience it caused himself.

Now, assuredly, Hemsworth requires some vindication at our hands. It had never entered into that worthy man's most imaginative conceptions to believe a visit from Sir Marmaduke to his Irish property within the reach of possibility; for although, as we have already said, he was in the constant habit of entreating Sir Marmaduke to bestow this mark of condescension on his Irish tenants, he ever contrived to accompany the recommendation with certain casual hints about the habits and customs of the na-

tives, as might well be supposed sufficient to deter a more adventurous traveller than the old baronet; and while he pressed him to come and see for
himself, he at the same time plied him with newspapers and journals, whose
columns were crammed with the fertile theme of outrage; the editorial com-
ments on which often indicated a barbarism even deeper than the offence
they affected to deplore. The accident which ultimately led to Sir Marmaduke's hurried journey was a casualty which Hemsworth had overlooked, and when he heard that the family were actually domesticated at
the Lodge, his regrets were indeed great. It was only on the day before
the intelligence reached him—for the letter had followed him from place to
place for a fortnight—that he had the misfortune to break his leg, by a fall
from a cliff in deer shooting. Whatever the urgency of the measure, he was
totally incapable of undertaking a journey to Ireland, whither, under other
circumstances, he would have hastened with all speed. Hemsworth's cor-
respondent, of whom we shall have occasion to speak more hereafter, was
the sub-agent of the estate—a creature of his own, in every sense, and far
more in his interest than in that of his principal. He told him, in forcible
terms, how Sir Marmaduke had commenced his work of Irish reformation;
that, already, both the baronet and his daughter had undertaken the task of
improvement among the tenantry; that rents were to be lowered, school-
houses erected, medical aid provided for the sick and suffering, more comfortable dwellings built, more liberal wages allowed; he narrated how
rapidly the people, at first suspicious and distrustful, were learning to feel
confidence in their benefactor, and anxious to avail themselves of his benevolence ; but more than all, he dwelt upon the conviction, which every hour
gained ground among them, that Hemsworth had misrepresented the landlord, and that, so far from being himself the instrument of, he had been the
obstacle to, their welfare and happiness. The letter concluded with a
pressing entreaty for his speedy return to the Lodge, as, should he be
longer absent, the mischief would become past remedy.

    Never did agent receive an epistle more alarming ; he saw the game, for
which he had been playing half a lifetime, slip from him at the very moment
of winning. For above twenty years his heart was set upon becoming the
owner of the estate ; all his plans, his plots, his machinations, had no other
end or object. From the deepest stroke of his policy, to the most trivial act
of his power, he had held this in view. By his artful management a veil
was drawn between the landlord and the people, which no acuteness on
either side could penetrate. The very acts intended as benefits by the
owner of the soil passed through such a medium that they diverged from
their destined direction, and fell less as blessings than inflictions. The
landlord was taught to regard the tenant as incurably sunk in barbarism,
ignorance, and superstition. The tenant to suppose the landlord a cruel,
unfeeling taskmaster, with no care but for his rent; neither sympathy for

their sufferings, nor sorrow for their calamities. Hemsworth played his game like a master; for while obtaining the smallest amount of rental for his chief, he exacted the most onerous and impoverishing terms from the people. Thus diminishing the apparent value of the property, he hoped one day to be able to purchase, and at the same time preparing it for becoming a lucrative and valuable possession; for although the rents were nominally low, the amount of fees and "duty-labour" were enormous. There was scarcely a man upon the property whose rent was paid to the day and hour; and for the favour of some brief delay, certain services were exacted which virtually reduced the tenants to a vassalage the most miserable and degrading.

If, then, the eye ranged over a district of poverty-struck and starving peasantry, with wretched hovels, naked children, and rude, unprofitable tillage, let the glance but turn to the farm around the Lodge, and there the trim fences, the well-weeded corn, and the nicely-cultivated fields, were an evidence of what well-directed labour could effect; and the astounding lesson seemed to say: "Here is an object for imitation. Look at yonder wheat: see that clover, and the meadow beyond it. They could all do likewise. Their land is the same, the climate the same, the rent the same; but yet ignorance and obstinacy are incurable. They will not be taught—prefer their own barbarous ways to newer and better methods—in fact, are beyond the lessons of either precept or example."

Yet, what was the real case? To till that model-farm, to make these fields the perfection you see them, families were starving, age left to totter to the grave uncared for, manhood pining in want and misery, and infancy to dawn upon suffering to last a life long. Duty-labour calls the poor man from the humble care of his own farm to come, with his whole house, and toil upon the rich man's fields, the requital for which is some poor grace of a week's or a month's forbearance ere he be called on for that rent these exactions are preventing him from earning. Duty-labour summons him from his own profitless ground to behold the fruits his exertions are raising for another's enjoyment, and of which he must never taste. Duty-labour culls the days of fair sky and sunshine, and leaves him the gloomy hours of winter, when, with darkness without and despair within, he may brood, as he digs, over the disproportioned fortunes of his tyrant and himself. Duty-labour is the type of a slavery that hardens the heart, by extinguishing all hope, and uprooting every feeling of self-confidence and reliance, till, in abject and degraded misery, the wretched man grows reckless of his life, while his vengeance yearns for that of his taskmaster.

Nor does the system end here. The agent must be conciliated by presents of various kinds : the humble pittance wrung from misery and hoarded up by industry must be offered to him, as the means of obtaining some poor and petty favour—most frequently one the rightful due of the asker. A tyranny like this spreads its baneful influence far beyond the afflictions of mere poverty—it breaks down the spirit, it demoralises the heart of a people; for where was black-mail ever extorted that it did not engender cruelty on the one hand and abject slavery on the other?

So far from regarding those placed above them in rank and station as their natural friends and protectors, the peasantry felt the great man as their oppressor. They knew him not as their comforter in sickness, their help in time of trouble—they only saw in him the rigid exactor of his rent, the merciless taskmaster who cared not for time or season, save those that brought round the period of repayment; and as year by year poverty and misery ate deeper into their natures, and hope died out, fearful thoughts of retribution flashed upon minds on which no prospect of better days shone; and, in the gloomy desolation of their dark hours, they wished and prayed for any change, come in what shape, and surrounded by what danger it might, if only this bondage should cease.

Men spoke of their light-heartedness, their gaiety of temper, their flashing and brilliant wit. How little they knew that such qualities, by some strange incongruity of our natures, are the accompaniments of deeply-reflective and imaginative minds, overshadowed by lowering fortune. The glittering fancy that seems to illumine the path of life is often but the wild-fire that dances over the bleak and desolate heath.

Their apathy and indifference to exertion was made a matter of reproach to them; yet, was it ever known that toil should be voluntary, when hopeless, and that labour should be endured without a prospect of requital?

We have been led almost unconsciously into this somewhat lengthened digression, for which, even did it not bear upon the circumstances of our story, we would not seek to apologise to our reader. Such we believe to have been, in great part, the wrongs of Ireland—the fertile source of those thousand evils under which the land was suffering. From this one theme have arisen most, if not all, the calamities of the country. Happy were it if we could say that such existed no longer—that such a state of things was a matter for historical inquiry, or an old man's memory—and that, in our own day, these instances were not to be found among us.

When Hemsworth perceived that the project of his life was in peril, he bethought him of every means by which the danger could be averted. Deep and well-founded as was his confidence in the cleverness of his deputy, his station was an insurmountable barrier to his utility at the present conjuncture. Sam Wylie, for so this worthy was called, was admirable as a spy, but never could be employed as minister plenipotentiary: it needed one, now, who should possess more influence over Sir Marmaduke himself. For this purpose, Frederick Travers alone seemed the fitting person; to him, therefore, Hemsworth wrote a letter marked "strictly confidential," detailing, with painstaking accuracy, the inevitable misfortunes Sir Marmaduke's visit would entail upon a people whose demands no benevolence could satisfy, whose expectations no concessions could content.

He narrated the fearful instances of their vengeance, whenever disappointment had chocked the strong current of their hopes; and told, with all the semblance of truth, of scenes of bloodshed and murder, no cause for which could be traced, save in the dark suspicions of a people long accustomed to regard the Saxon as their tyrant.

The night attack upon the Lodge furnished also its theme of terror; and so artfully did he blend his fact and fiction, his true statement aud his false inference, that the young man read the epistle with an anxious and beating heart, and louged for the hour when he should recal those he held dearest from such a land of anarchy and misfortune.

Not satisfied with the immediate object in view, Hemsworth ingeniously contrived to instil into Frederick's mind misgivings as to the value of an estate thus circumstauced, representing, not without some truth on his side, that the only chance of bettering the coudition of a peasantry so sunk and degraded, was by an actual residence in the midst of them—a penalty which, to the youth, scemed too dear for any requital whatever.

On a separate slip of paper, marked "to be burued when read," Frederick deciphered the following lines:

"Above all things, I would caution you regardiug a family who, though merely of the rank of farmer, affect a gentility which had its origin some dozen centuries back, and has had ample opportuuity to leak out in the mean time; these are the 'O'Donoghues,' a dangerous set, haughty, ill-conditioned, and scheming. They will endeavour, if they can, to obtain influence with your father, aud I cannot too strongly represent the hazard of such an event. Do not, I entreat you, suffer his compassion, or mistaken benevolence, to be exercised in their behalf. Were they merely unworthy, I should say nothiug on the subject; but they are highly aud eminently dangerous, in a land where their claims are regarded as only in abeyance—deferred, but not obliterated, by confiscation.

"E. H."

It would in no wise forward the views of our story were we to detail to our readers the affecting scenes which preluded Frederick's departure from London, the explanations he was called on to repeat, as he went from house to house, for a journey at once so sudden aud extraordinary; for even so late as fifty years ago, a visit to Ireland was a matter of more moment, and accompanied by more solemn preparation, thau mauy now bestow ou an overland journey to India. The Lady Marys and Bettys of the fashionable world regarded him pretty much as the damsels of old did some doughty knight, wheu setting forth on his way to Palestine. That filial affection could exact such an instance of devotion called up their astonishment even more than their admiration; and many were the cautions, many the friendly counsels, given to the youth for his preservation in a land so rife with danger.

Frederick was a soldier, and a brave one; but still he was not entirely divested of those apprehensions which the ignorance of the day propagated; and although only accompanied by a single servant, they were both armed to the teeth, and prepared to do valiant battle, if need be, against the Irish "rogues and rapparees."

Here, then, for the present, we shall leave him, having made his last "adieux" to his friends, and set out on his journey to Ireland.

CHAPTER XIV.

THE COMMENTS ON A HURRIED DEPARTURE.

BRIEF as has been the interval of our absence from Glenflesk, time's changes have been there. Herbert O'Donoghue had experienced a fortunate change in his malady, and on the day following Roach's eventful return, became actually out of danger. The symptoms of his disease, so suddenly subdued, seemed to reflect immortal honour on the doctor, who certainly did not scruple to attribute to his skill what, with more truth, was owing to native vigour and youth. Sir Archy alone was ungrateful enough to deny the claim of physic, and slightly hinted to Roach that he had at least benefited his patient by example, if not precept, since he had slept the entire night through, without awaking. The remark was a declaration of war at once; nor was Roach slow to accept the gage of battle—in fact, both parties were well wearied of the truce, and anxious for the fray. Sir Archibald had only waited till the moment Roach's services in the sick-room could be safely dispensed with, to reopen his fire; while Roach, harassed by so unexpected a peace, felt like a beleaguered fortress during the operation of the miners, and knew not when, and how, the dreaded explosion was to occur. Now, however, the signal-gun was fired—hesitation was at an end; and, of a verity, the champions showed no disinclination for the field.

"Ye'll be hungry this morning, doctor," said Sir Archy, "and I have ordered breakfast a bit early. A pick o' ham at twelve o'clock, and a quart of sherry, aye gives a man a relish for breakfast."

"Begad, so it might, or for supper too," responded Roach, "when the ham was a shank-bone, and the sherry-bottle like a four-ounce mixture."

" Ye slept surprisingly after your slight refection. I heerd ye snoring like a grampus."

" 'Twasn't the nightmare from indigestion, anyhow," said Roach, with a grin. " I'll give you a clean bill of health from that malady here."

" It's weel for us that we ken a cure for it—more than ye can say for the case you've just left."

" I saved the boy's life," said Roach, indignantly.

" Assuredly ye did na kill him, and folks canna a'ways say as muckle for ye. We maun thank the Lord for a' his mercies; and he vouchsafed you a vara sound sleep."

How this controversy was to be carried on further it is not easy to say, but at this moment the door of the breakfast-room opened cautiously, and a wild, rough head peeped stealthily in, which gradually was followed by the neck, and in succession the rest of the figure of Kerry O'Leary, who, dropping down on both knees before the doctor, cried out in a most lamentable accent,

" Oh! docther, darlint—docther dear—forgive me—for the love of Joseph, forgive me!"

Roach's temper was not in its blandest moment, and his face grew purple with passion as he beheld the author of his misfortunes at his feet.

" Get out of my sight, you scoundrel; I never want to set eyes on you till I see you in the dock—ay, with handcuffs on you."

" Oh, murther, murther, is it take the law of me for a charge of swan-drops? Oh, docther acushla, don't say you'll do it."

" I'll have your life, as sure as my name's Roach."

" Try him wi' a draught," interposed M'Nab.

" Begorra, I'm willin'," cried Kerry, grasping at the mediation. " I'll take anything, barrin' the black grease he gave the masther—that would kill the divil."

This exceptive compliment to his skill was not so acceptable to the doctor, whose passion boiled over at the new indignity.

" I'll spend fifty guineas but I'll hang you—there's my word on it."

" Oh, wirra! wirra!" cried Kerry, whose apprehensions of how much law might be had for the money made him tremble all over, " that's what I get for tramping the roads all night after the pony."

" Where's the pony—where's the gig?" called out Roach, suddenly reminded by material interests that he had more at stake than mere vengeance.

" The beast is snug in the stable—that's where he is, eating a peck of oats—last year's corn—divil a less."

" And the gig?"

" Oh, the gig is it? Musha, we have the gig, too," responded Kerry, but with a reluctance that could not escape the shrewd questioner.

"Where is it, then?" said Roach, impatiently.

"Where would it be, but in the yard? We're going to wash it."

The doctor did not wait for the conclusion of this reply, but hastening from the room, passed down the few stairs that led towards the old court-yard, followed by Sir Archy and Kerry, the one eager to witness the termination of the scene, the other muttering in a very different spirit, " Oh, but it's now we'll have the divil to pay !"

As soon as Roach arrived at the court-yard, he turned his eyes on every side to seek his conveyance; but although there were old harrows, broken ploughs, and disabled wheelbarrows in numbers, nothing was there that bore any resemblance to what he sought.

"Where is it?" said he, turning to Kerry, with a look of exasperation that defied all attempt to assuage by mere "blaruey"—"where is it ?"

"Here it is, then," said O'Leary, with the tone of one whose courage was nerved by utter despair, while, at the same time, he drew forth two wheels and an axle, the sole surviving members of the late vehicle. As he displayed the wreck before them, the ludicrous—always too strong for an Irish peasant, no matter how much it may be associated with his own personal danger—overcame his more discreet instincts, and he broke forth into a broad grin, while he cried, "'There's the inside of her now !' as Darby Cossoon said, when he tuk his watch in pieces, ' and, begorra, we'll see how she's made, any way.' "

This true history must not recount the expressions in which Roach permitted himself to indulge. It is enough to say that his passion took the most violent form of invective against the house, the glen, the family, and their retainers, to an extreme generation, while he stamped and gesticulated like one insane.

"Ye'll hae sma' space for yer luggage in yon," said M'Nab, with one of his driest laughs, while he turned back and re-entered the house.

"Where's my pony?—where's my pony ?" shouted out the Doctor, determined to face all his calamities at once.

"Oh, faix, he's nothing the worse," said Kerry, as he unlocked the door of the stable, and pointed with all the pride of veracity to a beast in the stall before him. " There he is, jumping like a kid out of his skin wid fun this morning."

Now, although the first part of Kerry's simile was assuredly incorrect, as no kid of which we have any record ever bore the least resemblance to the animal in question, as to the fact of being " out of his skin" there could not be a second opinion, the beast being almost entirely flayed from his shoulders to his haunches, his eyes being represented by two globular masses about the size of billiard-balls, and his tail bearing some affinity to an overgrown bamboo, as it hung down, jointed and knotted, but totally destitute of hair.

" The thief of the world," said Kerry, as he patted him playfully, " he stripped a trifle of hair off him with kicking, but a little gunpowder and butter will bring it on again in a day or two."

" Liar that thou art, Kerry—it would take a cask of one and a firkin of the other to make up the necessary ointment !"

There are some evils which no anticipation can paint equal to their severity, and these, in compensation, perhaps, are borne for the most part without the same violent exuberance of sorrow lesser misfortunes elicit. So it was—Roach spoke not a word : one menace of his clenched hand towards Kerry was the only token he gave of his malice, and he left the stable.

" I've a note here for Doctor Roach," said a servant, in Sir Marmaduke's livery, to Kerry, as he proceeded to close and lock the stable door.

" I'm the person," said the Doctor, taking the billet and breaking the seal. " Have you the carriage here now ?" asked he, when he had finished reading.

" Yes, sir, it's on the road. Sir Marmaduke desired me not to drive up, for fear of disturbing the sick gentleman."

" I'm ready, then," said the Doctor ; and never casting a look backward, nor vouchsafing another word, he passed out of the gate, and descended towards the high road.

" I'll take good care of the baste till I see you, sir !" shouted Kerry after him ; and then, as the distance widened, he added, " and may I never see your ould yallow wig agin, I pray this day. Divil take me, but I hope you've some of the slugs in ye, after all." And with these pious wishes, expressed fervently, Kerry returned to the house, his heart considerably lightened by the doctor's departure.

Scarcely was he seated beside the kitchen fire—the asylum he regarded as his own—when, all fears for his misconduct and its consequences past, he began speculating in a very Irish fashion on the reasons of the doctor's sudden departure.

" He's off now to the Lodge—divil fear him—faix if he gets in there, they'll not get him out so asy—they'll have a pain for every day of the week before he leaves them. Well, well, thanks be to God, he's out of this."

" Is he gone, Kerry ?" said Mrs. Branaghan. " Did he leave a 'cure' for Master Herbert before he went ?"

" Sorra bit," cried Kerry, as if a sudden thought struck him, " that's what he didn't !" And, without hesitating another moment, he sprang from his chair, and mounted the stairs towards the parlour, where now the O'Donoghue, Mark, and Sir Archy were assembled at breakfast.

" He's away, sir, he's off again," said Kerry, as though the nature of his tidings did not demand any more ceremonious preliminary.

" Who's away ! Who's gone ?" cried they all in a breath.

" The doctor, sir—Doctor Roach. There was a chap in a sky-blue livery
came up with a bit of a letter for him to go down there, and when he read
it, he just turned about, this way"—here Kerry performed a not over graceful pirouette—" and without saying 'By yer leave,' he walks down the road
and gets into the coach. ' Won't you see Master Herbert before you go,
sir,' says I; 'sure you're not leaving him that way?' but bad luck to one
word he'd say, but went away wid a grin on him."

" What !" cried Mark, as his face crimsoned with passion. " Is this
true ?—are you sure of what you're saying?"

" I'll take the book an it," said Kerry, solemnly.

" Well, Archy," said the O'Donoghue, addressing his brother-in-law.
" You are a good judge of these matters. Is this conduct on the part of
our neighbours suitable or becoming ? Was it exactly right and proper to
send here for one whose services we had taken the trouble to seek, and
might much have needed besides ? Should we not have been consulted,
think you ?"

" There's not a poor farmer in the glen would not resent it !" cried Mark,
passionately.

" Bide a wee, bide a wee," said Sir Archy, cautiously ; " we hae na heard
a' the tale yet. Roach may perhaps explain."

" He had better not come here to do so," interrupted Mark, as he strode
the room in passion; " he has a taste for hasty departures, and, by G—, I'll
help him to one; for out of that window he goes, as sure as my name is
Mark."

" 'Tis the way to serve him, divil a doubt," chimed in Kerry, who was
not sorry to think how agreeably he might thus be relieved from any legal
difficulties.

" I am no seeking to excuse the man," said Sir Archy, temperately.
" It's weel kenned we hae na muckle love for ane anither ; but fair play is
bonnie play."

" I never heard a mean action yet, but there was a Scotch adage to warrant it," muttered Mark, in a whisper inaudible by the rest.

" It's no improbable but that Sir Marmaduke Travers did ask if the
doctor could be spared, and it's no impossible, either, that Roach took the
answering the question in his ain hands."

" I don't think so," broke in Mark; " the whole thing bears a different
aspect. It smacks of English courtesy to an Irish kern."

" By Jove, Mark is right," said the O'Donoghue, whose prejudices,
strengthened by poverty, too readily chimed in with any suspicion of intended insult.

" They were not long learning the game," said Mark, bitterly ; " they
are, if I remember aright, scarce two months in the country, and, see, they
treat us as ' mere Irish' already."

" Ye'r ower hasty, Mark   I hae na muckle respect for Roach, nor wad I vouch for his good breeding; but a gentleman, as this Sir Marmaduke's note bespeaks him——"

" What note ?   I never heard of it."

" Oh! it was a polite kind of message, Mark, to say he would be obliged if I permitted him to pay his respects here.   I forgot to tell you of it."

" Does the enemy desire a peep at the fortress, that he may calculate how long we can hold out ?" said the youth, sternly.

" Begorra, with the boys from Ballyvourney and Inchigeela, we'll howld the place agin the English army," said Kerry, mistaking the figurative meaning of the speech; and he rubbed his hands with delight at the bare prospect of such a consummation.

Sir Archy turned an angry look towards him, and motioned with his hand for him to leave the room.   Kerry closed the door after him, and for some minutes the silence was unbroken.

" What does it matter, after all ?" said the O'Donoghue, with a sigh. " It is a mere folly to care for these things, now.   When the garment is worn and threadbare, one need scarce fret that the lace is a little tarnished."

" True, sir, quite true; but you are not bound to forget or forgive him who would strip it rudely off, even a day or an hour before its time."

" There is na muckle good in drawing inferences from imaginary evils. Shadows are a' bad enough; but they needna hae children and grandchildren; and so I'll even take a cup of tea to the callant."   And thus, wise in practice and precept, Sir Archibald left the room, while O'Donoghue and Mark, already wearied of the theme, ceased to discuss it further.

CHAPTER XV.

SOME OF THE PLEASURES OF PROPERTY.

In the small, but most comfortable apartment of the Lodge, which, in virtue of its book-shelves and smartly-bound volumes, was termed "the Study," sat Sir Marmaduke Travers.   Before him was a table covered with writing materials, books, pamphlets, prints, and drawings; his great armchair was the very ideal of lounging luxury, and in the soft carpet his slippered feet were almost hidden.   Through the window at his right hand an alley in the beech wood opened a view of mountain scenery it would have been difficult to equal in any country of Europe.   In a word, it was a very charming little chamber, and might have excited the covetousness of those whose minds must minister to their maintenance, and who rarely pursue their toilsome task save debarred from every sound and sight that might foster imagination.   How almost invariably is this the case !   Who has not seen, a hundred times over, some perfect little room, every detail of whose economy seemed devised to sweeten the labour of the mind, teeming with its many appliances for enjoyment, yet encouraging thought more certainly than ministering to luxury—with its cabinet pictures, its carvings, its antique armour, suggestive in turn of some passage in history, or some page in fiction;—who has not seen these devoted to the half-hour lounge over a newspaper, or the tiresome examination of house expenditure with the steward, while he, whose mental flights were soaring midway 'twixt earth and heaven, looked out from some gloomy and cobwebbed pane upon a forest of chimneys, surrounded by all the evils of poverty, and tortured by the daily conflict with necessity.

Here sat Sir Marmaduke, a great volume like a ledger open before him, in which, from time to time, he employed himself in making short memoranda.   Directly in front of him stood, in an attitude of respectful attention, a man of about five-and-forty years of age, who, although dressed in an humble garb, had yet a look of something above the common; his features were homely, but intelligent, and though a quick, sharp glance shot from his grey eye when he spoke, yet in his soft, smooth voice the words came forth with a measured calm, that served to indicate a patient and gentle disposition.   His frame betokened strength, while his face was pale and colourless, and without the other indications of active health in his gait and walk would have implied a delicacy of constitution.   This was Sam Wylie, the sub-agent—one whose history may be told in a few words :—His father had been a butler in the O'Donoghue house, where he died, leaving his son, a mere child, as a legacy to his master.   The boy, however, did not turn out well; delinquencies of various kinds—theft among the number—were discovered against him; and after many, but ineffectual, efforts to reclaim him, he was turned off, and advised, as he wished to escape worse, to leave the county.   He took the counsel, and did so; nor for many a year after was he seen or heard of.   A report ran that he passed fourteen years in transportation; but however that might be, when he next appeared in Kerry, it was in the train of a civil engineer, come to make surveys of the county. His cleverness and skill in this occupation recommended him to the notice of Hemsworth, who soon after appointed him as bailiff, and subsequently sub-agent on the estate; and in this capacity he had now served about fifteen years, to the perfect satisfaction, and with the full confidence of his chief.   Of his "antecedents" Sir Marmaduke knew nothing; he was only aware of the implicit trust Hemsworth had in him, and his own brief experience perfectly concurred in the justice of the opinion.   He certainly found him intelligent, and thoroughly well informed on all connected with the property. When questioned, his answers were prompt, direct, and to the purpose; and to one of Sir Marmaduke's business habits this quality possessed merit of the highest order. If he had a fault with him, it was one he could readily pardon—a leniency towards the people—a desire to palliate their errors and extenuate their failings—and always to promise well for the future, even when the present looked least auspicious. His hearty concurrence with all the old baronet's plans for improvement were also highly in his favour; and already Wylie was looked on as "a very acute fellow, and with really wonderful shrewdness for his station;" as if any of that acuteness or that shrewdness, so estimated, could have its growth in a more prolific soil than in the heart and mind of one bred and reared among the people, who knew their habits, their tone of thinking, their manners, and their motives—not through any false medium of speculation and theory, but practically, innately, instinctively—who had not studied the peasantry like an algebraic formula, or a problem in Euclid, but read them as they sat beside their turf fires, in the smoke of their mud hovels, cowering from the cold of winter, and gathering around the scanty meal of potatoes—the only tribute they had not rendered to the landlord.

"Roger Sweeney," said Sir Marmaduke—"Roger Sweeney complains of his distance from the bog; he cannot draw his turf so easily as when he lived on that swamp below the lake; but I think the change ought to recompense him for the inconvenience."

"He's a Ballyvourney man, your honour," said Sam, placidly, "and if you couldn't bring the turf up to his door, and cut it for him, and stack it, and carry a creel of it inside, to make the fire, he'd not be content."

"Oh, that's it, is it?" said Sir Marmaduke, accepting an explanation he was far from thoroughly understanding. "Then there's Jack Heffernan—what does this fellow mean by saying that a Berkshire pig is no good?"

"He only means, your honour, that he's too good for the place, and wants better food than the rest of the family."

"The man's a fool, and must learn better. Lord Mudford told me that he never saw such an excellent breed, and his swineherd is one of the most experienced fellows in England. Widow Mul—Mul—what?" said he, endeavouring to spell an unusually long name in the book before him—"Mulla——"

"Mallahedert, your honour," slipped in Wylie, "a very dacent crayture."

"Then why won't she keep those beehives? Can't she see what an excellent thing honey is in the house?—if one of her children was sick, for instance."

"True for you, sir," said Sam, without the slightest change of feature. "It is wonderful how your honour can have the mind to think of these things—upon my word, it's surprising."

" Samuel M'Elroy refuses to drain the field—does he?"

" No, sir ; but he says the praties isn't worth digging out of dry ground, nor never does grow to any size.   He's a Ballyvourney man, too, sir."

" Oh, is he?" said Sir Marmaduke, accepting this as a receipt in full for any degree of eccentricity.

" Shamus M'Gillicuddy—Heavens, what a name ! This Shamus appears a very desperate fellow; he beat a man the other evening, coming back from the market."

" It was only a neighbour, sir ; they live fornint each other."

" A neighbour ! but bless my heart, that makes it worse."

" Sure, sir, it was nothing to speak of ; it was Darby Lenahan said your honour's bull was a pride to the place, and Shamus said the O'Donoghue's was a finer baste any day; and from one word they came to another, and the end of it was, Lenahan got a crack on the skull that laid him quivering on the daisies."

" Savage ruffian, that Shamus ; I'll keep a sharp eye on him."

" Faix, and there's no need—he's a Ballyvourney man."

The old baronet looked up from his large volume, and seemed for a moment undecided whether he should not ask the meaning of a phrase, which, occurring at every moment, appeared most perplexing in signification ; but the thought that by doing so he should confess his ignorance before the sub-agent, deterred him, and he resolved to leave the interpretation to time and his own ingenuity.

" What of this old fellow, who has the mill?—has he consented to have the overshot wheel?"

" He tried it on Tuesday, sir," said Sam, with an almost imperceptible smile, " and the sluice gave way, and carried off the house and the end of the barn into the tail race.   He's gone in, to take an action again your honour for the damages."

" Ungrateful rascal! I told him I'd be at the whole expense myself, and I explained the great saving of water the new wheel would ensure him."

" True, indeed, sir ; but as the stream never went dry for thirty years, the ould idiot thought it would last his time.   Begorra, he had enough of water on Tuesday, anyhow."

" He's a Ballyvourney man, isn't he?"

" He is, sir," replied Wylie, with the gravity of a judge.

Another temptation crossed Sir Marmaduke's mind, but he withstood it, and went on :

" The mountain has then been divided as I ordered, has it?"

" Yes, sir; the lines were all marked out before Saturday."

" Well, I suppose the people were pleased to know that they have each their own separate pasturage?"

"Indeed, and, sir, I won't tell you a lie—they are not ; they'd rather it was the ould way still."

"What, have I taken all this trouble for nothing, then?—is it possible that they'd rather have their cattle straying wild about the country than see them grazing peaceably on their own land?"

"That's just it, sir; for you see, when they had the mountain among them, they fed on what they could get; one, had maybe a flock of goats, another, maybe a sheep or two, a heifer, an ass, or a bullsheen."

"A what ?"

"A little bull, your honour; and they didn't mind if one had more nor another, nor where they went, for the place was their own; but now that it is all marked out and divided, begorra, if a beast is got trespassing, out comes some one with a stick, and wallops him back again, and then the man that owns him, natural enough, wouldn't see shame on his cow, or whatever it was, and that leads to a fight ; and, faix, there's not a day now but there's blood spilt over the same boundaries."

"They're actually savages !" said Sir Marmaduke, as he threw his spectacles over his forehead, and dropped his pen from his fingers in mute amazement; "I never heard—I never read of such a people."

"They're Ballyvourney men," chimed in Wylie, assentively.

"D——d——"

Sir Marmaduke checked himself suddenly, for the idea flashed on him that he ought at least to know what he was cursing, and so he abstained from such a perilous course, and resumed his search in the big volume. Alas! his pursuit of information was not more successful as he proceeded. Every moment disclosed some case where, in his honest efforts to improve the condition of the people, from ignorance of their habits, from total unconsciousness of the social differences of two nations, essentially unlike, he discovered the failure of his plans, and unhesitatingly ascribed to the prejudices of the peasantry what with more justice might have been charged against his own unskilfulness. He forgot that a people long neglected cannot at once be won back—that confidence is a plant of slow growth ; but, more than all, he lost sight of the fact that to engraft the customs and wants of richer communities upon a people sunk in poverty and want, to introduce among them new and improved modes of tillage, to inculcate notions which have taken ages to grow up to maturity in more favoured lands, must be attended with failure and disappointment. On both sides the elements of success were wanting. The peasantry saw—for, however strange it may seem, through every phase of want and wretchedness their intelligence and apprehension suffer no impairment—they saw his anxiety to serve them ; they believed him to be kind-hearted and well-wishing, but they knew him to be also wrong-headed and ignorant of the country, and what he gained on the score of good feeling he lost on the score of good sense; and Paddy, however humble his lot, however hard his condition, has an innate reverence for ability, and can rarely feel attachment to the heart where he has not felt respect for the head. It is not a pleasant confession to make, yet one might explain it without detriment to the character of the people; but, assuredly, popularity in Ireland would seem to depend far more on intellectual resources than on moral principle and rectitude. Romanism has fostered this feeling, so natural is it to the devotee to regard power and goodness as inseparable, and to associate the holiness of religion with the sway and influence of the priesthood. If the tenantry regarded the landlord as a simple-hearted, crotchety old gentleman, with no harm in him, the landlord believed them to be almost incurably sunk in barbarism and superstition. Their native courtesy in declining to accept suggestions they never meant to adopt, he looked on as duplicity; he could not understand that the matter-of-fact sternness of English expression has no parallel here; that politeness, as they understood it, has a claim to which truth itself may be sacrificed; and he was ever accepting, in a literal sense, what the people intended to be received with its accustomed qualification.

But a more detrimental result followed than even these. The truly, well-conducted, and respectable portion of the tenantry felt ashamed to adopt plans and notions they knew inapplicable and unsuited to their condition; they, therefore, stood aloof, and by their honest forbearance incurred the reproach of obstinacy and barbarism; while the idle, the lazy, and the profligate became converts to any doctrine or class of opinion which promised an easy life and a rich man's favour. These, at first sight, found favour with him, as possessing more intelligence and tractability than their neighbours, and for them cottages were built, rents abated, improved stock introduced, and a hundred devices organised to make them an example for all imitation. Unhappily, the conditions of the contract were misconceived. The people believed that all the landlord required was a patient endurance of his benevolence; they never reckoned on any reciprocity in duty; they never dreamed that a Swiss cottage cannot be left to the fortunes of a mud cabin; that stagnant pools before the door, weed-grown fields, and broken fences, harmonise ill with rural palings, drill cultivation, and trim hedges. They took all they could get, but assuredly they never understood the obligation of repayment. They thought (not very unreasonably, perhaps), "It's the old gentleman's hobby that we should adopt a number of habits and customs we were never used to—live in strange houses, and work with strange tools. Be it so; we are willing to gratify him," said they; "but let him pay for his whistle."

He, on the other hand, thought they were greedily adopting what they only endured, and deemed all converts to his opinion who lived on his bounty.

Hence, each morning presented an array of the most worthless, irreclaimable of the tenantry around his door, all eagerly seeking to be included in some new scheme of regeneration, by which they understood three meals a day, and nothing to do.

How to play off these two distinct and very opposite classes, Mr. Sam Wylie knew to perfection; and while he made it appear that one portion of the tenantry whose rigid rejection of Sir Marmaduke's doctrines proceeded from a sturdy spirit of self-confidence and independence, were a set of wild, irreclaimable savages, he softly insinuated his compliments on the success in other quarters, while, in his heart, he well knew what results were about to happen.

"They're here now, sir," said Wylie, as he glanced through the window towards the lawn, where, with rigid punctuality, Sir Marmaduke each morning held his levee; and where, indeed, a very strange and motley crowd appeared.

The old baronet threw up the sash, and as he did so, a general murmur of blessings and heavenly invocations met his ears—sounds, that if one were to judge from his brightening eye and beaming countenance, he relished well. No longer, however, as of old, suppliant and entreating, with tremulous voice and shrinking gaze, did they make their advances. These people were now enlisted in his army of "regenerators;" they were converts to the landlord's manifold theories of improved agriculture, neat cottages, pigsties, dovecots, beehives, and Heaven knows what other suggestive absurdity, ease and affluence ever devised to plate over the surface of rude and rugged misery.

"The Lord bless your honour every morning you rise, 'tis the iligant little place ye gave me to live in. Musha, 'tis happy and comfortable I do be every night, now, barrin' that the slates does be falling betimes—bad luck to them for slates, one of them cut little Joe's head this morning, and I brought him up for a bit of a plaster."

This was the address of a stout, middle-aged woman, with a man's greatcoat around her in lieu of a cloak.

"Slates falling—why doesn't your husband fasten them on again? He said he was a handy fellow, and could do anything about a house."

"It was no lie, then; Thady Morris is a good warrant for a job any day, and if it was thatch was on it——"

"Thatch—why, woman, I'll have no thatch; I don't want the cabins burned down, nor will I have them the filthy hovels they used to be."

"Why would your honour?—sure there's rayson and sinse agin it," was the chorus of all present, while the woman resumed:

"Well, he tried that same too, your honour, and if he did, by my sowl, it was worse for him; for when he seen the slates going off every minit with the wind, he put the harrow on the top——"

I

" The harrow—put the harrow on the roof ?"

" Just so—wasn't it natural? But as sure as the wind riz, down came the harrow, aud stripped every dirty kippeen of a slate away with it."

" So the roof is off ?" said Sir Marmaduke, with stifled rage.

" 'Tis as clean as my five fingers, the same rafters," said she, with un-moved gravity.

" This is too bad—Wylie, do you hear this ?" said the old gentleman, with a face dark with passion.

" Ay," chorused in some half dozen friends of the woman—" nothing stands the wind like the thatch."

Wylie whispered some words to his master, and by a side gesture mo-tioned to the woman to take her departure. The hint was at once taken, and her place immediately filled by another. This was a short little old fellow, in yellow rags, his face concealed by a handkerchief, on removing which he discovered a countcnance that bore no earthly resemblance to that of a human being ; the eyes were entirely concealed by swollen masses of cheek and eyelid—the nose might have been eight noses—and the round, immense lips, and the small aperture between, looked like the opening in a ballot-box.

" Who is this?—what's the matter here ?" said Sir Marmaduke, as he stared in mingled horror and astonishment at the object before him.

" Faix, ye may well ax," said the little man, in a thick, guttural voice. " Sorra one of the neighbours knew me this morning. I'm Tim M'Garrey, of the cross-roads."

" What has happened to you, then ?" asked Sir Marmaduke, somewhat ruffled by the sturdy tone of the ragged fellow's address.

" 'Tis your own doing, then—divil a less—you may be proud of your work."

" My doing !—how do you dare to say so ?"

" 'Tis no darin' at all—'tis thruc, as I'm here. Them cursed beehives you made me take home wid me, I put them in a corner of the house, and by bad luck it was the pig's corner, and, sorra bit, but she rooted them out and upset them, and with that the varmint fell upon us all, and it was two hours before we killed them—divil such a fight ever ye seen : Peggy had the beetle, and I the griddle, for flattening them agin the wall, and maybe we didn't work hard, while the childer was roarin' and bawlin' for the bare life."

" Gracious mercy ! could this be credited ?—could any man conceive bar-barism like this ?" cried Sir Marmaduke, as with uplifted hands he stood overwhelmed with amazement.

Wylie again whispered something, aud again telegraphed to the applicant to move off ; but the little man stood his ground and continued : " 'Twas a

heifer you gave Tom Lenahan, and it's a dhroll day the M'Garreys warn't
as good as the Lenahans, to say we'd have nothing but bees, and them was
to get a dacent baste!"

"Stand aside, sir," said Sir Marmaduke; "Wylie has got my orders
about you. Who is this?"

"Faix, me, sir—Andrew Maher. I'm come to give your honour the key
—I couldn't stop there any longer."

"What! not stay in that comfortable house, with the neat shop I had
built and stocked for you? What does this mean?"

"'Tis just that, then, your honour—the house is a nate little place, and
barrin' the damp, and the little grate, that won't burn turf at all, one might
do well enough in it; but the shop is the divil entirely."

"How so—what's wrong about it?"

"Everything's wrong about it. First and foremost, your honour, the
neighbours has no money; and though they might do mighty well for want
of tobacco, and spirits, and bohea, and candles, and soap, and them trifles,
as long as they never came near them, throth they couldn't have them there
fornint their noses without wishing for a taste; and so one comes in for a
pound of sugar, and another wants a ha'porth of nails, or a piece of naygar-
head, or an ounce of starch—and divil a word they have, but 'Put it in the
book, Andy.' By my conscience, it's a quare book would hould it all."

"But they'll pay in time—they'll pay when they sell the crops."

"Bother! I ax yer honour's pardon—I was manin' they'd see me far
enough first. Sure, when they go to market, they'll have the rint, and the
tithe, and the taxes; and when that's done, and they get a sack of seed
potatoes for next year, I'd like to know where's the money that's to come
to me?"

"Is this true, Wylie?—are they as poor as this?" asked Sir Marmaduke.

Wylie's answer was still a whispered one.

"Well," said Andy, with a sigh, "there's the key, any way. I'd rather
be tachin' the gaffers again than be keeping the same shop."

These complaints were followed by others, differing in kind and complexion, but all agreeing in the violence with which they were urged, and
all inveighing against "the improvements" Sir Marmaduke was so interested in carrying forward. To hear them, you would suppose that the
grievances suggested by poverty and want were more in unison with comfort and enjoyment than all the appliances wealth can bestow; and that the
privations to which habit has inured us are sources of greater happiness
than we often feel in the use of unrestricted liberty.

Far from finding any contented, Sir Marmaduke only saw a few among
the number willing to endure his bounties, as the means of obtaining other

concessions they desired more ardently. They would keep their cabins clean if anything was to be made by it; they'd weed their potatoes if Sir Marmaduke would only offer a price for the weeds. In fact, they were ready to engage in any arduous pursuit of cleanliness, decency, and propriety, but it must be for a consideration. Otherwise, they saw no reason for encountering labour which brought no requital; and the *real* benefits offered to them came so often associated with new-fangled and absurd innovations, that both became involved in the same disgrace, and both sank in the same ridicule together. These were the refuse of the tenantry; for we have seen that the independent feeling of the better class held them aloof from all the schemes of "improvement," which the others, by participating in, contaminated.

Sir Marmaduke might, then, be pardoned if he felt some sinking of the heart at his failure; and, although encouraged by his daughter to persevere in his plan to the end, more than once he was on the brink of abandoning the field in discomfiture, and confessing that the game was above his skill. Had he but taken one-half the pains to learn something of national character that he bestowed on his absurd efforts to fashion it to his liking, his success might have been different. He would, at least, have known how to distinguish between the really deserving and the unworthy recipients of his bounty—between the honest and independent peasant, earning his bread by the sweat of his brow, and the miserable dependant, only seeking a life of indolence, at any sacrifice of truth or character; and even this knowledge, small as it may seem, will go far in appreciating the difficulties which attend all attempts at Irish social improvement, and explain much of the success or failure observable in different parts of the country. But Sir Marmaduke fell into the invariable error of his countrymen—he first suffered himself to be led captive by "blarney," and when heartily sick of the deceitfulness and trickery of those who employed it, coolly sat down with the conviction that there was no truth in the land.

CHAPTER XVI.

THE FOREIGN LETTER.

THE arrival of a post-letter at the O'Donoghue house was an occurrence of sufficient rarity to create some excitement in the household; and many a surmise, as to what new misfortune hung over the family, was hazarded between Mrs. Branaghan and Kerry O'Leary, as the latter poised and balanced the epistle in his hand, as though its weight and form might assist him in his divination.

After having conned over all the different legal processes which he deemed might be conveyed in such a shape, and conjured up in his imagination a whole army of sheriffs, sub-sheriffs, bailiffs, and drivers, of which the ominous letter should prove the forerunner, he heaved a heavy sigh at the gloomy future his forebodings had created, and slowly ascended towards his master's bedroom.

"How is Herbert?" said the O'Donoghue, as he heard the footsteps beside his bed, for he had been dreaming of the boy a few minutes previous. "Who is that? Ah! Kerry. Well, how is he to-day?"

"Troth there's no great change to spake of," said Kerry, who, not having made any inquiry himself, and never expecting to have been questioned on the subject, preferred this safe line of reply, as he deemed it, to a confession of his ignorance.

"Did he sleep well, Kerry?"

"Oh! for the matter of the sleep we won't boast of it. But here's a letter for your honour, come by the post."

"Leave it on the bed, and tell me about the boy."

"Faix, there's nothing particular, then, to tell your honour—sometimes he'd be one way, sometimes another—and more times the same way again. That's the way he'd be all the night through."

The O'Donoghue pondered for a second or two, endeavouring to frame some distinct notion from these scanty materials, and then said,

"Send Master Mark to me." At the same instant he drew aside the curtain, and broke the seal of the letter. The first few lines, however, seemed to satisfy his curiosity, although the epistle was written in a close hand, and extended over three sides of the paper; and he threw it carelessly on the bed, and lay down again once more. During all this time, however, Kerry managed to remain in the room, and, while affecting to arrange clothes and furniture, keenly scrutinised the features of his master. It was of no use, however. The old man's looks were as apathetic as usual, and he seemed already to have forgotten the missive Kerry had endowed with so many terrors and misfortunes.

"Herbert has passed a favourable night," said Mark, entering a few moments after. "The fever seems to have left him, and, except for debility, I suppose there is little to ail him. What!—a letter! Who is this from?"

"From Kate," said the old man, listlessly. "I got as far as 'My dear uncle;' the remainder must await a better light, and, mayhap, sharper eyesight too—for the girl has picked up this new mode of scribbling, which is almost unintelligible to me."

As the O'Donoghue was speaking, the young man had approached the window, and was busily perusing the letter. As he read, his face changed colour more than once. Breaking off, he said,

"You don't know, then, what news we have here? More embarrassment —ay, by Jove! and a heavier one than even it seems at first sight. The French armies, it appears, are successful all over the Low Countries, and city after city falling into their possession; and so, the convents are breaking up, and the Sacré Cœur, where Kate is, has set free its inmates, who are returning to their friends. She comes here."

"What!—here?" said the O'Donoghue, with some evidence of doubt at intelligence so strange and unexpected. "Why, Mark, by boy, that's impossible—the house is a ruin; we haven't a room; we have no servants, and have nothing like accommodation for the girl."

"Listen to this, then," said Mark, as he read from the letter: "'You may then conceive, my dear old papa—for I must call you the old name again, now that we are to meet—how happy I am to visit Carrignacurra once more. I persuade myself I remember the old beech wood in the glen, and the steep path beside the waterfall, and the wooden railings to guard against the precipice. Am I not right? And there's an ash-tree over the pool, lower down. Cousin Mark climbed it to pluck the berries for me, and fell in, too. There's memory for you!'"

"She'll be puzzled to find the wood now," said the O'Donoghue, with a sad attempt at a smile. "Go on, Mark."

"It's all the same kind of thing: she speaks of Molly Cooney's cabin, and the red boat-house, and fifty things that are gone many a day ago. Strange enough, she remembers what I myself have long since forgotten. 'How I long for my own little blue bedroom, that looked out on the Keim-an-eigh!——'"

"There, Mark—don't read any more, my lad. Poor dear Kate!—what would she think of the place now?"

"The thing is impossible," said Mark, sternly; "the girl has got a hundred faucies and tastes, unsuited to our rude life; her French habits would ill agree with our barbarism. You must write to your cousin—that old Mrs. Bedingfield—if that's her name. She must take her for the present, at least; she offered it once before."

"Yes," said the old man, with an energy he had not used till now, "she did, and I refused. My poor brother detested that woman, and would never, had he lived, have entrusted his daughter to her care. If she likes it, the girl shall make this her home. My poor Harry's child shall not ask twice for a shelter while I have one to offer her."

"Have you thought, sir, how long you may be able to extend the hospitality you speak of? Is this house now your own, that you can make a proffer of it to any one?—and if it were, is it here, within these damp, dis-

coloured walls, with ruin without and within, that you'd desire a guest—
and such a guest ?"

" What do you mean, boy ?"

" I mean what I say. The girl, educated in the midst of luxury, pampered and flattered—we heard that from the abbé—what a favourite she
was there, and how naturally she assumed airs of command and superiority
over the girls of her own age—truly, if penance were the object, the notion
is not a bad one."

" I say it again—this is her home. I grieve it should be so rude a one
—but I'll never refuse to let her share it."

" Nor would I," muttered Mark, gloomily, " if it suited either her habits,
or her tastes. Let her come, however ; a week's experience will do more
to undeceive her than if we wrote letters for a twelvemonth."

" You must write to her, Mark ; you must tell her that matters have not
gone so well with us latterly—that she'll see many changes here ; but mind
you say how happy we are to receive her."

" She can have her choice of blue bedrooms, too—shall I say that ?"
said Mark, almost savagely. " The damp has given them the proper tinge
for her fancy ; and as to the view she speaks of, assuredly there is nothing
to baulk it : the window has fallen out many a day ago that looked on
Keim-an-eigh."

" How can you torture me this way, boy ?" said the old man, with a look
of imploring, to which his white hairs and aged features gave a most painful
expression. But Mark turned away, and made no answer.

" My uncle," said he, after a pause, " must answer this epistle. Letter-
writing is no burden to him. In fact, I believe he rather likes it ; so here
goes to do him a favour. It is seldom the occasion presents itself."

It was not often that Mark O'Donoghue paid a visit to Sir Archibald in
his chamber ; and the old man received him as he entered with all the show
of courtesy he would have extended to a stranger—a piece of attention
which was very far, indeed, from relieving Mark of any portion of his former
embarrassment.

" I have brought you a letter, sir," said he, almost ere he took his seat
—"a letter which my father would thank you to reply to. It is from my
cousin Kate, who is about to return to Ireland, and take up her abode
here."

" Ye dinna mean she's coming here, to Carrignacurra ?"

" It is even so ! though I don't wonder at your finding it hard of belief."

" It's mair than that—it's far mair—it's downright incredible."

" I thought so too ; but my father cannot agree with me. He will not
believe that this old barrack is not a baronial castle ; and persists in falling
back on what is past, rather than look on the present, not to speak of the
future.

"But she canna live here, Mark," said Sir Archy, his mind ever dwelling on the great question at issue. "There's no a spot in the whole house she could inhabit. I ken something of these French damsels and their ways; and the strangers that go there for education are a' worse than the natives. I mind the time I was in Paris with his Royal——" Sir Archy coughed, and reddened up, and let fall his snuff-box, spilling all the contents on the floor. "Gude save us, here's a calamity! It was real macabaw, and cost twa shillings an ounce. I maun even see if I canna scrape it up wi' a piece of paper;" and so he set himself diligently to glean up the scattered dust, muttering, all the time, maledictions on his bad luck.

Mark never moved nor spoke the entire time; but sat with the open letter in his hand, patiently awaiting the resumption of the discussion.

"Weel, weel," exclaimed Sir Archy, as he resumed his seat once more; "let us see the epistle, and perhaps we may find some clue to put her off."

"My father insists ou her coming," said Mark, sternly.

"So he may, lad," replied Sir Archy; "but she may hae her ain reasons for declining—dinua ye see that? This place is a ruin. Wha's to say it is no undergoing a repair—that the roof is off, and will not be on for sax months to come. The country, too, is in a vara disturbed state. Folks are talking in a suspicious way."

Mark thought of the midnight march he had witnessed; but said nothing.

"There's a fever, besides, in the house, and wha can tell the next to tak' it. The Lord be mercifu' to us!" added he, gravely, as if the latter thought approached somewhat too close ou a temptation of Providence.

"If she's like what I remember her as a child," replied Mark, "your plan would be a bad one for its object. Tell her the place is a ruin, and she'd give the world to see it for bare curiosity; say there was a likelihood of a rebellion, and she would risk her life to be near it; and as for a fever, we never were able to keep her out of the cabins when there was sickness going. Faith, I believe it was the danger, aud not the benevolence, of the act charmed her."

"You are no far wrong. I mind her weel—she was a saucy cutty; and I canna forget the morning she gave me a bunch o' thistles on my birthday, and ca'ed it a ' Scotch bouqney.' "

"You had better read the letter in any case," said Mark, as he presented the epistle. Sir Archy took it, and perused it from end to end without a word; then laying it open on his knee, he said,

"The lassie's heart is no far wrang, Mark, depend upon it. Few call up the simple memories o' childish days if they have no retained some of the guileless spirit that animated them. I wad like to see her mysel'," said he, after a pause. "But what have we here in the postscript?" And he read aloud the following lines :

" ' I have too good a recollection of a Carrignacurra household to make any apology for adding one to the number below stairs, in the person of my maid Mademoiselle Hortense, from whose surprise and astonishment at our Irish mountains I anticipate a rich treat. She is a true Parisian, who cannot believe in anything outside the Boulevards. What will she think of Mrs. Branaghan and Kerry O'Leary?—and what will they think of her?'

"Lord save us, Mark, this is an awfu' business; a French waiting woman here ! Why, she might as weel bring a Bengal tiger ! I protest I'd rather see the one than the other."

"She'll not stay long; make your mind easy about her; nor will Kate either, if she need such an attendant."

"True enough, Mark ; we maun let the malady cure itsel'; and so, I suppose, the lassie must even see the nakedness o' the land wi' her ain eyes, though I'd just as soon we could 'put the cover on the parritch,' as the laird said, 'and make the fules think it brose.' It's no ower pleasant to expose one's poverty."

"Then you'll write the letter," said Mark, rising, "and we must do what we can in the way of preparation. The time is short enough too, for that letter was written almost a month ago. She might arrive this very week."

As he spoke, the shuffling sounds of feet were heard in the corridor outside; the young man sprang to the door and looked out, and just caught sight of Kerry O'Leary, with a pair of boots under his arm, descending the stairs.

"That fellow Kerry—listening as usual," said Mark. "I heard him at my door about a fortnight since, when I was talking to Herbert, and I sent a bullet through the panel—I thought it might cure him."

"I wonder it did na kill him !" exclaimed M'Nab, in horror.

"No, no, my hand is too steady for that. I aimed at least two inches above his head—it might have grazed his hair."

"By my word, I'll no play the eavesdropper wi' you, Mark; or, at least, I'd like to draw the charge o' your pistols first."

"She can have my room," said Mark, not heeding the speech. "I'll take that old tower they call the guard-room ; I fancy I shall not be dispossessed for a considerable time." And the youth left the chamber to look after the arrangements he spoke of.

" ' Tis what I tould you," said Kerry, as he drew his stool beside the kitchen fire; "I was right enough, she's coming back again to live here. I was listening at the door, and heerd it all."

"And she's laving the blessed nunnery !" exclaimed Mrs. Branaghan, with a holy horror in her countenance—"desarting the elegant place, with the priests, and monks, and friars, to come here again, in the middle of every wickedness and divilment—ochone! ochone!"

"What wickedness and what divilment are you spaking about?" said Kerry, indignantly, at the aspersion thus cast on the habits of the house.

Mrs. Branaghan actually started at the bare idea of a contradiction, and turned on him a look of fiery wrath, as she said,

"Be my conscience you're bould to talk that way to me!—What wicked-ness! Isn't horse-racing, card-playing, raffling, wickedness? Isn't drink-ing and swearing wickedness? Isn't it wickedness to kill three sheep a week, and a cow a fortnight, to feed a set of dirty spalpeens of grooms and stable chaps? Isn't it wickedness—— Botheration to you, but I wouldn't be losing my time talking to you! When was one of ye at his duties? Answer me that. How much did one of ye pay at Ayster or Christmas, these ten years? Signs on it, Father Luke hasn't a word for ye when he comes here—he trates ye with contimpt."

Kerry was abashed and terrified. He little knew when he pulled up the sluice-gate the torrent that would flow down; and now would have made any "amende" to establish a truce again; but Mrs. Branaghan was a wo-man, and, having seen the subjugation of her adversary, her last thought was mercy.

"Wickedness, indeed! It's fifty years out of purgatory, sorra less, to live ten years here, and see what goes on."

"Divil a lie in it," chimed in Kerry, meekly; "there's no denying a word you say."

"I'd like to see who'd dare deny it—and, signs on it, there's a curse on the place—nothing thrives in it."

"Faix, then, ye mustn't say that, anyhow," said Kerry, insinuatingly. "You have no rayson to spake again it. 'Twas Tuesday week last I heerd Father Luke say—it was to myself he said it—'How is Mrs. Branaghan, Kerry?' says he. 'She's well and hearty, your reverence,' says I. 'I'll tell you what she is, Kerry,' says he; 'she's looking just as I knew her five-and-thirty years ago; and a comelier, dacenter woman wasn't in the three baronies. I remember well,' says he, 'I seen her at the fair of Kil-larney, and she had a cap with red ribbons.' Hadn't ye a cap with red ribbons in it?"

A nod was the response.

"True for him, ye see he didn't forget it; and says he, 'She took the shine out of the fair; she could give seven pounds and half a distance to ere a girl there, and beat her after by a neck.'"

"What's that ye're saying?" said Mrs. Branaghan, who didn't comprehend the figurative language of the turf, particularly when coming from Father Luke's lips.

" I'm saying ye were the purtiest woman that walked the fair-green," said Kerry, correcting his phraseology.

" Father Luke was a smart little man then himself, and had a nate leg and foot."

" Killarney was a fine place, I'm tould," said Kerry, with a dexterous shift to change the topic. " I wasn't often there myself, but I heerd it was the iligant fair entirely."

" So it was," said Mrs. Branaghan; " there never was the kind of sport and divarsion wasn't there. It begun on a Monday, and went through the week; and short enough the time was. There was dancing, and fighting, and singing, and · stations,' up to Aghadoe and down again on the bare knees, and a pilgrimage to the holy well—three times round that, maybe after a jig two hours long; and there was a dwarf that tould fortunes, and a friar that sould gospels agin fever and fallin' sickness, and ballad-singers, and play-actors. Musha, there never was the like of it." And in this strain did she pour forth a flood of impassioned eloquence on the recollection of those carnal pleasures and enjoyments which, but a few minutes before, she had condemned so rigidly in others, nor was it till at the very close of her speech that she suddenly perceived how she had wandered from her text; then, with a heavy groan, she muttered, " Ayeh! we're sinful craytures, the best of us."

Kerry responded to the sentiment with a fac-simile sigh, and the peace was ratified.

" You wouldn't believe, now, what Miss Kate is bringing over with her— faix, you wouldn't believe it."

" Maybe a monkey," said Mrs. Branaghan, who had a vague notion that France lay somewhere within the tropics.

" Worse nor that."

" Is it a bear?" asked she again.

" No; but a French maid, to dress her hair, and powder her, and put patches on her face."

" Whisht, I tell you," cried Mrs. Branaghau, " and don't be talking that way. Miss Kate was never the one to turn to the likes of them things."

" 'Tis truth I'm telling ye, then; I heerd it all between the master and Master Mark, and afterwards with ould Sir Archy, and the three of them is in a raal fright about the maid; they say she'll be the divil for impidence."

" Will she, then !" said Mrs. Branaghan, with an eye glistening in anticipation of battle.

" The never a day's peace or ease we're to have again, when she's here— 'tis what the master says. ʽI pity poor Mrs. Branaghan,' says he; ʽshe's a quiet crayture that won't take her own part, and——ʼ "

" Won't I? Be my conscience, we'll soon see that."

"Them's his words—'and if Kerry and she don't lay their heads together to make the place too hot for her, she'll bully the pair of them.'"

"Lave it to myself—lave it to me alone, Kerry O'Leary."

"I was thinking that same, ma'am," said Kerry, with a droll leer as he
spoke; "I'd take the odds on you any day, and never ask the name of the
other horse."

"I'll lay the mark of my fingers on her av she says 'pays,'" said Mrs.
Branaghan, with an energy that looked like truth.

Meanwhile, Kerry, perceiving that her temper was up, spared nothing to
aggravate her passion, retailing every possible and impossible affront the
new visitor might pass off on her, and expressing the master's sorrows at
the calamities awaiting her.

"If she isn't frightened out of the country at once, there's no help for
it," said he, at last.   "I have a notion myself, but sure, maybe it's a bad
one."

"What is it, then?—spake it out free."

"'Tis just to wait for the chaise—she'll come in a chaise, it's likely——"

But what was Kerry's plan, neither Mrs. Branaghan nor the reader are
destined to hear, for at that moment a loud summons at the hall door—a
very unusual sound—announced the arrival of a stranger.   Kerry, therefore, had barely time for a hasty toilet with a pocket-comb, before a small
fragment of looking-glass he carried in his pocket, as he hastened to receive
the visitor.

CHAPTER XVII.

KATE O'DONOGHUE.

BEFORE Kerry O'Leary had reached the hall, the object around whose
coming all his schemes revolved was already in her uncle's arms.

"My dear, dear Kate," said the old man, as he embraced her again and
again, while she, overcome by a world of conflicting emotions, concealed her
face upon his shoulder.

"This is Mark, my dearest girl—cousin Mark."

The girl looked up, and fixed her large, full eyes upon the countenance
of the young man, as, in an attitude of bashful hesitation, he stood uncertain how far the friendship of former days warranted his advances.   She,
too, seemed equally confused; and when she held out her hand, and he took
it half coldly, the meeting augured but poorly for warmth of heart on either
side.

"And Herbert—where is he?" cried she, eagerly, hoping to cover the chilling reception by the inquiry; "and my uncle Archy——"

"Is here to answer for himsel'," said M'Nab, quietly, as he came rapidly forward and kissed her on either cheek; and, with an arm leaning ou each of the old men, she walked forward to the drawing-room.

"And are you alone, my dear child—have you come alone?" said the O'Donoghue.

"Even so, papa. My attached and faithful Hortense left me at Bristol. Sea-sickness became stronger than affection. She had a dream, besides, that she was lost, devoured, or carried off by a mermau—I forget what. And the end was, she refused to go further, and did her best to persuade me to the same opiniou. She didn't remember that I had sent ou my effects, and that my heart was here already."

"My own dearest child," said O'Donoghue, as he pressed her hand fervently between his own.

"But how have ye journeyed by yoursel'?" said Sir Archy, as he gazed on the slight and delicate figure before him.

"Wonderfully well, uncle. During the voyage every one was most polite and attentive to me. There was a handsome young Guardsman who would have been more, had he not been gentleman enough to know that I was a lady. And once at Cork, I met, at the very moment of landing, with a kind old friend, Father Luke, who took care of me hither. He only parted with me at the gate, not wishing to interfere, as he said, with our first greetings. But I don't see Herbert—where is he?"

"Poor Herbert has been dangerously ill, my dear," said the father; "I scarcely think it safe for him to see you."

"No, no," interposed Sir Archy, feelingly. "If the sight of her can stir the seared heart of an auld carle like mysel', it wadna be the surest way to calm the frenzied blood of a youth."

Perhaps Sir Archy was not far wrong. Kate O'Donoghue was, indeed, a girl of uo common attraction. Her figure—rather below than above the middle size—was yet so perfectly moulded that, for very symmetry and grace, it seemed as if such should have been the standard of womanly beauty, while her countenance had a character of loveliness even more striking and beautiful; her eyes were large, full, and of a liquid blue that resembled black; her hair a rich brown, through which a golden tinge was seen to run, almost the colour of an autumn sunset, giving a brilliancy to her complexion which, in its transparent beauty, needed no such aid; but her mouth was the feature whose expression, more than any other, possessed a peculiar charm. In speaking, the rounded lips moved with a graceful undulation, more expressive than mere sound, while, as she listened, the slightest tremble of the lip harmonising with the brilliant glance of her eyes, gave a character of rapid intelligence to her face well befitting the vivid temper of her nature. She looked her very self—a noble-hearted, high-spirited girl, without a thought save for what was honourable and lofty; one who accepted no compromise with a doubtful line of policy, but eagerly grasped at the right, and stood firmly by the consequence. Although educated within the walls of a convent, she had mixed, her extreme youth considered, much in the world of the city she lived in, and was thus as accomplished in all the "usage" and conventional habits of society, as she was cultivated in those gifts and graces which give it all its ornament. To a mere passing observer there might seem somewhat of coquetry in her manner; but very little observation would show, that such unerring gracefulness cannot be the result of mere practice, and that innate character had assumed that garb which best suited it, and not one to be merely worn for a season. Her accent, too, when she spoke English, had enough of foreign intonation about it to lay the ground for a charge of affectation; but he should have been a sturdy critic who could have persisted in the accusation. The fear was rather, that one leaned to the very fault of pronunciation as an excellence, so much of piquancy did it occasionally lend to expressions which, from other lips, had seemed tame and common-place. To any one who has seen the graceful coquetry of French manner engrafted on the more meaning eloquence of Irish beauty, my effort at a portrait will appear a very meagre and barren outline; and I feel how poorly I have endeavoured to convey any idea of one, whose Spanish origin had left a legacy of gracefulness and elegance, to be warmed into life by the fervid character of the Celt, and tempered again by the consummate attraction of French manner.

The ease and kindliness of spirit with which she sat between the two old men, listening in turn to each, or answering with graceful alacrity the questions they proffered—the playful delicacy with which she evaded the allusions they made from time to time to the disappointment the ruined house must have occasioned her—and the laughing gaiety with which she spoke of the new life about to open before her, were actually contagious. They already forgot the fears her anticipated coming had inspired, and gazed on her with the warm affection that should wait on a welcome. Oh! what a gift is beauty, and how powerful its influence, when strengthened by the rich eloquence of a spotless nature, beaming from beneath long-lashed lids, when two men like these, seared and hardened by the world's ills—broken on the wheel of fortune—should feel a glow of long-forgotten gladness in their chilled hearts as they looked upon her! None could have guessed, however, what an effort that seeming light-heartedness cost her. Poor girl! Scarcely was she alone, and had closed the door of her room behind her, when she fell upon the bed in a torrent of tears, and sobbed as if her heart was breaking. All that Father Luke had said as they came along—and the kind old man had done his utmost to break the shock of the altered state of her uncle's fortunes—was far from preparing her for the cold reality she witnessed. It was not the ruined walls, the treeless mountain, the desolate and dreary look of all around that smote upon her heart. Sad as these signs were, her grief had a higher source. It was the sight of that old man she called father, tottering feebly to the grave, surrounded by images of poverty and misfortune. It was the aspect of Mark, the cousin she had pictured to her mind as an accomplished gentleman in look and demeanour —the descendant of a house more than noble—the heir of a vast property; and now she saw him scarce in gesture and manner above the peasant—in dress, as slovenly and uncared for. She was prepared for a life of monotonous retirement and isolation. She was ready to face the long winter of dreary solitude—but not in such company as this. That she never calculated on. Her worst anticipations had never conjured up more than an unchequered existence, with little to vary or relieve it; and now, she foresaw a life to be passed amid the miserable straits and shifts of poverty, with all its petty incidents and lowering accidents, to lessen her esteem for those she wished to look up to and love. And this was Carrignacurra, the proud castle she had so often boasted of to her school companions, the baronial seat she had loved to exalt above the antique châteaux of France and Flanders; and these the haughty relatives, whose pride she mentioned as disdaining the alliance of the Saxon, and spurning all admixture of blood with a race less noble than their own. The very chamber she sat in, how did it contradict her own animated descriptions of its once comforts and luxuries! Alas! it seemed to be like duplicity and falsehood, that she had so spoken of these things. More than once she asked herself—" Were they always thus?" Poor child! she knew not that poverty can bring sickness, and sorrow, and premature old age. It can devastate the fields, and desolate the affections, and make cold both heart and home together.

If want stopped short at privation, men need not to tremble at its approach. It is in the debasing and degrading influence of poverty its real terror lies. It is in the plastic facility with which the poor man shifts to meet the coming evil, that the high principle of rectitude is sacrificed, and the unflinching course of honour deviated from. When the proud three-decker, in all the majesty of her might, may sail along her course unaltered, the humble craft, in the same sea, must tack, and beat, and watch for every casualty of the gale to gain her port in safety. These are the trials of the poor, but proud man. It is not the want of liveried lacqueys, of plate, of equipage, and all the glittering emblems of wealth, that smite his heart and break his spirit. It is the petty subterfuge he is reduced to that galls him —it is the sense of struggle between his circumstances and his conscience— between what he does, and what he feels.

It is true Kate knew not these things, but yet she had before her the results of them too palpably to be mistaken. Sir Archibald was the only one on whom reverse of fortune had not brought carelessness and coarseness of manner. He seemed, both in dress and demeanour, little changed from what she remembered him years before; nor had time, apparently, fallen on him with heavier impress in other respects. What was Herbert like? was the question ever rising to her mind, but with little hope that the answer would prove satisfactory.

While Kate O'Donoghue was thus pondering over the characters of those with whom she was now to live, they, on the other hand, were exerting themselves to the utmost to restore some semblance of its ancient comfort to the long neglected dwelling. A blazing fire of bog deal was lighted in the old hall, whose mellow glare glanced along the dark oak wainscot, and threw a rich glow along the corridor itself, to the very door of the tower. In the great chamber, where they sat, many articles of furniture, long disused and half forgotten, were now collected, giving, even by their number, a look of increased comfort to the roomy apartment. Nor were such articles of ornament as they possessed forgotten. The few pictures which had escaped the wreck of damp and time were placed upon the walls, and a small miniature of Kate, as a child—a poor performance enough—was hung up over the chimney, as it were to honour her, whose presence these humble preparations were made to celebrate. Sir Archy, too, as eager in these arrangements as Mark himself, had brought several books and illustrated volumes from his chamber to scatter upon the tables; while, as if for a shrine for the deity of the place, a little table of most elaborate marqueterie, and a richly carved chair beside the fire, designated the place Kate was to occupy as her own, and to mark which he had culled the very gems of his collection.

It is scarcely possible to conceive how completely even a few trifling objects like these can change the "morale" of a chamber—how that, which before seemed cumbrous, sad, and dispiriting, becomes at once lightsome and pleasant-looking. But so it is: the things which speak of human thought and feeling appeal to a very different sense from those which merely minister to material comfort; and we accept the presence of a single book, a print, or drawing, as an evidence that mental aliment has not been forgotten.

If the changes here spoken of gave a very different air and seeming to the old tower, Kate's own presence there completed the magic of the transformation. Dressed in black silk, and wearing a profusion of lace of the same colour—for her costume had been adapted to a very different sphere—she took her place in the family circle, diffusing around her a look of refinement and elegance, and making of that sombre chamber a spacious "salon." Her guitar, her embroidery, her old-fashioned writing-desk, inlaid with silver, caught the eye as it wandered about the room, and told of womanly graces and accomplishments, so foreign to the rude emblems of the chase and the field, henceforth to be banished to the old entrance hall.

The O'Donoghue himself felt the influence of the young girl's presence, and evidenced, in his altered dress and demeanour, the respect he desired to show; while Mark took from his scanty wardrobe the only garment he possessed above the rank of a shooting-jacket, and entered the room with a half-bashful, half-sullen air, as though angry and ashamed with himself for even so much compliance with the world's usages.

Although Kate was quick-sighted enough to see that these changes were caused on her account, her native tact prevented her from showing that knowledge, and made her receive their attentions with that happy blending of courtesy and familiarity so fascinating from a young and pretty woman. The dinner—and it was a "chef-d'œuvre" on the part of Mrs. Branaghan—passed off most pleasantly. The fear her coming had excited now gave way to the delight her presence conferred. They felt as if they had done her an injustice in their judgment, and hastened to make every "amende" for their unfair opinion. Never, for years long, had the O'Donoghue been so happy. The cold and cheerless chamber was once more warmed into a home. The fire beside which he had so often brooded in sadness was now the pleasant hearth surrounded by cheery faces. Memories of the past, soothing through all their sorrow, flowed in upon his mind, as he sat and gazed at her in tranquil ecstasy. Sir Archibald, too, felt a return to his former self, in the tone of good breeding her presence diffused, and evinced, by the attentive politeness of his manner, how happy he was to recur once more to the observances which he remembered with so much affection, associated, as they were, with the brightest period of his life.

As for Mark, although less an actor than the others in the scene, the effect upon him was not less striking. All his assumed apathy gave way as he listened to her descriptions of foreign society, and the habits of those she had lived amongst. The ringing melody of her voice, the brilliant sparkle of her dark eyes, the graceful elegance of gesture—the Frenchwoman's prerogative—threw over him their charm, a fascination never experienced before; and although a dark dread would now and then steal across his mind, How was a creature, beautiful and gifted like this, to lead the life of dreariness and gloom their days were passed in?—the tender feeling of affection she showed his father, the fondness with which she dwelt on every little incident of her childhood—every little detail of the mountain scenery—showed a spirit which well might harmonise with a home even humble as theirs, and pleasures as uncostly and as simple. "Oh! if she grow not weary of us!" was the heart-uttered sentence each moment as he listened; and, in the very anxiety of the doubt, the ecstasy of enjoyment was heightened. To purchase this boon there was nothing he would not dare. To think that as he trod the glens, or followed the wild deer along some cragged and broken mountain gorge, a home like this ever awaited him, was a picture of happiness too bright and dazzling to look upon.

K

"Now, then, 'ma belle,'" said Sir Archibald, as he rose from his seat, and, with an air of gallantry that might have done credit to Versailles of old, threw the ribbon of her guitar over her neck—"now for your promise, —that little romance ye spoke of."

"Willingly, dear uncle," replied she, striking the chords as a kind of prelude. "Shall I sing you one of our convent hymns?—or will you have the romance?"

"It is no fair to tempt one in a choice," said M'Nab, slyly; "but sin ye say so, I must hear baith before I decide."

"Your own favourite, the first," said she, smiling; and began the little chanson of the "Garde Ecossaise," the song of the exiled nobles in the service of France, so dear to every Scotchman's heart.

While the melody described the gathering of the clans in the mountains, to take leave of their departing kinsmen, the measured tramp of the music, and the wild ringing of the pibroch, the old chieftain's face lit up, and his eye glared with the fierce fire of native pride; but when the moment of leave-taking arrived, and the heartrending cry of "Farewell!" broke from the deserted, his eye became glazed and filmy, and with a hand tremulous from emotion, he stopped the singer.

"Na, na, Kate; I canna bear that the noo. Ye hae smote the rock too suddenly, lassie;" and the tears rolled heavily down his seared cheeks.

"You must let me finish, uncle," said she, disengaging her hand; and at the instant, sweeping the chord with a bold and vigorous finger, she broke into a splendid and chivalrous description of the Scottish valour in the service of France, every line swelling with their proud achievements, as foremost they marched to battle. To this succeeded the crash and turmoil of the fray, the ringing cheers of the plaided warriors mingling with the war-cries of the Gaul, till, in a burst of triumph and victory, the song concluded. Then the old man sprang from his chair, and threw his arms around her in transport, as he cried,

"It's a merciful' thing, lassie, ye didna live fifty years ago: by my saul, there's nae saying how many a brave fellow the like o' that had laid low!"

"If that be one of the hymns you spoke of, Kate," said the O'Donoghue, smiling, "I fancy Mark would have no objection to be a nun; but where is he?—he has left the room."

"I hope there is nothing in my song he disliked?" asked she, timidly; but before there was time for an answer the door opened, and Mark appeared with Herbert in his arms.

"There!" said he, laying him gently on the sofa; "if cousin Kate will only sing that once more, I'll answer for it, it will save you a fortnight in your recovery."

Kate knelt down beside the sick boy, and kissed him tenderly; while he, poor fellow, scarce daring to believe in the reality of all before him, played with the long tangles of her silky hair, and gazed on her in silence.

"We maun be cautious, Mark," whispered M'Nab, carefully; but Mark had no ears nor eyes save for her who now sat beside his brother, and in a low, soft voice, breathed her affectionate greetings to him.

In this way passed the first evening of her coming—a night whose fascination dwelt deep in every heart, and made each dreamer blest.

CHAPTER XVIII.

A HASTY PLEDGE.

WHILE these things were happening within the ruined castle of the O'Donoghue, a guest, equally unexpected as theirs, had arrived at the Lodge. Frederick Travers, delayed in Bristol by contrary winds, had come over in the same packet with Kate; but without being able either to learn her name, or whither she was going. His unlooked-for appearance at the Lodge was a most welcome surprise both to Sir Marmaduke and Sybella; and as he did not desire to avow the real object of his coming, it was regarded by them as the most signal proof of affection. They well knew how much London life engrossed him—how completely its peculiar habits and haunts possessed attractions for him—and with what a depreciating estimate he looked down on every part of the globe, save that consecrated to the fashionable follies and amusements of his own set.

He was not, in reality, insensible to other and better influences; his affection for his father and sister was unbounded; he had a bold, manly spirit, unalloyed with anything mean or sordid; a generous, candid nature, and straightforward earnestness of purpose, that often carried him further by impulse than he was followed by his convictions. Still, a conventional cant, a tone of disparaging, half-contemptuous indifference to everything which characterised his associates, had already infected him; and he felt ashamed to confess to those sentiments and opinions, to possess and to act upon which should have been his dearest pride.

"Well, Fred," said Sybella, as they drew around the fire after dinner, in that happy home circle so suggestive of enjoyment, "let us hear what you thought of the scenery. Is not Glenflesk fine?"

"Matlock on a larger scale," said he, coolly. "Less timber and more rocks."

" Matlock! dear Fred. You might as well compare Keim-an-eigh with Holborn—you are only jesting."

" Compare what? Repeat that droll name, I beg of you."

" Keim-an-cigh. It is a mountain pass quite close to us here."

" Admirably done! Why, Sybella dear, I shall not be surprised to see you take to the red petticoat and bare feet soon. You have indoctrinated yourself wonderfully since your arrival."

" I like the people with all my heart, Fred," said she, artlessly, " and if I could imitate many of their traits of forbearance and long suffering patience by following their costume, I promise you I'd don the scarlet."

" Ay, Fred," said Sir Marmaduke, with a sententious gravity, " they don't know these Irish at all at our side of the water. They mistake them totally. They only want teaching—a little example, a little encouragement, that's all—and they are as docile and tractable as possible. I'll show you to-morrow what improvements a few months have effected. I'll bring you over a part of the estate where there was not a hovel fit for a dog, and you shall see what comfortable dwellings they have. We hear nothing in England but the old songs about popery, and superstition, and all that. Why, my dear Fred, these people don't care a straw for the priest—they'd be anything I asked them."

" Devilish high principled that, any way," said Fred, dryly.

" I didn't exactly mean that; at least, in the sense you take it. I was about to say, that such is their confidence, such their gratitude to the land-lord, that—that——"

" That, in short, they'd become Turks, for an abatement in the rent. Well, Sybella dear, is this one of the traits you are so anxious to imitate?"

" Why will you misunderstand, Fred?" said Sybella, imploringly. " Cannot you see that gratitude may lead an uninstructed people far beyond the limits of reason?—my father is so good to them."

" With all my heart; I have not the slightest objection in life; indeed, I'm not sure, if all the estate be like what I passed through this afternoon, if *my* generosity wouldn't go further, and, instead of reducing the rent, make them an honest present of the fee simple."

" Foolish boy!" said Sir Marmaduke, half angrily. " There are forty thousand acres of reclaimable land——"

" Which might bear crops anno Domini 3095."

" There are mines of inexhaustible wealth."

" And would cost such to work them, sir, no doubt. Come, come, father —Hemsworth has passed a life among these people. He knows more than we do, or ever shall."

" I tell you, sir," said Sir Marmaduke, nettled by such a sarcasm on his powers of observation, " I know them perfectly; I can read them like a book. They are a guileless, simple-minded, confiding people; you may see every thought they have in their countenances. They only need the commonest offices of kindness to attach them; and, as for political or religious leanings, I have questioned them pretty closely, and, without a single exception, have heard nothing but sentiments of loyalty and attachment to the church."

"Well, I only hope you don't mean to prolong your stay here. I'm sure you have done enough for any ordinary call of conscience, and, if you have not, set about it in right earnest—convert the tens into hundreds—make them all as comfortable as possible—and then, in Heaven's name, get back again to England. There is no earthly reason why you should pass your time here; and as for Sybella——"

"Don't include me, Fred, in your reasons for departure. I never was so happy in my life."

"There, boy—there's an example for you; and if you need another, here am I, ready to confess the same thing. I don't mean that there are not little dampers and difficulties. There's that fool about the mill-wheel, and that fellow that persists in dragging the river with a net;" and so he muttered on for some minutes beneath his teeth, to the evident enjoyment of Fred, whose quivering lip and laughing eye told how he appreciated the conflicting evidence memory was eliciting.

Thus, for some time, the conversation continued, until Miss Travers retired for the night. Then Sir Marmaduke drew his chair closer to his son's, and, in an earnest manner, related the whole circumstance of Sybella's escape from the mountain torrent, dwelling with grateful eloquence on the young O'Donoghue's heroism in coming to her rescue. "The youth has narrowly escaped with his life. The doctor, who left this but a few hours ago, said he 'never witnessed a more dangerous case than the symptoms at one time presented.' He is well, however, now—the risk is past—and I want your aid, Fred, to devise some suitable mode of evincing our gratitude."

"These O'Donoghues are your tenants, are they not?" asked the young man.

"Yes, they are tenants; but on that score we must not say much in their favour. Wylie tells me that they have been at feud with Hemsworth for years past—they neither pay rent, nor will they surrender possession. The whole thing is a difficult matter to understand; first of all, there is a mortgage——"

"There, there, my dear father, don't puzzle my brain and your own with a statement we'll never get to the end of. The point I want to learn is, they are your tenants——"

"Yes, at least for part of the land they occupy. There is a dispute about another portion; but I believe Hemsworth has got the Attorney-General's opinion that their case cannot stand."

" Tush—never mind the Attorney-General. Give up the question at issue; send him, or his father, or whoever it is, the receipt for the rent due, and take care Hemsworth does not molest him in future."

" But you don't see, boy, what we are doing. We hope to obtain the whole of the Ballyvourney property—that is part of our plan; the tenants there are in a state of absolute misery and starvation."

" Then, in God's name, give them plenty to eat; it doesn't signify much, I suppose, whose tenantry they are when they're hungry."

The old gentleman was scarcely prepared for such an extended basis for his philanthropy, and, for a moment or two, seemed quite dumbfounded by his son's proposition, while Fred continued:

" If I understand the matter, it lies thus: you owe a debt of gratitude which you are desirous to acquit—you don't care to pay highly."

" On the contrary, I am quite willing," interposed Sir Marmaduke; " but let the price be one which shall realise a benefit equivalent to its amount. If I assure these people in the possession of their land, what security have I that they will not continue, as of old, the same useless, wasteful, spendthrift set they ever were—presenting the worst possible example to the other tenants, and marring the whole force of the lesson I am endeavouring to inculcate?"

" That, I take it, is more *their* affair than *yours*, after all," said Fred; " you are not to confer the boon and allocate its advantages afterwards— but come, what kind of people are they?"

" Oh! a species of half-gentry, half-farmer set, I believe—proud as they are poor—deeming themselves, as O'Donoghues, at least our equals; but living, as I believe, in every kind of privation."

" Very well; sit down there, and let me have a cheque on your banker for five hundred pounds, and leave the affair to me."

" But you mistake, Fred, they are as haughty as Lucifer."

" Just leave it to me, sir. I fancy I know something of the world by this time. It may require more money, but the result I will answer for."

Sir Marmaduke's confidence in his son's tact and worldly skill was one of the articles of his faith, and he sat down at the table and wrote the order on the bank at once. " Here, Fred," said he; " I only beg of you to re-member that the way to express the grateful sense I entertain of this boy's conduct is not by wounding the susceptibilities of his feelings; and if they be above the class of farmers, which I really cannot ascertain, your steps must demand all your caution."

" I hope, sir," said Fred, with some vanity in the tone, " that I have never made you blush for my awkwardness, and I don't intend to do so now. I promise for the success of my negotiation; but I must not say a word more of how I mean to obtain it."

Sir Marmaduke was very far from feeling satisfied with himself for having

even so far encouraged a plan that his own blind confidence in his son's cleverness had for a moment entrapped him into ; he would gladly have withdrawn his consent, but old experience taught him that Fred was never completely convinced he was right until he met opposition to his opinion. So
he parted with him for the night, hoping that sleep might suggest a wiser
counsel and a clearer head ; and that being left free to act, he might possibly feel a doubt as to the correctness of his own judgment.

As for Fred, no sooner was he alone than he began to regret the pledge
his precipitancy had carried him into. What were the nature of the advances he was to make—how to open the negotiation, in a quarter the habits
and prejudices of which he was utterly ignorant of, he had not the most
vague conception ; and, as he sought his chamber, he had half persuaded
himself to the conviction, that the safest, and the most honest course, after
all, would be to avow in the morning that he had overstated his diplomatic
abilities, and fairly abandon a task to which he saw himself inadequate.
These were his last sleeping thoughts ; for his waking resolves we must
enter upon another chapter.

CHAPTER XIX.

A DIPLOMATIST DEFEATED.

If Frederick Travers went to sleep at night with very considerable doubts
as to the practicability of his plans regarding the O'Donoghues, his waking
thoughts were very far from reassuring him, and he heartily wished he had
never engaged in the enterprise. Now, however, his honour was in a manner pledged ; he had spoken so confidently of success, there was nothing
for it but to go forward, and endeavour, as well he might, to redeem his
promise.

At the time we speak of, military men never for a moment divested them
selves of the emblems of their career ; the uniform and the sword, the plumed
hat and the high boot, formed a costume not to be worn at certain periods
and laid aside at others, but was their daily dress, varying merely in the degree of full or half dress, as the occasion warranted. There was no affectation of the happy freedom of "mufti"—no pretended enjoyment of the
incognito of a black coat and round hat ; on the contrary, the king's livery
was borne with a pride which, erring on the opposite side, suggested a degree of assumption and conscious importance in the wearer, which more or

less separated the soldier from the civilian in bearing, and gradually originated a feeling of soreness on the part of the more humbly clad citizen towards the more favoured order.

A certain haughty, overbearing tone of manner, was then popular in the
army, and particularly in those regiments which boasted of an unalloyed
nobility among the officers. If they assumed an air of superiority to the
rest of the service, so much the more did they look down upon the mere
civilian, whom they considered as belonging to a very subordinate class and
order of mankind. To mark the sense of this difference of condition in a
hundred little ways, and by a hundred petty observances, was part of a
military education, and became a more unerring test of the soldier in
society, than even the cockade and the cross-belt. To suppose that such a
line of conduct should not have inspired those against whom it was directed
with a feeling of counter hatred, would be to disbelieve in human nature.
The civilian, indeed, reciprocated with dislike the soldier's insolence, and,
in their estrangement from each other, the breach grew gradually wider—
the dominant tyranny of the one, and the base-born vulgarity of the other,
being themes each loved to dilate upon without ceasing.

Now this consciousness of superiority, so far from relieving Frederick
Travers of any portion of the difficulty of his task, increased it tenfold. He
knew and felt he was stooping to a most unwarrantable piece of condescension in seeking these people at all; and although he trusted firmly that his
aristocratic friends were very unlikely to hear of proceedings in a quarter so
remote and unvisited, yet how he should answer to his own heart for such a
course, was another and a far more puzzling matter. He resolved then, in
the true spirit of his order, to give his conduct all the parade of a most con-
descending act, to let them see plainly how immeasurably low he had volun-
tarily descended to meet them; and to this end he attired himself in his full
field uniform, and with as scrupulous a care as though the occasion were a
review before his Majesty. His costume of scarlet coat, with blue velvet
facings, separating at the breast so as to show a vest of white kerseymere,
trimmed with a gold border—his breeches, of the same colour and material,
met at the knee by the high and polished boot, needed but the addition of
his cocked-hat, fringed with an edging of ostrich feathers, to set off a figure
of singular elegance and symmetry. The young men of the day were just
beginning to dispense with hair powder, and Fred wore his rich brown locks,
long and floating, in the new mode—a fashion which well became him, and
served to soften down the somewhat haughty carriage of his head. There
was an air of freedom, an absence of restraint, in the military costume of the
period, which certainly contributed to increase the advantages of a naturally
good-looking man, in the same way as the present stiff Prussian mode of
dress will assuredly conceal many defects in mould and form among less-fa-

voured individuals. The loosely-falling flaps of the waistcoat—the deep hanging cuffs of the coat—the easy folds of the long skirt—gave a character of courtliness to uniform which, to our eye, it at present is very far from possessing. In fact, the graceful carriage and courteous demeanour of the drawing-room suffered no impediment from the pillory of a modern stock, or the rigid inflexibility of a coat strained almost to bursting.

"Are you on duty, Fred?" said Sir Marmaduke, laughing, as his son entered the breakfast-room thus carefully attired.

"Yes, sir; I am preparing for my mission; and it would ill become an ambassador to deliver his credentials in undress."

"To what court are you then accredited?" said Sybella, laughing.

"His Majesty The O'Donoghue," interposed his father, "King of Glenflesk, Baron of Inchigeela, Lord Protector of—of half the blackguards in the county, I verily believe," added he, in a more natural key.

"Are you really going to Carrignacurra, Fred?" asked Miss Travers, hurriedly; "are you going to visit our neighbours?"

"I'll not venture to say that such is the place, much less pretend to pronounce it after you, my dear sister, but I am about to wait on these worthy people, and, if they will permit me, have a peep at the interior of their stockade or wigwam, whichever it be."

"It must have been a very grand thing in its day: that old castle has some fine features about it yet," replied she, calmly.

"Like Windsor, I suppose," said Fred, as he replied to her; and then complacently glanced at the well-fitting boot which ornamented his leg. "They'll not be over ceremonious, I hope, about according me an audience."

"Not in the forenoon, I believe," said Sir Marmaduke, dryly; for he was recalling the description old Roach had given him of his own reception by Kerry O'Leary, and which circumstance, by-the-by, figured somewhat ostentatiously in his charge to the old baronet.

"Oh, then, they receive early," resumed Fred; "the old French style— the 'petit lever du roi'—before ten o'clock. Another cup of tea, Sybella, and then I must look after a horse."

"I have given orders already on that score. I flatter myself you'll rather approve of my stud; for, amongst the incongruities of Ireland, I have fallen upon an honest horse-dealer."

"Indeed!" said the young man, with more interest than he had yet shown in the conversation; "I must cultivate that fellow; one might exhibit him with great success in London."

"Unquestionably, Fred, he is a curiosity; for while he is a perfect simpleton about the value of an animal—an easy-tempered, good-natured, soft fellow—with respect to knowledge of a horse, his points, his performance, and his soundness, I never saw his equal."

"I'll give him a commission to get me two chargers," said Fred, delighted at the prospect of deriving so much benefit from his Irish journey. " What makes you look so serious, Sybella?"

"Was I so, Fred? I scarcely know—perhaps I was regretting," added she, archly, "that there were no ladies at Carrignacurra to admire so very smart a cavalier."

Frederick coloured slightly and endeavoured to laugh, but the conscious-ness that his "bravery" of costume was somewhat out of place, worried him, and he made no reply.

" You'll not be long, Fred," said his father; " I shall want you to take a walk with me to the lake."

" No, Fred—don't stay long away; it is not above two miles from this at farthest."

"Had I not better send a guide with you?"

" No, no ; if the place be larger than a mud hovel, I cannot mistake it. So here comes our steed. Well, I own, he is the best thing I've yet seen in these parts;" and the youth opened the window, and stepped out to ap-proach the animal. He was, indeed, a very creditable specimen of Lanty's taste in horseflesh—the model of a compact and powerfully-built cob horse.

" A hundred guineas, eh ?" said Fred, in a tone of question.

" Sixty—not a pound more," said the old man, in conscious pride. " The fellow said but fifty ; I added ten on my own account."

Frederick mounted the cob, and rode him across the grass, with that quiet hand and steady seat which bespeaks the judgment of one called upon to be critical. " A little, a very little over-done in the mouthing, but his ac-tion perfect," said he, as he returned to the window, and held the animal in an attitude to exhibit his fine symmetry to advantage. " The Prince has a passion for a horse of this class ; I hope you have not become attached to him ?"

"His Royal Highness shall have him at once, Fred, if he will honour you by accepting him." And as he spoke, he laid a stress on the *you*, to evince the pleasure he anticipated in the present being made by Frederick, and not himself.

" Now, then, with God and St. George!" cried Fred, laughingly, as he waved an adieu with his plumed hat, and cantered easily towards the high road.

It was a clear and frosty day in December, with a blue sky above, and all below bright and glittering in a thin atmosphere. The lake, clear as crystal, reflected every cliff and crag upon the mountain, while each island on its surface was defined with a crisp sharpness of outline, scarce less beautiful than in the waving foliage of summer. The many-coloured heaths, too, shone in hues more bright and varied than usual in our humid climate ; and the voices which broke the silence, heard from long distances away, came mellowed and softened in their tones, and harmonised well with the solitary grandeur of the scene. Nor was Frederick Travers insensible to its influence; the height of those bold mountains—their wild and fanciful outlines—the sweeping glens that wound along their bases—the wayward stream that flowed through the deep valleys, and, as if in sportiveness, serpentined their course, were features of scenery he had not witnessed before, while the perfect solitude awed and appalled him.

He had not ridden long, when the tall towers of the old castle of Carrignacurra caught his eye, standing proudly on the bold mass of rock above the road. The unseemly adjunct of farm-house and stables were lost to view at such a distance, or blended with the general mass of building, so that the whole gave the impression of extent and pretension to a degree he was by no means prepared for. These features, however, gradually diminished as he drew nearer; the highly-pitched roof, pierced with narrow windows, patched and broken—the crumbling battlements of the towers themselves—the ruinous dilapidation of the outer buildings, disenchanted the spectator of his first more favourable opinion; until at length, as he surveyed the incongruous and misshapen pile, with its dreary mountain background, he wondered how, at any point of view, he should have deemed it other than the gloomy abode it seemed at that moment.

The only figure Frederick Travers had seen, as he rode along, was that of a man carrying a gun in his hand, in a dress somewhat like a gamekeeper's, who, at some short distance from the road, moved actively across the fields, springing lightly from hillock to hillock with the step of a practised mountain walker, and seemingly regardless of the weight of a burden which he carried on one shoulder : so rapidly did he move, that Frederick found it difficult to keep pace with him, as the road was deeply cut up, and far from safe for horse travel. Curious to make out what he carried, Travers spurred eagerly forward; and at last, but not without an effort, came within hail of him at the iron-barred gate which formed the outer entrance to the castle from the high road. The burden was now easily seen, and at once suggested to Frederick's mind the reason of the bearer's haste. It was a young buck, just killed; the blood still trickled from the wound in its skull.

" Leave that gate open, my good fellow," cried Frederick, in a voice of command, as the other pushed the frail portal wide, and let it fall back heavily to its place again—" do you hear me ?—leave it open."

" We always leap it when mounted," was the cool reply, as the speaker turned his head round, and then, without deigning either another word or look, continued his way up the steep ascent.

Travers felt the rude taunt sorely, and would have given much to be near him who uttered it; but, whether disdaining to follow a counsel thus insolently conveyed, or, it might be, not over confident of his horse, he dismounted, and, flinging wide the gate, rode quickly up the causeway—not, however, in time to overtake the other; for, although the way was enclosed by walls on both sides, he had disappeared already, but in what manner, and how, it seemed impossible to say.

"My father has omitted poaching, it would seem, in his catalogue of Irish virtues," muttered the young man, as he rode through the arched keep, and halted at the chief entrance to the house. The door lay open, displaying the cheerful blaze of a pine-wood fire, that burned briskly within the ample chimney in the keen air of a frosty morning. "I see I shall have my ride for my pains," was Fred's reflection as he passed into the wide hall, and beheld the old weapons and hunting spoils arranged around the walls. "These people affect chieftainship, and go hungry to bed to dream of fourteen quarterings. Be it so. I shall see the old rookery, at all events;" and, so saying, he gave a vigorous pull at the old bell, which answered loudly in its own person, and also by a deep howl from the aged foxhound, then lying at the fire in the drawing-room. These sounds soon died away, and a silence deep and unbroken as before succeeded. A second time, and a third, Travers repeated his summons, but without any difference of result, save that the dog no longer gave tongue ; it seemed as if he were becoming reconciled to the disturbance, as one that needed no further attention from him.

" I must explore for myself," thought Fred ; and so, attaching his horse to the massive ring by which a chain used once to be suspended across the portal, he entered the house. Walking leisurely forward, he gained the long corridor. For a second or two he was uncertain how to proceed, when a gleam of light from the half-open door in the tower led him onward. As he drew near, he heard the deep tones of a man's voice recounting, as it seemed, some story of the chase ; the last words, at least, were, " I fired but one shot—the herd is wild enough already." Travers pushed wide the door, and entered. As he did so, he involuntarily halted: the evidences of habits and tastes he was not prepared for suddenly rebuked his unannounced approach, and he would gladly have retreated were it now practicable.

" Well, sir," said the same voice he heard before, and from a young man, who leaned with one arm on the chimney-piece, and with the other hand held his gun, while he appeared as if he had been conversing with a pale and sickly youth, propped and pillowed in a deep arm-chair. They were the only occupants of the room. " Well, sir, it would seem you have made a mistake; the inn is lower down the glen—you'll see a sign over the doorway."

The look which accompanied this insolent speech recalled at once to Frederick's mind the same figure he had seen in the glen; and, stung by impertinence from such a quarter, he replied,

" Have no fear, young fellow; you may poach every acre for twenty miles round—I have not tracked you on that score."

"Poach!—tracked me!" reiterated Mark O'Donoghue, for it is needless to say it was he; and then, as if the ludicrous were even stronger in his mind than mere passion, he burst into a rude laugh; while the sick boy's pale face grew a deep crimson, as, with faltering accents, he said,

"You must be a stranger here, sir, I fancy?"

"I am so," said Travers, mildly, and yielding at once to the respect ever due to suffering; "my name is Travers. I have come over here to inquire after a young gentleman who saved my sister's life."

"Then you've *tracked* him well," interposed Mark, with an emphasis on the word. "Here he is."

"Will you not sit down?" said Herbert, motioning with his wasted hand to a seat.

Frederick took his place beside the boy at once, and said, "We owe you, sir, the deepest debt of gratitude it has ever been our fortune to incur; and if anything could enhance the obligation, it has been the heroism, the personal daring——"

"Hold, there," said Mark, sternly. "It's not our custom here to listen to compliments on our courage—we are O'Donoghues."

"This young gentleman's daring was no common one," answered Travers, as if stung by the taunt.

"My brother will scarce feel flattered by your telling him so," was Mark's haughty answer; and for some seconds Frederick knew not how to resume the conversation; at last, turning to Herbert, he said,

"May I hope that, without offending you, we may be permitted in some shape to express the sentiment I speak of; it is a debt which cannot be requited; let us at least have some evidence that we acknowledge it."

"It is the more like some of our own," broke in Mark, with a fierce laugh; "we have parchments enough, but we never pay. Your father's agent could tell you that."

Frederick gave no seeming attention to this speech, but went on: "When I say there is nothing in our power we would deem enough, I but express the feelings of my father and myself."

"There, there," cried Mark, preventing Herbert, who was about to reply, "you've said far more than was needed for a wet jacket and a few weeks' low diet. Let us have a word about the poaching you spoke of."

His fixed and steady stare—the rigid brow, by which these words were accompanied, at once proclaimed the intention of one who sought reparation for an insult, and so instantly did they convey the sentiment, that Travers, in a second, forgot all about his mission, and, starting to his feet, replied in a whisper, audible but to Mark,

"True, it was a very hazardous guess; but when, in England, we meet with a fustian jacket and a broken beaver in company with a gun and a game-bag, we have little risk in pronouncing the owner a gamekeeper or a poacher."

Mark struck his gun against the ground with such violence as shivered the stock from the barrel, while he grasped the corner of the chimney-piece convulsively with the other hand. It seemed as if passion had actually paralysed him. As he stood thus, the door opened, and Kate O'Donoghue entered. She was dressed in the becoming half toilette of the morning, and wore on her head one of those caps of blue velvet, embroidered in silver, which are so popular among the peasantry of Rhenish Germany. The light airiness of her step as she came forward, unconscious of a stranger's presence, displayed her figure in its most graceful character. Suddenly her eyes fell upon Frederick Travers; she stopped and curtseyed low to him, while he, thunderstruck with amazement at recognising his fellow-traveller so unexpectedly, could scarcely return her salute with becoming courtesy.

" Mr. Travers," said Herbert, after waiting in vain for Mark to speak— " Mr. Travers has been kind enough to come and inquire after me. Miss O'Donoghue, sir ;" and the boy, with much bashfulness, essayed in some sort the ceremony of introduction.

" My cousin, Mr. Mark O'Donoghue," said Kate, with a graceful movement of her hand towards Mark, whose attitude led her to suppose he was not known to Travers.

" I have had the honour of presenting myself already," said Frederick, bowing ; but Mark responded not to the inclination, but stood still with bent brow and clenched lip, seemingly unconscious of all around him, while Kate seated herself, and motioned to Travers to resume his place. She felt how necessary it was that she should atone, by her manner, for the strange rudeness of her cousin's ; and her mind being now relieved of the fear which first struck her, that Frederick's visit might be intended for herself, she launched freely and pleasantly into conversation, recurring to the incidents of the late journey, and the fellow-travellers they had met with.

If Kate was not sorry to learn that the Lodge was tenanted by persons of such condition and class as might make them agreeable neighbours, Travers, on the other hand, was overjoyed at discovering one of such attractions within an easy visiting distance ; while Herbert sat by, wondering how persons, so little known to each other, could have so many things to say, and so many topics which seemed mutually interesting. For so it is ; they who are ignorant of the world and its habits, can scarcely credit the great extent of those generalities which form food for daily intercourse, nor with what apparent interest people can play the game of life with but counterfeit coinage. He listened at first with astonishment, and afterwards with delight, to the pleasant flippancy of each, as in turn they discussed scenes, and pleasures, and people, of whom he never so much as heard. The *gentillesse* of French manner—would that we had a name for the thing in English—imparted to Kate's conversation a graceful ease our more reserved habits rarely permit; and while in her costume and her carriage there was a certain coquetry discernible, not a particle of affectation pervaded either her opinions or expressions. Travers, long accustomed to the best society of London, had yet seen scarcely anything of the fascination of foreign agreeability, and yielded himself so insensibly to its charm, that an hour slipped away unconsciously, and he totally forgot the great object of his visit, and lost all recollection of the luckless animal he had attached to the door ring —luckless, indeed, for already a heavy snowdrift was falling, and the day had assumed all the appearance of severe winter.

" You cannot go now, sir," said Herbert, as Frederick rose to take his leave—" there's a heavy snow-storm without;" for the boy was so interested in all he heard, he could not endure the thought of his departure.

" Oh! it's nothing," said Travers, lightly. " There's an old adage—' Snow should not scare a soldier.' "

" There's another proverb in the French service," said Kate, laughing, as she pointed to the blazing hearth—' Le soldat ne tourne pas son dos au fcu.' "

" I accept the augury," cried Frederick, laughing heartily at the witty misapplication of the phrase, and resumed his seat once more.

" Cousin Kate plays chess," said Herbert, in his anxiety to suggest a plausible pretext for delaying Frederick's departure.

" And I am passionately fond of the game; would you favour me so far ?"

" With pleasure," said she, smiling; " I only ask one condition, *point de grace*—no giving back—the O'Donoghues never take or give quarter—isn't that so, Mark? Oh! he's gone." And now for the first time it was remarked that he had left the apartment.

In a few moments after they had drawn the little marqueterie table close to the fire, and were deeply interested in the game.

At first each party played with a seeming attention, which certainly imposed on Herbert, who sat eagerly watching the progress of the game. Frederick Travers was, however, far more occupied in observing his antagonist, than in the disposition of his rooks and pawns. While she, soon perceiving his inattention, half suspected that he did not deem her an enemy worth exerting his skill upon, and thus, partly in pique, she bestowed more watchfulness than at first.

" So, mademoiselle," cried Travers at length, recurring to his game, " I perceive you have only permitted me to advance thus far to cut off my retreat for ever. How am I to save myself now ?"

" It's hard to say, Sir Captain. It's the old tactique of Celts and Saxons on both sides; you would advance into the heart of the enemy's country, and as, unhappily, the men in ivory are truer than the natives were here, and won't take bribes to fight against their fellows, you must e'en stand or fall by your own deservings."

" Come, then, the bold policy for ever. Check."

" And you lose your castle."

" And you your bishop !"

" We must avenge the church, sir. Take care of your queen."

" *Parbleu,* mademoiselle, you are a fierce foe. What say you, if we draw the battle?"

" No, no, cousin Kate ; continue, and you win it."

" Be it so. And now for my turn," said Travers, who was really a first-rate player, and at length began to feel interested in the result.

The move he made exhibited so much of skill, that Kate foresaw that the fortune of the day was about to change. She leaned her brow upon her hand, and deliberated long on the move; and at length, lifting her head, she said,

" I should like much to beat you—but in fair fight, remember—no courtesy nor favour."

" I can spare neither," said Travers, smiling.

" Then defeat is no dishonour. There's my move."

" And mine," cried Fred, as rapidly.

" What prevents my taking you? I see nothing."

" Nor I either," said he, half chagrined, for his move was an oversight.

" You are too proud to ask quarter—of course you are—or I should say, take it back."

" No, Kate, no," whispered Herbert, whose excitement was at the highest.

" I must abide my fortune," said Frederick, bowing; " and the more calmly, as I have won the game."

" Won the game ! How ?—where ?"

" Check !"

" How tauntingly he says it now," said Kate, while her eyes sparkled brilliantly. " There is too much of the conqueror in all that."

Frederick's glance met hers at the instant, and her cheek coloured deeply. Who knows the source of such emotions, or of how much pleasure and pain they are made up ! " And yet I have not won," said he, in a low voice.

" Then be it a drawn battle," said Kate. " You can afford to be generous, and I can't bear being beaten—that's the truth of it."

" If I could but win !" muttered Travers, as he rose from the table ; and whether she overheard the words, and that they conveyed more than a mere allusion to the game, she turned hastily away, and approached the window.

" Is that snowball your horse, Captain Travers ?" said she, with a wicked smile.

" My father's favourite cob, by Jove !" exclaimed Frederick ; and, as if suddenly aroused to the memory of his lengthy visit, made his adieus with more confusiou than was exactly suitable to a fashiouablc Guardsman—and departed.

" I like him," said Herbert, as he looked out of the wiudow after him. " Don't you, cousin Katc ?"

But cousin Kate did not reply.

CHAPTER XX.

TEMPTATION IN A WEAK HOUR.

WHEN Mark O'Donoghuc left the room, his passion had become almost ungovernable—the entrance of his cousiu Kate had but dammed up the current of his anger—and, during the few moments he still remained afterwards, his temper was fiercely tried by wituessing the courtesy of her manner to the stranger, and the apparent intimacy which subsisted between them. " I ought to have known it," was the expression he muttered over and over to himself —" I ought to have known it ! That fellow's gay jacket aud plumed hat are dearer to her woman's heart than the rude devotion of such as I am. Curses be on them ! they carry persecution through everything—house, home, country, rank, wealth, station—ay, the very affection of our kindred they grudge us ! Was slavery ever like this ?" And with these bitter words, the offspring of bitterer thoughts, he strode down the causeway, and reached the high road. The snow was falling fast—a chilling north wind drove the thin flakes along—but he heeded it not. The fire of anger that burned within his bosom defied all sense of winter's cold ; and with a throbbing brow and fevered hand he went, turning from time to time to look up at the old castle, whence he expected each moment to see Travers take his departure. Now he hurried eagerly onward, as if to reach some destined spot—now he would stop, and retrace his steps, irresolutely, as though half determined to return home.

" Degraded, insulted, outraged on the very hearth of my father's house !" cried he, aloud, as he wrung his hands in agony, and gave his passion vent. Again he pressed forward, and at last arrived at that part of the gleu where, the road seems escarped between the two mountains, which rise several hundred feet, like walls, on either side. Here he paused, and after examining the spot for some seconds, he muttered to himself, " He has no choice here but stand or turn !" And so saying, he drew from the breast of his coat two

L

pistols, examined the priming of each, and then replaced them. The prospect of speedy revenge seemed to have calmed his vindictive spirit, for
now he continued to walk backwards and forwards, at a slow pace, like a
sentinel on his post, pausing occasionally to listen if a horse's hoofs could
be heard upon the road, and then resuming his walk once more. A rustling
sound in the brushwood above his head once startled him, but the granite
cliffs that overhung the road prevented his seeing from what it proceeded,
and his heart was now bent on a very different object than the pursuit of the
deer. At that moment the proudest of the herd might have grazed in safety
within pistol-shot of him, and he had not deigned to notice it. Thus passed
an hour—a second and a third succeeded—and already the dull shadows of
approaching night were falling, yet no one came. Tortured with strange
conjectures, Mark saw the day waning, and yet no sight nor sound of him
he looked for. Let not poets speak of the ardent longing of a lover's heart,
as in throbbing eagerness he waits for her whose smile is life, and hope, and
heaven. Compared with the mad impatience of him who thirsts for vengeance, his passion is but sluggish apathy. It is the bad that ever calls
forth the sternest energies of human nature. It is in crime that men
transcend the common attributes of mankind. Here was one, now, who
would have given his right hand beneath the axe for but one brief moment
of vengeance, and have deemed years of suffering cheaply bought for the
mere presence of his enemy before him.

"He must have guessed my meaning when I left the room," was the
taunting expression he now uttered, as his unsated anger took the shape of
an insolent depreciation of his adversary. "An Irishman would not need a
broader hint."

It grew darker—the mountains frowned heavily beneath the canopy of
clouds, and night was rapidly approaching, when, from the gloom of his
almost extinguished hope, Mark was suddenly aroused. He heard the
tramp of a horse's feet; the dull reverberation on the deep snow filled the
air, and sometimes they seemed to come from the opposite part of the glen,
when the pace slackened, and at last the sounds became almost inaudible.

"There is yet enough of daylight if we move into the broad road," was
Mark's soliloquy, as he stooped his ear to listen—and at the instant he beheld a man leading his horse by the bridle, while he himself seemed seeking
along the roadside, where the snowdrift had not yet fallen, as if for some
lost object. A glance, even by the imperfect light, and at some thirty paces
off, showed Mark it was not him he sought, and were it not that the attitude
attracted his curiosity, he had not wasted a second look on him; but the
horseman by this time had halted, and was scraping with his whip-handle
amid the pebbles of the mountain rivulet.

"I'll never see it again—it's no use!" was the exclamation of the seeker,
as he gathered up his reins and prepared to mount.

"Is that Lanty Lawler?" cried Mark, as he recognised the voice; "I say, did you meet with a young officer riding down the glen, in the direction of Carrignacurra?"

"No, indeed, Mr. Mark—I never saw living thing since I left Bantry."

The young man paused for a few seconds—and then, as if anxious to turn all thought from his question, said, "What have you lost thereabouts?"

"Oh, more than I am worth in the world!" was the answer, in a deep, heart-drawn sigh; "but, blessed Heaven! what's the pistols for? Oh, Master Mark, dear—sure—sure——"

"Sure what?" cried the youth, with a hoarse laugh—"sure I'm not turned highway robber! Is that what you want to say? Make your mind easy, Lanty, I have not reached that point yet; though, if indifference to life might tempt a man, I'd not say it is so far off."

"'Tis a duel, then," cried Lanty, quickly; "but I hope you wouldn't fight without seconds. Oh! that's downright murder. What did he do to you? Was it one of the fellows you met in Cork?"

"You are all wrong," said Mark, sullenly. "It is enough, however, that neither of us seem to have found what he was seeking. You have your secret; I have mine."

"Oh, faix, mine is soon told—'twas my pocket-book, with as good as seventy pounds in goold, I lost here a three weeks ago, and never set eyes on it since; and there was papers in it—ay, faix, papers of great value—and I daren't face Father Luke without them. I may leave the country when he hears what happened."

"Where are you going now?" said Mark, gloomily.

"I'm going as far as Mary's, for the night. Maybe you'd step down there and take a bit of supper? When the moon rises the night will take up fine."

The young man turned without speaking, and bent his steps in the direction Lanty was travelling.

The horse-dealer was too well versed in human nature to press for a confidence which he foresaw would be at last willingly extended to him; he therefore walked along at Mark's side, without uttering a word, and seeming to be absorbed in his own deep musings. His calculation was a correct one. They had not gone many paces forward when young O'Donoghue unburdened his whole heart to him—told him, with all the eloquent energy of a wounded spirit, of the insult he had received in his own home, before his younger brother's face. He omitted nothing in his description of the overbearing impertinence of Frederick Travers's manner — with what cool assurance he had entered the house, and with what flippant carelessness he treated his cousin Kate.

"I left home with an oath not to return thither unavenged," said he,

" nor will I, though this time luck seems against me. Had he but come, I should have given him his choice of pistols and his own distance. My hand is true from five paces to thirty; but he has not escaped me yet."

Lanty never interrupted the narrative except to ask from time to time some question, the answer to which was certain to develop the deeper indignation of the youth. A low, muttering commentary, intended to mean a heartfelt sympathy with his wrongs, was all he suffered to escape his lips; and, thus encouraged in his passionate vehemence, Mark's wrath became like a frenzy.

" Come in, now," said Lanty, as he halted at the door of Mary's cabin, " but don't say a word about this business. I have a thought in my head that may do you good service, but keep a fair face before people—do you mind me ?"

There was a tone of secrecy and mystery in these words Mark could not penetrate; but, however dark their meaning, they seemed to promise some hope of that revenge his heart yearned after, and with this trust he entered the house.

Mary received them with her wonted hospitality—Lanty was an expected guest—and showed how gratified she felt to have young O'Donoghue beneath her roof.

" I was afeard you were forgetting me entirely, Mr. Mark," said she; " you passed the door twice, and never as much as said, ' God save you, Mary.' "

" I did not forget you, for all that, Mary," said he, feelingly. " I have too few friends in the world to spare any of them; but I've had many things on my mind lately."

" Well, and to be sure you had, and why wouldn't you? 'Tis no shame of you to be sad and down-hearted—an O'Donoghue of the ould stock—the best blood in Kerry, wandering about by himself, instead of being followed by a troop of servants, with a goold-coat-of-arms worked on their coats, like your grandfather's men—the heavens be his bed. Thirty-eight mounted men, armed, ay, and well armed, were in the saddle after him, the day the English general came down here to see the troops that was quartered at Bantry."

" No wonder we should go afoot now," said Mark, bitterly.

" Well, well, it's the will of God," ejaculated Mary, piously; " and who knows what's in store for you yet ?"

" That's the very thing I do be telling him," said Lanty, who only waited for the right moment to chime in with the conversation. " There's fine times coming."

Mary stared at the speaker with the eager look of one who wished to derive a meaning deeper than the mere words seemed to convey, and then, checking her curiosity at a gesture from Lanty, she set about arranging the supper, which only awaited his arrival.

Mark eat but little of the fare before him, though Mary's cookery was not without its temptations; but of the wine—and it was strong Burgundy—he drank freely. Goblet after goblet he drained with that craving desire to allay a thirst, which is rather the symptom of a mind fevered by passion than by malady. Still, as he drank, no sign of intoxication appeared; on the contrary, his words evinced a tone of but deeper resolution, and a more settled purpose than at first, when he told how he had promised never to leave his father, although all his hopes pointed to the glorious career a foreign service would open before him.

" It was a good vow you made, and may the saints enable you to keep it," said Mary.

" And for the matter of glory, maybe there's some to be got nearer home, and without travelling to look for it," interposed Lanty.

" What do you mean?" said Mark, eagerly.

" Fill your glass. Take the big one, for it's a toast I'm going to give you —are you ready ? Here now, then—drink—

> A stout heart and mind,
> And an easterly wind,
> And the Devil behind
> The Saxon.' "

Mark repeated the doggerel as well as he was able, and pledged the only sentiment he could divine, that of the latter part, with all his enthusiasm.

" You may tell him what you plaze, now," whispered Mary in Lanty's ear ; for her ready wit perceived that his blood was warmed by the wine, and his heart open for any communication.

Lanty hesitated but a second, then drawing his chair close to Mark's, he said,

" I'm going now to put my life in your hands, but I can't help it. When Ireland is about to strike for liberty, it is not an O'Donoghue should be last in the ranks. Swear to me you'll never mention again what I'll tell you— swear it on the book." Mary, at the same moment, placed in his hand a breviary, with a gilt cross on the binding, which Mark took reverently, and kissed twice. " That's enough—your word would do for me, but I must obey them that's over me ;" and so saying, Lanty at once proceeded to lay before the astonished mind of young O'Donoghue the plan of France for an inva· sion of Ireland—not vaguely nor imperfectly, not in the mere language of rumour or chance allusion, but with such aids to circumstance and time, as gave him the appearance of one conversant with what he spoke on. The restoration of Irish independence—the resumption of forfeited estates—the return of the real nobility of the land to their long-lost position of eminence and influence, were themes he descanted upon with consummate skill, bringing home each fact to the actual effect such changes would work in the youth's own condition, who, no longer degraded to the rank of a mere peasant, would once again assert his own rightful station, and stand forth at the head of his vast property — the heir of an honoured name and house. Lanty knew well, and more, too, implicitly believed in all the plausible pretension of French sympathy for Irish suffering, which formed the cant of the day. He had often heard the arguments in favour of the success of such an expedition—in fact, the reasons for which its failure was deemed impossible. These he repeated fluently, giving to his narrative the semblance of an incontestable statement, and then he told him that from Brest to Dublin was "fifty hours' sail, with a fair breeze"—that same "easterly wind" the toast alluded to, that the French could throw thirty, nay fifty thousand troops into Ireland, yet never weaken their own army to any extent worth speaking of—that England was distracted by party spirit, impoverished by debt, and totally unable to repel invasion, and, in fact, that if Ireland would be but "true to herself," her success was assured.

He told, too, how Irishmen were banded together in a sworn union to assert the independence of their country, and that such as held back, or were reluctant in the cause, would meet the fate of enemies. On the extent and completeness of the organisation he dwelt with a proud satisfaction, but when he spoke of large masses of men trained to move and act together, Mark suddenly interrupted him, saying,

"Yes, I have seen them. It's not a week since some hundreds marched through this glen at midnight."

"Ay, that was Holt's party," said Mary, composedly; "and fine men they are."

"They were unarmed," said Mark.

"If they were, it is because the general didn't want their weapons."

"There's arms enough to be had when the time comes for using them," broke in Mary.

"Wouldn't you show him——" and Lanty hesitated to conclude a speech the imprudence of which he was already aware of.

"Ay will I," said Mary. "I never mistrusted one of his name;" and with that, she rose from the fireside, and took a candle in her hand. "Come here a minute, Master Mark." Unlocking a small door in the back wall of the cabin, she entered a narrow passage which led to the stable, but off which a narrow door, scarcely distinguishable from the wall, conducted into a spacious vault, excavated in the solid rock. Here were a vast number of packing-cases and boxes, piled on each other, from floor to roof, together with hogsheads and casks of every shape and size. Some of the boxes had been opened, and the lids laid loosely over them. Removing one of these, Mary pointed to the contents, as she said,

"There they are—French muskets and carbines. There's pistols in that case ; and all them, over there, is swords and cutlasses. 'Tis pike-heads that's in the other corner; and the casks has saddles and holsters and them kind of things."

Mark stooped down and took up one of the muskets. It was a light and handy weapon, and bore on its stock the words—"Armeé de Sambre-et-Meuse"—for none of the weapons were new.

" These are all French," said he, after a brief pause.

" Every one of them," replied Mary, proudly; "and there's more coming from the same place."

" And why can we not fight our own battles without aid from France?" said Mark, boldly. "If we really are worthy of independence, are we not able to win it?"

" Because there's traitors among us," said Mary, replying before Lanty could interpose—"because there's traitors that would turn again us if we were not sure of victory; but when they see we have the strong hand, as well as the good cause, they'll be sure to stand on the safe side."

" I don't care for that," said Mark. " I want no such allies as these. I say, if we deserve our liberty, we ought to be strong enough to take it."

" There's many think the same way as yourself," said Lanty, quietly. "I heard the very words you said from one of the delegates last week. But I don't see any harm in getting help from a friend, when the odds is against you."

" But I do; and great harm too. What's the price of the assistance?— tell me that."

" Oh, make your mind easy on that score. The French hate the English, whether they love us or no."

" And why wouldn't they love us," said Mary, half angry at such a supposition, "and we all Catholics? Don't we both belong to the ould ancient church? and didn't we swear to destroy the heretics wherever we'd find them? Ay, and we will, too!"

" I'm with you, whatever come of it," said Mark, after a few seconds of thought. " I'm with you; and if the rest have as little to live for, trust me they'll not be pleasant adversaries."

Overjoyed at this bold avowal, which consummated the success they desired, they led Mark back into the cabin, and pledged, in a bumper, the "raal O'Donoghue."

CHAPTER XXI.

SIR MARMADUKE TRAVERS and his daughter had passed a morning of great uneasiness at the delay in Frederick's return. Noon came, and yet no appearance of him. They wandered along the road, hoping to meet him, and at last turned homeward with the intention of despatching a servant towards Carrignacurra, fearing lest he should have missed his way. This determination, however, they abandoned, on being told by a countryman that he had seen the horse young Travers rode still standing at the gate of the " castle."

A feeling of curiosity to hear his son's account of the O'Donoghues mingled with the old man's excitement at his absence ; and, as the day declined, and still no sign of his return, he walked every now and then to the door, and looked anxiously along the road by which he expected his approach. Sybella, too, was not without her fears, and though vague and undefined, she dreaded a possible collision between the hot blood of Mark and her brother. The evening of her first arrival was ever present to her mind ; and she often thought of what might have then occurred had Frederick been present.

They had wearied themselves with every mode of accounting for his delay, guessed at every possible cause of detention, and were at length on the point of sending a messenger in search of him, when they heard the tramp of a horse coming, not along the high road, but, as it seemed, over the fields in front of them. A few minutes more of anxious expectancy, and Frederick, with his horse splashed and panting, alighted beside them.

" Well, you certainly have a very pretty eye for a country, father," said he, gaily. " That same line you advised has got three as rasping fences as I should like to meet with."

" What do you mean, boy ?" said Sir Marmaduke, as much puzzled at the speech as the reader himself may feel.

" Simply, sir, that though the cob is a capital horse, and has a great jump in him, I'd rather have daylight for that kind of thing ; and I really believe the ragged fellow you sent for me chose the stiffest places. I saw the rascal grinning when I was coming up to the mill-stream."

" Messenger !—ragged fellow ! The boy is dreaming."

" My dear Frederick, we sent no messenger. We were, indeed, very anxious at your delay, but we did not despatch any one to meet you."

Frederick stared at both the speakers, and then repeated, in astonishment, the last words, "Sent no messenger!" but when they once more assured him of the fact, he gave the following account of his return:

"It was very late when I left the castle. I delayed there the whole day; but scarcely had I reached the high road, when a wild-looking fellow, with a great pole in his hand, came up to me, and cried out,

"'Are you for the Lodge?' 'Yes,' said he, answering for himself, 'you are her brother. I'm sent over to tell you not to go back by the road, for the bridge is down; but you're to come over the fields, and I'll show you the way.'

"Supposing the fellow was what he assumed to be, your messenger, I followed him; and, by George, it was no joking matter; for he leaped like a deer, and seemed to take uncommon pleasure in pitting himself against the cob. I should have given up the contest, I confess, but that the knave had me in his power. For when it grew dark, I knew not which way to head, until, at length, he shouted out,

"'There's the Lodge now, where you see the light.' And after that, what became of himself I cannot tell you."

"It was Terry, poor Terry," cried Sybella.

"Yes, it must have been Terry," echoed her father.

"And is this Terry retained to play Will-o'-the-wisp?" asked Fred; "or is it a piece of amateurship?"

But both Sir Marmaduke and Sybella were too deeply engaged in canvassing the motive for this strange act to pay due attention to his question.

As Frederick was but little interested in his guide, nor mindful of what became of him, they were not able to obtain any clue from him as to what road he took; nor what chance there was of overtaking him.

"So then this was a piece of 'politesse,' for which I am indebted to your friend Terry's own devising," said Fred, half angrily. "The fellow had better keep out of my way in future."

"You will not harm him, Fred, you never could, when I tell you of his gallant conduct here."

"My sweet sister, I am really wearied of this eternal theme—I have heard of nothing but heroism since my arrival. Once for all, I concede the matter, and am willing to believe of the Irish, as of the family of Bayard, that all the men are brave—and all the women virtuous. And now, let us to dinner."

"You have told us nothing of your visit to the enchanted castle, Fred," said his sister, when the servants had withdrawn, and they were once more alone, "and I am all impatience to hear of your adventures there."

"I confess, too," said Sir Marmaduke, "I am not devoid of curiosity on the subject—let us hear it all."

"I have little to recount," said Frederick, with some hesitation in his manner; "I neither saw the O'Donoghue, as they call him, nor his brother-in-law—the one was in bed, the other had gone to visit some sick person on the mountain. But I made acquaintance with your preux chevalier, Sybella—a fine-looking young fellow, even though wasted with sickness; he was there with an elder brother, au insolent kind of personage—half peasant, all bully."

" He was not wanting iu proper respect to *you*," said Sir Marmadukc. " I trust, Fred, he was aware of who you were?"

" Faith, sir, I fancy he cared very little on the subject; aud had I been a much more important individual, he would have treated me in the same way—a way, to say the least of it, not overburdened with courtesy."

" Had you any words together, boy?" said Sir Marmaduke, with an evident anxiety in his look aud voice.

" A mere interchauge of greetiug," replied Fred, laughing, "in which each party showed his teeth, but did not bite withal. I uuhappily mistook him for a gamekeeper, and, worse still, told him so, aud he felt proportiouably angry at the imputation, preferring, probably, to be thought a poacher. He is a rude, coarse fellow," said he, with a changed voice, "with pride to be a gentlemau, but not breeding nor manner to enact the character."

" The visit was, after all, not au agreeable one," said Miss Travers, " aud I am only surprised how you came to prolong it. You speut the whole day there."

Although there was not the slightest degree of suspicion insinuated by this remark, Fred stole a quick glance at his sister, to see if she really intended more than the mere words implied. Then, satisfied that she had not, he said, in a careless way,

" Oh, the weather broke; it came on a heavy suow-storm; and as the younger brother pressed me to remain, and I had no fancy to face the hurricane, I sat down to a game of chess."

" Chess! Indeed, Fred, that souuds very humanising. And how did he play?"

" It was not with him I played," answered he, hesitatingly.

" What—with the elder?"

" No, nor him either; my antagonist was a cousin—I think they called her cousin."

" Call *her*," said Sybella, slyly. " So, then, Master Fred, there was a lady in the case. Well, we certainly have beeu a long while coming to her."

" Yes, she has lately arrived—a day or two ago—from some convent in the Low Countries, where she has lived since she was a child."

" A strange home for her," interposed Sir Marmaduke. " If I do not misconceive them greatly, they must be very unsuitable associates for a young lady educated in a Freuch couvent."

" So you would say if you saw her," said Fred, seizing with avidity at the opening then offered to coincide with an opinion he was half afraid to broach. "She is perfectly foreign in look, dress, and demeanour—with all the mannerism of Paris life, graceful and pleasing in her address; and they, at least one of them, a downright boor; the other, giving him credit for good looks and good nature, yet immeasurably *her* inferior in every respect."

"Is she pretty, Frederick?" said Sybella, not lifting her eyes from her work as she spoke.

"I should say pretty," replied he, with hesitation, as if qualifying his praise by a word which did not imply too much. "I prefer a quieter style of beauty, for my own part; less dazzle, less sparkling effect; something to see every day, and to like the better the more one sees it;" and he placed his arm around his sister's waist, and gazed at her, as if to give interpretation to his speech.

"You have made me quite curious to see her, Fred," said Sybella. "The very fact of finding one like her in such a place has its interest."

"What if you were to visit her, my dear?" said Sir Marmaduke; "the attention would only be a proper one; you have books and music here, besides, which she might be glad to have in a region so remote as this."

Frederick never spoke a word, but anxiously awaited his sister's answer.

"I should like it greatly; what says Fred to the notion?"

"I see nothing against it," replied he, with a well-affected indifference. "She is a most ladylike person, and if it be your intention to pass a few weeks longer in this solitude, would be of infinite value for companionship."

"A few weeks longer!—I shall remain till Christmas, boy," said his father, with determination. "I have taken a fancy to Ireland; and my intention is to go up to Dublin for a few months in winter, and return here in the spring."

This was at once approaching the very subject which Frederick had journeyed to determine; but whether it was that the time seemed unfavourable, or that his own ideas in the matter had undergone some modification since his arrival, he contented himself with simply a doubtful shake of the head, as if distrusting Sir Marmaduke's firmness, and did not endeavour to oppose his determination by a single argument of any kind. On the contrary, he listened with patience and even seeming interest to his father's detailed account of his project; how he had already given orders to secure a house in Stephen's-green for the winter, intending to make acquaintances with the gentry of the capital, and present himself and his daughter at the vice-regal court.

"Sybella may as well make her *début* in society here as in London," said Sir Marmaduke. "Indeed, I am not sure but the provincial boards are the best for a first appearance. In any case, such is the line I have laid down for myself; and if it only secured me against a sea voyage to England in such a season, I shall be amply repaid for my resolve."

Against the season of his return, too, Sir Marmaduke hoped to make such additions to the Lodge as should render it more comfortable as a residence; various plans for which were heaped upon the library table, and littered the chairs about the room.

Miss Travers had already given her hearty concurrence to all her father's schemes, and seconded most ably every one of his views by such arguments as she was possessed of; so that Frederick, even if disposed to record his opposition, saw that the present was not an opportune moment, and prudently reserved for another time what, if unsuccessful now, could never be recurred to with advantage.

The conversation on these topics lasted long. They discussed with interest every detail of their plans; for so it is, the pleasures of castle-building are inexhaustible, and the very happiest realities of life are poor and vague compared with the resources provided by our hopes and fancies. The slightest grounds of probability are enough to form a foundation, but there is no limit to the superstructure we raise above.

In the indulgence of this view, they continued to chat till a late hour, and parted for the night in high good humour with each other—a visit to the O'Donoghue being the plan for the succeeding day's accomplishment.

CHAPTER XXII.

A MORNING VISIT.

On the afternoon of the following day, Sir Marmaduke, accompanied by his son and daughter, bent their steps towards the castle of the O'Donoghue. The day was a fine and bright one, with a blue sky above, and a hard, frosty surface on the earth beneath, and made walking as pleasant as open air and exercise can render it. The carriage was ordered to meet them on their return, less, indeed, on account of the distance, than that the shortness of the day made the precaution reasonable.

Chatting agreeably, on they went. The time slipped rapidly away, now adverting to the bold and majestic scenery around them, now speaking of the people, their habits, their prejudices, and their leanings, or anon discussing the O'Donoghue family, which, of all the puzzling themes the land presented, was certainly not the least embarrassing to them.

"We must think of some means of evincing our gratitude to this boy, Fred," said Sir Marmaduke, in a whisper. "You appear to have found the matter more difficult than you anticipated."

"Very true, sir. In the early part of my visit, it was rendered impossible by the interruption of the elder brother; and, in the latter part, somehow, I believe I—I actually begin to fear I forgot it altogether. However, I have thought of one thing, and it should be done without a moment's loss of time. You must write to Carden, the law agent, and stop any proceedings Hemsworth may have begun against these people. It would be most disgraceful to think that, while professing sentiments of good feeling and friendliness, we were using the arm of the law to harass and distress them."

"I'll do it at once, Fred—by this night's post. In truth, I never understood the point at issue between us; nor can I clearly see Hemsworth's reason for the summary course he has taken with them. There must be more in it than I know of."

"The castle stands proudly, as seen from this point," said Sybella, who felt somewhat wearied of a conversation maintained in a voice too low for her to hear. And the remark had the effect of recalling them to other thoughts, in discussing which they arrived at the old keep of Carrignacurra.

Whether recent events had sharpened Kerry O'Leary to a more acute sense of his duties as butler, or that Kate O'Donoghue had exerted some influence in bringing about so desirable an object, we know not; but at the very first summons of the hall-door bell he made his appearance, his ordinary costume being augmented, if not improved, by a pair of very unwieldy top-boots of his master's, which reached somewhere to the middle of the thigh, and were there met by a green velvet waistcoat, from the same wardrobe, equally too large and voluminous for its present owner.

Visitors at the O'Donoghue house were generally of a character which Kerry felt necessary to close the door against. They unhappily came, not with the ceremonial of a visiting-card, but with some formidable missive of the law, in the shape of a distress warrant, a latitat, or that meeker and less dreaded engine, a protested bill. It was, then, with a considerable relief to his anxieties that his eye caught the flutter of a lady's dress, as he peeped from the small casement beside the door, and his heart expanded in a little thanksgiving of its own as he unbarred the portal to admit her.

Having informed his visitors that the family were at home, he preceded them to the drawing-room, with a step the noise of which happily drowned the tittering it was impossible to subdue at beholding him. To prevent the awkwardness which Sir Marmaduke foresaw might arise from the blundering announcement Kerry would inevitably make of their names, he having repeated over and over as he went along, by way of refreshing his memory, "Sir Marmaduke, Sir Marmaduke Travers," the old gentleman stepped forward as the door opened, and presented himself by name, introducing his daughter at the same time.

The O'Donoghue, seated in his chair, half rose, for it was one of his gouty days, and he could not stir without great difficulty, and with an air and voice which bespoke the gentleman, welcomed his guests.

Herbert's eyes gleamed with delight as he gazed on the party; and Sir Archibald, bowing with an ancient grace that would have suited a courtier of a century previous, presented chairs to each, going through the ceremonial of a new obeisance to every one of the group. Kate O'Donoghue was not in the room, nor Mark—the latter, indeed, had not returned to the castle since the day previous.

The ordinary greetings over, and Sir Marmaduke having expressed, in well-chosen phrase, the gratitude he had so long laboured to acquit, the conversation became easy and agreeable. Sir Marmaduke, seating himself next O'Donoghue, had entered into a discussion of the state of the country and the people—Frederick, beside Herbert's chair, was conversing with the boy by lively sallies and pleasant stories, that flowed the more rapidly as the listener was an eager one; while Sir Archibald, standing in an attitude of respectful attention, had engaged Miss Travers in a conversation about the glen and its scenery, to which his own correct taste and thorough appreciation of the picturesque gave a charm and piquancy that already interested her deeply. So naturally easy and unaffected was the tone of their reception, that all astonishment at finding their host so superior to their anticipation was merged in the pleasure that Travers felt in the interview. The good-tempered heartiness of the O'Donoghue himself, his frank speech, his ready humour, won each moment more and more on Sir Marmaduke. Frederick, too, never grew wearied of the fresh and joyous spirit which gleamed out at every look and word from Herbert, whose ardent temperament and high-hearted nature caught up the enthusiasm of a spirit like his own; and as for Sybella, the charm of Sir Archy's manner, whose perfection was its adaptation to the society of ladies, delighted her greatly, and she soon forgot any slight inclination to smile at the precision of language, where deep sound sense and high feeling were conveyed with only the fault of pedantry. While thus agreeably engaged on all sides, the door opened, and Kate entered, but so noiselessly withal, that she was in the midst of the party before they knew of her approach. Recognising Frederick Travers with a gracious smile, she received Sir Marmaduke's salutation with a deep curtsey, and then, as if similarity of years required a less ceremonious introduction, took her seat beside Miss Travers, with an air of mingled kindness and cordiality she so well knew how to assume. As in an orchestra, amid the swell of many instruments, where deep-toned thunders mingle with sounds of softer influence, some one strain will rise, from time to time, suggestive of feelings apart from the rest, with higher and nobler sympathies around it, so did her voice, heard among the others, sound thus sweetly. Her words came winged with a fine expression, which look and gesture could alone give them, and in the changing colour of her cheek, her brilliant brow, her lips, even in silence eloquent, there was a character of loveliness as much above mere beauty as life transcends the marble. The more perfect regularity of Sybella's features, their classic outline, their chaste correctness in every line and lineament, seemed cold and inanimate when contrasted with the more expressive loveliness of Kate O'Donoghue. The fearless character of her mind, too, was blended with so much of womanly delicacy and refinement, the wish to please so associated with a seeming forgetfulness of self, that every act and every gesture teemed with a charm of interest for which there is no word save "fascination;" even that slightly foreign accent, of which we have already spoken, served to individualise all she said, and left it graven on the heart long after the words were spoken.

Frederick Travers watched with eager delight the effects these gifts were producing upon his sister. He saw the pleasure with which Sybella listened; he recognised, even already, the symptoms of that conquest by which mind subdues mind, and was overjoyed as he looked.

To Sir Marmaduke's gracefully expressed hope that this visit should form a prelude to their nearer intimacy, the O'Donoghue, with a touch of sadness in his voice, replied that he himself was an invalid, whose steps never wandered beyond the precincts of his home; but his brother-in-law, and his niece, and the boys, they would all, he was certain, avail themselves of such a neighbourhood.

Sir Archibald bowed low, and somewhat stiffly, perhaps, in accordance with a pledge thus given without his concurrence; but Herbert's bright eyes grew brighter, and his cheek flushed with delight at the bare anticipation of the thought.

"And you, Miss O'Donoghue," said Sir Marmaduke, turning towards Kate, "our humble library at the Lodge is perfectly at your service; the only condition we ask is, that you come and choose from it in person."

"That promise is already most kindly made, father," interrupted Sybella, whose pleased look showed how she had been captivated by her new friend.

While their smiles and gracious words went round, the door was suddenly opened by Kerry O'Leary, who, forgetful of the visitors in his eager anxiety as the bearer of news, cried out,

"There's a shindy, master dear! Such a row! May I never die in sin if ever I seen the equal of it!"

"What does he mean?—is the fellow mad?" cried the O'Donoghue, angrily, while Sir Archy, bending on him a most ominous frown, muttered,

"Have ye lost a' decency together. Ye daft loon, what ails ye?"

"I ax your pardon, and the quality's pardon," said Kerry, with an expression of abject misery for his unceremonious "entrée;" "but, if you seen it, sorra bit but you'd forgive me."

" There has been good fun somewhere, I'm certain," cried out Frederick Travers, whose curiosity to learn Kerry's intelligence could no longer be repressed.

" What is it, then, Kerry?" said the O'Donoghue. " Let us hear it all."

" 'Tis Master Mark, good luck to him!" cried Kerry, overjoyed at the permission to speak out freely. " He was over at Ballyvourney with the greyhounds, when he seen that dirty spalpeen, Sam Wylie, wid a process-sarver along wid him, noticin' the tenants. The sarver was a stranger, and he didn't touch him ; but he made the boys put Sam on Nick Malone's mule, and give him a fair start, and they run him down the mountain, with a fine view, and ran into him here at the horse-pond, where the mule flung him head over heels ; and begorra, you wouldn't know 'twas a Christian, if you seen him this minit dripping wet, and the duckweed all hanging round him ; and he's running still, for he thinks Master Mark will take the life of him before he stops."

A roar of laughter from Frederick, joined in by Herbert, and at last by the O'Donoghue himself, for some moments prevented a word of commentary on this outrageous proceeding, when Sir Marmaduke, rising slowly, said,

" I am a stranger here, very ignorant of the country and its habits ; but I have yet to learn that any man, in the just discharge of his duty, should be thus treated. I call upon you, sir, to investigate this affair, and if it be as we have heard it, to make reparation——"

" Ye hae muckle reason for what ye say, sir," interposed Sir Archy ; " but the freaks and follies o' young men hae a license here I doubt ye are na used to."

" I'll lay my life on it Mark was right," called out the O'Donoghue. " The boy never makes any mistake in these matters."

" If the fellow were insolent," said Frederick, " your son has served him properly."

Kate smiled at the speaker a look of gratitude, which amply repaid him for coming thus promptly to the rescue.

" It may be so," said Sir Marmaduke, happy at such a means of escaping from a further prosecution of a most unpleasant topic.

" The captain's guessed it well," cried Kerry. " The spalpeen tould Master Mark that he'd be up here to-morrow wid a notice from the master himself, and it would go hard but he'd see us out of the place before Easter."

" Is this possible !" said Sir Marmaduke, blushing deeply. " I beg, my dear sir, that you will forgive any hasty expression I may have used."

" I can forgive the lad myself," said Sir Archy, proudly.

" Not I, then, uncle," interposed Kate—" not I. Mark should have horsewhipped the fellow within an inch of his life."

Sybella Travers started at the energy of voice and manner which accompanied these words; while the O'Donoghue, rising from his chair, came slowly across the hearth, and imprinted a kiss upon Kate's forehead.

" You're one of the raal stock—there's no denying it," muttered Kerry, as he gazed on her with an expression of almost worship. " 'Tis blood that never gives in—divil a lie in it !"

Herbert, who alone had witnessed the unfriendly meeting between his brother and young Travers, turned a pleasant smile at the latter, as he half whispered,

" This was very kind of *you*."

It would have been a difficult—nay, an almost impossible task, to recal the tone and temper of the party previous to this unhappy interruption. All Sir Marmaduke's efforts to resume the conversation had lost their former ease—the O'Donoghue himself was disconcerted; for he was not quite certain what were Sir Marmaduke's words on the occasion, and how far he should feel called upon to demand a retractation, and Sir Archibald, fretful and annoyed at the impression Mark's conduct would convey of the habits and temper of the house, felt his task a severe one to assume an air of serenity and quietude.

Frederick Travers alone seemed happy and delighted. The sudden expression of Kate O'Donoghue's opinion, so utterly unlike anything he had ever heard before from a young lady's lips, took him as much by surprise as the spirit pleased him; and he would willingly have engaged to horsewhip a dozen process-servers for another glance of her flashing eyes as she delivered the words; while Sybella could not help a sentiment bordering on fear, for one who, young as herself, gifted with every womanly attribute of grace and loveliness, had yet evinced a degree of impetuosity and passion she could not reconcile with such attractions. As for Kate, the sentiment had evoked no stir within her bosom. It was a wish as naturally expressed as it was felt, and all the surprise the others experienced at her words would have been nothing to her own to have known of their astonishment.

The visit soon came to a termination, and Sir Marmaduke, having succeeded in a great degree in restoring the favourable impression he had at first obtained, took his leave of the O'Donoghue, and then, addressing Sir Archy, said,

" You, sir, I rejoice to learn, are not an invalid. May I expect the happiness of seeing you sometimes ?"

Sir Archy bowed deeply, and, with a motion of his hand towards Miss Travers, replied,

" I have already made an engagement here, sir."

" Yes," said Sybella, to whom this speech seemed half addressed, " Sir Archibald has been kind enough to offer me his guidance up the glen, where there are several points of view finer than any I have seen."

Emboldened by the success of these advances, Sir Marmaduke, with a

M

courtesy he was perfect master of, requested the party would not delay their kind inteutions, but favour him with their company on the following day.

It is doubtful whether Sir Archy might not have declined a more formal invitation; but there seemed something so frank iu the abruptness of the preseut, that he acceded at once; and Kate having also pledged herself to accompany him, their greetings were iuterchanged, aud they parted.

CHAPTER XXIII.

SOME OPPOSITE TRAITS OF CHARACTER.

It may seem strauge, and almost paradoxical—but so it was—Kate O'Donoghue's preseuce appeared to have wrought a most magical change in the whole household of the O'Donoghue. The efforts they themselves made to ward off the semblance of their fallen estate induced a happier frame of miud than that which resulted from daily brooding over their misfortunes; the very struggle elicited a courage they had left long in disuse; and the cheerfulness which at first was but assumed, grew gradually more and more natural. To the O'Donoghue, who, for many a day, desired no more than to fend off the evil in his owu brief time—who, with the selfishness of an old age passed in continual conflict with poverty, only sought a life interest in their bettered fortuncs—she was a boon above all price. Her light step, her lighter laugh, her mirthful tone of conversation, with its many anecdotes and stories of places and people he had not heard of before, were resources agaiust gloom that never failed.

Sir Archy, too, felt a return to the old associations of his youth in the preseuce of a young, beautiful, and accomplished girl, whose gracefuluess and elegance threw a halo around her as she went, and made of that old and crumbling tower, dark with neglect, and sad with time, a salon, teeming with its many appliauces against depression, where she herself, armed with so many fasciuations, dispeused cheerfulness and bliss on all about her. Nor was he selfish in all this. He marked with delight the impression made upou his favourite Herbert by his cousin's attractive manners. How iusensibly, as it were, the boy was won from ruder pursuits and coarser pleasures, to sit beside her as she sang, or near her as she read; with what interest he pursued his lessons in French beneath her tuitiou, aud the ardour with which he followed every plau of study suggested by her. Sir Archibald saw all these thiugs, and calculated on their result with accuracy.

He foresaw how Kate's attractive gifts would throw into the shade the ruder tastes the boy's condition in life might expose him to adopt, and thus aid him in the great object of his whole existence—to save him, at least, from the wreck of his house.

Mark alone seemed untouched by her presence, save that the wild excesses of high spirit, to which from time to time he ever gave way, were now gone, and, in their place, a deep gloom, a moroseness of character succeeded, rendering him usually silent before her, or sunk in his own saddening reflections. Kate would sometimes adventure to disperse the dark clouds from his mind, but ever without success; he either felt annoyed at being the subject of remark, or left the room; so that at last she abandoned the effort, hoping that time and its changes would effect what the present denied. Perhaps, too, she had reasons for this hope. More than once, with womanly quickness, had she marked how he had stood with his eye fixed upon her, unconscious of being seen; how, when about to leave the room, he would loiter about, as if in search of something, but, in reality, to listen to the song she was singing. Still, she showed no sign of having seen these things, but always, in her air towards him, affected a careless ease of manner as like his own as possible. For days, sometimes for an entire week, he would absent himself from home; and, as he was never submissive to much questioning, his appearance called forth no other remark than some passing observation of what had occurred in his absence, but which drew from him no interchange of confidence.

These symptoms of Mark's altered character made a deeper impression on his father than events of greater moment could have done. He watched every movement and expression of his favourite son, to catch some clue to the change; but all in vain. The young man never, by any accident, alluded to himself, nor did he often now advert to the circumstances of the family difficulties; on the contrary, a lethargic carelessness seemed to brood over him, and he went about like one who had lost all zest for life, and all care for its enjoyments.

The O'Donoghue was too well versed in the character of his son to hope for any elucidation of the mystery by a mere inquiry; so that he was left to speculate on the many causes which might have operated the change, and divine, as well as he was able, the secret grief that affected him. In this pursuit, like all who have long suffered the pressure of a particular calamity, he ever felt disposed to ascribe Mark's suffering to the same cause which produced his own, namely, the fallen fortunes of the house, and the ruin that hung over them. Yet, somehow, of late, matters had taken a turn more favourable. His attorney at Cork had informed him, that from some informality in the proceedings, the ejectment was stopped, at least for the present term. The notices to the tenants not to pay were withdrawn, and the rents came in as before; and the only very pressing evil were the bills, the renewal of which demanded a considerable sum of ready money. That this one misfortune should occasion a gloom the accumulated griefs of former days had not done, he could not understand; but, by long musing on the matter, and deep reflection, he at last came to the conviction that such was the case, and that Mark's sorrow was the greater from seeing how near they were to a more favourable issue to their affairs, and yet how fatally debarred from such a consummation by this one disastrous circumstance.

The drowning man grasps not the straw with more avidity than does the harassed and wearied mind, agitated by doubts, and worn out with conjectures, seize upon some one apparent solution to a difficulty that has long oppressed it, and, for the very moment, convert every passing circumstance into an argument for its truthfulness. The O'Donoghue now saw, or believed he saw, why Mark would never accompany the others in their visits to the Lodge, nor be present when any of the Travers family came to the castle; he immediately accounted for his son's rejection of the proffered civilities, by that wounded pride which made him feel his present position so painfully, and, as the future head of the house, grieve over a state so unbecoming to its former fortunes.

"The poor fellow," said he, " is too high-spirited to be a guest to those he cannot be a host. Noble boy! the old blood flows strongly in *your* veins, at least."

How to combat this evil now became his sole thought. He mused over it by day—he dreamed of it by night. Hour by hour he endured the harassing tortures of a poverty whose struggles were all abortive, and whose repulses came without ceasing. Each plan he thought of was met by obstacles innumerable; and when, worn out with unprofitable schemes, he had resolved on abandoning the subject for ever, the sight of Mark's wasted cheek and sunken eye rallied him again to an effort, which, each time, he vowed should be the last.

The old and often successful remedies to rally him from his low spirits his father possessed no longer—the indulgence of some caprice, some momentary fancy for a horse or a hound—a boat or a fishing-rod. He felt, besides, that his grief, whatever it was, lay too deep for such surface measures as these, and he pondered long and anxiously over the matter. Nor had he one to share his sorrow, or assist him with advice. Sir Archibald he ever regarded as being prejudiced against Mark, and invariably more disposed to exaggerate than extenuate his faults. To have opened his heart to him would he to expose himself to some very plausible, but, as he would deem them, very impracticable remarks, on frugality and order—the necessity of submitting to altered fortunes—and, if need be, of undertaking some humble but honest occupation as a livelihood. These, and such like, had more than once been obtruded upon him; but to seek and court them, to invite their presence, was not to be thought of.

Kerry O'Leary was, then, the only one who remained; and they who know the intimacy to which old servants, long conversant with the fortunes of the family, and deemed faithful, because, from utter inutility, they are attached to the house that shelters them, are admitted in Irish households, will not be surprised at the choice of the confidant. He, I say, was the O'Donoghue's last resource; and from him he still hoped to gain some clue, at least, to the secret of this mystery. Scarcely had the O'Donoghue retired to his room at night, when Kerry was summoned to his presence, and after a few preliminaries, was asked if he knew where, how, or with whom his young master latterly spent his time.

" Faix, and 'tis that same does be puzzling myself," said Kerry, to whom the matter had already been one of considerable curiosity. " Sometimes I think one thing, and then I think another—but it beats me entirely."

" What were your thoughts then, Kerry?"

" 'Twas Tuesday last I suspected Joe Lenahan's daughter—the fair-haired girl, above at the three meadows; then I took it into my head it might be a badger he was after—for he was for ever going along by the bank of the river; but, twice in the week, I was sure I had him—and faix, I think, maybe I have."

" How is that, Kerry? Tell me at once, man!"

" It's a fine brown beast Lanty Lawler has—a strapping four-year-old, as likely a weight-carrier as ever I seen—that's what he's after—sorra lie in it. I observed him, on Friday, taking him over the big fences beyant the whin-field—and I measured his tracks—and may I never die in sin if he didn't stride nineteen feet over the yallow ditch."

" Do you know what he's asking for him, Kerry?" cried the old man, eagerly.

" His weight in goold, I heerd say; for the captain, up at the Lodge, will give him his own price for any beast will make a charger—and three hundred guineas Lanty expects for the same horse. Ayeh! he's a play-actor is Lanty, and knows how to rub the gentlemen down with a damp wisp."

" And you think that's it, Kerry?"

" I'll take the vestment it's not far off it. I never heerd Master Mark give a cheer out of him going over a fence that he hadn't a conceit out of the beast under him. 'Whoop!' says he, throwing up his whip hand, ' this way.' ' Your heart's in him,' says I, ' and 'tis a murther he isn't your own.' "

" You may leave me, Kerry," said the old man, sighing heavily; " 'tis getting near twelve o'clock."

" Good night, sir, and a safe rest to you."

" Wait a moment—stay a few minutes. Are they in the drawing-room still ?"

" Yes, sir ; I heerd Miss Kate singing as I came up the stairs."

" Well, Kerry, I want you to wait till she is leaving the room, and just whisper to her—mind now, for your life, that nobody sees nor hears you—just say that I wish to see her up here for a few seconds to-night. Do you understand me ?"

" Never fear, sir, I'll do it, and sorra one the wiser."

Kerry left the apartment as he spoke, nor was his master long doomed to suspense, for immediately after a gentle tap at the door announced Kate's presence there.

" Sit down there, my darling Kate," cried the O'Donoghue, placing a chair beside his own, " and let me have five minutes' talk with you."

The young girl obeyed with a smile, and returned the pressure of her uncle's hand with warmth.

" Kate, my child," said he—speaking with evident difficulty and embar-rassment, and fixing his eyes, not on her, but towards the fire, as he spoke—" Kate, you have come to a sad and cheerless home, with few comforts, with no pleasure for one so young and so lovely as you are."

" My dear uncle, how can you speak thus to me ? Can you separate me in your heart from your other children ? Mark and Herbert make no com-plaint—do you think that I could do so ?"

" They are very different from you, my sweet child. The moss-rose will not bear the storms of winter that the wild thorn can brave without danger. To you this dreary house must be a prison. I know it—I feel it."

" Nay, nay, uncle. If you think thus, it must be my fault—some piece of wilfulness of mine could alone have made you suppose me discontented ; but I am not so—far from it. I love dear old Sir Archy and my cousins dearly ; yes, and my uncle Miles too, though he seems anxious to get rid of me."

The old man pressed her fingers to his lips, and turned away his head.

" Come, Kate," said he, after a brief pause, " it was with no intention of that kind I spoke. We could none of us live without you now. My thoughts had a very different object."

" And that was——"

" Simply this"—and here he made a great effort, and spoke rapidly, as if fearing to dwell on the words—" lawsuits and knavish attorneys have wasted three-fourths of my estate—the remainder I scarcely know if I be its master or not ; on that portion, however, the old house stands, and the few acres that survive the wreck. At this moment heavy proceedings are pending in the courts, if successful in which, I shall be left in possession of the home of my father, and not turned adrift upon the world, a beggar.

There—don't look so pale, child—the story is an old one now, and has few terrors for us as long as it remains merely anticipated evil. This is a sad tale for your ears—I know it," said he, wiping away a tear that would come in spite of him.

Both were now silent. The old man paused, uncertain how he should proceed further. Kate spoke not; for as yet she could neither see the drift of the communication, nor, if it were in any way addressed to her, what part she was expected to take in the matter.

"Are you aware, my dear," resumed he, after a considerable delay, "that your father was married to your mother when she was but sixteen?"

"I have often heard she was scarcely more than a child," said Kate, timidly, for she had no recollection of having seen either of her parents.

"A child in years, love, she was; but a woman in grace, good sense, and accomplishments—in fact, so fortunate was my poor brother in his choice, he ever regarded the youthfulness of his wife as one of the reasons of that amiability of temper she possessed. Often have we talked of this together, and nothing could convince him to the contrary, as if, had the soil been un-fruitful, the tares and the thistles had not been as abundant a crop as the good fruit really was. He acted on his conviction, however, Kate; for he determined, if ever he had a daughter, she should be of age at sixteen—the period of life her mother was married at. I endeavoured to dissuade him. I did my best to expose the dangers and difficulties of such a plan. Per-haps, dearest, I should have been less obstinate in argument had I been pro-phetic enough to know what my niece would be; but it was all in vain. The idea had become a dominant one with him, and I was obliged to yield. And now, Kate, after the long lapse of years—for the conversation I allude to took place a great while ago—it is my lot to say, that my brother was right and I was wrong; that he foresaw with a truer spirit the events of the future than was permitted to me. You were of age two months since."

The young girl listened with eager curiosity to every word that fell from her uncle's lips, and seemed disappointed when he ceased to speak. To have gone thus far, and no farther, did not satisfy her mind, and she waited with impatience for him to continue.

"I see, my child," said he, gently, "you are not aware of the proceedings of coming of age; you have not heard, perhaps, that, as your guardian, I hold in my hands the fortune your father bequeathed to you. It was his portion as a younger son; for, poor fellow! he had the family failing, and never could live within his income. Your ten thousand—he always called it yours—he never encroached upon—and that sum, at least, is secured to you."

Although Kate knew that her uncle was her guardian, and had heard that some property would revert to her, what its amount was she had not the most remote idea of, nor that her power over it should commence so soon.

"I see, uncle—I understand all you say," said she, hurriedly; "I am of age, and the owner of ten thousand pounds."

The tone of decision she employed half terrified the O'Donoghue for the prudence of his communication, and he almost hesitated to answer her directly—"Yes, my child, it is a rent-charge—a——"

"I care not for the name, sir. Does it represent the value?"

"Unquestionably it does."

"Take it, then, dearest uncle," said she, flinging herself upon his neck— "take it, and use it, so that it may bring some comfort to yourself—some ease of mind, at least, and make your home a happier one. What need to think of the boys? Mark and Herbert are not of the mould that need fear failure, whatever path they follow; and as for me, when you grow weary of me, the Sacré Cœur will gladly take me back. Indeed, they feel their work of conversion of me but very imperfectly executed," added she, smiling; "and the dear nuns would be well pleased to finish their task."

"Kate, my child—my own darling," cried the old man, clasping her to his heart, "this may not—this cannot be."

"It must, and it shall be, uncle," said she, resolutely. "If my dear father's will be not a nullity, I have power over my fortune."

"But not to effect your ruin, Kate."

"No, sir, nor shall I. Will my dear uncle love me less for the consciousness in my own heart that I am doing right? Will he have a smile the less for me, that I can return it with an affection warmer from very happiness? I cannot believe this; nor can I think that you would render your brother's daughter unworthy of her father. You would not refuse *him*." Her lip trembled and her eyes grew full as she uttered the last few words, in a voice every word of which went to the old man's heart.

"There is but one way, Kate."

"What need of more, uncle? Do we want a choice of roads if we see a straight path before us?"

"Yes, dearest; but it will be said that I should not have suffered you to do this. That in accepting a loan——"

"A loan!" uttered she, reproachfully.

"As that, or nothing, can I ever touch a farthing of it," replied the O'Donoghue. "No, no! Distress and hardship have been a weary load this many a year; but all sense of honour is not yet obliterated in this poor heart!"

"Be it as you please, my dear, dear uncle," said the affectionate girl; "only let it not cost you another painful thought, to rob me of so many happy ones. There now, we must never speak of this any more;" and, so saying, she kissed him twice, and rose from her chair. "We are going to the Lodge to-morrow, to spend the day; Herbert is so well that he comes with us."

"And Mark—what of him, dearest?"

"Mark will be none of us, sir. We are either too gay, or too frivolous, or too silly, or too something or other, for his solemn humour, and he only frowns and stares at us; but all that will pass away soon; I shall find out the key to his temper yet, and then make him pay for all his arrears of sulkiness."

"It is our changed condition, my love, that has made him thus," said the father, anxious to excuse the young man's morose habits.

"The poorer courage his, then," replied the high-spirited girl; "I have no patience for a man who acts but the looking-glass to fortune—frowns when she frowns, and smiles when she smiles. No! Give me the temper that can enjoy the sunshine and brave the storm—take all the good the world affords, and show a bold heart to resist the evil."

"My own brother, my poor dear Mark, spoke there," cried the old man, in an ecstasy, as, springing up, he flung his arms about her; "and that's your philosophy, sweet Kate?"

"Even so; the stout heart to the stae brae, as Sir Archy would call it, and as he mutters every evening he has to climb the steep stair towards his bedroom. And now, good night, dear uncle, good night."

With an affectionate greeting the old man took his leave of her for the night, and sat down, in a frame of mingled happiness and shame, to think over what had passed.

The O'Donoghue was very far from feeling satisfied with himself for what he had done. Had Kate been at all difficult of persuasion—had she yielded to his arguments, or been convinced by any explanations of his views, he would soon have reconciled himself to the act, as one in which both parties concurred. Far from this, he saw that her only motive was affection; that she would listen to nothing save the promptings of her own warm heart; she would not let him even exculpate himself from the charge of his own conscience; and, although acquitted by her, he felt the guilt still upon him.

There was a time when he would not have stooped to such a course; but then he was rich—rich in the world's wealth, and the honour such affluence suggests; for, alas! humbling as the avowal may seem, the noble traits so often admired in prosperity, are but the promptings of a spirit revelling in its own enjoyment—open-handed and generous, because these qualities are luxuries; free to give, because the giving involves gratitude; and gratitude is the incense of weakness to power—of poverty to wealth. How often are the warm affections, nurtured by happy circumstances, mistaken for the evidence of right principles? How frequently are the pleasurable impulses of the heart confounded with the well-directed judgments of the mind? This man was less changed than he knew of—the world of his circumstances was, indeed, different, but he was little altered; the same selfishness that once made him munificent now made him mean; but, whether conferring or accepting favours, the spirit was one.

Besides, how ingenious is the mind in suggesting plausible reasons for its indulgences!—how naturally easy did it seem to borrow and repay! The very words satisfied his scruples on that score; but if he were indeed so contented with himself, why did he fear lest any one should ever learn the circumstance? Why cower with shame before himself, to think of his brother-in-law, or even Mark hearing of it? Were these the signs of conscious rectitude, or were they the evidence of a spirit seeking rest in casuistry and self-deception? In this conflict of alternate approval and condemnation he passed the greater part of the night—sometimes a struggling sense of honour urging him to regret a course so fraught with humiliations of every kind; and again a thrill of delight would run through his heart to think of all the pleasure he could confer upon his favourite boy—the indulgences he could once more shower upon him. He fancied the happiness of emancipation from pressing difficulties, and how instinctively Mark's buoyant temper would take the tone of their altered fortunes, and he once again become the gay and reckless youth he loved to see him.

" He must have that brown horse Kerry speaks of," muttered he to himself. " Sir Marmaduke shall not outbid us there, and we'll see which of the two best becomes his saddle. I'll back my own boy against his scarlet-coated fop for a thousand. They've got some couples of dogs, too, Kerry was telling me, up the mountains. We must inquire about them; with eight or ten couple Mark could have good sport in the glen. Then there's those bills of Callaghan's—but he'll not press hard when he sees we've money. Cassidy must get his 800l., and so he shall; and that scoundrel, Swaby, will be sending in his bill of costs; but a couple of hundred pounds ought to stop his mouth. Archy, too—by Jove, I forget how much I owe him now; but he doesn't, I'll warrant him. Well, well, if it won't stop the leak, it will at least give us time to work the pumps—ay, time, time!" He asked for no more; he only sought to reach the haven himself, and cared nothing what happened the craft nor the crew afterwards.

His next thought was how to effect all the legal arrangements in these complicated matters without the knowledge of Mark or Sir Archy; and on this difficult point he spent till nigh morning deliberating. The only mode he could think of was, by writing to Swaby himself, and making him aware of the whole proceeding. That, of course, would be attended by its own penalties, as Swaby would take care that his own costs were among the first things to be liquidated; but yet it seemed the sole course open to him, and with the resolve to do this on the morrow, he turned on his pillow and fell asleep.

The morning broke with happiness to the uncle and the niece; but it was a happiness of a very different order. To him, the relief of mind for the long harassing cares of debt and difficulty was a boon of inestimable price—life and liberty at once to the imprisoned spirit of his proud heart. To her, the higher and nobler sense of gratification which flows from having acted well, sent a thrill of ecstasy through her bosom, such as only gentle and generous youth can ever feel. And thus, while the O'Donoghue mused over the enjoyments and pleasures his new accession of wealth might place at his disposal, she revelled in the delight of having ministered to the happiness of one she had always regarded as a father, and even felt grateful to him for the emotions of her own heart.

The O'Donoghue's first thought on awaking was to employ this large sum to liquidate some of his most pressing debts, and to make such arrangements as might enable them to live economically but comfortably, paying off those creditors whose exorbitant interest was consuming all the remnant of his income, and entering into contracts with others for the gradual repayment of the loans. The more he reflected on these good intentions, the less pleasure did they yield him. He had for years past taught himself to regard a creditor as an implacable enemy. The very idea of succumbing smacked of defeat. He had defied the law so long, it looked like cowardice to surrender now; besides, the very complication of his affairs offered an excuse which he was not slow to catch at. How could he pay Cassidy in full, and only give Hickson a part? Would not the mere rumour of his paying off his debts bring down a host of demands that had almost slumbered themselves out of existence. He had often heard that his grandfather "muddled away his fortune paying small debts." It could not be supposed he would reject the traditions of his own house—nor did he.

He judged wisely, if not well, that new habits of expenditure would do more to silence the complaints of duns than the most accurately calculated system of liquidation. That entertainments and equipages, a stable full of horses, and a house crammed with guests, are a receipt in full for solvency, which, however some may distrust, none are bold enough to question openly.

If the plan had fewer excellences, it at least suited him better; and he certainly opened the campaign with vigour. No sooner had he decided on his line of acting, than he despatched Kerry O'Leary to Cork with a letter for Swaby, his attorney, requiring his immediate presence at Carrignacurra, and adding, "that if he brought a couple of hundred pounds over with him at the same time, he might include them with the costs, and get a cheque for the whole together."

As the old man sealed his epistle, he chuckled over the thoughts of Swaby's astonishment, and fancied the many guesses the crafty attorney would frame to account for such unexpected prosperity. The little remaining sorrow he felt for his share in the transaction gave way to the vulgar pleasure of this surprise; for so it is, the conflict with poverty can debase the mind, and make the very straits and stratagems of want seem straits of cleverness and ability.

It was a day of pleasure almost to all. Sir Archy, dressed in a suit which had not seen daylight for many a previous year, gave his arm to Kate, and, accompanied by Herbert, set out to pass the day at the Lodge. Mark alone had no participation in the general joy; he stood with folded arms at the window of the old tower, and gazed on the group that moved along the road. Although he never thought of accompanying them, there was a sense of desertion in his position of which he could not divest himself. With the idea of the pleasure their visit would afford them came the reflection that he was debarred from his share of such enjoyment, and the galling feeling of inferiority sent the blood with a throbbing current through his temples, and covered his face with a deep flush. He retorted his own isolation against those he had so strenuously avoided, and accused them of the very fault of which he was himself guilty. "My uncle is more distant to me than ever," muttered he, "and even Herbert, too—Herbert, that used to look up to and rely on me—even he shuns me." He did not utter his cousin's name, but a single tear, that rolled heavily down his cheek, and seemed to make it tremble as it passed, showed that another and a deeper spring of sorrow was opened in his heart. With a sudden gesture of impatience he roused him-self from his musing, and hastily descending the stair, he crossed the old court-yard, and, without any fixed resolve as to his course, walked down the road; nor was it until after proceeding some distance, that he perceived he was rapidly gaining on the little party on their way to the Lodge; then he quitted the high road, and soon lost himself in one of the mountain glens.

As for the others, it was indeed a day of unaccustomed pleasure, and such as rarely presented itself in that solitary valley. All that kindness and hos-pitality could suggest was done by the family at the Lodge to make their visit agreeable; and while Sir Marmaduke vied with his son and daughter in courteous attentions to his guests, they, on their part, displayed the happy consciousness of these civilities by efforts to please not less successful.

Sir Archy—albeit the faculty had long lain in disuse—was possessed of conversational powers of a high order, and could blend his observation of passing events with the wisdom derived from reflection, and the experience of long intercourse with the world; while, as if to relieve the sombre colour-ing of his thoughts, Kate's lively sallies and sparkling repartees lit up the picture, and gave it both brilliancy and action. The conversation ranged freely over the topics which form the staple of polite intercourse in the world of the cultivated and the fashionable; and, although Sir Archy had long been removed from such companionship, it was easy to perceive how naturally he could revert to a class of subjects with which he had once been familiar.

It was thus alternating remarks of the past with allusions to the present —mingling grave and gay, with that happy blending which springs from the social intercourse of different ages—they sat, after dinner, watching, through the unshuttered window, the bright moonlight that streamed across the glen and glittered on the lake, the conversation, from some reference to the scenery, turned to the condition of Ireland, and the then state of her people. Sir Marmaduke, notwithstanding his late experiences, fully maintaining the accuracy of his own knowledge in matters which have not ceased to puzzle even wiser heads, gained confidence from the cautious reserve of Sir Archy, who rarely ventured an opinion, and never hazarded a direct assertion.

"They would have me believe, in England," said Sir Marmaduke, "that Ireland was on the very brink of a rebellion; that the organisation of revolt was perfect, and only waiting French co-operation to burst forth; but how absurd such statements are to us who live amongst them."

Sir Archy smiled significantly, and shook his head.

"You, surely, have no fears on this head, sir? It is not possible to conceive a state of more profound peace than we observe around us. Men do not take up arms against a rightful authority without the working of strong passions and headlong impulses. What is there to indicate them here?"

"You'll allow, Sir Marmaduke, they are no overlikely to mak' ye a confidant, if they intend a rising," was the dry observation of M'Nab.

"True; but could they conceal their intentions from me—that is the question? Think you that I should not have discovered them long since, and made them known to the government?"

"I trust you'd have done no such thing, sir," interposed Fred. "I heard Maitland say there never was a chance of keeping this country down if we did not have a brush with them every thirty or forty years; and, if I don't mistake, the time for a lesson has just come round."

"Is it so certain on which side is to be the teacher?" said Kate, with a voice whose articulate distinctness actually electrified the party; and, as it drew their eyes towards her, heightened the flush that mantled on her cheek.

"It never occurred to me to doubt the matter," said Fred, with an air of ill-dissembled mortification.

"No more than you anticipated it, perhaps," retorted she, quickly; "and yet events are happening every day which take the world by surprise. See there!—look. That mountain peak was dark but a moment back; and now, see the blazing fire that has burst forth upon it!"

The whole party started to their feet, and drew near the window, from which, at a distance of about two miles, the red glare of a fire was seen. It burned brightly for some minutes, and then decaying, became extinguished, leaving the dark mountain black and gloomy as before.

"What can it mean?" said Sir Marmaduke, in amazement. "Can it be some signal of the smugglers? I understand they still venture on this coast."

"That mountain yonder is not seen from the bay," said Sir Archy, thoughtfully. "It can scarcely be that."

"I think we must ask Miss O'Donoghue for the explanation," said Fred Travers. "She is the only one here not surprised at its appearance."

"Miss O'Donoghue is one of those who, you assert, are to be taught, and, therefore, unable to teach others," said she, in a low whisper, only audible to Frederick, who stood beside her; and he almost started at the strange meaning the words seemed to convey.

CHAPTER XXIV

A WALK BY MOONLIGHT.

THE visit alluded to in the last chapter formed the first step to an acquaintance which speedily ripened into intimacy. Seldom a day passed without some interchange of civilities; and as they progressed in knowledge of each other they advanced in esteem, so that, ere long, they learned to regard themselves as members of a single family. The conventional usages of society are stronger barriers against friendship than the world deems them. The life of cities supplies a coinage of social intercourse which but very imperfectly represents the value of true feeling; while in remoter and less cultivated regions men are satisfied to disencumber themselves of this false currency, and deal frankly and openly with each other.

How little, now, did Sir Marmaduke remember of all Sir Archy's peculiarities of manner and expression! how seldom did Sybella think Kate's opinions wild and eccentric! and how difficult would it have been to convince the fastidious Guardsman that the society of St. James's possessed any superiority in tone or elegance over the evenings at the Lodge.

The real elements of mutual liking were present here : the discrepancy of character and taste—the great differences of age and habit of thought—yet moulded into one common frame of esteem from the very appreciation of qualities in others in which each felt himself deficient. If Kate admired the simple but high-minded English girl, whose thoughts were rarely faulty save when attributing to others higher and purer motives than the world abounds in, Sybella looked up with enthusiastic delight to the glittering talents of her Irish friend—the warm and generous glow of her imagination—the brilliant flashes of her wit—the ready eloquence of her tongue; and, perhaps, not least of all, the intrepid fearlessness of her nature, inspired her with sentiments of almost awe, which seemed to deepen and not diminish her affection for Kate O'Donoghue.

It might appear an ungenerous theme to dwell on, but how often are our friendships suggested by self-love?—how frequently are we led to think highly and speak praisingly of qualities the opposite to our own, from the self-satisfaction our apparent impartiality yields us. Justice must, indeed, be a great virtue when its very shadow can ennoble human nature. Not such, however, were the motives here. Kate's admiration for the unerring rectitude of Sybella's character was as free from taint as was Sybella's heartfelt enthusiasm for the Irish girl. As for Frederick Travers, the same dissimilarity in character which made him at first compare Kate with his sister disadvantageously, now induced him to be struck and fascinated by her qualities. The standard by which he had measured her she had long since passed, in his estimation; and any idea of a comparison between them would now have appeared ridiculous. It was true many of her opinions savoured of a nationality too strong for his admiration. She was intensely Irish—or, at least, what he deemed such. The traditions which, as a child, she had listened to with eager delight, had given a bias to her mind that grew more confirmed with years. The immediate circumstances of her own family added to this feeling, and her pride was tinctured with sorrow at the fallen condition of her house. All her affection for her cousins could not blind her to their great defects. In Mark she saw one whose spirit seemed crushed and stunned, and not awakened by the pressure of misfortune. Herbert, with all his kindliness of nature and open-heartedness, appeared more disposed to enjoy the sunshine of life than to prepare himself to buffet with its storms.

How often she wished she had been a boy—how many a day-dream floated before her of such a career as she might have struck out! Ireland a nation —her "own sons her rulers"—had been the theme of many an oft-heard tale; and there was a poetry in the sentiment of a people recalled to a long-lost, long-sought-for nationality, that excited and exalted her imagination.

Her convent education had stored her mind with narratives of native suffering and Saxon tyranny, and she longed for the day of retribution on the "proud invaders." Great was her disappointment at finding her cousins so dead to every feeling of this kind; and she preferred the chivalrous ardour of the French soldier to the sluggish apathy of Mark, or the happy indolence of Herbert O'Donoghue.

Had Frederick Travers been an Irishman, would he have borne his country's wrongs so meekly? was a reflection that more than once occurred to her mind, and never more powerfully than on parting with him the very evening we have mentioned. He had accompanied them on their return to Carrignacurra, which, as the night was fine and the moon nearly at her full, they did on foot. Kate, who rarely accepted an arm when walking, had, by some accident, taken his on this occasion, Sir Archy leaning on that of Herbert.

The young soldier listened with a high-beating heart as she related an incident of which the spot they were traversing had been the scene. It was a faithless massacre of a chieftain and his followers, seduced under pretences of friendship and a pledge of amity.

"They told him," said she, "that his young wife, who had been carried away by force, and imprisoned for two entire years, should on this spot be restored to him; that he had but to come, with twelve of his retainers, unarmed, save with their swords, and that here, where we now stand, she should once more become his own. The hour was sunset, and he waited, with anxious impatience, beneath that tall cliff yonder, where you can see the deep cleft. Strange enough, they have added a legend to the true story, as if their wrongs could derive any force from fiction! and they tell you still that the great rock was never split until that night. Their name for it, in Irish, is 'the rent,' or 'the ruptured pledge.' Do I weary you with these old tales?"

"No, no; go on, I entreat you. I cannot say how the scene increases its fascinations from connexion with your story."

"He stood yonder, where the black shadow now crosses the road, and having dismounted, he gave his horse to one of his attendants, and walked, with an anxious heart, up and down, waiting for their approach."

"There was less sympathy among his followers for their chieftain's sorrow than might be expected; for she was not a native born, but the daughter of an English earl. He, perhaps, loved her the more—her very friendlessness was another tie between them."

"Says the legend so, or is this a mere suspicion on your part?" whispered Travers, softly.

"I scarcely know," continued Kate, with an accent less assured than before. "I believe I tell you the tale as I have heard it; but why may she not have been his own in every sentiment and thought—why not have imbibed the right from him she learned to love?" The last words were scarcely uttered, when, with a sudden exclamation, less of fear than astonishment, Kate grasped Travers's arm, and exclaimed—"Did you see that?"

"I thought some dark object moved by the roadside."

"I saw a man pass, as if from behind us, and gain the thicket yonder: he was alone, however."

"And I am armed," said Travers, coolly.

"And if you were not," replied she, proudly, "an O'Donoghue has nothing to fear in the valley of Glenflesk. Let us join my uncle, however, for I see he has left us some distance behind him;" and while they hastened forward she resumed her story with the same unconcern as before the interruption.

Travers listened eagerly—less, it is true, in sympathy with the story than in delight at the impassioned eloquence of her who related it. "Such," said she, as they turned to bid him farewell at the old keep on the road side— "such are the traditions of our land; they vary in time, and place, and persons; but they have only one moral through all—what a terrible thing is slavery!"

Travers endeavoured to turn the application of her speech by some common-place compliment about her own powers of inflicting bondage; but she stopped him suddenly with—

"Nay, nay; these are not jesting themes, although you may deem them unsuited for one as ignorant and inexperienced as I am; nor will I speak of them again, if they serve but as matter for laughter."

Amid his protestations of innocence against this charge, which, in his ardour, he pushed further than calmer judgment might warrant, they shook hands cordially, and parted.

"He's a fine-hearted fellow, too," thought Kate, as she slowly moved along in silence. "Saxon though he be, there's a chord in his bosom that responds to the touch of truth and honour."

"Noble girl," said Frederick, half aloud, "it would be hard to rebuke treason, when spoken from such lips;" then added, with a smile, "it's no fair temptation to expose even a Guardsman to."

And thus each speculated on the character of the other, and fancied how, by their own influence, it might be fashioned and moulded to a better form; nor was their interest lessened in each other's fortune from the fact that it seemed to involve so much of mutual interposition.

"You should not walk this road so late," said Mark O'Donoghue, almost rudely, as he opened the door to admit them. "The smugglers are on the coast now, and frequently come up the glen at nightfall."

"Why not have come to be our escort, then?" said Kate, smiling.

"What? With the gay soldier for your guard," said he, bitterly.

"How knew you that, my worthy cousin?" said Kate, rapidly; and then, with a significant shake of the head, added, in a whisper, "I see there *are* marauders about."

Mark blushed till his face became scarlet, and turning abruptly away, sought his own room in silence.

CHAPTER XXV.

A DAY OF DIFFICULT NEGOTIATIONS.

THE time was now approaching when the Traverses were to remove to the capital, and, at Sybella's urgent entreaty, Sir Marmaduke was induced to request that Kate O'Donoghue might accompany them in their visit, and thus enjoy the pleasures of a winter in Dublin, then, second to no city of Europe in all that constituted social excellence.

The note of invitation, couched in terms the most flattering and cordial, arrived when the O'Donoghues were seated at breakfast, and, as was usual on all occasions of correspondence, was opened by Kate herself. Scarcely had she thrown her eyes over its contents, when, with a heightened colour, and a slight tremor in her voice, she passed the letter across the table to her uncle, and said, " This is for your consideration, sir."

" Then you must read it for me, Kate," replied he, " for my ears have outlived my eyes."

" Shall I do it ?" interposed Sir Archy, who, having remarked some hesitation in Kate's manner, came thus good-naturedly to the rescue.

" With all my heart, Archy," said the O'Donoghue ; " or rather, if you would do me a favour, just tell me what it is about — polite correspondence affects me pretty much as the ceremonies of bowing and salutation, when I have a fit of the gout. I become devilish impatient, and would give the world it was all over, and that I were back in my easy-chair again."

" The politeness in the present case lies less in the style than in the substance," said Sir Archy. " This is a vara civil, though, I must say, to me a vara unwelcome proposal, to take our darling Kate away from us, for a season, and show her some of the life and gaieties of the capital."

" Well, that is handsomely done, at least," said the O'Donoghue, whose first thought sprang from gratified pride at the palpable evidence of social consideration ; then suddenly changing his tone, he said, in a low voice, " but what says Kate herself ?"

Mark turned his eyes full upon her as his father said these words, and as a deadly pallor came over his face, he sat steadfastly awaiting her reply, like one expecting the decree of a judge.

" Kate feels too happy here, sir, to risk anything by a change," replied she, avoiding, even for a second, to look towards where Mark was sitting.

" But you must not lose such an opportunity, dearest Kate," whispered

Herbert eagerly into her ear. "These are the scenes, and the places you are used to, and best fitted to enjoy and to adorn, and besides——"

A stern frown from Mark, who, if he had not overheard the speech, seemed to have guessed its import, suddenly arrested the youth, who now looked overwhelmed with confusion.

"We are a divided cabinet, that I see plainly enough, Kate," said O'Donoghue; "though, if our hearts were to speak out, I'd warrant they would be of one mind. Still, this would be a selfish verdict, my dear girl, and a poor requital for all the happiness you have brought back to these old walls;" and the words were spoken with a degree of feeling that made all indisposed to break the silence that followed.

"I should like to see the capital, I own," said Kate, "if my absence were to be a short one."

"And I wad hae nae objection the capital should see yersel'," said Sir Archy, "albeit I may lose a sweetheart by my generosity."

"Have no fears of my fidelity," said Kate, laughing, as she extended her hand towards him, while, with antique gallantry, he pressed it to his lips. "The youth of this land are not, so far as my little experience goes, likely to supplant so true an admirer; they who have so little devotion to their country may well be suspected of having less for its daughters."

Mark's brow grew dark with the flush that covered his face and forehead in an instant; he bent his head almost to the table to avoid observation, and, as if in the distraction of the moment, he took up the note and seemed to pore over its contents; then suddenly crushing it in his hand, he arose from the table and left the room.

"My sweet Kate," said Sir Archy, as he led her within the deep recess of a window, "tak' care ye dinna light up a flame of treason where ye only hoped to warm a glow of patriotism; such eyes and lips as yours are but too ready teachers; be cautious, lassie. This country, however others may think, is on the eve of some mighty struggle; the people have abandoned many of their old grudges and seem disposed to unite."

"And the gentry—where are they who should stand at their head and share their fortunes?" cried Kate, eagerly; for the warning, so far from conveying the intended moral, only stimulated her ardour and excited her curiosity.

"The gentry," replied Sir Archy, in a firm, decided tone, "are better satisfied to live under a government they dislike than to be at the mercy of a rabble they despise. I hae lived langer than you in this dreary world, lassie, and trust me the poetry of patriotism has little relation to the revengeful fury of rebellion. You wish freedom for those who cannot enjoy the portion of it they possess. It is time to outlive the evil memories of the past, we want here—time, to blunt the acuteness of former and long-past sufferings—time, to make traditions so far forgotten as to be inapplicable to

the present—time, to read the homely lesson, that one half the energy a
people can expend in revolt will raise them in the rank of civilised and cul·
tivated beings."

"Time, to make Irishmen forget that the land of their birth was ever
other than an English province," added Kate, impetuously. "No, no, it
was not thus your own brave countrymen understood their ' devoirs.'"

"They rallied round the standard of a prince they loved, lassie," said
M'Nab, in a tone whose fervour contrasted with his former accent.

"And will you tell me that the principle of freedom is not more sacred
than the person of the sovereign?" said Kate, tauntingly.

"There can be nae mistake about the one, but folks may have vara unsettled notions of the other," said he, dryly; "but we maunna quarrel, Kate
dear; our time is e'en too short already. Sit ye down and sing me a sang."

"It shall be a rebel one, then, I promise you," replied she, with an air
of defiance which it was impossible to pronounce more real or assumed.
"But here comes a visitor to interrupt us, and so your loyalty is saved for
this time."

The observation was made in reference to a traveller, who, seated in a
very antique-looking dennet, was seen slowly labouring his wearied horse
up the steep ascent to the castle.

"It's Swaby, father," cried Herbert, who immediately recognised the
equipage of the Cork attorney, and felt a certain uneasiness come over him
at the unexpected appearance.

"What brings him down to these parts?" said the O'Donoghue, affecting
an air of surprise. "On his way to Killarney, perhaps. Well, well, they
may let him in."

The announcement did not, to all appearance, afford much pleasure to the
others, for scarcely had the door bell ceased its jingle, when each quitted the
drawing-room, leaving O'Donoghue alone to receive his man of law.

Although the O'Donoghue waited with some impatience for the entrance
of his legal adviser, that worthy man did not make his appearance at once,
his progress to the drawing-room being arrested by Sir Archy, who, with a
significant gesture, motioned him to follow him to his chamber.

"I will no detain you many minutes, Mr. Swaby," said he, as he made
signs for him to be seated. "I hae a sma' matter of business in which you
can serve me. I need scarcely observe I reckon ou your secrecy."

Mr. Swaby closed one eye, and placed the tip of his finger on his nose—a
pantomime intended to represent the most perfect fidelity.

"I happen," resumed Sir Archy, apparently satisfied with this pledge—"I
happen at this moment to need a certain sum of money, and would wish to
receive it on these securities. They are title-deeds of a property, which, for
reasons I have no leisure at this moment to explain, is at present held by a
distant relative in trust for my heir. You may perceive that the value is

considerable"—and he pointed to a formidable array of figures which covered one of the margins. "The sum I require is only a thousand pounds—five hundred at once—immediately—the remaiuder in a year heuce. Can this be arrauged ?"

"Money was never so scarce," said Swaby, as he wiped his spectacles and unfolded one of the cumbrous parchments. "Devil take me if I know where it's all gone to. It was only last week I was trying to raise five thousand for old Hoare on the Ballyrickau property, and I could not get any one to advance me sixpence. The country is unsettled, you see. There's a notion abroad that we'll have a rising soon, and who knows what's to become of landed property after."

"This estate is in Perth," said M'Nab, tapping the deeds with his finger.

"So I perccive," replied Swaby; "and they have no objection to a 'shindy' there too, sometimes. The Pretender got some of your country-men iuto a pretty scrape with his tricks. There are fools to be had for asking everywhere."

"We will no discuss this question just noo," said Sir Archy, snappishly; "and, to return to the main poiut, please to inform me, is this loan impracticable ?"

"I didu't say it was, all out," said Swaby. "In about a week or two——"

"I must know before three days," interrupted M'Nab.

"His honour's waiting for Mr. Swaby," said Kerry, who uow appeared in the room, without either of the others having noticed his entrance.

Sir Archy rose with an angry brow, but spoke not a syllable, while he motioned Kerry to leave the room.

"You must join my brother-in-law, sir," said he at last; "and if our conversation is not already become the gossip of the house, I entreat of you to keep it a secret."

"That, of course," said Swaby; "but I'm thinking I've hit ou a way to meet your wishes, so we'll talk of the matter again this evening;" and thus saying, he withdrew, leaving Sir Archy in a frame of miud very far indeed from tranquil or composed.

Swaby's surprise at his iuterview with Sir Archy, whom he never had the slightest suspicion of possessing any property whatever, was even surpassed by his astonishment on hearing the favourable turn of O'Donoghue's affairs; and while he bestowed the requisite attention to follow the old man's statement, his shrewd mind was also engaged in speculatiug what probable results might accrue from this unexpected piece of fortune, and how they could best be turned to his own benefit. O'Donoghue was too deeply interested in his own schemes to question Swaby respecting his business with M'Nab, of which Kerry O'Leary had already given him a hint. The attorney was, therefore, free to deliberate in his own mind how far he might most advautageously turn the prosperity of the oue to the aid of the other, for the sole beuefit of himself. It is not necessary, nor would it conduce to the object of this story, to ask the reader's atteutiou to this interview. It will be euough to say, that Swaby heard with pleasure O'Douoghue's disclosure, recoguising with practised acuteuess how far he could turn such uulooked-for prosperity to his own purposes, and subsidise one brother-in-law at the expeuse of both.

While thus each within the limit of this narrow household was follow-ing out the thread of his destiny, eagerly beut on his own object, Kate O'Douoghue sat aloue at the window of her chamber, buried in deep thought. The prospect of her approaching visit to the capital presented itself iu so many aspects, that, while offeriug pleasures aud eujoymeuts noue relished more highly than herself, she yet saw difficulties which might reuder the step unadvisable, if not perilous. Of all cousiderations, money was the one which least had occupied auy share in her calculations; yet now she bethought herself that expeuse must necessarily be incurred which her uucle's finances could but ill afford. No soouer had this thought occurred to her, than she was amazed it had not struck her before, aud she felt actually startled lest, in her eagerness for the promised pleasure, she had only listened to the suggestion of selfishness. Iu a moment more she deter-mined to decline the invitation. She was not one to take half measures when she believed a poiut of principle to be cugaged; aud the only difficulty uow lay, how and iu what mauuer to refuse au offer profferod with so much kinduess. The note itself must open the way, thought she, aud at the in-staut she remembered how Mark had taken it from the breakfast-table.

She heard his heavy step as he paced backwards and forwards in his chamber overhead, and without losing another moment, hastily asceuded the stairs to his door; her haud was already outstretched to knock, when suddenly she hesitated; a strauge confusion came over her faculties—how would Mark regard her request?—would he attribute it to over-eagerness on the subject of the iuvitatiou? Such were the questions which occurred to her; and as quick came the answer, "And let him think so. I shall certainly not seek to undeceive him. He alone of all here has vouchsafed me neither any show of his affection nor his confidence." The flush mounted to her cheek, aud her eyes darkened with the momentary excite-ment; and at the same instant the door was suddenly thrown open, and Mark stood before her.

Such was his astonishment, however, that for some seconds he could not speak; when at last he uttered, in a low, deep voice,

"I thought I heard a hand upon the lock, and I am so suspicious of that fellow Kerry, who frequently plays the eavesdropper here——"

"Not when you are alone, Mark?" said Kate, smiling.

"Ay, even then. I have a foolish habit of thinking aloud, of which I strive in vain to break myself; and he seems to know it, too."

"There is another absent trick you have acquired also," said she, laughing. "Do you remember having carried off the note that came while we were at breakfast?"

"Did I?" said he, reddening. "Did I take it off the table? Yes, yes; I remember something of it now. You must forgive me, cousin, if these careless habits take the shape of rudeness." He seemed overwhelmed with confusion, as he added, "I know not why I put it into my pocket; here it is."

And so saying, he drew from the breast of his coat a crushed and crumpled paper, and gave it into Kate's hand. She wished to say something in reply—something which would seem kind and good-natured; but, somehow, she faltered and hesitated. She twice got as far as, "I know, Mark—I am certain, Mark;" then unable to say what, perhaps, her very indecision rendered more difficult, she merely uttered a brief "thank you," and withdrew.

"Poor fellow," said she, as she re-entered her own chamber, "his is the hardest lot of all."

She had often wished to persuade herself that Mark's morose, sullen humour, was the discontent of one who felt the ignominy of an inglorious life—that habits of recklessness had covered, but not obliterated, the traces of that bold and generous spirit for which his family had been long distinguished; and now, for the first time, she believed she had fallen on the evidences of such a temper. She pondered long on this theme, and fancied how, under circumstances favourable to their development, Mark's good qualities and courageous temper had won for him both fame and honour. "And here," exclaimed she, half aloud—"here he may live and die a peasant!" With a deep sigh she threw herself into a chair, and, as if to turn her thoughts into some channel less suggestive of gloom, she opened the letter Mark had given her. Scarcely, however, had she cast her eyes over it, when she uttered a faint cry, too faint, indeed, to express any mere sense of fear, but in an accent in which terror and amazement were equally blended.

The epistle was a brief one, not more than a few lines, and she had read it at a glance, before ever there was time to consider how far her doing so was a breach of confidence; indeed, the intense interest of the contents left little room for any self-examinings. It ran thus:

"DEAR BROTHER,—No precipitation—no haste—nothing can be done without France. T. has now good hopes from that quarter, and if not 30,000, 20,000, or at least 15,000 will be given, and arms for double the number. Youghal is talked of as a suitable spot; and H. has sent charts, &c., over. Above all, be patient; trust no rumours, and rely on us for the

earliest and the safest intelligence. L. will hand you this. You must contrive to learn the cipher, as any correspondence discovered would ruin all.
                                        "Yours ever, and in the cause,
                                                            "H. R."

Here, then, was the youth she had been commiserating for his career of
lowly and unambitious hopes—here, the mere peasant! the accomplice of
some deep and desperate plot, in which the arms of France should be
employed against the government of England. Was this the secret of his
preoccupation and his gloom? Was it to concentrate his faculties on such
a scheme that he lived this lonely and secluded life? "Oh, Mark, Mark,
how have I misjudged you!" she exclaimed, and, as she uttered the words,
came the thought, quick as a lightning flash, to her mind—what terrible ha-
zards such a temperament as his must incur in an enterprise like this—without experience of men or any knowledge of the world whatever—without
habitual prudence or caution of any kind, the very fact of his mistaking
the letter a palpable evidence of his unfitness for trust. Reckless by
nature—more desperate still from the fallen fortunes of his house—what
would become of him? Others would wait the time and calculate their
chances. He would listen to nothing but the call of danger. She knew him
well, from boyhood upwards, and had seen him often more fascinated by
peril than others were by pleasure.
    As she reasoned thus, her thoughts insensibly turned to all the dangers of
such an enterprise as she believed him engaged in. The fascinating visions
of a speculative patriotism soon gave way before the terrors she now conjured up. She knew he was the only tie that bound his father to existence,
and that any misfortune to Mark would be the old man's death-blow. Nor
were these the most poignant of her reflections, for she now remembered
how often she had alluded tauntingly to those who lived a life of mean or
inglorious ambition; how frequently she had scoffed at the miserable part of
such as, endowed with high names and ancient lineage, evinced no desire to
emerge from an ignoble position, and assume a station of eminence and
power; could she, then, have contributed to this youth's rash step—had her
idle words and random speeches driven him to embrace a cause where his
passions and not his judgment were interested? What misery was in this
fear!
    Each moment increased the agony of this reflection, while her doubts as
to how she ought to act thickened around her. Sir Archy alone was capable
of advising her, his calm and unbiassed reason would be now invaluable, but
dare she, even to him, make use of a confidence thus accidentally obtained?
Would Mark—could he ever forgive her? And how many others might
such a disclosure compromise? In this dilemma she knew no course open
to her but one—to address herself at once to Mark, to explain how his

secret had become known, to learn from him as much as lay in her power
of the dangers and difficulties of the meditated revolt, and if unable to
dissuade him from participation, at least to mingle with his resolves all she
could of prudence or good counsel. The determination was scarcely formed
when she was once more at the door of his chamber; she knocked twice,
without any reply following, then gently opened the door. The room was
vacant, he was gone. "I will write to him," said she, hurriedly, and, with
this new resolve, hastened to her chamber, and began a letter.

The task she proposed to herself was not so easy of accomplishment; a
dozen times she endeavoured, while explaining the accident that divulged
his secret, to impress him with the hazard of an undertaking so palpably
depicted, and to the safe keeping of which his own carelessness might prove
fatal; but each effort dissatisfied her. In one place, she seemed not to have
sufficiently apologised for her unauthorised cognisance of his note; in
another, the stress she laid upon this very point struck her as too selfish
and too personal in a case where another's interests were the real consideration at issue; and even when presenting before him the vicissitudes of
fortune to which his venturous career would expose him, she felt how every
word contradicted the tenor of her own assertions for many a day and week
previous. In utter despair how to act, she ended by enclosing the letter
with merely these few words:

"I have read the enclosed, but your secret is safe with me.

"K. O'D."

This done, she sealed the packet and had just written the address, when,
with a tap at the door Sir Archy entered, and approached the table.

With a tact and delicacy he well understood, Sir Archy explained the object of his visit—to press upon Kate's acceptance a sum of money sufficient
for her outlay in the capital. The tone of half authority he assumed disarmed her at once, and made her doubt how far she could feel justified in
opposing the wishes of her friends concerning her.

"Then you really desire I should go to Dublin," said she.

"I do, Kate, for many reasons—reasons which I shall have little difficulty
in explaining to you hereafter."

"I half regret I ever thought of it," said Kate, speaking her thoughts
unconsciously aloud.

"Not the less reason, perhaps, for going," said Sir Archy, dryly; while at
the same moment his eye caught the letter bearing Mark O'Donoghue's
name.

Kate saw on what his glance was fixed, and grew red with shame and
confusion.

"Be it so then, uncle," said she, resolutely. "I do not seek to know the reasons you speak of, for if you were to ask my own against the project, I should not be able to frame them; it was mere caprice."

"I hope so, dearest Kate," said he, with a tone of deep affection—"I hope so, with all my heart;" and thus saying, he pressed her hand fervently between his own and left the room.

CHAPTER XXVI.

A LAST EVENING AT HOME.

WITH the experience of past events to guide us, it would appear now that a most unaccountable apathy existed in the English Cabinet of the period with regard to the plan of invasion meditated against Ireland by France; nor is it easy to determine whether this indifference proceeded more from ignorance of the danger, or that amount of information concerning it which disposed the Minister to regard it as little important.

From whatever cause proceeding, one thing is sufficiently clear—the emissaries of France pervaded the country in every part without impediment or molestation; statistical information the most minute was forwarded to Paris every week; the state of popular opinion, the condition of parties, the amount of troops disposable by Government, even the spirit which animated them, were reported and commented on, and made the subject of discussion in the "bureau" of the War Minister of France. To such an extent was this system carried, that more than once the French authorities became suspicious regarding the veracity of statements, from the very facility with which their details were communicated, and hinted that such regularity in correspondence might be owing to the polite attentions of the English Cabinet; and to this distrust is in a great measure to be attributed the vacillating and hesitating policy which marked their own deliberations.

Tone's letters show the wearisome toil of his negotiation; the assurances of aid, obtained after months of painful, harassing solicitation, deferred or made dependent on some almost impossible conditions; guarantees demanded from him which he neither could nor would accord; information sought, which, were they in actual possession of the country, would have been a matter of difficult acquisition; and, after all, when the promised assistance was granted, it came coupled with hints and acknowledgments that the independence of Ireland was nothing in their eyes, save as inflicting a death-blow to the power and greatness of England.

In fact, neither party was satisfied with the compact long before the time of putting it in operation arrived. Meanwhile the insurgents spared no efforts to organise a powerful body among the peasantry, and, at least numerically, to announce to France a strong and effective co-operation. Such reports were necessary to enable Tone to press his demand more energetically; and although he never could have deceived himself as to the inutility of such undisciplined and almost unarmed masses, still they looked plausible on paper, and vouched for the willingness of the people to throw off the yoke of England.

It is now well known that the French party in Ireland was really very small. The dreadful wrongs inflicted on the Roman Catholic church during the Revolution could not be forgotten or forgiven by that priesthood, who were their brethren; nor could it be supposed that they would lend a willing aid to further a cause which began its march to freedom over the ashes of their church. Such as were best capable of pronouncing on the project—those educated in France—were naturally fearful of a repetition at home of the horrible scenes they had witnessed abroad, and thus the "patriots" lost the aid which, more than any other, could have stirred the heart of the nation. Abstract principles of liberty are not the most effective appeals to a people; and although the French agents were profuse of promises, and the theme of English oppression could be chanted with innumerable variations, the right chord of native sentiment was never touched, and few joined the cause save those who, in every country and in every age, are patriots—because they are paupers. Some, indeed, like the young O'Donoghue, were sincere and determined. Drawn in at first by impulses more purely personal than patriotic, they soon learned to take a deep interest in the game, and grew fascinated with a scheme which exalted themselves into positions of trust and importance. The necessity of employing this lure, and giving the adherents of the cause their share of power and influence, was another great source of weakness. Diversity of opinion arose on every subject; personal altercations of the bitterest kind, reproaches and insinuations, passed continually between them, and it needed all the skill and management of the chiefs to reconcile, even temporarily, these discordant ingredients, and maintain any semblance of agreement among these " United Irishmen."

Among those who lived away from such scenes of conflict the great complaint was the delay. " What are we waiting for?" "When are we to strike the blow?" were the questions ever arising; and their inability to answer such satisfactorily to the people only increased their chagrin and disappointment. If the sanguine betrayed impatience, the despondent— and there are such in every cause—showed signs of vacillation, and threw out dark hints of treachery and betrayal; while between both were the great masses, moved by every passing rumour, and as difficult to restrain to-day as impossible to muster to-morrow.

Such, briefly, was the condition of the party into which Mark O'Donoghue threw his fortune in life, as reckless of his fate as he was ignorant of the precise objects in view, or the means proposed for their accomplishment.

His influence among the people was considerable. Independently of all claims resulting from his name and family, he was individually a great favourite with them. Personal courage and daring, skill in every manly exercise, and undaunted resolution, are gifts which, when coupled with a rough, good nature, and a really kind heart, are certain of winning their way among a wild and uncultivated people; and thus Herbert, who scarcely ever uttered a harsh word—whose daily visits to the sick were a duty Sir Archy expected from him—whose readiness to oblige was the theme of every tongue, was less their favourite than his brother.

This influence, which, through Lanty Lawler, was soon reported to the delegates in Dublin, was the means of Mark's being taken into special confidence, and of a command being conferred on him, for the duties and privileges of which, he was informed, a few days would sufficiently instruct him.

Nearly a week had elapsed from the day on which Kate addressed her note to Mark, and he had not yet returned home. Such absences were common enough; but now she felt an impatience almost amounting to agony at the thought of what treasonable and dangerous projects he might be engaged in, and the doubt became a torture how far she ought to conceal her own discovery from others.

At length came the evening before her own departure from Carrignacurra, and they were seated around the tea-table, thoughtful and silent by turns, as are they who meet for the last time before separation. Although she heard with pleasure the announcement that Herbert would be her companion to the capital, where he was about to take up his residence as a student in Trinity College, her thoughts wandered away to the gloomier fortunes of Mark, darker as they now seemed in comparison with the prospects opening before his brother.

Of all the party, Herbert alone was in good spirits. The career was about to begin which had engrossed all his boyish ambition—the great race of intellect his very dreams had dwelt upon. What visions did he conjure of emulative ardour to carry off the prize among his companions, and win fame that might reflect its lustre on all his after life. From his very childhood Sir Archy had instilled into him this thirst for distinction, wisely substituting such an ambition for any other less ennobling. He had taught him to believe that there would be more true honour in the laurels there won, than in all the efforts, however successful, to bring back the lost glories of their once proud house. And now he was on the very threshold of that career his heart was centred in. No wonder is it, then, if his spirits were high and his pulse throbbing. Sir Archy's eyes seldom wandered from him.

He scemed as if reading the accomplishment of all his long teaching, and as he watched the flashing looks and the excited gestures of the boy, appeared as though calculating how far such a temperament might minister to or mar his future fortune.

The O'Donoghue was more thoughtful than usual. The idea of approaching solitude, so doubly sad to those advanced in life, depressed him. His evenings of late had been passed in a happy enjoyment he had not known for years before. Separation to the young is but the rupture of the ties of daily intercourse; to the old, it has all the solemn meaning of a warning, and tells of the approach of the last dreadful parting, when adieus are said for ever. He could not help those gloomy forebodings, and he was silent and depressed.

Kate's attention wandered from the theme of Herbert's anticipated pleasures to think again of him, for whom none seemed now interested. She had listened long and anxiously for some sound to mark his coming, but all was still without, and on the road for miles the moonlight showed no object moving; and at last a deep reverie succeeded to this state of anxiety, and she sat lost to all around her. Meanwhile, Sir Archy, in a low, impressive voice, was warning Herbert of the dangers of involving himself in any way in the conflicts of party politics then so high in Dublin.

He cautioned him to reject those extreme opinions so fascinating to young minds, and which either give an unwarrantable bias to the judgment through life, or which, when their fallacy is detected, lead to a reaction as violent and notions as false. " Win character and reputation first, Herbert—gain the position from which your opinions will come with influence, and then, my boy, with judgment not rashly formed, and a mind trained to examine great questions, then you may fearlessly enter the lists, free to choose your place and party. You cannot be a patriot this way, in the newspaper sense of the term. It is possible, too, our dear Kate may deem your ambition a poor one——"

" Kate, did you say ?—Kate, uncle ?" said she, raising her head with a look of abstraction.

" Yes, my dear, I was speaking o' some of the dangers that beset the first steps in political opinion, and telling Herbert that peril does not always bring honour."

" True, sir—true; but Mark——" She stopped, and the blush that covered her face suffused her neck and shoulders. It was not till her lips pronounced the name that she detected how inadvertently she had revealed the secret of her own musings.

" Mark, my sweet Kate, is, I trust, in no need of my warnings. He lives apart from the struggle; and, were it otherwise, he is older, and more able to form his opinions than Herbert here."

These words were spoken calmly, and with a studious desire to avoid in-creasing Kate's confusion.

"What about Mark?" cried the O'Donoghue, suddenly aroused by the mention of the name. "It's very strange he should not be here to say 'good-by' to Kate. Did any one tell him of the time fixed for your de-parture?"

"I told him of it, and he has promised to be here," said Herbert. "He was going to Beerhaven for a day or two for the shooting, but, droll enough, he has left his gun behind him."

"The boy's not himself at all, latterly," muttered the old man. "Lanty brought up two horses here the other day, and he would not even go to the door to look at them. I don't know what he's thinking of."

Kate never spoke, and tried with a great effort to maintain a look of calm unconcern; when, with that strange instinct so indescribable and so inex-plicable, she felt Sir Archy's eyes fixed upon her, her cheek became deadly pale.

"There—there he comes, and at a slapping pace, too!" cried Herbert; and as he spoke the clattering sound of a fast gallop was heard ascending the causeway, and the next moment the bell sent forth a loud summons.

"I knew he'd keep his word," said the boy, proudly, as he walked to meet him. The door opened, and Frederick Travers appeared.

So unexpected was the disappointment, it needed all Sir Archy's practised politeness to conceal from the young Guardsman the discomfiture of the rest. Nor did he entirely succeed, for Frederick was no common observer, and failed not to detect in every countenance around that his was not the coming looked for.

"I owe a thousand apologies for the hour of my visit, not to speak of its abruptness," said he, graciously; "but we only learned accidentally to-day that Herbert was going up to Dublin, and my father sent me to request he would join our party."

"He is about to enter college," said Sir Archy, half fearing to divert the youth's mind from the great object of his journey.

"Be it so," said Fred, gaily; "we'll talk Virgil and Homer on the road."

"I'm afraid such pleasant companionship may put Greece and Rome in the background," said Sir Archy, dryly.

"I'll answer for it, he'll be nothing the worse for the brief respite from study. Besides, you'd not refuse me his company, when I tell you that otherwise I must travel alone, my father in his wisdom having decided to despatch me half a day in advance to make preparations for his arrival. Is that quite fair, Miss O'Donoghue?"

"I protest I think not, as regards us. As for you," added she, archly, "I should say so accomplished a traveller always finds sufficient to amuse him on the least interesting journey. I remember a little theory of yours on that subject; you mentioned it the first time I had the pleasure to meet you."

The allusion was with reference to the manner in which Travers made her acquaintance in the Bristol packet, and the cool assurance of which she, with most womanly pertinacity, had not yet forgiven. Travers, who had often felt ashamed of the circumstance, and had hoped it long since forgotten, looked the very picture of confusion.

"I perceive Sir Archibald has not taught you to respect his native proverb, Miss O'Donoghue, and let 'bygones be bygones.'"

"I hae taught her nothing Scotch, sir," replied Sir Archy, smiling, "but to love a thistle, and that e'en because it has a sting."

"Not for those that know how to take it, uncle," said she, archly, and with a fond expression that lit up the old man's face in smiles.

The Guardsman was less at his ease than usual; and, having arranged the matter of his visit satisfactorily, arose to take his leave.

"Then you'll be ready for me at eight, Herbert. My father is a martinet in punctuality, and the phaeton will not be a second behind time; remember that, Miss O'Donoghue, for he makes no exception, even for ladies."

He moved towards the door, then, turning suddenly, said,

"By-the-by, have you heard anything of a movement in the country here about us? The Government have apparently got some information on the subject, but I suspect without any foundation whatever."

"To what extent does this information go?" said Sir Archy, cautiously.

"That I can't tell you. All I know is, that my father has just received a letter from the Castle, stating that we are living in the very midst of an organised rebellion, only waiting the signal for open revolt."

"That same rebellion has been going on, to my knowledge, something more than forty years," said the O'Donoghue, laughing; "and I never knew of a lord-lieutenant or chief secretary who didn't discover the plot, and save the kingdom: always leaving a nest-egg of treason for his successor to make a character by."

"I'm no so sure it will no come to a hatching yet," said Sir Archy, with a dry shake of the head.

"If it is to come, I wish with all my heart it might while I have a chance of being a spectator," said Travers. Then, suddenly remembering that the levity of the remark might not please the others, he muttered a few words about a hope of better prospects, and withdrew.

During this brief colloquy, Kate listened with breathless interest to learn some fact, or even some well-grounded suspicion which might serve to put Mark on his guard; but nothing could be more vague and indecisive than Travers's information, and it was evident that he had not concealed anything he knew. Was he in a position to learn more? was the next question to herself; might he not be able to ascertain where the suspicion of Government rested, and on whom? Her decisions were seldom but the work of a second, and, as soon as this thought struck her, she determined to act upon it. Slipping noiselessly from the room, she hastily threw a shawl around her, and hurried from the house by a small postern door which, leading down to the high road, was considerably shorter than the causeway by which Travers must pass.

It was no time for the indulgence of bashfulness, and, indeed, her thoughts were far too highly excited by another's destiny to leave any room to think of herself; and, short as the path was, it sufficed to let her arrange her plan of procedure, even to the very words she should employ.

"I must not tell him it is for Mark," said she; "he must think it is a general desire to save any rash or misguided enthusiast from ruin. But here he comes." And at the same instant the figure of a man was seen approaching, leading his horse by the bridle. The dark shadow of the castle fell across the road at the spot, and served to make the form dim and indistinct. Kate waited not for his coming nearer, but, advancing hastily towards him, cried out,

"Captain Travers, I have a favour to ask of you—one which my coming thus to seek——"

"Say no more, Kate, lest I hear what was never intended for my ears," said a low, deep voice.

"Mark—cousin Mark, is this you?" cried she, with mingled pleasure and shame.

"Yes," replied he, in a tone of still deeper gravity; "I grieve to disappoint you—it is me."

"Oh! Mark, mistake me not—do not wrong me," said she, laying her hand affectionately on his arm. I have longed so much to see you—to speak to you, ere we went away."

"To see me—to speak to me," said he, stepping back, and letting the moonlight fall full upon his features, now pale as death; "it was not me you expected to meet here."

"No, Mark, but it was for you I came. I wished to serve—perhaps to save you. I know your secret, Mark, but it is safe with me."

"And I know yours, young lady," retorted he, bitterly. "I cannot say how far my discretion will rival your own."

As he spoke, a horseman darted rapidly past, and, as he emerged from the shadow, turned round in his saddle, stared fixedly at the figures before him, and then, taking off his hat, said,

"Good night, Miss O'Donoghue."

When Kate recovered the shock of this surprise, she found herself alone —Mark had disappeared; and she now returned slowly to the castle, her heart torn with opposing emotions, among which wounded pride was not the least poignant.

CHAPTER XXVII.

A SUPPER PARTY.

As we are about to withdraw our reader for a brief period from the scenes wherein he has so kindly lingered with us hitherto, we may be permitted to throw on them a last look ere we part.

On the evening which followed that recorded in our last chapter, the two old men were seated alone in the tower of Carrignacurra, silent and thoughtful, each following out in his mind the fortunes of him for whom his interest was deepest, and each sad with the sorrow that never spares those who are, or who deem themselves, forsaken.

Unaided memory can conjure up no such memorials of past pleasure as come from the objects and scenes associated with days and nights of happiness. They appeal with a force mere speculation never suggests, and bring back all the lesser but more touching incidents of hourly intercourse, so little at the time—so much when remembered years afterwards.

The brightest moments of life are the most difficult to recal; they are like the brilliant lights upon a landscape, which we may revisit a hundred times, yet never behold under the same favourable circumstances, nor gaze on with the same enthusiasm as at first. It was thus that both the O'Donoghue and Sir Archy now remembered her whose presence lightened so many hours of solitude, and even grafted hope upon the tree scathed and withered by evil fortune. Several efforts to start a topic of conversation were made by each, but all equally fruitless, and both relapsed into a moody silence, from which they were suddenly aroused by a violent ringing at the gate, and the voices of many persons talking together, among which Mark O'Donoghue's could plainly be heard.

"Yes, but I insist upon it," cried he; "to refuse will offend me."

Some words were then spoken in a tone of remonstrance, to which he again replied, but with even greater energy,

"What care I for that? This is my father's house, and who shall say that his eldest son cannot introduce his friends——"

A violent jerk of the bell drowned the remainder of the speech.

"We are about to hae company, I perceive," said Sir Archy, looking cautiously about to secure his book and his spectacles before retreating to his bedroom.

"Bedad, you just guessed it," said Kerry, who, having reconnoitred the

party through a small window beside the door, had now prudently adjourned
to take counsel whether he should admit them. "There's eight or nine at
laste, and it isn't fresh and fasting either they are."

"Why don't you open the door?—do you want your bones broken for
you," said the O'Donoghue, harshly.

"I'd let them gang the gate they cam," said Sir Archy, sagely; "if I
may hazard a guess from their speech, they arc no in a fit state to visit any
respectable house. Hear till that?"

A fearful shout now was heard outside.

"What's the rascal staring at?" cried the O'Donoghue, with clenched
teeth. "Open the door this instant."

But the words were scarcely uttered, when a tremendous crash resounded
through the whole building, and then a heavy noise like the fall of some
weighty object.

"'Tis the window he's bruk in—divil a lie," cried Kerry, in an accent of
unfeigned terror; and, without waiting a second, he rushed from the room
to seek some place of concealment from Mark's anger.

The clash of the massive chain was next heard, as it banged heavily
against the oak door; bolt after bolt was quickly shot, and Mark, calling
out, "Follow me—this way," rudely pushed wide the door and entered the
tower. A mere passing glance was enough to show that his excitement was
not merely the fruit of passion—his eyes wild and bloodshot, his flushed
cheek, his swollen and heavy lips, all betrayed that he had drunk deeply. His
cravat was loose and his vest open, while the fingers of his right hand were
one mass of blood, from the violence with which he had forced his entrance.

"Come along, Talbot—Holt, this way—come in boys," said he, calling
to those behind. "I told them we should find you here, though they insisted it was too late."

"Never too late to welcome a guest, Mark, but always too early to part
with one," cried the O'Donoghue, who, although shocked at the condition he
beheld his son in, resolved to betray for the time no apparent consciousness
of it.

"This is my friend, Harry Talbot, father—Sir Archy M'Nab, my uncle.
Holt, where are you? I'll be hanged if they're not slipped away;"and with
a fearful imprecation on their treachery, he rushed from the room, leaving
Talbot to make his own advances. The rapid tramp of feet, and the loud
laughter of the fugitives without, did not for a second or two permit of his
few words being heard; but his manner and air had so far assured Sir
Archy, that he stopped short as he was about to leave the room, and saluted
him courteously.

"It would be very ungracious in me," said Talbot, smiling, "to disparage
my friend Mark's hospitable intentions, but in truth I feel so much ashamed
for the manner of our entry here this evening, that I cannot express the

pleasure such a visit would have given me under more becoming circumstances."

Sir Archibald's surprise at the tone in which these words were delivered did not prevent him making a suitable reply, while, relinquishing his intention of retiring, he extinguished his candle, and took a seat opposite Talbot.

Having in an early chapter of our tale presented this gentleman to our reader's notice, we have scarcely anything to add on the present occasion. His dress, indeed, was somewhat different; then, he wore a riding costume —now, he was habited in a frock richly braided, and ornamented with a deep border of black fur; a cap of the same skin, from which hung a band of deep gold lace, he also carried in his hand—a costume which at the time would have been called foreign.

While Sir Archy was interchanging courtesies with the newly-arrived guest, the O'Donoghue, by dint of reiterated pulling at the bell, had succeeded in inducing Kerry O'Leary to quit his sanctuary, and venture to the door of the apartment, which he did with a caution only to be acquired by long practice.

"Is he here, sir?" whispered he, as his eyes took a rapid but searching survey of the apartment. "Blessed virgin, but he's in a dreadful temper to-night."

"Bring some supper here, directly," cried O'Donoghue, striking the ground angrily with his heavy cane; "if I have to tell you again, I hope he'll break every bone in your skin."

"I request you will not order any refreshment for me, sir," said Talbot, bowing; "we partook of a very excellent supper at a little cabin in the glen, where, among other advantages, I had the pleasure of making your son's acquaintance."

"Ah, indeed, at Mary's," said the old man. "There are worse places than that little ' shebeen ;' but you must permit me to offer you a glass of claret, which never tastes the worse in company with a grouse-pie."

"You must hae found the travelling somewhat rude in these parts," said M'Nab, who thus endeavoured to draw from the stranger some hint either as to the object or the road of his journey.

"We were not over particular on that score," said Talbot, laughing. "A few young college men, seeking some days' amusement in the wild mountains of this picturesque district, could well afford to rough it for the enjoyment of the ramble."

"You should visit us in the autumn," said O'Donoghue, "when our heaths and arbutus blossoms are in beauty; then, they who have travelled far, tell me that there is nothing to be seen in Switzerland finer than this valley. Draw your chair over here, and let me have the pleasure of a glass of wine with you."

The party had scarcely taken their places at the table, when Mark reentered the room, heated and excited with the chase of the fugitives.

"They're off," muttered he, angrily, "down the glen, and I only hope they may lose their way in it, and spend the night upon the heather."

As he spoke, he turned his eyes to the corner of the room, where Kerry, in a state of the most abject fear, was endeavouring to extract a cork from a bottle by means of a very impracticable screw.

"Ah, you there!" cried he, as his eyes flashed fire. "Hold the bottle up—hold it steady, you old fool!" and with a savage grin he drew a pistol from his breast-pocket, and levelled it at the mark.

Kerry was on his knees, one hand on the floor and in the other the bottle, which, despite all his efforts, he swayed backwards and forwards.

"O master, darlin'!—O Sir Archy, dear!—O Joseph and Mary!"

"I've drunk too much wine to hit it flying," said Mark, with a half-drunken laugh, "and the fool won't be steady. There!" and as he spoke, the crash of the report resounded through the room, and the neck of the bottle was snapped off about half an inch below the cork.

"Neatly done, Mark—not a doubt of it," said the O'Donoghue, as he took the bottle from Kerry's hand, who, with a pace a kangaroo might have envied, approached the table, actually dreading to stand up straight in Mark's presence.

"At the risk of being thought an epicure," said M'Nab, "I maun say I'd like my wine handled more tenderly."

"It was cleverly done, though," said Talbot, helping himself to a bumper from the broken flask. "I remember a trick we used to have at St. Cyr, which was, to place a bullet on a cork, and then, at fifteen paces, cut away the cork, and drop the bullet into the bottle."

"No man ever did that twice," cried Mark, rudely.

"I'll wager a hundred guineas I do it twice, within five shots," said Talbot, with the most perfect coolness.

"Done, for a hundred—I say done," said Mark, slapping him familiarly on the shoulder.

"I'll not win your money on such unfair terms," said Talbot, laughing; "and if I can refrain from taking too much of this excellent Bordeaux, I'll do the trick to-morrow without a wager."

Mark, like most persons who place great store by feats of skill and address, felt vexed at the superiority claimed by another, answered carelessly, "that, after all, perhaps the thing was easier than it seemed."

"Very true," chimed in Talbot, mildly; "what we have neither done ourselves nor seen done by another, has always the appearance of difficulty. What is called wisdom is little other than the power of calculating success or failure on grounds of mere probability."

"Your definition has the advantage of being sufficient for the occasion," said Sir Archy, smiling. "I am happy to find our glen has not disappointed you; but if you have not seen the Lake and the Bay of Glengariff, I anticipate even a higher praise from you."

"We spent the day on the water," replied Talbot; "and if it were not a heresy, I should affirm that these bold mountains are grander and more sublime in the desolation of winter than even when clothed in the purple and gold of summer. There was a fine sea, too, rolling into that great bay bounding upon the rocks, and swelling proudly against the tall cliffs, which, to my eye, is more pleasurable than the glassy surface of calm water. Motion is the life of inanimate objects, and life has always its own powers of excitement."

While they conversed thus, M'Nab, endeavouring, by adroit allusions to the place, to divine the real reason of the visit, and Talbot, by encomiums on the scenery, or, occasionally, by the expression of some abstract proposition, seeking to avoid any direct interrogatory, Mark, who had grown weary of a dialogue which, even in his clearer moments, would not have interested him, drank deeply from the wine before him, filling and refilling a large glass unceasingly, while the O'Donoghue merely paid that degree of attention which politeness demanded.

It was thus that, while Sir Archy believed he was pushing Talbot closely on the objects of his coming, Talbot was, in reality, obtaining from him much information about the country generally, the habits of the people, and their modes of life, which he effected in the easy, unconstrained manner of one perfectly calm and unconcerned. "The life of a fisherman," said he, in reply to a remark of Sir Archy's—"the life of a fisherman is, however, a poor one; for though his gains are great at certain seasons, there are days—ay, whole months—he cannot venture out to sea. Now it strikes me, that in that very Bay of Bantry the swell must be terrific when the wind blows from the west, or the nor'-west."

"You are right—quite right," answered M'Nab, who at once entered freely into a discussion of the condition of the bay, under the various changing circumstances of wind and tide. "Many of our poor fellows have been lost within my own memory, and, indeed, save when we have an easterly wind——"

"An easterly wind?" re-echoed Mark, lifting his head suddenly from between his hands, and staring in half-drunken astonishment around him. "Is that the toast—did you say that?"

"With all my heart," said Sir Archy, smiling. "There are few sentiments deserve a bumper better by any who live in these parts. Won't you join us, Mr. Talbot?"

"Of course I will," said Talbot, laughing; but with all his efforts to seem at ease, a quick observer might have remarked the look of warning he threw towards the young O'Donoghue.

" Here, then," cried Mark, rising, while the wine trickled over his hand from a brimming goblet—" I'll give it—are you ready ?"

" All ready, Mark," said the O'Donoghue, laughing heartily at the serious gravity of Mark's countenance.

" Confound it," cried the youth, passionately, " I forget the jingle."

" Never mind—never mind," interposed Talbot, slyly ; " we'll pledge it with as good a mind."

" That's—that's it," shouted Mark, as the last word clinked upon his memory. " I have it now," and his eyes sparkled, and his brows were met, as he called out,

> " A stout heart and mind,
> And an easterly wind,
> And the devil behind
> The Saxon.'

Sir Archy laid down his glass untasted, while Talbot, bursting forth into a well-acted laugh, cried out, " You must excuse me from repeating your amiable sentiment, which, for aught I can guess, may be a sarcasm on my own country."

" I'd like to hear the same toast explained," said Sir Archy, cautiously, while his looks wandered alternately from Mark to Talbot.

" So you shall, then," replied Mark, sternly, " and this very moment, too."

" Come, that's fair," chimed in Talbot, while he fixed his eyes on the youth with such a steady gaze as seemed actually to have pierced the dull vapour of his clouded intellect, and flashed light upon his addled brain. " Let us hear your explanation."

Mark, for a second or two, looked like one suddenly awakened from a deep sleep, and trying to collect his wandering faculties, while, as if instinctively seeking the clue to his bewilderment from Talbot, he never turned his eyes from him. As he sat thus he looked the very ideal of half-drunken stupidity.

" I'm afraid we have no right to ask the explanation," whispered Talbot into M'Nab's ear. " We ought to be satisfied if he give us the rhyme, even though he forget the reason."

" I'm thinking you're right, sir," replied M'Nab; " but I suspect we hae na the poet before us ony mair than the interpreter."

Mark's faculties, in slow pursuit of Talbot's meaning, had just at this instant overtaken their object, and he burst forth into a boisterous fit of laughter, which, whatever sentiment it might have excited in the others, relieved Talbot, at least, from all his former embarrassment: he saw that Mark had, though late, recognised his warning, and was at once relieved from any uneasiness on the score of his imprudence.

Sir Archy was, however, very far from feeling satisfied. What he had heard, brief and broken as it was, but served to excite his suspicions and make him regard this guest as at least a very doubtful character. Too shrewd a diplomatist to push his inquiries any further, he adroitly turned the conversation upon matters of comparative indifference, reserving to himself the part of acutely watching Talbot's manner, and narrowly scrutinising the extent of his acquaintance with Mark O'Donoghue. In whatever school Talbot had been taught, his skill was more than a match for Sir Archy's. Not only did he at once detect the meaning of the old man's policy, but he contrived to make it subservient to his own views by the opportunity it afforded him of estimating the influence he was capable of exerting over his nephew; and how far, if need were, Mark should become dependent on his will, rather than on that of any member of his own family. The frankness of his manner, the seeming openness of his nature, rendered his task a matter of apparent amusement; and none at the table looked in every respect more at ease than Harry Talbot.

While Sir Archy was thus endeavouring, with such skill as he possessed, to worm out the secret reason—and such, he well knew, there must be—of Talbot's visit to that unfrequented region, Kerry O'Leary was speculating, with all his imaginative ability, how best to account for that event. The occasion was one of more than ordinary difficulty. Talbot looked neither like a bailiff nor a sheriff's officer; neither had he outward signs of a lawyer or an attorney. Kerry was conversant with the traits of each of these. If he were a suitor for Miss Kate, his last guess, he was a day too late.

"But sure he couldn't be that: he'd never come with a throop of noisy vagabonds, in the dead of the night, av he was after the young lady. Well, well, he bates me out—sorra lie in it," said he, drawing a heavy sigh, and crossing his hands before him in sad resignation.

"On my conscience, then, it was a charity to cut your hair for you, anyhow!" said Mrs. Branaghan, who had been calmly meditating on the pistol-shot, which, in grazing Kerry's hair, had somewhat damaged his locks.

"See, then, by the holy mass! av he went half an inch lower, it's my life he'd be after taking; and av he was the fifty O'Donoghues, I'd have my vingince. Bad cess to me, but they think the likes of me isn't fit to live at all."

"They do," responded Mrs. Branaghan, with a mild puff of smoke from the corner of her mouth—"they do; and if they never did worse than extarminate such varmin, their sowls would have an easier time of it."

Kerry's brow lowered, and his lips muttered, but no distinct reply was audible.

"Sorra bit of good I see in ye at all," said she, with inexorable severity. "I mind the time ye used to tell a body what was doing above stairs; and,

though half what ye said was lies, it was better than nothing: but now yer
as stupid and lazy as the ould beast there fornint the fire—not a word
out of your head from morning to night. Ayeh, is it your hearin's
failin' ye?"

"I wish to the Blessed Mother it was," muttered he, fervently, to himself.

"There's a man now eatin' and drinkin' in the parlour, and the sorra
more ye know about him than if he was the Queen of Sheba."

"Don't I, thin—maybe not," said Kerry, tauntingly, and with a look of
such well-affected secrecy that Mrs. Branaghan was completely deceived
by it.

"What is he, then? spake it out free this minit," said she. "Bad cess to
you, do you want to trate me like an informer?"

"No, indeed, Mrs. Branaghan; it's not that same I'd even to you—sure
I knew your people—father and mother's side—two generations back.
Miles Buoy—Yellow Miles, as they called him—was the finest judge of a
horse in Kerry—I wonder, now, he didn't make a power of money."

"And so he did, and spint it after. 'Twas blackguards, with ould
gaiters, and one spur on them, that ate up every shilling he saved."

"Well, well! think of that, now," said Kerry, with the sententiousness
of one revolving some strange and curious social anomaly; "and that's the
way it wint?"

"Wasn't it a likely way enough?" said Mrs. Branaghan, with flashing
eyes; "feedin' a set of spalpeens that thought of nothing but chating the
world. The sight of a pair of top-boots gives me the heartburn to this
day."

"Mine warms to them, too," said Kerry, timidly, who ventured on his
humble pun with deep humility.

A contemptuous scowl was Mrs. Branaghan's reply, and Kerry resumed:

"Them's the changes of the world—rich yesterday—poor to-day. Don't
I know what poverty is well myself? Augh! sure enough they wor the fine
times when I rode out on a beast worth eighty guineas in goold, wid clothes
on my back a lord might envy; and now, look at me!"

Mrs. Branaghan, to whom the rhetorical figure seemed a direct appeal,
did look; and assuredly the inspection conveyed nothing flattering, for she
turned away abruptly, and smoked her pipe with an air of profound disdain.

"Faix, ye may say so," continued Kerry, converting her glauce into
words. "'Tis a poor object I am this blessed day. The coat on my back
is more like a transparency, and my small-clothes, saving your favour, is as
hard to get into as a fishing-net; and if I was training for the coorse I
couldn't be on shorter allowance."

"What's that yer saying about yer vittals?" said the cook, turning
fiercely towards him. "There's not your equal for an appetite from this to

Cork. It's little time a Kerry cow would keep you in beef; and it's an il. skin it goes into. Yer a disgrace to a good family."

"Well, I am, aud there's no denying it!" ejaculated Kerry, with a sigh that sounded far more like despair than resignation.

"Is it to hang yourself you have that piece of a rope there?" said she, pointing to the end of a stout cord that depended from Kerry's pocket.

"Maybe it might come to that same yet," said he; and then putting his hand into his pocket, he drew forth a great coil of rope, to the eud of which a leaden weight was fastened. "There now," resumed he, "yer a cute woman —can ye tell me what's the meanin' of that?"

Mrs. Branaghan gave one look at the object iu question, and then turned away, as though the inquiry was one beneath her dignity to investigate.

"Some would call it a clothes-line, and more would say it was for fishing; but sure there's no sign of hooks on it at all; aud what's the piece of lead for?—that's what bothers me out entirely."

These observations were so many devices to induce Mrs. Branaghau to offer her own speculations; but they failed utterly, that sage personage not deigning to pay the least attention either to Kerry or the subject of his re- marks.

"Well, I'll just leave it where I fouud it," said he, in a half soliloquy, but which had the effect of at least arousing the curiosity of his compauion.

"And where was that?" askcd she.

"Outside there, before the hall door," said he, carelessly, "where I got this little paper book too;" and he produced a small pocket almanack with blank pages interleaved, some of which had short pencil memoranda. "I'll leave them both there, for, somehow, I dou't like the look of either of them."

"Read us a bit of it first, anyhow," said Mrs. Branaghan, in a more con- ciliating tone than she had yet employed.

"'Tis what I can't do, then," said Kerry, "for it's writ in some out- landish tongue that's past me altogether."

"And you found them at the door, ye say?"

"Out there foruint the tower. 'Twas the chaps that run away from Master Mark that dropped them. Ye'r a dhroll bit of a rope as ever I seen," added he, as he poised the lead in his hand, "av a body knew ouly what to make of ye." Then turning to the book, he pored for several minutes over a page, in which thcre were some lines written with a pencil. "Be my couscience I have it," said he, at length; "and faix it wasn't bad of me to make it out. What do you think, now, the rope is for?"

"Sure I tould you afore I didn't know."

"Well, thcn, hear it, and uo lie in it—'tis for measurin' the say."

"Measurin' the say! What bother you're talking; isn't the say thousands and thousands of miles long?"

" And who says it isn't ?—but for measurin' the depth of it, that's what
it is.   Listen to this—' Bantry Bay, eleven fathoms at low water inside of
Whiddy Island ; but the shore current at half ebb makes landing difficult
with any wind from the westward ;' and here's another piece, half rubbed
out, about flat-bottomed boats being best for the surf."

" 'Tis the smugglers again," chimed in Mrs. Branaghan, as though sum-
ming up her opinion on the evidence.

" Troth, then, I don't think so ; they never found it hard to land, no matter
how it blew.   I'm thinking of a way to find it out at last."

" And what's that ?"

" I'll just go up to the parlour, wid an innocent face on me, and I'll lay
the rope and the little hook down on the table before the strange man there,
and I'll just say, ' There's the things your honour dropped at the door outside ;' and maybe ould Archy won't have the saycret out of him."

" Do that, Kerry avich," said Mrs. Branaghan, who at length vouchsafed
a hearty approval of his skill in devices—" do that, and I'll broil a bit o'
meat for ye agin ye come down."

" Wid an onion on it, av it's plazing to ye, ma'am," said Kerry, insinuatingly.

" Sure I know how you like it; and if ye have the whole of the saycret,
maybe you'd get a dhrop to wash it down besides."

" And wish you health and happy days, Mrs. Branaghan," added Kerry,
with a courteous gallantry he always reserved for the kitchen.   So saying,
he arose from his chair, and proceeded to arrange his dress in a manner becoming the dignity of his new mission, rehearsing at the same time the
mode of his entry.

" ' 'Tis the rope and the little book, your honour,' I'll say, ' that ye dropped
outside there, and sure it would be a pity to lose it afther all your trouble
measuring the places.'   That will be enough for ould Archy ; let him get a
sniff of the game once, and begorra he'll run him home by himself afterwards."

With this sensible reflection Kerry ascended the stairs in high good
humour at his own sagacity and the excellent reward which awaited it on
his return.   As he neared the door, the voices were loud and boisterous ; at
least, Mark's was such ; and it seemed as if Talbot was endeavouring to
moderate the violent tone in which he spoke, and successfully, too ; for a
loud burst of laughter followed, in which Talbot appeared to join heartily.

" Maybe I'll spoil your fun," said Kerry, maliciously, to himself ; and he
opened the door, and entered.

CHAPTER XXVIII.

THE CAPITAL AND ITS PLEASURES.

DUBLIN, at the time we speak of, possessed social attractions of a high order. Rank, beauty, intellect, and wealth, contributed their several influences; and while the tone of society had all the charms of a politeness now bygone, there was an admixture of native kindliness and cordiality as distinctive as it was fascinating.

Almost every Irishman of rank travelled in those days. It was regarded as the last finishing-touch of education, and few nations possess quicker powers of imitation, or a greater aptitude in adapting foreign habitudes to home usages, than the Irish; for, while vanity with the Frenchman—coldness with the Englishman—and stolid indifference with the German, are insuperable barriers against this acquirement, the natural gaiety of Irish character, the buoyancy, but still more than all, perhaps, the inherent desire to please, suggest a quality which, when cultivated and improved, becomes that great element of social success—the most precious of all drawing-room gifts—men call tact.

It would be a most unfair criterion of the tastes and pleasures of that day, were we to pronounce from our experience of what Dublin now is. Provincialism had not then settled down upon the city, with all its petty attendant evils. The character of a metropolis was upheld by a splendid Court, a resident Parliament, a great and titled aristocracy. The foreground figures of the time were men whose names stood high, and whose station was recognised at every Court of Europe. There was wealth more than proportioned to the cheapness of the country; and while ability and talent were the most striking features of every circle, the taste for gorgeous display exhibited within doors and without, threw a glare of splendour over the scene, that served to illustrate, but not eclipse, the prouder glories of mind. The comparative narrowness of the circle, and the total absence of English reserve, produced a more intimate admixture of all the ranks which constitute good society here than in London, and the advantages were evident; for while the aristocrat gained immeasurably from intercourse with men whose pursuits were purely intellectual, so the latter acquired a greater expansiveness, and a wider liberality in his views, from being divested of all the trammels of mere professional habit, and threw off his pedantry as a garment unsuited to his position in society. But what more than all else was the characteristic of the time, was the fact that social eminence—the *succès de salon*—was an object to every one. From the proud peer, who aspired to rank and influence in the councils of the State, to the rising barrister, ambitions of parliamentary distinction—from the mere fashionable idler of the squares, to the deeper plotter of political intrigue—this was alike indispensable. The mere admission into certain circles was nothing— the fact of mixing with the hundred others who are announced, and bow, and smile, and slip away, did not then serve to identify a man as belonging to a distinct class in society; nor would the easy platitudes of the present day in which the fool or the fop can always have the ascendant, suffice for the absence of conversational ability, ready wit, and sharp intelligence, which were assembled around every dinner-table of the capital.

It is not our duty, still less our inclination, to inquire why have all these goodly attractions left us, nor wherefore is it, that, like the art of staining glass, social agreeability should be lost for ever. So it would seem, how- ever; we have fallen upon tiresome times, and he who is old enough to re- member pleasanter ones has the sad solace of knowing that he has seen the last of them.

Crowded as the capital was with rank, wealth, and influence, the arrival of Sir Marmaduke Travers was not without its *éclat*. His vast fortune was generally known; besides that, there was a singularity in the fact of an Eng- lishman, bound to Ireland by the very slender tie of a small estate, without connexions or friends in the country, coming to reside in Dublin, which gratified native pride as much as it excited public curiosity ; and the rapidity with which the most splendid mansion in Stephen's-green was prepared for his reception vied in interest with the speculation as to what possible cause had induced him to come and live there. The rumours of his intended magnificence, and the splendour of his equipage, furnished gossip for the town and paragraphs for the papers.

It was, indeed, a wondrous change for those two young girls—from the stillness and solitude of Glenflesk, to the gaiety of the capital—from a life of reflection and retirement, to the dazzling scenes and fascinating pleasures of a new world. Upon Sybella the first effect was to increase her natural timidity—to render her more cautious, as she found herself surrounded by influences so novel and so strange ; and in this wise there was mingled with her enjoyment a sense of hesitation and fear that tinged all her thoughts, and even impressed themselves upon her manner. Not so with Kate: the instinct that made her feel at home in the world was but the consciousness of her own powers of pleasing. She loved society as the scene where, how- ever glossed over by conventionalities, human passions and feelings were at work, and where the power of influencing or directing others gave a stimulus to existence far higher and nobler than all the pleasures of retirement. It was life, in fact. Each day had its own separate interests, dramatising, as it were, the real, and making of the ordinary events of the world a romance, of which she felt herself a character. As much au actor as spectator, she threw herself into the pleasures of society with a zest which need only have the accompaniments of youth, beauty, and talents, to make it contagious. Thus differing in character as in appearance, these two young girls at once became the acknowledged beauties of the capital, and each was followed by a troop of admirers, whose enthusiasm exhibited itself in a hundred different ways. Their favourite colours at a ball became the fashionable emblems of the next day on the promenade, and even the ladies caught up the contagion, aud enlisted themselves into parties, whose rivalry amused none so much as those in whom it had its origin.

While the galling enmity of Celt to Saxon was then stirring in secret the hearts of thousands in the country, and fashioning itself into the elements of open insurrection, the city was divided by a more peaceful animosity, and the English and the Irish party were arrayed against each other in the cause of beauty.

It would be impossible to conceive a rivalry from which every ungenerous or unworthy feeling was more perfectly excluded. So far from any jealousy obtruding, every little triumph of one was a source of unalloyed heartfelt pleasure to the other; and while Sybella sympathised with all the delight of Kate's followers in an Irish success, so Kate, with characteristic feeling, enjoyed nothing so much as the chagrin of her own party when Sybella was unquestionably in the ascendant. Happily for us, we are not called upon to explain a phenomenon so novel and so pleasing—enough if we record it. Certain it is, the absence of all envy enhanced the fascinations of each, and exalted the objects in the eyes of their admirers. On this point alone opinion was undivided—none claimed any superiority for their idol by ascribing to her a greater share of this good gift; nor could even malice impute a difference in their mutual affection.

One alone among the circle of their acquaintances stood neutral—unable to divest himself enough of natural partiality to be a fair and just judge. Sir Marmaduke Travers candidly avowed that he felt himself out of court. The leaders of fashion, the great arbiters of *bon ton*, were happily divided, and if England could boast of a majority among the Castle party, Ireland turned the scale with those who, having enjoyed opportunities of studying foreign manner, pronounced Kate's the very perfection of French agreeability, united to native loveliness and attraction.

So much for "the sensation," to use the phrase appropriated by the newspapers, their entrance into the fashionable life of Dublin excited. Let us now return to the parties themselves. In a large and splendidly furnished apartment of Sir Marmaduke's Dublin residence, sat the baronet, his daughter, and Kate, at breakfast, alternately reading from the morning papers, and discussing the news as they ate.

" Well, but, my dear Kate"—Sir Marmaduke had emancipated himself from the more formal "Miss" a week before—" turn to another column, and let us hear if they have any political news."

" There's not a word, sir, unless an allusion to the rebel colour of my dress at the Chancellor's ball be such. You see, Sybella, Falkner fights not under my banner."

" I think you stole the Chancellor himself from me," replied Sybella, laughing, " and I must say most unhandsomely too : he had just given me his arm, to lead me to a chair, when you said something in a half whisper— I could not catch it if I would—he dropped my arm, burst out a laughing, and hurried over to Lord Clonmel—I suppose to repeat it."

" It was not worth relating, then," said Kate, with a toss of her head. " I merely remarked how odd it was Lady Ridgeway couldn't dance in time, with such beautiful clocks on her stocking."

" Oh, Kate, dearest !" said Sybella, who while she could not refrain from a burst of laughter, became deep scarlet at her friend's hardihood.

" Why Meddlicot told that as his own at supper," said Sir Marmaduke.

" So he did, sir; but I cautioned him that a license for wholesale does not permit the retail even of jokes. Isn't the worthy sheriff a druggist? But what have we here—all manner of changes on the staff—Lord Sellbridge to join his regiment at Hounslow, vice Captain—your brother, Sybella —Captain Frederick Travers ;" and she reddened slightly at the words. " I did not know he was appointed aide-de-camp to the Viceroy."

" Nor did I, my dear," said Sir Marmaduke. " I knew he was most anxious to make the exchange with Lord Sellbridge; but this is the first I have heard of the success of his negotiation."

" You see, Kate," said Sybella, while a sly glance shot beneath her long-lashed lids, " that even Fred has become a partisan of Ireland."

" Perhaps the prospect of the revolt he hinted at," replied Kate, with an air of scornful pride, " has made the Guardsman prefer this country for the moment."

" I incline to a very different reason," said Sybella, but in a voice so sub-dued as to be only audible to Kate herself, who again blushed deeply, and seemed greatly confused.

" Ha ! here it is," said Sir Marmaduke, reading aloud a long paragraph from a morning paper, which, descanting on the abortiveness of any effort to destroy the peace of the realm by enemies without or within its frontiers, concluded with a glowing panegyric on the blessings of the British consti-tution. " ' The Government, while confiding implicitly on the loyalty and bravery of his Majesty's people, have yet neglected no measures of precau-tion against the insane and rash attempts of our 'natural enemies,' whose temerity is certain of again receiving the same severe lesson which every attempt upon our shores has taught them.' Yes—yes—very prompt and active measures—nothing could be better," muttered he to himself.

"May I ask what they consist in, these precautionary movements ?" said Kate.

"A full organisation of the militia and yeomanry," replied Sir Marmaduke, proudly—for he commanded a regiment of Northamptonshire Fencibles—"strengthening the different garrisons in large towns, mounting guns of heavy calibre on the forts——"

A hearty burst of laughter broke from Kate, which she made no effort to control whatever.

"I cannot help laughing, because that same word recals a conversation I once heard between two French officers in Bruges. One of them, who seemed to know Ireland well, averred that these forts were so placed as only to be capable of battering down each other. I know he instanced two on the southern coast, which, in three discharges, must inevitably make a drawn battle of it."

"My dear young lady," said Sir Marmaduke, with an unusual gravity, "it is not exactly to our enemies we must look for any warm encomium on our means of defence ; nor has experience yet shown that British courage can be justly a subject for a Frenchman's laughter."

"And as to the militia and yeomanry," continued Kate, for she seemed bent on tormenting, and totally indifferent to the consequences regarding herself, "Colonel Delcamp called them ' arsenaux ambulants,' admirably contrived to provide an invading army with arms and ammunition."

"I heartily wish your friend Colonel Delcamp would favour us with a visit of inspection," said the baronet, scarcely able to control his anger.

"I should not think the occurrence unlikely," was the cool reply ; "and if so, I may be permitted to assure you that you will be much pleased with his manners and agreeability." Sybella's imploring look was all in vain. Kate, as she herself said, belonged to a race who neither gave nor took quarter, and such a controversy was the very conflict she gloried in. How it was to be carried on any further is not easy to foresee, had not the difficulty been solved by the entrance of Frederick Travers, come to communicate the news of his appointment. While Sir Marmaduke and Sybella expressed their joy at his success, Kate, half chagrined at the interruption to a game where she already deemed herself the winner, walked towards the window and looked out.

"Have I nothing like congratulation to expect from Miss O'Donoghue ?" said Frederick, as he placed himself at her side.

"I scarcely knew if it were a subject where congratulation would be suitable. To exchange the glories of London life, the fascinations of a great Court, and the society of the first people in the land, for the lesser splendours of a second-rate capital—perhaps you might have smiled at the simplicity of wishing you joy for all this;" and here her voice assumed a deeper, fuller accent. "I own that I do not feel Ireland in a position to bear even a smile of scorn without offence to one of her children."

"I was not aware till now that you could suspect me of such a feeling."

"You are an Englishman, sir—that's enough," said Kate, hurriedly. "In *your* eyes, we are the people you have conquered; and it would be too much to expect you should entertain great respect for the prejudices you have laboured to subdue. But, after all, there is a distinction worth making, and you have not made it."

"And that is—if I dare ask——"

"That is, there is a wide difference between conquering the territory and gaining the affections of a people. You have succeeded in one; you'll never, at least by your present courses, accomplish the other."

"Speak more plainly to me," said Travers, who felt a double interest in a conversation which every moment contained an allusion that bore upon his own fortune.

"There—there, sir," said Kate, proudly, "your very request is an answer to yourself. We here, who have known each other for some time, have had opportunities of interchanging opinions and sentiments, cannot understand a simple matter in the same way, nor regard it in the same light, how do you suppose that millions, separated by distance, habits, and pursuits, can attain to what we, with our advantages, have failed in? Can you not see that we are not the same people?"

"But need our dissimilitudes sever—may they not be made rather ties to bind us more closely together," said he, tenderly.

"Equality for the future, even if we obtained it, cannot eradicate the memory of the past. The penal laws——"

"Come—come. There is no longer anything there. See the University, for instance. By-the-by"—and here Travers caught eagerly at the opportunity of escape—"what of Herbert? is not this near the time for his examination?"

"The very day, the 28th of February," said she, reading from a small memorandum-book. "It is six weeks yesterday since we have seen him—poor boy!"

"How pale and sickly he looked, too. I wish with all my heart he had not set his mind so eagerly on college success."

"It is only for women to live without ambition of one sort or other," replied Kate, sadly; "and a very poor kind of existence it is, I assure you."

"What if we were to make a party, and meet him as he comes out? We might persuade him to join us at dinner, too."

"Well thought of, Fred," said Sir Marmaduke. "Herbert seems to have forgotten us latterly, and knowing his anxiety to succeed, I really scrupled at the thought of idling him."

" It is very kind of you all," said Kate, with one of her sweetest smiles, 'to remember the poor student, and there is nothing I should like better than the plan you propose."

" We must find out the hour they leave the Hall," said Frederick.

" I heard him say it was at four o'clock," said Sybella, timidly, venturing for the first time to interpose a word in the conversation.

" You have the best memory in the world, Sybella," whispered Kate in her friend's ear; and simple as the words were, they called the blush to her cheek in an instant.

The morning passed away in the thousand little avocations which affluence and ease have invented to banish "ennui" and render life always interesting. A few minutes before four o'clock the splendid equipage of Sir Marmaduke Travers, in all the massive perfection of its London appointments, drew up at the outer gate of the University; the party preferring to enter the courts on foot.

As Frederick Travers, with his two lady companions, appeared within the walls, the murmur of their names ran through the crowd of gownsmen already assembled in the court; for although by College time it still wanted fifteen minutes of the hour, a considerable number of students were gathered together, anxious to hear the result of the day. The simple but massive style of the buildings; the sudden change from the tumult and noise of a crowded city to the silence and quietude of these spacious quadrangles; the number of youths dressed in their University costume, and either gazing wistfully at the door of the Examination Hall, or conversing eagerly together, were all matters of curious interest to the Travers's party, who saw themselves in a world so different from that they daily moved in. Nor were the loungers the students only; mixed up with them, here and there, might be seen some of the leading barristers of the day, and one or two of the most distinguished members of the House of Commons—men who themselves had tasted the sweets of College success, and were fain, even by a passing moment, to refresh the memory of youthful triumphs, and bring back, by the sight of familiar objects, the recollection of days to which all the glories of after life are but poor in comparison. Many of these were recognised by the students, and saluted by them with marks of profound respect; and one, a small, mean-looking man, with jet-black eyes and olive complexion, was received with a cheer, which was with difficulty arrested by a waving motion with his hand and a gesture towards the door of the Hall, from which, with a hollow, cavernous sound, a heavy bolt was now drawn, and the wide portal opened. A general movement in the crowd showed how intense expectation then was; but it was destined to a further

P

trial, for it was only the head porter dressed in his crimson robe, and carrying his cap at arm's length before him, who, followed by the Provost, issued forth: the students removed their caps, and stood in respectful silence as he passed. Again the door was closed, and all was still.

"There is something in all this that stimulates curiosity strongly," said Kate. "When I came in here I could have waited patiently for an hour or two, but now, the sight of all these anxious faces, these prying looks, that seem eager to pierce the very door itself, those short sentences, broken by quick glances at the clock, have worked me up to an excitement high and fevered as their own."

"It wants but a minute now," said Fred.

"I think the hand has not moved for the last ten," said Sybella, smiling faintly.

"I hope he has gained the prize," muttered Kate, below her breath; and at the moment the bell tolled, and the wide doors, as if burst open by the sound, were flung wide, and the human tide poured forth, and mingled with that beneath; but what a different aspect did it present. The faces were mostly flushed and heated, the eyes flashing, the dress disordered, the cravats awry, the hair tangled—all the signs of mental excitement, long and arduously sustained, were there, and save a few, whose careless look and unmoved expression showed that their part had no high ambition at stake, all were impressed with the same character of mingled eagerness and exhaustion.

Many among these were quickly singled out and surrounded by troops of eager and anxious friends, and the passing stranger might easily read in the tone and accent of the speaker his fortune, whether good or evil.

"Where is Herbert?—where can he be?—I don't see him," said each of the Travers's party, as, mingling with the crowd, they cast their anxious looks on every side; but amid the bustle of the scene, the hurrying forms, and the babble of tongues, they felt bewildered and confused.

"Let us try at his chambers," said Frederick; "he will, in all likelihood, be there soon;" and at once they turned their steps towards the corner of the old square near the library, where Herbert lived his solitary life; for although nominally linked with a companion—a chum, in college parlance—he rarely made his appearance within the walls, and then only for a few days at a time.

When they reached the door they found it open, and without further waiting, or any notice of their approach, they entered, but so noiselessly and quietly withal, that the deep accents of grief—the heavy sound of broken sobs—struck at once upon their ears. They stopped and gazed in silence at each other, reading, as it were, their own heartfelt fears in the face of each.

"Poor fellow," said Kate, as her proud lip trembled with agitation; "this is a sad beginning."

"Let us go back," whispered Sybella, faintly, and her cheek was pale as death as she spoke.

"No, no," cried Frederick, hurriedly; "we must cheer him up. What signifies the whole affair—a piece of mere boyish ambition, that he'll only laugh at one of these days."

"Not so," said Kate; "the augury of success or failure in the outset of life is no such trifle as you deem it. If he be faint-hearted, the game is up with him for ever—if he be made of sterner stuff, as one of his name and house ought to be, he'll revenge his present fall by a great hereafter. Let me see him;" and, at once disengaging her arm, she walked forward and entered the chamber, while Frederick and his sister retired to the court to await her return.

When Kate O'Donoghue entered the room, Herbert was seated before a table, on which his head was leaning, with his hands pressed against his face. At his feet lay his cap, and the books he carried with him from the Hall. Unconscious of her presence, lost to everything save his overwhelming affliction, the sobs came with a convulsive shudder that shook his frame and made the very table rattle, while at intervals there broke from him a faint moan of heartrending sorrow.

"My dear brother," said Kate, placing her arm around his neck. The boy started and looked up, and prepared as she was to see the traces of suffering there, she started at the ravages long days and nights of study and deep grief had left behind them: his eyes were sunk, and surrounded by dark circles, that made them seem quite buried beneath his brows; his forehead, traversed by a network of blue veins, had that transparent thinness mental labour impresses, and his lips were thin and colourless; while on each cheek a burning spot of red looked like the mark of hectic. He made no answer, but the tears ran fast from his eyes, and his mouth quivered as he tried to say something.

She sat down beside him on the same chair, and bending her head till the silken curls touched his very cheek, she spoke to him—not in words of encouragement or good cheer, for such her own instinct told her were inapplicable, but in the soft accents of affection, neither undervaluing the source of his grief, nor yet suffering him to be carried away by his own sense of his calamity. "Remember, my dear brother," said she, "you are not less dear to our hearts for all this—remember that for the casualties of the world, and its chances, we can only do our utmost—that success is not for us to determine, but to strive for. Had you won to-day, some other must now have grieved like you, and who can tell if he could count as many fond and loving hearts to feel for and console him?"

"Oh, if you knew how I strived and longed—how I prayed for success," said he, in a voice almost stifled by convulsive throbs.

"And it will come yet, Herbert. The tree is only the more fruitful when the knife has cut down to its very heart. Yours is not the nature to be deterred by one repulse, nor yours the name to be stamped with failure because the contest is difficult. Ambitions are only noble when their path is steep. Who knows how indolent you might have become had you found the prize too easily won. Come, come, Herbert—enough for the past : look forward now, and with good courage and hope. The next struggle will end differently ; but, above all, wear a fair face before the world. I remember some French prisoners being brought into Courtray, who amused us so much by their gay and smiling air, and look of ease and satisfaction : their secret was, that defeat was never disgrace, save when it lowered the spirit and made the heart droop. Theirs never failed, and I promise you we thought all the better of them."

"But my uncle—who is to tell him——"

"Let me tell him. I see you have begun a letter already——"

"That was written last night," said the boy, as the tears gushed forth afresh—"last night, when hope was almost certainty."

"Then I'll finish it," said Kate, taking up the half-written letter.

"Say to him—I would wish him to know all—say that I had beaten my opponents down to one, and that he, too, almost gave up the contest, when, somehow—I cannot now say exactly how or wherefore—I got into a dispute with the examiner about the meaning of a word in Terence. He seemed to enjoy the eagerness with which I defended my opinion for a time, and actually encouraged my persistance, until at length, my temper excited and my brain on fire, I said something—I know not what ; but it was evidently an offence, for he closed the book, and merely replied, ' Enough, sir ; I give your opponent the premium. His temper more than compensates for any deficiency in his scholarship ;' and I was beaten." The last words evoked all his sorrow once more, and the youth burst into tears.

"That, then, I call unfair," said Kate, passionately, "unless the gentleman were the arbiter of temperament as well as talent. Come, Herbert, even this should reconcile you to your fortune ; you have not failed unworthily."

"But my uncle, Kate—my uncle will deem it far otherwise. To guard against this very error of my temper was almost the last pledge I made him ; and here, in my first trial, see how I have kept my promise."

"Leave the explanation to me ; only promise one thing—and mind, Herbert, this is a pledge there must be no forgetting—do all in your power— spare nothing to win the next time. I care not whether you ever earry away another prize within these walls ; but one you must have. Is this agreed?—give me your hand upon it. There, that's like your own self, and now don't waste another thought on what's bygone. The Traverses invited you to dine with them to-day."

" Oh, no—no."

" No, I have not any intention to press you, only come soon to see us— to see *me*." She kissed his forehead tenderly as she spoke the last word, and glided rapidly from the room.

CHAPTER XXIX.

FIRST IMPRESSIONS.

KATE O'DONOGHUE was more deeply affected by Herbert's failure than she had let appear to the youth, or even confessed to herself. It was not that the character of his ambition enlisted her sympathies or engaged her interest. Far from it: she thought too meanly of such triumphs, and knew not how far they shed an influence on a future career. The habits of her education—all her early prejudices—disposed her to regard the life of a soldier as the only one becoming a gentleman. The passion for military glory which the great victories of the Republic and the Consulate had spread throughout Europe, penetrated into every remote village of the Continent; and even the prison-like walls of the convent did not keep out the spirit-stirring sounds of drum and trumpet, the tramp of marching hosts, and the proud clangor of war. It was a time when the soldier was everything. There was but one path in life by which to win honour, rank, fame, and fortune. Even the humblest might strive, for the race was open to all; or, in the phrase of the period, every conscript left a spare corner in his knapsack for his future *bâton de maréchal*.

All she had ever seen of foreign society partook of this character; for, strangely enough, on the ruin of an aristocracy a new and splendid chivalry was founded—a chivalry whose fascinations covered many a wrong, and made many a bad cause glorious by the heroism it evoked! The peaceful path in life was then, in her estimate, the inglorious one. Still, her proud nature could not brook defeat in anything. It was not without its influence upon the hearts and minds of her house that the eagle figured as their crest. The soaring bird, with outstretched wing, careering high above his compeers, told of a race who once, at least, thought no ambition above their daring; and she was worthy of the haughtiest of her ancestors.

Too proud to enter into any detail of Herbert's failure, she dismissed the subject as briefly as she could, and made her appearance in the drawing-room without any perceptible change of manner; nor did she appear to take any

notice of the announcement made by Sir Marmaduke to his son, that Hemsworth, who had just arrived from Scotland, would join the family circle at
dinner.   Kate had never seen him, but his name was long associated in her
mind with anecdotes of oppression and cruelty to her uncle—of petty insults
and annoyances which the letters from Carrignacurra used constantly to tell
of, and of which her relatives abroad had often descanted in her hearing.
The picture she had drawn of him in her own mind was not a flattering one
—composed of features and ingredients which represented all that was base,
low-minded, and treacherous—a vulgar sycophant, and a merciless tyrant.
What was her astonishment, almost her chagrin, to discover that Hemsworth entered the room a gentleman-like person, of about five-and-forty, tall,
and well-formed, with regular features, rather melancholy in their expression
than otherwise, with a voice singularly low, soft, and pleasing, his manner a
mixture of well-bred ease, and that excessive deference so often seen in
those who have passed a long portion of life about persons of rank superior
to their own, but without the slightest trace, that she could discover, of anything subservient.   With all her disposition to be critical, she could find
little fault with either his manner or his conversation, nor could she detect
any appearance of affectation.   On the contrary, he seemed affable, like one
who felt himself among friends, and need set no limits to his natural frankness.   On the several topics he talked he spoke with good sense and fair-
ness; and even when the often agitated question of the state of Ireland was
alluded to, he surprised Kate by the absence of any violent or exaggerated
tone, speaking of the people in terms of kindliness and even affection—
lauding the native virtues of their character, and dwelling with pleasure on
the traits which advantageously distinguish them from the peasantry of
other lands.

    She listened at first with suspicion and distrust, then, by degrees, with
interested attention, and, at last, with actual delight, to the narrative he
gave of the social condition of Ireland; in which he laboured to show that
a mistaken estimate of the people by England—a misconception of the
national character, a contempt of it, perhaps—had perpetuated usages
which, by their injustice, had excited the hatred and animosity of the country, and led to that condition of insulting depreciation on one side, and
proud defiance on the other, which the two people exhibited towards each
other.

    So well and ably did he sustain his part—so powerfully support each po-
sition by reference to some fact with which his ample memory supplied him
—that Sir Marmaduke was eventually obliged to confess himself vanquished,
though unconvinced—who ever was when worsted?—and Frederick, chagrined at the favour Kate bestowed on the speaker, merely remarked, as he
concluded,

    "Very conclusive and satisfactory, I have no doubt it is; but, in my mind, all you have said goes to prove that we English are a very inferior nation, and very unworthily placed in rule and governance over a people so much our superiors."

Kate's eyes flashed with an unwonted fire, and for an instant she felt almost unable to control the temptation to answer this taunt; but a quiet smile of half acquiescence on Hemsworth's face so adequately expressed what she wished, but dared not say, that she merely returned the smile, and was silent.

Had Hemsworth's whole object been on that evening to disabuse Kate O'Donoghue of her dislike to him—to obliterate all memory of the wrongs with which she had heard him charged towards her family—he could not have chosen a more successful path. There was the very degree of firmness and decision she admired in the manner he gave his opinions, and yet all the courtesy of one who would not be supposed capable of advancing them as incontrovertible or irrefutable. They were merely his sentiments—his mode of seeing and estimating particular events, of which another might judge differently. For all he advanced he was ready to show his reasons—they might be shallow, they might be inconclusive—but they were *his*, and, fortunately for his chance of winning her favour, they were *her* opinions also.

" So you think we shall have no outbreak, Hemsworth," said Sir Marmaduke, as they sat at tea.

"I scarcely go so far," said he, gravely. " There are too many reasons for an opposite fear, to say so much, even if the Secretary of State did not assure us that the danger is over. The youth of Ireland will always be dangerous when left without a career or a road to their ambition; and from them any peril that may now be apprehended will certainly come. Many young men of the best families of the country, whose estates are deeply encumbered—heavy mortgages and large dowries weighing them down—are ready to join in any bold attempt which promises a new order of things. They see themselves forgotten in the distribution of all patronage—excluded from every office—sometimes for reasons of religion—sometimes for family, even for a mere namesake. They are ready to play a bold game, where losing is only quicker ruin, and to gain would be a glorious victory."

" But what could a few rash and desperate young men like these effect against a power so great and so consolidated as England ?"

"Little, perhaps, as regards the overthrow of a government ; but a world of injury to the prospect of future quiet. The rebellion of a week—ay, a day—in Ireland, will sow the seeds of fifty years of misery, and retard the settlement of peaceful relations at least another century. Had the minister made the same concessions here he was glad to accord to Scotland—had he, without insulting a nationality, converted it into a banner under which loyalty was only rendered more conspicuous—you might have, perchance, seen a different order of things in Ireland."

"For the life of me, I cannot see the evils and wrongs these people labour under. I have a very large Irish acquaintance in London, and pleasanter, happier fellows cannot exist than they are."

"All the young men of family in Ireland are not in the Guards," said Hemsworth, with a smile, which, with all its blandishment, very thinly covered over the sarcasm of his remark.

Frederick's face flushed angrily, and he turned away without speaking.

"Should we not ask pardon of the ladies for this subject of our conversation?" said Hemsworth. "I am sure neither Miss Travers nor Miss O'Donoghue deem the topic interesting or amusing."

"On the contrary, sir, I believe I may reply for both of us," said Kate, "whatever concerns the fortunes of a country we have so near at heart has all our sympathy; and, as an Irish girl, I feel grateful for your explanation of motives which, while I appreciate, I should still be unable so satisfactorily to account for."

"How happy I am to meet my countrywoman's approval," said Hemsworth, bowing courteously, and with a marked emphasis directing his speech to Kate.

The manner in which he spoke the words was so palpably intended for herself, that she felt all the charm of a flattery to which the disparity of their years imparted force.

Soon after tea, Sir Marmaduke retired with Hemsworth to his study. Frederick took his leave at the same time, and Sybella and Kate were left alone together.

"I have a long letter to write this evening, my dear Sybella," said Kate, after they had talked some time. "Poor Herbert has failed in his examination, and I have promised to break the news to my uncle; not so difficult a task as the poor boy deems, but one to which he is himself unequal."

"Does he then feel it so deeply?" said Sybella, timidly.

"Too much, as regards the object of the ambition; but no more than he ought as a defeat. It is so bad to be beaten, Sybella," said she, with a sharp distinctness on each word. "I shall hate the sight of that University until he carries off the next prize; and then—then I care not whether his taste incline him for another effort;" and so saying, she embraced her friend, and they parted for the night.

The epistle which Kate had promised to conclude was in itself a lengthy one—written at different intervals during the week before the examination, and containing a minute account of his progress, his hopes and his fears, up to that very moment. There was little in it which could interest any but him to whom it was addressed, and to whom every allusion was familiar, and the reference to each book and subject thoroughly known—what difficulties he had found here, what obscurity there—how well he had mastered this, how much he feared he might have mistaken the other—until on the evening of the first day's examination, when the following few lines, written with a trembling hand, appeared:

"They say I shall gain it. H—— called my translation of Horace a brilliant one, and asked the Vice-Provost to listen to my repeating it. I heard I gave it in blank verse. Oh, my dearest uncle, am I deceiving myself, and deceiving you? Shall I be able to write thus to-morrow night?"

Then came one tremulous line, dated "Twelve o'clock:"

"Better and better—I might almost even now say, victory; but my heart is too much excited to endure a chance."

"And it remains for me, my dear uncle," wrote Kate, after these words, "to fulfil the ungrateful task of bearing bad tidings; and I, who have never had the good fortune to bring you happiness, must now speak to you of misfortune.—My dear cousin has failed."

She followed these few lines by a brief narrative Herbert had given her—neither seeking to extenuate his errors, nor excuse his rashness—well knowing in her heart that Sir Archy would regard the lesson thus conveyed an ample recompense for the honour of a victory so hardly lost.

"It is to you he looks for comfort—to you, sir, whom his efforts were all made to please, and for whose praise his weary nights and toilsome days were offered. You, who know more of the human heart than I do, can tell how far so severe a discouragement may work for good or evil on his future life; for myself, I feel the even current of prosperity is but a sluggish stream, that calls for no efforts to stem its tide; and, were his grief over, I'd rather rejoice that he has found a conflict, because he may now discover he has courage to meet it.

"Even I, to follow a theme so dispiriting—even I grow weary of pleasure, and tired of gaiety. The busy world of enjoyment leaves not a moment free for happiness, and already I am longing to be back in the still valley of Glenflesk. It is not that Dublin is not very brilliant, or that society has less of agreeability than I expected—both have exceeded my anticipations; nor is it that I have not been what we should call in France 'successful' in my 'début'—far from that, I am the fashion, or rather half the fashion, Sybella dividing public favour with me; but, somehow, nobody contradicts me here—no one has courage to tell me I'm wrong—no one will venture to say, what you have often said, and even oftener looked, that 'I talked of what I knew nothing;' and, in fact, my dear uncle, every one is so very much in love with me, that I am beginning to detest them, and would give the world to be once more at home before I extend the hatred to myself, which I must inevitably end by doing, if nobody anticipates me in the sentiment.

"You told me I should prove faithless to you. Well, I have refused Heaven knows how many 'brilliant offers,' for such even the proposers called them. Generals of fourscore, guardsmen of twenty, dignitaries in the church, serjeants learned in the law, country gentlemen in hordes, two baronets, and one luckless viscount, have asked for the valueless hand that writes these lines; and yet—and yet, my dear chevalier, I shall still write myself at the bottom of this page, 'Kate O'Donoghue.' I have no doubt you are very vain of my constancy, and will be so when you read this; and it is right you should be, for I promise you, in my *robe, coleur de cerise*, looped with white roses, and my *chapeau de paysane*, I am a very pretty person indeed—at least, it seems a point the twelve judges agree upon, and the Master of the Rolls tells me, 'that with such long eyelashes I might lift my eyes very high indeed.'

"And now, my dear, kind uncle, divide your sorrow between your niece who is dying of vanity, and your nephew who is sick of grief—continue your affection to both—and believe me, in all sincerity of heart, your own fond and faithful

"KATE O'DONOGHUE.

"I have met Hemsworth, and, strange to say, found him both pleasant and agreeable."

Such were the concluding lines of an epistle, in which few who did not possess Sir Archy's acuteness could successfully trace anything of the real character of the writer.

CHAPTER XXX.

OLD CHARACTERS WITH NEW FACES.

AT the time we speak of, Clontarf was the fashionable watering-place of the inhabitants of Dublin; and, although it boasted of little other accommodation than a number of small thatched cabins could afford, and from which the fishermen removed to give place to their more opulent guests, yet thither the great and the wealthy of the capital resorted in summer to taste the pleasures of a sea-side, and that not inferior one, the change of life and habit entailed by altered circumstances and more restricted spheres of enjoyment.

If, with all the aid of sunshine and blue water, waving foliage and golden beach, this place had an aspect of modest poverty in its whitened walls and net-covered gardens in summer, in winter its dreariness and desolation were great indeed. The sea swept in long waves the narrow road, even to the doors of the cabins, the muddy foam settling on the window-sills, and even drifting to the very roofs; the thatch was fastened down with strong ropes, assisted by oars and spars, to resist the wild gale that generally blew from the south-east. The trim cottages of summer were now nothing but the miserable hovels of the poor—their gardens waste, their gay aspect departed, even the stirring signs of life seemed vanished. Few, if any, of the inhabitants stirred abroad, and, save some muffled figure that moved past, screening his face from the beating storm, all was silent and motionless. The little inn, which in the summer-time was thronged from morning till night, and from whose open windows the merry laugh and the jocund sound of happy voices poured, was now fast shuttered up, and all the precautions of a voyage were taken against the dreaded winter; even to the sign of a gigantic crab, rudely carved in wood and painted red, everything was removed, and a single melancholy dip-candle burned in the bar, as if keeping watch over the sleeping revelry of the place.

If such were the gloomy features without, within doors matters wore a more thriving aspect. In a little parlour behind the bar a brisk fire was burning, before which stood a table neatly prepared for supper; the covers were laid for two, but the provision of wine displayed seemed suited to a larger number. The flashy-looking prints upon the walls shone brightly in the ruddy blaze; the brass fender and the glasses sparkled in its clear light, and even to the small, keen eyes of Billy Corcoran, the host, who kept eternally running in and out, to see all right, everything presented a very cheering contrast to the bleak desolation of the night without.

It was evident that Mr. Corcoran's guests were behind time; his impatience was not to be mistaken. He walked from the kitchen to the parlour and back again without ceasing, now adding a turf to the fire, now removing the roasting chickens a little farther from the blaze, and anon bending his ear to listen if perchance he could catch the sound of approaching wheels. He had sat down on every chair of the parlour, he had taken a half-glass out of each decanter on the table, he had sharpened every knife in turn, and in fact resorted to every device to cheat time, when suddenly the sound of a carriage was heard on the road, and the next moment he unbarred the door and admitted two persons, whose dripping hats and soaked great-coats bore evidence to the downpour without.

"Well, Billy," said the first who entered, "this rain will beat down the wind at last, and we shall be able to get some fish in the market."

"Sorra bit, sir," said Billy, as he assisted the speaker to remove his wet garments, leaving the other stranger to his own devices. "The wind is coming more round to the east, and I know from the noise on the Bull we'll have plenty of it. I was afeard something happened you, sir; you're an hour behind the time you said yourself."

"Very true—so I am. I was detained at a dinner party, and my friend here also kept me waiting a few minutes for him."

"It was not my fault," interposed the other; "I was ready wheu——"

"Never mind—it was of no consequence whatever; the only misfortune was, we could find no coach, and were forced to put up with a car, and got wet for our pains. But the supper, Bill—the supper."

"Is smoking hot on the table," was the reply; and, as he opened the door into the parlour, the fact declared itself to their senses.

The strangers were soon seated at the meal, aud like men who could relish its enjoyment not the less for the merit of what they had quitted without doors. It is not necessary to consume much time in presenting them to our readers; they are both already known to him. One was Mr. Hemsworth; the other no less a person than Lanty Lawler, the horse-dealer. One only remark is necessary. Familiar as these characters already are, they here appeared in aspect somewhat different from what they have hitherto exhibited. Hemsworth, no longer the associate of fashionable company, had exchanged his silken deferential manner for an air of easy confidence that seemed to fit him even better; Lanty, on the other hand, had lost all his habitual self-possession, looked abashed and sheepish, and seemed for all the world as though he were in the hands of one who could dispose of his destiny as he willed it. All the got-up readiness of his wit, all his acquired frankness, were now gone, and in their place a timid, hesitating manner that bespoke the most abject fear aud terror; it was evident, too, that he struggled hard to conceal these signs of trepidation. He ate voraciously of all before him, and endeavoured, by the preoccupation of the table, to cover his real sentiments at the moment; he drank, too, freely, filling a large goblet to the brim with sherry several times during the meal; nor was this unnoticed by Hemsworth, who at last interposed, in a calm but commanding tone, as he laid his hand on the decanter:

"A pipe of it, if you please, Lanty; you may have a whole bank of the Guadalquiver for your own drinking at another time; but now, if you please, let us have calm heads and cool judgments. It is some time since we met, and it may be longer cre we have another opportunity like the present."

"Very true, sir," said Lanty, submissively, as he pushed his untasted glass before him. "It was the wetting I was afeard of; my clothes were soaked through."

Hemsworth paid no attention to the excuse, but sat for some minutes deeply sunk in his reflections; then lifting his head suddenly, he said,

"And so these papers have never been found?"

"Never, sir. I did my best to get them. I spent days at the place, and had others looking besides. I said I'd give five guineas—aud you know what a reward that is down there—to the man who would bring them to me; but from that hour to this I uever set eyes ou them."

While he was speaking these words, Hemsworth's eyes never turned from him. They were fixed on him, not with any expression of severity or harshness, neither did the glance indicate suspicion. It was a steady, passionless stare, rather like one seeking an explanation than prejudging a motive.

"You were quite certain that they were the papers we wanted?"

"Sure I opened them—sure I read the writing myself when I took them out of the old man's desk."

"They had better have remained there," said Hemsworth to himself, but loud enough for the other to hear; then, rallying quickly, he added, "no matter, however; we have evidence enough of another kind. There are the letters Mark wrote to the Delegates."

"I think Mr. Morrissy has most of them, sir," said Lanty, hesitating; "he is the man that keeps all the writings."

"So he may be, Lanty; but you have some of them yourself: three or four are as good as thirty or forty, and you may have as many as that—ay, and here in your pocket, too, this minute. Come, my worthy friend, you may cheat me in horseflesh whenever I'm fool enough to deal with you, but at this game I'm your master. Let me see these letters."

"How would I have them, captain, at all?" said Lanty, imploringly; "sure you know as well as me that I'm not in the scheme at all."

"Save so far as having a contract to mount five hundred men of the French on their landing in Ireland, the money for which you have partly received, and for which I hold the cheque, countersigned by yourself, Master Lanty. Very pretty evidence in a court of justice—more than enough to hang you, that's all."

"There's many a one sould a horse, and didn't know what use he was for," replied Lanty, half rudely.

"Very true; but a contract that stipulates for strong cattle, able to carry twelve-stone men with full cavalry equipments, does not read like an engagement to furnish plough-horses." Then altering his tone, he added, "No more of this, sir; I can't afford time for such fencing. Show me these letters—show me that you have done something to earn your own indemnity, or by G—d I'll let them hang you as I'd see them hang a dog."

Lanty became lividly pale as Hemsworth was speaking; a slight convulsive tremor shook his lip for a moment, and he seemed struggling to repress a burst of passion, as he held the chair with either hand; but he uttered not a word. Hemsworth leisurely drew forth his watch, and placed it on the table before him, saying,

"It wants eleven minutes of one o'clock; I'll give you to that hour to make up your mind, whether you prefer five hundred pounds in your hand, or take your place in the dock with the rest of them; for, mark me, whether we have your evidence or not, they are equally in our hands. It is only an economy of testimony I'm studying here, and I reserve my other blackguards for occasions of more moment."

The taunt would appear an ill-timed one at such a minute; but Hemsworth knew well the temperament of him he addressed, and did not utter a syllable at random. Lanty still preserved silence, and looked as though doggedly determined to let the minutes elapse without speaking; his head slightly sunk on his chest, his eyes bent downwards, he sat perfectly motionless. Hemsworth meanwhile refilled his glass, crossed his arms before him, and seemed awaiting, without impatience, the result of the other's deliberation. At length the hand approached the figure; it wanted but about half a minute of the time, and Hemsworth, taking up the watch from the table, held it before Lanty's eyes, as he said,

" Time is nearly up, Master Lawler; do you refuse?"

" I only ask one condition," said Lanty, in a faint whisper.

" You shall make no bargains: the letters, or ——. It is too late now;" and with these words he replaced his watch in his pocket, and rose from the table.

Lanty never moved a muscle, while Hemsworth approached the fireplace, and rang the bell. In doing so, he turned his back to the horse-dealer, but commanded a view of him through means of the little glass above the chimney. He stood thus for a few seconds, when Lanty—in whose flashing eyes and darkened colour inward rage was depicted—suddenly thrust his arm into the breast of his coat. Hemsworth turned round at once, and seizing the arm in his powerful grasp, said in a cool, determined voice,

" No, no, Lanty; I'm armed too."

" It was the pocket-book I was feeling for, sir," said Lanty, with a sickly effort at a smile, while he drew forth a black leather case, and handed it towards Hemsworth. "They are all there—seventeen letters—besides two French commissions signed by young Mark, and a receipt for four hundred pounds in French gold."

" You must find it hard to get bullets for those pistols I gave you, Lanty," said Hemsworth, in a tranquil voice. "I forgot to let you have the bullet-mould with them. Remind me of it to-morrow or next day."

Lanty muttered a faint "I will," but looked the very picture of abject misery as he spoke.

" Let me see them, Lanty," said Hemsworth, in a manner as calm and unconcerned as could be. "If I don't mistake, they are nearly a quarter of an inch in the bore."

" About that same, sir," replied Lawler, while he drew forth the two pistols from the same breast-pocket he had taken the letters.

Hemsworth first examined one, and then the other, leisurely, passing the ramrod into each in turn, and then opening the pans, inspected the priming, adjusting the powder carefully with his finger. "You spoil such pistols as these by loading with two bullets, Lanty," said he, as he handed them back to him. "The bore is too perfect for such coarse usage. Now, this is a less delicate weapon, and will bear harder usage," and he drew forth a short pistol, containing four revolving barrels, each as wide as the bore of a musket. Lanty gazed in astonishment and terror at the murderous implement, into which the hand fitted by a handle like that of a saw. Hemsworth played the spring by which the barrels moved with a practised finger, and seemed to exult in the expression of Lanty's terror as he watched them. Then quickly replacing the weapon, he resumed: "Well, I am glad, for your own sake, that you are more reasonable. You ought to know that I never place dependence on only one man for any single service. Such would be merely to play the part of slave instead of master. But, first of all, how did you become possessed of these letters?"

"I was charged by Mark to deliver them to the Delegates, and as they never saw his handwriting, I just copied the letters, and kept all the originals, so that he has received his answers regularly, and never suspects what has happened."

"All right so far. And the younger brother—what of him?"

"Oh, he is too much under old M'Nab's influence to be caught. I wouldn't say but that he's a Protestant this minute."

"You appear to be greatly shocked at your suspicion, Lanty," said Hemsworth, smiling. "Well, well; we must hope for the best. And now as to this other fellow—where and how can I see him—this Talbot, I mean?"

"Ay, that's the puzzle," replied Lanty, with a greater appearance of ease in his manner than before. "You never can meet him when you look for him; but he's at your elbow every day twenty times if you don't want him."

"Could you not manage a meeting for me with him down here, Lanty?—I'll take care of the rest."

"I don't think so; he's a wary fellow; he gave me a fright once or twice already, by a word he let drop. I am not easy in his company at all."

"False or true, he would be an immense service to us," said Hemsworth, musingly. "If I only could see and speak with him, I'd soon convince him that he incurred no risk himself. It's a bad sportsman shoots his decoy duck, Lanty," and he pinched his cheek good-humouredly as he spoke. Lanty endeavoured to laugh, but the effort was a feeble one. Meanwhile, the host, now summoned for the second time, made his appearance, and by Hemsworth's orders the car was brought round to the door; for, severe as the night was, he determined to return to the city.

"You are coming back to town, too, Lanty?" said he, in a tone of inquiry.

"No, sir; I'm going to stop here with Billy, if your honour has no objection."

"None whatever. Remember to let me see you on Tuesday, when I shall have everything in readiness for your journey south—till then, good-by." So saying, and handing Corcoran two guineas in gold, for he paid liberally, Hemsworth mounted the car and drove off.

Lanty looked after him till the darkness shut out the view, and then, buttoning his rough coat tightly around his throat, set out himself towards town, muttering, as he went, "I wish it was the last I was ever to see of you."

CHAPTER XXXI.

SOME HINTS ABOUT HARRY TALBOT.

We must beg of our reader to retrace his steps once more to the valley of Glenflesk, but only for a fleeting moment. When last we left Carrigna-curra it was at night, the party were at supper in the old tower, and Kerry stood outside, rehearsing to himself for the tenth time the manner in which he should open his communication. The sound of Mark's voice, raised above its ordinary pitch, warned him that his mission might not be without danger, if perchance anything on his part might offend the youth. None knew better than Kerry the violent temper of the young O'Donoghue, and how little restraint he ever put upon any scheme he thought of to vent his humour on him who crossed him. It was an account of debtor and creditor then with him how he should act; on the one side lay the penalties, on the other the rewards of his venture—how was he to escape the one and secure the other? A moment's reflection suggested the plan.

"I'll not go in, divil a step, but I'll tell I was convarsin' with them this half hour, and that the rope and the bit of lead is a new way they do have for catching mermaids and other faymale fishes in the bay; and sure if I only say that there's an act of Parliment agin doin' it, she'll not only believe it all, but 'she'll keep the sayeret to her dying bed." And with this profound reflection on Mrs. Branaghan's character, and a face of very well got up surprise, Kerry re-entered the kitchen to announce his discovery.

It is not our intention to dwell on the scene that followed; we have merely adverted to the fact, inasmuch as that on the trivial circumstances of Kerry's resolve depended the discovery of a plot which, if once known to M'Nab, would immediately have been communicated to the Government. The fates willed it otherwise; and when the party separated in the old tower, Sir Archy was as little satisfied concerning Talbot's character as ever, and as eager to ascertain whence and wherefore he came, and with what intention he had made Mark's acquaintance. With many a wily scheme for the morrow, the old man went to rest, determining to spare no pains to un-ravel the mystery; a fruitless resolve after all, for when day broke Talbot and Mark were already away, many miles on the road to Dublin.

The O'Donoghue's first act, on completing his arrangements with Swaby, was to place at Mark's disposal a sum of five hundred pounds, an amount far greater than ever the young man had at any time possessed in his life. Talbot, to whom the circumstance was told by Mark, readily persuaded him to visit Dublin, not merely for the pleasures and amusements of the capital, but that he might personally be made known to the Delegates, and see and confer with those who were the directors of the threatened rebellion. Talbot understood perfectly the kind of flattery which would succeed with the youth, and by allusion to his ancient lineage, his more than noble blood, the rights to which he was entitled, and to which he would unquestionably be restored, not only stimulated his ardour in the cause, but bound him in a debt of gratitude to all who encouraged him to engage in it.

Mark's character, whatever its faults, was candid and frank in every-thing. He made no secret to his new friend of his present unhappiness, nor did he conceal that an unpaid debt of vengeance with respect to young Travers weighed heavily on his spirits. It was the first time in his life he had tasted the bitterness of an insult, and it worked like a deadly poison within him, sapping the springs of his health, and rendering miserable the hours of his solitude. The thought rarely left him day or night—how was he to wipe out this stain? When Talbot, therefore, spoke of a visit to the capital, Mark cheerfully acceded, but rather from a secret hope that some opportunity might arise to gratify this cherished passion than from any de-sire of witnessing the splendour of the metropolis; and while the one pictured the glittering scenes of festive enjoyment to which youth and money are the passports, the other darkly ruminated on the chances of meeting his enemy and provoking him to a duel.

It was on the evening of the third day after they left Carrignacurra that they drew near the capital, and after a promise from Mark that in every-thing he should be guided by his friend, nor take any step without his counsel and advice, they both entered the city.

"You see, Mark," said Talbot, as, after passing through some of the wider and better-lighted thoroughfares, they approached a less frequented and more gloomy part of the town—"you see, Mark, that the day is not come when we should occupy the place of honour: an humble and quiet hotel will best suit us for the present; but the hour is not very distant, my boy, when the proudest mansion of the capital will throw wide its doors to receive us. The Saxon has but a short tenure of it now."

Q

"I don't see any reason for secrecy," said Mark, half doggedly; "we have good names, and a good purse, why then must we betake ourselves to this gloomy and desolate quarter?"

"Because I am the guide," said Talbot, laughing; "and if that's not reason enough, that's the only one I will give you just now. But come, here we are, and I do not think you will complain of your entertainment." And, as he spoke, the carriage entered the spacious court-yard of an old-fashioned inn, which, standing in Thomas-street, commanded a view of the river through one of the narrow streets leading down to the quay.

"This was the fashionable house, some fifty years back," said Talbot, as he assisted his friend to alight; "and though the heyday of its youth is over, there are many generous qualities in its good old age—not your father's cellar can boast a better bottle of Burgundy."

Talbot's recommendation was far from being unmerited. The "Black Jack," as the inn was named, was a most comfortable house of the old school, with large, low-ceilinged rooms, wide stairs, and spacious corridors; the whole furnished in a style which, though far from pretending to elegance or fashion, possessed strong claims for the tired traveller seeking rest and repose. Here, then, our young travellers alighted; Talbot being received with all the courteous urbanity due to an old acquaintance; the landlord himself appearing to do the honours of the house, and welcome a valued guest.

"We must get our host, Billy Crossley, to sup with us, Mark. No one can tell us so much of how matters are doing here; for, however it happens, Billy knows all the gossip of the day—fashionable, political, or sporting, he keeps himself up to what is going forward everywhere." And so saying, Talbot at once hastened after the landlord to secure his company for the evening.

Billy was somewhat fastidious about bestowing his agreeability in general, but on the present occasion he acceded at once, and in less than half an hour the three were seated at a meal which would not have disgraced an hotel of more pretentious exterior; Mr. Crossley doing the honours of the table, like a host entertaining his friends.

"I scarcely had expected to see you so soon, Mr. Talbot," said he, when the servants had left the room, and the party drew round the fire. "They told me you would pass the winter in the country."

"So I had intended, Billy; but as good luck would have it, I made an acquaintance in the south, which changed my plans, my friend, Mr. O'Donoghue here; and as he had never seen the capital, and knew nothing of your gay doings, I thought I'd just take a run back, and show him at least the map of the land."

"My service to you, sir," said Billy, bowing to Mark; "it would be hard to have got a better guide than you have in Master Harry. I can assure you, so far as wickedness goes, he's a match for anything here—from the Royal Barracks to Trinity College."

"Flattery, gross flattery, Bill. I was your own pupil, and you can't help partiality."

"You are a most favourable specimen of private tuition, there's no doubt of it," said Crossley, laughing; "and I have reason to be proud of you. Did Mr. O'Donoghue ever hear of your clearing out Hancey Hennessy at hazard—the fellow that carried the loaded dice?"

"Have done, Bill. None of these absurd stories now."

"Nor what a trick you played Corny Mehan at the spring meeting with the roan cob that knew how to limp when you wanted him?—as great a devil as himself, Mr. O'Donoghue. You'd swear the beast had a bad blood spavin if you saw him move, and he all the time a three-quarter bred horse, without a stain or a blemish about him."

Talbot seemed for a second or two somewhat uneasy at these familiar reminiscences of his friend Crossley, not knowing precisely how Mark might take them; but when he saw that a hearty laugh was the reception they met with, he joined in the mirth as freely as the others.

"The best of all was the Wicklow steeple-chase; sorrow doubt about it, that was good fun;" and Crossley laughed till his eyes streamed again with the emotion.

"You must tell me that," said Mark.

"It was just this:—Mister Henry there had a wager with Captain Steevens, of the staff, that he'd reach the course before him, each starting at the same moment from Quin's door at Bray. Well, what does he do but bribes one of the boys to let him ride postilion to Steevens's chaise, because that way he was sure to win his wager. All went right. The blue jacket and boots fitted him neatly—they were both new—got on purpose for the day; and Mr. Talbot lay snug in the stable, waiting for the chaise to be ordered round, when down comes the word, 'Number four, two bays, you're wanted;' and up he jumps into the saddle, and trots round to the door, afraid of his life to look round, and keeping his chin sunk down in his cravat to hide his face. He never once looked back, but let the boys harness the cattle without saying a word.

"'My lord says you're to drive slow,' said one of the boys.

"He looked round, and what did he see but an old man in the chaise with a horseshoe wig, and in the full dress of a bishop.

"'Who is he at all?' said Talbot.

"'The Bishop of Cloyne,' whispered the boy; 'he's going up to the levee.'

"'By my conscience he is not,' said Talbot, for at that moment he spied

Q 2

Steevens starting from the door at a round trot, and with that he turned the bishop's horses sharp round, laid the whip heavily over them, and took the lead towards Wicklow.

" Never such cries were heard as the bishop's. Some say that he swore hard; but it isn't true—he prayed, and begged, and shouted—but no use. Talbot gave them the steel at every stride; and after a long slapping gallop, he drew up at the stand-house, with a cheer that shook the course; and a fine sight it was to see the little man in the lawn sleeves stepping out, his face red with shame and passion.

" ' Twelve miles in forty-two minutes, my lord,' said Talbot, showing his watch; ' hope your lordship won't forget the boy.' "

If Mark O'Donoghue enjoyed heartily the story, he was not the less sur-prised that Harry Talbot was the hero of it—all his previous knowledge of that gentleman leading him to a very different estimate of his taste and pursuits. Indeed, he only knew Talbot from his own lips, and from them he learned to regard him as the emissary despatched by the Irish party in France to report on the condition of the insurgents in Ireland, and, if necessary, to make preparations for the French landing on the Irish shores. Mark could not well understand how any one charged with such a mission could have either wasted his time or endangered his safety by any ridiculous adventures, and did not scruple to show his astonishment at the circum-stance.

Talbot smiled significantly at the remark, and exchanged a glance with Crossley, while he answered,

" Placed in such a position as I have been for some years, Mark, many different parts have been forced upon me; and I have often found that there is no such safe mask against detection as following out the bent of one's humour in circumstances of difficulty. An irresistible impulse to play the fool, even at a moment when high interests were at stake, has saved me more than once from detection; and from habit I have acquired a kind of address at the practice, that with the world passes for cleverness. And so, in turn, I have been an actor, a smuggler, a French officer, an Irish refugee, a sporting character, a man of pleasure, and a man of intrigue; and however such features may have blended themselves into my true character, my real part has remained undetected. Master Crossley here might furnish a hint or two towards it; but—but, as Peachem says, ' we could hang one another' —eh, Bill ?"

A nod and a smile, more grave than gay, was Crossley's answer; and a silence ensued on all sides. There was a tone of seriousness, even through the levity of what Talbot said, very unlike his ordinary manner; and Mark began, for the first time, to feel that he knew very little about his friend. The silence continued unbroken for some time; for while Mark speculated on the various interpretations Talbot's words might bear, Talbot himself was reflecting on what he had just uttered. There is a very strange, but not wholly unaccountable tendency in men of subtle minds, to venture near cnough to disclosures to awaken the suspicions without satisfying the curiosity of others. The dexterity with which they can approach danger, yet not incur it, is an exercise they learn to pride themselves upon; and as the Indian guides his canoe through the dangerous rapids of the St. Lawrence—now bending to this side and to that—each moment in peril, but ever calm and collected—so do they feel all the excitement of hazard in the game of address. Under an impulse of this kind was it that Talbot spoke, and the unguarded freedom of his manner showed, even to so poor an observer as Mark, that the words contained a hidden meaning.

"And our gay city of Dublin—what of it, Billy?" said he, at length rallying from his mood of thought, as he nodded his head, and drank to Crossley.

"Pretty much as you have always known it. 'A short life and a merry one,' seems the adage in favour here. Every one spending his money and character——"

"Like gentlemen, Bill—that's the phrase," interrupted Talbot; "and a very comprehensive term it is, after all. But what is the Parliament doing?"

"Voting itself into Government situations."

"And the Viceroy?"

"Snubbing the Parliament."

"And the Government in England?"

"Snubbing the Viceroy."

"Well, they are all employed at least; and, as the French say, that's always something. And who are the play men now?"

"The old set. Tom Whaley and Lord Drogheda—your old friend Giles Daxon—Sandy Moore——"

"Ah, what of Sandy? They told me he won heavily at the October races."

"So he did—beggared the whole club at hazard, and was robbed of the money the night after, when coming up through Naas."

"Ha! I never heard of that, Billy. Let us hear all about it."

"It's soon told, sir. Sandy, who never tries economy till he has won largely, and is reckless enough of money when on the verge of ruin, heard, on leaving the course, that a strange gentleman was waiting to get some one to join him in a chaise up to Dublin. Sandy at once sent the waiter to open the negotiations, which were soon concluded, and the stranger appeared—a fat, unwieldly-looking old fellow, with a powdered wig and green goggles—not a very sporting style of travelling companion; but no matter for that, he had a dark chesnut mare with him, that looked like breeding, and with strength enough for any weight over a country.

" ' She'll follow the chaise—my son taught her that trick,' said the old fellow, as he hobbled out of the inn, and took his place in the carriage.

" Well, in jumped Sandy, all his pockets bursting with guineas, and a book of notes crammed into his hat, very happy at his adventure, but prouder of saving half the posting than all besides.

" ' Keep to your ten miles an hour, my lad, or not a sixpence,' said the old gentleman; and he drew his nightcap over his eyes, and was soon snoring away as sound as need be.

" That was the last was seen of him, however, for when the postilion drew up for fresh horses at Carriek's, they found Sandy alone in the chaise, with his hands tied behind him, and his mouth gagged. His companion and the dark chesnut were off, and all the winnings along with them. "

" Cleverly done, by Jove!" cried Talbot, in an ecstasy of admiration.

" What a contemptible fellow your friend Sandy must be," exclaimed Mark, in the same breath. " Man to man—I can't conceive the thing possible."

" A bold fellow, well armed, Mark," observed Talbot, gravely, " might do the deed, and Sandy be no coward after all."

Chatting in this wise the first evening was spent; and if Mark was, at times, disposed to doubt the morality of his new friend, he was very far from questioning his knowledge of mankind. His observations were ever shrewd and caustic, and his views of life those of one who looked at the world with a scrutinising glance; and although the young O'Donoghue would gladly have seen in his young companion some traces of the enthusiasm he himself experienced in the contemplated rising, he felt convinced that a cooler judgment, and a more calculating head than his, were indispensable requisites to a cause beset with so many dangers. He, therefore, implicitly yielded himself to Talbot's guidance, resolving not to go anywhere, nor see any one, even his brother, save with his knowledge and consent.

If the scenes into which Talbot introduced Mark O'Donoghue were not those of fashionable life, they were certainly as novel and exciting to one so young and inexperienced. The taverns resorted to by young men of fashion, the haunts of sporting characters, the tennis-court, but, more frequently still, the houses where high play was carried on, he was all familiar with— knew the precise type of company at each, and not a little of their private history; still it seemed as if he himself were but little known, and rather received for the recommendation of good address and engaging manners than from any circumstance of previous acquaintance. Mark was astonished at this, as well as that, although now several weeks in Dublin, Talbot had made no advance towards introducing him to the leading members of the insurgent party, and latterly had even but very rarely alluded to the prospect of the contemplated movement.

The young O'Donoghue was not one to harbour any secret thought long unuttered in his breast, and he briefly expressed to Talbot his surprise— almost his dissatisfaction—at the life they were leading. At first, Talbot endeavoured to laugh off such inquiries, or turn them aside by some passing pleasantry; but when more closely pressed, he avowed that his present part was a duty imposed upon him by his friends in France, who desired, above all things, to ascertain the feeling among young men of family and fortune in the metropolis how they really felt affected towards England, and with what success, should French republicanism fail to convert them, would the fascinations of Parisian elegance and vice be thrown around them.

"There must be bribes for all temperaments, Mark," said he, at the end of a very lengthened detail of his views and stratagems. "Glory is enough for such as you, and happily you can have wherewithal to satisfy a craving appetite; but some must be bought by gold, some by promises of vengeance upon others, some by indemnities for past offences, and not a few by the vague hope of change, which disappointed men ever regard as for the better. To sound the depths of all such motives is part of my mission here, and hence I have rigidly avoided those by whom I am more than slightly known; but, in a week or two, I shall exchange this part for another, and then, Mark, we shall mix in the gayer world of the squares, where your fair cousin shines so brilliantly. Meanwhile, have a little patience with me, and suffer me to seem sometimes inconsistent, that I may be least so in reality. I see you are not satisfied with me, Mark, and I am sorry to incur a friend's reproach, even for a brief season; but come—I make you a pledge. To-day is the 12th; in five days more the Viceroy gives his St. Patrick's ball, at which I am to meet one of our confederates. You seem surprised at this; but where can man speak treason so safely as under the canopy of the throne?"

"But how do you mean to go there? You do not surely expect an invitation?"

"Of course not; but I shall go, notwithstanding, and you with me. Ay, Mark, never frown and shake your head. This same ball is a public assembly, to which all presented at the levees are eligible, without any bidding or invitation. Who is to say that Harry Talbot and Mark O'Donoghue have not paid their homage to mock royalty? If you mean that there is some danger in the step, I agree with you there is; but you are not the man, I take it, to flinch on that account."

This adroit stroke of Talbot's settled the matter, and Mark felt ashamed to offer any objection to a course which, however disinclined to, he now believed was accompanied by a certain amount of peril.

CHAPTER XXXII.

A PRESAGE OF DANGER.

WHEN the long-wished-for evening drew nigh in which Talbot had pledged himself to reveal to Mark the circumstances of their enterprise, and to make him known to those concerned in the plot, his manner became flurried and excited ; he answered, when spoken to, with signs of impatience, and seemed so engrossed by his own thoughts, as to be unable to divert his attention from them. Mark, in general the reverse of a shrewd observer, perceived this, and attributing it to the heavy losses he had latterly incurred at play, forebore in any way to notice the circumstance, and from his silence Talbot became probably more indifferent to appearances, and placed less restraint on his conduct. He drank, too, more freely than was his wont, and appeared like one desirous by any means to rid himself of some unwelcome reflections.

" It is almost time to dress, Mark," said he, with an effort to seem easy and unconcerned. "Let us have another flask of Burgundy before we go."

" I'll have no more wine, nor you, if you will be advised by me, either," said Mark, gravely.

" Ha! then you would imply I have drunk too much already, Mark ? Not far wrong there, perhaps, and under ordinary circumstances such would be the case; but there are times when the mind, like the body, demands double nourishment, and with me wine strengthens, never confuses thought. Do you know, Mark, that I have a presentiment of some evil before me ;— whence, and in what shape it is to come, I cannot tell you ; but I feel it as certain as if it had been revealed to me."

" You are despondent about our prospects," said Mark, gloomily.

Talbot made no answer, but leaned his head on the chimney-piece, and seemed buried in deep thought ; then recovering himself, he said, in a low, but distinct accent,

" Did you take notice of a fellow at the tennis-court the other day, who stood beside me all the time I was settling with the marker ? Oh! I forgot —you were not there. Well, there was such a one—a flashy-looking, vulgar fellow, with that cast of countenance that betokens shrewdness and cunning. I met him yesterday in the Park, and this evening, as I came to dinner, I saw him talking to the landlord's nephew, in the hall."

" Well, and what of all that? If any one should keep account of where and how often he had seen either of us, this week past, might he not conjure up suspicions fully as strong as yours? Let us begin to take fright at shadows, and we shall make but a sorry hand of it when real dangers approach us."

" The shadows are the warnings, Mark, and the wise man never neglects a warning."

" He who sees thunder in every dark cloud above him is but the fool of his own fears," said Mark, rudely, and walked towards the window. " Is that anything like your friend, Talbot?" added he, as he beheld the dark outline of a figure, which seemed standing, intently looking up at the window.

" The very fellow!" cried Talbot; for at the moment a passing gleam of light fell upon the figure, and marked it out distinctly.

" There is something about him I can half recognise myself," said Mark; " but he is so muffled up with great-coat and cravat, I cannot clearly distinguish him."

" Indeed! Do, for Heaven's sake, think of where you saw him, and when, Mark; for I own my anxiety about him is more than common."

" I'll soon find out for you," said Mark, suddenly seizing his hat;—but at the same instant the door opened, and a waiter appeared.

" There's a gentleman below stairs, Mr. Talbot, would be glad to speak a few words with you."

Talbot motioned, by an almost imperceptible gesture, that Mark should retire into the adjoining room; and then, approaching the waiter, asked, in a low, cautious voice, if the stranger were known to him.

" No, sir—never saw him before. He seems like one from the country; Mr. Crossley says he's from the south."

" Show him up," said Talbot, hurriedly; and, as the waiter left the room, ne seated himself in his chair, in an attitude of well-assumed carelessness and ease. This was scarcely done, when the stranger entered, and closed the door behind him.

" Good evening to you, Mr. Talbot. I hope I see your honour well," said he, in an accent of very unmistakable Kerry Doric.

" Good evening to you, friend," replied Talbot. " My memory is not so good as yours, or I'd call you by your name also."

" I'm Lanty Lawler, sir—that man that sold your honour the dark chesnut mare down in the county Kerry last winter. I was always wishing to see your honour again, by reason of that same."

" How so?" said Talbot, getting suddenly paler, but with no other appearance of emotion in his manner. " Was not our contract honestly concluded at the time?"

" It was, sir—there's no doubt of it. Your honour paid like a gentleman,

aud in goold besides; but that's just the business I come about here. It
was French money you gave me, and I got into trouble about it—some
saying that I was a spy, and others making out that I was, maybe, worse;
and so I thought I wouldn't pass any more of it till I seen yourself, and
maybe you'd change it for me."

While he was speaking, Talbot's eye never wandered from him—not fixed,
indeed, with any seeming scrutiny, but still intently watching every play of
his features.

" You told me at the time, however, that French gold was just as convenient to you as English," said he, smiling good-humouredly, " and from tho
company I met you in I found no difficulty in believing you."

" The times is changed, sir," said Lanty, sighing. " God help us!—we
must do the best we can."

This evasive answer seemed perfectly to satisfy Talbot, who assented with
a shake of the head, as he said,

" Very well, Lanty; if you will come here to-morrow, I'll exchange your
gold for you."

" Thank your honour kindly," said Lanty, with a bow; but still making
no sign of leaving the room, where he stood, changing from one foot to the
other, in an attitude of bashful diffidence. " There was another little matter,
sir, but I'd be sorry to trouble you about it—and sure you couldn't help
it, besides."

" And that is——Let us hear it, Lanty."

" Why, sir, it's the horse—the mare with the one white fetlock. They
say, sir, that she was left at Moran's stables by the man that robbed Mr.
Moore, of Moore-croft. Deaf Collisou, the postboy, can swear to her; and
as I bought her myself at Dycer's, they are calling me to account for when
I sold her, and to whom."

" Why, there's no end to your trouble about that unlucky beast, Lanty,"
said Talbot, laughing; " and I confess it's rather hard that you are not only
expected to warrant your horse sound, but must give a guarantee that the
rider is honest."

" Devil a lie in it, but that's just it," said Lanty, who laughed heartily at
the notion.

" Well, we must look to this for you, Lanty; for although I have no
desire to have my name brought forward, still you must not suffer on that
account. I remember paying my bill at Rathmallow with that same mare.
She made an overreach coming down a hill, and became dead lame with me;
and I gave her to the landlord of the little inn in the square in lieu of my
score."

" See, now, what liars there's in the world!" said Lanty, holding up his
hauds in pious horror. " Ould Finn, of the Head Inn, tould me she ate a
feed of oats at the door, and started again for Askeaton with a gentleman

just like your honour the night after I sold her. He knew the mare well; and by the same token he said she was galled on the shoulder with holsters that was fixed to the saddle. Now, think of that, and he after buying her! Is it early in the morning I'm to come to your honour?" said he, moving towards the door.

" Yes—that is—no, Lanty, no—about twelve o'clock. I'm a late riser. Wait a moment, Lanty; I have something more to say to you, if I could only remember it." He passed his hand across his brow as he spoke, and looked like one labouring to recal some lost thought. " No matter," said he, after a pause of some minutes; " I shall, perhaps, recollect it before to-morrow."

" Good night to you, then, sir," said Lanty, with a most obsequious bow, as he opened the door.

Their eyes met: it was only for a moment; but with such intelligence did each glance read the other, that they both smiled significantly. Talbot moved quickly forward at the instant, and closing the door with one hand, he laid the other gently on Lanty's shoulder.

" Come, Lanty," said he, jocularly, " I can afford to sport ten pounds for a whim. Tell me who it was sent you after me this evening, and I'll give you the money."

" Done, then!" cried Lanty, grasping his hand; " and you'll ask no more than his name?"

" Nothing more. I pledge my word; and here's the money."

" Captain Hemsworth, the agent to the rich Englishman at Glenflesk."

" I don't think I ever saw him in my life—I'm certain I don't know him. Is he a tall, dark man?"

" I'll tell you no more," said Lanty. " The devil a luck I ever knew come of speaking of him."

" All fair, Lanty—a bargain's a bargain; and so, good night." And with a shake-hands of affected cordiality they parted.

" Your conference has been a long one," said Mark, who waited with impatience until the silence without permitted him to come forth.

" Not so long as I could have wished it," was Talbot's reply, as he stood in deep thought over what had passed. " It is just as I feared, Mark; there is danger brewing for me in some quarter, but how, or in what shape, I cannot even guess. This same horse-dealer, this Lanty Lawler——"

" Lanty Lawler, did you say?"

" Yes. You know him, then?"

" To be sure I do. We've had many dealings together. He's a shrewd fellow, and not over-scrupulous in the way of his trade; but, apart from that, he's a true-hearted, honest fellow, and a friend to the cause."

" You think so, Mark," said Talbot, with a smile of significant meaning.

" I know it, Talbot. He is not an acquaintance of yesterday with me. I have known him for years long. He is as deep in the plot as any, and perhaps has run greater risks than either of us."

" Well, well," said Talbot, sighing, as though either weary of the theme or disinclined to contradict the opinion ; " let us think of other matters. Shall we go to this ball or not ?   I incline to say nay."

" What !   Not go there ?" said Mark, starting back in astonishment. " Why, what in Heaven's name have we been waiting for but this very opportunity ?—and what reason is there now to turn from our plans ?"

" There may be good and sufficient ones, even though they should be purely personal to myself," said Talbot, in a tone of ill-dissembled pique. "But come ; we will go.   I have been walking over a mine too long to care for a mere petard.   And now, let us lose no more time, but dress at once."

" Must I really wear this absurd dress, Talbot ?   For very shame's sake, I shall not be able to look about me."

" That you must, Mark.   Remember that your safety lies in the fact that we attract no notice of any kind.   To be as little remarked as possible is our object ; and for this reason I shall wear the uniform of an English militia regiment, of which there are many at every levee.   We shall separate on entering the room, and meet only from time to time ; but as we go along, I'll give you all your instructions.   And now to dress as quickly as may be."

CHAPTER XXXIII.

THE ST. PATRICK'S BALL.

Much as O'Donoghue marvelled at the change effected in his own appearance by the court dress, he was still more surprised at finding what a complete transformation his friend Talbot had undergone.   The scarlet uniform seemed to make him appear larger and fatter ; while the assumption of a pair of dark whiskers added several years to his apparent age, and totally changed the character of his countenance.

" I see by your face, Mark," said he, laughing, "that the disguise is complete.   You could scarcely recognise me—I may safely defy most others."

" But you are taller, I think ?"

" About an inch and a half only—false heels inside my boots give me a slight advantage over you.   Don't be jealous, however ; I'm not your match on a fair footing."

This flattery seemed successful, for Mark smiled and reddened slightly. As they drove along, Talbot entered minutely into an account of the people they should meet with—warning Mark of the necessity there existed to avoid any, even the most trivial, sign of astonishment at anything he saw —to mix with the crowd, and follow the current from room to room, carefully guarding against making any chance acquaintance—and, above all, not to be recognised by his cousin Kate, if by any accident he should be near her.

In the midst of these directions, Talbot was interrupted by the sudden stoppage of the carriages in the line, already extended above a mile from the Castle gate.

"Here we are at last, Mark, in the train of the courtiers—does your patriotism burn for the time when your homage shall be rendered to a native sovereign? Ha! there goes one of the privileged class—that carriage, with the two footmen, is the Lord Chancellor's; he has the right of the private 'entrée,' and takes the lead of such humble folk as we are mixed up with."

A deep groan from the mob burst forth as the equipage, thus noticed, dashed forward. Such manifestations of public feeling were then frequent, and not always limited to mere expressions of dislike. The very circumstance of quitting the regular line and passing the rest, seemed to evoke popular indignation, and it was wonderful with what readiness the mob caught up allusions to the public or private life of those thus momentarily exposed to their indignation. Some speech or vote in Parliament, some judicial sentence, or some act or event in their private history, was at once recalled and criticised in a manner far more frank than flattering. None escaped this notice, for, notwithstanding the strong force of mounted police that kept the street clear, some adventurous spirit was always ready to rush forward to the carriage window, and in a moment announce to the others the name of its occupant. By all this Mark was greatly amused; he had few sympathies with those in little favour with the multitude, and could afford to laugh at the sallies which assailed the members of the Government. The taunting sarcasms and personal allusions, of which the Irish members were not sparing in the House, were here repeated by those who suffered the severity to lose little of its sting in their own version.

"Look at Flood, boys—there's the old vulture with broken beak and cadaverous aspect—a groan for Flood!" And the demand was answered by thousands.

"There's Tom Connolly," shouted a loud voice; "three cheers for the Volunteers—three cheers for Castletown!"

"Thank you, boys, thank you," said a rich, mellow voice, as in their enthusiasm the mob pressed around the carriage of the popular member, and even shook hands with the footmen behind the carriage.

" Here's Luttrel, here's Luttrel!" cried out several together; and in a moment the excitement, which before was all joy, assumed a character of deepest execration.

Aware of the popular feeling towards him, this gentleman's carriage was guarded by two troopers of the horse police. Nor was the precaution needless, for no sooner was he recognised, than a general rush was made by the mob, and for a moment or two the carriage was separated from the rest of the line.

" Groan him, boys, groan him, but don't touch the traitor!" shouted a savage-looking fellow, who stood a head and shoulders above the crowd.

" Couldn't you afford to buy new liveries with the eighty thousand pounds the Government gave you?" yelled another; and the sally was responded to with a burst of savage laughter.

" Throw us out a penny," called a third; "it will treat all your friends in Ireland. Let him go, boys, let him go—he's only stopping the way of his betters!"

" Here's the man that knows how to spend his money—three cheers for the Englishman from Stephen's-green—three cheers for Sir Marmaduke Travers!" And the cheers burst forth with an enthusiasm that showed how much more a character for benevolence and personal kindness conciliated mob estimation than all the attributes of political partisanship.

" Bring us a lamp here, bring us a lamp!" cried a miserable object in tattered rags; "take down a lamp, boys, till we have a look at the two beauties;" and, strange as the suggestion may seem, it was hailed with a cry of triumphal delight, and in another moment a street lamp was taken from its place and handed over the heads of the mob to the very window of Sir Marmaduke's carriage; while the old baronet, kindly humouring the eccentricities of the people, lowered the glass to permit them to see in. A respectful silence extended over that crowd, motley and miserable as it was, and they stood in mute admiration, not venturing upon a word nor a remark, until, as it were, overcome by a spontaneous feeling of enthusiasm, they broke forth into one loud cheer that echoed from the College to the very gates of the Castle; and with blessings deep and fervent, as they would have bestowed for some real favour, the carriage was allowed to proceed on its way once more.

" Here's Morris, here's the colonel!" was now the cry; and a burst of as merry laughter as ever issued from happy hearts welcomed the new arrival. " Make him get out, boys, make him get out, and show us his legs; that's the fellow ran away in Flanders!" And before the mirth had subsided, the unhappy colonel had passed on.

" Who's this in the hackney-coach?" said one, as the carriage in which Talbot and Mark were seated came up. The window was let down in a moment, and Talbot, leaning his head out, whispered a few words in a low voice; whatever their import, their effect was magical, and a hurra, as wild as the war-cry of an Indian, shook the street.

" What was it you said?" cried Mark.

" Three words in Irish," said Talbot, laughing; "they are the only three in my vocabulary, and their meaning is, 'Wait awhile;' and, somehow, it would seem a very significant intimation to Irishmen."

The carriage moved on, and the two friends soon alighted in the brilliantly-illuminated vestibule, now lined with battleaxe-guards, and resounding with the clangor of a brass band. Mixing with the crowd that poured up the staircase, they passed into the first drawing-room without stopping to write their names, as was done by the others, Talbot telling Mark, in a whisper, to move up and follow him closely.

The distressing impression that he himself would be an object of notice and remark to others, and which had up to that very moment tortured him, gave way at once, as he found himself in that splendid assemblage, where beauty, in all the glare of dress and jewels, abounded, and where, for the first time, the world of fashion and elegance burst upon his astonished senses. The courage that, with dauntless nerve, would have led him to the cannon's mouth, now actually faltered, and made him feel faint-hearted, to find himself mixing with those among whom he had no right to be present. Talbot's shrewd intelligence seemed to divine what was passing in Mark's mind, for he took him by the arm, and as he led him forward, whispered, from time to time, certain particulars of the company, intended to satisfy him that, however distinguished by rank and personal appearance, in reality their characters had little claim to his respect. With such success did he demolish reputations — so fatally did his sarcasms depreciate those against whom they were directed—that, ere long, Mark moved along in utter contempt for that gorgeous throng, which at first had impressed him so profoundly. To hear that the proud-looking general, his coat a blaze of orders, was a coward; that the benign and mild-faced judge was a merciless, unrelenting tyrant; that the bishop, whose simple bearing and gentle quietude of manner were most winning, was in reality a crafty place-hunter and a subtle *intrigant*—such were the lessons Talbot poured into his ear, while amid the ranks of beauty still more deadly calumnies pointed all he said.

" Society is rotten to the very core here, Mark," said he, bitterly. " There never was a land nor an age when profligacy stood so high in the market. It remains to be seen if our friends will do better—for a time, at least, they are almost certain to do so; but now, that I have shown you something of the company, let us separate, lest we be remarked. This pillar can always be our rallying spot. Whenever you want me, come here;" and so saying, and with a slight pressure of his hand, Talbot mixed with the crowd, and soon was lost to Mark's view.

Talbot's revelations served at first to impair the pleasure Mark experienced in the brilliant scene around him; but when once more alone, the magnetic influence of a splendour so new, and of beauty so dazzling, appealed to his heart far more powerfully than the cold sarcasms of his companion. Glances which, directed to others, he caught in passing, and felt with a throb of ecstasy within his own bosom; bright eyes, that beamed not for him, sent a glow of delight through his frame. The atmosphere of pleasure which he had never breathed before, now warmed the current of his blood, and his pulse beat high and madly. All the bitter thoughts he had harboured against his country's enemies could not stand before his admiration of that gorgeous assemblage, and he felt ashamed to think that he, and such as he, should conspire the downfal of a system whose very externals were so captivating. He wandered thus from room to room in a dream of pleasure—now stopping to gaze at the dancers, then moving towards some of the refreshment-rooms, where parties were seated in familiar circles, all in the full enjoyment of the brilliant festivity. Like a child roaming at will through some beauteous garden, heightening enjoyment by the rapid variety of new pleasures, and making in the quick transition of sensations a source of more fervid delight, so did he pass from place to place, and in this way time stole by, and he utterly forgot the rendezvous he had arranged with Talbot. At last, suddenly remembering this, he endeavoured to find out the place, and in doing so was forced to pass through a card-room, where several parties were now at play. Around one of the tables a greater crowd than usual was assembled. There, as he passed, Mark thought he overheard Talbot's voice. He stopped and drew near, and, with some little difficulty, making his way through, perceived his friend seated at the table, deeply engaged in what, if he were to judge from the heap of gold before him, seemed very high play. His antagonist was an old, fine-looking man, in the uniform of a general officer; but while Mark looked, he arose, and his place was taken by another—the etiquette being, that the winner should remain until he ceased to win.

"He has passed eleven times," said a gentleman to his friend, in Mark's hearing; "he must at least have won four hundred pounds."

"Do you happen to know who he is?"

"No; nor do I know any one that does. There!—see!—he has won again."

"He's a devilish cool player—that's certain. I never saw a man more collected."

"He studies his adversary far more than his cards—I remark that."

"Oh! here's old Clangoff come to try his luck:" and an opening of the crowd was now made to permit a tall and very old man to approach the table. Very much stooped in the shoulders, and with snow-white hair, Lord Clangoff still preserved the remains of one who in his youth had been the handsomest man of his day. Although simply dressed in the Windsor uniform, the brilliant rings he wore upon his fingers, and the splendour of a gold snuff-box surrounded by enormous diamonds, evinced the taste for magnificence for which he was celebrated. There was an air of dignity with which he took his seat, saluting the acquaintances he recognised about him, very strikingly in contrast with the familiar manners then growing into vogue, while in the courteous urbanity of his bow to Talbot, his whole breeding was revealed.

" It is a proud thing even to encounter such an adversary, sir," said he, smiling. "They have just told me that you have vanquished our best players."

" The caprice of Fortune, my lord, that so often favours the undeserving," said Talbot, with a gesture of extreme humility.

" Your success should be small at play, if the French adage have any truth in it," said his lordship, alluding to Talbot's handsome features, which seemed to indicate favour with the softer sex.

" According to that theory, my lord, I have the advantage over you at present."

This adroit flattery at the other's earlier reputation as a gallant, seemed to please him highly; for, as he presented his box to one of his friends near, he whispered, " A very well-bred fellow indeed." Then turning to Talbot, said, " Do you like a high stake ?"

" I am completely at your service, my lord—whatever you please."

" Shall we say fifty ? or do you prefer a hundred ?"

" If the same to you, I like the latter just twice as well."

The old lord smiled at having found an adversary similarly disposed with himself, and drew out his pocket-book with an air of palpable satisfaction; while in the looks of increased interest among the bystanders could be seen the anxiety they felt in the coming struggle.

" You have the deal, my lord," said Talbot, presenting the cards. " Still, if any gentleman cares for another fifty on the game——"

" I'll take it, sir," said a voice from behind Lord Clangoff's chair; and Mark, struck by the accent, fixed his eyes on the speaker. The blood rushed to his face at once, for it was Hemsworth who stood before him—the ancient enemy of his house—the tyrant, whose petty oppressions and studied insults had been a theme he was familiar with from boyhood. All fear of his being recognised himself was merged in the savage pleasure he felt in staring fixedly at the man he hated.

He would have given much to be able to whisper the name into Talbot's ear; but remembering how such an attempt might be attended by a discovery of himself, he desisted, and with a throbbing heart awaited the result of the game. Meanwhile Hemsworth, whose whole attention was concentrated on Talbot, never turned his eyes towards any other quarter. The

R

moment seemed favourable for Mark, and gently retiring through the crowd, he at last disengaged himself, and sat down on a bench near a doorway. His mind was full of its own teeming thoughts—thoughts that the hated presence of his enemy sent madly thronging upon him; he lost all memory of where he was, nor did he remark that two persons had entered and seated themselves near him, when a word, a single word, fell upon his ear. He turned round and saw his cousin Kate sitting beside Frederick Travers. The start of surprise he could not restrain attracted her notice. She turned also, and as a deadly pallor came over her features, she uttered the one word, "Mark." Travers immediately caught the name, and, leaning forward, the two young men's eyes met, and for some seconds never wandered from each other.

"I should have gone to see you, cousin Kate," said Mark, after a momentary struggle to seem calm and collected, "but I feared—that is, I did not know——"

"But, Mark, dear Mark, why are you here?" said she, in a tone of heartfelt terror. "Do you know that none save those presented at the levees, and known to the Lord-Lieutenant, dare to attend these balls?"

"I came with a friend," said Mark, in a voice where anger and self-reproach were mingled. "If he misled me, he must answer for it."

"It was imprudent, Mr. O'Donoghue, and that's all," said Travers, in a tone of great gentleness; "and your friend should not have misled you. I'll take care that nothing unpleasant shall arise in consequence. Just remain here for a moment."

"Stay, sir," said Mark, as Travers arose from his seat; "I hate accepting favours, even should they release me from a position as awkward as this is. Here comes my friend Talbot, and he'll perhaps explain what I cannot."

"I have lost my money, Mark," said Talbot, coming forward, and perceiving with much anxiety that his young friend was engaged in a conversation. "Let us move about and see the dancers."

"Wait a few seconds first," said Mark, sternly, "and satisfy this gentleman that I am not in fault in coming here, save so far as being induced by you to do so."

"May I ask how the gentleman feels called on to require the explanation?" said Talbot, proudly.

"I wish him to know the circumstances," said Mark.

"And I," said Travers, interrupting, "might claim a right to ask it as first aide-de-camp to his Excellency."

"So, then," whispered Talbot, with a smile, "it is the mere impertinence of office."

Travers's face flushed up, and his lips quivered, as, in an equally low tone of voice, he said,

"Where and when, sir, will you dare to repeat these words?"

" To-morrow morning, at seven o'clock, on the strand below Clontarf, and in this gentleman's presence," said Talbot, into his ear.

A nod from Travers completed the arrangement, and Talbot, placing his arm hurriedly within Mark's, said,

" Let us get away from this, Mark. It is all settled. We meet to-morrow."

Mark turned one look towards Kate, who was just in the act of accepting Travers's arm to return to the ball-room. Their glances met for a second, but with how different a meaning!—in *hers*, a world of anxiety and interest —in *his*, the proud and scornful defiance of one who seemed to accept of no compromise with fortune.

"So, then, it is your friend Travers, Mark, with whom I am to have the honour of a rencontre. I'm sorry, for your sake, that it is so."

" And why so ?" asked Mark, sternly, for in his present mood he was as little satisfied with Talbot as with Travers.

"Because, if I don't mistake much, you will not have the opportunity of wiping out your old score with him. I'll shoot him, Mark !" These last words were uttered between his almost closed teeth, and in a tone of scarce restrained anger. " Are either of us looking very bloody-minded or savage, Mark, I wonder ? for see how the people are staring and whispering as we pass !"

The observation was not made without reason, for already the two young men were regarded on all sides as they passed—the different persons in their way retiring as they approached.

" How do you do, my lord ? I hope I see you well," said Talbot, bowing familiarly to a venerable old man who stood near, and who as promptly returned his salute.

" Who is it you bowed to ?" said Mark, in a whisper

" The Chief Justice, Mark. Not that I know him, or he me; but at this critical moment such a recognition is a certificate of character, which will at least last long enough to see us down stairs. There, let me move on first, and follow me;" and as he spoke, he edged his way through a crowded door, leaving Mark to follow how he could. This was, however, a task of more difficulty than it seemed, for already a number of persons blocked up the doorway, eager to hear something which a gentleman was relating to those about him.

" I can only tell you," continued he, " that none seems to know either of them. As Clangoff has lost the diamond snuff-box the Emperor of Austria presented him with—he missed it after leaving the card-table—the presumption is, that we are favoured with somewhat doubtful company."

" Carysford says," cried another, " that he knows one of them well, and has often seen him in Paris at the playhouses."

A low whisper ran around after these words, and at the instant every eye

was directed to Mark O'Donoghue. The young man sustained their looks
with a frown of resolute daring, turning from one to the other to see if, perchance, by any gesture or expression, he could single out one to pay the
penalty for the rest : his blood boiled at the insulting glances that fell upon
him, and he was in the very act of giving his temper vent, when an arm was
slipped within his, and Frederick Travers whispered in his ear,

"I hope your friend has got safely away. There are some fellows here
to-night of notoriously bad character, and Mr. Talbot may get into trouble on
that account."

"He has just left this. I hope before now he has reached the street."

"Let me be your convoy, then," said Travers, good-naturedly. "These
talking fools will cease their scandal when they see us together;" and,
affecting an air of easy intimacy, he led Mark through the crowd, which even
already bestowed very altered glances as they passed.

"Good night, sir," said Mark, abruptly, as they arrived at the room by
which he remembered to have entered; "I see my friend yonder, awaiting
me." Travers returned the greeting, and half extended his hand, but Mark
coolly bowed and turned away. The moment after he was at Talbot's side.

"Thank Heaven, we are breathing the free air again!" he exclaimed, as
they issued forth into the street; "a little longer would have suffocated me."

"It was with Travers you parted at the head of the stairs?" said Talbot,
inquiringly.

"Yes; he was polite enough to come up when you left me, and the company and myself have reason to be thankful to him, for assuredly we were,
both of us, forgetting our good manners very much at the moment. They
were pleased to look at me in a fashion of very questionable civility, and I,
I greatly fear, was scarcely more polite. It would seem, Talbot, that some
swindlers or pickpockets had introduced themselves at the assembly, and we
had the honour of being confounded with them—so much for the prudence
of our first step."

"Come, come, Mark, don't lose temper about trifles."

"Would it have proved a trifle if I had thrown one of those gold-laced
fops out of the window into the court? I promise you the temptation was
devilish strong in me to act so at one moment. But what have we gained
by all this? where were the friends you should have met? whom have you
seen? what have you learned?"

Talbot made no reply, but walked on in silence.

"Or have we exposed ourselves to the taunting insolence of these people
for the mock pleasure of mixing with them? Is that our gain here?"

Still Talbot made no reply, and Mark, as if his passion had expended itself,
now became silent also, and in this wise they reached the hotel, each sunk
in his own personal reflections.

"Now, Mark," said Talbot, when they had gained their room, "now let us set ourselves to think over what is to be done, and not waste a thought on what is bygone. At seven to-morrow I am to meet Travers; before nine I must be on the way to France, that is, if he do not issue a leaden *ne exeat* against me. I shall certainly fire at him—your pretty cousin will never forgive me for it, that I know well"—here he stole a side look at Mark, across whose features a flash of passion was thrown—"still, I am sorry this should have occurred, because I had many things to settle here; among others, some which more nearly concerned yourself."

" Me!—concerned me!" said Mark, in surprise.

" Yes; I am deeper in your secrets than you are aware of—deeper than you are yourself, perhaps. What would you say, Mark, if I could ensure you the possession of your property and estate, as it was left to you by your grandfather, without debt or incumbrance of any kind, free from mortgage?"

" Free from Hemsworth?" cried Mark, passionately.

" Even so—I was just coming to that."

" I know not what I should say, Talbot, but I know what I should do— throw every farthing of it into the scale where I have thrown life and hope —the cause of my country."

Talbot shook his head doubtfully for a second or two, then said:

" It is not money is wanting to the enterprise, it is rather what no money can buy—the reckless courage of men willing to devote themselves to a cause which they must never hope to live to see successful, but whose graves must be the ramparts over which others will achieve liberty. No, my hopes for you point otherwise. I wish to see you as the head and representative of an ancient name and house, with the influence property and position would confer, taking your place in the movement, not as a soldier of fortune, but as a man of rank and weight." Talbot paused for a moment to enjoy, as it were, the delight this brilliant picture of coming greatness produced upon the youth, and then went on, " Such a place I can offer you, Mark."

" How, and on what terms?" cried Mark, bursting with impatience.

" I make no conditions—I am your friend, and ask nothing but your friend-ship. A lucky chance has given me the opportunity to serve you—all I bar-gain for is, that you do not inquire further how that chance arose."

Mark stood in mute amazement, while Talbot, unlocking his writing-desk, drew forth a dark leather pocket-book, tied with a string, and laid it leisurely on the table before him.

" There is a condition I will bargain for, Mark," said Talbot, after a pause, " although I'm sure it is a weakness I scarcely ever thought to feel. We shall soon be separated; who knows when we shall meet again, if ever. Now, if men should speak of me in terms unworthy of one who has been your friend, laying to my charge acts of dishonour——"

" Who will dare to do so before me?" said Mark, indignantly.

" It will happen, nevertheless, Mark; and I ask not your defence of me when absent, as much as that you will yourself reject all belief in these calumnies. I have told you enough of my life to let you know in what circumstances of difficulty and danger different parts have been forced upon me, and it may be that, while I have personated others, they in revenge have masqueraded under my name. This is no mere suspicion. I know it has already happened; bear it well in mind, and when your friend Henry Talbot is assailed, remember the explanation and your own promise."

Mark grasped Talbot's hand firmly, and shook it with the warmth of true friendship.

"Sit down beside me, Mark," said he, placing the chairs at the table, "and read this."

With these words he unfastened the string of the pocket-book, and took forth a small paper from an envelope, of which the seal was already broken.

"This is addressed to your father, Mark," said he, showing him the superscription.

"I know that handwriting," said Mark, gazing fixedly at it; "that is Father Rourke's."

"Yes, that's the name," said Talbot, opening the letter. "Read this," and he handed the paper to Mark, while he himself read aloud:

"'Mark O'Donoghue, son of Miles O'Donoghue, and Mary his wife, born 25th December, 1774, and christened on the morning of the 27th December, same year, by me, Nicholas Rourke, P.P., Ballyvourney and Glengariff. Witnessed by us, Simon Gaffney, steward, and Sam. Wylie, butler.'"

"And what of all that?" said Mark, with a voice of evident disappointment. "Do you think I wanted this certificate of birth or baptism to claim my name or my kindred?"

"No; but to claim your estate and fortune," said Talbot, hurriedly. "Do you not perceive the date of this document—1774—and that you only attained your majority on last Christmas Day——"

"That cannot be," interrupted Mark. "I joined my father in a loan upon the estate two years ago; the sale to Hemsworth was made at the same time, and I must have been of age to do so."

"That does not follow," said Talbot, smiling. "It suited the objects of others to make you think so; but you were little more than nineteen at the time. Here's the certificate of your mother's marriage, and the date is February, 1773."

Mark's countenance became perfectly bloodless, his lips grew livid, while his nostrils were alternately distended and contracted violently as he breathed with a heaving effort.

"You have your choice, therefore," said Talbot, flippantly, "to believe your father a man of honour, or your mother——"

"Stop!" cried Mark, as he seized his arm and shook it in his strong grasp; "speak the word, and, by Heaven, you'll never leave this spot alive!"

Talbot seemed to feel no anger at this savage threat, but calmly said,

"It was not my wish to hurt your feelings, Mark. Very little reflection on your part might convince you that I can have no object to serve here save my regard for you. You seemed to doubt what I said about your age, and I wished to satisfy you at once that I was correct. You were not of age till last December. A false certificate of birth and baptism enabled your father to raise a considerable sum of money with your concurrence, and also permitted him to make a sale to Hemsworth of a property strictly entailed on you and yours. Both these acts were illegal and unjust. If Hems-worth be the rightful owner of that estate, your birth is illegitimate—nay, nay—I am but putting the alternative, which you cannot, dare not accept. You must hear me with temper, Mark—calmly and patiently. It is a sad lesson when one must learn to think disparagingly of those they have ever looked up to and revered. But remember, that when your father did this act, he was surrounded with difficulties on every hand. There seemed no escape from the dangers around him—inevitable ruin was his lot. He doubtless intended to apply a considerable portion of this money to the repair of his shattered fortunes. Of his affection for you there can be no question——"

"There, there," said Mark, interrupting him rudely; "there is no need to defend a father to his son. Tell me, rather, why you have revealed this secret to me at all, and to what end have you added this to the other calamities of my fortune."

He stood up as he said these words, and paced the room with slow steps, his head sunk upon his bosom, and his arms dropped listlessly at his side. Talbot looked upon the figure, marked with every trait of despondency, and for some moments he seemed really to sorrow over the part he had taken; then, rallying with his accustomed energy, he said,

"If I had thought, Mark, that you had neither ambition for yourself, nor hatred for an enemy, I would never have told you these things. I did fancy, however, that you were one who struggled indignantly against an in-glorious fortune, and, still more, believed that you were not of a race to repay injury with forgetfulness. Hemsworth, you have often told me, has been the insulting enemy of your family. Not content with despoiling you of fortune, he has done his utmost to rob you of fair fame—to reduce an honoured house to the ignoble condition of peasants, and to break down the high and haughty spirit of a noble family by the humiliating ills of poverty. If you can forgive his injuries, can you forget his insults and his taunts?"

"Would you have me repay either by arraigning my father as a criminal?"

"Not so, Mark; many other courses are open to you. The knowledge of this fact by you places you in a position to make your own terms with Hemsworth. He who has spent thirty thousand pounds on a purchase without a title, must needs yield to any conditions you think fit to impose. You have but to threaten——"

"That I will expose my father in a court of justice," said Mark, between his teeth—"that I will put money in one scale, and the honour of my house in the other—that I will truck the name and credit of my race against the acres that were theirs. No, no; you mistake me much; you know little of the kind of vengeance my heart yearns for, or you would never have tempted me with such a bait as this."

"Be it so," said Talbot, coolly; "Hemsworth is only the luckier man that has met such a temperament as yours to deal with; a vulgar spirit like mine would have turned the tables upon him. But I have done; keep the paper, Mark; there might come a time when it should prove useful to you. Hark!—what's that noise below? Don't you hear that fellow Lawler's voice in the court-yard?"—and, as he spoke, the voice of the host, Billy Crossley, raised very high above its usual pitch, called out,

"I tell you, gentlemen, Mr. Talbot is not in the house; he dined out to-day, and has not returned since dinner."

A confused murmur followed this announcement; and again Crossley said, but in a still louder tone,

"You have perfect liberty to look for him wherever you please; don't say that I gave you any impediment or hindrance; follow me—I'll show you the way."

Talbot knew in a moment the intention of the speaker, and recognised in Crossley's vehemence an urgent warning to himself.

"I'm tracked, Mark," cried he; "there, take that key—burn the papers in that desk—all of them. At seven to-morrow, meet me on the strand; if all be safe, I'll be true to time; if not——"

The remainder of the sentence was cut short by the hurrying sounds of feet upon the stairs, and Crossley's voice, which in its loudest key continued to protest that Talbot was not in the house, nor had he seen him since dinner.

Mark hastily unlocked the desk and took out the papers, but when he turned round Talbot was gone; a tremulous motion of the tapestry on the wall seemed to indicate that his escape had been made through some secret door behind it. He had no time, however, to think further of the circumstance, for scarcely had he applied the lighted candle to the papers when the door was burst violently open, and three strange men, followed by Lanty Lawler, entered the room, while Crossley, whom they had pushed roughly aside, stood without, on the lobby, still talking as loudly as before.

"Is that him?" said one of the fellows, who seemed like a constable in plain clothes.

"No," whispered Lanty, as he skulked behind the shoulder of the speaker; "that's another gentleman."

"Were you alone in this apartment?" said the same man who spoke first, as he addressed Mark in the tone of authority.

"It is rather for me to ask what business you have to come here?" replied Mark, as he continued to feed the flames with the letters and papers before him.

"You shall see my warrant when you have answered my question. Meanwhile these may be of some consequence," said the other, as, approaching the hearth, he stooped down to seize the burning papers.

"They do not concern you," said Mark, as he placed his foot in the very middle of the blaze.

"Stand back, sir," cried the constable, half raising his arm to enforce the command.

"Lay but a finger on me," said Mark, scornfully, "and I'll dash your head against the wall."

The insolence of this threat might have been followed by ill consequences, had not Lanty sprung hastily forward, and, catching the constable by the arm, cried out,

"It is the O'Donoghue of Glenflesk, a young gentleman of rank and fortune."

"What do we care for his rank or fortune?" said the other, passionately. "If he obstructs the King's warrant for the arrest of a traitor or a felon, I value him no more than the meanest beggar in the street. Those papers there, for all I know, might throw light on the whole plot."

"They are at your service, now," said Mark, as with a kick of his foot he dashed the blackened embers from him, and sent them in floating fragments through the room.

Unwilling as he seemed to continue a contest in which his authority had met only defiance, the constable gave the order to his underlings to make a strict search of the apartment and the bedroom which opened into it, during which Mark seated himself carelessly in an arm-chair, and taking a newspaper from the table, affected to read it.

Lanty stood for a few seconds, irresolute what to do; then stealing softly behind Mark's chair, he muttered, in a broken voice,

"If I thought he was a friend of yours, Master Mark——But it's no matter—I know he's off. I heard the gallop of a beast on the stones since we came in. Well, well, I never expected to see you here."

Mark made no other reply to this speech than a steady frown, whose contemptuous expression Lanty cowered under, as he said once more,

"It wasn't my fault at all, if I was obliged to come with the constables. There's more charges nor mine against him, the chap with the black whiskers says——"

"It's quite clear," said the chief of the party, as he re-entered the room—"it's quite clear this man was here a few minutes since, and equally so that you know of his place of concealment. I tell you plainly, sir, if you continue to refuse information concerning him, I'll take you as my prisoner. I have two warrants against him—one for highway robbery, the other for treason."

"Why the devil have you no informations sworn against him for murder?" said Mark, insolently, for the language of the bailiff had completely aroused his passion. "Whoever he is you are looking for seems to have a clear conscience."

"Master Mark knows nothing at all about him, I'll go bail to any amount."

"We don't want your bail, my good friend; we want the man who calls himself Harvey Middleton in Herts, Godfrey Middleton in Surrey, the Chevalier Duchatel in France, Harry Talbot in Ireland, but who is better known in the police sheet;" and here he opened a printed paper, and pointed to the words, "full description of John Barrington, convicted at the Maidstone assizes, and sentenced to fifteen years' transportation."

The smile of insolent incredulity with which Mark listened to these imputations on the honour of his friend, if it did not assuage the anger of the constable, served to satisfy him that he was at least no practised colleague in crime, and turning to Lanty, he talked to him in a low whisper for several minutes.

"I tell ye," said Lanty, eagerly, in reply to some remark of the other, "his worship will never forgive you if you arrest him; his time is not yet come, and you'll get little thanks for interfering where ye had no business."

Whether convinced by these arguments, or deterred from making Mark his prisoner by the conscious illegality of the act, the man collected his party, and having given them his orders in a low voice, left the room, followed by the others.

A gesture from Mark arrested Lanty as he was in the act of passing out. "A word with you, Lanty," said he, firmly. "What is the information against Talbot?—what is he accused of?"

"Sure didn't you hear yourself," replied Lanty, in a simpering, mock bashful voice. "They say he's Barrington the robber, and faith, they're strong evidence that they're not far out. 'Tis about a horse I sold him that I came here. I didn't want to harm or hurt anybody, and if I thought he was a friend of yours——"

"He is a friend of mine," said Mark, "and therefore these stories are but one tissue of falsehoods. Are you aware, Lanty"—and here, as the youth

spoke, his voice became low and whispering—"are you aware that Talbot is
an agent of the French Government—that he is over here to report on the
condition of our party, and arrange for the rising?"

"Is it in earnest you are?" cried Lanty, with an expression of admirably
dissembled astonishment. "Are you telling me truth, Master Mark?"

"Yes, and more still—the day is not far distant now when we shall strike
the blow."

"I want you here, my worthy friend," said the constable, putting his
head into the room, and touching Lanty's shoulder. The horse-dealer looked
confused, and for a second seemed undetermined how to act; but suddenly
recovering his composure, he smiled significantly at Mark, wished him a
good night, and departed.

CHAPTER XXXIV.

THE DAYBREAK ON THE STRAND.

It was with an impatience almost amounting to madness that Mark
O'Donoghue awaited the dawn of day; long before that hour had arrived
he had made every preparation for joining his friend. A horse stood ready
saddled awaiting him in the stable, and his pistols—the weapons Talbot
knew so well how to handle—were carefully packed in the heavy holsters.
The time settled for the meeting was seven o'clock, but he was certain that
Talbot would be near the place before that hour, if not already there. The
scene which followed Talbot's escape also stimulated his anxiety to meet
with him; not that any, even the faintest, suspicion of his friend's honour
ever crossed Mark's mind, but he wished to warn him of the dangers that
were gathering around him, for were he arrested on a suspicion, who was to
say what material evidence might not arise against him in his real character
of a French spy? Mark's was not a character long to brood over doubtful
circumstances, and seek an explanation for difficulties which only assumed
the guise of suspicions. Too prone always to be led by first impressions of
everybody and everything, he hated and avoided whatever should disturb
the opinions he thus hastily formed. When matters too complicated and
knotty for his immediate comprehension crossed him, he turned from them
without an effort, and rather satisfied himself that it was a point of honour
to "go on believing," than harbour a doubt even where the circumstances
were calculated to suggest it. This frame of mind saved him from all uneasiness on the score of Talbot's honour; he had often heard how many dis-

guises and masks his friend had worn in the events of his wild and dangerous career, and if he felt how incapable he himself would have been to play so many different parts, the same reason prevented his questioning the necessity of such subterfuges. That Harry Talbot had personated any or all of the persons mentioned by the constable, he little doubted, and therefore he regarded their warrant after him as only another evidence of his skill and cleverness; but that his character was in the least involved was a supposition that never once occurred to him. Amid all his anxieties of that weary night not one arose from this cause; no secret distrust of his friend lurked in any corner of his heart; his fear was solely for Talbot's safety, and for what he probably ranked as highly—the certainty of his keeping his appointment with Frederick Travers; and what a world of conflicting feelings were here! At one moment a sense of savage, unrelenting hatred to the man who had grossly insulted himself, at the next a dreadful thrill of agony that this same Travers might be the object of his cousin's love, and that on *his* fate *her* whole happiness in life depended. Had the meeting been between himself and Travers—had the time come round to settle that old score of insult that lay between them—he thought that such feelings as these would have been merged in the gratified sense of vengeance, but now, how should he look on, and see him fall by another's pistol?—how see another expose his life in the place he felt to be his own? He could not forgive Talbot for this, and every painful thought the whole event suggested embittered him against his friend as the cause of his suffering. And yet, was it possible for him ever himself to have challenged Travers? Did not the discovery of Kate's secret, as he called it to her, on the road below the cliff, at once and for ever prevent such a catastrophe? Such were some of the harassing reflections which distracted Mark's mind, and to which his own wayward temper and natural excitability gave additional poignancy; while jealousy, a passion that fed and ministered to his hate, lived through every sentiment and tinctured every thought. Such had been his waking and sleeping thoughts for many a day—thoughts which, though lurking, like a slow poison, within him, had never become so palpable to his mind before; his very patriotism, the attachment he thought he felt to his native country, his ardent desire for liberty, his aspirations for national greatness, all sprang from this one sentiment of hate to the Saxon, and jealousy of the man who was his rival. Frederick Travers was the embodiment of all those feelings he himself believed were enlisted in the cause of his country.

As these reflections crowded on him they suggested new sources of suffering, and in the bewildered frame of mind to which he was now reduced there seemed no possible issue to his difficulties. Mark was not, however, one of those who chalk out their line in life in moments of quiet reflection, and then pursue the career they have fixed upon. His course was rather to throw passion and impulse into the same scale with circumstances, and take his chance of the result. He had little power of anticipation, nor was his a mind that could calmly array facts before it, and draw the inferences from them. No, he met the dangers of life, as he would have done those of battle, with a heart undaunted and a spirit resolved never to turn back. The sullen courage of his nature, if it did not suggest hope, at least supplied resolution—and how many go through life with no other star to guide them !

At last the grey dawn of breaking day appeared above the house-tops, and the low distant sounds that prelude the movement of life in great cities, stirred faintly without.

" Thank Heaven, the night is over at last !" was Mark's exclamation, as he gazed upon the leaden streak of cloud that told of morning.

All his preparations for departure were made, so that he had only to descend to the stable and mount his horse. The animal, he was told, had formerly belonged to Talbot, and nothing save the especial favour of Billy Crossley could have procured him so admirable a mount.

" He has never left the stable, sir," said Billy, as he held the stirrup himself—" he has never left the stable for ten days, but he has wind enough to carry you two-and-twenty miles within the hour, if you were put to it."

" And if I were, Billy," said Mark, for a sudden thought just flashed across him—" if I were, and if I should not bring him back to you, his price is——"

" I wouldn't take a hundred guineas for him from any man living, save Mr. Talbot himself; but if it were a question of saving him from danger, or any man he deems his friend, then, then, sir, I tell you fairly, Billy Crossley isn't so poor a man but he can afford to do a generous thing. Take him. I see you know how to sit on him ; use him well and tenderly, keep him until you find the time to give him back. And now a good journey to you wherever you go; and go quickly," whispered Billy, " for I see two fellows at the gate, who appear listening attentively to our conversation."

" Take that, in any case, as a pledge," said Mark, as he pitched a purse, containing above a hundred pounds in gold, towards Crossley; and, before the other could interpose to restore it, Mark had dashed his spurs into the beast's flanks, and in another minute was hastening down Thomas-street.

Mark had not proceeded far, when he slackened his pace to a walk—he remembered that it was yet two hours before the time, and, with the old spirit of a horseman, he husbanded the qualities of the noble animal he bestrode. Whether it was that, as the moment approached which should solve some of the many difficulties that beset him, or that the free air of the morning, and the pleasure he felt on being once more in the saddle, had rallied his mind and raised his courage, I know not, but so it was, Mark's spirits grew each instant lighter, and he rode along revolving other ones, if not happier thoughts, such as were at least in a frame more befitting his youth and the bold heart that beat within his bosom. The streets were

deserted, the great city was sleeping; the thoroughfares he had seen
crowded with brilliant equipages and hurrying masses of foot passengers
were still and vacant ; and as Mark turned from side to side to gaze on the
stately public edifices, now sleeping in their own shadows, he thought or
the dreadful conflict which, perchance, it might be his own lot to lead in that
same city—he thought of the wild shout of the insurgent masses, as with
long-pent-up but now loosened fury they poured into the devoted streets—
he fancied the swelling clangor which denoted the approach of troops,
ringing through the various approaches, and the clattering sounds of distant musketry as post after post, in different parts of the town, was
assailed. He halted before the Castle gate, where a single dragoon sat
motionless in his saddle, his carbine at rest beneath his long cloak, the very
emblem of peaceful security; and as Mark gazed on him, his lip curled with
an insolent sneer, as he thought over the false security of those within ;
and that proud banner, whose lazy folds scarce moved with the breath of
morning, "How soon may we see a national flag replace it !" were the
words he muttered, as he resumed his way as slowly as before. A few
minutes after brought him in front of the College. All was still silent in
that vast area, along which at noonday the wealth and the life of the city
poured. A single figure here appeared—a poor miserable object in tattered
black, who was occupied in fixing a placard on the front of the Post-office.
Mark stopped to watch him—there seemed something sad and miserable in
the lot of this one poor creature, singled out as it were to labour while
others were sunk in sleep. He drew near, and, as the paper was unfolded
before him, read, in large letters, the words "Capital Felony—£500 Reward ;" and then followed a description of John Barrington, which in
every particular of height, age, look, and gesture, seemed perfectly applicable to Talbot.

"Then, sorra one of me but would rather be tearing you down than
putting you up," said the bill-sticker, as, with his arms folded leisurely on
his breast, and his ragged hat set sideways on his head, he apostrophised his
handiwork.

"And why so, my good fellow?" said Mark, replying to his words.

He turned round rapidly, and pulling off his hat, exclaimed, in an accent
of unfeigned delight, "Tear an ages, captain, is it yourself? Och! och!
no," added he, in a tone of great despondency; "it is the black horse that
deceived me. I beg your honour's pardon."

"And you know this horse?" said Mark, with some anxiety of manner.

The bill-sticker made no answer, but carefully surveyed Mark for a few
moments from head to foot, and then, as if not perfectly satisfied with the
result of his scrutiny, he slowly resumed the implements of his trade, and
prepared to move on.

"Stop a moment," said Mark ; "I know what you mean, this horse beιonged to——" and he pointed with his whip to the name on the placard. "Don't be afraid of me, then, for I am his friend, perhaps the nearest friend he has in the world."

"Av you were his brother you don't like him better than I do myself. I'll never forget the night he got his head laid open for me on the bridge there beyant. The polis wanted to take me up for a bit of a ballad I was singing about Major Sirr, and they were hauling me along through the gutter, and kicking me at every step, when up comes the captain, and he sent one flying here, and the other flying there, and he tripped up the chief, calling out to me the whole time, ' Run for it, Dinny—run for it like a man! I'll give you five minutes fair start of them any way.' And he kept his word, though one of them cut his forehead clean down to the boue; and here I am now sticking up a reward to take him, God pardon me!" And the poor fellow uttered the last words in a voice of self-reproach that actually brought the tears into his eyes.

Mark threw him a crown, and pressed on once more; but somehow the convictions which he had resisted before, were now shaken by this chance meeting. The recognition of the horse at once identified Talbot with Barrington, and although Mark rejected altogether any thought which impugned the honour of his friend, he felt obliged to believe that, for some object of intrigue, Talbot had assumed the name and character of this celebrated personage. The very fact of his rescuing the bill-sticker strengthened this impression. Such an act seemed to Mark far more in unison with the wayward recklessness of Talbot's character, than with the bearing of a man who might thus expose himself to capture. With the subtlety which the will supplies to furnish arguments for its own conviction, Mark fancied how readily Talbot might have made this personation of Barrington a master-stroke of policy; and while thus he ruminated, he reached the sea shore, and could see before him that long bleak track of sand, which, uncovered save at high tide, is called "the Bull." This was the spot appointed for the meeting, and, although now within half an hour of the time, no figure was seen upon its bleak surface. Mark rode on, and crossing the narrow channel of water which separates "the Bull" from the mainland, reached the place over which, for above two miles in extent, his eye could range freely. Still no one was to be seen; the light ripple of the ebbing tide was the only sound in the stillness of the morning; there was a calmness over the surface of the sea, on which the morning sunbeams were slanting faintly, and glittering like freckled gold, wherever some passing breeze or shore-current stirred the waters. One solitary vessel could be seen, and she, a small schooner, with all her canvas bent, seemed scarcely to move.

Mark watched her, as one watches any object which relieves the dreariness of waiting. He gazed on her tall spars and white sails reflected in the sea, when suddenly a bright flash burst from her side, a light-blue smoke, followed by a booming sound, rolled forth, and a shot was seen skimming the surface of the water for above a mile in her wake; the next moment a flag was run up to her peak, when it fluttered for a moment and was then lowered again. Mark's experience of a smuggling life taught him at once to recognise these signs as signals, and he turned his gaze towards the land to discover to whom they were made; but although for miles long the coast lay beneath his view, he could see nothing that corresponded with this suspicion. A single figure on horseback was all that he could detect, and he was too far off to observe minutely. Once more Mark turned towards the ship, which now was feeling a fresher breeze and beginning to bend beneath it. The white curl that broke from her bow, and rushed foaming along her sides, showed that she was making way through the water, not as it seemed without the will of those on board, for as the wind freshened they shook out their mainsail more fully, and continued at every moment to spread sail after sail. The hollow tramp of a horse's feet galloping on the strand made Mark turn quickly round, and he saw the rider, whom he had observed before, bending his course directly towards him. Supposing it must be Talbot, Mark turned to meet him, and the horseman, who never slackened his speed, came quickly within view, and discovered the features of Frederick Travers. He was unaccompanied by friend or servant, and seemed, from the condition of his horse, to have ridden at the top of his speed. Before Mark could think of what apology he should make for, or how explain Talbot's absence, Travers addressed him:

"I half feared that it might not be you, Mr. O'Donoghue," said he, as he wiped the perspiration from his brow, for he seemed no less exhausted than his horse.

"I'm alone, sir," said Mark; "and were you not unaccompanied by a friend, I should feel the difficulty of my present position more severely."

"I know—I am aware," said Travers, hurriedly, "your friend is gone. I heard it but an hour since; you, in all likelihood, were not aware of the fact till you saw the signal yonder."

"What!—Talbot's signal! Was that his?"

"Talbot, or Barrington," said Travers, smiling; "perhaps we should better call him by the name he is best known by."

"And do you concur in the silly notion that confounds Harry Talbot with a highwayman?" said Mark, sternly.

"I fear," said Travers, "that in doing so I but follow the impression of all the world. It was not the least clever thing he has ever done, his deception of you. Be assured, Mr. O'Donoghue, that the matter admits of no doubt. The warrant for his apprehension, the informations sworn against him, are not only plain and precise, but I have myself read certain facts of his intimacy with you, the places you have frequented, the objects for which, it is alleged, you were confederated—all these are at this moment in the nands of the Secretary of State. Forgive me, sir, if I tell you that you appear to have trusted too implicitly to men who were not guided by your own principles of honour. This very day a warrant for your own arrest will be issued from the Privy Council, on the information of a man whom, I believe, you never suspected. He is a horse-dealer named Lawler—Lanty Lawler."

"And he has sworn informations against me?"

"He has done more; he has produced letters written by your hand, and addressed to different leaders of the United Irish party—letters whose treasonable contents do not admit of a doubt."

"And the scoundrel has my letters?" said Mark, as his face grew purple with passion.

"He has them no longer," said Travers. "Here they are, sir. They were shown in confidence to my father, by one who certainly is not your friend. Sir Marmaduke asked permission to let me see them, and I have taken on myself, without permission, to give them back to you."

"At whose suggestion," said Mark, proudly, "comes this act of grace? Is it your father, who extends his protection to a tenant, or is it yourself, whose wish is to humble me by an obligation?"

"There is none," said Travers, frankly. "I believe that scoundrels without heart or courage have laid a trap for a man who has both one and the other. I do not desire you should accept my conduct as a favour, still less as offering any bar to such a reckoning between us as two gentlemen of equal place and standing may demand or expect from one another."

"Say you so, indeed!" cried Mark, as his eyes flashed with joy. "Is that your meaning?"

"There's my hand on it," said Travers, "as friend or foe!"

Mark grasped his hand, and wrung it with a convulsive pressure.

"Then you are aware that you owe me such a reparation?" said he, in a voice tremulous with emotion. "You do not forget the day at Carrignacurra —beside the hearth—before my brother?"

"I remember it well," said Travers. "I ask your pardon for the insult. It was unworthy of me to have made the speech, nor have I been on good terms with myself since I uttered it."

Mark dropped his head, and uttered not a word. He could better have looked on Travers wounded and bleeding than have seen him thus elevated above himself by temper and manly candour. The vengeance he had yearned after so long was not only snatched from his grasp, but in the bitterness of disappointment its sting was turned against himself.

"This would be an unworthy cause of quarrel," said Travers; "one of which I could not but feel ashamed, and wherein you could have no pride. If we are not to be friends—and I seek no man's friendship who is not as willing to accept of mine—if we are not to be friends, let our enmity be ratified on some better cause—we surely can have little difficulty in finding one."

Mark nodded assentingly, and Travers resumed:

"There is something still more pressing than this. My father will be able to defer the issue of the warrant against you for three days, when the Privy Council will again be summoned together. Until that time you are safe. Make good use of it, therefore. Leave the capital—reach some place of security; and, after some time, when the excitement of the affair has passed away——"

"By a due expression of sorrow and penitence I might be fortunate enough to obtain the King's pardon. You were about to say so much. Is't not so?"

"Not exactly," said Frederick, smiling; "but now that the Government are in possession of the secret details of this plot, and thoroughly aware of the men engaged in it, and what their objects are, to persist in it would be hopeless folly. Believe me, the chances were never in your favour, and at present you have not a single one left. For your sake, Mr. O'Donoghue, this is most fortunate. The courage that would seem madness in a hopeless cause, will win you fame and honour where the prospects are fairer. There is a new world beyond the seas, where men of hardy minds and enterprising spirits achieve rank and fortune—in India, where war has all the features of chivalry, where personal daring and heroism are surer roads to distinction than influence and patronage; no prize will be too high for your aspirations."

Mark was silent, and Travers, conjecturing that his words were sinking into his heart, with a persuasive power went on to repicture the adventurous life which should open to him if he would consent to leave his country, and seek fortune beyond the seas. As he continued to speak, they rode along side by side, and at last came to that part of the shore where a road branched off. Here Mark suddenly drew up, and said,

"I must say good-by here, Mr. Travers. My path will lie this way for the present. Do not suspect me of want of feeling because I have not thanked you for the part you have taken; but in truth you have averted the evil from one whose life has nothing worth living for. You have saved me from a danger, but I am without a hope. Betrayed and cheated by those I trusted, I have little care for the future, because I have no confidence in anything. Nay, nay—don't speak of that again. I will not go to India— I will not accept of favours from a country that has been the enemy of my own. The epaulette which *you* wear with honour would be a badge of disgrace upon *my* shoulder. Good-by; I can afford to thank you, because you have not made a service take the form of an 'amende.'"

Travers forbore to press him further. He wisely judged that enough had been done for the present, and that his safety being provided for, time and opportunity would both present themselves for the remainder. He shook his proffered hand with cordiality, and they separated, Frederick to return to Dublin, Mark to wander wherever chance might incline him.

"He said truly," exclaimed Mark, as soon as he once more found himself separated from his companion—"he said truly, the chances were never in our favour, and at present we have not a single one left. The cause which depends on such elements as these is worse than hopeless." Such were the words that broke from him as, in sorrow and humiliation, he remembered the character of his associates, and felt, in deep shame, the companionship he had fallen into. "Had there been but one true to me!" exclaimed he, in accents of misery, "I could have stood against the shock, stout-hearted; but to find all false—all!"

Seeking out some of the least frequented lanes, he rode on for several miles, caring little which way, so long as he turned from the capital; for although as yet no personal danger threatened him, a nervous sense of shame made him dread the sight of his former acquaintances. Again and again did the thought recur to him—"How will Kate hear me spoken of? In what light will my actions be displayed to her? Is it as the miserable dupe of such a wretch as Lawler, or is it as the friend and chosen companion of Barrington, I would be known? And yet, what have I to fear, to whom no hope is left?"

Among the many sources of his sorrow one recurred at every moment, and mingled itself with every other thought: "What would their noble-hearted friends in France say of them?—how would they speak of a land whose struggle for freedom is stained with treachery, or which cannot number in the ranks of its defenders but the felon or the outlaw?"

For the deceit practised on the people he felt bitterly. He knew with what devotedness they followed the cause—the privations they had borne in silence, awaiting the time of retribution—how they had forborne all ebullitions of momentary passion, in expectation of the day of a greater reckoning—with what trust they obeyed their leaders—how implicitly they confided in every direction given for their guidance. Can patriotism like this survive such a trial? Will they ever believe in the words of their chief again? were questions which his heart answered despondingly.

The day wore over in these sad musings, and by evening Mark, who had made a wide circuit of the country, arrived at the village of Lucan, where he passed the night. As day was breaking, he was again on the road, directing his steps towards Wicklow, where, in the wild district near Blessington, he had acquaintance with several farmers, all sincerely devoted to the "United party." It was as much to rescue his own character from any false imputations that might be cast on it, as from any hope of learning

favourable tidings, that he turned hither. The mountain country, too, promised security for the present, and left him time to think what course he
should follow.

Mark did not miscalculate the good feeling of the people in this quarter.
No success, however triumphant, would have made him one half so popular
as his disasters had done. That he had been betrayed, was an appeal
stronger than all others to their best affections ; and had the deliverance of
Ireland depended on his safety, there could not have been greater efforts to
provide for it, nor more heartfelt solicitude for his own comfort. He found,
too, that the treachery of individuals did not shake general confidence in the
success of the plot, so much hope had they of French assistance and co-
operation. These expectations were often exaggerated, because the victories
of the French armies had been represented as triumphs against which no
opposition availed; but they served to keep up national courage ; and the
theme of all their discourses and their ballads was the same—" The French
will do us right."

If Mark did not fully concur in the expectations so confidently formed,
he was equally far from feeling disposed to throw any damper on them ; and
at length, as by daily intercourse these hopes became familiarised to his
mind, he ended by a partial belief in that future to which all still looked,
undismayed by past reverses. And in this way time rolled on, and the embers of rebellion died not out, but smouldered.

CHAPTER XXXV.

THE WANDERER'S RETURN.

It was about two months after the events detailed in the last chapter, on
the evening of a bright day in midsummer, that a solitary traveller was seen
descending one of the mountain passes which lead from Macroom to Glengariff, and which were only known to those well acquainted with the place.
He led his horse by the bridle, for the ground did not admit of riding; but
were it otherwise, the beast showed too many signs of a hard journey not
to make the course advisable, and, in this respect, both horse and rider well
agreed. The man, though young and athletic, was emaciated and weary-
looking. His clothes, once good, seemed neglected, and his beard, unshaven
and uncared for, gave an air of savage ferocity to a face pale and careworn,
while his horse, with as many evidences of better days, exhibited unquestionable signs of fatigue and bad feeding. The path by which he descended
was the cleft worn by a mountain torrent, a rough and rugged road, with

many spots of difficulty and danger, but neither these nor the scene which unfolded itself in the glen beneath, attracted any share of his attention; and yet few scenes were fairer to look upon. The sun was just setting, and its last glories were lighting up the purple tints upon the mountains, and shedding a flood of golden hue over lake and river. The bright yellow of the furze, and the gay colours of the foxglove, contrasted with the stern grandeur of the dark rocks, while in the abundance of wild holly and arbutus which grew from even the most precipitous places, the scene had a character of seeming cultivation to an eye unpractised to the foliage of this lovely valley. The traveller, who, for above an hour, had pursued his way, treading with the skill of a mountaineer over places where a false step might have perilled life, and guiding his horse with a caution that seemed an instinct, so little of his attention did it exact, at last halted, and leaning his arm over his saddle, stood for some time in contemplation of the picture. From the spot on which he stood, one solitary cabin was discernible on the side of the road that wound through the valley, and from whose chimney a thin blue smoke slowly curled, and floated along the mountain side. On this little habitation the traveller's eyes were fixedly bent, until their gaze was dimmed by a passing emotion. He drew his hand roughly over his face, as if angry at his own weakness, and was about to proceed on his way, when a shrill whistle from a cliff above his head arrested his step. It was a mountain recognition he well knew, and was about to reply to, when suddenly, with a bounding speed that seemed perilous in such a place, a creature clad in the most tattered rags, but with naked legs and bare head, came springing towards him.

" I knew you from the top of Goorhaun Dhub—I knew you well, Master Mark. There's not many with a good coat on their back could venture over the way you came, and I said to myself it was you," cried Terry the Woods, as, with his pale features lit up in smiles, he welcomed the young O'Donoghue to his native hills.

"How are they all yonder?" asked Mark, in a voice scarcely above a whisper, pointing with his finger up the glen in the direction of Carrignacurra, but which was not visible from where they were.

"I saw the master yesterday," replied Terry, who applied to the O'Donoghue the respected title by which he was known in his own household. " He was sitting on a big chair at the window, and the young girl with the black eyes was reading to him out of a book—but sorra much he was mindin' it, for when he seen me he beckoned this way, and says he, 'Terry, you villain, why don't you ever come up here now and talk to me?' 'Faix,' says I, 'I haven't the heart to do it. Since Master Mark was gone, I didn't like the place;' and the master wiped his eyes, and the young girl made a sign to me not to speak about that any more."

" And who is at the Lodge now?" asked Mark, endeavouring to restrain any semblance of emotion, even before Terry.

"There's nobody but the agent. The family is over in England till the house is ready for them. Oh, then, but you'll wonder to see the illigant place it is now, wid towers and spires all over it—the ground all gardens, with grass walks as fine as a carpet, and the beautifullest flowers growin' against the walls and up against the windows, and a fountain, as they call it, of cool water spouting up in the air, and coming down like rain."

"And my brother—where is he?"

"He's over in England with the family from the Lodge; the black-eyed girl, Miss Kate, wouldn't go. They say—but there's no knowing if it's true—they say she likes Hemsworth better than the captain—and, troth, if she does, it's a dhroll choice."

"Like Hemsworth! Do they say that my cousin likes Hemsworth?" said Mark, whose anger was only kept down by gazing on the tranquil features of the poor witless object before him.

"They do," said Terry, quietly, "and it's rasonable, too, seein' that he's never out of the house from morning till night."

"What house?—where do you mean?"

"What house but Carrignacurra—your father's house."

Mark passed his hand across his forehead, and over his closed eyelids, and for a second or two seemed trying to dispel some horrible vision, for deep-rooted as was his jealousy of Frederick Travers, his most gloomy forebodings had never conjured up the thought of such a rival as Hemsworth, nor did he now credit it. His indignation was, however, scarcely less to think that this man should now be received on terms of intimacy, perhaps of friendship, by those he so long pursued with insult and oppression. He paid no attention to Terry, as he continued to narrate the changes effected in his absence, and the various surmises current among the people to account for his long absence, when at length they approached the high road that led up the valley. Here Terry halted, and, pointing in the direction of Mary's cabin, about half a mile distant, said,

"I can't go any further with you. I dar'n't go there."

"And why not, my poor fellow?" said Mark, compassionately, for the terror depicted in his face too plainly indicated the return of some hallucination.

"They're there, now," said Terry, in a faint whisper, "watching for me. They're five weeks waiting to catch me, but if I keep in the mountains I needn't care."

"And who are they, Terry?"

"The soldiers," said Terry, trembling all over. "I ran away from them, and they want to shoot me for desarting."

"And there are soldiers quartered at Mary's now?"

"Ay, and at Macroom, and at Bantry, and Kinsale—they have them all round us; but divil a one o' me cares; so long as they keep to the towns, I'll never trouble them."

"And how does poor Mary bear it ?" said Mark.

"Bad enough, I hear, for nobody ever goes into the house at all since she had the red-coats, and then she's pining away every day; but I must be going. I'll come down and see you soon, Master Mark, and I hope you won't lave us in a hurry again." Terry did not wait for any rejoinder to this speech, but with the agility of his wild life, sprang lightly up the mountain, from whence his voice was heard gaily carolling as he went, long afterwards.

Mark looked after him for a few moments, and probably amid the compassionate feelings with which he regarded the poor creature, there were mingled others of actual envy, so light-hearted and happy did he seem amidst all his poverty.

"I could even change with him," said Mark, aloud; and then, as if he had unburdened his heart of its weary load, he resumed his way.

The grey twilight was fast merging into night as he approached the little inn, nor was it without emotion that he watched the light that streamed from the windows across the road. Many an evening of his happy boyhood had been passed beside that humble hearth—many a thrilling tale and many a merry story had he listened to, there. Beneath that roof it was he first imbibed the proud thoughts of his house and family, and learned to know the estimation in which men held his name. It was there he first felt the spirit of chieftainship, and there, too, he had first devoted himself to the cause of his country. Alas! these were but sad memories, how he had lived to find himself deceived, by every one he had trusted; falsehood and treachery in so many shapes surrounded him, that it needed only the extinction of hope to make him feel his life a weary and unprofitable load. He stood for a few seconds before the door, and listened with an indignant spirit to the coarse revelry of the soldiers who caroused within. Their very laughter smote upon his ear like derision, and he turned away from the spot, angry and impatient. Some vague resolve to return home and take a last farewell of his father, was the only plan he could fix on; whither, afterwards, or how, he knew not, nor did he care. Like most men who attribute their failures in life to evil destinies that sway them, and not to their own faults and follies, his fatalism urged him to a recklessness of the future, and in place of hope there sprang up in his heart a strange feeling of wonder to think what trials and straits fortune might yet have in store for him. He often deliberated with himself how he should meet, and how part with his father—whether acknowledge that he knew the secret of the deceit that had been practised upon him, or whether he should conceal that knowledge within his own bosom. To do the latter was his final resolve. To spare the old man the added misery of knowing that his son had detected his criminality, was the suggestion of his better and purer feeling, and even though his leaving him should thus be wanting in the only excuse he could proffer, he preferred this to the misery another course would entail.

At last he reached the old gateway, and often as it had been his lot to bring beneath its shadow a heavy and sorrow-struck heart, never had he passed it so deeply depressed as now.

"Come on, good beast," he said, patting the wearied horse, "you shall have rest here; and that," said he, with a sigh—"that is more than I can promise to myself."

With these sad words he toiled up the steep ascent, and gained the terrace in front of the castle. There were lights burning in the old tower and in the hall, but all the rest of the building was in darkness. The door lay open, and, as Mark stood within it, he could hear the mellow sounds of a harp which came floating softly through the long-vaulted corridor, blended with a voice that stirred the fibres of his strong heart, and made him tremble like a child.

"Why should I not linger here?" thought he—"why not stay and listen to these sweet sounds? I shall never hear them more!" And he stood and bent his ear to drink them in, and stirred not until they ceased. The last chord had died away in silence, then, hastily fastening his horse to the door ring, he entered the long passage unnoticed by any, and reached the door. The sound of voices, as of persons talking pleasantly together, struck harshly on his ear, and the loud laughter that burst forth grated strangely on his senses.

"They have little sorrow for the outcast, that is certain," said he, as, with a swelling heart and proud step, he opened the door and entered.

This part of the room lay in deep shadow, and while Mark could distinctly perceive the others, they could but dimly discern the outline of his figure, without being able to recognise him. His father and Sir Archy were seated, as of old, on either side of the chimney; Kate was leaning over her harp, which she had just ceased to play, while, seated near her, and bending forward in an attitude of eager attention, was Hemsworth himself, the man of all others he least wished to see at such a moment.

"Who is that?" cried the O'Donoghue—"who is standing yonder?" And they all turned their eyes towards the door.

"Why don't you speak?" continued the old man. "Have you any tidings from my son?—is it news of Mark you bring me?"

"Even so, sir," responded the other, as he slowly advanced into the strong light, his arms folded upon his breast, and his brow stern and contracted.

"Mark!—my boy! my child!" cried the old man, springing from his chair, and, with a strength that seemed at once to defy age and infirmity, rushed towards him, and threw his arms about him. "He's here—he's with us once more!" said he, in accents half-choked by sobs—"my son! my hope! my pride!" And while the old man poured forth these words of happiness, the young one stood pale, cold, and seemingly apathetic. His eyes bent on vacancy, and his features devoid of all expression of passion, he turned from Sir Archy, who grasped one hand, and looked at Kate, who held the other between hers, but in his gaze there was rather the look of one suddenly recalled to consciousness out of some long-fevered sleep than the healthful aspect of waking life.

"You are not ill, Mark—you're only fatigued," said Kate, as a tear slowly trickled down her cheek, and fell upon his hand.

Mark started as he felt the drop, and looked at her with a searching glance; then turned his eyes towards Hemsworth, and back again to her, and, for the first time, a stern and scornful smile curled upon his lip. Kate seemed to read the glance, and returned it with a look proud and haughty as his own, while, dropping his hand, she walked towards her chair without speaking.

"We maun let him hae a bit supper as soon as may be," said Sir Archy, whose practical good sense saw how much bodily fatigue influenced the youth's demeanour.

"Supper!" said the O'Donoghue. "Ay, faith, every bottle in the cellar would be too little to celebrate the boy's return! Ring that bell, Archy. Where is Kerry? What are the people doing not to know that their young master is here?"

"At another moment, I should beg that Mr. O'Donoghue might remember me," said Hemsworth, with a deferential bow. "And I hope the time is coming when I may be permitted to renew my acquaintance. For the present, I feel how unsuited the presence of a stranger is, on an occasion like this, and cannot better show how deeply I appreciate feeling than by taking my leave."

So saying, he courteously saluted the O'Donoghue, Sir Archy, and Kate; while, turning to Mark, he proffered his hand, as he said,

"Pray, sir, let the occasion excuse the liberty, and permit me to add my welcome also."

"You do the honours of this house too early, sir," was Mark's savage reply, while he folded his arms upon his breast, and measured Hemsworth with a glance of withering scorn. "I'm beneath my father's roof. It is not for a stranger to bid me welcome here."

Hemsworth smiled and muttered some words in mild acquiescence; their tone and accent were apologetic, and the manner in which he spoke them humble even to humility. When they were uttered, he bowed deeply, and with a look towards the others that seemed to indicate the absence of any feeling of offence, withdrew.

"You are unco severe on Mister Hemsworth, Mark," said Sir Archy, gravely. "If his politeness was na altogether correct, it was weel intended."

"Mark was all right, whatever he said," cried the old man, exultingly. "Egad! I'll not dispute with the boy to-night, if he thought proper to throw the fellow out of the window."

"I am sorry my rudeness should have offended others," said Mark, with a sidelong glance at Kate. "As for Mr. Hemsworth, we understand each other. He neither thinks better nor worse of me than he did before."

"D—n Hemsworth!" said the O'Donoghue. "Why are we talking of him at all? Sit down beside me, Mark. Let me see you again, my boy, in your old place. Give me your hand, and let me think that my three months of fretting have only been a dream."

"Would it had been a dream to me," said Mark, with a deep sigh, as he seated himself beside the old man.

"Come, come, Mark," said Sir Archy; "ye hae often laughed at my Scotch adage about 'byganes,' let me have my revenge now, by applying it to your own fortunes."

"So, you have come at last," cried the O'Donoghue, as Kerry O'Leary at length made his appearance at the door. "Is Master Mark to go supperless to bed?"

"Master Mark!" shouted Kerry. "Oh, murther alive! and is it himself that's in it? Oh, blessed honr! but I'm glad to see you home again, and your honour looking so well and hearty. Maybe we won't have bonfires over the hills, when the boys hear it."

"The supper! the supper! Confound the fellow! the boy is famished, and the rascal stands prating there about bonfires."

"My horse is far more in need of care than I am," said Mark, suddenly remembering the wearied animal he left fastened to the door. "I must look to the poor beast before I take anything myself." And so saying he left the room, none wishing to gainsay anything he desired to do.

"Poor fellow!" said the O'Donoghue, "how pale and careworn he looks —he appears to have suffered heavily."

"Depend upon it," said Sir Archy, gravely, "the lad has learned much since we saw him last. I dinna mislike the look his features have, although it be one of sorrow. What says Kate?" No answer followed this appeal, but the young girl turned away her head, and affected to assist in arranging the table.

"Mind, Archy," said the O'Donoghue, eagerly; "remember, not a word about his absence—no questioning whatever; the boy has gone through too many troubles already to bear the penalty of relating them. Take care, too, that there be no allusion to Hemsworth; Mark does not yet know the friendly part he has taken, and only knows him as we used to think and speak of him of old. But hush! here he comes."

When Mark re-entered the room, he seemed at least easier, if not happier than before. The cloud that Hemsworth's presence threw over him had passed away, and he felt anxious to show himself in more favourable colours than his first appearance had displayed. While, therefore, he did his utmost to repay to his father and uncle the kind and affectionate greetings by which they met him, to his cousin Kate he was either sternly distant, or totally indifferent in manner; and when at last, repulsed in many efforts to attract his notice, she arose to retire for the night, he took a formal leave of her, and seemed relieved by her departure. This was not remarked by the O'Donoghue; but Sir Archy was a shrewd observer, and noted the circumstance with displeasure; still, too careful of consequences to show that he had observed it, he reserved his interference for another and more favourable moment, and soon afterwards wished them good night, and left the room.

"It is time for me to go also," said Mark, as, after a silence of some moments, he arose, and lighted a candle. "I have not been accustomed to a good bed latterly, and I feel that one sound night's sleep is due to me."

"But for that, Mark, I could not part with you just yet. I have so much to say—so much to hear from you. There have been many things during your absence I must tell you of."

"And, first of all," said Mark, rapidly, "how comes that man Hemsworth so intimate here? What claim has he to darken our door with his presence?"

"The strong claim of true friendship," said the old man, firmly—"a claim I have not met so much of in life that I can afford to undervalue it when it does present itself. But for him, the ejectment would have been sued out last assizes—he saved us also from a foreclosure of Drake's mortgage—advanced me five thousand pounds upon my own bond, Archy being a co-surety, which you well know was a matter of form. This, besides saving us from any proceedings the Traverses might have taken, in revenge for their own disappointment about Kate——"

"Speak more plainly, I beg you, sir, and, above all, please to remember that I am ignorant of everything you allude to. What of Kate?"

"Oh, I forgot you were not with us then. It was a proposal of marriage. Young Travers made your cousin a brilliant offer, as far as money was concerned, which Kate refused. There was some negotiation about leaving the thing open. Something about the future—I forget exactly what—but I only know she was peremptory and decided, as she always is, and wrote to me to take her home. Archy went up for her to Dublin, and the Traverses soon after left Ireland in high indignation with us, and determined, as we soon found, to let us feel their enmity. Then it was that we learned to appreciate Hemsworth, whom all along we had so completely mistaken; and, indeed, but for him, we should never have heard of you."

"Of me! What did he know of me?"

"Everything, Mark—all," said the old man, in a low whisper, as he stole a prying glance through the room to satisfy himself that they were not overheard.

"Once more, sir, speak out, and intelligibly—say what this man assumes to know of me."

"He knew Talbot—Barrington rather," said the O'Donoghue, in a low voice—"knew of your intercourse with him—knew of the plot that fellow laid to entangle you in his schemes—knew all about the robbery at the Curragh, and saved you, without your knowing it, from being there. But for him, Mark, your name would have figured in the *Hue and Cry*. A reward for your apprehension was actually deliberated at the Privy Council. Hemsworth rescued you from this——"

"The scoundrel—the base, black-hearted villain," exclaimed Mark, "did he dare to speak thus of *me?*"

"You mistake, Mark, he never said you were culpable—he only deplored the fatal accident of your intimacy with Barrington—a man twice convicted and sentenced—that in company with this man you frequented certain houses of high play, where more than one large robbery was effected. Then came the Castle ball—was it not true that you went there? Well, the diamond snuff-box stolen from Lord Clangoff, at the card table——"

"Hell and confusion! you will drive me mad," cried Mark, stamping his foot with passion. "This infernal mixture of truth and falsehood—this half-fact and all-lying statement is more than my brain can bear. What does this scoundrel mean—is it that I am guilty of a robbery?"

"Heaven forbid, boy, but that you lived on terms of closest friendship with one branded as a felon, and that information of your intimacy with him was obtained by the police, who, for political reasons—you are aware of what I mean—would strain a point to have caught you within their grasp. There were letters, too, Mark, written by you, and of such a character as would, if proved against you, have cost your life; these, Hemsworth, by some means, obtained and destroyed."

"Ah! did he so?" cried Mark, eagerly, for now a sudden light broke in upon him of the game that Hemsworth had played; "and so, he burned my letters?"

"You know now, then, something of the services he rendered you," said the old man, who began at last to be satisfied that conviction was coming home to Mark's mind.

"I do," replied he, calmly ; "I believe that I can appreciate his kindness, and I believe also I may promise that I shall not prove ungrateful. And Kate, sir, what said she to those revelations concerning me?"

"What we all said, Mark, that nothing dishonourable would ever lie at

your door—there might be rashness, imprudence, and folly, but guilt or dishonour, never."

" And my uncle, he is generally a shrewd and cautious judge—what was
his opinion ?"

" Faith, it is hard to say, Mark, but I think with all his affected freedom
from prejudice, he nourishes his old notions about Hemsworth as strong as
ever, and persists in thinking the Travers family everything amiable and
high-minded ; indeed, he forced me to let Herbert accompany them to
England—for I let him take the boy into his own hands—and so, as the invitation had been made and accepted before Kate had refused the captain's
offer, I thought it would look better even to suffer matters to take their
course quietly, as if nothing had happened."

" It was well done," said Mark, assentingly ; " and now I have heard
enough to dream over for one night at least, and so I'll to bed."

" Remember, Mark," said the O'Donoghue, grasping his son's arm—"remember, I am solemnly pledged to Hemsworth never to tell you anything
of these matters—it was a promise he exacted from me; I rely upon you,
Mark, not to betray me."

" My discretion is above price, sir," said Mark, smiling dubiously, and
left the room.

CHAPTER XXXVI.

SUSPICIONS ON EVERY SIDE.

EARLY on the following morning Mark O'Donoghue was on his way to
the Lodge. To see Hemsworth, and dare him to a proof of his assertions
regarding him, or provoke him, if possible, to a quarrel, were his waking
thoughts throughout the night, and not even all his weariness and exhaustion could induce sleep. He did not, indeed, know the full depth of the
treachery practised against him ; but in what he had discovered there were
circumstances that portended a well-planned and systematic scheme of
villany. The more Mark reflected on these things, the more he saw the
importance of proceeding with a certain caution. Hemsworth's position at
Carrignacurra, the advances he had made in his father's esteem, the place he
seemed to occupy in Kate's good graces, were such that any altercation
which should not succeed in unmasking the infamy of his conduct, would
only be regarded as a burst of boyish intemperance and passion; and
although Mark was still but too much under the influence of such motives,

he was yet far less so than formerly; besides, to fix a duel on Hemsworth might be taken as the consequences of a sense of rivalry on his part, and anger that his cousin had preferred him to himself. This thought was intolerable; the great effort he proposed to his heart was to eradicate every sentiment of affection for his cousin, and every feeling of interest. To be able to regard her as one whose destiny had never crossed with his own— to do this, was now become a question of self-esteem and pride. To return her indifference as haughtily as she bestowed it, was a duty he thought he owed to himself, and therefore he shrank from anything which would have the faintest semblance of avenging his own defeat.

Such were some of the difficulties of his present position, and he thought them over long and patiently, weighing well the consequences each mode of acting might entail, and deliberating with himself as to what course he should follow. His first resolve, then, which was to fasten a hostile meeting upon Hemsworth, was changed for what seemed a better line of procedure—which was simply to see that gentleman, to demand an explanation of the statements he had made concerning him, calling upon him to retract whenever anything unfounded occurred, and requiring him to acknowledge that he had given a colouring and semblance to his conduct at total variance with fact. By this means, Mark calculated on the low position to which Hemsworth would be reduced in Kate's estimation, the subterfuges and excuses he would be forced to adopt,—all the miserable expedients to gloss over his falsehood, and all the contemptible straits to conceal his true motives. To exhibit him in this light before Kate's eyes, she whose high sense of honour never brooked the slightest act that savoured of mere expediency, would be a far more ample revenge than any which should follow a personal rencontre.

"She shall see him in his true colours," muttered he to himself, as he went along; "she shall know something of the man to whom she would pledge honour and affection; and then, when his treachery is open as the noonday, and the blackness of his heart revealed, she shall be free to take him, unscathed and uninjured. I'll never touch a hair of his head."

Mark had a certain pride in thus conducting himself on this occasion; to show that he possessed other qualities than those of rash and impetuous courage, that he could reason calmly and act deliberately, was now the great object he had at heart. Nor was the least motive that prompted him the desire he felt to exhibit himself to Kate in circumstances more favourable than any mere outbreak of indignant rage would display him.

The more he meditated on these things, the more firm and resolute were his determinations not to suffer Hemsworth to escape his difficulties, by converting the demand for explanation into an immediate cause of quarrel. Such a tactique he thought it most probable Hemsworth would at once adopt, as the readiest expedient in his power.

"No," said Mark to himself, "he shall find that he has mistaken me; my patience and endurance will stand the proof; he must and shall avow his own baseness, and then, if he wish for fighting——"

The clenched lip and flashing eye the words were accompanied by, plainly confessed that, if Mark had adopted a more pacific line of conduct, it certainly was not in obedience to any temptations of his will.

Immersed in his reveries, he found himself in front of the Lodge before he was aware of it; and, although his thoughts were of a nature that left him little room for other considerations, he could not help standing in surprise and admiration at the changes effected in his absence. The neat but unpretending cottage had now been converted into a building of Elizabethan style; the front extended along the lake side, to which it descended in two terraced gardens. The ample windows, thrown open to the ground, displayed a suite of apartments furnished with all that taste and luxury could suggest—the walls ornamented by pictures, and the panels of both doors and window-shutters formed of plate glass, reflecting the mountain scenery in every variety of light and shadow. The rarest flowers, the most costly shrubs, brought from long distances, at great risk and price, were here assembled to add their beauties to a scene where nature had already been so lavish.

While Mark was yet looking about in quest of the entrance to the building, he saw a man approach, with whose features he was well acquainted. This was no other than Sam Wylie, the sub-agent, the same he had treated so roughly when last they met. The fellow seemed to know that, though in certain respects the tables were now turned, yet, with such a foe as Mark O'Donoghue, any exhibition of triumph might be an unsafe game; so he touched his hat, and was about to move past in silence, when Mark cried out,

"I want to speak with your master—can I see him?"

"Master!" said Wylie, and his sallow face grew sallower and sicklier. "If ye mean Mr. Hemsworth, sir——"

"Of course I do. If I spoke of Sir Marmaduke Travers, I should mean *his* master. Is he at home?"

"No, sir; he has left the Lodge."

"Left it!—since when? I saw him last night at ten o'clock."

"He left here before eleven," was Wylie's answer.

"When is he expected back?"

"Not for a week, at soonest, sir. It may be even longer, if, as he said, it were necessary for him to go to England."

"To England!" exclaimed Mark, in bitter disappointment, for in the distance the hope of speedy vengeance seemed all but annihilated. "What is his address in Dublin?" said he, recovering himself.

"To the office of the Upper Secretary, sir, I am to address all his letters," said Wylie, for the first time venturing on a slight approach to a smile. "His hotel, I mean. Where does he stop in the city?"

"He usually stays in the Lower Castle-yard, sir, when in town, and probably will be there now, as the Privy Council is sitting, and they may want to examine him."

The slow, measured tone in which these few words were uttered gave them a direct application to Mark himself, which made him flush deeply. He stood for a few seconds, seemingly in doubt, and then turned his steps towards home.

"Did you hear what the young O'Donoghue said, there, as he passed?" said Wylie to a labouring man who stood gazing after the youth.

"I did, faix," replied the other; "I heerd it plain enough."

"Tell me the words, Pat—I'd like to hear them."

"'Tis what he said—'He's escaped me this time; but, by G——, he'll not have the same luck always.'"

"It was Mr. Hemsworth he was after," said Wylie. "It was him he meant."

"To be sure it was; didn't I hear him asking after him?"

"All right—so you did," added Wylie, nodding. "Take care you don't forget the words, that's all, and here's the price of a glass to keep your memory fresh."

And he chucked a sixpence to the man, who, as he caught it, gave a look of shrewd intelligence, that showed he felt there was a compact between them.

Mark moved homewards in deep thought. There was a time when disappointment would have irritated him rather than have suggested any new expedient for success. Now he was changed in this respect. If baffled, he did not feel defeated. His first anger over, he began to think how best he should obtain a meeting with Hemsworth, and a retractation of his calumnies against himself. To venture back to Dublin would have been unsafe on every account. The informations sworn against him by Lanty Lawler might be at any moment used for his capture. In Glenflesk alone was he safe; so long as he remained there, no force Government would think of sending against him could avail; nor was it likely, for the sake of so humble an individual as himself, that they would take measures which would have the effect of disclosing their knowledge of the plot, and thus warn other and more important persons of the approaching danger. Mark's first determination to leave home at once was thus altered by these casual circumstances. He must await Hemsworth's return, since, without the explanation he looked for, he never could bring himself to take leave of his friends. As he pondered thus, a servant in Hemsworth's livery rode rapidly past him. Mark looked suddenly up, and perceived, with some surprise, from the train of dust upon the road, that the man was coming from Carrignacurra. Slight as the incident was, he turned his thoughts from his own fortunes to fix them on those of his cousin Kate. By what magic this man Hemsworth had won favour in her eyes he could not conceive. That he should have overcome all the prejudices of his father was strange enough ; but that Kate, whose opinions of people seldom or ever underwent a change, and who of all others professed to dislike that very plausibility of manner which Hemsworth possessed, that she could forgive and forget the tyrannies with which his name was associated—she whose spirit no sordid bait could tempt, nor any mean object of personal ambition bias—this was, indeed, inexplicable. Twice or thrice a thought flashed across him, if it should not be true—if it was merely one of those rumours which the world builds on circumstances—that Hemsworth's intimacy was the sole foundation for the report, and the friendly interchange of visits the only reason for the story.

"I must know this," said Mark ; "it may not be too late to save her. I may have come back in the very nick of time, and, if so, I shall deem this piece of fortune more than enough to requite all the mischances of my life."

As he spoke thus he had reached the little flower-garden, which, in front of the tower, was the only spot of cultivation around the old building. His eye wandered over the evidences of care, few and slight as they were, with pleasant thoughts of her who suggested the culture, when at the turn of a walk he beheld his cousin coming slowly towards him.

"Good morrow, Mark," said she, extending her hand, and with a smile that betokened no angry memory of the preceding night ; "you took but little sleep for one so much fatigued as you were."

"And you, cousin, if I mistake not, even as little. I saw a light burning in your room when day was breaking."

"An old convent habit," said she, smiling. " Our matins used to be as early."

A low, soft sigh followed this speech.

"Yes," said Mark, "you have reason to regret it; your life was happier there ; you had the pleasure of thinking that, many a mile away in this remote land, there were relatives and friends to whom you were dear, and of whom you might feel proud. Sad experience has told you how unworthy we are of your affection, how much beneath your esteem. The cold realities that strip life of its ideal happiness are only endurable when age has blunted our affections and chilled our hearts. In youth their poignancy is agony itself. Yes, Kate, I can dare to say it, even to you, would that you had never come amongst us."

"I will not misunderstand you, Mark ; I will not affect to think that in your speech there is any want of affection for me; I will take it as you mean it, that it had been better for me; and, even on your own showing, I tell you, nay. If I have shed some tears within these old walls, yet have my brightest hours been passed within them. Never, until I came here, did I know what it was to minister to another's happiness; never did I feel before the ecstasy of being able to make joy more pleasurable, and sorrow less afflicting. The daughter feeling has filled up what was once a void in my poor heart; and when you pity me for this life of loneliness, my pulse has throbbed with delight to think how a duty, rendered by one as humble and insignificant as I am, can ennoble life, and make of this quiet valley a scene of active enjoyment."

" So you are happy here, Kate," said he, taking her hand, "and would not wish to leave it ?"

" No, Mark, never. There would be no end to my ambition were the great world open to me, and the prizes all glittering before me—ambitions which should take the shape, not of personal aggrandisement, but high hope for objects that come not within a woman's sphere. Here, affection sways me ; there, it might be prejudice or passion."

"Ambition !" muttered Mark, catching at the word—"ambition! The penalty you pay for it is far too high ; and, were the gain certain, it is dearly bought by a heart dead to all purer emotions, cold to every affection of family and kindred, and a spirit made suspecting by treachery. No, Kate, no; the humblest peasant on that mountain, whose toil is for his daily bread, whose last hope at night is for the health that on the morrow shall sustain more labour, he has a nobler life than those who nourish high desires by trading on the crimes and faults of others. I had ambition once; God knows, it grew not in me from any unworthy hope of personal advantage. I thought of myself then as meanly as I now do; but I dreamt that, by means humble and unworthy as mine, great events have been sometimes set in motion. The spark that ignites the train is insignificant enough in itself, though the explosion may rend the solid masonry that has endured for ages. Well, well, the dream is over now ; let us speak of something else. Tell me of Herbert, Kate. What success has he met with in the University ?"

" He failed the first time, but the second trial made ample amends for that defeat. He carried away both prizes from his competitors, Mark, and stands now, confessedly, the most distinguished youth of his day; disappointment only nerved his courage. There was a failure to avenge, as well as a goal to win, and he has accomplished both."

" Happy fellow, that his career in life could depend on efforts of his own making—who needed but to trust his own firm resolve, and his own steady pursuit of success, and cared not how others might plot, and plan, and intrigue around him."

" Very true, Mark; the prizes of intellectual ambition have this advantage, that they are self-won; but, bethink you, are not other objects equally noble—are not the efforts we make for others more worthy of fame than those which are dictated by purely personal desire of distinction ?"

Mark almost started at the words, whose direct application to himself could not be doubted, and his cheek flushed, partly with pride, partly with shame.

"Yes," said he, after a brief pause, "these are noble themes, and can stir a heart as sorrow-struck as mine; but the paths that lead upwards, Kate, are dark and crooked—the guides that traverse them are false and treacherous."

"You have, indeed, found them so," said Kate, with a deep sigh.

"How do you mean, I have found them so?" cried Mark, in amazement at the words.

"I mean what I have said, Mark, that betrayal and treachery have tracked you for many a day. You would not trust me with your secret, Mark, nor yet confide in me, when an accident left it in my possession. Chance has revealed to me many circumstances of your fortune, and even now, Mark, I am only fearful lest your own prejudices should hazard your safety. Shall I go on? May I speak still more plainly?"

Mark nodded, and she resumed:

"One who never favoured the cause you adopted, probably from the very confederates it necessitated, yet saw with sympathy how much truth and honour were involved in the struggle, has long watched over you, stretching out, unseen, the hand to help, and the shield to protect you. He saw in you the generous boldness of one whose courage supplies the nerve, that mere plotters trade upon but never possess. He saw that, once in the current, you would be swept along, while they would watch you from the shore. He, I say, saw this, and with a generosity the greater because no feelings of friendship swayed him, he came forward to save you."

"And this unseen benefactor," said Mark, with a proud look of scornful meaning, "his name is——"

"I will not speak it, if you ask me thus," said Kate, blushing, for she read in his glance the imputation his heart was full of. "Could you so far divest yourself of prejudice as to hear calmly, and speak dispassionately, I could tell you anything—everything, Mark."

"No, Kate, no," said he, smiling dubiously; "I have no right to ask—perhaps not to accept of such a confidence."

"Be it so, then," said she, proudly, "we will speak of this no more;" and, with a slight bow, and a motion of her hand, she turned into another alley of the garden, and left Mark silently musing over the scene. Scarcely, however, had she screened herself from his view by the intervening trees, than she hastened her steps, and soon gained the house. Without stopping to take breath, she ascended the stairs, and tapped at Sir Archy's door.

"Come in, my sweet Kate," said he, in his blandest voice; "I should

know that gentle tap amid a thousand.   But, my dear child, why so pale?—
what has agitated you?   Sit down and tell me."

"Read this, sir," said she, taking a letter from the folds of her handkerchief; "this will tell you all, shorter and more collectedly than I can.   I
want your advice and counsel, and quickly, too, for no time is to be lost."

"This is Mr. Hemsworth's writing," said Sir Archy, as he adjusted his
spectacles to read.   " When did you receive it ?"

" About an hour ago," answered Kate, half impatient at the unhurried
coolness of the old man's manner, who at last proceeded to examine the
epistle, but without the slightest show of anxiety or eagerness.   His apathy
was, however, short-lived; short expressions of surprise broke from him,
followed by exclamations of terror and dismay, till at length, laying down
the letter, he said,

"Leave me, sweet Kate—leave me to read and reflect on this alone.   Be
assured I'll lose no time in making up my mind about it, for I see that hours
are precious here."   And as she glided from the room Sir Archy placed the
open letter on a table before him, and sat down diligently to reconsider its
contents.

CHAPTER XXXVII.

HEMSWORTH'S LETTER.

THE letter over which Sir Archy bent in deep thought was from Hemsworth.   It was dated the night before, and addressed to Kate O'Donoghue,
and, although professing to have been hurriedly written, an observer as acute
as Sir Archy could detect ample evidence of great care and consideration in
its composition.   Statements seemingly clear and open, were in reality confused and vague ; assertions were qualified, and, in lieu of direct and positive information, there were scattered throughout hopes and fears, wishes
and expectations, all capable of being sustained, whatever the issue of the
affair they referred to.

The letter opened with a respectful apology for addressing Miss O'Donoghue, but pleading that the urgency of the case, and the motives of the
writer, might be received as a sufficient excuse.   After stating, in sufficiently
vague terms to make the explanation capable of a double meaning, the
reasons for selecting her, and not either of her uncles, for the correspondence, it entered at once upon the matter of the communication in these
words :

"I have hesitated and doubted, Miss O'Donoghue, how far my inter-ference in the affairs of your family may be misconstrued, and whether the prejudices which were once entertained to my disadvantage might not now be evoked to give a false colouring to my actions. These doubts I have resolved, by reflecting that they are for the most part personal, and that if I succeed in rendering real service, the question is comparatively indifferent what light or shadow it may seem to throw on my conduct. A candid and impartial judgment I certainly look to from *you*, and I confess myself at liberty to lay less store by the opinions of others."

Continuing for a brief space in this strain, the letter went on to mention that the sudden return of Mark had left the writer no alternative but to venture on this correspondence, whatever the consequences—consequences which, the writer palpably inferred, might prove of the last moment to him-self. The explanation—and, for the reader's sake, it is better to spare him Hemsworth's involved narrative, and merely give its substance—was chiefly that information of Mark O'Donoghue's complicity in the plot of the United Irish party had been tendered to Government, and supported by such evi-dence that a judge's warrant was issued for his apprehension and the seizure of all his papers ; partly from friendly interference—this was dubiously and delicately put by Hemsworth—and partly from the fact that his extreme youth and ignorance of the real views of the insurgents were pleaded in his favour, the execution of this warrant was delayed, and the young man suffered to go at large. So long as he withdrew himself from the company of the other conspirators, and avoided publicity, the Government was willing to wink at the past. It had been, however, determined on, that, should he either be found mixed up with any of the leaders of the movement in future, or should he venture to return to Glenflesk, where his influence amongst the peasantry was well known to, and apprehended by, the Govern-ment, then there should no longer be any hesitation in the line to be fol-lowed. He was immediately to be apprehended, and sent up under a sufficient escort to Dublin, to take his trial, with five others, for high treason. The proofs of his guilt were unquestionable, consisting of letters written and received, conversations to which witnesses could depose, as well as an inti-macy, for months long, with Barrington, whose active participation in the schemes of rebellion was as well known as the notorious fact of his being a convicted felon. To found a hope upon his innocence was thus shown to be perfectly impossible. His most trusted associates were the evidence against him ; documents in his handwriting were also in the hands of the law officers of the Crown, and, in fact, far more than enough to bring him to the scaffold.

Hemsworth, who gently hinted all through how far his interference had been beneficial, was one of those entrusted with Mark's arrest, should he ever dare to reappear in his native country. The orders of the Privy

278 THE O'DONOGHUE.

Council on this score were positive and clear, aud admitted of no possible misconception.

"You may judge, then," continued he, "what were my feelings on seeing him suddenly euter the house last night—to think that, while I was enjoying the pleasure of your society and the hospitable attentions of your home, I had actually in my pocket at the moment the official order to apprehend the eldest sou of my entertainer—the friend and companion of your child-hood—to bring grief and mourning beueath the roof where I had passed so many happy hours—to dispel all the dreams I had begun to nourish of a neighbourhood connected by ties of kindness and good will. I had to choose between the alternative of this, or else, by a palpable avoidance of my duty, criminate myself, and leave my conduct open to the most dangerous com-ments of my enemies. The latter involved only myself. I have adopted it, and before this letter reaches your hands, I shall be on my way up to Dublin, nominally to attend the Council, but in reality to escape the neces-sity my onerous position would impose. Noue save those beneath your roof know that I have met Mr. Mark O'Douoghue, and I shall be half way to Dublin before his arrival in the country is suspected. So much, in brief, for the past and the present. Now for the future. There are two courses open to this young gentleman, or to those who would serve and befriend him. One is, by a free aud unlimited confession to the Government of all the circumstances of the plot, so far as they have come to his knowledge, the parties interested, their several shares iu the undertaking, with every detail of date and time, to sue for a pardon for himself—a grace which, I need scarcely say, I will use all my influence to obtain. The other mode is, by a temporary exile, to withdraw himself from the notice of the Govern-ment, until the danger having perfectly passed over, political acrimony will have abated, and the necessity for making severe examples of guilt be no longer urgent. This latter course I opine to be preferable, on many grounds. It demands no sacrifice of private feeling — no surrender of honour. It merely provides for safety, reserving the future untrammelled by any pledge. Neither need the absence be long; a year or two at farthest; the probabilities are, that with their preseut knowledge of the schemes of the insurgents, the Government can either precipitate eveuts, or retard and protract them at will; their policy, in this respect, depending on the rauk and importauce of those who, by either line of procedure, would be delivered into their hands. Arguing from what they have already done, I should pronounce it likely that their game will be to wait, to weaken the hopes and break the spirit of the United party, by frequent defectious to sow distrust and suspicion amougst them, and thus, while avoiding the ne-cessity of bloodshed, to wear out rebellion by a long and lingering fear. If, then, others, whose age aud position involved a greater promiueuce in these schemes, would require a longer banishment to erase the memory of the acts, your young relative, who has both youth and its rashness to plead for him, need not reckon on so lengthened an absence from his native land.

"Above all things, however, remember that not an hour is to be lost. Any moment may disclose to the Crown some new feature of the plot, and may call forth measures of stringent severity. The proclamation offering a reward for the apprehension of four persons, of whom your cousin is one, is already printed, and in the office of the Secretary. An hour would see it all over the walls of the capital, in a day or two more it would reach every remote corner of the land. Then, all efforts on my part would be ineffectual, were they even possible. Reflect on this. It is not a mere question of fine or even imprisonment. It is life itself is on the issue, and life which, in surrendering, will blast a great name with dishonour, and a great house with obloquy and shame; for there has been no struggle, no effort, no bold and generous exposure to danger, to palliate treason, and gloss over its faults. All has been plotting and contriving for alien assistance and foreign help; no self-reliance, no patriotism, which, if mistaken, was still sincere and manly. Reflect on all this, and think a life offered up in such a cause has no martyrdom to throw lustre on the grave shared with the felon and the highwayman. Forgive me if, in the warmth of my zeal, I have said one word which may offend. If I had not spoken thus forcibly, I should be a traitor to my own heart.

"I have written hurriedly, and I doubt not, in some respects, unadvisedly; but the sincerity of my purpose will plead for me, should the indiscretion of my zeal require apology. You will, perhaps, ask why I should have imposed a task difficult as this upon you—why I should have loaded you with a responsibility so weighty? My answer is simply, I dared not write to the O'Donoghue on the subject of his son's indiscretion—to impugn the acts of the young man, would be to forfeit all influence with the old one. You will then say, why not address Sir Archibald? For the simple reason, that the prejudices of his country are too strong in him to make due allowances for those who err from excitable or impetuous natures; not only would he judge too harshly of Mark, but he would be anxious to record that judgment as a warning to Herbert, for whom alone he is interested. I therefore make it a strenuous request—nay, more, I esteem it as the term of a compact between us, that you do not show this letter either to the O'Donoghue or to his brother. I have expressed myself openly and candidly to you, but with a tacit assurance that my confidence is not to be extended to others. In the part I have taken, I already incur considerable risk. This is a period when loyalty cannot afford to be even suspected; yet have I jeoparded mine in befriending this youth. I now conclude, dear madam, assuring you that any danger I incur, or any anxiety I feel, will be amply repaid if I only know that you think not unworthily of

"WILLIAM HEMSWORTH."

Sir Archy studied this letter with the patient care a lawyer bestows upon a brief. He thought over each sentence, and weighed the expressions in his mind with deep thought. It had been his fortune, in early life, to have been thrown into situations of no common difficulty, and his mind had, in consequence, acquired a habit of shrewd and piercing investigation, which, though long disused, was not altogether forgotten ; by the aid of this faculty, Hemsworth's letter appeared to him in a very different light from that in which Kate viewed it. The knowledge of every circumstance concerning Mark evinced an anxiety which he was very far from attributing to motives of friendship. Sir Archy well knew the feelings of dislike which subsisted between these two men—how then account for this sudden change on Hemsworth's part ?—to what attribute this wonderful interest concerning him ?

" Let us see," said the old man to himself—" let us see the fruit, and then we may pronounce upon the tree. Where and to what does Hemsworth's benevolence point ? Dishonour or banishment ! Such are the terms he offers; such are the alternatives his kindness suggests. Might these have no other motive than friendship ?—might they not be the offspring of feelings very different indeed ? What benefit might he derive from Mark's expatriation ?—that is the question. Does he anticipate easier terms with the old man for the little remnant of property that still pertains to him—or is it merely the leaven of the old hate that still rises in his nature ?—or"— and here his eye flashed with brilliancy as a new thought crossed his brain —" or does he suspect Mark of occupying a place in his cousin's affection, and is rivalry the source of this mysterious good-nature ?"

This suspicion no sooner occurred to him than Sir Archy recalled to mind all the circumstances of Hemsworth's recent behaviour—the endeavours he had made to recommend himself to their favourable notice—all his acts to ingratiate himself with Kate—the ample views he affected in politics—the wide-spread generosity of his plans for the amelioration of the people. That his conduct was unreal, that his principles were but assumed for the occasion, the shrewd Scotchman had long suspected; and this letter, so far from dispelling the doubts, increased them tenfold. Besides this, there seemed some reason to fear that Kate was not quite indifferent to him. The disparity of years was so far in his favour, as she could not but feel flattered by the notice of one so conversant with the world and its ways, who had travelled and seen so much, and might in every respect be deemed a competent judge in matters of taste. Any comparison of him with Mark must redound with great advantage to the former. The accomplished scholar, the agreeable and well-bred man of society, was a severe competitor for the half-educated and slovenly youth, whose awkward and bashful manner seemed rather ill-temper than mere diffidence. Mark was himself conscious of the disadvantages he laboured under, and although Sir

Archy had few fears that such an admirer was likely to win favour with the gay and capricious girl, whose foreign habits had taught her to value social qualities at the highest price, still there was a chance that Hemsworth might have thought differently, and that jealousy was the secret of the whole scheme. Kate, with her ten thousand pounds of a rent-charge, might be a very reasonable object of Hemsworth's ambition; and when already he had absorbed so large a portion of the family estates, this additional lien would nearly make him master of the entire. It was, then, perfectly possible that this was his game, and that in withdrawing Mark from the scene, he both calculated on the gratitude his generosity would evoke, and more securely provided for his own success.

While Sir Archy thus pondered over Hemsworth's motives, he did not neglect the more pressing consideration of Mark's danger. It was evident that he had taken an active part in the insurrectionary movement, and without the slightest precautions for his personal safety. The first care, therefore, was to see and learn from him the full extent of his danger, what proofs there existed against him, and what evidence, either in writing or otherwise, might be adduced to his disadvantage.

"Tell me, frankly and freely, Mark," said he, aloud, as he arose and paced the room; "tell me, openly, how you stand, who are your betrayers, what your dangers, and I'll answer for it the peril may be averted."

"I have come to do so, sir," said a voice behind him—and Mark O'Donoghue was standing at the door.

CHAPTER XXXVIII.

TAMPERING AND PLOTTING.

WHILE they who meditated the invasion of Ireland were thoroughly informed on the state of parties and the condition of public opinion in that kingdom, the English Government were satisfied with vague and insufficient rumours of those intentions, derived from sources of questionable accuracy, or communicated by persons in the pay of their opponents. Certain it is, neither the magnitude of the peril was appreciated, nor its nearness suspected. Many, in England, regarded the whole in the light of a menace, and believed that the embarrassments of the French Directory were quite sufficient to withdraw their thoughts from foreign aggression to troubles nearer home. Their great want of money, arms, and all the munitions of war, was well known and trusted to as a guarantee of security. Others supposed that a rash attempt might be made, but were equally sure of its being defeated by our naval forces before a landing could be effected; and many more believed that the pretence of foreign aid was but a threat of the malcontents at home to enforce compliance with their demands. The event itself was to show how unfounded were all these calculations, and how little reason we had to regard our security as derived from our own measures of foresight and precaution.

Constituted as the French Government of the day was, nothing would have been easier than to have ample knowledge of all the projects. The men in high situations were newly elevated to power from positions of very humble pretension, with no habits of public business, no experience of the mode of conducting difficult affairs, and many of them of very questionable character for integrity; and yet, with these opportunities at our disposal, a few scattered facts, ill-authenticated and vague, were all that our Government attained to; and even these were unattended to, save when they implicated the conduct of some suspected character nearer home; then, indeed, party violence assumed an appearance of statesmanlike vigilance, and Crown prosecutions and ex-officio informations seemed the safeguard of the empire.

On occasions of this kind the activity of the Government was most remarkable, and while the great question of national security was overlooked, no pains were spared to track out the narrow path where some insignificant treason was plodding, and bring the plotter to the scaffold. Large sums of money were spent in obtaining secret information, and the whole science of government was reduced to a system of espionage. This little-minded and narrow policy was, in a great measure, the consequence of entrusting so much of the government to the influence of the lawyers, who, regarding everything through the light of their own profession, placed the safety of the empire on the success of a Crown prosecution.

It was at a moment when this favourite policy was in the ascendant that Hemsworth reached Dublin, little aware, indeed, how far events there were hastening forward the catastrophe for which he was interested. Lanty Lawler, who for a long time had never communicated, save to Hemsworth, his knowledge of the United Irish movement, had at length become alarmed for his own safety; and putting but slight trust in Hemsworth's good faith, should any calamity befal him, had come forward and revealed to Major Sirr all that he knew of the plot, the names of several parties implicated, and in particular the whole history of Mark O'Donoghue's complicity. The information came well-timed. The Crown lawyers were desirous of exhibiting the parade of a state prosecution, and all the ordinary measures were taken to secure its success. Lanty, now a prisoner in Newgate, but with the promise of a free pardon and a reward, had been repeatedly examined by the Attorney and Solicitor-General, and his statement found perfectly accurate and consistent. He narrated the various interviews he had been present at among the Delegates in Dublin—the messages he had conveyed from them to different individuals through the country—the depôts where pikes and muskets were stored—and the several places of rendezvous agreed upon whenever the rising should take place. He also revealed many facts of the feeling prevalent among the people, and exemplified the conflicting state of opinion then in the country—how that many were worn out and discouraged by delay, and believed themselves betrayed by France—while others were full of hope and confidence, eager for the time to come, and ready to incur any peril. While in all these disclosures he was most candid and explicit, he never once betrayed the name of Mary M'Kelly, nor even alluded in any way to her cabin as the resort of the French spies and the secret depôt of arms and ammunition. It might have been that, in the blackness of his treachery to others, this one spark of better feeling survived towards her—that some lurking affection lingered in a heart dead to every other noble sentiment, or perhaps the lesser motive swayed him, that in excepting her from the general ruin, he was securing to himself one who, as a wife, would bring him no small share of worldly wealth. Either may be the explanation of his conduct, for, strange as it may seem, the vilest actions are sometimes con-ceived with a reserve of conscience that shows what casuistry guilt requires, and how much the spirit of evil lacks of courage, when it has to borrow the energy to act from even the semblance of something good.

It was not without reluctance at first that Lanty ventured on the betrayal of Mark O'Donoghue, nor did he even consent to do so until his own safety had been threatened by Hemsworth, and also a solemn promise given that he should never be brought forward to give evidence against him, nor exhi-bited before the world as an informer. This was the character he most dreaded—it was the only reproach that had any terror for his mind. Gra-dually, however, and by the frequency of his revelations to Hemsworth, this dread diminished, and in proportion the fears for his own safety increased. Hemsworth's game was to make him believe that such depended solely on him—that at any moment he could give information of a character sufficient to convict him—and by this tie was he bound to a man he detested with all his hatred. After much vacillation and doubt it was that Lanty deter-mined, whatever the consequences to his fame, to make a full disclosure to Government, and only bargain for his own life. Hemsworth's absence from Dublin afforded the opportunity, and he seized it at once. Such, then, was the position of affairs when Hemsworth reached the capital, and learned that his agent, Lanty, was no longer at his disposition, but at that very mo-ment a prisoner in the gaol of Newgate, strict orders being given that nobody was to be admitted to converse with him without the special leave of the law officers of the Crown. Now, although Hemsworth had personally little to fear from any disclosure Lanty might make, yet his information might thwart all the plans he had so artfully devised regarding the O'Donoghues, the events impending that family being, up to that moment, perfectly at his own discretion and disposal, to delay or precipitate which constituted the essence of his policy. Mark could not be brought to trial, he well knew, without exhibiting himself in the light of an enemy and an accuser, he being the person to whom Lanty originally communicated his informations. This hostile part would form an impassable obstacle to any success with Kate, and consequently to his great plan of obtaining the Glenflesk estate.

Hemsworth lost not a moment, after his arrival in town, in his endeavours to have an interview with Lanty; and, being on terms of old intimacy with the sheriff, at length persuaded him to grant him a brief opportunity of speaking to him—a permission, under the circumstances, most reluctantly acceded. It was near nine o'clock—the latest hour at which a visit to the gaol was practicable—when Hemsworth presented himself with a sheriff's order at the gate. A brief delay ensued, for even on such an authority the gaoler scrupled to deviate from the directions given him, and he was admitted. Following the turnkey for some minutes, through passages and across courts, they reached an angle of the building dedicated to the reception of those who were held over by the Crown as "approvers" against their former friends and associates. Many of these had been in confinement several months, the time not having arrived when the evidence which they were to corroborate was perfected, and not a few preferring the security of a prison to the dangers the character of an informer would expose them to without doors. A confused noise of voices and coarse laughter was heard as they came near, and the turnkey, striking his bunch of keys against a heavy door, called, "Be silent there, b——t ye ; there's more trouble with six of ye than we have with the whole condemned ward;" then, turning to Hemsworth, he added, in a lower voice, "Them chaps is awaitin' a passage over seas. They've given their evidence long ago, and they're not wanted now. That one with the cracked voice is Cope, the fellow that tracked Parson Jackson ; but here, this is your man's cell—we cannot give you more than a quarter of an hour, and so don't lose any more time."

Hemsworth laid his hand on the gaoler's arm as he extended it with the key. "One second—just wait one second," said he, as he pressed his finger across his brow, and seemed to reflect ; then added, "Yes, that will do— open it now, and I shall be ready to retire whenever you please."

Whether the sound without had drowned the noise, or that his attention was too much engaged to notice it, Lanty never stirred nor looked round, as the heavy door was unbarred and fastened again behind Hemsworth. Seated in a recess of the window, and with his face pressed against the iron bars, he was watching with interest the movement in the street below, where a considerable number of people went past, their eyes directed upwards to the front of the building, but all view of which was impossible to him. Hemsworth stood and looked at him for some minutes without speaking—he was as if calculating the very thoughts of the other's brain—then, advancing gently, he laid his hand on Lawler's shoulder, as he said,

" Ay, Lanty, that's the reward they get. Two of them are to be turned off to-morrow."

" Two of whom, sir ?" asked Lanty, as, starting at the voice, his face became the colour of death.

" I thought you knew !" said he, affecting astonishment ; " they are the approvers against Bond. The Government has no use for the rascals now, and it saves expense to hang them, and so they tried them for a murder at Sallins in March last. I hear they were not there; but, no matter, they've enough to answer for without that."

" But, sure, Mr. Hemsworth, they'll never treat their own friends that way ?"

" Wouldn't they, Lanty! You don't know them as well as I do. They keep little faith with scoundrels, and more fools the scoundrels for being caught ; but I mustn't lose time ; it was that very thing brought me here. I heard this evening the scrape you were in."

" Me in a scrape !" exclaimed Lanty, his eyes growing wider with terror.

" To be sure it is ; and a devilish ugly scrape, too, my friend. Haven't you given information to the Attorney-General against the young O'Donoghue ?"

Lanty nodded, and he went on :

" Haven't you confessed the whole of the plot, and told them everything ?"

" Very nearly, faix !" said Lanty, dropping his head, and sighing.

" And what do you expect to gain by that, Master Lanty? Is it by showing that you are of no use to them—that you've nothing more left in you—that you hope for a reward? Is it for the sake of your family and friends, or on account of your remarkable honesty, they're so fond of you ?" Then, checking this sneering tone, he added, in a slow and solemn voice, " Are you a fool, man ?—or don't you see what you are bringing yourself to? What will be your claim when the trial of the young O'Donoghue is over ? The Crown lawyers will have you up in the witness-box till they've drained you dry. Devil a drop they'll leave in you ; and when they say, ' Go down,' take my word for it, it's down you'll go, in earnest, and all the world wouldn't lift you up afterwards."

Hemsworth permitted the words to sink into his heart for a few seconds in silence, and then went on :

" So long as you trusted *me*, you were safe. I'd never expose you in open court."

"No, sir, nor the Attorney-General neither. He said that all they wanted was my information on oath."

"And you gave it!" exclaimed Hemsworth, in a voice of ill-dissembled anxiety.

"Not all out, sir," said Lanty, with a shrewd glance of malicious intelligence. "I asked them for a copy, to read it over before I signed it, and they gave me one"—here he produced a roll of paper from his breast-pocket, and showed it to Hemsworth—"and I'm to give it back to-morrow, with my name to it."

"They've played you off well, Lanty," said Hemsworth, while, carelessly opening the paper, he affected not to pay it any attention. "The lawyers have got round you nicely; and, faith, I always thought you a clever fellow before. Your evidence, so long as it was your own, was worth five thousand pounds, and I wouldn't give five for your chance of escape, now that they know your secret."

"What would you say if they didn't know it?" said Lanty, with a look of impudent familiarity he had never ventured on before. "What would you say, now, if the best of my evidence was to come out yet?—that I never told one word about the French clipper that landed the muskets in Glengariff Bay, and left two pipes of wine at your own house the same night?"

"Ah! you'd try that game, would you?" said Hemsworth, with a smile of deadly malice; "but I've thought of that part, my honest Lanty. I've already given information on that very matter. You don't suppose that I afforded those fellows my protection for the sake of the bribe. No, faith; but I made them pay for the very evidence that can any day convict them —ay, *them* and *you*; you, a paid spy of France, a sworn United Irishman, who have administered the oaths to eighteen soldiers of the Roscommon militia, and are at this moment under a signed and witnessed contract, bound to furnish horses for a French cavalry force on their landing here in Ireland. Are these truths, Mr. Lanty, or are they mere matters of fancy?"

"I'm a Crown witness," said Lawler, sturdily, "and if I speak out all I know, they're bound to protect me."

"Who is to bind them?" said Hemsworth, jeeringly; "is it your friends, the United Irishmen, that you betrayed?—is it they are to watch over your precious life?—or do you think your claims are stronger with the other party, that you only swore to massacre? Where's the sympathy and protection to come from? Tell me that, for I'm curious on the point."

Lanty turned a fierce look upon him—his eyeballs glared, and his nether lip shook convulsively, while his hands were firmly clenched together. Hemsworth watched these evidences of growing anger, but without seeming to regard them, when the key grated roughly in the lock, the door opened, and the gaoler called out, with a savage attempt at laughter,

" Time's up. I must turn you off, sir."

" A short reprieve," said Hemsworth, humouring the ruffian jest, and he pitched his purse into the fellow's hand.

" To settle family matters, I suppose," said the turnkey, with a grin, as he retired, and closed the door once more.

The interruption seemed to offer a favourable opportunity to Hemsworth of giving an amicable turn to the interview, for, with a changed voice, and a look of well-assumed friendship, he said,

" I have misspent my moments here sadly, Lanty. I came to befriend you, and not to interchange words of angry meaning. If I had been in Dublin, I'm certain you would never have fallen into this perilous position. Let us see how best to escape from it. This information—I see it is all confined to young O'Donoghue's business—is of no value whatever, until signed by you. It is just as if it were never spoken. So that, if you steadily determine not to sign it, you need give no reason whatever, but simply refuse when asked. Do this, and all's safe."

" Couldn't they transport me ?" said Lanty, in a feeble voice, but whose very accent betrayed the implicit trust he reposed in Hemsworth's answer.

" They'll threaten that, and worse too ; but never flinch; they've nothing against you, save your own evidence. When the time comes—mark me, I say, when the time comes—your evidence is worth five thousand pounds ; but now, all it will do is to convict young O'Donoghue, and warn all the others not to go forward. I don't suppose you want that; the young fellow never did you any harm."

" Never," said Lanty, dropping his head with shame, for even in such a presence his conscience smote him.

" Very well—there's no use in bringing him to trouble. Keep your own counsel, and all will be well."

" I'm just thinking of a plan I've a notion in my head will do well," said Lanty, musingly. " I'm to see Father Kearney, the priest of Luke's Chapel, to-morrow morning—he's coming over to confess me. Well, when the Attorney-General and the others come for me to write my name, I'll just say that I dar'n't do it. I'll not tell why nor wherefore—sorra word more, but this, ' I dar'n't do it.' They'll think at once it's the priest set me against it. I know well what they'll say—that Father Kearney put me under a vow ; and so they may. They'll scarcely get *him* to say much about it, and I'll take care they won't make *me*."

" That thought was worthy of you, Lanty," said Hemsworth, laughing, "but take care that you don't swerve from your determination. Remember that there is no accusation against you—not a word nor a syllable of testimony. Of course they'll threaten you with the worst consequences. You'll be told of prosecutions for perjury, and all that. Never mind—wait patiently your time. When the hour arrives, *I'll* make your bargain for you, and it will not be merely the evidence against an individual, but the disclosure of a great plot of rebellion, they must pay you for. Cockayne got four thousand pounds and a free pardon. *Your* services will rank far higher."

"If they won't bring me up in open court," said Lanty, timidly, "I'll do whatever they please."

"For that very reason you must adhere to my advice. There, now, I perceive the fellow is about to lock up for the night, and I must leave this. You may want some money from time to time. I'll take means of sending whatever you stand in need of. For the present, ten pounds will, I suppose, be sufficient."

Lanty took the money with a mixture of humility and sullenness. He felt it as a bribe rather than a gift, and he measured the services expected of him by the consideration they were costing. The turnkey's presence did not admit of further colloquy, and they parted in mutual suspicion and distrust, each speculating how far self-interest might be worked upon as the guiding principle to sway the other's actions.

"I'm scarcely sure of him yet," said Hemsworth, as he slowly returned to his hotel. "They'll stop at nothing to terrify him into signing the informations, and if the prosecution goes on, and the young O'Donoghue is convicted, the plot is blown up. The others will escape, and all my long-projected disclosures to the Government become useless. Besides, I fail where failure is of more consequence. It was to little moment that I prevented a marriage between Travers and the girl if I cannot make her my own; but yet, that alliance should have been thwarted on every ground of policy. It would have been to plant the Traverses here on the very spot I destine for myself. No, no. I must take care that they never see Ireland more. Indeed this breaking off the marriage will prove a strong obstacle to their returning." Thus did he review his plans, sometimes congratulating himself on the success of the past, sometimes fearing for the future, but always relying with confidence on the skill of his own negotiations—an ingenuity that never yet had failed him in his difficulties.

The next day was the time appointed for Lanty's final examination, and on which he was to affix his name to the informations, and Hemsworth loitered in one of the offices of the Castle, where the gossip of the morning was discussed, in no common anxiety to hear how his *protégé* had acquitted himself. As the clerks and underlings conversed among themselves on the dress or equipage of the officials who at intervals drove off towards the Park, Hemsworth, who affected to be engaged in reading a morning paper, overheard one remark to another,

"There's the devil to pay at the Council. That fellow they have in Newgate against Coyle and M'Nevin, and the rest of them, it seems, now refuses to confirm his informations. They have good reason to believe all he said was true, but they can't go on without him."

"What's the meaning of that? He was willing enough yesterday."

"They say a priest from Luke's Chapel was with him this morning, and forbid him, under any number of curses and anathemas in case of disobedience, to reveal a syllable against the 'United party.' "

"They can compel him, however. Don't you remember Cockayne did the same thing about Jackson's business, and they brought him over to Lord Clonmel's house, and made him sign there?"

"That they did, but they'll not try the same game twice. Curran brought it out in the cross-examination, and made it appear that the witness was terrified by the Crown by a threat of consequences to himself as an accomplice, and the point went very far with the jury in Jackson's favour."

Hemsworth did not wait to hear more. The great fact that Lanty was firm, was all that he cared for, and, after a few casual remarks on the morning news, he strolled forth with all the lazy indifference of an idle man.

CHAPTER XXXIX.

THE BROTHERS.

AMONG the unexplained phenomena of the period is one very remarkable and, doubtless, pregnant circumstance—the species of lull or calm in the movements of the United Irish party, which was conspicuous throughout the entire of the summer and autumn of 1796. The spring opened on them with hopes high and expectations confident. Tone's letters from Paris breathed encouragement; the embarrassments of England promised favourably for their cause; and many who wavered before were found now willing to embrace the enterprise. To this state of ardent feeling succeeded an interval of doubt and uneasiness; conflicting statements were circulated, and men's minds were shaken, without any apparent cause. A vague fear of betrayal and treachery gained ground; yet no one was able to trace this dread to any definite source. The result, however, was evident in the greater caution of all concerned in the scheme—a reserve which seemed to threaten a total abandonment of the undertaking; such, at least, it appeared to those who, like Mark O'Donoghue, having few or no opportunities of intercourse with the leaders, were disposed to take their impressions from the surface of events. As for him, his correspondence had ceased with Lanty's

U

treachery. He neither knew the real names nor addresses of those to whom he had formerly written, and had not a single acquaintance to whom he could look for advice and assistance.

All Sir Archy's endeavours to win his confidence had failed, not from any distrust either in his judgment or his good faith, but because Mark regarded his secret as a sacred depository, in which the honour of others was concerned; and however disposed to seek advice for himself, he would not compromise their safety for the sake of his own advantage. Unable to extort a confidence by entreaty, and well aware how little efficiency there lay in menace, Sir Archy abandoned the attempt, and satisfied himself by placing in Mark's hands Hemsworth's letter, significantly hinting his own doubts of the writer's integrity.

Mark sat himself down in the garden to study the epistle, and, however artfully conceived, the experience his own career opened displayed the dishonesty of the writer at every sentence.

"I am the obstacle to his plans—my presence here is somehow a thwarting influence against him," said he, as he folded up the paper. "I must remain at every hazard; nor is there much, so long as I bound my wanderings by these great mountains—he will be a bolder than Hemsworth who captures me here."

Guided by this one determination, and trusting that time might clear up some of the mysteries that surrounded him, Mark waited, as men wait for an event that shall call upon their faculties or their courage for some unusual effort. The same reverses of fortune that had taught him distrust, had also inculcated the lesson of patience; but it was the patience of the Indian warrior, who will lie crouching in concealment for days long, till the moment of his vengeance has arrived. And thus, while to others he seemed an altered character, less swayed by rash impulses, and less carried away by anger, the curbed up passions became only more concentrated by repression. He mixed little with the others, rarely appearing save at meal times, and then seldom taking any part in the conversation around. He did not absent himself from home, as before, for whole days or weeks long, but spent his time mostly in his own chamber, where he read and wrote for hours—strange and unusual habits for one who had never sought or found amusement save in the fatigues of the hunting-field. His manner, too, was no longer the same. Calmer, and more self-possessed than before, he neither seemed to feel momentary bursts of high spirits nor depression. The tone of his mind was indeed sad, but it was the sadness that indicated strength and constancy to endure, fully as much as it betrayed the pain of suffering. The altered features of his character impressed themselves on everything he did; and there was an air of quiet gentleness in his demeanour quite foreign to his former rough and abrupt manner. Upon none did these things make so great an impression as on Kate: her woman's tact enabled her to see them differently and more correctly than the rest. She saw that a mighty change had come over him; that no mere check of disappointment, no baffled ambition could have done this; neither could she attribute it to any feeling towards herself, for he was never more coolly distant than now. She guessed, then, rightly, that it was the first step towards freedom of a mind enthralled by its own strong passions. It was the struggling energy to be free of a bold and daring spirit, that learned at length to feel the lowering influences of ill-directed ambition. How ardently she wished that some career were open to him now—some great path in life: she did not fear its dangers or its trials—his nature suggested anything save fear! How sad to think that energy like his should be suffered to wane, and flicker, and die out for want of the occasion to display its blaze. She could not avoid communicating these thoughts to Sir Archy, who for some time past had watched the growing change in the youth's manner. The old man listened attentively as she spoke, and his glistening eye and heightened colour showed how her girlish enthusiasm moved him; and while some reminiscence of the past seemed to float before him, his voice trembled as he said,

"Alas! my sweet child, the world offers few opportunities like those you speak of, and our political condition rejects them totally. The country that would be safe must give little encouragement to the darings of youthful energy. His rewards are higher here who seeks out some path well trod and beaten, and tries by industry and superior skill to pass by those who follow it also. The talents men prize are those available for some purpose of every-day life. Gifts that make mankind wiser and happier, these bring fame and honour; while the meteor brilliancy of mere heroism can attract but passing wonder and astonishment."

"You mistake Mark, my dear uncle—you undervalue the change that is worked in his character. He is not deficient in ability, if he but suffer himself to rely upon it, rather than on the casual accidents of fortune. If Herbert were but here——"

"Herbert comes home to-night. I had thought to keep my secret for a surprise, but you have wrested it from me."

"Herbert coming home! Oh, how happy you have made me! The brothers once more together, how much each may benefit the other. Nay, uncle, you must not smile thus. Superior as Herbert is in the advantages that training and study impart, Mark has gifts of determination and resolve as certain to win success. But, here he comes—may I not tell him of Herbert's coming?"

Sir Archy smiled and nodded, and the happy girl was the next moment at Mark's side, relating with delight her pleasant news.

Mark listened with pleasure to the intelligence. Any little jealousy he once felt for acquirements and attainments above his own had long since given way to a better and more brotherly feeling ; and he ardently desired to meet and converse with him again.

" And yet, Kate, how altered may he be from what we knew him. Who is to say the changes time may not have wrought in him ?"

" Such are not always for the worse, Mark," said Kate, timidly, for she felt how the allusion might be taken.

A slight tinge of red coloured Mark's cheek, and his eye was lighted with a look of pleasure. He felt the flattery in all its force, but did not dare to trust himself with a reply.

" I wonder," said he, after a lengthened pause—" I wonder how Herbert may feel on seeing once more our wild glen. Will these giant rocks and bold ravines appeal to his heart with the same sympathies as ever, or will the habits of the life he has left cling to him still, and make him think this grandeur only desolation ?"

" You did not feel so, surely, Mark ?" said Kate, as she turned upon him a look of affectionate interest.

" Me ?—I think so ? No ! This valley was to me a place of rest—a long-sought-for haven. I came not here from the gay and brilliant world, rich in fascinations and pleasures. I had not lived among the great and learned, to hear the humble estimate they have of our poor land. I came back here like the mariner whose bark puts back shattered by the storm and baffled by the winds, unable to stem the tide that leads to fortune. Yes, shipwrecked in everything."

" Herbert, Herbert !" cried Kate.

At the same moment a chaise, advancing at full gallop, turned from the road into the avenue towards the house. The boy caught sight of the figures in the garden, flung open the door, and springing out, rushed towards them.

" My dear, dear Kate !" was his first exclamation, as he kissed her affectionately; his next, in a tone of unqualified surprise, was, " What a fine fellow you have grown, Mark !" And the two brothers were locked in each other's arms.

The sentiment which thus burst from him in the first moment of surprise was the very counterpart of Mark's own feeling on beholding Herbert. Time had worked favourably for both. On the elder brother, the stamp of manhood more firmly impressed, had given an elevation to the expression of his features, and a character of composure to his air; while with Herbert, his career of study alternating with a life passed among cultivated and polished circles, had converted the unformed stripling into a youth of graceful and elegant demeanour. The change was even greater in him than in his brother. In the one case it was, as it were, but the growth and development of original traits of character ; in the other, new and very different features were distinguishable. His thoughts, his expressions, his very accent were changed; yet through this his old nature beamed forth, bright, joyous, and affectionate as ever. It was the same spirit, although its flights were bolder and more daring—the same mind, but its workings more powerful and more free. The one had placed his ambition so high he scarcely dared to hope; the other had already tasted some of the enjoyments of success—life had even already shed around him some of its fascinations and quickened the ardour of his temper. A winner in the race of intellect, he experienced that thrilling ecstasy which acknowledged superiority confers; he knew what it was to feel the mastery over others, and, even now, the flame of ambition was lighted in his heart, and its warm glow tingled in his veins and throbbed in every pulse. In vain should they who knew him once seek for the timid, bashful boy, that scarcely dared to make an effort from very dread of failure. His flashing eye and haughty brow told of victory; still around his handsome mouth the laughing smile of happy youth showed that no ungenerous feeling, no unworthy pride, had yet mingled with his nature.

" They tell me you have swept the University of its prizes, Herbert—is not this so?" said Mark, as he leaned his arm affectionately on his shoulder.

" You would think but poorly of my triumphs, Mark," replied Herbert, with a smile. "The lists I fight in peril not life or limb."

" Still, there is honour in the game," said Mark. " Wherever there is success on one side, and failure on the other—wherever there is hope to win and dread to lose—there, the ambition is never unworthy."

" But what of you, Mark? Tell me of yourself? Have you left a buck in the glen, or is there a stray grouse on the mountain? What have you been doing since we met?"

Mark coloured and looked confused, when Kate, coming to the rescue, replied,

" How can you ask such a question, Herbert? What variety does life afford in this quiet valley? Is it not the very test of our happiness that we can take no note of time? But here comes my uncle."

Herbert turned at the words, and rushed to meet the old man.

" Have you won baith, Herbert," cried he—"baith premiums? Then I must gie you twa hands, my dear boy," said he, pressing him in a fond embrace. "Were the competitors able ones? Was the victory a hard one? Tell me all, everything about it."

And the youth, with bent down head and rapid utterance, related in a low voice the event of his examination.

" Go on, go on," said Sir Archy M'Nab, aloud—"tell me what followed." And Herbert resumed in the same tone as before.

" Ha!" cried Sir Archy, in an accent of irrepressible delight, "so they said your Latin smacked of Scotland. They scented Aberdeen in it. Well, boy, we beat them—they canna deny that. The prize is ours; the better that it was hardly fought for."

And thus they continued for some time to talk, as they walked side by side through the garden, the old man's firm step and joyous look telling of the pride that filled his heart, while Herbert poured forth in happy confidence the long-treasured thoughts that crowded his brain; nor did they cease their converse till Kerry came to summon the youth to his father's room.

"He's awake now," said Kerry, gazing with undisguised rapture on the tall and handsome youth; "and it's a proud man he ought to be this day, that has the pair like ye."

The young men smiled at the flattery, and arm in arm took their way towards the house.

CHAPTER XL.

THE LULL BEFORE THE STORM.

ONCE again assembled beneath that old roof, the various members of the family seemed more than ever disposed to make present happiness atone for any troubles of the past. Never was the old O'Donoghue so contented; never did Sir Archy feel a lighter heart. Herbert's spirits were buoyant and high as present success and hope could make them; and Kate, whatever doubts might secretly have weighed upon her mind, did her utmost to contribute to the general joy; while Mark, over whose temperament a calmer and less variable habit of thought prevailed, seemed at least more reconciled to his fortunes.

The influences of tranquillity that prevailed over the land appeared to have breathed their soothing sway over that humble dwelling, where life rolled on like an unruffled stream, each day happy with that monotony of enjoyment, so delicious to all whose minds have ever been tortured by the conflicting cares of the world.

For many a year long the O'Donoghue had not been so free from troubles. The loan he had contracted on Kate's fortune had relieved him from his most pressing embarrassments, and left him money enough to keep other creditors at bay. Sir Archy felt already he had received the earnest of that success he so ardently desired for Herbert, and in the calm of political life hoped that the rash scheme in which Mark had embarked was even now becoming forgotten, and that the time was not far remote when no memory of it would be treasured against him. His own experience taught him that sage lessons may be gathered from the failures and checks of youthful ambition, and in the changed features of Mark's character he argued most favourably for the future. But of all those on whom happier prospects shone, none revelled in the enjoyment so much as Herbert. The fascinations of that new world, of which he had only caught a glimpse, hung over him like a dream. Life opened for him at a moment when he himself had won distinction, while a new passion stirred his heart, and stimulated hope to the utmost. Kate, his companion throughout every day, was not slow to perceive the lurking secret of his thoughts, and soon led him to confide them to her. Herbert had never heard of Frederick Travers's attachment to his cousin, still less suspected he had made a proposal of marriage to her. The studied avoidance of their names among his own family was a mystery he could not solve, and he referred to Kate for the explanation.

"How strange, Kate," said he, one day, as they wandered along the glen somewhat further than usual—"how singular is this silence respecting the Traverses! I can make nothing of it. If I speak of them, no one speaks again; if I allude to them, the conversation suddenly stops. Tell me, if you know it, the secret of all this."

Kate blushed deeply, and muttered something about old and half-remembered grudges, but he interrupted her quickly, saying,

"This can scarcely be the reason; at least their feelings show nothing of the kind towards us. Sybella talks of you as a sister nearest to her heart. Sir Marmaduke never spoke of you but with the warmest terms of affection, and if the gay Guardsman did not express himself on the subject, perhaps it was because he felt the more deeply."

Kate's cheek grew deeper scarlet, and her breathing more hurried, but she made no reply.

"My explanation," continued Herbert, more occupied with his own thoughts than attentive to his companion, "is this—and, to be sure, it is a very sorry explanation which elucidates nothing—that Hemsworth is somehow at the bottom of it all. Sybella told me what persuasions he employed to prevent her father returning to Glenflesk; and when everything like argument failed, that he actually, under pretence of enlarging the house, rendered the existing part uninhabitable."

"But what object could he have in this?" said Kate, who felt that Herbert was merely nourishing the old prejudices of his family against Hemsworth. "He is anxious for the peace and welfare of this country—he grieves for the poverty and privations of the people—and, whether he be correct or not, deems the remedy the residence among them of a cultivated and wealthy proprietary, with intelligence to perceive and ability to redress their grievances."

"Very true, Kate," replied Herbert; "but don't you see that in these very requisites of a resident gentry he does not point at the Travers family, whose ignorance of Ireland he often exposed when affecting to eulogise their knowledge. The qualities he recommends he believes to be his own."

"No, Herbert, you wrong him there," said she, warmly; "he told me himself the unceasing regret he suffered, that, in his humble sphere, all efforts for the people's good were ineffectual; that, wanting the influence which property confers, benefits from his hands became suspected, and measures of mere justice were regarded as acts of cruelty and oppression."

"Well, I only know that such is Frederick Travers's opinion of him," said Herbert, not a little piqued at Kate's unexpected defence of their ancient enemy. "Frederick told me himself that he would never cease until his father promised to withdraw the agency from him. Indeed, he is only prevented from pressing the point because Hemsworth has got a long lease of part of the estate, which they desire to have back again on any terms. The land was let at a nominal rent, as being almost valueless. The best part of the valley it turns out to be!—the very approach to the Lodge passes through it—so that, as Frederick says, they could not reach their hall door without a trespass, if Hemsworth pleased to turn sulky."

Kate felt there might be another and more correct explanation of Frederick's dislike, but she did not dare to hint at it.

"You are too favourable in your opinion of Hemsworth, Kate. Sybella said as much to me herself."

"Sybella said so?" said Kate, as a flush, half of shame, half of displeasure, mantled her cheek.

"Yes," cried Herbert, for he felt that he was in a difficulty, and there was no way out save the bold one, of right through it—"yes, she saw what you did not, that Hemsworth had dared to lift his eyes to you—that all his displays of patriotic sentiment were got up to attract your favourable notice, and that in his arguments with Frederick about Ireland, his whole aim was to expose the Guardsman's ignorance, and throw ridicule upon it, neither seeking to convey sound notions, nor combat erroneous impressions."

"Captain Travers was but too easy a mark for such weapons," said Kate, angrily. "It was his pleasure to make Ireland the object of his sarcasm."

"So Hemsworth contrived it!" cried Herbert, eagerly, for it was a subject of which he had long been anxious to speak, and one he had heard much of from Sybella. "I know well the game he played, and how successfully, too."

Kate blushed deeply. For a moment she believed that her own secret was known to Herbert, but the next instant she was reassured that all was safe.

"Sybella told me how he actually lay in wait for opportunities to entice

Frederick into discussion before you, well knowing the theme that would irritate him, and calculating how far petty refutations and half-suppressed sneers would embarrass and annoy him—the more, because Frederick saw how much more favourably you regarded Hemsworth's sentiments than his own; and, indeed, sometimes I fancied, Kate, it was a point the Guardsman was very tender about;—nay, sweet cousin, I would not say a word to offend you."

" Then do not speak of this again, Herbert," said she, in a low voice.

" It is a luckless land," said Herbert, sighing. " They who know it well are satisfied with the cheap patriotism of declaiming on its wrongs. They who feel most acutely for its sorrows are, for the most part, too ignorant to alleviate them. I begin to think my uncle is quite right—that the best thing we could do would be to make a truce—to draw the game—for some twenty or thirty years, and try if the new generation might not prove wiser in expedients than their fathers."

" A luckless land, indeed !" said Mark, who, coming up at the moment, had overheard the last words. " You were right to call it so—where the son of an O'Donoghue sees no more glorious path to follow than that of a hollow compromise !"

Kate and Herbert started as he spoke, and while her face flashed with an emotion of mingled pride and shame, Herbert looked abashed, and almost angry at the reproach.

" Forgive me, Herbert," said Mark, in a voice of deep melancholy. " Not even this theme should sow a difference between us. I came to bid you good-by."

" Good-by, Mark !" cried Kate, starting with terrified surprise.

" Going to leave us, Mark !" exclaimed Herbert, in an accent of true sorrow.

" It is but for a few days—at least I hope that it will be no more," said Mark. " But I have received intelligence that makes it necessary for me to remain in concealment for a short time. You see, Herbert," said he, laughing, " that your theory has the advantage on the score of prudence. Had I followed it, the chances are, I should not have occupied the attention of his Majesty's Privy Council."

" The Privy Council ! I don't understand this, Mark."

" Perhaps this is the easiest mode of explaining it," said Mark, as he unfolded a printed paper, headed " Treason—Reward for the apprehension of Mark O'Donoghue, Esq., or such information as may lead to his capture." " Is that enough ? Come, come—I have no time for long stories just now. If you want to hear mine about the matter, you must visit me at my retreat —the low shealing at the west of Hungry Mountain. At least, for the present I shall remain there."

" But is this necessary, Mark? Are you certain that anything more is meant than to threaten?" said Kate.

" I believe that Carrignacurra will be searched by a military force to-night, or to-morrow at furthest—that the bribe has tempted three or four—none of our people—don't mistake me—to set on my track. If my remain-ing would spare my father's house the indignity of a search—or if the country had any better cause at heart than that of one so valueless as I am, I would stay, Kate——"

" No, no, Mark. This were but madness, unworthy of you, unjust to all who love you."

The last few words were uttered so faintly, as only to be heard by him alone ; and, as she spoke them, a heavy tear rolled down her cheek, now pale as marble.

" But surely, Mark," said Herbert, who never suspected anything of his brother's intrigues, " this must proceed on mere falsehood. There is no charge against you—you, whose life of quiet retirement here can defy any calumny."

" But not deny the truth," said Mark, with a sorrowful smile. " Once for all, I cannot speak of these things now. My time is running fast ; and already my guide, yonder, looks impatient at my delay. Remember the shealing at the foot of the mountain. If there be any mist about, you have but to whistle."

" Is poor Terry your guide, then?" said Kate, affecting to smile with some semblance of tranquillity.

" My guide and my host both," said Mark, gaily. " It's the only invita-tion I have received for Christmas, and I accept it most willingly, I assure you."

An impatient gesture of Terry's hand, as he stood on a small pinnacle of rock, about fifty feet above the road, attracted Mark's attention, and he called out,

" Well!—what is it?"

" The dragoons !" shouted Terry, in a terrified voice. " They're crossing the ford at Caher-mohill, two miles off—eight, nine, ten—ay, there's twelve now, over ; and the fellow in the dark coat, he's another. Wait! they're asking the way : that's it, I'm sure. Well done!—my blessing be an ye this day, whoever ye are. May I never ! if he's not sending them wrong ! They're down the glen towards Killarney ;" and as he finished speaking he sprang from the height, and hastened down the precipice at a rate that seemed to threaten destruction at every step.

" Even so, Terry, we have not more time than we need. It's a long journey to the west of the mountain ; and so, good-by, my dear cousin—good-by, Herbert—a short absence it will be, I trust ;" and, tearing him-self away hurriedly, lest any evidence of emotion might be seen, the young man ascended the steep pathway after Terry; nor did he turn his head round until distance enabled him to look down unnoticed, when again he cried out "Farewell! Remember the west side of Hungry!" and waving his cap, disappeared, while Herbert and his cousin wended their sorrowful way homeward.

CHAPTER XLI.

A DISCOVERY.

WHEN Kate arrived at home, she found a note awaiting her, in Hemsworth's handwriting, and marked "Haste." Guessing at once to what it must refer, she broke the seal with an anxious heart, and read:

" MY DEAR MADAM,—I have been unable to retard any longer the course of proceedings against your cousin. It would seem that the charges against him are far more grave and menacing than either of us anticipated, at least so far as I can collect from the information before me. The Privy Council was determined on arresting him at once. Orders to support the warrant by a military force have been transmitted to officers commanding parties in different towns of the south, and there is no longer a question of the intentious of the Crown regarding him. But one of two chances is now open to him: to surrender and take his trial, or, should he, as he may, without any imputation on his courage, dread this, to make his escape to the coast, near Kenmare, where a lugger will lie off on Wednesday night. By this means he will be able to reach some port in France or Flanders; or, probably, should the wind change, obtain protection from some of the American vessels, which are reported as cruising to the westward.

" In making this communication to you, I need scarcely observe the implicit faith I repose in the use you make of it. It is intended to be the means of providing for your cousin's safety—but should it, by any accident, fall under other eyes than yours, it would prove the inevitable ruin of your very devoted servant,

" WM. HEMSWORTH."

"And they will not believe this man's integrity!" exclaimed Kate, as she finished reading the note. "He who jeopardies his own station and character for the sake of one actually his enemy! Well, *their* injustice shall not involve *my* honour.—Was it you brought this letter?" said she to Wylie, who stood, hat in hand, at the door.

" Yes, my lady, and I was told there might, perhaps, be an answer."

" No—there is none ; say, 'Very well—that I have read it.' Where is Mr. Hemsworth ?"

" At Macroom. There was a meeting of magistrates there, which de·layed him, and he wrote this note, and sent me on, instead of coming himself."

" Say that I shall be happy to see him—that's enough," said Kate, hur-riedly, and turned back again into the house.

Through all the difficulties that beset her path hitherto, she had found Sir Archy an able and a willing adviser ; but now the time was come when not only must she act independently of his aid, but, perhaps, in actual opposi-tion to his views—taking for her guidance one distrusted by almost every member of her family. Yet what alternative remained ?—how betray Hems-worth's conduct in a case which, if known, must exhibit him as false to the Government, and acting secretly against the very orders that were given to him ? This she could not think of; and thus, by the force of circumstances, was constrained to accept of Hemsworth as an ally. Her anxious delibera-tions on this score were suddenly interrupted by the sound of horses gallop-ing on the road, and as she looked out the individual in question rode up the causeway, followed by his groom.

The O'Donoghue was alone in the drawing-room, musing over the sad events which necessitated Mark's concealment, when Hemsworth entered, heated by a long and fast ride.

" Is your son at home, sir—your eldest son ?" said he, as soon as a very brief greeting was over.

" If you'll kindly ring that bell, which my gout won't permit me to reach, we'll inquire," said the old man, with a well-affected indifference.

" I must not create any suspicion among the servants," said Hemsworth, cautiously ; " I have reason to believe that some danger is impending over him, and that he had better leave this house for a day or two."

The apparent frankness of the tone in which he spoke, threw the O'Donoghue completely off his guard, and taking Hemsworth's hand, he said,

" Thank you sincerely for this, the poor boy got wind of it this morning, and I trust before now has reached some place of safety for the present. But what steps can we take ? Is there anything you can advise us to do ? I'm really so bewildered by all I hear, and so doubtful of what is true and what false, that I'm incapable of an opinion. Here comes the only clear head amongst us. Kate, my sweet child, Mr. Hemsworth, like a kind friend, has come over about this affair of Mark's—will you and Sir Archy talk it over with him ?"

"I beg your pardon for the interruption, sir, but I must recal to your memory that I am a magistrate, charged with your son's arrest, and if by an unguarded expression," here he smiled significantly, "I have betrayed my instructions, I rely on your honour not to expose me to the consequences."

The O'Donoghue listened without thoroughly comprehending the distinction the other aimed at, and then, as if disliking the trouble of a thought that puzzled him, he shook his head and muttered, "Ay, very well —be it so—my niece knows these matters better than I do."

"I agree with that opinion perfectly," said Hemsworth, in an under tone, "and if Miss O'Donoghue will favour me with her company for a few minutes in the garden, I may be able to assist her to a clear understanding of the case." Kate smiled assentingly, and Hemsworth moved towards the door and opened it; and then, as if after a momentary struggle with his own diffidence, he offered her his arm; this Kate declined, and they walked along side by side.

They had nearly reached the middle of the garden before Hemsworth broke silence. At last he said, with a deep sigh, "I fear we are too late, Miss O'Donoghue. The zeal, real or affected, of the country magistrates, has stimulated them to the utmost. There are spies over the whole country— he will inevitably be taken."

Kate re-echoed the last words in an accent of deep anguish, and was silent.

"Yes," resumed he, "escape is all but impossible—for even if he should get to sea, there are two cruisers on the look-out for any suspicious sail.

"And what if he were to surrender and stand his trial?" said Kate, boldly.

Hemsworth shook his head sorrowfully, but never spoke.

"What object can it be with any Government to hunt down a rash, inexperienced youth, whose unguarded boldness has led him to ruin? On whom would such an example tell, or where would the lesson spread terror, save beneath that old roof yonder, where sorrows are rife enough already?"

"The correspondence with France—that's his danger. The intercourse with the disturbed party at home might be palliated by his youth—the foreign conspiracy admits of little apology."

"And what evidence have they of this?"

"Alas! but too much—the table of the Privy Council was actually covered with copies of letters and documents—some written by himself— almost all referring to him as a confidential and trusty agent of the cause. This cannot be forgiven him! When I heard a member of the Council say, 'Jackson's blood is dried up already,' I guessed the dreadful result of this young man's capture."

Kate shuddered at these words, which were uttered in a faint tone, tremulous through emotion. "Oh, God!" she cried, "do not let this calamity fall upon us. Poverty, destitution, banishment, anything save the death of a felon!"

Hemsworth pressed his handkerchief to his eyes, and looked away, as the young girl, with upturned face, muttered a brief but fervent prayer to Heaven.

"But you, so gifted and experienced in the world's ways," cried she, turning on him a glance of imploring meaning, "can you not think of any-thing? Is there no means, however difficult and dangerous, by which he might be saved? Could not the honour of an ancient house plead for him? Is there no pledge for the future could avail him?"

"There is but one such pledge—and that"—here he stopped and blushed deeply, and then, as if by an effort, resumed—"do not, I beseech you, tempt me to utter what, if once spoken, decides the destiny of my life?"

He ceased, and she bent on him a look of wondering astonishment. She thought she had not heard him aright, and amid her fears of some vague kind, a faint hope struggled that a chance of saving Mark yet remained. Perhaps, the mere expression of doubt her features assumed, was more chilling than even a look of displeasure, for Hemsworth's self-possession, for several minutes, seemed to have deserted him; when, at last recovering himself, he said,

"Pray, think no more of my words, I spoke them rashly. I know of no means of befriending this young man. He rejected my counsels when they might have served him. I find how impossible it is to win confidence from those whose prejudices have been fostered in adverse circumstances. Now, I am too late—my humble task is merely to offer you some advice, which the day of calamity may recal to your memory. The Government intends to make a severe example of his case. I heard so much, by accident, from the Under Secretary. They will proceed, in the event of his conviction—of which there cannot be a doubt—to measures of confiscation regarding his property; timely intervention might be of service here."

This additional threat of misfortune did not seem to present so many terrors to Kate's mind as he calculated on its producing. She stood silent and motionless, and appeared scarcely to notice his words.

"I feel how barbarous such cruelty is to an old and inoffensive parent," said Hemsworth, "whose heart is rent by the recent loss of a son."

"He must not die," said Kate, with a hollow voice; and her pale cheek trembled with a convulsive motion. "Mark must be saved. What was the pledge you hinted at?"

Hemsworth eyes flashed, and his lip curled with an expression of triumph. The moment, long sought, long hoped for, had at length arrived, which should gratify both his vengeance and his ambition. The emotion passed rapidly away, and his features assumed a look of subdued sorrow.

"I fear, Miss O'Donoghue," said he, "that my hope was but like the straw which the drowning hand will grasp at; but, tortured as my mind has been by expedients, which more mature thought has ever discovered to be impracticable, I suffered myself to believe that possible which my own heart forbids me to hope for."

He waited a few seconds to give her an opportunity of speaking, but she was silent, and he went on:

"The guarantee I alluded to would be the pledge of one whose loyalty to the Government stands above suspicion; one, whose services have met no requital, but whose reward only awaits the moment of demanding it; such a one as this might make his own character and fortune the recognisance for this young man's conduct, and truck the payment of his own services for a free pardon."

"And who is there thus highly placed and willing to befriend us?"

Hemsworth laid his hand upon his heart, and bowing with deep humility, uttered, in a low, faint voice,

"He who now stands before you!"

"You!" cried Kate, as clasping her hands in an ecstasy, she fixed her tearful eyes upon him—"you would do that?" Then growing suddenly pale, as a sick shudder came over her, she said, in a deep and broken voice, "At what price, sir?"

The steady gaze she fixed upon him seemed to awe and abash him, and it was with unfeigned agitation that he now spoke.

"A price which the devotion of a lifelong could not repay. Alas! a price I dare no more aspire to than hope for."

"Speak plainly, sir," said Kate, in a firm, collected tone, "this is not a moment for misconception. What part have I to play in this compact, for by your manner I suppose you include me in it?"

"Forgive me, young lady, I have not courage to place the whole fortunes of my life upon one cast; already I feel the heaviness of heart that heralds in misfortune. I would rather live on with even this faint glimmer of hope than with the darkness of despair for ever." His hands dropped powerless at his side, his head fell forward on his bosom, and as if without an effort of his will, almost unconsciously his lips muttered the words, "I love you."

Had the accents been the sting of an adder, they could not have called up an expression of more painful meaning than flashed over Kate's features.

"And this, then, is the price you hinted at—this was to be the compact."

The proud look of scorn she threw upon him evoked no angry feeling in his breast; he seemed overwhelmed by sorrow, and did not dare even to look up.

"You judge me hardly, unfairly too; I never meant my intercession should be purchased. Humble as I am, I should be still more unworthy, had I harboured such a thought. My hope was this: to make my intervention available, I should show myself linked with the fortunes of that house I tried to save—it should be a case where, personally, my own interest was at stake, and where my fortune—all I possessed in the world—was in the scale, if you consented." Here he hesitated, faltered, and finally became silent; then, passing his hands across his eyes, resumed more rapidly, " But I must not speak of this; alas, that my tongue should have ever betrayed it ! You have forced my secret from me, and with it my happiness for ever. Forget this, I beseech you—forget that, even in a moment so unguarded, I dared to lift my eyes to the shrine my heart has worshipped. I ask no pledge, no compact; I will do my utmost to save this youth; I will spare no exertion or influence I possess with the Government; I will make his pardon the recompense due to myself, but, if that be impossible, I will endeavour to obtain connivance at his escape, and all the price I ask for this is your forgiveness of my presumption."

Kate held out her hand towards him, while a smile of bewitching loveliness played over her features.

" This is to be a friend indeed," said she.

Hemsworth bent down his head till his lips rested on her fingers, and, as he did so, the hot tears trickled on her hand; then, suddenly starting up, he said,

" I must lose no time. Where shall I find your cousin?—in what part of the country has he sought shelter?"

" The shealing at the foot of Hungry Mountain, he mentioned to Herbert as the rendezvous for the present."

" Is he alone—has he no companion?"

" None ; save, perhaps, the idiot boy who acts as his guide in the mountains."

" Farewell, then," said Hemsworth; "you shall soon hear what success attends my effort—farewell;" and, without waiting for more, he hastened from the spot, and was soon heard descending the causeway at a rapid pace.

Kate stood for a few moments lost in thought, and as the sound of the retreating hoofs aroused her, she looked up, and muttering to herself, " It was nobly done !" returned with slow steps to the house.

As Hemsworth spurred his horse, and urged him to his fastest speed, expressions of mingled triumph and vengeance burst from him at intervals. "Mine at last !" cried he—"mine, in spite of every obstacle ! Fortune is seldom so kind as this—vengeance and ambition both gratified together—me, whom they despised for my poverty and my low birth—that it should be my destiny to crush them to the dust." These words were scarcely uttered, when his horse, pressed beyond his strength, stumbled over a rut in the road, and fell heavily to the ground, throwing his rider under him.

For a long time no semblance of consciousness returned, and the groom, fearing to leave him, had to wait for hours until a country car should pass, in which his wounded master might be laid. There came one by at last, and on this Hemsworth was laid, and brought back to the Lodge. Before he reached home, however, sense had so far returned as that he felt his accident was attended with no serious injury; the shock of the fall was the only circumstance of any gravity.

The medical man of Macroom was soon with him, and partly confirmed his own first impressions, but strictly enjoining rest and quiet, as, in the event of any unusual excitement, the worst consequences might ensue. Hemsworth bore up under the injunction with all the seeming fortitude he could muster, but in his heart he cursed the misfortune that thus delayed the hour of his long-sought vengeance.

"This may continue a week, then?" cried he, impatiently.

The doctor nodded an assent.

"Two—three weeks, perhaps?"

"It will be a month, at least, before I can pronounce you out of danger," said the physician, gravely.

"A month! Great Heaven!—a month! And what are the dangers you apprehend, in the event of my not submitting?"

"There are several, and very serious ones—inflammation of the brain, fever, derangement even."

"Yes, and are you sure this confinement will not drive me mad?" cried he, passionately. "Will you engage that my brain will hold out against the agonising thoughts that will not cease to torture me all this while?—or can you promise that events shall stand still for the moment when I can resume my place once more among men?"

The hurried and excited tone in which he spoke was only a more certain evidence of the truth of the medical fears; and, without venturing on any direct reply, the doctor gave some directions for his treatment, and withdrew.

The physician's apprehensions were well founded. The first few hours after the accident seemed to threaten nothing serious, but, as night fell, violent headache and fever set it, and before daybreak he was quite delirious.

No sooner did the news reach Carrignacurra, than Kerry was despatched to bring back tidings of his state; for, however different the estimation in which he was held by each, one universal feeling pervaded all—of sorrow for his disaster. Day after day Sir Archy or Herbert went over to inquire after him; but some chronic feature of his malady seemed to have succeeded, and he lay in one unvarying condition of lethargic unconsciousness.

In this way week after week glided over, and the condition of the country seemed like that of the sick man—one of slumbering apathy. The pursuit of Mark, so eagerly begun, had, as it were, died out. The proclamations of reward, torn down by the country people on their first appearance, were never renewed, and the military party, after an ineffectual search through Killarney, directed their steps northwards towards Tralee, and soon after returned to head-quarters. Still, with all these signs of security, Mark, whose short experience of life had taught him cautiou, rarely ventured near Carrignacurra, and never passed more than a few moments beneath his father's roof.

While each had a foreboding that this calm was but the lull that preludes a storm, their apprehensions took very different and opposing courses. Kate's anxieties increased with each day of Hemsworth's illness. She saw the time gliding past in which escape seemed practicable, and yet knew not how to profit by the opportunity. Sir Archy, coupling the activity with which Mark's pursuit was first undertaken with the sudden visit of Hemsworth to the country, and the abandonment of all endeavours to capture him which followed on Hemsworth's accident, felt strong suspicion that the agent was the prime mover in the whole affair, and that his former doubts were well founded regarding him; while Herbert, less informed than either on the true state of matters, formed opinions which changed and vacillated with each day's experience.

In this condition of events, Sir Archy had gone over one morning alone, to inquire after Hemsworth, whose case, for some days preceding, was more than usually threatening, symptoms of violent delirium having succeeded to the dead lethargy in which he was sunk. Buried deeply in his conjectures as to the real nature of the part he was acting, and how far his motives tallied with honourable intentions, the old man plodded wearily on, weighing every word he could remember that bore upon events, and carefully endeavouring to divest his mind of everything like a prejudice. Musing thus, he accidentally diverged from the regular approach, and turned off into a narrow path which led to the back of the Lodge; nor was he aware of his mistake till he saw, at the end of the walk, the large window of a room he remembered as belonging to the former building. The sash was open, but the curtains were drawn closely, so as to intercept any view from within or without. He observed these things as, fatigued by an unaccustomed exertion, he seated himself for some moments' rest on a bench beneath the trees.

A continuous low moaning sound soon caught his ear. He listened, and could distinctly hear the heavy breathing of a sick man, accompanied as it was by long-drawn sighs. There were voices, also, of persons speaking cautiously together, and the words, "He is asleep at last," were plainly audible, after which the door closed, and all was still.

The solemn awe which great illness inspires was felt in all its force by the old man, as he sat like one spell-bound, and unable to depart. The labouring respiration that seemed to bode the ebb of life made his own strong heart tremble, for he thought how, in his last hours, he might have wronged him. "Oh! if I have been unjust—if I have followed him to the last with ungenerous doubt—forgive me, Heaven; even now, my own heart is half my accuser;" and his lips murmured a deep and fervent prayer for that merciful benevolence which, in his frail nature, he denied to another. He arose from his knees with a spirit calmed, and a courage stronger, and was about to retire, when a sudden cry from the sick-room arrested his steps. It was followed by another more shrill and piercing still, and then a horrid burst of frantic laughter. Dreadful as are the anguish-wrung notes of suffering, how little do they seem in comparison with the sounds of mirth from the lips of madness!

"There,—there," cried a voice he at once knew as Hemsworth's—that's him, that's your prisoner—make sure of him now; remember your orders, men!—do you hear. If they attempt a rescue, load with ball, and fire low—mind that, fire low. Ah! you are pale enough now;" and again the savage laughter rang out. "Yes, madam," continued he, in a tone of insolent sarcasm, "every respect shall be shown him—a chair in the dock—a carpet on the gallows. You shall wear mourning for him—all the honey-moon, if you fancy it. Yes," screamed he, in a wild and frantic voice, "this is like revenge! You struck me once—you called me coarse plebeian, too! We shall be able to see the blood you are proud of—ay, the blood! the blood!" And then, as if worn out by exhaustion, he heaved a heavy sigh, and fell into deep moaning as before.

Sir Archy, who felt in the scene a direct acknowledgment of his appeal to Heaven, drew closer to the window, and listened. Gradually, and like one awaking from a heavy slumber, the sick man stretched his limbs, and drew a long sigh, whose groaning accent spoke of great debility, and then, starting up in bed, shouted:

"It is, it is the King's warrant—who dares to oppose it? Ride in faster, men—faster; keep together here, the west side of the mountain. There, there, yonder, near the beach. Who was that spoke of pardon? Never; if he resists, cut him down. Ride for it, men, ride!" and in his mad excitement he arose from his bed and gained the floor. "There—that's him yonder; he has taken to the mountains; five hundred guineas to the hand that grasps him first!" And he tottered to the window, and tearing aside the curtain, looked out.

Worn and wasted, with beard unshaven for weeks long, and eyes glistening with the lustre of insanity, the expression of his features actually chilled the heart's blood of the old man, as he stood almost at his side, and unable

to move away.   For a second or two Hemsworth gazed on the other, as if
some struggling effort of recognition was labouring in his brain; and then,
with a mad struggle, he exclaimed,

"They were too late ; the Council gave but eight days. I suppressed the
proclamation in the south. Eight days—after that, no pardon—in this world
at least"—and a fearful grin of malice convulsed his features ; then, with an
altered accent, and a faint smile, from which sickness tore its oft-assumed
dissimulation, he said, "I did everything to persuade him to surrender—to
accept the gracious favour of the Crown; but he would not—no, he would
not!"—and, with another burst of laughter, he staggered back into the
room, and fell helpless on the floor.   Sir Archy was in no compassionate
mood at the moment, and without bestowing a thought on the sufferer, he
hastened down the path, and with all the speed of which he was capable,
returned to Carrignacurra.

CHAPTER XLII.

THE SHEALING.

Sir Archy's manner, so precise and measured in every occasion of life,
had undergone a very marked change before he had arrived at Carrignacurra ; exclamations broke from him at every moment, mingled with fervently expressed hopes that he might not be yet too late to rescue Mark
from his peril.   The agitation of his mind and the fatigue of his exertions
completely overcame him ; and when he reached the house, he threw himself
down upon a seat, utterly exhausted.

"Are you unwell, my dear uncle?" broke from Kate and Herbert together, as they stood at either side of his chair.

"Tired, wearied, heated, my dear children; nothing more.   Send me
Kerry here ; I want to speak to him."

Kerry soon entered, and Sir Archy, beckoning him to his side, whispered
a few words rapidly into his ear.   Kerry made no reply, but hastened from
the room, and was soon after seen hurrying down the causeway.

"I see, my dear uncle," whispered Kate, with a tremulous accent—"I
see you have bad tidings for us this morning—he is worse."

"Waur he canna be," muttered Sir Archy, with a significance that gave
the words a very equivocal meaning.

"But there is still hope.   They told us yesterday that to-morrow would be
the crisis of the malady—the twentieth day since his relapse."

"Yes, yes!" said the old man, who, not noticing her remark, pursued aloud the track of his own reflections. "Entrapped—ensnared—I see it all now. And only eight days given!—and even of these to be kept in ignorance. Poor fellow! how you have been duped."

"But this delirium may pass away, uncle," said Kate, who, puzzled at his vague expressions, sought to bring him again to the theme of Hemsworth's illness.

"Then comes the penalty, lassie," cried he, energetically. The Government canna forgie a rebel, as parents do naughty children, by the promise of doing better next time. When a daring scheme——But wait a bit, here's Kerry. Come to the window, man—come over here;" and he called him towards him.

Whatever were the tidings Kerry brought, Sir Archy seemed overjoyed by them; and taking Herbert's arm, he hurried from the room, leaving the O'Donoghue and Kate in a state of utter bewilderment.

"I'm afraid, my sweet niece, that Hemsworth's disease is a catching one. Archy has a devilish wild, queer look about him to-day," said the O'Donoghue, laughing.

"I hope he has heard no bad news, sir. He is seldom so agitated as this. But what can this mean? Here comes a chaise up the road. See, it has stopped at the gate, and there is Kerry hastening down with a portmanteau."

Sir Archy entered as she spoke, dressed for the road, and approaching his brother-in-law's chair, whispered a few words in his ear.

"Great Heaven protect us!" exclaimed the O'Donoghue, falling back, half unconscious, into his seat. While, turning to Kate, Sir Archy took her hand in both of his, and said,

"My ain dear bairn, I have no secrets from you, but time is too short to say much now. Enough, if I tell you Mark is in danger—the greatest and most imminent. I must hasten up to Dublin and see the Secretary, and, if possible, the Lord-Lieutenant. It may be necessary, perhaps, for me to proceed to London. Herbert is already off to the mountains, to warn Mark of his peril. If he can escape till I return, all may go well yet. Above all things, however, let no rumour of my journey escape. I'm only going to Macroom, or Cork, mind that, and to be back to-morrow evening, or next day."

A gesture from Kerry, who stood on the rock above the road, warned him that all was ready; and, with an affectionate but hurried adieu, he left the room, and gaining the high road, was soon proceeding towards Dublin, at the fastest speed of the posters.

"Them's the bastes can do it," said Kerry, as he watched them, with the admiration of a connoisseur; "and the little one wid the rat-tail isn't the worst either."

"Where did that chaise come from, Kerry?" cried the O'Donoghue, who could not account for the promptitude of Sir Archy's movements.

"'Twas with Dr. Dillon from Macroom it came, sir; and it was to bring him back there again; but Sir Archibald told me to give the boy a pound note to make a mistake, and come over here for himself. That's the way of it."

While we leave the O'Donoghue and his niece to the interchange of their fears and conjectures regarding the danger which they both concurred in be-lieving had been communicated to Sir Archy by Hemsworth, we must follow Herbert, who was now on his way to the mountains, to apprise Mark that his place of concealment was already discovered, and that mea-sures for his capture were taken in a spirit that indicated a purpose of per-sonal animosity.

Herbert knew little more than this, for it was no part of Sir Archy's plan to impart to any one his discovery of Hemsworth's treachery, lest, in the event of his recovery, their manner towards him would lead him to a change of tactique. Hemsworth was too cunning an adversary to concede any ad-vantage to. Indeed, the only chance of success against him lay in taking the opportunity of his present illness to anticipate his movements. Sir Archy, therefore, left the family at Carrignacurra in ignorance of this man's villany, as a means of lulling him into security. The expressions that fell from him half unconsciously in the drawing-room, fortunately contributed to this end, and induced both the O'Donoghue and Kate to believe that, whatever the nature of the tidings Sir Archy had learned, their source was no other than Hemsworth himself, of whose good intentions towards Mark no suspicion existed.

Herbert's part was limited to the mere warning of Mark, that he should seek some more secure resting-place; but what kind the danger was, from whom or whence it came, the youth knew nothing. He was not, indeed, unaware of Mark's political feelings, nor did he undervalue the effect his principles might produce upon his actions. He knew him to be intrepid, fearless, and determined; and he also knew how the want of some regular pursuit or object in life had served further to unsettle his notions and increase the discontent he felt with his condition. If Herbert did not look up to Mark with respect for his superior qualities of mind, there were traits in his nature that inspired the sentiment fully as strongly. The bold rapidity with which he anticipated and met a danger, the fertile resources he evinced at moments when most men stand appalled and terror-struck, the calmness of his spirit when great peril was at hand, showed that the passionate and wayward nature was the struggle which petty events create, and not the real germ of his disposition.

Herbert foresaw that such a character had but to find the fitting sphere for its exercise, to win an upward way; but he was well aware of the risks to which it exposed its possessor. On this theme his thoughts dwelt the entire day, as he trod the solitary path among the mountains; nor did he meet with one human thing along that lonely road. At last, as evening was falling, he drew near the glen which wound along the base of the mountain, and as he was endeavouring to decide on the path, a low whistle attracted him. This, remembering it was the signal, he replied to, and the moment after Terry crept from a thick cover of brushwood, and came towards him.

" I thought I'd make sure of you before I let you pass, Master Herbert," cried he, "for I couldn't see your face, the way your head was hanging down. Take the little path to the left, and never turn till you come to the white-thorn tree—then straight up the mountain for a quarter of a mile or so, till you reach three stones, one over another. From that spot you'll see the shealing down beneath you."

" My brother is there now ?" said Herbert, inquiringly.

" Yes ; he never leaves it long now ; and he got a bit of a fright the other evening, when the French schooner came into the bay. "

" A French schooner here, in the bay?"

"Ay, just so ; but with an English flag flying. She landed ten men at the point, and then got out to sea as fast as she could. She was out of sight before dark."

" And the men—what became of them ?"

" They stayed an hour or more with Master Mark. One of them was an old friend, I think; for I never saw such delight as he was in to see your brother. He gave him two books, and some paper, and a bundle—I don't know what was in it—and then they struck off towards Kenmare Bay, by a road very few know in these parts."

All these particulars surprised and interested Herbert not a little ; for although far from implicitly believing the correctness of Terry's tidings as to the vessel being a French one, yet the event seemed not insignificant, as showing that Mark had friends who were aware of his present place of concealment. Without wasting further time, however, he bade Terry good-by, and started along the path down the glen.

Following Terry's directions, Herbert found the path, which, in many places was concealed by loose furze bushes, evidently to prevent detection by strangers, and at last, having gained the ridge of the mountain, perceived the little shealing at the distance of some hundred feet beneath him. It was merely a few young trees, covered over with loose sods, which, abutting against the slope of the hill, opened towards the sea, from whence the view extended along thirty miles of coast on either hand.

At any other moment the glorious landscape before him would have engrossed Herbert's entire attention. The calm sea, over which night was slowly stealing—the jutting promontories of rock, over whose sides the white foam was splashing—the tall dark cliffs, pierced by many a cave, through which the sea roared like thunder—all these caught his thoughts but for a second, and already with bounding steps he hurried down the steep, where the next moment a scene revealed itself of far deeper interest to his heart.

Through the roof of the shealing, from which, in many places, the dry sods had fallen, he discovered his brother, stretched upon the earthen floor of the hut, intently gazing on a large map which lay wide-spread before him. The figure was indeed Mark's. The massive head, on either side of which, in flowing waves, the long and locky hair descended, there was no mistaking. But the costume was one Herbert saw for the first time. It was a simple uniform of blue and white, with a single silver epaulette, and a sword, hilted with the same metal. The chako was of dark fur, and ornamented with a large bouquet of tri-colored ribbons, whose gay and flaunting colours streamed with a strange contrast along the dark earthen floor. Amid all his terror for what these emblems might portend, his heart bounded with pride at the martial and handsome figure, as leaning on one elbow he traced with the other hand the lines upon the map. Unable to control his impatience longer, he cried out,

"Mark, my brother!" and the next moment they were in each other's arms.

"You passed Terry on the mountain? He was at his post, I trust?" said Mark, anxiously.

"Yes; but for his directions I could never have discovered the path."

"All's well, then. Until I hear a certain signal from him, I fear nothing. The fellow seems neither to eat nor sleep. At least, since I've been here, he has kept watch night and day in the mountains."

"He always loved you, Mark."

"He did so; but now it is not me he thinks of. His whole heart is in the cause—higher and nobler than a mere worthless life like mine."

"Poor fellow! he is but half-witted at best," said Herbert.

"The more reason for his fidelity now," said Mark, bitterly. "The men of sense are traitors to their oaths, and false to their friends. The enterprise cannot reckon save on the fool or the madman. I know the taunt you hint at, as——"

"My dearest brother," cried Herbert, with streaming eyes.

"My own dear Herbert, forgive me," said Mark, as he flung his arm round his neck. "These bursts of passion come over me after long and weary thoughts. I am tired to-day. Tell me, how are they all at Carrignacurra?"

"Well, and I would say happy, Mark, were it not for their anxieties about you. My uncle heard some news to-day so threatening in its nature, that he has set out for Dublin post haste, and merely wrote these few lines, which he gave me for you before he started."

Mark read the paper twice over, and then tearing it, threw the fragments at his feet, while he muttered,

"I cannot, I must not leave this."

"But your safety depends on it, Mark—so my uncle pressed upon me. The danger is imminent, and, he said, fatal."

"So would it be were I to leave my post. I cannot tell you, Herbert —I dare not reveal to you what our oath forbids me—but here I must remain."

"And this dress, Mark—why increase the risk you run by a uniform which actually designates treason?"

"Who will dare to tell me so?" cried Mark, impetuously. "The uniform is that of a French grenadier, the service whose toil is glory, and whose cause is liberty. It is enough that I do not wear it without authority. You can satisfy yourself on that head soon. Read this;" and he unfolded a paper which, bearing the arms and seal of the French Republic, purported to be a commission as lieutenant in Hoche's own regiment of Grenadiers, conferred on Mark O'Donoghue in testimony of esteem for his fidelity to the cause of Irish independence. "You are surprised that I can read the language, Herbert," said he, smiling; "but I have laboured hard this summer, and, with Kate's good aid, have made some progress."

"And is your dream of Irish independence brought so low as this, Mark, that the freedom you speak of must be won by an alien's valour?"

"They are no aliens whose hearts beat alike for liberty. Language, country, seas may divide us, but we are brothers in the glorious cause of humanity. Their swords are with us now, as would be ours for them, did the occasion demand them. Besides, we must teach the traitors, boy, that we can do without them; that if her own sons are false, Ireland has friends as true; and then, woe to them who have betrayed her. Oh, my brother, the brother of my heart, how would I kneel in thankfulness to Heaven if the same hopes that stirred within me were yours also; if the genius you possess were enlisted in the dear cause of your own country; if we could go forth together, hand in hand, and meet danger side by side, as now we stand."

"My love for you would make the sacrifice, Mark," said Herbert, as the tears rolled heavily along his cheek; "but my convictions, my reason, my religion, alike forbid it."

"Your religion, Herbert? Did I hear you aright?"

"You did. I am a Protestant."

Mark fell back as his brother spoke; a cold, leaden tinge spread over his features, and he seemed like one labouring against the sickness of an ague.

"Oh, is it not time," cried he, as he clasped his hands above his head, and shook them in an agony of emotion—"is it not time to strike the blow, ere every tie that bound us to the land should be rent asunder! Rank, place, wealth, and power they have despoiled us of; our faith degraded, our lineage scoffed; and now the very links of blood divided—we have not brothers left us!"

Herbert bent down his head upon his knees and wept bitterly.

"Who will tell me I have not been tried now?" continued Mark, in a strain of impassioned sorrow; "deceived on every hand—robbed of my heritage—my friends all false—my father——" He stopped short, for at the moment Herbert looked up, and their eyes met.

"What of our father, Mark?"

"My brain was wandering then," said Mark, in a broken voice. "Once more I ask forgiveness: we are brothers still; if we be but true of heart to Him who knows all hearts, He will not suffer us to be divided. Can you remain a while with me, Herbert? I know you don't mind a rough bivouac."

"Yes, Mark, I'll not leave you. All is well at home, and they will guess what cause detained me." So saying, the two brothers sat down side by side, and with hands clasped firmly in each other, remained sunk in silent thought.

The whole night through they talked together. It was the first moment for many a long year since they had unburdened their hearts like brothers, and in the fulness of their affection the most secret thoughts were revealed, save one topic only, of which neither dared to speak, and while each incident of the past was recalled, and friends were mentioned, Mark never once alluded to Kate, nor did Herbert utter the name of Sybella Travers.

Of his plans for the future Mark made no secret; he had accepted a commission in the French army, on the understanding that an invasion of Ireland was determined on, in the event of which his services would be of some value. He hoped to reach France by the schooner, which, after landing her cargo near the mouth of the Shannon, was to return at once to Cherbourg; once there, he was to enter the service and learn its discipline.

"I have made my bargain with them; my face is never to turn from England till Ireland be free; after that I am theirs, to march on the Rhine or the Danube—where they will. Personal ambition I have none; to serve as a simple grenadier in the ranks of that army that shall first plant the standard of liberty here, such is my only compact. Speak to me of defeat or disaster if you will, but do not endeavour to persuade me against an enterprise I have resolved to go through with, nor try to argue with me where my impulses are stronger than my reason."

In this strain Mark spoke, and while Herbert listened in sorrow, he knew too well his brother's nature to offer a word of remonstrance in opposition to his determination.

Mark, on his side, led his brother to talk of many of his own plans for the future, where another and a very different ambition was displayed. Herbert had entered the lists where intellect and genius are the weapons, and in his early triumphs had conceived that passion for success which, once indulged, only dies with life itself. The day broke upon them thus conversing, and already the sunlight was streaming over the western ocean, as they lay down side by side, and slept.

CHAPTER XLIII.

THE CONFEDERATES.

The paroxysm which Sir Archibald had witnessed formed the crisis of Hemsworth's malady; and ou the evening of the same day his disease had so far abated of its violence, that his delirium had left him, and excessive debility was now the only symptom of great danger remaining. With the return of his faculties came back his memory, clear and unclouded, of every incident up to the very moment of his accident; and as he lay, weak and wasted on his bed, his mind reverted to the plans and projects of which his illness had interrupted the accomplishment. The excitement of the theme seemed rather to serve than be hurtful to him; and the consciousness of returning health gave a spring to his recovery; fatigue of thought induced deep sleep, and he awoke on the following day refreshed and recruited.

The lapse of time iu illness is, probably, one of the most painful thoughts that await upon recovery. The lethargy in which we have been steeped simulates death; while the march of events around us shows how insignificant our existence is, and how independently of us the work of life goes on.

When Wylie was summoned to his master's bedside, the first question put to him was, what day of the month it was? and his astonishment was, indeed, great, as he heard it was the 16th of December, and that he had been above two months on a sick-bed.

" Two months here !" cried he; "and what has happened since ?"

" Scarcely anything, sir," said Wylie, well knowing the meaning of the question. " The country is quiet—the people tranquil. Too much so, perhaps, to last. The young O'Donoghue has not been seen up the glen for several weeks past; but his brother passes frequently from Carrignacurra to the coast, and back again, so that there is little doubt of his still being in his old hiding-place. Talbot—Barrington, I mean—has been here again, too."

" Barrington !—what brings him back ? I thought he was in France."

" The story goes that he landed at Bantry with a French agent. One thing is certain, the fellow had the impudence to call here and leave his card for you, one day I was at Macroom."

"That piece of boldness bodes us no good," said Hemsworth.   "What of the others ?   Who has called here from Carrignacurra ?"

"A messenger every day; sometimes twice in the same day."

"A messenger !—not one of the family ?"

"For several weeks they have had no one to come.   Sir Archy and the younger brother are both from home."

"Where, then, is Sir Archy ?" said Hemsworth, anxiously.

"That would seem a secret to every one.   He left this one morning at a moment's notice, taking the chaise that brought the doctor here.   The post-boy pretended he was discharged; but I say that the excuse was made up, and that the fellow was bribed.   On reaching Macroom, the old man got fresh horses, and started for Cork."

"And what's the report in the country, Wylie ?"

"There are two stories.   One, that he heard some rumours of an accusa tion against himself, for intriguing with the United people, and thought best to go over to Scotland for a while."

"That's folly; what is the other rumour ?"

"A more likely one," said Wylie, as he threw a shrewd glance beneath his half-closed eyelids.   "They say that he determined to go up to Dublin and see the Lord-Lieutenant, and ask him for a. free pardon for Mark."

Hemsworth sprang up in the bed at these words, as if he had been stung "And who says this, Wylie ?"

"I believe I was the first that said so myself," said Wylie, affecting modesty, "when Kerry told me that the old man packed up a court dress and a sword."

"You're right, Sam ; there's not a doubt of it.   How long is this ago ?'

"Five weeks on Tuesday last."

"Five weeks !—five weeks lost already !   And have you heard what has been done by him ?—what success he's met with ?"

"No, sir; but you can soon know something about it yourself."

"How do you mean?   I don't understand you."

"These are the only two letters he has written as yet.   This one came on Saturday.   I always went down in the mornings to Mary M'Kelly's before the bag came in, and as she could not read over well, I sorted the letters for her myself, and slipped in these among your own."

Hemsworth and his companion exchanged looks.   Probably never did glances more rapidly reveal the sentiments of two hearts.   Each well knew the villany of the other; but Hemsworth, for the first time, saw himself in another's power, and hesitated how far the advantage of the discovery was worth the heavy price he should pay for it; besides that, the habits of his life made him regard the breach of confidence, incurred in reading another man's letter, in a very different light from his under-bred associate, and he made no gesture to take them from his hand.

"This has an English post-mark," said Wylie, purposely occupying himself with the letter to avoid noticing Hemsworth's hesitation.

"You have not broken the seals, I hope?" said Hemsworth, faintly.

"No, sir; I knew better than that," replied Wylie, with well-assumed caution. "I knew your honour had a right to it if you suspected the correspondence was treasonable, because you're in the commission, and it's your duty, but I couldn't venture it of myself."

"I'm afraid your law is not very correct, Master Wylie," said Hemsworth, who felt by no means certain as to the sincerity of the opinion.

"It's good enough for Glenflesk, anyhow," said the fellow, boldly; for he saw that in Hemsworth's present nervous condition audacity might succeed where subserviency would not.

"By which you mean that we have the case in our own hands, Wylie; well, you're not far wrong in that; still I cannot break open a letter.'

"Well, then, I'm not so scrupulous when my master's interests are concerned;" and, so saying, he tore open each in turn, and threw them on the bed. "There, sir, you can transport me for the offence whenever you like."

"You are a strange fellow, Sam," said Hemsworth, whose nerves were too much shaken by illness to enable him to act with his ordinary decision; and he took up one of the letters and perused it slowly. "This is merely an announcement of his arrival in Dublin; he has waited upon, but not seen, the Secretary—finds it difficult to obtain an audience—press of parliamentary business for the new session—no excitement about the United party. What tidings has the other? Ha! what's this?" and his thin and haggard face flushed scarlet. "Leave me, Sam; I must have a little time to consider this. Come back to me in an hour."

Wylie said not a word, but moved towards the door, while in his sallow features a savage smile of malicious triumph shone.

As Hemsworth flattened out the letter before him on the bed, his eyes glistened and sparkled with the fire of aroused intelligence; the faculties which, during his long illness, had lain in abeyance, as if refreshed and invigorated by rest, were once more excited to their accustomed exercise; and over that face, pale and haggard by sickness, a flush of conscious power stole, lighting up every lineament and feature, and displaying the ascendancy of mental effort over mere bodily infirmity.

"And so this Scotchman dares to enter the list with *me*," said he, with a smile of contemptuous feeling; "let him try it."

CHAPTER XLIV.

A LITTLE lower down the valley than the post occupied by Terry as his look-out, was a small stream, passable by stepping-stones; this was the usual parting place of the two brothers whenever Herbert returned home for a day or so, and this limit Mark rarely or never transgressed, regarding it as the frontier of his little dominion. Beside this rivulet, as night was falling, Mark sat, awaiting with some impatience his brother's coming, for already the third evening had passed in which Herbert promised to be back, and yet he had not come.

Alternately stooping to listen, or straining his eyes to see, he waited anxiously; and while canvassing in his mind every possible casualty he could think of to account for his absence, he half resolved on pushing for-ward down the glen, and, if necessary, venturing even the whole way to Carrignacurra. Just then a sound caught his ear—he listened, and at once recognised Terry's voice, as, singing some rude verse, he came hastening down the glen at his full speed.

"Ha! I thought you'd be here," cried he, with delight in his coun-tenance; "I knew you'd be just sitting there on that rock."

"What has happened, then, Terry, that you wanted me?"

"It was a message a man in sailor's clothes gave me for your honour this morning, and somehow I forgot to tell you of it when you passed, though he charged me not to forget it."

"What is it, Terry?"

"Ah, then, that's what I misremember, and I had it all right this morn-ing. Let me think a bit."

Mark repelled every symptom of impatience, for he well knew how the slightest evidences of dissatisfaction on his part would destroy every chance of the poor fellow regaining his memory, and he waited silently for several minutes. At last, thinking to aid his recollection, he said,

"The man was a smuggler, Terry?"

"He was, but I never saw him before. He came across from Kinsale, over the mountains. Botheration to him, why didn't he say more, and I wouldn't forget it now."

"Have patience, you'll think of it all by-and-by."

"Maybe so. He was a droll-looking fellow, with a short cutlash at his side, and a hairy cap on his head, and he seemed to know yer honour well, for he said,

"'How is the O'Donoghues—don't they live hereabouts?'

"'Yes,' says I, 'a few miles down that way.'

"'Is the eldest boy at home?' says he.

"'Maybe he is, and maybe he isn't,' says I, for I wouldn't tell him where you were.

"'Could you give him a message,' says he, 'from a friend?'

"'Av it was a friend,' says I.

"'A real friend,' says he. 'Tell him—just tell him——' There it is now—divil a one o' me knows what he said."

Mark suffered no sign of anger to escape him, but sat without speaking a word, while Terry recapitulated every sentence in a muttering voice, to assist him in remembering what followed.

"I have it now," said he, at last; and clapping his hands with glee, he cried out, "them's the very words he said:

"'Tell Mr. Mark it's a fine sight to see the sun rising from the top of Hungry Mountain; and if the wind last it will be worth seeing to-morrow.'"

"Were those his words?" asked Mark, eagerly.

"Them, and no other—I have it all in my head now."

"Which way did he take when he left you?"

"He turned up the glen, towards Googawn Barra, and I seen him crossing the mountain afterwards. But here comes Master Herbert." And at the same instant he was seen coming up the valley at a fast pace.

When the first greetings were over, Herbert informed Mark that a certain stir and movement in the glen and its neighbourhood for the last few days had obliged him to greater caution; that several strangers had been seen lurking about Carrignacurra; and that in addition to the military posted at Mary's, a sergeant's guard had that morning arrived at the Lodge, and taken up their quarters there. All these signs of vigilance combined to make Herbert more guarded, and induced him to delay for a day or two his return to the shealing.

"Hemsworth has been twice over to our house," continued Herbert, "and seems most anxious about you; he cannot understand why we have not heard from my uncle. It appears to me, Mark, as if difficulties were thickening around us; and yet this fear may only be the apprehension which springs from mystery. I cannot see my way through this dark and clouded atmosphere."

"Never fret about the dangers that come like shadows, Herbert. Come up the mountain with me to-morrow at sunrise, and let us take counsel from the free and bracing air of the peak of old Hungry."

Herbert was but too happy to find his own gloomy thoughts so well combated, aud iu mutual converse they each grew lighter in heart; and when at last, wearied out, they lay down upon the heather of the shealing, they slept without a dream.

It was still dark as midnight when Mark awoke and looked at his watch —it wanted a quarter of four. The night was a wild and gusty one, with occasional showers of thin sleet, and along the shore the sea beat heavily, as though a storm was brewing at a distance off.

The message of the smuggler was his first thought on waking, but could he venture sufficient trust iu Terry's version to draw any inference from it? Still, he resolved to ascend the mountain, little favourable as the weather promised for such an undertaking. It was not without reluctance that Herbert found himself called upon to accompany his brother. The black and dreary night, the swooping wind, the wet spray, drifting up to the very shealing, were but sorry inducements to stir abroad; aud he did his utmost to persuade him to defer the excursion to a more favourable moment.

"We shall be wet through, and see nothing for our pains, Mark," said he, half sulkily, as the other overruled each objection in turn.

"Wet we may possibly be," said Mark; "but with the wind, northing by west, the mist will clear away, and by sunrise the coast will be glorious; it is a spring tide, too, and there will be a sea running mountains high."

"I know well we shall find ourselves in a cloud on the top of the mountain; it is but one day in a whole year anything can be seen favourably."

"And who is to say this is not that day? It is my birthday, Herbert—a most auspicious event, when we talk of fortunate occurrences."

The tone of sarcasm he spoke these words in, silenced Herbert's scruples, and without further objection he prepared to follow Mark's guidance.

The drifting rain, and the spongy heavy ground iu which at each moment the feet sank to the very instep, made the way toilsome and weary, and the two brothers seldom spoke as they plodded along the steep ascent.

Mark's deep preoccupation of mind took away all thought of the dreary road; but Herbert followed with reluctant steps, half augry with himself for compliance with what he regarded as an absurd caprice. The way was not without its perils, and Mark halted from time to time to warn his brother of the danger of some precipice, or the necessity to guard against the slippery surface of the heather. Except at these times he rarely spoke, but strode on with firm step, lost in his own reflections.

"We are now twelve hundred feet above the lake, Herbert," said he, after a long silence on both sides, "and the mountain at this side is like a wall. This same island of ours has noble bulwarks for defence."

Herbert made no reply; the swooping clouds that hurried past, heavily charged with vapour, shut out every object; and to him the rugged path was a dark and cheerless way. Once more they continued their ascent, which here became steeper and more difficult at every step; and although Mark was familiar with each turn and winding of the narrow track, more than once he was obliged to stop and consider the course before him. Herbert, to whom these interruptions were fresh sources of irritation, at length exclaimed,

"My dear Mark, have we not gone far enough yet, to convince you that there is no use in going farther. It is dark as midnight this moment—you yourself are scarcely certain of the way—there are precipices and gullies on every side—and grant that we do reach the top for sunrise, what shall we be able to see amid the immense masses of cloud around us?"

"No, Herbert, that same turning-back policy it is which thwarts success in life. Had you yourself followed such an impulse, you had not gained the honours that are yours. Onward, is the word of hope to all. And what if the day should not break clearly, it is a fine thing to sit on the peak of old Hungry, with the circling clouds wheeling madly below you, to hear the deep thundering of the sea, far, far away, and the cry of the curlew mingling with the wailing wind—to feel yourself high above the busy world, in the dreary region of mist and shadow. If at such times as this the eye ranges not over leagues of coast and sea, long winding valleys and wide plains, the prophetic spirit fostered by such agencies looks out on life, and images of the future flit past in cloudy shapes and changing forms. There, see that black mass that slowly moves along, and seems to beckon us with giant arms. You'd not reject an augury so plain."

"I see nothing, and if I go on much farther this way, I shall feel nothing either, I am so benumbed with cold and rain already."

"Here, then, taste this—I had determined to give you nothing until we reached the summit."

Herbert drained the little measure of whisky, and resumed his way more cheerily.

"There is a bay down here beneath where we stand—a lovely little nook in summer, with a shore like gold, and waves bright as the greenest emerald. It is a wild and stormy spot to-day—no boat could live a moment there; and so steep is the cliff, this stone will find its way to the bottom within a minute."

And as Mark spoke he detached a fragment of rock from the mountain, and sent it bounding over the edge of the precipice, while Herbert, awe-struck at the nearness of the peril, recoiled instinctively from the brink of the cliff.

"There was a ship of the Spanish Armada wrecked in that little bay—they show you still some mounds of earth upon the shore they call the Spaniards' graves," said Mark, as he stood peering through the misty darkness into the depth below. "The peasantry had lighted a fire on this rock, and the ves-

Y

sel, a three-decker, decoyed by the signal, held on her course, in shore, and
was lost.   Good Heavens!" cried he, after a brief pause, "why has this
fatality ever been our lot?   Why have we welcomed our foes with smiles,
and our friends with hatred and destruction?   These same Spaniards were
our brethren and our kindred, and the bitter enemies of our enslavers;
and even yet we can perpetuate the memory of their ruin, as a thing of
pride and triumph.   Are we for ever to be thus, or is a better day to dawn
upon us?"

Herbert, who by experience knew how much more excited Mark became
by even the slightest opposition, forbore to speak, and again they pursued
their way.

They had continued for some time thus, when Mark, taking Herbert's arm,
pointed to a dark mass, which seemed to loom straight above their heads,
where, towering to a considerable height, it terminated in a sharp pinnacle.

"Yonder is the summit, Herbert—courage for a quarter of an hour more,
and the breach is won."

The youth heaved a heavy sigh, and muttered,

"Would it were so."

If Herbert became dispirited and worn out by the dark and dreary way,
where no sight nor sound relieved the dull monotony of fatigue, Mark's
spirit seemed to grow lighter with every step he went.   As if he had left his
load of care with the nether world, his light and bounding movement, and
his joyous voice, spoke of a heart which, throwing off its weight of sorrow,
revelled once more in youthful ecstasy.

"You are a poet, Herbert—tell me if you have faith in those instinctive
fancies which seem to shadow forth events?"

"If you mean to ask me whether, from my present sensations, I anticipate a heavy cold, or a fit of rheumatism, I say, most certainly," replied
Herbert, half doggedly.

Mark smiled, and continued:

"No, those are among the common course of events.   What I asked for
was an explanation of my own feelings at this moment.   Why, here upon
this lone and gloomy mountain, a secret whispering at my heart tells me to
hope—that my days and nights of disaster are nigh over—and that the
turning point of my life is at hand, even as that bold peak above us."

"I must confess, Mark, this is a strange time and place for such rose-
coloured visions," said Herbert, as he shook the rain from his soaked garments; "my imagination cannot carry me to such a lofty flight."

Mark was too intent upon his own thoughts to bestow much attention on
the tone and spirit of Herbert's remark, and he pressed forward towards the
summit with every effort of his strength.   After a brief but toilsome exertion he reached the top, and seated himself on a little pile of stones that
marked the point of the mountain.   The darkness was still great; faint outlines of the lesser mountains beneath could only be traced through the

masses of heavy cloud that hung, as it were, suspended above the earth; while over the sea an unusual blackness was spread. The wind blew with terrific force arouud the lofty peak where Mark sat, and in the distant valleys he could hear the sound of crashing branches as the storm swept through the wood; from the sea itself, too, a low booming noise arose, as the caves along the shore re-echoed to the swelling clangor of the waves.

Herbert at last reached the spot, but so exhausted by the unaccustomed fatigue, that he threw himself down at Mark's feet, and with a wearied sigh exclaimed,

"Thank Heaven! there is no more of it."

"Day will not break for half an hour yet," said Mark, pointing westward; "the grey dawn always shows over the sea. I have seen the whole surface like gold, before the dull mountains had oue touch of light."

The heavy breathing of the youth, as he lay with his head on Mark's knees, attracted him; he looked down, aud perceived that Herbert had fallen into a calm and tranquil sleep.

"Poor fellow," cried Mark, as he smoothed the hair upon his brow, "this toil has been too much for him."

Placing himself iu such a positiou as best to shelter his brother from the storm, Mark sat awaiting the breaking dawn. The hopes that in the active ascent of the mountain were high iu his heart, already began to fail; exer·tion had called them forth, and now, as he sat silently amid the dreary waste of darkness, his spirit fell with every moment. One by one the bright visions he had conjured up faded away, his head fell heavily on his bosom, and thoughts gloomy and dark as the dreary morning crowded on his brain.

As he remaiued thus deep sunk in sad musiugs, the grey dawn broke over the sea, aud gradually a pinkish hue staiued the sky eastward. The rain, which up to this time drifted in heavy masses, ceased to fall; aud instead of the gusty storm, blowing in fitful blasts, a geutle breeze rolled the mists along the valleys, as if taking away the drapery of Night at the call of Morning. At first the mountain peaks appeared through the deuse clouds, and then, by degrees, their steep sides, begirt with rock, and fissured with many a torrent. At length the deep valleys and gleus began to open to the eye, and the rude cabins of the peasants, markcd out by the thin blue wreath of smoke that rose iuto the air ere it was scattered by the fresh breeze of morning. Over the sea the sunlight glittered, tipping the glad waves that dauced and sported towards the shorc, and making the white foam upon the breakers look fairer than snow itself. Mark looked upon the scene thus suddenly changed, and shaking his brother's arm, he called out,

"Awake, Herbert! see what a glorious day is breakiug. Look, that is Sugarloaf, piercing the white cloud; and youder is Castlctown. See how the shore is marked out in every jutting point and cliff. I can see the Kenmare river as it opens to the sea."

" It is indeed beautiful!" exclaimed Herbert, all fatigue forgotten in the ecstasy of the moment. " Is not that Garran Thual, Mark, that rears its head above the others?"

But Mark's eyes were turned in a different direction, and he paid no attention to the question.

" Yes," cried Herbert, still gazing intently towards the land, " and that must be Mangerton. Am I right, Mark?"

" What can that mean?" said Mark, seizing Herbert's arm, and pointing to a distant point across Bantry Bay. " There, you saw it then."

" Yes, a bright flash of flame. See, it burns steadily now."

" Ay, and there's another below Beerhaven, and another yonder at the Smuggler's Rock."

And while he was yet speaking, the three fires blazed out, and continued to burn brilliantly in the grey light of the morning. The dark mist that moved over the sea gave way before the strong breeze, and the tall spars of a large ship were seen as a vessel rounded the point, and held on her course up Bantry Bay. Even at the distance Mark's experienced eye could detect that she was a ship of war; her ports, on which the sun threw a passing gleam, bristled with guns, and her whole trim and bearing bespoke a frigate.

"She's a King's ship, Mark, in pursuit of some smuggler," said Herbert; " and the fires we have seen were signals to the other. How beautifully she sails along; and see, is not that another?"

Mark made no reply, but pointed straight out to sea, where now seven sail could be distinctly reckoned, standing towards the bay with all their canvas set. The report of a cannon turned their eyes towards the frigate, and they perceived that already she was abreast of Whitty Island, where she was about to anchor.

" That gun was fired by her; and see, there goes her ensign. What does that mean, Mark?"

" It means Liberty, my boy!" screamed Mark, with a yell that sounded like madness. " France has come to the rescue! See, there they are—eight —nine of them!—and the glorious tricolor floating at every mast! Oh, great Heaven! in whose keeping the destinies of men and kingdoms lie, look favourably upon our struggle now! Yes, my brother, I was right—a brighter hour is about to shine upon our country! Look there—think of those gallant fellows that have left home and country to bring freedom across the seas, and say if you will be less warm in the cause than the alien and the stranger. How nobly they come along! Herbert, be with us—be of us, now !"

" Whatever be our ills here," said Herbert, sternly, " I know of no sympathy to bind us to France; nor would I accept a boon at such hands, infidel and blood-stained as she is."

" Stop, Herbert ; let us not here, where we may meet for the last time, interchange aught that should darken memory hereafter. My course is youder."

"Farewell, theu, Mark; I will not vainly endeavour to turn you from your rash project. The reasons that seemed cold and valueless iu the hour of tranquil thought, have few chances of success in the moment of your seeming triumph."

"Seeming triumph!" exclaimed Mark, as a slight change coloured his cheek. "And will you not credit what your eyes reveal before you? Are these visions? Was that loud shot a trick of the imagination? Oh! Herbert, if the loyalty you boast of have no better foundation than these fancies, be with your country—stand by her in the day of her peril."

"I will do so, Mark, and with no failing spirit either," said Herbert, as he turucd away, sad and sorrow-struck.

"You would not betray us," cried Mark, as he saw his brother preparing to desceud the mountain.

"Oh, Mark, you should not have said this."

And in a torrent of tears he threw himself upon his brother's bosom. For some minutes they remained close locked in each other's arms, and then Herbert, tearing himself away, clasped Mark's hand in both of his, and kissed it. The last "Good-by" broke from each lip together, and they parted.

Mark remained on the spot where his brother had left him, his eyes fixedly directed towards the bay, where already a second ship had arrived— a large three-decker, with an admiral's pennon flyiug from the mast-head. The first burst of wild euthusiasm over, he began to reflect ou what was next to be doue. Of course, he should lose no time in presenting himself to the officers in commaud of the expedition, and making known to them his name, and the place he occupied in the confidence of his countrymen. His great doubt was, whether he should not precede this act by measures for assembling and rallying the people, who evideutly would be as much taken by surprise as himself at the sudden arrival of the French.

The embarrassment of the positiou was great; for, although deeply implicated in the danger of the plot, he never had eujoyed either intimacy or intercourse with its leaders. How, then, should he satisfy the French that his position was such as entitled him to their confidence? The only possible escape to this difficulty was by marshalliug around him a considerable body of the peasantry, ready and willing to join the arms and follow the fortunes of the invaders.

"They caunot long distrust me with a force of three hundred men at my back," exclaimed Mark, aloud, as he descended the mountain with rapid strides. "I know evcry road through these valleys—every place where a stand could be made, or an escape effected. We will surprise the party of soldiers at Mary M'Kelly's, and there there are arms enough for all the peasantry of the country."

Thus saying, and repeating to himself the names of the different farmers whom he remembered as true to the cause, and on whose courage and readiness he depended at this moment, he hastened on.

"Holt at the cross-roads promised eighteen, all armed with firelocks. M'Sweeny has six sons, and stout fellows they are, every man of them ready. Then, there are the O'Learys, but there's a split amongst them—confound their petty feuds, this is no time to indulge them—they shall come out, and they must—ah! hand in hand, too, though they have been enemies this twelvemonth. Black O'Sullivan numbers nigh eighty—pikemen every one of them. Our French friends may smile at their ragged garments, but our enemies will scarce join in the laugh. Carrignacurra must be occupied—it is the key of the glen. The Lodge we'll burn to the ground—but no, we must not visit the sin of the servant on the master. Young Travers behaved nobly to me. There is a wild time coming, and let us, at least, begin our work in a better spirit, for bloodshed soon teaches cruelty."

Now, muttering these short and broken sentences, now, wondering what strength the French force might be—how armed—how disposed for the enterprise—what spirit prevailed among the officers, and what hopes of success animated the chiefs—Mark moved along, eager for the hour to come when the green flag should be displayed, and the war-cry of Ireland ring in her native valleys.

CHAPTER XLV

THE PROGRESS OF TREACHERY.

LEAVING, for the present, Mark O'Donoghue to the duties he imposed on himself of rallying the people around the French standard, we shall turn to the old castle of Carrignacurra, where life seemed to move on in the same unbroken tranquillity. For several days past, Hemsworth, still weak from his recent illness, had been a frequent visitor, and although professing that the great object of his solicitude was the safety of young O'Donoghue, he found time and opportunity to suggest to Kate that a more tender feeling influenced him. So artfully had he played his part, and so blended were his attentions with traits of deference and respect, that, however little she might be disposed to encourage his addresses, the difficulty of repelling them without offence was great indeed. This delicacy on her part was either mistaken by Hemsworth, or taken as a ground of advantage. All his experiences in life pointed to the fact, that success is ever attainable by him who plays well his game; that the accidents of fortune, instead of being obstacles and interruptions, are, in reality, to one of quick intelligence, but so many aids and allies. His illness alone had disconcerted his plans; but now, once more well, and able to conduct his schemes, he had no fears for the result. Up to this moment, everything promised success. It was more than doubtful that the Traverses would ever return to Ireland. Frederick would be unwilling to visit the neighbourhood where his affections had met so severe a shock. The disturbed state of the country, and the events which Hemsworth well knew must soon occur, would in all likelihood deter Sir Marmaduke from any wish to revisit his Irish property. This was one step gained. Already he was in possession of a large portion of the Glenflesk estate, of which he was well aware the title was defective, for he had made it a ground of considerable abatement in the purchase-money to the O'Donoghue, that his son was in reality under age at the time of sale. Mark's fate was, however, in his hands, and he had little fear that the secret was known to any other. Nothing, then, remained incomplete to the accomplishment of his wishes, except his views regarding Kate. Were she to become his wife, the small remnant of the property that pertained to them would fall into his hands, and he become the lord of the soil. His ambitions were higher than this. Through the instrumentality of Lanty Lawler, he had made himself master of the conspiracy in all its details. He knew the names of the several chiefs, the parts assigned them, the places of rendezvous, their hopes, their fears, and their difficulties. He was aware of the views of France, and had in his possession copies of several letters which passed between members of the French executive and the leaders of the United party in Ireland. Far from communicating this information to the Government, he treasured it as the source of his own future elevation. From time to time, it is true, he made known certain facts regarding individuals whom he either dreaded for their power, or suspected that they might themselves prove false to their party and betray the plot; but, save in these few instances, he revealed nothing of what he knew, determining, at the proper moment, to make this knowledge the groundwork of his fortune.

"Twenty-four hours of rebellion," said he—" one day and night of massacre and bloodshed, will make me a peer of the realm. I know well what terror will pervade the land when the first rumour of a French landing gains currency. I can picture to myself the affrighted looks of the Council; the alarm depicted in every face, when the post brings the intelligence that a force is on its march towards the capital; and then—then, when I can lay my hand on each rebel of them all, and say, this man is a traitor, and that a rebel—when I can show where arms are collected and ammunition stored —when I can tell the plan of their operation, their numbers, their organisation, and their means—I have but to name the price of my reward."

Such were the speculations that occupied the slow hours of his recovery, and such the thoughts which engrossed the first days of his returning health.

The latest letters he had seen from France announced that the expedition would not sail till January, and then, in the event of escaping the English force in the Channel, would proceed to land fiftcen thousand men on the banks of the Shannon. The causes which accelerated the sailing of the French fleet before the time originally determined on were unknown to Hemsworth, and on the very morning when the vessels anchored in Bantry Bay, he was himself a visitor beneath the roof of Carrignacurra, where he had passed the preceding night, the severity of the weather having detained him there. He, therefore, knew nothing of what had happened, and was calmly deliberating on the progress of his own plans, when events were occurring which were destined to disconcert and destroy them.

The family was seated at breakfast, and Hemsworth, whose letters had been brought over from the Lodge, was reading aloud such portions of news as could interest or amuse the O'Donoghue and Kate, when he was informed that Wylie was without, and most anxious to see him for a few minutes. There was no communication which, at the moment, he deemed could be of much importance, and he desired him to wait. Wylie again requested a brief interview—one minute would be enough—that his tidings were of the deepest consequence.

"This is his way ever," said Hemsworth, rising from the table. "If a tenant has broken down a neighbour's ditch, or a heifer is impounded, he always comes with this same pressing urgency ;" and, angry at the interruption, he left the room to hear the intelligence.

"Still no letter from Archy, Kate," said the O'Donoghue, when they were alone ; "once more the post is come, and nothing for us. I am growing more and more uneasy about Mark. These delays will harass the poor boy, and drive him perhaps to some rash step."

"Mr. Hemsworth is doing everything, however, in his power," said Kate, far more desirous of offering consolation to her uncle than satisfied in her own mind as to the state of matters. "He is in constant correspondence with Government. The only difficulty is, they demand disclosures my cousin neither can, nor ought to make. A pardon is no grace, when it commutes death for dishonour. This will, I hope, be got over soon."

While she was yet speaking, the door softly opened, and Kerry, with a noiseless step, slipped in, and, approaching the table unseen and unheard, was beside the O'Donoghue's chair before he was perceived.

"Whisht, master dear—whisht, Miss Kate," said he, with a gesture of warning towards the door. "There's great news without. The French is landed—twenty-eight ships is down in Bantry Bay. Bony himself is with them. I heard it all, as Sam Wylie was telling Hemsworth ; I was inside the pantry door."

"The French landed !" cried the O'Donoghue, in whom amazement overcame all sensation of joy or sorrow.

"The French here in Ireland!" cried Kate, her eyes sparkling with enthusiastic delight; but before she could add a word, Hemsworth re-entered. Whether his efforts to seem calm and unmoved were in reality well devised, or that, as is more probable, Hemsworth's own preoccupation prevented his strict observance of the others, he never remarked that the O'Donoghue and his niece exhibited any traits of anxiety or impatience; while Kerry, after performing a variety of very unnecessary acts and attentions about the table, at last left the room, with a sigh over his inability to protract his departure.

Hemsworth's eye wandered to the door to see if it was closed before he spoke; and then leaning forward, said, in a low, cautious voice,

"I have just heard some news that may prove very important. A number of the people have assembled in arms in the glen, your son Mark at their head. What their precise intentions, or whither they are about to direct their steps, I know not; but I see clearly that young Mr. O'Donoghue will fatally compromise himself, if this rash step become known. The Government never could forgive such a proceeding on his part. I need not tell you that this daring must be a mere hopeless exploit; such enterprises have but one termination—the scaffold."

The old man and his niece exchanged glances—rapid, but full of intelligence. Each seemed to ask the other, "Is this man false? Is he suppressing a part of the truth at this moment, or is this all invention? Why has he not spoken of the great event—the arrival of the French?"

Kate was the first to venture to sound him, as she asked,

"And is the rising some mere sudden ebullition of discontent, or have they concerted any movement with others at a distance?"

"A mere isolated outbreak—the rash folly of hairbrained boys, without plan or project."

"What is to become of poor Mark?" cried the O'Donoghue, all suspicions of treachery forgotten in the anxiety of his son's safety.

"I have thought of that," said Hemsworth, hastily. "The movement must be put down at once. As a magistrate, and in the full confidence of the Government, I have no second course open to me, and therefore I have ordered up the military from Macroom. There are four troops of cavalry and an infantry regiment there. With them in front, this ill-disciplined rabble will never dare to advance, but soon scatter and disband themselves in the mountains—the leaders only will incur any danger. But, as regards your son, you have only to write a few lines to him, and despatch them by some trusty messenger, saying that you are aware of what has happened—know everything—and without wishing to interfere or thwart his designs, you desire to see and speak with him, here, at once. This he will not refuse. Once here safe, and within these walls, I'll hasten the pursuit of these foolish country fellows; and even should any of them be taken, your son will not be of the number. You must take care, however, when he is here, that he does not leave this until I return."

"And are these brave fellows, misguided though they be, to be kidnapped thus, and by our contrivance, too?" said Kate, on whom, for the first time, a dread of Hemsworth's duplicity was fast breaking.

"I did not know Miss O'Douoghue's interest took so wide a range, or that her sympathies were so catholic," said Hemsworth, with a smile of double meaning. "If she would save her cousin, however, she must adopt my plan, or at least suggest a better one."

"Yes, yes, Kate, Mr. Hemsworth is right," said the O'Donoghue, in whom selfishness was always predominant; "we must contrive to get Mark here, and to keep him when we have him."

"And you may rely upon it, Miss O'Donoghue," said Hemsworth, in a whisper, "that my pursuit of the others will not boast of any excessive zeal in the cause of loyalty. Such fellows may be suffered to escape, and neither King nor Constitution have any ground of complaint for it."

Kate smiled gratefully in return, and felt angry with herself for even a momentary injustice to the honourable nature of Hemsworth's motives.

"Mr. Hemsworth's horse is at the door," said Kerry, at the same moment.

"It is, then, agreed upon that you will write this letter at once," said Hemsworth, leaning over the old man's chair, as he whispered the words into his ear.

The O'Donoghue nodded an assent.

"Without knowing that," continued Hemsworth, "I should be uncertain how to proceed. I must not let the Government suppose me either ignorant or lukewarm. Lose no time, therefore; send off the letter, and leave the rest to me."

"You are not going to ride, I hope," said Kate, as she looked out of the window down the glen, where already the rain was falling in torrents, and the wind blowing a perfect hurricane. Hemsworth muttered a few words in a low tone, at which Kate coloured and walked away.

"Nay, Miss O'Donoghue," said he, still whispering, "I am not one of those who make a bargain for esteem; if I cannot win regard, I will never buy it."

There was a sadness in his words, and an air of self-respect about him, as he spoke them, that touched Kate far more than ever she had been before by any expression of his feelings. When she saw him leave the room, her first thought was, "It is downright meanness to suspect him."

"Is it not strange, Kate," said the O'Donoghue, as he took her hand in his, "he never mentioned the French landing to us? What can this mean?"

"I believe I can understand it, sir," said Kate, musingly; for already she had settled in her mind, that while Hemsworth would neglect no measures for the safety of Carrignacurra, he scrupled to announce tidings which might overwhelm them with alarm and terror. "But let us think of the letter; Kerry, I suppose, is the best person to send with it."

"Yes, Kerry can take it; and as the way does not lead past Mary's door, there's a chance of his delivering it without a delay of three hours on the road."

"There, sir, will that do?" said Kate, as she handed him a paper, on which hastily a few lines were written.

"Perfectly—nothing better; only, my sweet Kate, when a note begins 'My dear son,' it should scarcely be signed 'Your own affectionate Kate O'Donoghue.'"

Kate blushed deeply, as she tore the paper in fragments, and without a word reseated herself at the table.

"I have done better this time," said she, as she folded the note and sealed it; while the old man, with an energy quite unusual for him, arose and rang the bell for Kerry.

"Did I ever think I could have done this?" said Kate to herself, as a tear slowly coursed along her cheek and fell on the letter; "that I could dare to recal him, when both honour and country demand his services? that I could plot for life, when all that makes life worth having is in the opposite scale?"

"You must find out Master Mark, Kerry," said the O'Donoghue, "and give him this letter; there's no time to be lost about it."

"Sorra fear; I'll put it into his hand this day."

"This day!" cried Kate, impatiently. "It must reach him within three hours' time. Away at once—the foot of Hungry Mountain—the shealing—Bautry Bay—you cannot have any difficulty in finding him now."

Kerry waited not for further bidding, and though not by any means determined to make any unusual exertion, left the room with such rapidity as augured well for the future.

"Well," said Mrs. Branaghan, whose anxiety for news had led her to the head of the kitchen stairs, an excursion which, at no previous moment of her life, had she been known to take—"well, Kerry, what's going on now?"

"Faix, then, I'll tell ye, ma'am," said he, sighing; "'tis myself they're wanting to kill. Here am I setting out wid a letter, and where to, do you think? the top of Hungry Mountain, in the Bay of Bantry, that's the address—divil a lie in it."

"And who is it for?" said Mrs. Branaghan, who, affecting to bestow a critical examination on the document, was inspecting the superscription wrong side up.

"'Tis for Master Mark; I heard it all outside the door; they don't want him to go with the boys, now that the French is landed, and we're going to have the country to ourselves. 'Tis a dhroll day when an O'Donoghue wouldn't have a fight for his fathers' acres."

"Bad cess to the weak-hearted, wherever they are," exclaimed Mrs. Branaghan; "don't give him the letter, Kerry avich; lie quiet in the glen till evening, and say you couldn't find him by any manner of means. Do that, now, and it will be a good sarvice to your country this day."

"I was just thinking that same myself," said Kerry, whose resolution wanted little prompting; "after I cross the river, I'll turn into the Priest's Glen, and never stir out till evening."

With these honest intentions regarding his mission, Kerry set out, and if any apology could be made for his breach of faith, the storm might plead for him; it had now reached its greatest violence; the wind, blowing in short and frequent gusts, snapped the large branches like mere twigs, and covered the road with fragments of timber; the mountain rivulets, too, were swollen, and dashed madly down the rocky cliffs with a deafening clamour, while the rain, swooping past in torrents, concealed the sky, and covered the earth with darkness. Muttering in no favourable spirit over the waywardness of that sex, to whose peculiar interposition he ascribed his present excursion, Kerry plodded along, turning, as he went, a despairing look at the barren and bleak prospect around him. To seek for shelter in the glen he knew was out of the question, and so he at once determined to gain the priest's cottage, where a comfortable turf fire and a rasher of bacon were certain to welcome him.

Dreadful as the weather was, Kerry wondered that he met no one on the road. He expected to have seen groups of people, and all the signs of that excitement the arrival of the French might be supposed to call forth; but, on the contrary, everything was desolate as usual, not a human being appeared, nor could he hear a signal nor a sound that betokened a gathering.

"I wouldn't wonder, now, if it was a lie of Sam Wylie's, and the French wasn't here at all," said he to himself; "'tis often I heerd that Hemsworth could have the rebellion break out whenever he liked it, and sorra bit but that may be it now, just to pretend the French was here, to get the boys out, and let the army at them."

This reflection of Kerry's was scarcely conceived, when it was strengthened by a boy who was coming from Glengariff with a turf car, and who told him that the ships which came in with the morning's tide had all weighed anchor, and sailed out of the bay before twelve o'clock, and that nobody knew anything about them, what they were, and whence from. "We thought they were the French," said the boy, "till we seen them sailing away; but then we knew it wasn't them, and some said it was the King's ships coming in to guard Bantry."

"And they are not there now!" said Kerry.

"Not one of them; they're out to say, and out of sight, this hour back." Kerry hesitated for a second or two whether this intelligence might not entitle him to turn homeward; but a sceond thought, the priest's kitchen, seemed to have the advantage, and thither he bent his steps accordingly.

CHAPTER XLVI.

THE PRIEST'S COTTAGE.

WHEN Mark and Herbert separated on the mountain, each took a different path downward. Mark, bent on assembling the people at once, and proclaiming the arrival of their friends, held his course towards Glengariff and the coast, where the fishermen were, to a man, engaged in the plot. Herbert, uncertain how to proceed, was yet equally anxious to lose no time, but could form no definite resolve what course to adopt amid his difficulties. To give notice of the French landing, to apprise the magistrates of the approaching outbreak, was, of course, his duty; but, in doing this, might he not be the means of Mark's ruin; while, on the other hand, to conceal his knowledge would be an act of disloyalty to his sovereign, a forfeiture of the principles he held dear, and the source, perhaps, of the most dreadful evils to his country. Where, too, should he seek for counsel or advice? His father, he well knew, would only regard the means of his brother's safety, reckless of all other consequences; Kate's opinions, vague and undefined as they were, would be in direct opposition to his own; Hemsworth he dared not confide in. What then remained? There was but one for miles round in whose judgment and honour together he had trust; but from him latterly he had kept studiously aloof. This was his old tutor, Father Rourke. Unwilling to inflict pain upon the old man, and still unable to reconcile himself to anything like duplicity in the matter, Herbert had avoided the occasion of meeting him, and of avowing that change in his religious belief which, although secretly working for many a year, had only reached its accomplishment when absent from home. He was aware how such a disclosure would afflict his old friend—how impossible would be the effort to persuade him that such a change had its origin in conviction, and not in schemes of worldly ambition; and to save himself the indignity of defence from such an accusation, and the pain of an interview, where the matter should be discussed, he had preferred leaving to time and accident the disclosure, which from his own lips would have been a painful sacrifice to both parties. These considerations, important enough as they regarded his own happiness, had little weight with him now. The graver questions had swallowed up all others—the safety of the country—his brother's fate. It was true the priest's sympathies would be exclusively with one party; he would not view with Herbert's eye the coming struggle; but still might he not regard with him the results? Might he not, and with prescience stronger from his age, anticipate the dreadful miseries of a land devastated by civil war? Was it not possible that he might judge unfavourably of success, and prefer to endure what he regarded as evils, rather than incur the horrors of a rebellion, and the re-enactment of penalties it would call down?

The hopes such calculations suggested were higher, because Mark had himself often avowed that the French would only consent to the enterprise on the strict understanding of being seconded by the almost unanimous voice of the nation. Their expression was, "We are ready and willing to meet England in arms, provided not one Irishman be in the ranks." Should Father Rourke, then, either from motives of policy or prudence, think unfavourably of the scheme, his influence, unbounded over the people, would throw a damper on the rising, and either deter the French from any forward movement, or at least delay it, and afford time for the Government to take measures of defence. This alone might have its effect on Mark, and perhaps be the means of saving him.

Whether because he caught at this one chance of succour, when all around seemed hopeless, or that the mind fertilises the fields of its own discovery, Herbert grew more confident each moment that this plan would prove successful, and turned with an eager heart towards the valley where the priest lived. In his eagerness to press forward, however, he diverged from the path, and at last reached a part of the mountain where a tremendous precipice intervened, and stopped all further progress. The storm, increasing every minute, made the way slow and perilous, for around the different peaks the wind swept with a force that carried all before it. Vexed at his mistake, he resolved, if possible, to discover some new way down the mountain; but, in the endeavour, he only wandered still further from his course, and finally found himself in front of the sea once more.

The heavy rain and the dense drift shut out for some minutes the view; but when, at last, he saw the bay, what was his surprise to perceive that the French fleet was no longer there. He turned his eyes on every side, but the storm-lashed water bore no vessel on its surface, and save some fishing craft at anchor in the little nooks and bays of the coast, not a mast could be seen.

Scarcely able to credit the evidence of his senses, he knelt down on the cliff, and bent his gaze steadily on the bay; and when, at length, reassured and certain that no deception existed, he began to doubt whether the whole had not been unreal, and that the excitement of his interview with Mark had conjured the images his wishes suggested. The faint flickering embers of an almost extinguished fire on the Smuggler's Rock decided the question, and he knew at once that all had actually happened.

He did not wait long to speculate ou the reasons of this sudden flight—enough for him that the most pressiug danger was past, and time afforded to rescue Mark from peril; aud, without a thought upon that armament whose menace had already filled him with apprehension, he sped down the mountain in reckless haste, and never halted till he reached the glen beneath. The violence of the storm, the beating rain, seemed to excite him to higher efforts of strength and endurance, aud his courage appeared to rise as difficulties thickened around him. It was late in the day, however, before he came in sight of the priest's cottage, and where, as the gloom was falling, a twinkling light now shone.

It was with a last effort of strength, almost exhausted by fatigue and hunger, that Herbert gained the door; this lay, as usual, wide open, and eutcring, he fell overcome upon a seat. The energy that had sustained him hitherto seemed suddenly to have given way, and he lay back scarcely conscious, and unable to stir. The confusion of sense, so general after severe fatigue, prevented him for some time from hearing voices in the little parlour beside him; but, after a brief space, he became aware of this vicinity, when suddenly the well-known accents of Mark struck upon his ear. He was speaking louder than was his wont, and evidently with an effort to control his rising temper, while the priest, in a low, calm voice, seemed endeavouring to dissuade aud turn him from some purpose.

A brief silence ensued, during which Mark paced the room with slow and heavy steps; theu, ceasing suddenly, he said,

" Why was it, then, that we never heard of these scruples before, sir ?—why were we not told that unbelieving France was no fittiug ally for saintly Ireland ? But why do I ask ? Had the whole fleet arrived in safety—were there not thirteen missing vessels—we should hear less of such Christian doubts."

" You are unjust, Mark," said the priest, calmly. " You know me too well and too long to put any faith in your reproaches. I refuse to address the people, because I would not see them fall, or even conquer, in an un-just cause. Raise the banner of the Church——"

" The banner of the Church !" said Mark, with a mocking laugh.

" What does he say ?" whispered a third voice, in French, as a new speaker mingled in the dialogue.

" He talks of the banner of the Church !" said Mark, scoffingly.

" Oui, parbleu, if he likes it," replied the Frenchman, laughingly ; " it smacks somewhat of the middle ages ; but the old proverb is right, ' a bad etiquette never spoiled good wine.' '

" Is it then in full canonicals, and with the smoke of censers, we are to march against the Saxon ?" said Mark, with a taunting sneer.

" Hear me out, Mark," interrupted the priest; " I didn't say that we were yet prepared even for this; there is much to be done—far more, indeed, than you wot of. Every expedition insufficiently planned and badly supported must be a failure; every failure retards the accomplishment of our hopes; such must this enterprise be, if now——"

" Now, or never !" interposed Mark, as he struck the table violently with his clenched hand; " now, or never—for me, at least. You have shown me to these Frenchmen as a fool, or worse—one with influence, and yet without a man to back me—with courage, and you tell me to desert them—with the confidence of my countrymen, and I come alone, unaccompanied, unaccredited, to tell my own tale amongst them. What other indignities have you in store for me, or in what other light am I next to figure? But for that, and perhaps you would dare to go further, and say I am not an O'Donoghue ;" and in his passion Mark tore open a pocket-book, and held before the old man's eyes the certificate of his baptism, written in the priest's hand. " Yes, you have forced me to speak of what I ever meant to have buried in my own heart. There it is, read it, and bethink you how it becomes him who helped to rob me of my inheritance to despoil me of my honour also."

" You must unsay these words, sir," said the priest, in an accent as stern and commanding as Mark's own. " I was never a party to any fraud, nor was I in this country when your father sold his estates."

" I care not how it happened," cried Mark, passionately. " When my own father could do this thing, it matters little to me who were his accomplices ;" and he tore the paper in fragments, and scattered them over the floor. " Another and a very different cause brought me here. The French fleet has arrived."

The priest here muttered something in a low tone, to which Mark quietly replied,

" And if they have, it is because their anchors were dragging; you would not have the vessels go ashore on the rocks ; the next tide they'll stand up the bay again. The people that should have been ready to welcome them, hold back. The whole country round is become suddenly craven; of the hundreds that rallied round me a month since, seventeen appeared this morning, and they were wretches more eager for pillage than the field of honourable warfare. It is come then to this : you either come forth at once to harangue the people and recal them to their sworn allegiance, or the expedition goes on without you—go on it shall."

Here he turned sharply round, and said a few words in French, to which the person addressed replied,

" Certainly ; the French Republic does not send a force like this for the benefit of a sea voyage."

" Desert the cause, then," continued Mark, in a tone of denunciation ;

" desert us, and by G—d your fate will be worse than that ot our more open enemies. To-night the force will land; to-morrow we march all day, ay, and all night, too : the blazing chapels shall light the way !"

" Take care, rash boy, take care ; the vengeance of outraged Heaven is more terrible than you think of. Whatever be the crime and guilt of others, remember that you are an Irishman ; that what the alien may do in reck-lessness, is sacrilege in him who is the son of the soil."

" Save me, then, from this guilt—save me from myself," cried Mark, in an accent of tender emotion. "I cannot desert this cause, and oh ! do not make it one of dishonour to me."

The old man seemed overcome by this sudden appeal to his affections, and made no reply, and the deep breathing of Mark, as his chest heaved in strong emotion, was the only sound in the stillness. Herbert, who had hitherto listened with that vague half consciousness of reality excessive fatigue inflicts, became suddenly aware that the eventful moment was come, when, should the priest falter or hesitate, Mark might succeed in his request, and all hope of rescuing him be lost for ever. With the energy of a desperate resolve he sprang forward, and entered the room just as the priest was about to reply.

" No, father, no," cried he, wildly ; " be firm, be resolute; if this un-happy land is to be the scene of bloodshed, let not her sons be found in opposing ranks."

" This from you, Herbert !" said Mark, reproachfully, as he fixed a cold, stern gaze upon his brother.

" And why not from him ?" said the priest, hastily. " Is he not an Irish-man in heart and spirit ? Is not the land as dear to him as to us ?"

" I give you joy upon the alliance, father," said Mark, with a scornful laugh. " Herbert is a Protestant."

" What !—did I hear aright ?" said the old man, as, with a face pale as death, he tottered forwards, and caught the youth by either arm. " Is this true, Herbert ? Tell me, boy, this instant, that it is not so."

" It is true, sir, most true ; and if I have hitherto spared you the pain it might occasion you, believe me it was not from any shame the avowal might cost *me*."

The priest staggered back, and fell heavily into a chair ; a livid hue spread itself over his features, and his eyes grew glassy and lustreless.

" We may well be wretched and miserable," exclaimed he, with a faint sigh. " When false to Heaven, who is to wonder that we are traitors to each other ?"

The French officer—for such he was—muttered some words into Mark's ear, who replied,

" I cannot blame you for feeling impatient. This is no time for fooling. Now for the glen. Farewell, father. Herbert, we'll meet again soon ;"

and, without waiting to hear more, he hasteued from the room with his companion.

Herbert stood for a second or two undecided. He wished to say something, yet knew not what, or how. At last, approaching the old man's chair, he said,

"There is yet time to avert the danger. The people are irresolute—many actually averse to the rising. My brother will fall by his rashuess."

"Better to do so than survive in dishonour," said the priest, snatching rudely away his hand from Herbert's grasp. "Leave me, young man—go; this is a poor and an humble roof, but never till now has it sheltered the apostate."

"I never thought I should hear these words here," said Herbert, mildly; "but I cannot part with you in anger."

"There was a time when you never left me without my blessing, Herbert," said the priest, his eyes swimming in tears as he spoke; "kneel now, my child."

Herbert knelt at the priest's feet, when, placing his hand on the young man's head, he muttered a fervent prayer over him, saying, as he concluded,

"And may He who knows all hearts, direct and guide yours, and bring you back from your wanderings, if you have strayed from truth."

He kissed the young man's forehead, and then, covering his eyes with his hands, sat lost in his own sorrowful thoughts.

At this moment Herbert heard his name whispered by a voice without : he stole silently from the room, and, on reaching the little porch, fouud Kerry O'Leary, who, wet through aud wearied, had reached the cottage, after several hours' endeavour to cross the watercourses, swollen into torrents by the rain.

"A letter from Carriguacurra, sir," said Kerry ; for, heartily sick of his excursion, he adopted the expedient of pretending to mistake to which brother the letter was addressed, and thus at once terminate his unpleasant mission.

The note began "My dear son," and, without the mention of a name, simply entreated his immediate return home. Thither Herbert felt both duty and inclination called him, and, without a moment's delay, left the cottage, and, accompanied by Kerry, set out for Carriguacurra.

The night was dark and starless as they plodded onward, and as the rain ceased, the wind grew stronger, while for miles inland the roaring of the sea could be heard like deep, continuous thunder. Herbert, too much occupied with his own thoughts, seldom spoke, nor did Kerry, exhausted as he felt himself, often break silence as they went. As they drew near the castle, however, a figure crossed the road, and, advancing towards them, said,

"Good night."

"Who could that be, Kerry?" said Herbert, as the stranger passed on. "I know the voice well," said Kerry, "though he thought to disguise it. That's Sam Wylie, and it's not for anythiug good he's here."

Scarcely were the words spoken, when four fellows sprang down upon and seized them.

"This is our man," said one of the party, as he held Herbert by the collar, with a grasp there was no resisting; "but secure the other also."

Herbert's resistance was vain, although spiritedly made, and, stifling his cries for aid, they carried him along for some little distance to a spot where a chaise was standing with four mouuted dragoons on either side. Into this he was forced, and, seated between two men in plain clothes, the word was giveu to start.

"You know your orders if a rescue be attempted," said a voice Herbert at once knew to be Hemsworth's.

The answer was lost in the noise of the wheels; for already the horses were away at the top of their speed, giving the escort all they could do to keep up beside them.

CHAPTER XLVII.

THE DAY OF REOKONING.

NEVER had the O'Donoghue aud Kate passed a day of more painful anxiety, walking from window to window, whenever a view of the glen might be obtained, or listening to catch among the sounds of the storm for something that should announce Mark's return; their fears increased as the hours stole by, and yet no sign of his coming appeared.

The old castle shook to its very foundations as the terrific gale tore along the glen, and the occasional crash of some old fragment of masonry would be heard high above the roaring wind—while in the road beneath were scattered branches of trees, slates, and tiles, all evidencing the violence of the hurricane. Under shelter of the great rock a shivering flock of mountain sheep were gathered, with here and there amidst them a heifer or a wild pony, all differences of habit merged in the common instinct of safety. Within doors everything looked sad and gloomy; the kitchen, where several country people, returning from the market, had assembled, waiting in the vain hope of a favourable moment to proceed homeward, did not present any of its ordinary signs of gaiety. There was no pleasant sound of happy voices; no laughter, no indulgence in the hundred little narratives of personal adventure by which the peasant can beguile the weary time. They all sat around the turf fire, either silent, or conversing in low, cautious whispers, while Mrs. Branaghan herself smoked her pipe in a state of moody dignity, that added its shade of awe to the solemnity of the scene.

It was a strange feature of the converse, nor would it be worth mentioning here, save as typifying the wonderful caution and reserve of the people in times of difficulty, but no one spoke of the "rising," nor did any allude, except distantly, to the important military preparations going forward at Macroom. The fear of treachery was at the moment universal; the dread that informers were scattered widely through the land prevailed everywhere, and the appearance of a stranger, or of a man from a distant part of the country, was always enough to silence all free and confidential intercourse. So it was now—none spoke of anything but the dreadful storm—the injury it might do the country—how the floods would carry away a bridge here, or a mill there—what roads would be impassable—what rivers would no longer be fordable—some had not yet drawn home their turf from the bog, and were now in despair of ever reaching it—another had left his hay in a low callow, and never expected to see it again—while a few, whose speculations took a wider field, ventured to expatiate on the terrible consequences of the gale at sea, a topic which, when suggested, led to many a sorrowful tale of shipwreck on the coast.

It was while they were thus, in low and muttering voices, talking over these sad themes, that Kate, unable any longer to endure the suspense of silent watching, descended the stairs and entered the kitchen, to try and learn there some tidings of events. The people stood up respectfully as she came forward, and while each made his or her humble obeisance, a muttered sound ran through them, in Irish, of wonder and astonishment at her grace and beauty; for, whatever be the privations of the Irish peasant, however poor and humble his lot in life, two faculties pertain to him like instincts— a relish for drollery, and an admiration for beauty; these are claims that ever find acknowledgment from him, and, in his enjoyment of either, he can forget himself and all the miseries of his condition. The men gazed on her as something more than mortal; the character of her features, heightened by costume strange to their eyes, seemed to astonish almost as much as it captivated them—while the women, with more critical discernment, examined her more composedly, but, perhaps, with not less admiration; Mrs. Branaghan, at the same time, throwing a proud glance around, as though to say, "You didn't think to see the likes of that in these parts."

Kate happened on this occasion to look more than usually handsome. With a coquetry it is not necessary to explain, she had dressed herself most becomingly, and in that style which distinctly marks a French woman. The only time in his life Mark had ever remarked her costume was when she wore this dress, and she had not forgotten the criticism.

"I didn't mean to disturb you," said Kate, with her slightly foreign accent; "pray sit down again. Well, then, I must leave you, if you won't. Every one lets me have my own way—is it not true, Mrs. Branaghan?"

Mrs. Branaghan's reply was quite lost in the general chorus of the others, as she said,

"And why wouldn't you, God bless you for a raal beauty!" while a powerful looking fellow, with dark beard and whiskers, struck his stick violently against the ground, and cried out in his enthusiasm,

"Let me see the man that would say agin it—that's all."

Kate smiled at the speaker, not all ungrateful for such rude chivalry, and went on: "I wanted to know if you have any news from the town—was there any stir among the troops, or anything extraordinary going forward there?"

Each looked at the other as if unwilling to take the reply upon himself, when at last an old man, with a head as white as snow, answered,

"Yes, my lady, the soldiers is all under arms since nine o'clock; then came news that the French was in the bay, and the army was sent for to Cork."

"No, 'tis Limerick, I heerd say," cried another.

"Limerick, indeed! sorra bit; 'tis from Dublin they're comin', wid cannons; but it's no use, for the French is sailed off again as quick as they come."

"The French fleet gone!—left the bay! Surely you must mistake," said Kate, eagerly.

"Faix, I won't be sure, my lady; but here's Tom M'Carthy seen them going away, a little after twelve o'clock."

The man thus appealed to seemed in no wise satisfied with the allusion to him, and threw a quick, distrustful look around, as though far from feeling content with the party before whom he should explain,—a feeling that increased considerably, as every eye was now turned towards him.

Kate, with a ready tact that never failed her, saw his difficulty, and approaching close to where he stood, said, in a voice only audible by himself,

"Tell me what you saw in the bay—do not have any fear of me."

M'Carthy, who was dressed in the coarse blue jacket of a fisherman, possessed that sharp intelligence so often found among those of his calling, and seemed as once to have his mind relieved by this mark of confidence.

"I was in the boat, my lady," said he, "that rowed Master Mark out to the French frigate, and waited for him alongside to bring him back. He was more than an hour on board talking with the officers, sometimes down in the cabin, and more times up on the quarter-deck, where there was a fierce-looking man, with a blue uniform, lying on a white skin—a white bear,

Master Mark tould me it was. The officer was wounded in the leg before he left France, and the sea voyage made it bad again, but, for all that, he laughed and joked away like the others."

"And they were laughing, then, and in good spirits?" said Kate.

"'Tis that you may call it. I never heerd such pleasant gentlemen before; and the sailors, too, were just the same—sorra bit would sarve them, but making us drink a bottle of rum apiece, for luck, I suppose. Devil a one had a sorrowful face on him but Master Mark, whatever was the matter with him. He wouldn't eat anything either, and the only glass of wine he drank you'd think it was poison, the face he made at it—more by token, he flung the glass overboard when he finished it. And to be sure the Frenchmen weren't in fault—they treated him like a brother. One would be shaking hands wid him—another wid his arm round his shoulders, and——" Here Tom blushed and stammered, and at last stopped dead short.

"Well, go on, what were you going to say?"

"Faix, I'm ashamed then—but 'tis true enough—saving your presence, I saw two of them kiss him."

Kate could not help laughing at Tom's astonishment at this specimen of French greeting; while for the first time, perhaps, did the feeling of the peasant occur to herself, and the practice she had often witnessed abroad without remark, became suddenly repugnant to her delicacy.

"And did Master Mark come back alone?" asked she, after a minute's hesitation.

"No, my lady; there was a little dark man wid gould epaulets, and a sword on him, that came too. I heerd them call him Mr. Morris, but sorra word of English or Irish he had."

"And where did they land, and which way did they take afterwards?"

"I put them ashore at Glengariff, and they had horses there to take them up the country. I heerd they were going first to Father Rourke's, in the glen."

"And then, after that?"

"Sorra a one of me knows. I never set eyes on them since. I was trying to get a warp out for one of the French ships, for the anchors was dragging. They came to the wrong side of the island, and got into the north channel, and that was the reason they had to cut their cables and stand out to sea till the gale is over, but there's not much chance of that for some time."

Kate did not speak for several minutes, and at length said,

"The people—tell me of them. Were they in great numbers along the coast?—were there a great many of them with Mr. Mark when he came down to the shore?"

"I'll tell you no lie, my lady; there was not. There was some boys from Castletown, and down thereabouts, but the O'Learys and the Sullivans, the

M'Carthys—my own people—and the Neals wasn't there; and sure enough it was no wonder if Master Mark was angry, when he looked about and saw the fellows was following him. ' Be off,' says he; 'away wid ye; 'tis for pillage and robbery the likes of ye comes down here. If the men that should have heart and courage in the cause won't come forward, I'll never head ruffians like you to replace them.' Them's the words he said, and hard words they were."

" Poor fellow !" said Kate, as she wiped away a tear from her eye, " none stand by him, not one. And why is this the case ?" asked she, eagerly; " have the people grown faint-hearted—are there cowards amongst them ?"

" There's as bad," said M'Carthy, in a low, cautious whisper—"there's traitors, that would rather earn blood-money than live honestly; there's many a one among them scheming to catch Master Mark himself, and he's lucky if he escapes at last."

" There's horses now coming up the road, and fast they're coming, too," said one of the country people; and the quick clattering of a gallop could be heard along the plashy road.

Kate's heart beat almost audibly, and she bounded from the spot, and up the stairs. The noise of the approaching horses came nearer, and at last stopped before the door.

" It is him—it is Mark," said she to herself, in an ecstasy of delight ; and with trembling fingers withdrew the heavy bolt, and undid the chain, while, with an effort of strength the emergency alone conferred, she threw wide the massive door, clasped and framed with iron.

" Oh, how I have watched for you," exclaimed she, as a figure, dismounting hastily, advanced towards her, and the same instant the voice revealed Hemsworth, as he said,

" If I could think this greeting were indeed meant for me, Miss O'Donoghue, I should call this moment the happiest of my life."

" I thought it was my cousin," said Kate, as, almost fainting, she fell back into a seat ; " but you may have tidings of him—can you tell if he is safe ?"

" I expected to have heard this intelligence from you," said he, as, recovering from the chagrin of his disappointment, he resumed his habitual deference of tone ; " has he not returned ?"

" No, we have not seen him, nor has the messenger yet come back. Herbert also is away, and we are here alone."

As Hemsworth offered her his arm to return to the drawing-room, he endeavoured to reassure her on the score of Mark's safety, while he hinted that the French, who that morning had entered Bantry Bay with eleven vessels, unprepared for the active reception his measures had provided, had set sail again, either to await the remainder of the fleet, or perhaps return to France. " I would not wish to throw blame on those whose misfortune is already heavy, but I must tell you, Miss O'Donoghue, that every step of this business has been marked by duplicity and cowardice. I, of course, need not say, that in either of these, your friends stand guiltless, but your cousin has been a dupe throughout—the dupe of every one who thought it worth his while to trick and deceive him; he believed himself in the confidence of the leaders of the expedition—they actually never heard of his name; he thought himself in a position of trust and influence—he is not recognised by any; unnoticed by his own party, and unacknowledged by the French, his only notoriety will be the equivocal one of martyrdom."

Every word of this speech, uttered in a voice of sad, regretful meaning, as though the speaker were sorrowing over the mistaken opinions of a dear friend, cut deeply into Kate's heart; she knew not well, at the instant, whether she should not better have faced actual danger for her cousin, than have seen him thus deceived and played upon. Hemsworth saw the effect his words created, and went on :

"Would that the danger rested here, and that the fate of one rash, but high-spirited boy, was all that hung on the crisis." As he spoke, he threw a cautious look around the roomy apartment to see that they were, indeed, alone.

"Great Heaven! there is not surely worse than this in store for us," cried Kate, in a voice of heartrending affliction.

"There is far worse, Miss O'Donoghue; the ruin that threatens is that of a whole house—a noble and honoured name. Your uncle is, unhappily, no stranger to these mischievous intentions. I was slow to put faith in the assertion."

"It is false—I know it is false," said Kate, passionately. "My poor dear uncle, overwhelmed with many calamities, has borne up patiently and nobly, but of any participation in schemes of danger or enterprise he is incapable ; think of his age—his infirmity."

"I am aware of both, young lady, but I am also aware that for years past his pecuniary difficulties have been such that he would hesitate at nothing which should promise the chance of extrication. Many have imagined, like him, that even a temporary triumph over England would lead to some new settlement between the two countries—concessions of one kind or other, laws revoked and repealed, and confiscations withdrawn; nor were the expectations, perhaps, altogether unfounded. Little has ever been accorded to Ireland as a grace—much has been obtained by her by menace."

"He never calculated on such an issue to the struggle, sir; depend upon it, no unworthy prospect of personal gain ever induced an O'Donoghue to adopt a cause like this. You have convinced me, now, that he is unconnected with this plot."

"I sincerely wish my own convictions could follow yours, madam; but it is an ungrateful office I have undertaken. Would to Heaven I knew how to discharge it more fittingly. To be plain, Miss O'Donoghue, the statute of high treason, which will involve the confiscation of your uncle's estate, will, if measures be not speedily taken, rob you of your fortune; to prevent this——"

"Stay, sir; I may save you some trouble on my account. I have no fortune, nor any claim upon my uncle's estate."

"Pardon me, young lady, but the circumstance of my position has made me acquainted with matters connected with your family ; your claim extends to a very considerable, and a very valuable property."

"Once more, sir, I must interrupt you—I have none."

"If I dare contradict you, I would say——"

"Nay, nay, sir," cried she, blushing, partly from shame, and partly from anger—"this must cease; I know not what right you have to press the avowal from me. The property you speak of is no longer mine ; my uncle did me the honour to accept it from me. Would that the gift could express the thousandth part of the love I bear him."

"You gave over your claim to your uncle!" said Hemsworth, leaving a pause between every word of the sentence, while a look of malignant anger settled on his brow.

"Who dares to question me on such a subject?" said Kate, for the insulting expression so suddenly assumed by Hemsworth roused all her indignation.

"Is this, then, really so?" said Hemsworth, who, so unaccustomed as he ever was to be overreached, felt all the poignancy of a deception in his disappointment.

Kate made no answer, but moved towards the door, while Hemsworth sprang forward before her, and placed his back against it.

"What means this, or how comes it, that you dare to treat me thus beneath my uncle's roof?"

"One word only, Miss O'Donoghue," said Hemsworth, with an effort to assume his habitual tone of deference. "May I ask, was this transfer of property made legally and formally?"

"Sir!" said Kate, as, drawing herself up, she stared full at him, without another word of reply.

"I see it all," said Hemsworth, rapidly, and as if thinking aloud. "This was the money that paid off Hickson—in this way the mortgage was redeemed, and the bond for two thousand also recovered—duped and cheated at every step. And so, madam"—here he turned a look of insulting menace towards her—"I have been the fool in your hands all this time ; and not content with thwarting my views, you have endeavoured to sap the source of my fortune. Yes, you need not affect ignorance; I know of Sir Archibald's kind interference in my behalf. Sir Marmaduke Travers has withdrawn his agency from me; he might have paused to inquire where was the property from which he has removed me—how much of it owns him the master or me. This was your uncle's doing. I have it under his own hand, and the letter addressed to yourself."

"And you dared, sir, to break the seal of my letter!"

"I did more, madam—I sent a copy of it to the Secretary of State, whose warrant I possess. The young officials of the Home Office will, doubtless, thank me for the amusement I have afforded them in its contents. The match-making talents of Sir Archy, and his niece's fascinations, have, however, failed for once. The Guardsman seems to have got over his short-lived passion."

"Stand back, sir, and let me pass."

"One moment more, madam. If I have suffered some injuries from your family, I have at least one debt of gratitude to acknowledge. But for your note, written by your own hand, I should scarcely have succeeded in capturing a rebel, whose treason will not long await its penalty; but for your able assistance, your cousin might have escaped. Indeed, it may be worth while to inform you that Sir Archibald had good hopes of obtaining his pardon—a circumstance which will, doubtless, be satisfactory to the surviving members of his family."

"My cousin Mark taken!" cried Kate, as she clasped her hands to either side of her head in a paroxysm of agony.

"Taken, and on his way to Dublin under a military escort. On Wednesday he will be tried by court-martial. I hope and trust on Thursday—— But, perhaps, it would be cruel to tell you of Thursday's proceedings."

Kate reeled, and endeavoured to support herself by a chair; but a sickness like death crept over her, and, with a faint, low sigh, she sank lifeless on the floor; at the same instant the door was burst open by a tremendous effort, and Hemsworth sent forward into the room. It was Mark, splashed and dripping, his face flushed with violent exertion, that entered. With one glance at Hemsworth, and another at the fainting form before him, he seemed to divine all.

"Our day of reckoning is come at last, sir," said he, in a low, distinct voice; "it has been somewhat tardy, however."

"If you have any claim on me, Mr. O'Donoghue," said Hemsworth, with a forced calmness, "I am ready, at the proper time and place, to offer you every satisfaction."

"That time and place is here, sir," said Mark, as, without the slightest sign of passion, he bolted the door, and drew a heavy table across it. "Here, in this room, from which both of us shall never walk forth alive."

"Take care, sir, what you do; I am armed," said Hemsworth, as he threw a quick glance around, to see if any hope of escape should present itself.

"And so am I," said Mark, coolly, who still busied himself in removing every object from the middle of the room, while, gently lifting Kate, he laid her, still unconscious as she was, upon a sofa. "We have neither of us much time to throw away, I fancy," said he, with a bitter laugh. "Choose your place now, sir, and fire when you please—mine is yonder;" and, as he spoke, he turned half round to walk towards the spot indicated. With the quickness of lightning, Hemsworth seized the moment, and, drawing a pistol from his bosom, aimed and fired. The ball grazed Mark's shoulder, and made him stagger forwards; but in a moment he recovered himself. The casualty saved him, for, while falling, a second bullet whizzed after the first. With a cry of vengeance that made the old walls ring again, Mark sprang at him. It was the deadly leap of a tiger on his prey. The impulse was such, that, as he caught him in his arms, both rolled over together on the floor. The struggle was but brief. Mark, superior in youth, strength, and activity, soon got him under, and, with his knee upon his chest, pinioned him down to the ground. There was a pause, the only sounds being the quick-drawn breathings of both, as, with looks of hate, they gazed at each other. While with one hand he grasped Hemsworth by the throat, with the other he felt for his pistol. Slowly he drew forth the weapon, and cocked it; then, laying the cold muzzle upon the other's forehead, he pressed the trigger; the cock snapped, but the priming burned. He flung the weapon from him in passion, and drew another; but, ere he could adjust it, Hemsworth ceased to breathe; a cold, livid colour spread over his features, and a clammy sweat bedewed his forehead—he had fainted.

Mark dropped the uplifted weapon as he muttered, "It was a fitting fate —the death of a coward." Then, standing up, he approached the window that overlooked the road, and threw it wide open. The storm still blew with all its force, and in a second extinguished the lights in the room, leaving all in darkness. With cautious steps, Mark moved towards where the body lay, and, lifting it in his powerful arms, carried it towards the window; with one vigorous effort he hurled the lifeless form from him, and the heavy mass was heard as it fell crashing among the brushwood that covered the precipice.

Mark gazed for a few seconds into the black abyss beneath, and then withdrawing, he closed the window, and barred it. By the aid of his pistol he struck a light and relighted the candles, and then approached the sofa where Kate lay.

"Have I been ill, Mark?" said she, as she touched his hand—"have I been ill, and dreaming a horrid dream? I thought Hemsworth was here, and that—that——But he was here—I know it now—you met him here. Oh, Mark! dearest Mark! what has happened—where is he?"

Mark pointed to the window, but never spoke.

"Is he killed—did you kill him?" cried she, as her eyes grew wild with the expression of terror. "Oh, merciful Heaven! who has visited us so heavily, why will reason remain when madness would be mercy! You have killed him!"

"He did not die by my hand, though he well deserved to have done so," said Mark, sternly; "but are our hours to be so many now, that we can waste them on such a theme? The French are in the bay—at least a portion of the fleet. Sixteen vessels, nine of which are ships of the line, are holding by their anchors beneath our cliffs; twenty more are at sea, or wrecked, or captured by the English, for who can tell the extent of our disasters? All is against us; but against all we might succeed, if we had not traitors amongst us."

"The Government is aware of the plot, Mark—knows every man engaged in it, and is fully prepared to meet your advance."

"Such is the rumour; but there's no truth in it. The people hold back, and give this as the excuse for their cowardice. The priests will not harangue them, and the panic spreads every moment wider, of treachery and betrayal. Lanty Lawler, the fellow who should have supplied horses for the artillery, is an informer; so are half the others. There's nothing for it but a bold plunge—something to put every neck in the halter, and then will come the spirit to meet all difficulties. So thinks Tone, and he's a noble-hearted fellow, and ready for any peril."

A loud knocking at the door of the tower now broke in upon the converse, and Kerry O'Leary called aloud,

"Open the door, Master Mark; be quick, the soldiers is comin'."

Mark speedily withdrew the heavy table from its place across the door, and opened it. Kerry, his clothes reduced to rags, and his face and hands bleeding, stood before him, terror in every feature. "They took me prisoner at the gate there, but I contrived to slip away, and took to the mountain, and a fine chase they gave me for the last hour."

"But the soldiers—where are they, and in what place?"

"There's two troops of horse about a mile below Mary's in the glen, waiting for Hemsworth's orders to advance."

"Go on," said Mark, with a stern smile; "they're not likely to move for some time."

"I do not know that, then," said Kerry, "for I saw Hemsworth pass up the road, with two men holding him on his horse. He seemed to have got a bad fall, for the blood was running down his face, and his cheeks was as pale as a corpse."

"You saw Hemsworth, and he was living!"

"Faix he was, and no doubt of it; there never was the man in these parts could curse and swear the way he does, barrin' himself, and I heerd him blaspheming away as he went along what he wouldn't do down here."

"Oh, fly, Mark; don't lose a second, for Heaven's sake——"

" And leave you here to the mercy of this scoundrel and his blood-hounds !"

" No, no; we are safe here ; he dare not wreak his vengeance on us; but you are his greatest enemy."

" 'Tis thrue she's sayin'," cried Kerry, eagerly; " I heerd Hemsworth say to Sam Wylie that Captain Travers is up at Macroom with his regiment, and was coming down to guard the castle here; but that there was plenty of time to take you before he came, and there was a tree standing to hang you, besides."

" I leave you, then, in safe keeping," said Mark, with a touch of sarcasm in his voice ; " one word of good-by to my father, and I am gone."

It was some moments before the O'Donoghue could rally from the deep stupor grief and anxiety induced, and recognise Mark as he leaned over his chair ; and then, as he felt his hands and clutched his arms, he seemed endeavouring to persuade himself that it was not some passing dream he laboured under.

" The pursuit is too hot, father," said Mark, after two or three efforts to arouse his mind to what was going forward, " and I must be off. Hems- wortn nas a strong party in the glen; but fear nothing; he cannot molest you; and, besides, his time is brief now."

" And will you leave me, Mark—will you desert me now ?" said the old man, with all the selfishness of age, forgetting everything save his own feelings.

" Not if you wish me to remain; if you think there is more honour in my being taken prisoner under your own roof, I'm just as willing."

" Oh, no, uncle," cried Kate, rushing forward; " do not keep him. Say good-by, and speedily ; the dragoons are advancing already."

" There goes a shot ! that was a cannon," cried Mark, in ecstasy, as he lifted his hand to catch the sound. " Another ! another ! they're landing— they're coming. You'll see me again before daybreak, father," said he, embracing the old man tenderly, while he turned to bid Kate adieu. She stood with her hands before her eyes, her bosom heaving violently. Mark gazed at her for a moment, and, pressing his lips to her cheek, merely whispered one word, and was gone.

Hemsworth's horse, which Kerry had found in the stable, stood ready awaiting Mark, and without a moment's loss of time he sprang on the animal's back, and dashed down the road at full speed. Meanwhile the loud firing of cannon continued at intervals towards the bay, and more than one rocket was seen to throw its bright glare through the blackness of the night.

" They're landing at last," cried Mark, as every report set his heart bounding with eager hope, and forward he rode through the storm.

CHAPTER XLVIII.

KERRY O'LEARY's intelligence was correct in every particular. Hemsworth was not only living, but, save some bruises, and a cut upon his forehead, was little the worse for his adventure. The brushwood had caught him in his descent, and broken the fall; and although the height was considerable, when he reached the ground he was merely stunned and not seriously injured. After a little time he was able to walk, and had succeeded in advancing about half a mile up the glen, when he was met by Wylie and a party of his followers, returning after escorting the chaise some miles on the road.

Neither our space nor our inclination permit us to dwell on the scene that followed, where Hemsworth, outwitted and duped as he believed himself, gave way to the most violent passion, accusing every one in turn of treachery, and vowing a deep and bloody vengeance on the whole house of O'Donoghue.

Seated on Wylie's horse, and supported on each side by two men—for at first his weakness increased as he found himself in the saddle—he went along at a foot's pace. He would not listen to Wylie's proposal of returning to the Lodge, but constantly called out—"To Keim-an-eigh as fast as possible—to the dragoons!" And at last passion had so far supplied energy, that he was able to press on faster, when suddenly a twinkling light through the gloom apprised him that he was near the little wayside inn.

"Get me some wine, Wylie, and be quick!" cried he, as they reached the door.

"You had better get off, and rest a few moments, sir," said the other.

"Rest!—I'll never rest," shouted he, with an infamous oath, "till I see that fellow waving from the gallows! Some wine this instant!"

To the loud summons of Wylie no answer was returned, and the light that shone so brightly a moment before was now extinguished.

"Break open the door! B—t you! what do you delay about?" shouted Hemsworth. "There are some rebel tricks at work here."

At the same instant the light reappeared, and Mary's voice was heard from within:

"Who's that, at this hour of the night, making such a noise?"

" Open the door, and be d—d to you !" cried Hemsworth, who, having got off his horse, was now endeavouring with his foot to force the strong door.

" It will take a better man than you to stave that panel in," said Mary, who, although recognising the voice, affected not to know the speaker. And she said truly : the door once made part of the rudder of an Indiaman, and was strong oak belted with iron.

" Put a light in the thatch! Snap your pistol, Wylie, and set fire to it !" cried Hemsworth, savagely ; for any opposition to him at this moment called forth all the malignity of his nature.

"Oh, is it you, captain?" said Mary, with a voice of well-affected respect; "the Lord pardon me for keeping you out in the cold !" And with that she opened the door, and, with many a low curtsey, saluted her guest.

Rudely pushing her aside, and muttering an oath, Hemsworth entered the cabin, followed by the others.

" Why was the light put out," said he, "when you heard us knocking at the door ?"

" I did not hear the knocking," said Mary. "I was in the little room there, and goin' to bed. The saints be good to me ! since the soldiers were here, the hearing is knocked out of me—the noise and the ballyragging they went on with, from mornin' till night ! And now that they are gone— thanks to your honour, that ordered them away two days ago up to the Lodge—I do be thinking they are here still."

" Bring us some wine," said Hemsworth, " and the best in your house. You need not spare the tap to-night, for it's the last you will ever draw beneath this roof. There—don't look surprised and innocent—you know well what I mean. This is a rebel den, but I will leave it a heap of ashes before I quit the spot."

" You'll not burn my little place down, captain ?" said Mary, with a look in which a shrewd observer might have read a very different expression than that of fear. " You'll not take away the means I have of earning my bread ?"

" Bring the wine, woman; and, if you don't wish to wait for the bonfire, be off with you up the glen. I'll leave a mark on this spot as a good warning to traitors. People shall talk of it hereafter, and point to it as the place where rebellion met its first lesson."

" And who dares to say that there was any treason in this house ?"

"If my oath," said Wylie, "won't satisfy you, Mrs. M'Kelly——"

" Yours !" interrupted Mary—" yours !—a transported felon's oath !"

" What do you think of your old sweetheart, Lanty Lawler?" said Hemsworth, as he drank off goblet after goblet of the strong wine. " Wouldn't you think twice about refusing him now, if you knew the price it was to cost you ?"

"I would rather see my bones as black as his own traitor's heart," cried Mary, with flashing eyes, "than I would take a villain like that! There, captain, there's the best of the cellar, and there's the house for you; and there," said she, throwing herself on her knees, "and there's the curse of the lone woman that you turn out this night upon the road, without a roof to shelter her, and may it light on you now, and follow you hereafter!"

"Clear your throat, and cool it, after your hot wishes," said Hemsworth, with a brutal laugh; for in this ebullition of the woman's passion was the first moment of his enjoyment.

With a gesture of menace, and a denunciation uttered in Irish, with all the energy the native language possesses, Mary turned into the road, and left her home for ever.

"What was that she said?" said Hemsworth, turning to one of the men that stood behind the chair.

"It was a saying they do have in Irish, sir," said the fellow, with a simper, "and the meaning of it is, that it isn't them that lights a bonfire that waits to dance round the ashes."

"Ha! that was a threat, then! She will bring the rebels on us; but I have taken good care for that. I have sent a strong party by the other road to cut off their advance from the bay, and we'll hear the firing time enough to warn us. And that party," said Hemsworth, muttering to himself, "should be at their post by this time"—here he looked at his watch—"it is now eleven o'clock. You took the order, Wylie, for Captain Travers to go round by Googawn Barra, and occupy the pass between Carriguacurra and Bantry Bay?"

"I did, sir, and he set off the moment I gave the letter."

"Then the fellow Mark cannot escape me," said Hemsworth. "If he leave the castle before I come, he falls into the hands of the others. Still, I would rather be judge and jury myself, and you shall be the hangman, Sam. There's little love between you: it is an office you'll like well."

"If I don't do it nate," said Wylie, "the young gentleman must forgive me, as it is my first time." And they both laughed heartily at the ruffian jest.

"But what are we staying for?" said Hemsworth, while he drained his glass. "Let us get up the dragoons, and make sure of him at once. I am strong now, and ready for any exertion."

"'Tis a pity to burn the little place, captain," said one of the fellows of the party. "There's many a dacent boy would think himself well off to get the likes of it for his reward."

"Make yourself at home," said Hemsworth, "for I'll give you a lease for three lives of it—yours, Wylie's, and mine own—will that satisfy you?"

The fellow stared at the speaker, and then looked at Wylie, as if not knowing whether to place any faith in the words he heard.

"I didn't say you were to get the premises in good repair, however," said Hemsworth, with a bitter laugh—"I didn't boast much about the roof;" and at the same moment he took a lighted turf from the hearth, and thrust it into the thatch, while Wylie, to curry favour with his patron, imitated his example.

"Where does that door lead to?" said Hemsworth, pointing to the small portal which led into the rock towards the stable.

"That's the way to the stable," said Wylie, as he opened it, and looked down the passage; "and here's another door that I never saw before."

"That's where she do keep the spirits, sir," said one of the men; "'tis there she do have all the liquor."

"There's nothing like whisky for a blaze," said Hemsworth, with a half-drunken laugh. "Burst open that door!" But all their efforts were vain: it was made with every precaution of strength, and studded over with strong nails.

"Stop!" said Hemsworth, as he pushed the others rudely away, "there's a readier plan than yours to force it. I'll blow the lock to pieces!" And, so saying, he took the pistol from Wylie's hand, and having leisurely examined the priming and the flint, placed the muzzle in the lock.

"Be quick, sir, be quick!" said Wylie; "the place is filling with smoke!"

And so it was: the crackling of the thatch, and the dense masses of black smoke that filled the cabin, showed that the work of destruction was begun.

"Here, then: this is to put the seal to your lease, Peter," said Hemsworth, as he pulled the trigger.

A quick report followed, and then a crashing sound, as of splintered timber, and sudden as the lightning flash itself a noise burst forth louder than thunder, and at the same moment the house, and all that were in it, were blown into the air, while the massive rock was shattered from its base full fifty feet up above the road. Report after report followed, each accompanied by some new and fearful explosion, until at length a great portion of the cliff was rent asunder, and scattered in huge fragments across the road, where, amid the crumbling masonry and the charred rafters, lay four black and lifeless bodies, without a trait which should distinguish one from the other.

All was silent on the spot, but through every glen in the mountains the echoing sounds sent back in redoubled peals the thunder of that dreadful explosion, and through many a far-off valley rung out that last requiem over the dead.

For some time the timbers and the thatch continued to burn, emitting at intervals lurid bursts of flame, as more combustible matter met the fire, while now and then a great report, and a sudden explosion, would announce that some hitherto untouched store of powder became ignited, until, as day was breaking, the flames waned and died out, leaving the rent rocks and the ruined cabin the sad memorials of the event.

Nor were these the only occurrences of which the glen was that night the witness. Mark, his brain burning for the moment when the fray should commence, rode on amid the storm, the crashing branches and the loud brawling torrents seeming to arouse the wild spirit within him, and lash his enthusiasm even to madness. The deafening clamour of the hurricane increased as he came nearer the bay, where the sea, storm-lashed and swollen, beat on the rocks with a din like artillery.

But louder far than all other sounds were the minute peals of cannon from the bay, making the deep valleys ring with their clangor, and sending their solemn din into many a far-off glen.

"They are coming—they are coming!" cried Mark, as he bounded madly in his saddle. "What glorious music have they for their march!"

"Stop!—pull in!—hould hard, Master Mark!" screamed a voice from the side of the road, as a fellow jumped from a cliff, and made towards the rider.

"Don't delay me now, Terry—I cannot stay," said Mark, as he recognised the youth; "the French are landing!"

"They are not!" cried Terry, with a yell of despair; "they are going off, leaving us for ever, and the glen is full of soldiers. The dragoons is there; ay, not half a mile from you," as he pointed through the gloom in the direction of the glen.

"The dragoons there!—what treachery is this?"

"I saw them coming round the head of the lake this evening, and I thought it was after me they were coming; but they never turned off the road, but went on to the gap of the glen, and there they are now, waiting; I suppose, for the French to go."

"The French are not going, fool!—they are landing! Don't you hear the guns—there! and there again! There is but one way now, but a bold heart needs no more. Let go the bridle, Terry."

"I can't—I won't let go. 'Tis cut to pieces you'll be. I seen them looking at their swords a while ago. Och, don't twist my hand that way!"

"Leave me free! There is no such armour of proof as recklessness!"

As he spake, he reined in his horse, and, dashing the spurs into his flanks, sprang beyond Terry, and the next moment was out of sight. A very few minutes showed that Terry was but too accurate. Around a blazing fire beneath the rock a party of dragoons were dismounted, vainly seeking to dry their soaked clothes, while in front two mounted men could be seen with their carbines unslung, ready for action.

A bold dash to force his way through was the only chance remaining. To depend on his horse's speed, and his own dexterous hand to guide him, was all his hope. He resolved, therefore, neither to draw sword nor pistol, but attempt to pass by sheer horsemanship. Few men were either better suited for a venture so daring, or better equipped at the moment. The animal he rode was a powerful thorough-bred, trained and managed to perfection.

Without the slightest noise Mark dismounted, and, ungirthing his saddle, readjusted and fastened it further back. He then looked carefully to his bridle, to see all was safe there, and loosened the curb, to give the horse free play of his head. This done, and with his cap pressed firmly down upon his brow, he sprang into his saddle once more.

The bright blaze enabled him to see the party in front, and, while he himself escaped all observation, to devise his plans at leisure. He advanced, therefore, at a slow walk, keeping the horse's feet in the deep ground, where no noise was made. He counted seven figures around the fire, and two as sentinels, and suspected at once that the whole party was not there. Still there was no other chance. To attempt the mountain would delay him a day at least, and a day now was a lifetime. Creeping noiselessly forward, he came within a few yards of the outposts, and could distinctly hear the voices as they talked together. He halted for a second or two, and looked back down the glen. It was an involuntary action, for even had all not been dark around him, his home, to which he wished to bid a last adieu, was out of-sight.

A cannon-shot rang out at the instant, and, taking it for a signal, Mark reined in his horse sharply, and then, dashing the spurs to his sides, made him plunge madly forward, and, with the bound, shot through the space between the two sentinels, each of whom presented, but feared to fire, lest he should injure his comrade.

" Come on—follow me !" cried Mark, waving his hand as if encouraging others on ; and the action turned every look down the glen in the direction from whence he came, and whence now came a wild, shrill yell, the most savage and appalling.

" Fire !—down with him !—fire !" shouted the soldiers to one another, as Mark, leaning flat on his horse's mane, rode on; and the balls whistled quick, above and around, but not one struck him. " After him, Jack—after him !" cried one of the sentinels, who, perceiving that Mark was not followed, turned his horse to the pursuit ; but another yell, wilder than the first, arrested him, and he heard a voice screaming, " This way, boys, this way—we have them here !" and Terry, waving his cap, bounded forward, and called out unceasingly for others to come on. In an instant the whole attention was turned to the front, while with the stroke of a sabre poor Terry was stretched upon the ground, bleeding and senseless.

" It is only that cursed fool we used to see at Macroom about the barrack gates," said one of the dragoons, as he held a piece of lighted wood beside his face, " and the other fellow cannot have had much more sense, or he would never have tried to ride through a squadron of horse. But there! —he's down now! Did you hear that crash?—that was a horse that fell."

So it was; Mark had but passed the first party to fall on a much more formidable body farther on, and his horse, twice wounded, was at last struck in the shoulder, and fell headlong to the ground, pinioning the rider beneath him. With a dexterity that seemed magical, Mark disengaged himself from the wounded animal, and drawing his pistols, prepared to sell his life dearly.

"You are a prisoner, sir," called out the sergeant, as with fearless step he marched towards him.

"Another pace nearer, and I'll send a bullet through you," said Mark; "you may have my corpse for your booty, but you'll never lay hands on me living."

"Don't fire, don't fire, men!" cried a voice, as the officer rode up at the speed of his horse, and then throwing himself from the saddle, commanded the men to fall back. With looks of astonishment and even of anger the dragoons retired, while the captain, sheathing his sword, approached Mark.

"Thank Heaven, Mr. O'Donoghue, you have not fired at my men."

"Am I your prisoner, Captain Travers?" said Mark, replacing his weapon.

"No, far from it; it was to serve you I accepted the command of this party. I knew of the plot by which you were threatened. Hemsworth——"

"He is gone to his reckoning now," said Mark, who never gave credit to Kerry's story.

"Not dead—you do not mean that?"

"Even so, sir, but not as I see you suspect."

"No matter now," cried Travers, wildly, for a thousand dreadful fears came crowding on his mind; "you must escape at once; this will be worse than the charge of treason itself. Was there any witness to his death?"

"None," said Mark, for he remembered that Kate was still fainting during the struggle he believed fatal.

"You must escape at once," repeated Travers, for without directly attributing guilt to Mark, he feared the consequence of this dreadful event. "Keep in the mountain for some little time, and when this mad enterprise has blown over——"

"The country then will be in other hands," interrupted Mark; "ay, sir, you may look and feel incredulous, but the time is, perhaps, not distant when I may be able to return your present courtesy. The French are landing——"

"They are putting out to sea—flying—not advancing," said Travers, proudly.

"No, no, you mistake them," said Mark, with a smile of incredulity.

" I heard the guns not a quarter of an hour since—would I had never left them."

" There, take my horse, mount quickly, and make for the bay, and turn him loose on the shore. Reach the fleet if you can—in any case, escape; there is no time to lose."

" And you—how are you to account for this?" said Mark. " Will your loyalty stand so severe a trial as that of having assisted a rebel's escape?"

" Leave me to meet my difficulties my own way; turn your thoughts to your own—Heaven knows they are enough."

The tone he spoke in appealed to Mark's feelings more strongly than all he said before, and grasping Travers's hand, he said,

" Oh, if I had but had your friendship once, how different I might be this day; and my father, too—what is to become of him?"

" Spare him at least the sorrow of seeing his son arraigned on a charge of treason, if not of worse."

Fortunately Mark heard not the last few words, which rather fell from Travers inadvertently, and were uttered in a low voice.

" There!" cried Mark, as the loud report of several guns pealed forth— "they have landed—they will soon be here."

As he spoke, a mounted dragoon rode up to Travers, and whispered a few words in his ear. Frederick motioned the man to fall back, and then, approaching Mark, said,

" I was correct, sir—the French fleet is under weigh—the expedition is abandoned. Away, then, before your chance is lost—down to the bay, and get on board; you will at least find a path where there is glory as well as peril; there—away."

" They cannot have done this," cried Mark, in an agony of passion; "they would not desert the cause they have fostered, and leave us to our fate here."

Mark vaulted on Travers's horse as he said this, all feeling for his own safety merged in his anxiety for the issue of the plot.

"Treachery we have had enough of—we may be well spared the curse of cowardice. Good-by; farewell. Few, either friends or foes, have done me the services that you have. If we are to meet again, Travers——"

" Farewell—farewell!" cried Travers; " we shall never meet as enemies."

And he hastened from the spot, while Mark, bending forward in the saddle, pressed the spurs to his horse, and started.

With the speed of one who cares for nothing less than his own safety, Mark urged his horse onward, and, deserting the ordinary road, he directed his course to the shore along the base of the mountain—a rough and dangerous path, beset with obstacles, and frequently on the very edge of the cliff. At last he reached the bay, over which the dark storm was raging in all its violence; the wind, blowing with short and sudden gusts, sent the great waves thundering against the rocks, and with fearful roar through the caves and crevices of the coast. Riding madly on till the white foam dashed over him, he turned on every side, expecting to see the boats of the fleet making for the land; but all was dreary and desolate. He shouted aloud, but his voice was drowned in the uproar of the elements; and then, but not till then, came over him the afflicting dread of desertion. The vivid lightning shot to and fro over the bleak expanse of sea, but not a sail was there —all, all were gone.

There was a projecting promontory of rock which, running out to a considerable distance in the bay, shut out all view beyond it. The last hope he cherished was, that they might have sought shelter in the bay beneath this, and, plunging into the boiling surf, he urged his horse forward; now madly rearing as the strong sea struck him, now buffeting the white waves with vigorous chest, the noble beast braved the storm-lashed water, and bore him, alternately bounding and swimming, as the tide advanced or receded.

The struggle, with all its peril to life, brought back the failing courage to Mark's heart, and he cheered his horse with a cry of triumphant delight as each great wave passed over them, and still they went on undaunted. It was a short but desperate achievement to round the point of the promontory, where the sea beat with redoubled fury; but the same daring intrepidity seemed to animate both horse and rider, and, after a moment of extreme danger, both gained the beach in safety. At the very same instant that the animal touched the strand, a quick flash broke over the sea, and then came the thundering report of a cannon. This was answered by another farther out to sea, and then a blue light burst forth on high, and threw its lurid glare over the spars and canvas of a large ship—every rope and block, every man, and every gun, were displayed in the spectral light. It was a grand, but still an appalling sight, to see the huge mass labouring in the sea, and then the next moment to strain the eyes through the black canopy of cloud that closed around her; for so it was, as the light went out, no trace of the vessel remained, nor was there aught to mark the spot she had occupied.

From time to time the flash and the report of a gun would show where some ship struggled with the raging sea; but to Mark all was mystery. He knew not what it might portend, and hesitated between hope and despair, whether these might prove the preparations for disembarking, or the last signal before sailing.

In the low hut of a fisherman, not far from where he was, a light still twinkled, and thither he hastened. It belonged to the man who had rowed him on board of the frigate, and with whom Kate had spoken in the kitchen. As Mark reached the door, he heard the sound of several voices talking in a low, half-suppressed tone; pushing open the door, he entered, and found about a dozen fishermen standing over the lifeless body of a man in a French uniform.

"Who is this?—what has happened?" said Mark, hurriedly.

"It's one of the French officers, sir," said Tom M'Carthy; "he came ashore with us this morning, and to-night, when it came on to blow, and he saw the signals to sail, he insisted on going on board again, and we did our best for him. We twice put out, and twice were sent back again; but the last time we tried the craft was upset, and the poor fellow could not swim, and we never saw him more, till we found his body on the strand about an hour ago."

Mark held the light beside the pale features, and saw that he was a youth of not more than eighteen years. There was no distortion whatever, and the features were calm and tranquil, as if in sleep.

"Let us lay him in the earth, boys," said Mark, as his voice trembled with emotion; "it is the least we can do to let him sleep in the land he came to save."

The men lifted the body without a word, and, preceded by Mark, who carried a lantern, issued from the hut. A few paces brought them to a little grassy mound, where the cliff, descending between the rocks, preserved its rich verdure untrodden and untouched.

"Here, this will do, boys," said Mark; "this rock will mark the spot."

The work was soon over, and, as the last turf was laid over him, a deafening peal of artillery thundered over the sea, and suddenly lights shone here and there through the dark atmosphere.

"He has had a soldier's burial," said Mark; "may his rest be tranquil. And now"—and his voice assumed a firm and determined tone at the moment —"and now, who will put me on board of any ship in that fleet? I have neither gold to offer, nor silver to bribe you. I am poor and powerless, but if the broad lands that were once our own were mine now, I'd give them all for that one service."

"No boat could live ten minutes in that surf. There's a sea running there would swamp a schooner," said an old man, with white hair.

"We'd never get outside the breakers yonder," said another.

"I think we've had enough of it for one night," muttered a third, with a sidelong glance towards the recent grave.

"And you," said Mark, turning fixedly round to Tom M'Carthy, "what words of comfort have you for me?"

"Faix, that I'm ready and willin' to go with you, divil may care who the other is," said the stout-hearted fellow. "I seen the day you jumped into a boat yourself to take the crew off a wreck below the point there, and I took an oath that night I'd never see you wanting for two hands at an oar as long as I could pull one. The waves that isn't too high for you is not a bit too big for me either."

"Well done, Tom," said a powerful-looking young fellow beside him, "and I'll be the bow oar for you, an you'll take me."

"And here's two more of us," said another, as he held a comrade by the hand, "that will never see his honour at a loss, no matter how it blows."

The doubt and hesitation which prevailed but a moment before, were at once changed for confidence and resolution, and eight men now hurried to the beach to launch the boat, and make ready for the enterprise.

"If we could only see a flash, or hear a shot now, we'd know which way to bear down," said Tom, as he stood on the shore, with his eyes turned seaward.

"There—there goes one!" cried Mark, as a red flame shot forth and glittered for a second over the dark water.

"There's the frigate—she's holding on still by her anchors."

"I knew they would not desert us, boys," cried Mark, with wild enthusiasm, for hope gained on him every moment as peril increased.

"Now for it, and all together!" said Tom, as he bent forward against the whistling storm, and the craft, as if instinct with life, bounded over the wave, and cleft her way through the boiling surf, while the hardy fishermen strained every nerve, and toiled with all their energy. Mark, kneeling in the bow, his eyes strained to catch any signal, seemed perfectly delirious in the transport of his joy.

"Luff her—luff her—here comes a large wave! Nobly done, lads!—how she mounts the sea!—here's another." But the warning was this time too late, for the wave broke over the boat, and fell in torrents over the crew. With redoubled vigour, the stout fellows bent to their work, and once more the boat sped on her course, while Mark cheered them with a shout heard even above the storm, and, with a deep, mellow voice, chanted out the rude verses of a song:

"The fisherman loves the rippled stream,
And the lover the moonlit sea,
But the darkening squall,
And the sea-bird's call,
Are dearer far to me.

"To see on the white and crested wave
The stormy petrel float,
And then to look back
On the stormy track
That glitters behind our boat."

"Avast there, Master Mark; there's wind enough without singing for more," cried one of the fishermen, who, with the superstition of his craft, felt by no means pleased at Mark's ditty; "and there comes a sea to poop a line-of-battle ship!" And, as he said the words, a wave, mountains high, rolled past, and left them labouring in the deep trough of the sea, while the lurid glare of sheet lightning showed all the ships of the fleet, as, with top-sails bent, they stood out to sea.

"There they go," said one of the fishermen; "and that's all the good they've done us."

" Pull hard, boys !" cried Mark, passionately, "it may not be yet too late ; strain every arm—the fate of our country may rest upon those bending spars ; together, men, together ! it is not for life now, it is Ireland is on the struggle !" Thus cheering the drooping courage of the men, and eagerly oending his glance towards the sea, his own heart glowed with enthusiasm that made every danger forgotten ; and at last, after an hour of desperate ex-ertion, with strength all but exhausted, and nearly overcome by fatigue, they beheld the dark hull of a large ship looming above them. By firing his pistol, Mark attracted the notice of the watch on deck; his signal was replied to, and the next moment the boat was alongside, and Mark, clam-bering up the steep side, stood on the quarter-deck.

"Will the troops not land ?" said Mark, as the officers crowded eagerly around him—"is the expedition abandoned ?"

"Don't you think the hurricane might answer the question, young man ?" said a weatherbeaten officer, who appeared in command; "or are you so ig-norant of naval matters as to suppose that a force could disembark in a gale like this ?"

"It might scare a pleasure party," said Mark, rudely, "but for men who have come to give and get hard knocks, methinks this need not disconcert them."

"And who is to aid us if we land ?" said the first speaker ; "what forces are in arms to join us?—what preparations for ourselves ? Have you a musket ? have you a horse ? or do you yourself, in your own person, repre-sent the alliance we seek for ?"

Mark hung down his head, abashed and ashamed. Too well he knew how treachery had sapped the foundation of the plot; that, betrayed and aban-doned by their chiefs, the people had become either apathetic or terror-stricken, and that, if a blow were to be struck for Irish independence, it must be by the arm of the stranger.

"It is needless to waste words, sir," said the French captain, for such he was ; "the admiral has twice made the signal to stand out to sea. The French Republic will have suffered loss enough in some of the finest ships of her navy, without hazarding fifteen thousand brave fellows upon an exploit so hopeless."

"The captain says truly," interposed another; "Ireland is not ripe for such an enterprise. There may be courage enough among your countrymen, but they know not how to act together. There's no slavery like dissension."

"That boat will be swamped," said the officer of the watch, as he pointed to the fishing craft, which still held on to the leeward of the ship. "If you are going back to shore, sir, let me advise you, for your own sake, and your comrades', too, to lose no time about it."

"Far better to come with us," said a powerful-looking man in the uniform of an infantry regiment; "the young gentleman seems inclined to see service. *Ma foi*, we seldom lack an opportunity of showing it."

"I will never go back," said Mark; "I have looked at my country for the last time."

With many a welcome speech the officers pressed round and grasped his hands, and for a moment all their misfortunes were forgotten in the joy with which they received their new comrade.

"Who will be my banker for some gold?" said Mark. "Those brave fellows have risked their lives for me, and I have nothing but thanks to give them."

"Let this go to the expenses of the expedition," said the captain, laughing, as he threw his purse to Mark. The young man leaned over the bulwark and hailed the boat, and, after a moment of great difficulty, one of the fishermen reached the deck.

"I wish to bid you good-by, Tom," said Mark, as he grasped the rough hand in his. "You are the last thing I shall see of my country. Farewell, then; but remember, that however deeply wrongs may gall, and injuries oppress you, the glory of resistance is too dearly bought at the cost of companionship with the traitor and the coward. Good-by for ever!" He pressed the purse into the poor fellow's hand; nor was it without a struggle he could compel him to accept it. A few minutes after the boat was cleaving her way through the dark water, her prow turned to the land which Mark had left for ever.

Seated on the deck, silent and thoughtful, Mark seemed indifferent to the terrible storm, whose violence increased with every moment, and as the vessel tacked beneath the tall cliffs, when every heart beat anxiously, and every eye was fixed on the stern rocks above them, his glance was calm, and his pulse was tranquil; he felt as though fate had done her worst, and that the future had no heavier blow in store for him.

CHAPTER XLIX.

THE END.

The storm of that eventful night is treasured among the memories of the peasantry of the south. None living had ever witnessed a gale of such violence—none since have seen a hurricane so dreadful and enduring. For miles along the coast the scattered spars and massive timbers told of shipwreck and disasters, while inland, uptorn trees and fallen rocks attested its power.

The old castle of Carrignacurra did not escape the general calamity. The massive walls that had resisted for centuries the assaults of war and time, were shaken to their foundations; and one strong, square tower, the ancient keep, was rent by lightning from the battlements to the base, while far and near might be seen fragments of timber, and even of masonry, hurled from their places by the storm. For whole days after the gale abated the air resounded with an unceasing din—the sound of the distant sea, and the roar of the mountain torrents, as, swollen and impetuous, they tore along.

The devastation thus wide-spread, seemed not to have been limited to the mere material world, but to have extended its traces over man. The hurricane was recognised as the interposition of Heaven, and the disaster of the French fleet looked on as the vengeance of the Almighty. It did not need the superstitious character of the southern peasants' mind to induce this belief: the circumstances in all their detail were too strongly corroborative not to enforce conviction on sterner imaginations, and the very escape of the French ships from every portion of our Channel fleet, which at first was deemed a favour of fortune, was now regarded as pointing out the more signal vengeance of Heaven. Dismay and terror were depicted in every face; the awful signs of the gale which were seen on every side suggested gloom and dread, and each speculated how far the anger of God might fall upon a guilty nation.

There was no reason to doubt the fact that, whatever the ultimate issue of the struggle, the immediate fate of the country was decided on that night. Had the French fleet arrived in full force, and landed the troops, there was neither preparation for resistance, nor means of defence, undertaken by the Government.

How far the peasantry might or might not have associated themselves with a cause to which the Romish clergy were then manifestly averse, may be a matter of uncertainty; but there are a sufficient number in every land,

and every age, who will join the ranks of battle with no other prospect than the day of pillage and rapine. Such would have flocked around the tricolor in thousands, and meet companions such would have been to that portion of the invading army called the "Legiou des Francs"—a battalion consisting of liberated felons and galley-slaves—the murderers and robbers of France, drilled, armed, and disciplined to carry liberty to Ireland! With this force, and a company of the "Artillerie Légère," Wolfe Tone proposed to land; and as the expedition had manifestly failed, any further loss would be inconsiderable; and, as for the "Legion," he naïvely remarked, "The Republic would be well rid of them."

Let us, however, turn from this theme to the characters of our tale, of which a few words only remain to be told. By Terry, who made his escape after being wounded by the dragoons, was the first news brought to Carrignacurra of Mark's rencontre with the dragoons; and while the O'Donoghue and Kate were yet speculating in terror as to the result, a small party of cavalry were seen coming up the causeway at a brisk trot, among whom rode a person in coloured clothes.

"It is Mark—my boy is taken!" cried the old man, in a burst of agony; and he buried his head in his hands, and sobbed aloud. Kate never spoke, but a sick, cold faintness crept over her, and she stood almost breathless with anxiety. She heard the horses as they drew up at the door, but had not strength to reach the window and look out. The bell was rung violently —every clank sent a pang to her bosom. The door was opened, and now she heard Kerry's voice, but could not distinguish the words. Then there was a noise as of some one dismounting, and the clatter of a sabre was heard along the flagged hall. This ceased, and she could recognise Kerry's step as he came up the corridor to the door of the tower.

"Come in," cried she to his summons, but her utmost effort could not make the words audible. "Come in," said she again.

Kerry heard it not, but, opening the door cautiously, he entered.

"'Tis the captain, Miss Kate, wants to know if he could see the master."

"Yes," said she, in a voice scarcely above a whisper. "Who is with him? Is there a prisoner there?"

"Faix, there is then; but Captain Travers will tell you all himself."

"Captain Travers!" cried Kate, a deep flush covering her face.

"Yes, madam," said Frederick, as he entered at the same moment. "I am but too happy to bear pleasant tidings, to think of my want of courtesy in intruding unannounced."

"Leave the room—shut the door, Kerry," said Kate, as, with eyes fixed on Travers, she waited for him to continue.

"Your cousin is safe, Miss O'Donoghue—he has reached the fleet, and is already on his way to France."

" Thank God !" cried Kate, fervently, as she fell upon her uncle's shoulders, and whispered the tidings into his ear.

The old man looked up, and stared wildly around him.

" Where's Mark, my love—where did you say he was ?"

" He's safe, uncle—he's on board of a French ship, and bound for France, beyond the reach of danger."

" For France ! And has he left me—has he deserted his old father ?"

" His life was in peril, sir," whispered Kate, who, stung by the old man's selfishness, spoke almost angrily.

"My boy has abandoned me," muttered the O'Donoghue. The one idea, absorbing all others, occupied his mind, and left him deaf to every explanation or remonstrance.

" You are right, Miss O'Donoghue," said Travers, gently; " his danger was most imminent. The evidence against him was conclusive and complete ; and although one of the principal witnesses could not have appeared, Lanty Lawler——"

" And was he an informer ?"

" He was, madam ; but amid the mass of treachery he has met a just fate. Barrington, determined to punish the fellow, has come forward and given himself up, but with such evidence of the horse-dealer's guilt that his conviction is certain. The sums he received from France are all proved under his own hand, and now that Hemsworth is no more, and Lawler's treachery has no patron, his case has little hope. He is at this moment my prisoner ; we took him on the mountain where he had gone with a party to secure Mr. Mark O'Donoghue, for whose capture a large reward was offered."

As Kate listened to this recital, delivered in a tone which showed the contempt the speaker entertained for an enterprise undertaken by such actors, her own indignant pride revolted at the baseness of those with whom her cousin was associated.

"Yes," said she, at length, and speaking unconsciously aloud, "no cause could prosper with supporters like these. There must be rottenness in the confederacy that links such agencies as these together. And had my cousin not one friend ?—was there not one to wring his hand at parting ?" said she, hurriedly, changing the theme of her thoughts.

"There was one," said Travers, modestly. " Mr. O'Donoghue was noble-hearted enough, even in the hour of calamity, to forget an ancient grudge, and to call me his friend. He did more—he wished we had been friends for many a day before."

"Would that you had," said Kate, as the tears burst forth, and ran down her cheeks.

" And we might have been such," continued Travers, "had not deceit and malevolence sowed discord between our families. You know not, Miss

O'Donoghue, how deeply this treachery worked, and how artfully its plans were conceived. The very hopes whose disappointment has darkened my life, were fed and fostered by him who knew how little reason I had to indulge them—forgive me, I pray, if I allude to a subject I ought never to recal. It was Hemsworth persuaded me that my suit would not prove unsuccessful; it was by his advice and counsel I risked the avowal which has cost me the happiness of my future life. I will speak of this no more," said Travers, who saw in the deep blush that covered Kate's features the distress the theme occasioned her. "It was a selfish thought that prompted me to excuse my hardihood at the cost of your feelings."

"I will not let you speak thus, sir," said Kate, in a voice faint from excessive emotion. "There was no such hardihood in one favoured by every gift of fortune stooping to one humble as I am ; but there were disparities wider than those of rank between us, and if I can now see how greatly these were exaggerated by the falsehood and treachery of others, yet I know that our opinions are too wide apart to make agreement aught else than a compromise between us."

"Might not time soften, if not obliterate, such differences ?" whispered Travers, timidly.

"It could not with me," said Kate, resolutely; "this is the losing side ever, and my nature is a stubborn one—it has no sympathies save with those in misfortune. But we can be friends," said she, extending her hand frankly towards him—"friends firm and true, not the less strong in regard because our affections have not overcome our convictions."

"Do not speak so decisively, Miss O'Donoghue," said Travers, as his lip trembled with strong emotion; "even at this moment how much has misrepresentation clouded our knowledge of each other. Let time, I entreat of you, dissipate these false impressions, or give me, at least, the opportunity of becoming more worthy of your esteem."

"While I should become less so," interrupted Kate, rapidly. "No, no ; my duties are here ;" and she pointed to the old man, who, with an expression of stupid fatuity, sat with his hands clasped, and his eyes fixed on vacancy. "Do not make me less equal to my task by calling on me for such a pledge. Besides," added she, with a smile, "you are too truly English to suggest a divided allegiance ; we are friends, but we can never be more."

Travers pressed the white hand to his lips without a word, and the moment after his horse was heard descending the causeway, as with desperate speed he hurried from the spot so fatal to all his hopes.

Scarcely had Frederick left the castle, when a chaise and four, urged to the utmost speed, dashed up to the door, and Sir Archy, followed by Herbert, jumped out. The old man, travel-stained and splashed, held an open paper in his hand, and cried aloud, as he entered the drawing-room,

" He's pardoned, he's pardoned—a free pardon to Mark !"

" He's gone, he's away to France," said Kate, as, fearing to awaken the O'Donoghue to any exertion of intelligence, she pointed cautiously towards him.

" All the better, my sweet lassie," cried M'Nab, folding her in his arms; " his arm will not be the less bold in battle because no unforgiven treason weighs upon his heart. But, my brother, what ails him ?—he does not seem to notice me."

" He is ill—my father is ill," said Herbert, with a terrified accent.

" He is worse," whispered M'Nab to himself, as passing his hand within the waistcoat, he laid it on his heart.

It was so. The courage that withstood every assault of evil fortune—every calamity which poverty and distress can bring down—failed at last. The strong heart was broken—the O'Donoghue was dead.

———————————

We will once more ask our readers to accompany us to the glen, the scene of our story. It was of an evening, calm and tranquil as that on which our tale opened, on a day in August, in the year 1815, that two travellers, leaving the postilion of their carriage to refresh his horses, advanced alone and on foot for above a mile into this tranquil valley. The air had all that deathlike stillness so characteristic of autumn, while over the mountains and the lake the same rich mellow light was shed. As the travellers proceeded slowly, they stopped from time to time, and gazed on the scene; and although their looks met, and glance seemed to answer glance, they neither of them spoke. From their appearance, it might have been conjectured that they were foreigners. The man, bronzed by weather and exposure, possessed features which, in all their sternness, were yet eminently handsome. He wore a short, thick moustache, but the armless sleeve of his coat, fastened on the bosom, was a sign still more indisputable than even his port and bearing that he was a soldier. His companion was a lady in the very pride and bloom of beauty, but her dress more remarkably than his betrayed the foreigner. In the rapid look she turned from the bold scenery around them to the face of him at whose side she walked, one might read either a direct appeal to memory, or the expression of wonder and admiration of the spot. Too much engrossed by his own thoughts, or too deeply occupied by the scene before him, the man moved on, until at last he came in front of a low ruined wall, beneath a tall and overhanging cliff. He stopped for some seconds, and gazed at this with such intentness as prevented him from noticing the figure of a beggar, who, in all the semblance of extreme poverty, sat crouching among the ruins. She was an old, or at least seemed a very old woman. Her hair, uncovered by cap or hood, was white as snow, but her features still preserved an expression of quick intelligence, as, lifting her head from the attitude of moping thought, she fixed her eyes steadfastly on the travellers.

"Give her something, *mon cher*," said the lady to her companion in French; but the request was twice made before he seemed conscious of it. The woman, meanwhile, sat still, and neither made any demand for charity nor appeal to their compassion.

"This is Glenflesk, my good woman," said he at length, with the intonation of a foreign accent on the words.

The woman nodded assentingly, but made no reply.

"Whose estate is all this here?" said he, pointing with his hand to either side of the valley.

"Sorra one o' me knows whose it is," said the woman, in a voice of evident displeasure. "When I was a child it was the O'Donoghues, but they are dead and gone now—I don't know whose it is."

"And the O'Donoghues are dead and gone, you say? What became of the last of them?—What was his fate?"

"Is it the one that turned Protestant, you mean?" said the woman, as an expression of fiendish malignity shot beneath her dark brows. "He was the only one that ever prospered, because he was a heretic, maybe."

"But how did he prosper?" said the stranger.

"Didn't he marry the daughter of the rich Englishman, that lived there beyant? and wasn't he a member of Parlimint? and sure they tell me that he went out beyond the says to be a judge somewhere in foreign parts—in India, I believe."

"And who lives in the old castle of the family?"

"The crows and the owls lives in it now," said the woman, with a grating laugh—"the same way as the weasels and the rats burrow in my own little place here. Ay, you may stare and wonder, but here, where you see me sit, among these old stones and black timbers, was my own comfortable home—the house I was born and reared in—and the hearth I sat by when I was a child."

The man whispered a few words to his companion in a deep, low voice. She started, and was about to speak, when he stopped her, saying, "Nay, nay, it is better not;" then, turning to the woman, asked, "And were there, then, no others, whose fortunes you remember?"

"It is little worth while remembering them," said the crone, whose own misfortunes shed bitterness over all the memory of others. "There was an old Scotchman that lived there long after the others were gone, and when the niece went back to the nunnery in France he stayed there still alone by himself. The people used to see him settling the room, and putting books here, and papers there, and making all ready agin she came back—and that's the way he spent his time to the day of his death. Don't cry, my lady; he was a hard-hearted old man, and it isn't eyes like yours should weep tears for him ; if you want to pity any one, ' pity the poor, that's houseless and friendless.' ''

" And the Lodge," said the stranger—" is not that the name they gave the pretty house beside the lake ?"

" 'Tisn't a pretty house now, then," said the nag, laughing. " It's a ruin like the rest."

" How is that ?—does the Englishman never come to it ?"

" Why should he come to it ? Sure it's in law ever since that black-hearted villain Hemsworth was killed. Nobody knows who owns it, and they say it will never be found out ; but," said she, rising and gathering her cloak around her as she prepared to move away, " there's neither luck nor grace upon the spot. God Almighty made it beautiful and lovely to look upon, but man and man's wickedness brought a curse down upon it."

The man drew his purse forth, and while endeavouring to take some pieces of money from it by the aid of his single remaining hand, she turned abruptly about, and, staring him steadfastly in the face, said,

" I'll not take your money—'tisn't money will serve me now—them that's poor themselves will never see me in want."

" Stop a moment," said the stranger, " I have a claim on you."

" That you haven't," said the woman, sternly. " I know you well, Mark O'Donoghue—ay, and your wife, Miss Kate there ; but it isn't by a purse full of gold you'll ever make up for desarting the cause of ould Ireland."

" Don't be angry with her," whispered a low, mild voice behind. He turned, and saw a very old man dressed in black, and with all the semblance of a priest. " Don't be angry with her, sir ; poor Mary's senses are often wandering ; and," added he, with a sigh, " she has met sore trials, and may well be pardoned if, in the bitterness of her grief, she looks at the world with little favour or forgiveness. She has mistaken you for another, and hence the source of her anger."

THE END.

2 B

THE
SELECT LIBRARY OF FICTION,
PRICE TWO SHILLINGS EACH.

Vol. IX.
CRANFORD.
By the Author of "Mary Barton," &c.

"This is not a book to be described or criticized other than by a couple of words of advice—*Read it.* It is a book you should judge for yourself. If we told you it contained a story, that would be hardly true—yet read only a dozen pages, and you are among real people, getting interested about them, affected by what affects them, and as curious to know what will come of it all as if it were an affair of your own. * * * The writer of this unpretending little volume, with hardly the help of any artifice the novelist most relies upon, and showing you a group of the most ordinary people surrounded by the commonest occurrences of human life, has yet had the art to interest you, as by something of your own experience, a reality you have actually met with, and felt yourself the better for having known. *Cranford* is the most perfect little book of its kind that has been published for many a day. * * * * Every page of *Cranford* is as good or better than the things we have quoted—so let no reader be satisfied with extracts, but get the little book and straightway read every bit of it."—*Examiner.*

Vol. X.
TWO YEARS' RESIDENCE IN A LEVANTINE FAMILY.
By BAYLE ST. JOHN.

"The lovers of fictional literature will be glad to find that Messrs. Chapman and Hall have issued 'cheap editions' of the works of Mr. Bayle St. John—a writer who has the tact of always sustaining the interest of his readers. 'Maretimo' and the experiences of a 'Two Years' Residence in a Levantine Family,' are among the most popular works of this author. They are full of incident, and written with the pen of a man who is a keen observer of character and an excellent story-teller."—*Morning Post.*

Vol. XI.
MARY BARTON.
A Tale of Manchester Life. By the Author of "Ruth," "Cranford," &c.

"This deeply-interesting work appears before us in a new shape, viz. as a single volume, and at the astonishingly low price of two shillings. The genuine philanthropy which dictates this tale, and the talent, vigour, and good sense which pervade it, induce us to hope that a very wide circulation will prove the public's appreciation of its merits."—*Britannia.*

London: CHAPMAN AND HALL; and at all Railway Bookstalls.

THE WORKS OF CHARLES LEVER.

Reprinted from Blackwoods' Magazine,
April, 1862.

THE name of Charles Lever is still chiefly associated with those novels by which his popularity as a writer was first secured, and by which, perhaps, his subsequent literary reputation has been in some measure overpowered. These works have probably met with a more cordial reception from the public than from the critics. Their author may, in a certain sense, defy criticism, by exclaiming like Horace, " *Pueris canto !*" He has been the biographer of boyhood. In all his earlier works he especially addresses himself to that happy portion of mankind whose digestion is yet unimpaired, whose nerves are unshaken, in whom the breath of life has no resemblance to a sigh, and who (as he himself portrays them) are every ready to risk, with unabated ardour, a broken neck or a broken heart at every turn in the joyous chase of existence. To the verdict of such an audience Mr. Lever has every right to appeal as gaily and as confidently as Anacreon appealed to the Loves. It would undoubtedly be as ungracious to reproach the author of ' Charles O'Malley ' with the absence of those pretensions to literary dignity which he himself disclaims with so merry a laugh at dignities of every sort, as to denounce the Greek lyrist for his resolute refusal to celebrate the exploits of Atrides. To the most captious critic Mr. Lever may fairly say,—

" Non potes in nugas dicere plura meas
Ipse ego quam dixi."

And he that can follow the adventures of Harry Lorrequer, Charles O'Malley, Jack Hinton, and Tom Burke, without the frequent interruption of hearty laughter, has probably survived all sense of enjoyment in the society of the young. In any case he is not a man to be envied. To us, indeed, there is something of pathos in the reperusal of these books. It is like reading one's old love-letters, or hearing an old friend recount the frolics of one's own youth. We turn the pages with a certain tender incredulity, and there steals over us a sensation like that

" Smell of violets hidden in the green,"

which the poet declares to have

" Poured back into his empty soul and frame
The times when he remembers to have been
Joyful, and free from blame."

Mr. Lever's blooming young heroes, if not invariably blameless, are at least exceedingly joyful. Like the first mariners, they launch into the sea of life with breasts fortified by oak and triple brass : their constitutions are Titanic. To watch them from the beaten high-road of tame and ordinary experience, dashing and glittering through a stupendous steeple-chase of astounding and never-ending adventure, literally takes away our breath. We cannot but sigh as we ask ourselves, " Was life indeed, then, at any time, such an uncommonly pleasant holiday ? " Has not the world itself grown older and colder since those jaunty days when the dazzling Mr. Lorrequer drove his four-in-hand through all the proprieties ? Is it possible that Mr. Lorrequer's son and heir, whom we presume to be now a hopeful cornet in the Blues, can be such a merry dog as we all remember his father to have been ? Would not any such artless, but not invariably harmless, ebullitions of youthful mirth as those recorded with infinite gusto in the biography of the elder gentleman, be now visited with the severest penalties at the disposal of Bow Street, and denounced with the angriest eloquence at the command of the 'Times' ? We suspect that the younger Mr. Lorrequer is a man of much sadder complexion. It would not, alas ! surprise us to learn that, notwithstanding a prudent regard for his health, he is occasionally not altogether free from low spirits, especially when his natural hilarity is tempered by the prospective shadow of a competitive examination, or vexed by the aggressive attentions of the Civil Service Commissioners. The fact is, that times are changed with us. Napoleon's Paladins are *pulvis et umbra*. Beau Brummel has paid his last debt. Duelling is a thing forsworn. Notwithstanding Dr. Parr's celebrated receipt for the gout, consisting of " prayer, patience, and port-wine," this latter source of human comfort is all but extinct. The epitaph of it is already written by Mr. Cobden in the French Treaty. The Union is an historical reminiscence. The Encumbered Estates Bill has done its work. " After life's fitful fever," O'Connell agitates no more. And Harry Lorrequer, and Charles O'Malley, and Jack Hinton, and Tom Burke, and Bagenal Daly, look down upon us from the distance of an age no longer ours. We have no hope ever again to meet them cantering in the Phoenix Park or swaggering down Sackville Street, or dancing at Dublin Castle. They are all " gone *proiapsoi* to the Stygian shore." Like Achilles, and Ajax, and all the *fortes ante Agamemnonem*, they rest in an elysium of which the beatitude appears to us shadowy and unreal. But they have quaffed their last bumper, and shot their last shot—

" They lie beside their nectar, and their bolts are hurled."

And although their glittering ghosts yet hover about the fading splendour of the " good old times," as the Scandinavian warriors are said by the

Swedish poet to hover in the light of sunset over the horizon of the Baltic, yet we can no more recall them to tangible existence than we can renew the race of the Anakim.

Mr. Lever has himself survived his first progeny. That in growing an older, he has also grown a wiser, and in some respects a sadder man, his more recent writings bear witness. Job's second batch of sons and daughters, who were, doubtless, a much steadier set of young people than the first, could not have differed from that jovial crew who were overwhelmed in a whirlwind whilst "eating and drinking wine," more strongly than Mr. Lever's later works differ from his earlier ones.

The author of 'Harry Lorrequer' has given unquestionable proof of powers matured by time and enriched by cultivation. His more recent novels evince a greater mastery in the craft of authorship, a larger experience, and more skilled faculty of construction. But whether these qualities exist in so great a degree as entirely to compensate the reader for the absence of that vivacity, freshness, and continuous flow of high animal spirits, which have rendered Mr. Lever's first books so widely and so justly popular, is a question which we shall presently have occasion to consider. Meanwhile, to say of such novels as 'Harry Lorrequer' and its immediate successors that they abound in extravagance, is to detract nothing from the merit of them. Youth is in itself the grandest of all extravagances; and these books are an emanation from, and an embodiment of, all the joyous audacity of young manhood. We cannot too largely estimate the extent to which Mr. Lever possesses the merit most essential to popularity in narrative composition—viz., *gusto*. He relates incidents with a relish, and accumulates them with a fecundity of invention and a rapidity of movement that never flag. Of all qualities in the genius of an author, this is the most necessary to the successful conduct of narrative interest; and we must the more admire it, wherever it is displayed, because it is innate, and neither to be acquired by labour, nor replaced by experience. It is to this rush and flow of vigorous animal life that we must attribute the indescribable attraction exerted by Homer upon the sympathies of all ages and conditions of men; and we accord to the Father of Verse a supremacy felt to be unattainable by any other poet, in recognition (which is perhaps partly unconcious) of the completeness with which he has expressed the high spirits and dauntless health of the boyhood of mankind. A recent poet, who deserves to be better known, has said that "the old gods were only men and wine." Their godship is certainly the extravagant idealisation of the merely human faculties at their highest pitch. The same extravagance gives to the Homeric heroes their colossal proportions. Achilles and Hector will, to the end of time, be a head-and-shoulders taller than all other men, because it is impossible that any man should realize so intensely, or define so distinctly, as Homer, the supernatural dimensions of all natural faculties and sensations. To represent human

THE WORKS OF CHARLES LEVER.

beings precisely as they are, is not a necessary condition of art of any
kind. A deformed saint by Massaccio may be truer in art than a correct
anatomical study by Mr. Etty. Nor is there any reason why that extravagance of design which dilates either human actions or human emotions, or even the situations of human life, to perfectly impossible
proportions should be in itself a defect. For what is impossible in fact
may be proper in art. Ariosto is undoubtedly one of the greatest narrative poets, and it is probably in his extravagance that we shall find the
secret of his indefinable power. The humour of Quevedo is often most
irresistible when it consists entirely of what might be called pure extravagance of expression. And such extravagance as is to be found in
Mr Lever's earlier novels is occasioned by the overflow of that exuberant
vitality which constitutes their special excellence. The plan and
character of these books are obviously panoramic rather than dramatic.
It is by the narration of humorous incident that the interest of the
reader is to be carried on. For this, rapidity and gusto are the best of
all qualifications. No great writer of narrative fiction has ever been
wholly without them. Le Sage possessed them largely ; they are to be
detected in the sadder and more profound genius of Cervantes ; they are
not wanting to the elaborate minuteness of De Foe ; they give vigour to
the most envenomed creations of Swift ; they are remarkable in Sir
Walter Scott, than whom, certainly, there is no happier master of the art
of telling a story. Fielding, though his genius philosophises while it
frolics, was far from neglecting those means of exciting interest which
depend upon the rapid movement and striking effect of incident. But
Smollett certainly possessed the gift of high spirits to a pre-eminent degree. The extraordinary impulse and animation of his genius is such,
that his narrative, though often extremely digressive, always rushes
away with the reader, and carries him, like a runaway horse, over
every obstacle, "*turbine raptus ingenii.*"

In this respect Mr. Lever, of all modern novelists, most resembles the
author of 'Roderick Random.' There is, indeed, not only much
similarity of character between the works of Charles Lever and those of
Tobias Smollett, but also no inconsiderable coincidence in the circumstances which may possibly have given to the genius of both authors
something of the same tendency.

The Irish humorist, like his great Scotch predecessor, was, we believe,
brought up for the medical profession, and for some years practised as a
doctor. Whether indeed Mr. Lever found his profession as little profitable to him as it would appear to have proved to Dr. Smollett, or whether
he was simply impelled to abandon so sober a career by the consciousness
of those powers of humour and that facility of composition which he
evinced at an early age, we do not know ; but it is difficult to believe
that the pen which wrote 'Charles O'Malley,' or that which wrote 'Peregrine Pickle,' would have been equally well employed in signing pre-

scriptions. To the experience of medical life, however, to the opportunities for the study of character thereby afforded, and the quickness of penetration and habits of observation thus acquired, it is highly probable that both Smollett and Lever have owed much excellent material for humorous fiction. Both authors appear to have early evinced, and long retained, an extreme predilection for a military life. Smollett, indeed, never forgave his grandfather for thwarting his inclination to enter the army; and he never omits an occasion for introducing into his novels some description of martial scenes and events. There is fair reason to attribute to both Smollett and Lever some carelessness, not so much of composition, as of writing. They both appear to have written hastily. Of Smollett it is told that (whilst writing the 'Adventures of Sir Launcelot Greaves'), "when post-time drew near he used to retire for half-an-hour or an hour to prepare the necessary quantity of *copy*, as it is technically called in the printing-house, which he never gave himself the trouble to correct, or even to read once." And we may assume that Mr. Lever, speaking through the mask of Harry Lorrequer, is not very wide of the truth when he says, "I wrote as I felt—sometimes in good spirits, sometimes in bad—always carelessly—for, God help me! I can do no better." Smollett is, indeed, the more correct writer of the two ; his style, though often hasty, is never inaccurate, and, for the most part, his English is very pure. Mr. Lever's language, on the contrary, is in places so heedless that the grammar of it is sometimes more conventional than correct. In one place he speaks of "purchasing a boon," and in another he describes an Irish member waiting "till the House was done prayers." Nevertheless he has great powers of description. He represents objects and actions with a touch that is always vivid, often masterly. He is always happy in the open air; in his love of nature and hearty relish of out-of-door life, as well as in the force and fidelity with which he depicts them, he is certainly unsurpassed, and perhaps unequalled, by Smollett himself. The veracity, freshness, and power with which he describes scenery is deserving, we think, of higher appreciation than it has yet received. His pictures of Irish landscape, sea scenery, and all effects of wind and weather, are full of the truth and intensity which belong to poetry. It is for such reasons all the more to be regretted that an author entitled on so many grounds to hold a permanent place in literature should ever be forgetful of the duty which is owed by eminent writers to the language they bequeath to posterity. Some expressions throughout Mr. Lever's works, so incorrect as to be obvious oversights, have passed through so many editions that we must believe the ὃ γέγραφα γέγραφα sentiment to be in him unusually strong, and that what he writes he never revises. The bent of such minds as those of Mr. Lever and Dr. Smollett is instinctively conservative, loyal, and inclined to the maintenance of institutions which have been tested and endeared by time. On the one hand, a shrewd appreciation of life as it is, and a keen sense of the ludicrous and incongruous, indisposes them to indulge in the dreams of democracy ; whilst, on the other hand, a certain chivalry of disposition induces them to side with a cause which, by the very nature of it, must always be that of the party attacked. Conservatism, therefore, has found in each of these writers a warm and ready adherent. To continue any further this passing comparison between the two authors would be tedious and pedantic ; but if we turn to the books themselves, we cannot but remark a resemblance which in many respects, is striking.

The merits as well as the defects of both writers are, for the most part, of the same kind. Their humour does not always rise above fun, their fun sometimes degenerates into farce. Criticism, which is applicable to such books as ' Harry Lorrequer' and ' Charles O'Malley' may equally be applied to ' Roderick Random' and 'Peregrine Pickle.' We can feel little sympathy for the heroes themselves, and still less for the greater part of the personages by whom we find them surrounded. Roderick Random is a low-minded, selfish, unamiable character. Harry Lorrequer is not much more thoughtful of the feelings of others, and his various misdeeds are only not amenable to the gravest censure because they render gravity impossible, and compel the reader himself to become an accomplice in their impish frolic. Peregrine Pickle is a brutal savage, indulging an almost fiendish delight in the prosecution of the most barbarous practical jokes. Charles O'Malley, though much less repulsive, is certainly a brawling mischievous fellow, whose acquaintance we, for our own part, must confess we should little desire out of a book. The female characters are often too merely animal, or else too shadowy and indistinct, to inspire much interest. Of the rest of the *dramatis personæ* the larger portion is often made up of adventurers, blacklegs, practical jokers, and such oddities and odds and ends of humanity as seem only made to furnish material for practical jokes. The heroes ramble from page to page, through scenes and situations almost unconnected, and characters which crowd one portion of the book hardly appear in another.

Yet, when the critic has summed up all such apparent grounds of objection, he will find that they constitute no real defect in the art of these romances, which can only be criticised in accordance with the laws which they themselves create. The fact is, Art does not make Genius, but Genius makes Art. '' Genius,'' says Kant, in his ' Analysis of the Sublime,' '' is the talent to produce that of which one cannot give the determinating rule, and not the ability that one can show in doing that which one can learn by a rule. Hence originality is its first quality.'' Every writer of original genius has his own object, and his own way of carrying it out ; and his success or failure can only be fairly estimated by reference to the object which he has himself had in view, not that which the critic expects him to have had in view. The barbarous conduct of the clown in the pantomime, the elfish perversity and duplicity of the Pierot in ·the French Harlequinade, and the excessive profligacy of the Don Juan in the play, inspire no disgust, outrage no moral sentiment, revolt no sympathy, but only excite innocent and hearty laughter.

When a clown trips up a baker in the street, wheels him off in his own barrow, trundles him into his own oven, and there bakes him alive, the fate of the baker excites no pity, and the inhumanity of his persecutor no indignation. And when Harry Lorrequer initiates his proceedings in Dublin, by gratuitously detailing to a perfectly inoffensive stranger an elaborate falsehood, and afterwards shoots the man he has insulted, without the least consciousness of any reason why he should fight him at all, we laugh at the drollery of the misdeed described, without for a moment attributing either to ourselves or the author any participation in the immorality of the conduct which causes our merriment. We know beforehand that all such victims are only men of straw, purposely so contrived as to minister to the flitting spirit of mischievous fun which presides over that entirely fantastical world wherein all that passes is too impossible in fact to come within the jurisdiction of any moral law, and yet sufficiently real in art to enthral attention and create pleasurable emotion. It is in securing this result that the art and genius of the author consist; and we believe it is no less an authority than Sir Walter Scott who has said, " If it be the highest praise of pathetic composition that it draws forth tears, why should it not be esteemed the greatest excellence of the ludicrous that it compels laughter ? The one tribute is at least as genuine an expression of natural feeling as the other." Certainly, in the power of producing effects irresistibly ludicrous, and instantaneously destructive of all gravity, Mr. Lever is pre-eminent, and may challenge comparison with any writer, living or dead. Nor is even the broad fun of Mr. Lever's earliest novels destitute of passages which indicate powers of thoughtful humour and subtle irony. Sparks's story, in ' Charles O'Malley,' and the description in it of the man who loves a mad girl—his sensations on discovering her insanity, and hers on finding that he is not the Ace of Spades, and that she has taken "the nephew of a Manchester cottonspinner, with a face like printed calico, for a trump card, and the best in the pack," is told with an irresistible drollery which only partially conceals a depth of grave sad satire and pathetic allegory. The story of the Knight of Kerry's conversation with the Irish tenant, who earns his "rints" by personating a wild man in a London showroom, has in it much more than the merely ludicrous. The origin of the story would undoubtedly appear to be Hibernian, but it has also been told by Paul de Kock, with little more alteration than that of substituting Frenchmen for Irishmen, and Paris for London. Mr. Lever's version of the story, however, is far more humorous, and in all respects infinitely better, than that of the French novelist. But of all the characters in Mr. Lever's earlier romances, that which affords most evidence of this higher kind of humour is undoubtedly Mickey Free; and the story (as recounted by himself) of how he got his father's soul out of purgatory, is so excellently well told, and is so admirable a specimen of that sly wit which is characteristic of the Irish peasant, that it is with great reluctance we refrain from extracting it.

The whole character of Mickey Free is indeed inimitable. We have no hesitation in affirming it to be the most perfect type of Irish humour that has ever been given to the world. It is perfectly sustained from first to last, and nothing in the conception of it is exaggerated or in-congruous. Mickey Free is the Irish Sam Weller. He has, in fact, this advantage over Sam Weller, that he is the more thoroughly national and comprehensive type of the two. It is impossible but what this creation, which is in many respects the most felicitous of all Mr. Lever's creations, should live for ever as a distinct embodiment of national character. It must always have a historical value ; and it is indeed so truthfully and so comprehensively drawn, that whoever has since at-tempted to describe in future the Irish peasant, has appeared to copy rather from Lever than from nature. Mickey Free, however, is but one (although to our thinking, the best) picture in Mr. Lever's large gallery of Irish portraits. The Knight of Gwynne is another equally character-istic ; and it is perhaps more delicately, although less vividly, de-lineated. Nothing can be more complete than this elaborate picture of a character which has ceased to exist—the high-bred, ill-starred Irish gentleman of the days before the Union. It is a strange anomaly, combining all the courtly grace and refinement of a Sir Charles Grandi-son with the rude, half-civilized life of a Rob Roy ; at once splendid and spendthrift ; chivalrous in all things, careful in nothing ; alienating prosperity, yet elevating misfortune, and always débonnaire in the midst of disaster; every inch a gentleman, yet just such a gentleman as seems destined by Providence to ruin himself, and hasten the ruin of the class to which he belongs. The Knight of Gwynne is certainly one of the most lovable characters that Mr. Lever has ever drawn; and he monopolises so much of our sympathy, that we hope to be forgiven for extending less of it than he probably deserves to Bagenal Daley, not-withstanding the vigour with which that character is drawn, the remarkable originality of it, and the fidelity with which it represents and sustains a most peculiar combination of qualities, intellectual as well as moral.

We may, however, note here by the way, that this singular character is the first of Mr. Lever's earlier creations, in which he has given evidence of that shrewd experience of mankind, that practical worldly wit, and power of philosophical epigram, into which his natural humour has developed itself in more recent works; and there are passages of dialogue between "the Howling Wind" and his Irish Scot which not unfrequently remind one of the dry humorous wisdom which abounds in such creations as Dalgetty and Sancho Panza. This work is indeed a most complete and varied picture of Irish life and manners. The book is written with a profound knowledge of the subject of it; and, without overloading the narrative with political or philosophical discussion, the author never loses sight of a thoughtful purpose; he penetrates beneath the surface of the society which he describes, and lays bare, with the ease and accuracy of a skilful anatomist, all the minutest causes and remotest effects of those social and political phenomena which in Ireland preceded the Union. The Castlereagh policy is sketched with the masterly hand of a man who has thoroughly comprehended both the nature of the measure itself, and that of the country to which it referred. The whole epoch of that time is indeed reproduced, investigated, and criticised by Mr. Lever, with an accuracy of delineation and depth of reflection which show him to be not only an admirable novelist, but something also of a philosophical politician. What is especially to be noted in this book is, that all the principal characters therein are the representatives of *genera* rather than of *species*—that is to say, they image and embody large aggregates of national character rather than individual and special peculiarities. Creation of this kind necessitates many high powers of thought as well as of fancy; and although Mr. Lever has not attempted it so often as he gives us reason to wish, yet, wherever he has done so, his success cannot be disputed. The old Irish proprietor, the old Irish domestic, the petty usurer, the Irish attorney, founders of a new race of landlords; the Irishman of the north, and the Irishman of the south—are all admirably described in the 'Knight of Gwynne.' Freeny the robber is also a very well-drawn character; and the escape of Freeny from the burning jail is a scene which in power and terror fully justifies the admiration of it formerly entertained by Miss Edgeworth. Mr. Lever has, indeed, given many proofs that he is by no means deficient in the faculty of exciting terror, and some of his night-rides, his battle-scenes, and robber-meetings have about them a palpability and intensity which may fairly entitle them to compete for praise with Smollett's much-admired sea-engagements. It is as having given the completest and most intense expression to Irish humour, and furnished familiar types of almost every distinction of Irish character, that Mr. Lever, whatever may be his other merits, will, in our opinion, maintain a solid and permanent reputation as a humorist. Scenes which, in such novels as ' O'Malley '

and 'Hinton,' may perhaps appear to Cockney critics as simple impossi-
bilities, are truly facts of Irish life ; and Mr. Lever has so little carica-
tured or exaggerated the habits and characters of Irishmen, that those
parts of his Irish novels which appear absurdly unreal are only ridi-
culously *true*. It would be entirely beyond the scope and purpose of
these remarks to discuss the relative value of any really original conception ; but we see no reason to doubt why Mickey Free, and Major Mon-
soon, and Kerry O'Leary, and Baby Blake, Mary Martin, and Kate
O'Donoghue, and Kenny, and Mrs. Dodd, should not live as long as
Jeanie Deans, or Mathew Bramble, or Squire Western, or any other
distinctly-recognized type of national character.

That conviction which is entertained by Irishmen, not without a
certain self-satisfaction, that their characters are all but incomprehen-
sible to Englishmen ; the humorous enjoyment which they derive from
the consciousness that their ways and habits are a continual source
of dismay and bewilderment to their fellow-subjects over the water ;
and a certain sense of not unnatural resentment, with which, some
years ago, the Irish people must have been disposed to regard every
attempt on the part of Government to shape out or constrain the
pattern of their national life into formal accordance with the modes and
manners of an alien and dominant race,—have furnished Mr. Lever with
many opportunities for drollery at the expense of Cockney critics. An
amusing piece of good-humoured caricature in this sense occurs in the
story of the gentleman who never saw daylight in Ireland, which
occupies the twenty-fourth chapter of 'Jack Hinton.' Equally comi-
cal in its way is the quiz upon Mr. Prettyman, the "intelligent
traveller."

As instances of easy and natural Irish humour, we may refer, by the
way, to the oration delivered by Kerry O'Leary over the ruins of the
doctor's gig, in the fourteenth chapter of 'The O'Donoghue,' and
the priest's moonlit ride in 'Jack Hinton.' Mr. Lever has also shown,
in the death of Mary Martin, that he can, when he pleases, be pathetic
as well as humorous. His female characters are seldom very refined
or very interesting. In depicting a romping "wild Irish-girl," a wily
adventuress, a Continental demirep, or a pretentious petticoated par-
venu, he is never at fault ; but his women are for the most part either
rouées, romps, or Xantippes ; and the majestic visions which animate
old Chaucer's 'Legend of Good Women,' and inspired Wordsworth's
picture of the "perfect woman, nobly planned," never flit across his
pages. If, indeed, modern mothers and daughters are only half as
knowing, vigilant, and unscrupulous in their designs upon that portion
of humanity who have not only breeches but breeches-pockets, no
bachelor can have a chance against the female foe ; all unmarried men

are marching through an enemy's country, in which they must expect at every step to have their flank turned by some astute matrimonial manœuvre.

We cannot, however, sufficiently praise Mr. Lever for his evidently hearty abhorrence of all sentimentality and false writing. The most tempting occasion never betrays him into this—he is always manly, simple, and sincere in his treatment of sentiment and passion. This is no small virtue in a modern novelist—many of our modern writers, like our modern singers, are always in *falsetto*; and the public is in both cases always entrapped into applause.

Nor can we pass from the consideration of Mr. Lever's earlier romances without according our cordial approbation of the admirable ballads, fighting songs, and drinking songs, which are interspersed throughout the pages of those books. These songs are full of spirit—they have all the drollery, dash, and devilry peculiar to the land of the shamrock and shillelah. If they have here and there a flavour of poteen, the scent of the heather and the breath of the mountain breeze are equally strong in them. It is almost impossible to read them without singing them, and almost impossible to hear them sung without wishing to fight, drink, or dance. They bubble forth without premeditation from the depth of a most joyous conviction in the

> " Nunc est bibendum, nunc pede libero
> Pulsanda tellus."

We believe that Mr. Lever's later novels are, on the whole, less generally popular than those by which his reputation as a writer was first acquired. This is natural, for many reasons quite independent of the merits or defects of the works themselves. The public is seldom of one mind with an author in comparing the relative merit of his works, especially where such comparison is between early and subsequent efforts. The author is naturally inclined to esteem most highly those of his works upon which he is conscious of having expended most labour; the public, on the contrary, are inclined to prefer those to the enjoyment of which they have given the least labour. The first works of an original writer take us by surprise. They issue unexpectedly from the unknown, our enjoyment of them is spontaneous, and the delight occasioned by the freshness of feeling with which the author writes is increased by the freshness of sympathy with which the public reads. Every man's favourite poet is the poet he first learned to love under the summer trees in his boyhood. New poets only address new generations. The authors which most agreeably impress us are those which we read when most capable of receiving agreeable impressions ; that is to say, in youth. We cannot even entirely renew for the subsequent works of the same author those sensations of delight which we derived from our first acquaintance with him, when he was young to us, and we were young to ourselves : and in proportion as we experience this difficulty on our own part, we are inclined to resent more naturally than justly the inability of the author to overcome it. Long familiarity, moreover, with the name of an author, often indisposes the public to expect much novelty from increased familiarity with the mind of him. Nothing is so reluctantly conceded to a popular writer as superiority to *himself*. The more readily his claim to attention and sympathy has been admitted in one direction, the more resolutely is it resisted in every other. A previous success is often the greatest hindrance to a subsequent reputation. People are sometimes startled into applause by the first revelation of an original mind; they are generally on their guard against any inconsiderate approval of a second. And as the process by which the mind of an author passes from one phase into another is usually gradual, and marked by various stages of development more or less imperfect and unsatisfactory, the advance made is not always immediately noticeable, and the recognition accorded to it is naturally slow and dubious. This must be especially the case with an author who has introduced himself to the public rather as a boon-companion than a moralist. We have often heard it said of Mr. Lever that he is much less funny than he used to be ; which is indeed true. But when it is asked why he does not resort to the style and matter of his early novels, and implied that he should write nothing but ' Harry Lorrequer's ' and ' Charles O'Malley's,' we must express the conviction that compliance with any such demand, even if it were not purely impossible, would be altogether unadvisable. We could not ourselves bring to the perusal of repeated ' Harry Lorrequers ' an undiminished capacity to be amused by them. *Consuetudine vilescunt.* The piper might pipe as of old, but who would dance to his piping ? *Non eadem est ætas, non mens.* We cannot blame Mr. Lever for abandoning a vein of humour which he has the merit of having exhausted ; but it is nevertheless obvious, that in relinquishing that particular kind of fiction in which he is allowed to have excelled, Mr. Lever has withdrawn from a territory of which he was sole and undisputed proprietor, and entered upon one in which, whatever the acquirements he may bring to the cultivation of it, he is not without competitors.

It must be conceded that what we miss in Mr. Lever's later publications is that freshness, vivacity, and exuberant wealth of animal spirits, which gave to his earlier novels their chief charm. Although the relative merit of his recent works is decidedly unequal, some of them being much better than others, and all of them being better in one part than in another ; yet there is in the majority of them a sameness of subject and material which does not give fair play to the powers employed upon them. Upon this point we shall speak more fully by-and-by ; but whatever objections we may presently have to make in detail to some of Mr. Lever's last books, we have no hesitation in expressing the opinion, that amongst these books are to be found proofs of a genius richer, maturer, and more pleasing than any which is apparent in the earlier works of the same author. Indeed, 'The Dodd Family Abroad,' which has not been published many years, is in our opinion the best of all Mr. Lever's works. He has written nothing at any time comparable to the letters of Henry Dodd; nor could there be any better evidence than what is afforded throughout the pages of this delightful and good-humoured satire, that the genius of the author, if it has lost much of that physical animation which is the arbitrary gift of youth, has acquired with years that thoughtful and more pleasing humour which is the result of enlarged experience and deeper sympathy with mankind. This chronicle of the adventures of 'The Dodd Family Abroad,' like 'The Expedition of Humphrey Clinker,' Smollett's last and most pleasing fiction, is a narrative thrown into epistolary form, and related by the actors themselves, who are thus made with great skill to be, as it were, the unconcious exponents of their own characters, follies, and foibles, as well as the historians of their own fates. We do not desire to suggest even a critical comparison between this clever romance and that masterpiece of Smollett, which will doubtless remain unrivalled as long as the English literature endures. But the most conspicuous merit in 'The Dodd Family' is, that each character in the story is so contrived as to evoke, in the most humorous form, the peculiarities of all the others, without any violation of the individuality assigned to itself. The book, which is a sort of prose 'Fudge Family,' deeper, broader, and more comprehensive than Moore's clever satire, is a good-humoured but unsparing mockery of "false pretences" all over the world. If the dramatic power exist in the capacity to realise and express with an accuracy, too great for mere conjecture, other people's habits of thought and feeling, Mr. Lever has shown in this book more of such power than in anything else he has ever written. The humour of his earlier books is almost entirely superficial. It deals purely with external things, and is little more than an extraordinarily acute sense of the ludicrous in situation and circumstance. In this book the humour is of that rarer kind which plays less with external and accidental peculiarities than with men's modes of thought, and the manner in which different minds are impressed by the same facts, or operated on by the same influences. The difference of the result in each case is great. The highest humour is inseparable from a profound sympathy with human nature, and is therefore always tinged with sadness. For man is too grand a subject, after all, for eternal practical jokes, and even the most defaced and misfeatured humanity should be safe from unmitigated laughter. The fun which abounds, however, in Mr. Lever's more youthful writings, ignores the existence of sorrow in any sense but that of hateful deformity, to be contemplated as little as possible : and consequently this sort of fun, incompatible as it is with any deep sympathy, is never quite free from a certain element of cruelty, inherent to the strong animal life of early youth. But what is most delightful in the letters of "K. I." is that loving, tender capacity to feel for and with humanity in all the forms of its imperfection and weakness—that tendency to live in the life of others, and to draw from the various thoughts and acts and manners of mankind constant food for reflection, which breathe through the playful satire, and furnish material to the genial humour of those charming letters. And though the author appears to have given fuller scope both to his own sentiments and his own experience in the letters of "K. I.," yet the same spirit of kindly humour, and the same shrewd appreciation of social characteristics, are apparent in all the epistles, even where the drollery most approaches to caricature, as in those of the Irish servant-girl who complains to her friends at home of being like "a pelican on a dissolute island."

Of all Mr. Dodd's numerous misfortunes, those under which his patience is most pathetic, and which enlist our warmest sympathies, are certainly his domestic and conjugal afflictions. Who that remembers or anticipates matrimonial experience can read without a cold shudder this description of the household tactics adopted on great occasions by Mrs. Dodd ?—

"For the last week Mrs. D. had adopted a kind of warfare, at which she, I'll be bound to say, has few equals and no superior—a species of irregular attack, at all times and on all subjects, by innuendo and insinuation, so dexterously thrown out as to defy opposition; for you might as well take your musket to keep off the mosquitoes! What she was driving at I never could guess, for the assault came on every flank and in all manner of ways. If I was dressed a little more carefully than usual, she called attention to my 'smartness;' if less so, she hinted that I was probably going out 'on the sly.' If I stayed at home, I was waiting for somebody; if I went out, it was to 'meet them.' But all this guerilla warfare gave way at last to a grand attack, when I ventured to remonstrate about some extravagance or other. 'It came well from me,' she burst forth with indignant anger—'it came well from me to talk of the little necessary expenses of the family —the bit they ate, and the clothes on their backs.' She spoke as if they were Mandans or Iraquois, and lived in a wigwam !"

Poets, we are told by one of them, "learn in suffering what they teach in song," and philosophers acquire wisdom from their own afflictions. Mr. Dodd, in the true spirit of the philosophy preached by Æschylus, παρ' ἔκοντας ἦλθε σωφρονεῖν, thus moralises on his own misfortune :—

" Ah, Tom, my boy, it's all very good fun to laugh at Keeley, or Buckstone, or any other of those diverting vagabonds who can convulse the house with such a theme, but in real life the Farce is downright Tragedy. There is not a single comfort or consolation of your life that is not kicked clean from under you! A system of normal agitation is a fine thing, they tell us, in politics, but it is a cruel adjunct of domestic life! Everything you say, every look you give, every letter you seal, or every note you receive, are counts in a mysterious indictment against you, till at last you are afraid to blow your nose, lest it be taken for a signal to the fat widow lady that is caressing her poodle at the window over the way!"

But his greatest trial of all is the prospect of a sudden accession of fortune to the ambitious partner of his bosom. His excessive alarm at the possibility of a contingency so fatal to domestic happiness is very humorous, and his opinions upon the subject of legacies to married ladies in small circumstances are evidently the result of profound and painful experience.

"To tell you the plain truth, Tom, I don't know a greater misfortune for a man that has married a wife without money, than to discover at the end of some fifteen or twenty years that somebody has left her a few hundred pounds! It is not only that she conceives visions of unbounded extravagance, and raves about all manner of expense, but she begins to fancy herself an heiress that was thrown away, and imagines wonderful destinies she might have arrived at, if she hadn't had the bad luck to meet you. For a real crab-apple of discord, I 'll back a few hundreds in the Three per Cents. against all the family jars that ever were invented.

"Save us, then, from this, if you can, Tom. There must surely be twenty ways to avoid the legacy; and so that Mrs. D. doesn't hear of it, I 'd rather you 'd prove her illegitimate, than allow her to succeed to this bequest. I 'll not enlarge upon all I feel about this subject, hoping that by your skill and address we may never hear more of it; but I tell you, frankly, I 'd face the small-pox with a stouter heart than the news of succeeding to the M'Carthy inheritance."

The adventures of a vulgar Irish family abroad in search of economy combined with pretension and display, afford Mr. Lever a good opportunity for satirising the social and political condition of a great number of foreign States. In doing this he has shown not only an affluent experience of Continental life, and a quick perception of all social phenomena, but also a very uncommon amount of shrewd common-sense and sound political judgment. We must say the satire is well deserved and unerringly aimed. Nothing escapes. The state of society, the conduct of government, the foreign and domestic policy, the administration of justice, the civil and military jurisdictions, the morals and manners of Continental capitals are sharply canvassed. The character, too, of Kenny Dodd, in its strange admixture of childishness and wisdom, ignorance of the world and knowledge of mankind, and that subdued humorous consciousness which it betrays of the utter worthlessness of those influences to which it is ever an easy victim, greatly facilitates the indulgence of that moralising vein in which Mr. Lever reviews almost every possible aspect of society. From the moment in which K. I. discovers that "shamelessness is the grand characteristic of foreign life," and that "one picks up the indecency much easier than the irregular verbs," the wisdom of his private reflections keeps pace with the folly of his public proceedings.

We extract the following passage from Mr. Dodd's reflections upon geology and the sciences, viewed in their relation to education and politics, because it is a favourable sample of a particular kind of humour in which Mr. Lever's later writings (and especially the work from which the passage is taken) are equally fertile and felicitous. It is a humour which consists in turning some indisputable truth upside down or inside out when the reader is least expecting it. The effect is often irresistible.

"For a man who has daughters abroad, my advice is—stick to the sciences. Grey sandstone is safer than the polka, and there's not as dangerous an experiment in all chemistry as singing duets with some black-bearded blackguard from Naples or Palermo. Now mind, Tom, this counsel of mine applies to the education of the young, for when people come to the forties, you may rely upon it, if they set about learning anything, they'll have the devil for a schoolmaster. What does all the geology mean? Junketting, Tom—nothing but junketting! Primitive rock is another name for a Pic-nic, and what they call Quartz is a figurative expression for iced champagne. Just reflect for a moment and see what it comes to. You can enter a protest against family extravagances when they take the shape of balls and soirees, but what are you to do against botanical excursions and anti-quarian researches? It's like writing yourself down Goth at once to oppose these. 'Oh, papa hates chemistry; he despises natural history,' that's the cry at once, and they hold me up to ridicule just in the way the rascally Protestant newspapers did Dr. Cullen, for saying that he didn't believe the world was round. If the liberty of the subject be worth anything—if the right for which these same Pro-testants are always prating, private judgment, be the great privilege they deem it —why shouldn't Dr. Cullen have his own opinion about the shape of the earth? He can say, 'It suits me to think that I'm walking erect on a flat surface, and not crawling along with my head down, like a fly on the ceiling! I'm happier when I believe what doesn't puzzle my understanding, and I don't want any more mira-cles than we have in the Church.' He may say that, and I'd like to know what harm does that do you or me? Does it endanger the Protestant succession or the State religion? Not a bit of it, Tom. The real fact is simply this: private judg-ment is a boon they mean to keep for themselves, and never share with their neighbours! So far as I have seen of life, there's no such tyrant as your Pro-testant, and for this reason: it's bad enough to force a man to believe something that he doesn't like, but it's ten times worse to make him disbelieve what he's well satisfied with; and that's exactly what they do. Even on the ground of common humanity it is indefensible. If my private judgment goes in favour of saints' toe-nails and martyrs' shin-bones, I have a right to my opinion, and you have no right to attack it. Besides, I won't be badgered into what it may suit somebody else to think. My opinion is like my flannel-waistcoat, that I'll take off or put on as the weather requires; and I think it very cruel that I must wear mine simply because you feel cold."

When Mr. Dodd moralises on the field of Waterloo, his words are the words of wisdom. Could Mr. Mill himself be more logical on the subject of Divine Right? All the political philosophers in the world could add but little to this pithy summary of the case, as between kings and peoples:—

" I know you 'll reply to me with your old argument about Legitimacy and Divine Right, and all that kind of thing. But, my dear Tom, for the matter of that, haven't I a divine right to my ancestral estate of Tullylicknaslatterley; and look what they 're going to do with it, to-morrow or next day ! 'T is much Commissioner Longfield would mind, if I begged to defer the sale on the ground of 'divine right.' *Kings are exactly like landlords; they can't do what they like with their own, hard as it may seem to say so.* *They have their obligations and their duties; and if they fail in them, they come into the Encumbered Estates Court just like us—* ay, and just like us, they 'take very little by their motion.'

" I know it's very hard to be turned out of your 'holding.' I can imagine the feelings with which a man would quit such a comfortable quarter as the Tuileries, and such a nice place for summer as Versailles; Dodsborough is too fresh in my mind to leave any doubt on this point : but there 's another side of the question, Tom. What were they there for? You 'll call out, ' This is all Socialism and Democracy, and the devil knows what else.' Maybe I 'll agree with you. Maybe I 'll say, I don't like the doctrine myself. Maybe I 'll tell you that I think the old time was pleasantest, when if we pressed a little hard to-day, why, we were all the kinder to-morrow, and both ruler and ruled looked more leniently on each other's faults. But say what we will—do what we will—these days are gone by, and they 'll not come back again. There 's a set of fellows at work, all over the world, telling the people about their rights. Some of these are very acute and clever chaps, that don't overstate the case; they neither go off into any flights about Universal Equality, or any balderdash about our being of the same stock; out they stick to two or three hard propositions, and they say, ' *Don't pay more for anything than you can get it for—that's free trade; don't pay for anything you don't want—that's a blow at the Church Establishment; don't pay for soldiers if you don't want to fight—that's at a 'standing army;' and above all, when you haven't a pair of breeches to your back, don't be buying embroidered small-clothes for Lords-in-Waiting or Gentlemen of the Bedchamber.'* But here I am again, running away from Waterloo, just as if I was a Belgian."

K. I. has certainly no pretension to be a faultless philosopher, but he is a very pleasant one. Montaigne would have chosen him for a companion. Molière would have sympathised with and loved him. He has so large a sympathy for human nature, that his own claim upon that of the reader is irresistible ; and so kindly and compassionate a feeling for the imperfections of mankind, that we follow him with undiminished affection through all the faults and follies that he so frankly attributes to himself. He so innocently pleads guilty to the occasional " delight of doing wrong ;" there is something so natural in the touch of envy with which he remarks that " India-rubber itself is not so elastic as a bad character," and so sly an appeal to commiseration in his candid avowal, " I don't want to disparage principle, no more than I do a great balance at Coutts's, or anything else that I don't possess myself," that all such good-humoured self-accusations are at once understood to be among the philosophical paradoxes peculiar to that vein of banter which proves all pro-

b

blems by the *ad absurdum* argument, and which he frequently indulges at his own expense. Mr. Lever is, indeed, so happy in the management of dialogue, and in the art of allowing his characters to evolve themselves without interference from the author, that there is every reason to think he would be successful in the comic drama ; and were he to exercise his genius in that direction we have little doubt but what he would do much to rescue the English stage from its present discreditable obligation to the charity of third-rate French play-wrights. Our extracts from ' The Dodd Family' have extended over a larger space than we could well afford, because it is our sincere opinion that Mr. Lever has written nothing comparable to this book ; and without ample reference to the work itself, it was hardly possible to justify the opinion which we have not hesitated to express about it.

The 'Dodd Family' is an elaborate denunciation of the folly of "people living upon false pretences ;" and 'Davenport Dunn,' which deals with the crimes rather than the follies of society, exposes with considerable power, and an extraordinary knowledge of the dark side of modern civilisation, the innumerable "fraudulent pretences" of roguery in every rank of life. The character of Dunn himself, which is that of the brilliant commercial swindler, the Robert Law of these days, whose roguery is on a magnificent scale, is carefully drawn ; and Mr. Lever has certainly the merit of never allowing himself to be tempted into conventional exaggeration of this character. Davenport Dunn is a rascal of genius, and throughout all his roguery he remains sufficiently human and natural (the good being never entirely obliterated by the evil in his complex character) to justify to the last the interest which his career excites in the mind of the reader. His ambition, before it comes in contact with distracting and debasing influences, is legitimate, and even noble ; and the gradual deterioration of a character whose power is uncontrolled by principle, is finely worked out. But the best and most powerful character in this book—a character in which Mr. Lever has shown, in addition to his ordinary knowledge of the world, no ordinary knowledge of human nature—is that of Grog Davis, the professional " sporting swindler." This man, a vulgar blackleg, and in all his dealings with society a most unmitigated scoundrel, nevertheless affects us with a sense of power, and secures from us a degree of interest which it would be impossible to feel for a character of which the delineation was less true to the deepest realities of nature. The whole conception of this character is, indeed, of the highest order. The one redeeming point in the much-defaced humanity of this man, and the secret of the strong dramatic interest which he excites, lies in his devoted and absorbing affection for his daughter.

Whatever he has in him better than the fiend, or above the brute, is concentrated in this affection, of which the pathos is all the more poignant from the power of nature which it indicates, and the contrast which it suggests with the prostitution of that power in the habitual life of the man. The professional associations of Grog Davis with the turf and the fashionable gambling-houses of Europe, bring him into daily contact with the most worthless and demoralised members of the upper ranks of society. Their ambition to be knaves renders them only the dupes of a knavery more practised and audacious than their own; and the contempt of the professional swindler for those who, though his superiors in social rank, are only his equals in infamy, and his inferiors in the dexterity which renders infamy partially profitable, is embittered by his haunting consciousness that they are by birthright the inheritors of what a man may desecrate but cannot transfer, and that the sphere from which they descend into connection with him is one into which, by no possible connection with them, is he able to elevate himself. His dreary and restricted experience teaches him that there is no moral degradation which men will not incur for the sake of money, and from this he argues to the conclusion that there is no social disability which may not be overcome by that all-powerful agent. He therefore labours to accumulate wealth dishonestly, in order that he may make his child rich enough to be honest. What matter though his own hands be soiled?—hers shall be stainless! What matter though he heap infamy on himself, if it be to bequeath to her the purity and innocence which, the further it is removed from the depths of his own degradation, the more he delights to contemplate and revere in the future of his child? The profligate gentlemen who are his boon-companions may laugh away, in the course of a night's debauch, the reputation of every duchess in England; but where is he, so bold of tongue, or so sure of his pistol-practice, as shall dare to find a spot on the character of the daughter of the "infamous Grog Davis?" Whilst he, for her sake, is plotting nefarious plunder, in the company of men whose presence is pollution, she, an innocent happy girl, in her convent at Brussels, shall be learning all that can refine and elevate life—the associate of spotless maidens, and the pupil of the most accomplished teachers that money can secure. And in all this notable scheme nothing is overlooked save that alone which involves the inevitable failure of it. It never occurs to the remarkable natural shrewdness of a man whose experience, however varied, is limited exclusively to evil, that in this world, where the consequences of evil are endless, the sins of the fathers are visited upon the children, and that, in the eye of society, the daughter of the "infamous Grog Davis," were she wise as Sheba and pure as Ruth, can never be other than the child of infamy, and the inheritor of shame. And so complete is his inability to realize or comprehend any but social distinctions between right and wrong, that although there is no self-sacrifice of which he is not capable to secure the happiness of his child, and no barbarity in which he would scruple to

indulge his vengeance on the man who should injure her, yet he is himself a conspirator to sell her in marriage to the most abjectly worthless
and contemptible of all his infamous associates, simply because that man
is brother and heir to a peer of the realm. That the daughter of Grog
Davis should be a peeress, for this Grog Davis schemes to secure as his
son-in-law a man whom he knows to be guilty of forgery, and whom he
himself despises as a poltroon. This is the summit of his ambition. And
how a theory of life which insults human nature is defeated by human
nature itself; how the human heart vindicates its inherent birthright to
the control of its own destinies, and avenges upon itself the wrongs inflicted by itself upon its better aspirations; how, out of the utter wreck
and failure of all that unscrupulous ingenuity can devise for the attain-
ment of unworthy desires, arises at the last, in the mere might of man's
common instinct to be good, something which reconciles the fact of
human sin to our faith in human nature, and seems to vindicate the hope
of a distant but ultimate salvation,—is shadowed forth in the development and destiny of these two characters, with a masterly power and
depth of insight which not unfrequently reminds us of Balzac.

Before we pass from the consideration of this work, we may remark,
as regards the entire conception of it, that considerable skill is evinced
in the mechanism by which Mr. Lever contrives to show that every rogue
is limited, in his power to do mischief, to the use, as it were, of a single
engine, and that he who assails honest men with one kind of weapon is
liable to be himself overthrown by his ignorance of the fence peculiar
to some other species of rascality. Thus, for instance, the amateur
blackguard Annesley Beecher, is no match for the professional blackleg
Grog Davis; and Grog Davis, in turn, with all his craft and audacity,
is no match against the more astute tactics of Davenport Dunn, the refined and comprehensive rascal; whilst even Dunn is overreached at last
by the combined common-sense of the honest portion of society; so that,
with this species of vermin as with all others, the rhyme holds good, that

> " Greater fleas have little fleas,
> Upon their legs to bite 'em ;
> And little fleas have lesser fleas,
> And so *ad infinitum.*"

There are some admirable characters in Mr. Lever's last novel. Mrs.
Penthony Morris is excellent. So, in another way, is Mr. Ogden, the
bully of a public office, the sycophant of secretaries of state, and the
tyrant of junior clerks, the pedant of Downing-street, and the bore of all
society. There is nothing more delightful than to see a bully cowed ;
and the absolute terror and anguish of Ogden when he unexpectedly en-
counters, on the Continent, the fascinating wife from whom he has been
divorced, the groan of positive pain into which his pompous compliment

is sudddenly converted by a single glance at the person for whom it was destined with the most approved conventional gallantry, is inimitable. There is something even which claims our sympathy in the capacity for common human suffering thus revealed beneath all the small formalities of the man. Layton, the lost man of genius, is of a higher range, and there is considerable power, and not a little pathos, in Mr. Lever's vigourous sketch of this character. But, perhaps, the best-sustained character in the book is that of the Yankee, Leonidas Shaver Quakenboss.

In the delineation of this character Mr. Lever has evinced one merit, for which, perhaps, he can hardly hope to receive due appreciation from the majority of readers. Quakenboss is, so far as we know, almost the only Yankee of English manufacture in whose figures of speech the purely Yankee idiom, peculiar to the New England States, is not constantly confounded with the slang of the South and West. Mr. Lever is also deserving of approval for not having allowed the merely ludicrous in a subject so obviously open to coarse caricature, to overpower his finer perception of what are the better and worthier qualities of the Yankee character. In this respect, however, he has been anticipated by Sir E. Lytton.

There is certainly no lack of power in Mr. Lever's later novels. On the contrary, they contain writing of greater power, and evince qualities which belong to genius of a higher order, than we discover in his earlier and still, perhaps, more popular books. Had he never written anything but the 'Dodd Family,' that work alone would have entitled him to take undisputed rank amongst the humorists of England; and had that work been the first of a hitherto unknown writer, the sensation it would have excited must have been very great. But familiarity, if it does not breed contempt, often induces indifference. If Aristides had taken to rope-dancing, perhaps he would not have been ostracised by the Athenians. Popularity is an alms which, the more cheerfully it is accorded to a first appeal, the more churlishly is it conceded to a second from the same quarter. When we see a boy in the street standing on his head, if we are in a good humour we fling him a penny, but the next time we see him turning a somersault, we only say "There's that boy again!" and button up our pockets. Still, there are undoubtedly drawbacks to the claim of Mr. Lever's later works on general sympathy and approval for which he is himself responsible; and we have reserved to the last the few remarks which we have to make of an unfavourable nature in reference to these works, because the cordial recognition which we have already expressed of their author's ability will be the best guarantee for our sincerity in objecting to the subjects on which that ability is sometimes exercised. There is a sameness of subject about the majority of Mr. Lever's younger novels, which is partly counterbalanced by the fact that such sameness lies at least within the sphere of a more or less national interes t, such as the portraiture of Irish life. But the continued repe

tition of scenes representative of a kind of society which is neither familiar nor pleasing to a large class of English readers, which is the characteristic of nearly all Mr. Lever's later works, is under any circumstances
a mistake. The frivolity of Continental society, the vulgarity and mis-
takes of English travellers abroad, and the tricks and deceptions of
sharpers and adventurers, is a very legitimate subject for satire ; but it
has really been exhausted with great success in the 'Dodd Family,'
and we regret to see it enter so largely into the staple material of Mr.
Lever's subsequent novels. However excellent may be the cookery, and
skilful the arrangement of the dishes, we object to continual invitations
to dine off the leavings of any feast, however good ; it is not hospitality,
but thrift, which would force us to drain the last flagon and swallow
the last crumb.

> " The funeral baked meats
> But coldly furnish forth the marriage-feast."

In such works as 'Davenport Dunn' and 'One of Them,' the
genius of the author carries everything before it. But the subject of
such a story as 'The Daltons' can, we should think, have little interest for the mass of the public. We need not defend these remarks
from the imputation of a false and vulgar morality which would ex-
clude from fiction its legitimate sources of interest in the delineation of
crime and the analysis of evil. Nothing in human nature can be alien
to art, which derives from nature all its materials. All we ask from an
author is to preserve the balance and proportion of the emotions to which
he appeals. To be continually poring over the blots and failures of
humanity, or the vices and corruption of any social state, is neither
profitable nor pleasant. And the perusal of a series of fictions which
present to us only the deformities of nature, and detain us without
relief or intermission in the society of sharpers and vagabonds, and
all manner of vicious or vulgar persons, becomes fatiguing and painful.
As we close one after the other of such books, we feel like men returning
from a hell. Our gains are not equivalent to the unpleasurable process of
their acquirement, and we long for some more wholesome intercourse with
mankind. The highest and most truthful art must occasionally hold intercourse with evil, but it is a mistake in art to make that intercourse
habitual. When an author continually presents to our view one side only
either of society or of man's heart, and that the most unpleasant of all,
he appears to imply—not that this is to be found in society or human
nature, and is worth looking at—but that nothing else is to be found in
society or human nature, and that this is worth looking at ; and we revolt
from acquiescence in any such view of a cause which is, after all, our own.
Our estimation of the genius of Le Sage would be much lower if he had
written half-a-dozen small 'Gil Blas;' and if Fielding had written
many 'Jonathan Wilds,' we should be disposed to think less highly of

the mind that made 'Tom Jones.' We attribute this defect to what is perhaps in itself a conscientious quality. We think that Mr. Lever is apt to be content to draw his materials for fiction too exclusively from *observation.* Human nature is indeed inexhaustible, but no one man's observation of human nature can be so. The widest experience is limited, and the limit of it must be reached at last. There is only one inexhaustible source for fiction, and that is the Imagination.

But the imagination itself is an engine which cannot be kept in frequent operation without being frequently supplied with fuel. It cannot act without being first acted upon. And the fault we are inclined to attribute to the majority of our modern writers of romance is, that they give out too much and take in too little. Let men say what they will about native originality, man is not really a creator. He changes, improves, and extends, that is all. *Ex nihilo nihil fit;* and the best new ideas are the product of a large accumulation of old ones. Those authors who rely chiefly upon personal observation and experience for the materials of fiction, cannot be too careful to vary their point of sight pretty often. Every imaginative writer must at some period have experienced the feelings expressed by Cowley, when he wrote—

> " The fields which sprang beneath the ancient plough,
> Spent and outworn, return no harvest now,
> And we must die of want,
> Unless new lands we plant."

If Mr. Lever is disposed to dispute the justice of these observations, or, at any rate, their special application to himself, he may certainly refer to the extraordinary sameness of a vast number of his contemporary novelists, who do not seem, on that account, to enjoy less popularity. One set of writers can talk of nothing but governesses, tutors, and athletic curates, who love fly-fishing and abhor Strauss. The domestic novel happens to be in fashion, and we certainly have enough of it. Others are never happy out of the precincts of Pall-Mall and the clubs, unless it be at a fashionable watering-place; and some can give no flavour to English fiction without importing it from Florence or Rome, or borrowing their intrigue from the secret societies, and their sentiment from Mazzinian manifestoes. But Mr. Lever is immeasurably richer in imagination and power than all such writers; and if he would occasionally emigrate to "fresh fields and pastures new," he has already all that is needful in the way of stock and capital. He may be contented with his present reputation, which is extensive, and likely to be permanent; but we believe that it is in his own power to elevate and enlarge it.

" Count no man happy till he has ceased to live," says the Greek proverb. Sum up the attributes of no genius till it has ceased to act or to write. The last work of an author may sometimes be the first which gives a just idea of his mind as a whole.